FORKED HEAD PASS

ALSO BY TOM TRABULSI

Sandaman's Riposte

Bearing Down

FORKED
HEAD
PASS

TOM TRABULSI

Dedicated to Diamond Dave Delery
The Ragin' Cajun
(1969-2004)

For my parents, Raymond and Leila Trabulsi.

"All men climb the ladder of death."
African proverb

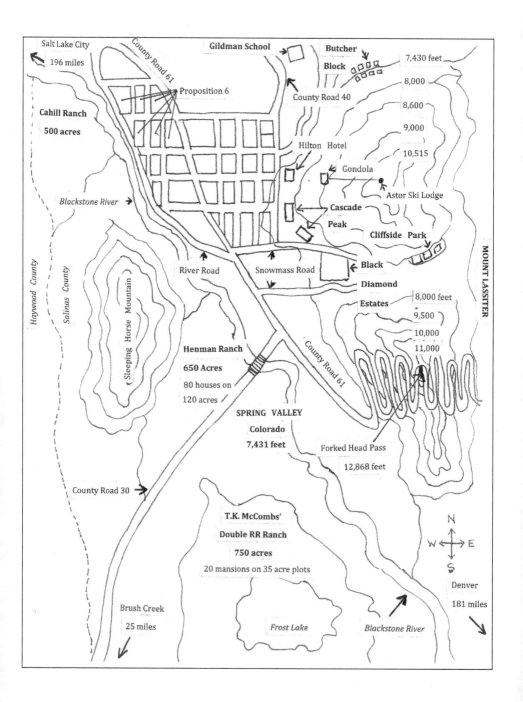

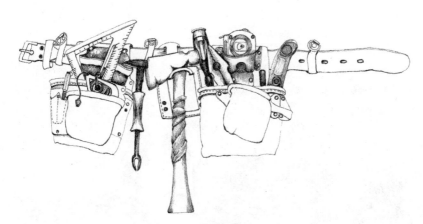

Toolbelt

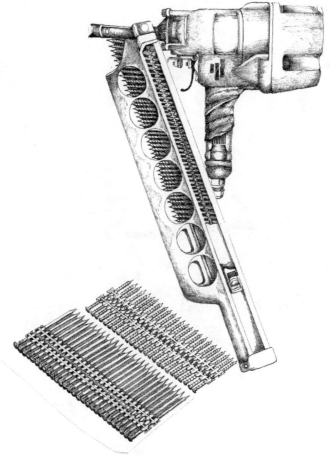

Nail gun

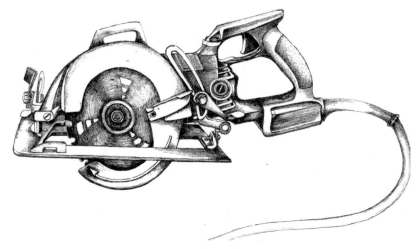

Saw

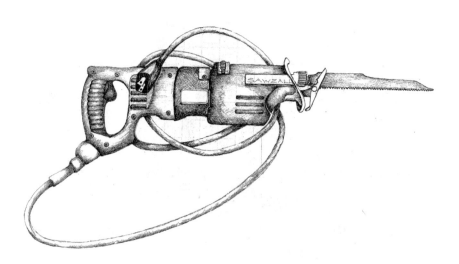

Sawzall

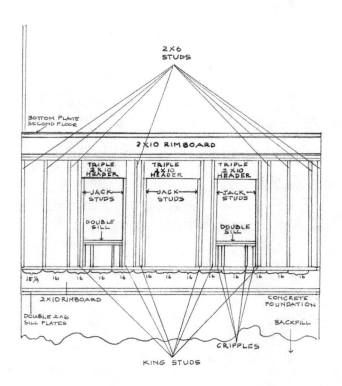

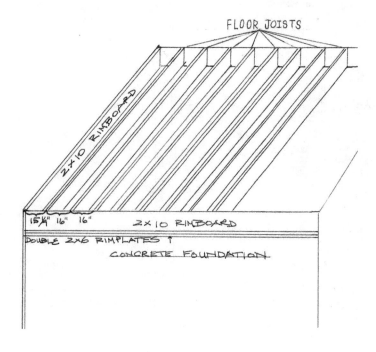

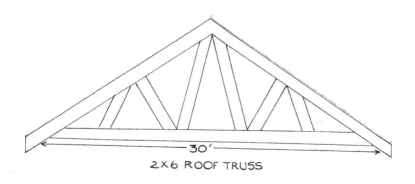

2X6 ROOF TRUSS

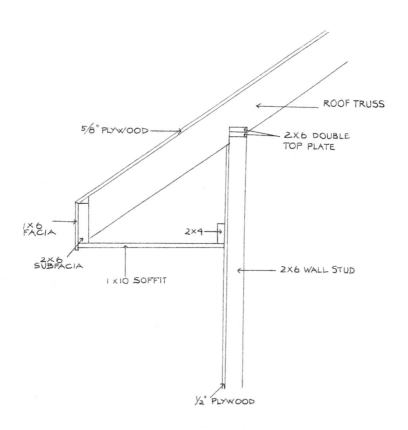

ROOF TRUSS

5/8" PLYWOOD

2X6 DOUBLE
TOP PLATE

1X6
FACIA

2×4

2X6
SUBFACIA

2X6 WALL STUD

1 X10 SOFFIT

1/2" PLYWOOD

Characters—

HARRIS FRAMING—Spring Valley, Colorado

Nolan Harris—Owner and Lead Carpenter
Randall Holmscomb—"Fabio"—Lead Carpenter
Neal Killea—"Rigor Mortis"—Lead Carpenter
Thomas Elias—Carpenter
Brian Osmanski—"O-Zone"—Carpenter
James Wyatt—"Cooter"—Carpenter
Neil Abbot—"Baby New Year"—Apprentice

EAGER BEAVER FRAMING—Vail, Colorado

Cameron Rogers—Owner and Lead Carpenter
James Spooner— "Spoons"—Lead Carpenter
Rick Cadmus—"Uno"—Carpenter
Steven Bunncamper— "Bunny"—Carpenter
Luís and Hector Soldano—Apprentices

Nolan's Siding Teams—
Dan Delaney "Showtime"
Robert Campbell "Soup"
Chris Carmichael "Red Death"

Kara Harris—Colorado Preservation Society, Community Relations
   Committee
Sarah Vaughn—Colorado Preservation Society, Head Legal Council
Rebecca Johns—National Ecological and Geographical Association,
   Biologist

T.K. McCombs—20 houses on 35 acre lots
Eugene Henman—80 houses on 1.5 acre lots—105 acres put into conservation easement
William Cahill—175 acres placed into conservation easement

Proposition 6—the annexation by eminent domain statutes of five square blocks of downtown Spring Valley

CONTENTS

PROLOGUE

MOUNT PERSHING
Peak 4 Resort, 14,351 feet
October 28, 2000

Virtually invisible in the predawn hour, three Yamaha snowmobiles carried six men up the mountainside like wraiths on twin-cylinder four-stroke engines. They were dressed in black and wore black masks and dark goggles to protect their faces from the snow-filled wind. Because of the steep ascent, they used caution but still rode the throttle. Around them, the darkness was only hacked open by the lead vehicle's snow-choked headlight. It was an 8,000-foot climb straight up the leeward side of Mt. Pershing, and launched from a dirt trail few traveled.

Up top, they smashed open the front doors of the ski lodge. Three teams of two went separate directions. They unslung their backpacks, tore through their individual tasks, and rendezvoused back at the snowmobiles. At the bottom, once they reloaded the Yamahas onto trailers in total darkness, they heard an explosion and paused to watch a distant fireball incinerate the sky.

Then the pickup trucks disappeared into the night.

Section One

———

The Astor Lodge was not really a lodge at all but actually a three-story building filled with restaurants and ski shops. To reach it, the primary gondola line scrawled up Mt. Lassiter's eastern face like a seam between the trees. The main kitchen was on the second-floor and fed a thousand people in the cafeteria. From there food was distributed by freight elevator to the first-floor bar and third-floor eatery/cafe.

Thomas Elias had punched in at 6:30 A.M. and was halfway through his shift. He was an average size with an average face, but his hazel eyes fiercely glowed. That gaze, combined with his black goatee and shaved head, gave him a somewhat forbidding appearance. At twenty-eight, he had spent the last ten years slaving in Manhattan kitchens, so his skill-set superseded his current role as "re-heater in chief." Originally, he had taken this job for the free ski-pass. But after a rash of firings with only two months left in the season, Elias quickly went from prep cook to sous chef under head chef Pete Billen.

With lunch rapidly approaching, the morning prep work was coming to an end. Next to the stack ovens, twin forty-gallon steam kettles simmered with meat and vegetarian chili. Inside the ovens, Elias checked the fifteen-pound top rounds slowly cooking, then consulted a clipboard to make sure all was coordinated for their 11:30 A.M. opening. Since Chef Billen was running late again, and one of the other cooks had already banged out sick with a hangover, crunch time loomed.

When Clara Biggs entered the kitchen, Elias frowned but quickly said, "Morning, Clara."

"Hello, Thomas." Biggs was in her late fifties and a proper woman from Havens, Kansas. "It's especially cold this morning, don't you think?"

"It sure is." Elias expertly julienned a stack of green peppers despite the half-cast on his right forearm, his knife-hand. "Listen, I want to apologize for yesterday. I know my mouth gets a little filthy, but Pete sat me down and told me you'd been complaining about that and, well, I can respect that. I'm gonna try to watch it, okay? Even though you work in the front of the house serving, you're in the kitchen as well, and I'm sorry if I offended you or made you uncomfortable."

Clara smiled warmly. Attired in the blue denim shirt and pants uniform, she wore her AMERICAN RESORTS visor like a crown tucked into her curls.

"I appreciate that, Thomas, thank you." She reached for a cluster of utensils to equip the steam table out front. "I don't mean to be such a nudge—"

"Clara—"

"But I thank you nonetheless."

"No problem." Elias shifted his focus back to the green peppers. "And by the way, there's no chowder today. We got chicken veggie, mushroom, Italian noodle and tomato."

"Okay." Biggs carried an armload of spoons and ladles through the swinging doors just as Chef Pete Billen walked in off the freight elevator.

"Tommy kid, what is up?"

"Morning, chef." Elias nodded to the left. "Got the chilies done, top rounds are in the oven, soups are fired, and I got those two morons down by the fridges cutting up salad mix."

"Nice, Tommy, nice." Pete Billen had the thin stained teeth of a two-pack-a-day smoker. He was an ex-drill sergeant twenty years removed from the Army, and his bulbous eyes at times surveyed his employees as if they were mere recruits begging for the whip. Like any good drill sergeant, his booming voice contained alternating levels of aggression. "How's that arm feeling?"

"Today's the day." Elias lifted his half-cast. "Seeing the doc at three o'clock."

"Nice." Billen was thin, but he tied an apron around the beer-fed basketball his stomach had become. "Bet it'll feel good to finally jerk off right-handed again."

"Frankly, just wiping my ass will be plenty cool for me."

Billen laughed as he grabbed a stack of recipes.

"Chef ..." Elias paused. "Before you go, think you could give me a hand getting lunch out?"

Billen frowned. "I got a lot to do today, Tommy."

"I know. So do I. Hooper called out sick, those two idiots down there are taking all fucking—"

"Tommy." Billen crossed his arms. "What did we discuss yesterday?"

Elias rolled his eyes. "She's not even in the kitchen, man."

"Doesn't matter. I told you, no more cussing. That comes from the top down."

"But you swear all the time!"

"That may be true." Billen spread a stained grin. "But I'm the *fucking* boss."

"Yeah, right ..." Chopping vegetables once again, Elias murmured, "Thanks to guys like me."

"What was that?"

"Nothing. I didn't say anything."

"Naw, I'm pretty sure I heard you say something."

"Nope." Elias looked him in the eye. "I didn't say a *fucking* word."

"That's it." Billen slammed the recipes on the table. "Maybe you should take the rest of the day off!"

"Oh yeah?" Elias' expression seemed amused by this challenge. Not usually one to quit a job, he also knew he could not survive this hypocrisy much longer. "I'll do you one better and take off the rest of the *fucking* week."

"You do that!"

"Deadbeat." Elias picked up the cutting board and tossed all the recently chopped vegetables into the garbage. "I'm sick of carrying your dead ass anyway!"

"Oh, is that what you've been doing?"

"Yup." Elias ripped off his apron. "You come strolling in here at ten o'clock every day. Even one-handed I get more done in a single shift then you do all week!"

Billen's eyes, already bulging from all of the cigarettes, widened exponentially. "Clean out your locker!"

"Fuck you!" Elias grabbed his set of knives and headed for the door. "I hope you remember how to cook."

"Get the hell out of here before I call security!"

"Go ahead. I get high with those guys every day." Elias made his way to the employee locker room and collected his jacket and extra gear. Enraged, he slammed the door and descended two flights to where the gondola disgorged skiers.

"Hey, Elias!"

Elias turned and caught sight of one of his neighbors, a stoner named Joey Rossi, who worked in Lift Operations.

Rossi said, "What's up, kid, you look all jacked up."

"Man ... I think I just quit my job."

"Oh yeah? Want me to quit mine? Jimmy says there's some killer pow-pow on the backside of C-basin."

"Naw, man." Elias lifted his cast. "I gotta get this thing dealt with today."

"Well, suit yourself. Here—" Rossi wedged aside a line of skiers waiting to descend. "Excuse me, people, we have an injured employee here, please step aside."

Elias settled into the empty gondola car as its door crisply closed. For the hundredth time since his arrival three months earlier, the beauty of the surrounding valley killed his rage with awe.

———

Two days later, Elias was at a gas station filling up his '86 Skylark. Long past its prime, the car had so far survived a 2,300-mile road trip and brutal winter, so he kept his complaints in check.

Despite being under contract until the ski season ended in April, Elias was now jobless in January. His right hand, just freed from its cast, was a shrunken pale hook on the gas pump nozzle. Looking at it now made it seem entirely emblematic of his decision to leave New York City. After he had abandoned a nightmarish situation with a trauma-tized girlfriend who needed her space, he originally envisioned a fresh start on the slopes surrounded by freaks and tourists. But Spring Valley was small, too small to have any unskilled jobs outside of the restaurant/ hotel business and construction, which he had never worked a single day in his life. There was no new girlfriend, and the crystal powder he had hoped to ski was all but forgotten after he got the job cooking on the mountain. His days off were Saturday and Sunday, which meant commuters from Boulder and Denver flooded the already tourist-filled slopes. Worse, he had traded in his skis for a snowboard and promptly fractured his wrist in two places.

The girlfriend in New York was long gone but, after speaking with his landlord, Elias found his old apartment might soon be on the market again. He did the math. Even after he pawned off his snowboard, gear, and stereo, he would still need cash for bills, rent, and the three-day car ride home. Once there, he would also need another $1500 for the apartment.

His mind was a haze of gloomy possibilities as he finished pumping gas. Inside the store, he poured himself a soda. By chance, he noticed a large man wearing a grimace and a soaked Carhartt jumpsuit. Stone-faced, this stranger stood behind a woman as she paid at the counter.

Elias sipped his drink. He considered the guy's trashed outfit and knew he worked outside doing something miserable in the freezing cold. That fact ensured a probable high rate of employee turnover, so Elias nonchalantly approached. The guy was tall, about six-foot-four, and emanating a distinct hostility. His size sixteen boots disappeared beneath the battle-scarred jumpsuit destroyed through previous winters. The face was ruddy and wind-whipped, a tanned blister from the winter sun. His green eyes constantly swept his surroundings as if cataloging possible threats. That same glance pinged like sonar off Elias when he was still twenty-feet out, and as sometimes happens when strangers meet, neither one could have known the implications of this encounter.

"Excuse me." Elias looked up at him, undeterred. "I know this is out of the blue, but I'm looking for work."

The guy gnawed on a piece of jerky. "What do you do?"

"Nothing."

"What? You've got to do something."

"I'm a cook."

"Jesus ..." A full ten seconds passed. "Can you carry wood?"

"Mister, for cash I'll carry whatever the fuck you want."

"Hey, my wife's standing right here."

"No offense, miss."

"You know where the old high school's at?"

"Kind of."

"We're right behind it. Be there at seven tomorrow." The guy stuck out his hand. "I'm Nolan."

"Thomas." Elias' wounded hand withered inside the grip. "So that's it?"

"Yep." Nolan put an arm around his wife. "No experience means you start at ten bucks an hour. And if you're not there at seven o'clock exactly, don't even bother to show."

They pushed through the doors and cold air rushed in as if an arctic hatch had blown wide open. Elias watched until they gained the shelter of their pickup truck and then wondered if he had just made a huge mistake.

———

At 6:55 A.M. the next morning, he punched his beat-up Skylark through a snowbank and parked next to the same pickup he recognized from yesterday's introduction. As Elias stepped outside, the realization that he would be working in this freezing cold for the remainder of the day almost caused him to leave.

"Hey!"

Elias saw an arm waving from one of the eight small houses clustering this hillside.

"Yeah!" he yelled back, and the clouded steam from his words blew across the air like smoke.

Nolan called out, "What's your name again?"

"Thomas!"

"Grab a sawzall from the boxes and get up here. Hurry up!"

Elias pulled on a pair of ski gloves and headed toward a pile of cardboard boxes. Peeling back the lids, he saw they were totally empty.

"Hey!" Nolan screamed again and pointed from the second-floor window. "Are you fucking kidding me? The *tool* boxes are over there! And the sawzall looks like a pissed-off swordfish. Hurry up!"

Elias spotted two large rectangular metal chests with KNACK stenciled on their sides and felt like a moron. He found a shoveled-out path and thirty-feet later threw open their lids. Searching through a crowded jumble of tools, he spied a two-foot-long rectangular device with a thin, wickedly serrated twelve-inch blade extending from its nose.

He double-timed it to the house where he had last seen Nolan. The snow was shoveled three-feet high on either side of the icy trench. Elias saw whole systems of trenches connecting the parking lot, the eight houses, the wood stacks, and portajohn. As he passed each structure, they seemed unremarkable, like 30'x30' tissue boxes with simple, steep-pitched roofs. The last two were unfinished, and from the one on the left, in an upstairs window, Nolan suddenly reappeared.

"Nice job, Thomas, hurry up."

Elias entered the doorway and saw the first-floor was only gravel and sand. There were no interior walls, and the second-floor landing was a giant loft holding two bedrooms and a bath. He looked around for the staircase until he saw Nolan smiling down from the edge of the floor above. "Shove that thing into your jacket and start climbing. Someone stole my extension ladders and we haven't cut the stairs in yet."

Elias saw a makeshift ladder of 2x4s nailed into a pair of wall studs. He struggled climbing it because his right wrist was still too weak. Once he reached the landing, he saw someone else hanging upside down from the top of the second-floor wall and said, "Holy shit ..."

"Say hello to Rand." Nolan took the sawzall out of Elias' grasp. "Rand, this is Thomas."

From his awkward position, Rand Holmscomb nailed off the block line before rappelling the nailgun to the deck by its airhose. Then he dropped himself off the wall and stuck the landing right beside it. He held out a hand and said, "Heard you were a cook." The voice was flat, but his appraising glance was not.

"Used to be." Elias seemed embarrassed by the admission.

Rand was about the same height as Elias but had curly blond hair framing a strong jaw and light blue eyes. Despite the layered clothing and heavy jacket, the shape of his powerful physique was still apparent.

His movements were fluid, confident and, as just witnessed, not without considerable strength.

Elias nodded at their surroundings and said, "Listen, I don't know if he told you, but I don't have a single clue about what you guys are doing."

"Can you carry wood?"

"Like a mindless moron, all day long."

Rand cracked a smile and then looked over to where Nolan was at war with a knot-filled extension cord. "Hear that?"

"Yeah." Nolan pointed outside while still wrestling with the cord. "Near those boxes, and not the fucking cardboard boxes neither, is a stack of half-inch plywood sheets. Start humping that shit over and stack it against this wall. You're gonna be hoisting them up like a motherfucker in a minute."

"Yep. Can I ask you something? What's the deal with those?" Elias pointed at the red and green stripes spray-painted on every tool.

"Theft. You ever see those stripes on someone else's site, you tell me and then we'll all bathe in their blood."

Elias descended the ladder and backtracked until he found the 4'x8' plywood sheets beneath a giant afro of snow. After hacking away the ice, he hoisted one of these rectangles into his right hand, which, atrophied from the cast, immediately buckled. Careful with his feet, he shuffled down the trench because the ice was like glass beneath his boots. Reaching the house, he slammed the plywood up against the wall.

"Thomas."

Startled, Elias looked up at Nolan in the upstairs window as Nolan said, "Guess what?"

"Jesus, man, you scared the hell out of me."

"Twenty more of those and then you can start carrying 2x4s."

"Awesome." Elias cleared a nostril into the snow. "My doctor told me I needed to get more fresh air."

"Yeah, well, you came to the right fucking place. Hurry up."

"Hurry up," Elias echoed, and then he did just that.

———————

At noon, Nolan and Rand told him he had thirty minutes for lunch. They took off in Nolan's F-250 as Elias cranked the heat and ate a frozen sandwich. His hands and toes were numb, his nose a running mess. His right arm hurt from barely using it for two months, and his left was ablaze from overcompensation. Stomping his ice-crusted boots, Elias cursed and said, "I can't believe this is actually a job."

He had time for two Marlboros and tried a quick nap, but his body was already aching. Having done the math last night, he needed two hundred dollars for the car ride home, another two hundred for bills and utilities, and an additional $1500 for a deposit on his old apartment—$1900 was the only thing standing between himself and sweet freedom. If he got paid under the table, his remaining sentence inside this frozen hell was only a month or two at best.

"Another month," he said just as the F-250 abruptly reappeared. "One more frozen month."

Nolan shouted, "Up!"

From his ladder, Elias hoisted the plywood sheet up to Rand, who was standing inside the wall line on the second-floor. Rand and Elias held the plywood in place so Nolan could nail it off from another ladder to the left. The first-floor exterior walls were already sheeted before the second-floor walls were built. Now they applied the plywood to the second-floor walls as well. Firing crisply in the cold air, Nolan paced the Hitachi stripnailer like an automatic weapon. After he reset and climbed his ladder, he called out, "Up!"

Elias fed the machine until eventually, with arms at full extension, his withered grip began to fail.

Sensing trouble, Rand asked, "You all right?"

"No." Elias' arm shook. "I'm sorry. I can't hold it anymore."

Rand pulled the next sheet up into place alone. Cursing, Elias climbed down and repeatedly kicked a snowbank.

Nolan reloaded the nailgun. "What's the problem?"

"Nothing. My arm was kind of broken."

"When?"

"Just got the cast off three days ago."

"Jesus Christ. Don't you think that might've been important information to tell me before I hired you?"

"Don't worry about me." Elias shook his right wrist. "I'm fine."

"Good. Then I need more gunner 8's."

"What the hell does that mean?"

Rand smiled at the attitude, but Nolan was not a fan. "It means you're gonna go get them. As the honorary gopher, that's exactly what you're gonna do all day long. Go-fer anything I tell you to."

"Gopher, huh?" Elias grinned at the demotion. "From wood bitch to gopher in a single day?"

"These are 8's, and these are 16's." Nolan held up two different sized nail clips. "The 8's are 2½-inches long and have rings along the shaft. The 16's are 3¼-inches but smooth. The 8's are for sheeting, the 16's are for framing."

"Okay."

"There's a box of 8's inside. Go fer it."

As Elias set off, Nolan barely waited until he was around the corner to ask, "What do you think?"

"Well ..." Rand paused as the afternoon began to darken. "The kid's weaker than fuck, but I like his attitude."

"It's horrible, isn't it?"

"Almost bad enough to last the week."

"Wanna bet?"

Rand chuckled, watching his partner nail off the stud line beneath the sheet. "Let's at least get these last two houses sheeted, have him drag over all those fucking trusses, and then you can fire him."

"Fire him?" The nailgun was empty, so Nolan reached into the tool bags around his waist. "This motherfucker won't even last long enough for that."

"I don't know about that. He's got that certain look of desperation in his eye."

"If by desperation you mean stupidity, than I wholeheartedly agree."

Elias turned the corner into their immediate silence and set down a small cardboard box with a big thud.

"Man," he said, "I can't believe that little thing weighs fifty pounds."

"Nails." Nolan held out a gloved hand. "Hurry up."

"Hurry up." Elias ripped open the lid and handed up a dozen racks. The nails came twenty to a rack and were held in place by two thin rows of plastic. Since the Hitachi held two racks, and its safety had been wrenched off, Nolan's deft touch from years of experience, had the nailgun sounding like a Marine Corps assault team.

Elias held up a rack of 8's. "What's with the rings?"

"No more questions."

"Not again," Rand said. "You gotta teach the ones that want to learn, man, or we ain't never gonna keep anyone good."

"We don't know anything about this guy. No offense." But Nolan frowned. "Alright. The ringshanks are for plywood because the rings prevent the nail from working itself out over time. Kind of like an arrowhead. We don't want any part of the house to move, so the plywood acts like skin around the bones."

"Was that so painful?" Rand turned to Elias. "The 16's are for framing. They're smooth so you can pull them out. Some framers need that because they fuck shit up."

"We're not those guys." Nolan climbed down and reset his ladder. "I'm ready for another sheet."

They worked in rhythm until the second-floor was finished. Elias moved slower as dusk approached, but redoubled his efforts since they seemed insulted if kept waiting. Finally, at 4:30 P.M., Nolan detached the nailgun from the pressurized airhose with a loud pop. "That's it." He handed the hose to Elias. "Roll this up, kill the compressor and the gas feed, and then meet us by the boxes."

"Yep." Exhausted, Elias followed the hose like an old man pulling on a string. It led him into another unfinished house where an ancient gasoline air compressor loudly rattled and hissed. Kneeling down, squinting at the oil-spattered gauges, he flipped the power toggle and the engine ground to a stop. He switched off the gasoline feed, gathered up the hose, and stumbled back outside. With full dark expected by five o'clock, the temperature was already in freefall.

At the job boxes, Nolan and Rand unbuckled their tool bags. Elias handed over the hose and noticed their curious expressions. "What?"

"You good?" Nolan stuck a Marlboro Light between his lips. "Can we expect you here tomorrow?"

Elias flinched. "My arm's fine. I ain't no pussy."

"Excuse me? Who are you talking to—"

"Hey! Hey now," Rand said. "This ain't no way to break for home. Come on, let's get ghost of this place." Rand lowered the job-box lids with a crash before snapping closed the Master locks. "The good news is that at seven o'clock we get to do it all over again. The bad news is that we're just stupid enough to be here."

"Thanks," Nolan dryly said. "As if the noose wasn't already tight enough ..."

Single file, they hunched their shoulders into the wind and marched through the best trench of all—the one that led to the heated ride home.

The town of Spring Valley had been founded in 1878 by pioneers unable to press onward into Utah. Caught in the mountain passes by an October start to an early winter, they eventually built small cabins along the Blackstone River that later became Main Street. Thirty miles from the nearest town, and 180 miles northwest of Denver, Spring Valley's initial generations enjoyed anonymity for fifty years until the first ski trails were carved through Mt. Lassiter's pine wood forests. At 11,563 feet, the mountain loomed nearly a mile above the valley floor, which was already 7,500 feet above sea level. Facing west into the jet stream, tucked into the twin paths of Canadian cold air and Pacific Northwest moisture, the entire region was like a giant snowmaking machine averaging thirty-five to fifty-feet per season. But the serious commercialization of winter did not begin until the 1970s. After recreational skiing collided with tourism, the Rocky Mountains was never the same. Places like Vail, Breckenridge, and Steamboat Springs got swamped with East Coast skiers seeking uncrowded, pristine conditions, and West Coasters spoiled enough to be sick of Lake Tahoe and Mammoth.

Spring Valley, one of Colorado's most remote vacation sites, waited until the 1980s to share in this bonanza. Then, almost overnight, it doubled to 7,000 year-round residents. Another 3,000 seasonal workers and vacationers hit town for the winter months. The quaint downtown strip of old saloons and antique storefronts blossomed into western-influenced eateries adjacent to boutiques and curio shops catering to an increasingly upscale clientele. The locals, who warily regarded the tourists as an unpleasant though necessary affliction, and who had previously only worked in agriculture and ranching, created businesses to grab a slice of this six-month windfall. Besides, as the bottom fell out of the cattle industry, and county-wide bankruptcies mounted, economic alternatives were nonexistent.

It was past five o'clock when Elias hit Main Street. Little more than a ten-block row of bars, restaurants, and shops, the surrounding vistas remained the real attraction. Two other mountains to the north and east, as well as Mt. Lassiter to the west, reminded people of their exact meaninglessness in the face of Mother Nature's billion-year-old architecture.

Over the past decade, the eastern edge of town had transformed into a series of one and two-story condominium developments. In accordance with strict zoning, they were spread along the hillside like alcoves tucked amongst the trees. Mt. Lassiter, on whose lower rim these developments infringed, tolerated this encroachment like a gracious host ungraciously repaid. The constant parade of hotel vans and town-owned buses spewing skiers at the main gondola line did nothing to assuage this scourge. After scrolling up to the giant lodge where Elias had recently lost his job, the gondola then fed four other lifts which climbed to the mountain's furthest reaches.

He took a left onto Snowmass Road. The Skylark continued defying the odds and clawed up the icy incline. He swung into Pine Ridge Estates. Ten split-level condos were stacked like stairs uphill. With year-round residents as well as a changing mix of time-share renters, the development's most prized feature, especially in a ski town, was the ten-minute walk to the gondola. He parked in front of the unit he shared with four other roommates, and unfolded himself from the car as every body part already screamed in pain.

He staggered through the sliding glass door and found roommates Billy and James strewn in front of the television. Since the PlayStation was their master, they spent whole days groveling before it like paralyzed crackheads.

"What's up, big T?" Soft-spoken but sarcastic, James had short brown hair and a face with delicate features. "How was your first day?"

"Awful." Barely able to lean over to dislodge his boots, Elias grunted and said, "It was unbelievable."

Billy Dunn asked, "Did you make a good first impression?" Stork-like at six-foot-two, he had a screaming demon tattoo covering the crown of his shaved head. "That's important, you know."

Completely exhausted, Elias could do little more than shrug out of his jacket and soaked ski pants before collapsing onto the sofa behind them.

"So, what'd they have you do?" James, after hearing about Spring Valley's ample restaurant work and skiing, had lined up the condominium back in late October.

Elias rolled onto his side, wincing from the effort. "Actually, I carried wood."

"Wood for what? I thought you said he was a landscaper?"

"Landscaper? It's the middle of freaking winter, dumbass."

"Yeah, really," Billy concurred. "How could you be so stupid?"

"Anyway," Elias said, "these guys build houses."

"Carpenters?" James asked.

"Well, yeah, I guess. But they call themselves framers."

"Framers?"

"Yeah. As in house framers."

"So you a framer now too?"

"Naw, man, I'm the official wood bitch." Elias did a slow roll onto his back. "Honestly, every muscle in my body feels torn."

"That's rough," Billy said, but he was smiling as he said it. "Big T's getting his toolbelt on."

"Tools," James repeated and then quickly laughed. "Man, who're you kidding? You're a mother-humping cook, bitch."

"Seriously, dude." Billy's gaze was incredulous. "What're you doing to yourself? We got a slot in sauté at thirteen bucks an hour to start, man, drop this other shit."

"I don't know ..." Elias, a born city-dweller, could not remember ever working outside for an entire day, not even as a kid. "It was definitely some horrible shit but ... I don't know ..."

"Well, know this." Billy threw him a wink. "Since you're such a blue-collar motherfucker, dinner's on me."

"Hey!" James screamed, hands thrust in angst toward the frozen screen. "What're you doing, dude?"

"Dude. Relax. I gotta check on the meatloaf and taters. They're world famous, bro."

"Goddamn," Elias said in mock disgust. "After busting my ass all day I have to come home to *that*?"

"Yeah, we'll see who's bitching soon enough." Billy hopped up the six stairs leading to the kitchen.

"I better shower before my whole body seizes up." Elias moved himself into a seated position. "If it hurts this bad already, imagine how I'm gonna feel in the morning."

James' smile was not exactly sympathetic. "Sucks to be you, bitch."

"I hate you." Elias shuffled toward the basement where he and Dennis Mitchell, a boisterous Texan, lived. He waded through Dennis' assorted crap before reaching the back bedroom where his own crap was likewise spread. He stripped naked and caught sight of Lisa's picture. Why had he not already taken it down? He thought of New York City and where she might be, but knew she had probably moved on. Having shouldered the majority of their relationship for as long as he had, his departure from New York had been more like a last-ditch escape from the flaming train wreck of their lives. She, on the other hand, could make no such gesture. Instead, she walled him off to asphyxiate their relationship. But today, whether it was just the change in scenery or surviving the frozen conditions, something jarred loose the endless loop their ruined union constantly played inside his head.

Grabbing a towel off the doorknob, he pulled her picture from the wall and dropped it in the corner. Then he limped into the bathroom.

CHAPTER TWO

At 6:00 A.M. the following morning, Elias gasped as he reached for the alarm clock. While his back felt more or less okay, the pain everywhere else was ungodly. Sudden movements shot shards of glass through his muscles, so he was careful with his motions. He dressed and stepped quietly through the darkness of Dennis' room, heard his snores, and felt a jealous burst of anger.

Upstairs, the darkness was complete. The thought of spending the next nine-and-a-half hours in that frozen hell seemed outside the bounds of reason. He chugged two mason jars of coffee and set off for the jobsite at 6:45 A.M. The worst part was that even though the Skylark had been idling for a full ten minutes before he left, it still felt like a rolling icebox.

At this hour, downtown was a vacant strip of snowy street. The Northwest Bank clock flashed the temperature at twenty-one degrees. Pulling in at 6:56 A.M., Elias saw the F-250 and another Ford pickup truck already parked side-by-side. As a city boy, Elias didn't know anything about pickup trucks except for the fact that Colorado was apparently Ford country. Inside the battered F-150 pickup, Elias saw a giant unfamiliar man with red hair and a plain expression wave hello. Barely nodding back, Elias staggered through the chill dawn air until he found Nolan Harris and Rand Holmscomb already rolling out the tools.

"Wow," Nolan said. "You all right?"

"I'm fine." Elias was not flattered by the remark or its blunt assumption, but did not necessarily want a repeat of yesterday either. "Couldn't be better. What do you need me to do?"

"Did you see that big red-headed moron parked out there?"

Elias nodded. "Who is he?"

"Fucking Frank." Nolan fired up the compressor as its parts complained against the cold. He dialed back the choke once it settled into a groove of sputtered wheezing. Nolan scanned the makeshift parking lot, watching Frank change into his boots.

"Motherfucker." Nolan looked at his watch. "Every day this guy pulls in at six-fifty-five and then waits until seven o'clock exactly to switch into his boots."

"So what?"

Nolan shot Elias a blisteringly unpleasant look. "So work starts at seven A.M., not seven-oh-three."

"Who is he, anyway?"

"The guy you're about to replace."

"Oh yeah?" Elias cinched his hood, smiling through the cold. "He a wood bitch too?"

"Worse." Nolan connected another hose to the original, then heaved the remainder up over the second-floor wall. "As far as idiot savants go, this moron's mostly idiot."

Rand appeared walking down the snow trench with an armload of saws, a sawzall, and wearing electrical extension cords like necklaces. "Did you see him?"

"Of course." Nolan aimed his disgust to where Frank suddenly caught all three of them staring directly at him. "Motherfucker's already slipping into borrowed time." He turned toward Elias. "We need a box of gunner 16's. You remember what they are?"

"8's are for sheeting, and 16's are for framing."

"Great. Thanks for listening. We also need one more airhose from the boxes. Think you can round all that up without blowing out a brain cell?"

"Does the Pope like blowjobs?" Elias trudged off for the requested items.

As Elias faded down the trench, Nolan shared a smile with Rand. "Think he's gonna make it through today?"

"I'm in pain just watching him walk."

"Yeah, well, we're about to see what he's made of. I'm gonna ride this motherfucker 'til he forgets his own name ..." Nolan turned back toward the pickup trucks and screamed, "Hey Frank! I gave you the day off yesterday and now you're gonna take a half hour just to put on your fucking boots!"

"Frank sucks."

"Motherfucker!" Nolan lightened Rand's load by taking two of the saws. "We'll let him help Thomas drag all those trusses up here and then I'm gonna fire his ass."

"The sooner the better. We should probably beat him before you fire him."

"Yeah, that's also a good way to stay warm."

They set off down the trench.

Rand said, "I actually wasn't kidding."

"Neither was I."

They continued on in silence.

———————

By 8:00 A.M., they were ready to roll the roof even though the forecast called for blizzard-like conditions by ten o'clock. Nolan stuck the tenth Marlboro Light of the day into the corner of his mouth and surveyed the huge black clouds rolling in with a mixture of awe and impending doom. The steam created by the combination of cigarette smoke and his frozen breath made him look like Pig Pen from *Peanuts*.

"Thomas!" he yelled, watching until Elias poked his head out of an upstairs window. "Grab Fabulous Frank and meet me by the trucks!"

Nolan stalked down the trench that led to the parking lot. In the corner was a blue tarp over a giant shapeless mound. He grabbed one end and tore the tarp away like a massive bed sheet in the breeze. Beneath it were twenty roof trusses banded together with metal straps. Yanking out the combination hammer and hatchet he carried instead of a hammer, Nolan hacked through the straps which popped and snapped like hissing snakes suddenly released. As Elias and Frank approached, Nolan said, "Listen up, new guy. When you pop these bands stand the fuck back, because they'll rip you wide open. Also, say hello to the rest of your morning."

Elias scanned the monstrous triangles. "What are they?"

"Trusses. These are what hold up every roof in the world. There are two gable ends and the rest are commons." Nolan pointed. "We're gonna need one of the gables first."

"What's a gable?"

Nolan frowned but said, "It's smaller than the regular trusses. They're on either end because we have to roll 2x10 outriggers to keep the snow off the house."

He left them staring at the stack forlornly. Frank, who was thick through the middle and a good four-inches taller than Elias, gamely snugged up his gloves. Until last month, he had been logging in Wyoming but now, laid off for the third time in two years, Frank was looking to trade in his chainsaw for a new career.

"Well, Thomas," he said, and seemed eager for the challenge, "no better time than the present."

"Fuck me."

They positioned themselves and hoisted the first truss. Made from 2x6 instead of the usual 2x4, the weight was at first ungainly. Slipping on the ice, straining through Elias' weakness, they navigated the trench while maneuvering the thirty-foot triangle around snowbanks and trees. Once they finally got it to the house, Nolan looked down from the top of the second-floor wall and said, "Nice job, girls. Now you only got nineteen more."

"Shouldn't we have a crane?" Elias asked.

"Yeah, you're it. Hand that thing up."

Rand climbed up onto the wall next to Nolan. They both stood balanced on the 2x6 top-plate twenty-five feet in the air. While Elias and Frank grunted and strained, the truss slid up the wall until Nolan and Rand could get a grip, then they hauled it up hand over hand. With the four of them working together, the triangle finally hit a pivot point and teetered on the wall.

"Hang on." Rand strolled along the top-plate as if certain death was not awaiting his first misplaced step. Elias watched the highwire-act in awe.

Rand said, "Okay."

Nolan grunted and shoved until the truss reached Rand's outstretched hand. Carefully balanced, Rand lifted and dragged the truss, walking along the side wall backwards.

"Jesus Christ." Elias turned to Frank. "They've done all these houses like this?"

"I guess." Frank shrugged, his smile as plain as the job he was about to lose. "I've only been on board for a few weeks."

Nolan screamed, "One of you morons get up here!"

Elias jumped through a window and scaled the interior wall like a spider to the second-floor. The truss was lying flat from wall to wall. The snow was landing on Elias' face as he glanced up and heard Nolan say, "Grab one of those twenty-footers, blast it onto the middle vertical and then, once we've got this thing in the air, you're gonna nail it to the floor."

"I have no idea what you just said."

"Jesus Christ." Nolan compressed his mounting fury. "I need to keep reminding myself that it's only your second day before I kill everything around me. Grab that nailgun, take one of those twenty-foot 2x4s, and nail it into the truss near the peak. Then me and Rand are gonna tilt this fucker up until it's standing straight in the air. Once we've leveled it, you're gonna nail that 2x4 to the floor as a brace, got it?"

"Yes." Elias quickly picked up the Hitachi stripnailer. He pulled over one of the 2x4s and was still looking at the gun inquisitively when Nolan called out, "You ever fire one of those things before?"

"Yeah."

"Stop lying. Listen to me—and listen good. We yanked the safeties on all the guns, so watch out for double shots. Big boy rules apply. Place the muzzle flush against the board and squeeze the trigger once. Don't get cute or you'll be pulling three-and-a-half-inch nails out of your hand. Got it?"

"Yeah." Elias scaled a step-ladder. He held the end of the 2x4 against the center post of the truss near its peak and, as instructed, fired a single nail through both boards.

"Put two more bones in a tight circle near the first so it can pivot as we lift."

Elias did and then set down the nailgun. "Good to go."

"All right." Nolan glanced across at Rand. "Ready, Fabio? You know what they say—safety last."

"Safety last." Elias grabbed the brace. "That should be the name of your company."

They counted to three in unison before slowly raising the truss. Elias used the 2x4 like a giant arm to stabilize the peak from falling in or out, and once the truss was stood, Nolan and Rand gently kicked it to the outside edge of the wall.

"Thomas, you've got the weight." Nolan pulled the hatchet from his belt and bent over to bang a single nail through the truss into the top-plate of the wall. Rand looked down at Elias and said, "Gimme that gun."

"But I'm holding—

"I got it. It'll be fine."

Elias let go of the 2x4, quickly handed up the gun, and then scurried back to his position. Rand walked the remaining three inches of top-plate trusting that Elias' grip would not waver. Neither one spoke, but Elias was fully aware of the stakes as Rand moved and balanced like a cat on the balls of his feet. He nailed the truss into the top-plate and, within six-feet of Nolan, swung him the Hitachi by its hose. After Nolan nailed off the remainder, he repelled the gun to the deck by its hose and said, "Hand up that six-foot level." He then placed it vertically along the truss. "Nail those two blocks into a stack on the floor, and when I tell you to, nail the 2x4 brace into the blocks."

Elias was about to nail them when Rand called down, "Make sure the first block is nailed into a floor joist, otherwise just nailing it into plywood ain't gonna hold shit."

"How do I know where the floor joist is?"

"Follow the nail lines."

Frowning like that should have been obvious, Elias kicked aside snow until he found a string of indented dimples along the deck. Checking where the brace would land, he then nailed the blocks into a stack. "Okay."

"Push it out." Nolan nodded toward the parking lot. Elias knelt down and slowly pushed on the brace until Nolan said, "Stop." He checked the level. "Out a cunt hair more." Elias shoved until Nolan screamed, "I said a cunt hair!"

"Sorry." Elias eased back on the brace.

"Stop! Okay, hold that pose … nail it!"

Elias fired the 2x4 brace into the blocks.

"More nails, goddamnit!"

He fired four more and then stood up.

Nolan handed down the six-foot level, stuck the eleventh Marlboro Light of the morning into his mouth and said, "Just broke your cherry, didn't ya?"

"Great. Does that mean I get a raise?"

"A fucking cook," Rand cracked. He knelt, dangled from the top-plate of the wall, and then dropped to the floor in one fluid movement. "We'll make a framer out of you yet."

"Don't do me any favors."

"Hey you absolute bag of shit!" Nolan screamed down at Frank. "You've been standing there holding your cock for the last ten minutes! Get out there and get that next truss ready!"

Elias met Frank at the trusses and, like two robots on a conveyor belt, they lifted and carried until the stack gradually disappeared. By mid-morning, the sky unzipped and by noon four-inches was on the deck as the snow blew sideways.

The trusses were set and nailed on a two-foot layout. Two rows of 2x4 blocks were added between every truss to stabilize the un-sheeted structure. Once the last truss was handed up, Elias was out of breath and looking at the skeleton of the roof with a small measure of pride.

Staring down through the gathering blizzard, Nolan said, "Half hour for lunch, and then we're gonna sub-fascia and sheet this bitch."

"What's he talking about?" Elias could barely stand up.

Frank pat him on the shoulder and said, "Good times, man, that's what he's talking about."

Watching Frank fade into the falling snow, Elias suddenly hated him more than anything else in the world.

CHAPTER THREE

Nolan's wife, Kara, was growing angrier by the second. It was their sixth anniversary and he was late. Stanford educated, Kara had a bachelor's in mathematics and a master's in finance. After college she moved to Manhattan and worked for Merrill Lynch on Wall Street. Despite her rising star on the International Acquisitions desk, she eventually forced a transfer to their San Francisco office. New York was not entirely to blame, but being surrounded by all that towering brick and steel made her crave a return to the forests and small towns of northern California. Also, the manic, class-climbing free for all left even her closest friends comparing incomes, apartment sizes, and other obsessions like thieves on an endless pillage.

She told Nolan all of this the night they met at a New Year's Eve bash in Crescent Lake, Oregon. Her Greek-Italian mix meant he was instantly attracted to her olive skin and long black hair. She never wore makeup, and her dark brown eyes were her prettiest feature. Instead of small talk, he saw the steaming hot tub on the outside deck and brashly proclaimed she did not have the balls. Ten seconds later, she was out the door and in her bra and panties.

In addition to the fact that he towered a foot above her, his bold demeanor and charisma felt like a freight train bearing down. She also sensed a certain lawlessness that caused her to be wary. He briefly told her about his past—the middle-class upbringing and year of college before he got expelled—the ex-wife and daughter that, because of his work, he did not see nearly enough.

Once they started dating, Nolan bounced between San Francisco and Lake Tahoe where he and Rand were building. His quirks and mood shifts could not remain hidden for long. Volatile, explosive, he was also generous to the point of absurdity. Then there was the violence. Having seen it unleashed on others, and while she did not necessarily think of herself as that kind of woman, there certainly was an animalistic passion created by such turmoil.

But she learned to live with his faults, turned a blind eye when his only means of communication was slamming doors or mumbled curses. He was fiery but never physical with her because he was also a total drama queen, nit-picking and wailing at perceived slights before storming off like a baby. Then, as per ritual, he would immediately call her, battle for a bit, and hang up half a dozen more times until they either found resolution, or he returned for a face to face. After these eruptions, the ensuing cleanup often involved dinner out and a week or two of his undivided attention.

They traveled across the west as part of their new life. That, combined with Nolan's transient job, meant she surrendered her financial career to become a bank teller in whichever town they moved to. Her biological clock, now in its thirty-second year, was only recently concerning. It made her realize that her never-ending indecision might soon be making the choice in her stead.

As for their actual relationship, they were now more like roommates dividing up the chores. She constantly complained about his inattention to their lives, much less herself, and if they were not going to have kids, what exactly was the point in being married?

Like tonight—they were supposed to be going out for their *anniversary* and where was Nolan? With the new guy, Elias, cleaning tools in the rented storage space that doubled as his office and shop.

But she also knew her growing commitment to the Colorado Preservation Society was not exactly helping her case. Founded in 1967 to halt the clearing of land that eventually became the Denver suburbs, the CPS had grown into a full-blown movement in response to the sudden construction boom that now made Colorado the nation's fastest growing state. Loosely affiliated with the Sierra Club, the Nature Conservancy, and the Audubon Society, the CPS' goal was community-based management of undeveloped lands. Backed by a huge trust funded by private donations, the CPS achieved success one of two ways—either they bought the undeveloped land outright and placed it into a trust, or they pleaded with the landowner, usually an aged rancher or farmer who was desperate for cash but did not necessarily want to leave his land, to sell them the development rights only. This left the rancher free to carry on with his livelihood but legally castrated from selling to developers. The proper term for this arrangement was "conservation easement," and in Spring Valley, where plans for three different subdivisions totaling 345 houses had been submitted to the town Planning Commission, and where almost 1,100 prime acres was heading to the highest bidder, the hard sell from opposing sides was raucously underway.

Kara knew this influx of construction would kill the only reason most folks moved up here to begin with, which was mainly to escape once scenic locales now overrun by people, taxes, and nuisance. As far as Kara was concerned, this was not about to happen in their own back-yard without a fight.

At stake were three vast ranches owned by families as old as the town itself. Their reasons for selling, however, were totally incomparable. As a member of the Community Relations Committee for the local chapter of the CPS, Kara knew each side was already probing the other for weakness. She had also been in close contact with Sarah Vaughn, the CPS' chief legal counsel for northwest Colorado. Soon, the CPS Advisory Committee would be selecting a delegation to speak with each of the three ranchers trying to sell their lands. Kara planned on being a part of that delegation, so any extra time spent alongside Sarah Vaughn would make Kara's inclusion that much harder to deny.

As for now, she hoped Nolan knew that if he took much longer cleaning tools, he might end up spending their anniversary with the biggest tool of all—himself.

———

Rand Holmscomb was drinking in one of the three bars downtown that held little allure for tourists. The Broken Spoke Saloon had a worn-out bar and an even more haggard woman pouring drinks behind it. Happy hour was almost over, but Rand had nowhere else to go.

Shaking a Marlboro from the pack, he thanked the bartender for the shot and cold Budweiser beside it. A lifetime of hard labor and physical fitness had created the sort of physique women salivated over, but with his bulky winter clothes, misjudgment came easy. His square jaw, blond hair, quick blue eyes, and beach boy looks were a no-brainer once Nolan nicknamed him Fabio.

It had been a long afternoon through the blizzard, even longer for the new guy Elias. Rand knew how much the kid was hurting, and then remembered his own transformation. After quitting high school, he hit his first jobsite at sixteen. He apprenticed for two years before cutting in his first staircase, and, by twenty-one, had his own company with three older employees. But framing nonstop for seven years left him burnt out by twenty-three, so he moved from Grand Junction to the South Dakota oil fields where an even worse level of hell awaited. Carrying three-hundred-pound pipes with equally miserable partners, pulling sixty-hour weeks, and making incredible money was little reward for the vast dangers stalking every conceivable action. Exploding well-heads, burst pipes, and blown out spinal columns were just a few of the hazards Rand circumvented to escape intact. Bunking with guys for weeks at a time also meant fuses were short, especially with no alcohol, drugs or women allowed. Perceived slights and ridiculous exchanges led to all out brawls rarely broken up until the last possible instant. One was expected to hold his own, and if not, that man's time in the fields could usually be measured by the ticking of the closest clock.

After three years wrenching pipe, Rand beat up the boyfriend of the local prom queen before they both took off for Los Angeles. That's when things began to change. He became loosely affiliated with the Vandals MC and started running cocaine from L.A. to Chicago, and returning with kilos of meth. He spent the cash on women and liquor before his lawyers took the rest to save his ass.

But he did not want to think about that now. Instead, his reverie jumped a decade to that night in a bar outside Silverthorne, Colorado. He was minding his own business until the guy next to him, a massive Southern Californian, insulted half a dozen bikers and their equally portly women. Rand, a reckless man back then, jumped in with this stranger just to even up the odds. The bikers stood fierce until one of them took a whiskey bottle to the center of his face, which caved in, and the smashed nose and squirting blood showed the other five that what approached was no idle bar-fight. The twosome beat their way to the door. Outside, they hopped into Rand's pickup and off-roaded until the biker posse lost heart for the chase. That night had been Nolan's twenty-seventh birthday, and the following day he and Rand paired up to spend the next seven years building throughout the southwest and western United States. Yet their extreme work ethic and differing personalities barely survived their volatile partnership. Rand was the brooder no one approached. But Nolan, obstreperous beyond offense, made a loud point of his opinions. And while equally short-tempered, an actual conflict between them was inconceivable since the Cold War doctrine of Mutual Assured Destruction applied.

Rand smashed the cigarette into the ashtray. His blue eyes calmly scanned the bar, noting the usual assortment of drunks and misfits the Broken Spoke inevitably attracted. None of them had any money or jobs and seemed to exist by some fluke of evolution. The meth heads were easy to spot with their geeked-out eyes and chattering nonsense behind grins of grinding teeth. He knew he should have been at one of the other, trendier places with at least some pretty women to look at, but he could not stomach tourists. Or crowds. Or people he did not know or like, or just people in general.

Which he also knew was a pretty big problem.

Slamming the shot, he chased it with the Bud before quickly ordering another round.

Rand, Nolan, and Elias were assembled by 6:50 A.M. Friday morning. After yesterday's blizzard, with all three of them shoveling, the old trench quickly reappeared.

The padlocks were iced over, so Nolan used his lighter like a torch. Rand joined him on the other lock, blinking through his hangover until Frank's truck skid to a stop in the makeshift parking lot.

"This motherfucker," Nolan growled.

"Must be six-fifty-five," Elias cracked, but no one laughed.

They tried the locks again but had no luck. Nolan checked his watch. "Six-fifty-eight."

Rand said, "Easy, Noll."

"Man ..." He tried refocusing on the lock but burned his finger instead. A minute later he said, "It's seven o'clock. I can't even look. Please tell me he's getting out of his truck with his boots on."

"Noll—"

"Yes or no?"

"He's changing into them now."

Nolan shot up out of his crouch and screamed, "Hey, fuckface!" He started running toward the parking lot but slipped, and so quickly began waddling over the uneven icescape like a deranged penguin.

"Boy," Elias said. "This ain't gonna go too good for fuckin' Frank, is it?"

"I told you yesterday about those fucking boots!"

At first, unsure of whether Nolan might be joking, Frank let a big smile teeter across his face until he heard, "*Seven o'clock means seven o'clock, motherfucker!*"

Now briefed accordingly, Frank fled for his truck as Nolan started fast-balling chunks of ice. Miraculously, Frank took one off the head, fell down, but then quickly regained his feet.

"Get out of my sight before I rip off one of those goddamn boots and beat you to death with it!"

Frank hit reverse and slammed through part of a snowbank as the barrage of ice chunks rained down like Armageddon.

"Faster!" Nolan screamed, bending over to grab what looked to be a small boulder of ice.

Back at the tool chests, Elias could only smile. "Just think, ten more hours of this and then we get to go home."

"If you're lucky." Rand returned to work on the lock with his lighter. "Here." He fished an extra from his pocket. "Start burning. In case you haven't noticed, Schizo's already losing his shit and it's not even five past seven."

"Awesome." Kneeling at the lock, Elias watched Frank speed away as Nolan, vapor-locked with rage, continued the chase in vain.

———

Even though the January sun had set nearly thirty minutes before, they worked until five o'clock. Climbing into the cab of the F-250, Nolan fired up the high beams so Rand and Elias could find the tool chests. He cranked the heat and then took a moment to pull his purple hands from the frozen gloves. The digital thermometer on the rearview mirror read five degrees. As Nolan watched them ferrying tools, cords, and hoses toward the chests, his guilt became overwhelming. Mustering the nerve to open the door, he checked his cellphone for new messages, but no calls from Mike Conyers, the general contractor, had been missed.

"Well, fuck me standing." Nolan stepped out into the freezing dusk. "A Friday no-call no-show again."

He stalked down the trench and saw Rand throw him an inquisitive look, so he said, "Nothing. Can you believe the balls on this guy? Guess he thinks we work for free."

Rand paused, chewing on the end of a cigarette. "Son of a bitch."

"Even after we had it out with him last week, too. I swear, I'm about ready to cut this fucker off at the knees. He can't even call me?"

Rand grunted and then peeled off into the darkness.

"Where's Thomas?" Nolan asked.

"Rolling up the rest of the shit. Come on."

They gathered up the last of the tools before all three trudged in silence toward the chests. Nolan locked up and then led the way to the vehicles. After he and Rand climbed into the truck, he saw Elias standing and staring at them expectantly. Powering down his window, Nolan said, "I'm waiting on a call."

"So ..." Elias glanced self-consciously toward his car. "So I'm not getting paid?"

"I should have it by—"

"That's fine." Elias did not even bother to fake it. "See you Monday."

Rand watched him cross through the high beams. "Man ..."

"What?" Nolan snapped, raising his window. "What am I supposed to do? Ass-face didn't drop off our check, man, what the fuck?"

"That kid busted his ass *all week*. If that was you or me, we'd never set foot in this place again, man, and he won't either."

"Fuck!" Knowing Rand was right, Nolan repeatedly punched the dashboard and then the horn, easing down the passenger side window. "Thomas!"

Elias paused at his car. "What?"

"Get in. We're going for a ride."

Elias hopped into the pickup and, like Nolan, carefully peeled the gloves off his throbbing fingers.

Nolan cranked Slayer as the pickup chewed down the mountain toward town. No one spoke until they swooped into the driveway of a nondescript colonial with all of its landscape lights lit in welcome. Nolan parked alongside two panel trucks with CONYERS CONSTRUC-TION emblazoned on their sides.

"Well." He killed the engine. "Here we go."

"Who's this?" Elias quickly joined them in the freezing night.

"The general contractor we're framing for."

At the front door, still upset that it had finally come to this, Nolan rang the bell. A tense minute elapsed until a pretty face peeked out from the seam of the barely opened door.

"Nolan?" Betty Conyers asked, and then glanced cautiously at the other two. "Is everything all right?"

"Everything's fine." Nolan cocked his head to peek around her. "Is Mike in there?"

"Um, yes, hold on one second." She nervously smiled before closing the door. They stood in silence until a large man in a flannel shirt and handlebar mustache eventually appeared. After he pulled on a pleasing grin, he held open the door and said, "Come on in, guys."

"We're in a bit of a rush." Nolan tapped the snow from his boot. "Guess I missed your call."

"Hey, Rand." Mike Conyers made as if to shake his hand until Rand's gaze abruptly ended that assumption. Conyers placed both hands on his hips and said, "I guess I know why you fellas are here."

"Kind of sucks, Mike, don't ya think?" Nolan laughed sarcastically. "On a Friday night too, after busting ass all week, we got to chase you down *again* for our fucking money?"

"I was actually just waiting for the bank—"

Nolan held up a hand like a stop sign. "On me, Mike? You're actually gonna try and pull that bullshit on me? Again?" Smiling sadly, Nolan seemed poised for something worse. "You know what? We're gonna finish out this contract because I'm a man of my word. And after that, I'm never swinging a hammer for you ever again. Believe me, once I'm done telling every other framer in this valley what a deadbeat fuck you are, hopefully you'll be forced back out into the cold to work for your money instead of playing dodgeball with your phone."

"I can cut you a partial check—"

"Naw, Mike, I don't think so." Nolan zipped up his jacket. "Between what's left over from the last draw and finishing the final house, you owe me ten thousand dollars. Me and the fellas here are gonna work all weekend, so that come Monday I don't ever have to look at your fucking face again."

Turning to leave, Nolan encountered the pure awe on Elias' windburnt face.

Conyers called out, "Nolan, please be reasonable. I promise, by tomorrow I'll have you paid in full."

"Then what, Mike?"

Once inside the pickup, Nolan punched the gas and reversed into the street. He glanced out at the still stunned countenance of their soon-to-be ex-employer, but found no satisfaction.

Rand smiled and said, "Think he got the picture?"

"That douchebag's got seventy-two hours to pay in full before we bust out the sawzalls."

"Sawzalls for what?" Elias asked.

Rand turned and said, "You can't cut that place down with bad language."

"Oh ..." Elias digested the threat and seemed to like it. "*Nice.*"

As they returned to the completely blackened jobsite, Nolan said, "Are you guys on board? Can you give me forty-eight hours in hell so that we never have to set foot in this place again?"

"Why not?" Rand answered.

"I guess," Elias said. "I'll help you guys out for as long as I can."

"Why? Where you going?" Nolan asked.

"New York. I don't know when yet." Elias seemed surprised by his own answer. "I mean, I was kind of supposed to, but ..."

"But what?" Rand added.

"But I'm not real sure there's anything left for me to go back to."

The silence became uncomfortable without elaboration, so Nolan opened his checkbook instead. "What were your hours this week, Thomas?"

"Thirty-two hours for three days work."

"I made you work that much in three days? I'm a real dick, huh?"

"I'll answer that after I get the check."

"Ten bucks an hour is what we agreed on, right?"

"Yup."

Nolan detached the check and handed it into the backseat. "You're 1099. Responsible for your own taxes. Tomorrow's Saturday. Eight o'clock start okay with you?"

"Sure."

"See you then."

Elias took the check and grabbed his hat and gloves. "Thanks." He hopped out into the cold.

Nolan watched him make his way through the high beams before turning to Rand. "What do you think?"

"About this joke of a job or him?"

"Take your pick."

Rand shrugged and said, "I hope the kid stays on."

"Why?"

"Because I think he gets it."

"Gets what?"

"That you gotta feed on this misery. The cold, the snow, the ice, the asshole boss—"

"Hey!"

"I mean even when he was half dead, he never stopped." Rand lit a cigarette. "We put up a lot of wood through zero-degree weather and two freaking blizzards."

"We sure did." Nolan drummed his fingers on the steering wheel as Elias' Skylark faded down the road. "If he doesn't sketch out, we might just have something to work with."

"Maybe."

"Let's get out of here." Nolan pointed the Ford toward town.

———————

Nolan dropped Rand off at the motel where he rented a room by the week. Then he headed to his apartment on the western edge of town. Because of its proximity, Mt. Lassiter was like a neighbor looming through the windows.

At 6:30 P.M. on a tourist-packed Friday night, traffic downtown was a slow crawl. Since it was date night, his wife was waiting, a fact that was now only slightly less enticing. He kept telling himself it was the normal ebb and flow, but everything just felt stuck. The same routines, the same meals, the same sex—after a while, she had somehow turned into his friend.

In the parking lot, he killed the engine and grabbed his gear. He stepped out into the frozen chill for one last blast of pain. Crunching up the salt-strewn staircase, he banged into their kitchen and heard the TV from around the corner.

He called out, "Hey, babe."

"Hi, Noll."

He stiffly shrugged off his size sixteen boots, dropped the jacket and soaked Carhartt jumpsuit, and then peeled off two turtlenecks, a thermal shirt, and long-johns. Turning the corner, he found her curled up on the couch like a cat.

"Where were you?" she asked, dialing down the volume by remote.

"Fucking Mike, man," Nolan scratched himself through his boxers, looking down at her nestled shape. "You look awful comfy."

"And you look cold and miserable."

He grunted.

"Your poor face." Kara unfolded herself from the couch. "It looks like a chapped blister." She hugged him and then looked up. "I made beef stew."

"Awesome."

"Do you want some coffee?"

"Naw." Still inside the circumference of her arms, he gave her a kiss and said, "Today wasn't such a good day, babe."

"What happened?"

"Mike ..."

"Again? On back-to-back weeks?"

"That's part of it. But lately every job with him ..." Nolan disengaged from the embrace. "I said some shit."

"Uh-oh."

"Yeah."

"How bad? You didn't beat him, did you?"

"No. But we've got to finish up in the next two days because come Monday, I'm never swinging another hammer for that idiot ever again."

"Honey ..."

"I'll find something quick."

"But it's the dead of winter."

"Kara ..."

"Seriously." She returned to the couch, refolding her legs beneath her. "And not only that, but Junior called up today."

"Oh yeah? How is she?" Nolan sat at the kitchen table. "Please tell me we have some good news."

"I didn't really get to talk to her before you-know-who got on the line."

At the mention of his ex-wife, Nolan's expression twisted into a grimace. "Lemme guess."

"She says the tests are getting expensive, and the insurance company is rejecting half of every bill they receive."

"Jesus. Did it sound like she was fishing?"

Kara frowned and said, "Not particularly."

"On top of the alimony and child support ..." Nolan worked a facial tic and then immediately stood up. He exhumed his cellphone out of the mountain of shed clothes and a moment later said to his ex-wife, "Stacy, it's me ... Yeah, I got the message ... How's she doing? ... How tired? ... Yeah? What are the doctors saying? I mean I thought last week they said they were getting a handle on this thing? ... Jesus Christ ... Overnight stay for what? ... Uh-huh ... Right, I remember ...Well how many tests do they need before they find out what's wrong with her? ... You can save the lectures, okay? Believe me, I know it doesn't grow on trees ... I'm not shouting ... No, *you're* the one who is getting on *my* nerves ... Oh sure, Stace," he said. "Why don't I just sign the whole thing over to you every week and I'll just starve to death ... Because it sounds like that would be the only thing that would finally make you happy ... Yeah, well, she's my kid too, okay, so put away the violin ... *Believe* me this is not shouting. You, out of anyone, should know the difference ... Because we spent three freaking years screaming at each other! ... Yeah, you're right. *That* was shouting ... Listen, if you want to get the lawyers all wound up again, be my guest. But I'm telling you straight up, I'm barely making it on what I got. Besides that, I quit my job today … Straight up done … Jesus Christ …" He held the phone out at arm's distance and took a deep breath. "Listen, I can't do this now, okay? I just can't … Stace … Stacy, please, I swear to God I'm gonna flip out … I promise I'll dig up whatever I can, and then I'm gonna call those insurance assholes on Monday, okay? Now can you please put our daughter on the phone?" Nolan headed for the refrigerator to retrieve a Diet Coke. "Hi, honey … Yeah, it's snowing like crazy here … How's the weather in dreary old California? … Oh yeah? … Ha-ha … How're you feeling, baby? … Yes, I know, your mom told me." Nolan looked at Kara and repeated, "The doctors said you were brave, huh? … That's great, little bud, that's my girl … Your birthday's only a month away, too. You'll be here for that … Well, I'm sure you'll be feeling fine enough to get on a plane … Of course, we'll go skiing. I got your stuff out of storage last week … Okay … No, little B, you can't drive my truck … I know I did last time, whoa, wait a second—make sure your mom doesn't hear you or daddy's gonna take a beating … Okay, love you too … Talk to you Sunday." Nolan flipped closed the phone and stared at his feet.

A minute elapsed before Kara said, "I hate to say it, but Stacy's right."

"Excuse me?"

"You're the vacation and good time while she does all the yelling."

"Guess what? She can move the fuck back then, how about that?"

"What are the doctors saying?"

"Same thing as always—nothing. Now they think it might be some kind of bacteria.

"Bacteria?"

"Jesus Christ, where does it end?"

Kara eyeballed him from the couch. "I'm sure she'll be fine, whatever it is. And I'm still in line for that raise at the bank."

With his elbows on his knees, Nolan stretched his neck toward the floor. "It'll be good to see her."

"Yep."

"I've been thinking, seriously thinking, about starting up my own company." He watched for her reaction. "I'm just so sick of making everybody else rich."

"I think you're right. Actually, I like that idea a whole lot. Who knows? Maybe I can even get you a loan for more equipment."

"Hmmm."

"You might as well, Noll. Just the time you could save chasing these bastards around for money ..."

"Ain't that the truth."

"And if you can keep Rand out of jail long enough, the two of you might just make a run of it. Stranger things have happened."

"I can't even think about that now." He rubbed his belly. "I'm dying over here."

"Give me a few minutes to reheat it," she said. "Mind setting the table?"

The beef stew went down like molten gravy. Afterwards, he sat in the half-light of the kitchen, his finances spread before him. The ledger did not read pretty. The left side of the page contained his monthly responsibilities. As with any venture, this one did not come without serious risks. First and foremost was the liability and worker's compensation insurance, both of which would now be his to shoulder. And since a miscalculation by even a week might mean the difference between profit and loss, assembling bids for particular jobs would almost instantly determine his survival. If he successfully budgeted for the inevitable setbacks and delays every job encounters, he stood to make halfway decent money. The average house was 2,000 square feet. Right now, as a subcontractor to Conyers, Nolan was billing out at five dollars per square foot. On his own, by shouldering the risks and expenses, he could eventually raise his rate to fifteen dollars and walk away with $30,000 per building. He needed to make a statement, to take a job and completely blow the doors off in record time, because word like that, in a town this small, traveled at the speed of light.

He powered off the calculator and rubbed his bleary eyes. Closing the ledger, he stared into the pitch-black shadows of Mt. Lassiter's western face. Since his independence was now a foregone conclusion, he planned to utterly destroy this entire valley, and every sorry ass carpenter in it. Behind him, Kara watched TV beneath a blanket on the couch, so he rose stiffly and shoe-horned in beside her.

CHAPTER FOUR

A bitter frost overnight turned the morning roads into a skating rink. Nolan was doing 30 miles per hour in four-wheel drive, and even with the ¼-inch steel knobs, the tires barely gripped the ice. After the car ahead of him jerked to a stop, Nolan took a bath in his coffee. Already cursed by a manic overdrive, he spent most days in a caffeine-soaked twitch fumigated by his pack and a half a day habit. A longtime horrible sleeper, his insomnia only worsened after he went sober seven years ago. Since then, sleep remained elusive and sadistic, usually lingering just out of reach or, at best, manifesting in some semi-catatonic crash that never lasted more than a couple of hours. For someone his size, combined with the fervor which had become part of his existence, the agitation of chronic exhaustion made his nights a torment.

With the thirty-two-ounce coffee steaming on his knee, his other hand juggled the wheel, a cigarette, and his cellphone. He was already hip-deep in an argument with Kara, who had awakened to find the bathroom utterly destroyed.

While waiting for a pause to return fire, he came to a stop at the Ski Bunny Motor Inn. It was a single-story row of twelve rooms rented by the week. It housed locals, transients, and people like Rand, who basically looked upon leases as ridiculous technicalities. After a long string of ransacked apartments and evictions, Spring Valley's three efficiency motels were now home to Randall Holmscomb.

Not caring about sleeping neighbors, Nolan blasted the horn as he said, "Look, you're right about the bathroom, okay? But I can't do this now, babe. It's four degrees outside, I'm already starving, and fucking Fabio isn't even awake." Nolan leaned on the horn again but knew it was futile. "I gotta go, babe, sorry." He flipped closed the phone and jumped down from the truck. Without gloves on, his hands immediately froze. He cursed, shrugged the jacket sleeves over his fists, and then pounded on the door like a cop looking for suspects.

Finding it unlocked, he pushed in and saw the TV lying on its side as the picture danced like a fluttering pulse. He kicked his way through a foot-deep layer of dirty clothes and said, "Wake up, dipshit."

There was a groan from somewhere beneath a pillow. Rand's muscular body twisted around a single sheet.

"It's almost eight, dude, wake the hell up."

The pillow slowly lifted. Rand peered up at Nolan's scowl and laughed. "Oh my God. Are you the ghost of brain cells past?"

Nolan grimaced at the surrounding devastation. "What a disgrace. Nice work with the TV, by the way. I can't believe it's even lasted this long."

"It's a tough one, all right." Rand coughed like someone who had spent the previous evening drinking and smoking. "Did you bring any coffee?"

"Oh, I sure did. It's outside in the truck with the Playboy Playmate who's also holding a plate of scrambled eggs and home fries between her tits."

"Does she have any weed? Cause it feels like my freaking head's ready to explode."

"Good." Nolan kicked him again. "Let's go, man, Thomas is gonna be waiting."

"So?"

"So get the fuck up, man."

Rand chuckled, and when he coughed again, a shifting in coverage occurred.

"Oh no." Nolan held up a hand to block his view. "Dude, are you naked?"

Rand cackled loudly as Nolan turned for the door and said, "Hurry up, Fabio, because we're already late enough."

"Oh, yes sir." Rand stood, dangerously askance. He scavenged through the mess until locating his long johns and jeans below the same pair of turtlenecks worn all week. When the temperature barely broke ten degrees, six days in the same outer garments meant he could do laundry twice a month. Lacing up his inch-tread logger boots, Rand scrubbed a hand through his curly blond hair and slipped on a black knit cap. There was a crumpled pile of money on top of a two-inch stack of twenties. He pocketed the pile and hid the stack in a dirty sock. He grabbed tomato juice and a lemon from the fridge before killing the lights.

They took a left out of the motel. CR 61 doubled as Main Street before stretching out a hundred miles in either direction. Heading northwest meant a flat sprint ninety miles to the Utah border, with Salt Lake City another two hours beyond that. Choosing south meant climbing the western edge of Mt. Lassiter and six miles of switchbacks and straight-aways pirouetting 12,000 feet up to Forked Head Pass. Then, after descending through a nasty thirty-mile stretch of nearly uninhabited land, it took another hour to reach Interstate 70. Denver was still another ninety miles from there, so total drive time to the capital city in good conditions with no stops was three and a half hours.

But in the dead of winter, through fifty feet of snow and temperatures that rarely broke zero degrees, negotiating Forked Head Pass was never taken for granted. Remarkably, even after seventy years of vehicular trauma, there was still no center divider between the lanes. Infamous for icy conditions that ran from October until May, and in a place where snow in July was not unheard of, accidents were usually spectacular head-on collisions caused by downhill traffic skidding into the uphill lane. Or crashing into the side of the mountain. Or spinning completely off the mountain altogether. Depending on the severity of the season, the last two miles leading to and from the pass could claim as many as twenty lives per year. The local towing companies had captured all aspects of this automotive rodeo in gruesome snapshots tacked to their walls. There was the VW Beetle that had launched from the road and gotten wedged into a pine tree eighty feet in the air. Or the gas tanker that jackknifed and burst, spilling ten thousand gallons of flaming jet fuel into the Northfork National Forest.

Despite the carnage, nothing seemed to impede Spring Valley's growth. It was projected to double within the next five years. Riding atop this booming economy, land prices continued soaring as the big money investors salivated at the year-round tourist potential. Because once the winter melted into the mess of spring's Mudseason, world-class kayakers, mountain bikers, and professional road cyclists burst outdoors to lay siege upon the summer. After fighting through a six-month winter, the eighty-degree days and cloudless blue skies were a hard-earned, intoxicating reward.

Wherever one glanced, the whole town now seemed under construction. South on CR 61, they passed a large commercial job where Big Valley Ironworks had thirty workers erecting a supermarket. On the right, Shelby's crew was framing a gasoline/convenience store. And closer to the ski base, at a half-built thirty-floor Sheraton Hotel and conference center, two Paulsen cranes reached hundreds of feet into the sky. It made Nolan sick that he had not declared his independence sooner. Now, the shameful stupidity of having busted his ass for Mike Conyers was nearly unbearable. He took a left by the post office and, at the next stop sign, glanced at Randall Holmscomb.

"Hey."

"Yeah?"

"I was serious last night. It's over for Mike."

"Yeah?" Rand sunk his teeth into the lemon and scraped out the meat before chucking the rind out the window. He popped two Tylenols and finished off the tomato juice. "Good."

"We pound this motherfucker out and come Monday we make a grab for our own slice. You know how we thought this boom wasn't gonna last?"

"Yeah."

"We were wrong."

"Awesome." Rand lit a Marlboro and began coughing like a jackhammer. "At least we're consistent."

"Listen, don't ever do that again."

"Do what?"

"Bite into a lemon in front of me. Who does that? Your taste buds must be as dead as your soul."

They crested a bend leading to Mt. Lassiter and the sunlight abruptly ricocheted off the icy morning dawn. Pulling down their visors and sunglasses, they grimaced at the rapidly approaching jobsite. They both considered it to be the ugliest, most unimaginative project they had so far undertaken in their seven-year acquaintance.

"Six fucking months," Nolan groaned as he wheeled them in. "Somebody shoot me in the head."

"No kidding." Rand cocked back the seat, enjoying the last of his smoke before what lay ahead ruined the rest of the day. "Eight lame-ass boxes stacked on a hillside."

"Shithole." Nolan threw it into park next to Elias' Skylark. "If I ever get us involved in another project like this ..."

"Don't worry, bro. It'll be a murder/suicide."

"Thank you."

They soaked up a few more minutes of heat as the diesel loudly idled.

"Where is he?" Rand squinted into the empty Skylark.

"He ain't in there?"

"Nope."

"Huh." Nolan glanced at the temperature gauge on the rearview mirror. "We just lost a degree."

"Oh yeah?"

"We're now down to three."

"You trying to cheer me up?" Rand pointed. "There he is. Looks like he's scrapping out."

They watched Elias round the corner with an armload of cut-offs and scrap wood. The clock read 7:58 A.M.

"I'll be damned." Nolan killed the engine. "You think this kid's bucking for promotion or what?"

"Yeah, he can be Vice-President of Carrying Wood."

Nolan burst out laughing. "What does that make you?"

"Secretary of Pain." Rand rubbed his aching head and then pulled on a pair of gloves. "Here we go again."

Once they stepped outside, their feet cracked the glass of the crystallized surface.

———————

It took three of them working in total concert to raise the last truss on the last house two hours later. Once it was leaned against the wall, Nolan and Rand went back upstairs. From the top-plate, they hauled it up hand over hand in a ridiculous maneuver so fraught with catastrophe Elias wondered how they had survived this long.

Nolan peeked down from the top of the wall and said to Elias, "Guess what?"

"What?"

Nolan held the giant triangle as Rand toe-nailed the truss into the wall. Nolan told him, "All we have left is to sub-fascia and sheet the entire roof."

Elias squinted up through the sun and said, "Then we're outta here for good?"

"No." Nolan stuck a Marlboro Light into his grin. "Then we can go home for the day."

Bent at the waist, still intoxicated as he cat-walked the top-plate, Rand cackled and said, "Dear God ..."

"Like that?" Nolan laughed at the sheer horror of it. "Ain't that some of the sickest shit you've ever heard?"

"Hey." Elias snapped his gum. "What's next?"

"We're gonna brace this gable end and then sheet the roof." Nolan repelled his nailgun to the floor by its hose. "Start hauling over the ⅝-inch plywood."

"Yep." Elias set off for the 4'x8' sheets.

Because of his size, Nolan carefully climbed down to the floor. Rand, however, stepped off the truss, snagged its bottom cord on the way by like a gymnast, dangled, and then dropped to the deck with a bang.

"Fucking Fabio." Nolan tore into a box of 8's. As he and Rand cleared the 16's from the nailguns and reloaded, they shared a look of exhilaration since the end was finally near.

Rand dug out a pack of smokes. "What time you got?"

"Little after ten."

"We got some great momentum going, man, good thing we scaffed up yesterday."

They had nailed 2x6 arms out of every second-floor window. These held planks that ran the length of the house twenty feet in the air. Rand grabbed a saw and said, "I'll get a line snapped. Then you can feed me sheets."

"That'll work. I'll help Thomas hump that shit until you're ready."

On the scaffold, Rand butted his tape against the wall and marked 22½ inches on the first and last truss. He snapped a chalkline, used a two-foot level to plumb down each mark, and then cut every truss.

Down below, out near the parking lot, Elias watched in horror as Nolan shouldered two sheets before setting off for the house. Two sheets. Now challenged, Elias hoisted a pair while trying not to kill himself along the icy trench.

Fifteen minutes later Nolan poked his head out a window and asked Rand, "What do you need?"

"A 2x4 at 115⅜, and a 2x6, 172½."

"Yep."

"Hey."

"Yeah?"

Crouched on the plank, Rand punched his hands together and said, "It's pretty fucking cold, man."

"Ya think?" Nolan peeled frozen mucus from his own nose. "So what?"

"So how's he doing?"

"Who? Thomas?" Nolan scanned the yard until he saw their laborer. "Thomas!"

"What?"

"There's a blizzard coming and the temperature's gonna bottom out at minus ten degrees!"

"Oh yeah?" Elias heaved another pair of sheets against the growing stack propped against the corner of the house. "Guess we better hurry the fuck up then, right?"

"Thatta girl." Nolan winked at Rand. "You were right. He likes the misery. Hell, I might even buy you morons lunch. Now keep moving, old man, and stop trying to hide your gaping vagina behind the new guy."

"Fucker." Rand scowled and picked up the nailgun. Seconds later, the cold from the freezing metal seeped through his gloves.

———

They broke for lunch at noon, and as Elias headed for his Skylark, Nolan said, "Thomas."

"Yeah?"

"What're you doing for grub?"

"Sandwich and chips. I was gonna crank the heat in my rig and smoke a bone."

"Sounds nutritious. Bring the bone for you and your sister and hop in. We got an errand to run."

Ten minutes later they pulled into a hardware store. Sitting in the blasting heat, all three looked outside forlornly.

"All right, ladies." Nolan threw it into park. "It ain't gonna get any warmer out there."

"What the fuck are we doing here?" Rand asked.

"You'll see. Grab your purse and follow me."

Inside, a clerk was reading a book in the service department until Nolan said, "Here to pick up for Harris."

The clerk was aggravated at being disturbed, until he then looked up and saw the three humorless expressions staring back. Or it might have been the mere presence of Nolan, whose manic impatience now cascaded across what might have been a high school kid at best.

"Um ..." The clerk jerked closed his book. "There were three of them, right?"

"You got it."

After Rand threw him another look of annoyance, Nolan said, "Easy, sweet-meat. You'll see."

The clerk returned with three brown Carhartt jackets. He held one up and asked, "Look okay?"

"You did a nice job with the lettering."

On the back was stenciled HARRIS FRAMING. Below that was a hatchet and ladder-crossed logo above the next line, which read, SPRING VALLEY, COLORADO, alongside Nolan's phone number.

"Well." Nolan proudly held up the jacket and looked at Rand. "What do you think?"

"Um ..." Rand cracked a smirk. "Didn't you forget a name?"

"You're the silent partner." Nolan turned to Elias. "You get one too, but that means you're not allowed to leave."

"Am I missing something?" Elias looked from one boss to the other. "Don't I already work for you?"

"Yes. But now we work for ourselves. We're gonna incorporate this bitch."

"Sweet."

Nolan took the jackets, thanked the clerk, and headed for the register. As they walked out, Nolan tossed a jacket to Elias. "It is what it is, right? You're not going anywhere now."

"Oh yeah? I'm officially on the team?"

"Yes. So now it's time to call a company meeting."

"The Lodge has breakfast specials on Saturday—"

"No, Rand, sit down lunches are for the spoiled, privileged upper classes. Instead, we will partake in three bags of grease from the local McShits and, while we're there, you two girls can model your nice new jackets."

Rand rolled his blue eyes onto Elias and said, "I think the joint sounds more appetizing."

"No back talk." Nolan opened the driver side door. "Gentlemen, on behalf of this solemn occasion, shall we super-size our grease?"

"Oh God."

"Wow." Elias pulled on his jacket. "A fat joint, a new jacket, and a bag of puke from McFist's ... boy, that's almost enough to keep a guy from killing himself."

"There will be no suicides unless you're off the clock." Nolan fired up the F-250. "Hurry up."

"Hurry up," Rand and Elias replied in unison.

———————

The only thing worse than hauling over forty sheets of plywood was then having to shove them up to where Nolan waited on the landing. Over the past week, growing accustomed to their grueling pace on the fly, every inch of Elias' body buzzed in pain. Entire muscle groups were forced to mend while absorbing even more abuse.

Motivated by the paralyzing cold, combined with the looming Monday deadline, the three of them fed off each other's sheer perseverance and will. Rand carefully set his feet on the freshly laid roof sheeting he had just nailed down. He pulled the plywood up from Nolan, slapped it down, and nailed it off in a hail of flying steel. However, after two more rows, Nolan could no longer reach, so Elias balanced in the trusses to serve as go-between. It went fast, an hour per side, and the last sheet was being cut just as a Conyers Construction truck pulled to a stop out front.

On the roof, Rand reloaded his nailgun while he waited for a fresh sheet. "Hey, Thomas."

"Yeah?" In the trusses, Elias looked up at Rand through the last spot of roof that remained unsheeted.

Rand said, "Tell Nolan ass-face is here."

Elias waited for the screeching saw to stop before he called down, "Hey, Rand says ass-face is here."

"Jesus, which one?" Nolan handed the cut sheet up to Elias. He walked to the window, took one look, and winced. "Thomas, come on down. Once Fabio's done up there, we're gonna fascia this bitch." Nolan's cellphone read 2:20 P.M. He did the math and knew it would be close. With the fascia on, tomorrow they would nail in the soffit boards, which covered the two-foot overhang between the house and fascia. The end was drawing near. He said to Elias, "The fascia boards are downstairs. They're 1x8 finished cedar and already primed for painting, so don't wreck them." Nolan stuck a Marlboro Light between cracked lips. "I'm also gonna need the finish gun and half-a-dozen racks of Brad nails."

"I have no idea what any of that means."

Nolan held his hands a foot apart. "The finish gun is about this big and in a gray Porter Cable case. The nails are thin and two inches long. They're like slender needles for finish work."

"Yep." Elias stepped to the edge of the loft, grabbed a wall stud with his left hand, jammed the left boot around the same stud, and then grabbed the next stud over with his right. Still a new move he had stolen from Rand, Elias's feet were not wedged hard enough to control his descent. He slid down both studs and hit the bottom-plate just as Mike Conyers trudged in.

"Wall-sliding's a great way to drive a splinter straight through your hand." Conyers stomped his boots into the gravel. He smashed an over-sized pair of mittens together and twitched his handle bar mustache. "You fellas are really tearing it up on a Saturday, God bless ya."

"Nolan's upstairs." Elias stepped past on his errand.

Conyers' expression read as if it pained him to be the first to cave, so he scanned the loft above. "Nolan! Where you at?"

A saw exploded the silence. From the scaffold, Rand hopped in through the window, tossed Conyers a nod, and then likewise disappeared into the rear of the loft.

After the saw stopped, Conyers backed against the wall, straining for a glimpse upstairs. "Nolan?"

"Yeah." He finally appeared, the sunglasses propped onto his forehead. "What's up?"

Conyers mustered an unctuous grin. "Cold one today, ain't it?"

Nolan puffed on the cigarette, silent.

"Came by to drop off your check," Conyers said. "Mine cleared last night."

"That's nice."

"I've also got the prints for the DeSoto job. Thought maybe you could be ready by midweek."

"Oh yeah?" Nolan ground ice with his boot. "I don't think that's gonna be possible, Mike."

"If it's about the rate, I want you to know I've found a new flexibility on the price."

"Really? You mean the five dollar per square foot slave days are over?"

"Well, of course everything's negotiable—"

"It sure is, Mike. It surely is."

"That what the jackets are for?" Conyers' expression assumed a new glint. "Formalizing the declaration of independence?"

"I know you're getting old, Mike, but I didn't realize your memory was going too."

"Why should it? How many times over the last year and a half have you fellas quit and then changed your minds?"

"Not this time."

"Eight bucks a square foot."

"Not good enough."

"What?"

"To be treated like *this*?" Nolan swung an arm across their surroundings. "To work on this god-awful shit fuck of a development for six months, hand-loading from the parking lot since you were too cheap to level and fill before winter, meeting every single deadline, and then having to chase you down on a Friday for our pay?"

"That's—"

"Are you part of the real world or what?"

"It was an aberration."

"You're getting sloppy, Mike. Aberrations don't last two fucking months, man, fuck that."

"You know what? The worst part is that you guys really know your shit." Conyers shook his head like a dismayed parent. "But your jobsite reputation ain't exactly something to brag about."

"What the fuck does that mean?"

"That before I took both of you on, and kept you fed with work, and put up with your insane mood swings, tempers, and horrible treatment of the other subs, there wasn't a single G.C. left in this valley who would even take your calls."

"Times change."

"Oh really?" Conyers ruefully smiled. "Abandoning me, I can assure you, will not go unnoticed."

Nolan crossed his arms. "After the next job, once we blow the doors off for someone who actually gives a fuck, they'll be calling *me*."

"Not if I have anything to say about it."

Nolan paused, flicking the cigarette butt through the window. "Is there anything else, Mike, or are you unwisely going to threaten me again?"

"I'll leave the check in your truck." Conyers paused, unable to muster an appropriate rebuttal. "Well, good luck to you then." He stomped out the door.

Rand watched from the window until Conyers deposited the check into Nolan's truck. "Fuck that deadbeat."

"I really wanted to beat him."

"Me too."

Nolan lit another cigarette, joining Rand by the window. "We just dropped a match ..."

"Burn, baby, burn." Rand smiled warmly. "Now it's gonna get interesting."

"It sure is. We've either just doubled our incomes or fucked ourselves for good."

CHAPTER FIVE

Years earlier, Rand met and fell for a redhead named Lena Marie. Originally from Union, Tennessee, Lena grew up with three older brothers who quickly taught her that competition equaled survival. She was twice crowned state champion in the 400 meters, found a kayak, and then became an instant white-water junkie. She earned a scholarship to Yale and anchored the women's eight rowing team. After twice failing to make the Olympics, she won silver at the 1987 Pan Am games in Indianapolis before going on a three-day bender that ended at dawn in the Market East District. She came back to New Haven well-tanned and packed what was left at her off-campus apartment. To her parents' chagrin, her sociology degree returned home in a box simply labeled, in the top right corner, "Stuff." Her parents, however, framed it and drove a nail into her bedroom wall in case she ever came back to use it.

She set off for Arizona and tended bar in Phoenix, Flagstaff, and tiny Jerome. She apprenticed with a glazier in Missoula, Montana, and guided white-water trips down the Snake River in Idaho. She spent two seasons as a ski instructor in Mammoth, California, before training at the National Park Services' School for Forest Rangers at Yosemite National Park. The men, like the towns she lived in, came and went until that fateful day at Soccorro National Park. Having donned the ranger's cap, she was dragging a dour tour of unconditioned East Coast tourists through the patented New Mexican mix of desert and mountains. As they paused for water, a man suddenly swung over the ridge and descended the rock-strewn slope in a rapid sideways gait. On his back must have been eighty pounds of gear because she recognized the long steel pry bars, pickaxe, and coal chisels the serious diggers carried. She also noticed, holstered on each hip, two small pistols that immediately prompted her to say, "Excuse me, sir?"

She could tell he wanted no part of her because he merely waved and called out hello before he somehow, beneath all of that weight, jumped to the trail below.

"Could you hold up, sir?" she actually ordered instead of asked.

As he turned, she got a full broadcast of muscle groups, the veins like tubes bored through stone.

She could feel the dozen tourists watching this interdiction between swigs of water and labored breathing. Another story for them to tell. His blue eyes, behind the curly blond hair, never left her face.

She slowly approached. "Do you have a permit for those?"

"It's in my wallet." He shrugged off the massive pack. It hit the ground with a dusty thud. Because of the pistols, she watched his hands until he produced the necessary documentation.

"This is only a state ID." She looked up. "Did you stop in at reception to register them?"

"Yes, ma'am." He bent back over, poking through cans of food and crumpled maps and something stinking like rotted cheese.

She examined the next paper he proffered while asking, "Why are you carrying sidearms?"

"I'm usually off-map."

"So?"

"Well, I've been up there digging before."

"Cypress Peak?"

"And Cottler Valley." He nodded to the northeast. "Got lucky the last time because I heard it rattling at the last second, coiling up near my boot."

"A Mojave?"

"No." His eyes went wide. "No, no, no. Thank God. But it was a big old Western rattler, though."

"Is that why the holsters are open-ended?" she asked, now more curious than alarmed.

"Yep. They swivel, too, so I don't even have to waste time pulling them out."

"Lucky you haven't blown off a foot, though, huh?"

"Lucky or just good, I haven't yet decided."

She examined the permit again but everything seemed in order. It was completely filled out and stamped, and the state ID had not expired. "Well," she said, "I guess you're on your way."

He shouldered into the pack and centered the weight in a series of shrugs. Looking at the tourists, he offered her a sympathetic grin. "Looks like you got your hands full today."

"Tell me about it." She turned toward their curious, haggard expressions. "Okay people, it's only six more miles, so let's get moving."

As they collectively groaned, she watched Rand Holmscomb continue his descent after he dropped off the other side of the trail.

Since there were only three bars in town, it was no coincidence that they crossed paths again that night. Along Route 21, outside the National Park entrance, a string of quaint motels had names like The Sleepy Eye Inn and The Last Light Out. Curio shops stuffed with tourist paraphernalia stood darkened as the bars, located within a block of each other, played nursemaid to a restless citizenry. It was Friday night, so the locals eyed the tourists and seasonal workers like gargoyles from their stools.

The Sunday Lady was crowded but manageable. Lena arrived early to meet a friend and found a seat at the bar as the opening riff to "Can't You Hear Me Knocking" poured from the speakers. She ordered a margarita and checked her outfit. It was modest but, with the short-cut skirt and simple white T-shirt, more than suggestion enough. Come October, after her rotation up to Grand Teton, Wyoming, it would already be time for jeans and flannel shirts.

She sipped her drink and started a slow scan while nodding at a few familiar faces. It did not take long to recognize Rand, seated as he was against the wall at the far end of the bar. He stared at a television, motionless, the smoke from his cigarette corkscrewing up to the ceiling.

She replayed their introduction and wondered what he had been up there digging for. Besides fossils, there were stones and gems in select areas of the park, but not readily accessible. She thought of that monstrous pack he had been carrying, plus the foodstuffs and ripeness of his odor, and decided he could have been up there for days.

Currently, his gaze did not wander. He was still as stone and seemingly locked into his chunk of space. She was halfway through her margarita when Florencia Macazaga appeared. A medic at the ranger station, Flo hailed from Sacramento, California. She was an undersized dervish in a tiny dress draped across her toned body. Her long black hair and beaming smile always made her entrance a grand event.

Flo came over and cocked a hand on her hip. "It better get a whole lot more interesting than this."

"Or what?" Lena challenged. "I guess we could always go line-dancing at the VFW."

"God help us." Flo grabbed the stool beside her. "*Dios mio*. My rotation to Yosemite can't happen soon enough."

Their drinks emptied and got refilled. The music grew louder through the night. Lena checked in on Rand a couple of times, but at the end of the bar, he remained stoically unapproachable. So she danced with Flo, which caused a crowd of would-be suitors to clumsily appear.

Once the crowd thinned out after midnight, and Flo was drunkenly holding court at a booth near the window, Lena found her chance. As she left the restroom, the stool next to his was empty, so she boldly zeroed in. She tapped her beer toward the bartender before glancing at Rand. "Not much of a dancer, are you?"

"I got weak ankles."

"Must be hell then, lugging all that equipment around." She paid the bartender. "What do you dig for?"

He sipped his pint, refocusing on the cigarette. "Crystals." He ground out the butt. "Smokies, mostly."

"Really?"

"Yep." He blinked, seemingly self-conscious. "I like ... well, I guess it just relaxes me."

"You don't dig full time?"

"God, no. With digging, relaxation and exhaustion go hand in hand."

"So what do you do?"

"I'm in construction." He retreated toward the safety of his beer. "Carpentry mostly."

"Local?"

"Nope." He gave her a businesslike glance, as if gauging the sincerity of late-night small talk from an overly curious park ranger. "I live in Colorado."

"Huh." She started peeling her beer label, now regretting even coming over.

"What about you?" He lit another cigarette. "With that accent, I know you ain't a local."

"Tennessee." She scanned the bar, suddenly bored. "Yep, been lots of different places."

"Me too. Boy, ain't that the truth."

"Well, it's been nice talking—"

"Whoa, wait a second. I know I'm not Tom Cruise, but at least stay for a single beer."

She cocked her head, unimpressed by the offer. He stuck out a calloused hand and said, "I'm Rand. Randall Holmscomb."

"I know." Curious, she examined the gnarled claw clasping her hand. "I saw your ID, remember?"

"Oh yeah."

"I'm Lena."

"Here's to it." He raised his glass and she clinked it with her longneck. He said, "I've been here since last Thursday, and I got one more week left."

"For what?"

"Well, I've got a dealer friend in Albuquerque who pays real well. Doesn't even matter what kind of stone, either. Clear crystal, smoky crystal, turquoise—he'll buy anything."

"Does he pay for your expenses?"

"It ain't that serious." Rand killed the cigarette. "But we'll see. If I keep coming in like I have the past six months, he might just put me on retainer. Doesn't matter either way because I keep the best stuff for myself."

"It must be quite a collection."

"Crystals are my favorite. When the tips are perfect, meaning all five sides taper into a pointed cone, you can get almost five times more than if it's broken, cracked, or chipped. And if both ends are plum perfect, well, that's even rarer. Forget about the price. Money, with something that beautiful ..." He reached into his jacket and pulled out a chunk.

"I found a pocket two days ago with some sweet, deep-toned purple. Check it out."

She took the three-inch piece. The color and shape reminded her of a hexagon-shaped candy.

He said, "Hold it up to the light."

In the fluorescent light above the bar, she peeked and blinked, stunned. "Wow. What's that black stuff?" She squinted as she rolled it over. "I mean it looks like a wave through the entire crystal."

"Could be charcoal or some other impurity. I might've pulled ten thousand pounds of crystal in my life, and can't remember ever seeing the same thing twice. Color, designs, those little imperfections actually end up making the piece even more unique ..."

Lena spun it one more time before trying to hand it back, but he said, "Keep it."

"Is it worth anything?"

"You might get twenty bucks for it."

"It's beautiful, thank you." She slid it into her purse. "How long have you been doing this?"

"Oh, man, since I was a kid. My mom, she used to spend weeks in the mountains. Wyoming, Utah, Arizona, even here ... my brothers and sisters would come and go but I ... I really loved it, just following along behind her as she named every weed, flower, tree, bush ... tracing along the ground for clues, like changes in vegetation or soil, until she would finally say, 'This is it.' And then we'd just start digging."

"She must have been a very fit woman."

"You got that right. Mom was no joke."

After the bartender arrived with their refills, she went for her purse but Rand drew first. Holding out a twenty, he said, "I'm also gonna have a shot."

"Another whiskey?" the bartender asked.

"Yeah." He looked at Lena. "Game?"

"Absolutely." She felt sure she meant it. "So mom passed it on to you?"

"Pretty much. Crystals were one thing, but everything else ... she just knew so much about the outdoors. We must have walked out of our yard and into the forest a thousand times, but something different always caught her eye. Our property bordered Teton, so growing up I got personally toured through just about every square foot of that place. Why are you shaking your head?"

"It's just funny ... Teton's my next assignment."

"Well, hell. You're just about the luckiest person I've met today."

"What about your dad? Was he an outdoorsman as well?"

"Yeah, but going out with pops was way different."

"How so?"

"He was a hunter. A good one, too. For a couple of seasons he hired out as a guide, mainly for middle-aged fat guys from the Midwest or East Coast. I mean most of them were too drunk or stupid to shoot anything other than each other, which happens more frequently than you might think. Finally got so bad, Pop just said fuck it. The money was good but he got sick of killing the animals and then handing them over to these morons, you know? The ritual of it ... It became disrespectful. He felt like he was perverting the odds."

Lena watched the shots arrive and immediately questioned her earlier decision. He, though, raised his glass. "Thanks for coming over."

"Well, I sure wasn't gonna wait on you." She tossed it back, trying not to gag. "Wow. Well done, cowboy."

"Bars are where I do some of my best work."

She laughed and it seemed easy, or it could have been all the beer.

"What about you?" he asked. "How long you been a ranger?"

"A decade off and on. My problem is that I just absolutely love being outside."

"Only place I ever felt comfortable."

"Yes." She pointed at the cigarettes. "Mind? Don't usually smoke, but that whiskey ..."

"Say no more." He shelled two out.

As she leaned in for the flame, she could feel his close-quarter observation as he asked, "So what else have you been?"

"Let's see." She gave him the list and locations like a resume. After her last job—organizing rodeos for the Laramie branch of the National Rodeo Association—she folded her hands and said, "That's it. I quit Laramie a year ago and signed back up to ranger, and besides a six-month stint at Badlands National Park, I've been here ever since."

"I love that place."

"Isn't it something? And Black Hills and Buffalo Gap ..."

"Yeah." He shoved the ashtray between them. "Fucking South Dakota, man."

"It can't be shaken off."

"Nope. So you were a Tennessee high school girl and then what?"

"College. I was a rower for Yale."

"Really? Some of the best-conditioned athletes on the planet."

"Yup ..." She found nothing else to add. "You're right."

"Were you good?"

"That depends. Of my three years as a starter on the women's eight, we won nationals twice. Trounced Harvard both times, which felt *really* good. But I had two tryouts for the Olympic team and didn't make it."

"Why not?"

"I just didn't. The first one was nerves. I got so riled up I was blown out three-quarters of the way through." She motioned for two more shots. "And the second, well, I wrecked my bike in training, second-degree shoulder separation, and three weeks later I injured it even worse at tryouts. I finished, though. Tore the capsule to shreds but I kept my pace. That whole boat though ..." She grimaced. "Politics fucked that boat up from the beginning."

"Politics fuck up everything."

"You would have made a horrible philosopher."

The bartender arrived with their shots. She hoisted hers and said, "Thanks for being a good sport."

They chain-smoked through their histories as the night moved on, the crowd thinned out, and Flo's drunken laugh screeched through the bar. Rand did a lot more talking than normal, and by one o'clock, after last call was announced, they pounded a final shot.

Flo stumbled over with two men more inebriated than herself, then the threesome babbled incoherently. It was obvious the guys thought at least one of them might still have a shot, but Flo was turning mean. She cracked jokes about their appearance and pathetic seductions until they finally got the message and filed out the door. Rand thought it might be his turn next, but Lena stated, "We need to get her out of here."

"You got that right."

Flo was all over the bartender, but he was too busy closing to even glance her way.

Lena said, "I should get her home. Give us a lift? I'll put her to bed and then we can hang out."

"Where does she live?"

"We'll go to my place. It's only a mile away. Believe me, once she's crashed, she's done til morning."

They drained their drinks as Flo drunkenly approached. Her long black hair had been run through by the night. She asked Lena in a straight slur, "Is that who you're taking home tonight?" She squinted at Rand. "He's cute."

"Flo—"

"He's real cute, but the cute ones always turn out to be stupid." She gave him a curious expression. "Are you stupid?"

"I don't like to think so."

"I'm sorry." Lena frowned. "Flo, no more talking."

"Says who? You ain't my master."

Rand was already headed for the door.

CHAPTER SIX

THE GILDMAN SCHOOL BUILD
February, 1998

Nolan met Elias in a supermarket parking lot at 7:00 A.M. Monday morning. Elias was right on time. As Nolan pulled up puffing on his fifth cigarette of the morning, he was, as usual, balancing the steering wheel, a half-gallon jug of coffee, and a cellphone as he parked next to the Skylark.

Elias climbed into the passenger seat.

"Hey, Ted," Nolan said into the phone, pinching it with a shoulder to free up a hand as he turned onto CR 61. "Hope I didn't wake ya."

Nolan shoved the coffee-jug at Elias and said, "Yeah, well, like I was saying yesterday, my calendar's wide open ... No, Conyers didn't say much of anything. You know how it is, after a while, one party might start to take advantage and that's just not gonna work for me ..." Nolan laughed at the response. "Right? Call me crazy, Ted, but life's a whole lot simpler than that ... I hear ya. Let the reunion begin. You were one of the best bosses I ever had, man, straight up ... Oh God, how many years ago was that? We're old now, Ted, I can't hate like that anymore." There was another round of laughter until an offer was apparently tendered, because Nolan said, "Of course. Hell, we can start today. Two week draws on a ten percent down payment and we'll be rolled out by noon ... Not a problem ... Hit me up, I'll have it on me all day."

He flipped the phone closed and puffed on his neglected smoke. The glare off the ice made both of them squint behind their sunglasses. The temperature gauge on the rearview mirror read six degrees.

Elias asked, "So where's Rand?"

"Drunk." Nolan tossed the butt and quickly closed the window. "We're grabbing all the shit, getting something to eat, and then waiting for this moron to call me back."

"That the next gig?"

"*Gig*?" Nolan frowned, swiping back his coffee. "Seems more like a show to me."

Elias smiled. "What kind of show?"

"The kind that has idiotic, lazy-ass, ex-con drunks for workers, architects who draw pretty pictures but have never built a single fucking thing in their entire lives, and whose blueprints I don't get paid nearly enough to fix, not to mention the fat-cat owners who come strolling through like fat, slimy, bloated sows ..."

"Jesus, that sounds awful."

"It surely is,"

"Welcome to the fuckshow."

"Ha-ha! Fuckshow! That, it surely is." He drove up Silver Mine Road until their old jobsite swung into view. "Look at this disgrace." He nodded at the eight boxes with simple twelve-pitch roofs. "Butcher Block. That's the new name for this weak-ass development."

"Butcher what?"

"A butcher. A wood butcher. Only a fucking hack would take on this shit-fuck assignment."

The Ford crunched through the opening in the three-foot berm created by the plow. Of the two trucks parked amid the drifts, Felding Electricians was painted on one and Conyers Construction adorned the other.

"Speaking of fuckshows ..." Nolan threw it into park and tossed Elias the keys. "Start burning those locks. The yellow Master opens both boxes."

Elias set off for the tool chests. Nolan dialed up Kara and made small talk until Mike Conyers' Stetson rounded a doorway. The rest of him appeared as he tripped coming up the same slippery path Nolan had been forced to trudge up and down for the last six months. Since Conyers had left the jobsite an unprepared mess of boulders, tree stumps, and frozen mud, Nolan had also had to carry every single board down it as well. Actually, there had been a long line of laborers paid for just that task, but their resolve usually collapsed somewhere between the hellish pace and relentless verbal abuse.

Still on the phone as he clandestinely watched Conyers approach, Nolan tried gauging the upcoming encounter. It could go smooth and easy between two adult men or, more likely, dissolve into a bitch-fest over money. Either way, with their business relationship finished, Nolan only wanted his last draw for $8,000 and the remaining ten percent con-tractually held as retainer until completion. But the fact that Conyers was about to nickel-and-dime him with the usual small talk and procras-tination, forced Nolan's lips into a tight and readied line.

"Honey, I got to go. Mike's on the way up ... I do so have self-control! ... Love you too. Talk to you later."

He snapped the phone closed and fished his pockets for a smoke. Lighting up, he stomped his size sixteens to thaw his freezing legs.

"Saw the rest of number five," Conyers said, and threw a nod at the last house. "Boy, that gable fascia came out sweet."

"That's good to know. It was getting dark when we finished."

Conyers came to a stop a few feet away and they both awkwardly surveyed the house.

"Carries a nice line, don't ya think?"

"Yup." Nolan knocked one boot against the other, dying to escape. "I got my guy Thomas out there at the locks, so after we load up, that should be about it."

"I was meaning to talk to you about that." Conyers' handlebar mus-tache twitched against the breeze.

It was then that Nolan finally saw it, understood what had been nag-ging him about the other man's entire manner for the length of their acquaintance. Conyers was originally from Atlanta, had come from old money that made new money in the construction business and, after making quite enough of it, set off for the great wide West. To his credit, Conyers knew how to frame and was a decent builder, but after arriving in Spring Valley, he settled into a gentleman's position of buying land and lining up owners. To fit more perfectly into this new entrepreneur-ial role, he grew the mustache and bought the denim, even creating an affected gait in the new cowboy boots he preferred. The accent as well, though noticeably southern, had been bastardized with a Western twang. That this weak amalgamation of so many bad character traits could blend so smoothly behind this mask, and that a guy like Nolan could bust his ass for a poser who stalled and lied and slid the numbers in his favor, made Nolan crave a confrontation, if only out of therapeutic release.

Conyers said, "I really think it's in both our interests to find a way through this impasse so our partnership can continue."

"Our what?" Nolan's disinterest was made obvious by his tapered smile, which seemed dangerously close to a sneer. "Listen, Mike, like we agreed on Friday, the work would be completed today and I would get my check."

"I've got it right here. I included your bill for the nails as well."

Nolan took it, and then his nostrils flared. "What the fuck is this?"

"Excuse me? There's seven grand there—"

"First of all, we both know it's eight. Plus, five hundred more for the nails, and another ten grand on the retainer."

"Nolan ..." Conyers held out both arms. "That retainer only comes after the final inspection. You know that."

"Jesus Christ ..." Nolan ripped up the check. "Then I want a new one for eighty-five hundred. And since you insist on being such a bitch about the percentage, the inspection better happen by tomorrow latest."

"Or else?"

"Or else I'm gonna put a lien on this whole fucking place, and not one of these units will be released until I'm paid in full."

"Who said you wouldn't be paid? You got some nerve, you know that? When have I ever not paid you what I owe?"

"I'm done playing games, Mike. I want that check. Now, please."

"Unbelievable." Conyers turned for his truck.

Nolan's cellphone rang but he ignored it. He only wanted his tools packed and a full payment, and was practically counting the seconds until he could quit this place for good.

"Nolan!"

He turned and saw Elias waving from where he now had both chests open.

"Start hauling that shit over here!" Nolan shouted back and Elias held one thumb into the air.

Seven grand plus an inspection, Nolan thought, and ground out the cigarette. *Motherfucker must think I'm a moron.*

Conyers walked over with a dour expression and held out the check. "You know, your work speaks for itself, Noll, but your mouth just ruins it all."

"Get me my inspection, Mike, or else you've got forty-eight hours until you hear from my attorney."

———————

After shoveling out a small patch of ground next to the F-250, Elias and Nolan made painstaking hundred-yard round trips to and from the tool chests. There were three framing guns, two finish guns, 200 pounds of nails, three worm-drive skillsaws, two sawzalls, a compound miter DeWalt chop-box that weighed fifty pounds, a collective 500 feet of coiled hose and electrical extension cords, an air-driven impact wrench with accompanying sockets, tool boxes, two framing squares, a thirty-pound sledgehammer, three Stabila levels, two Husqvarna chainsaws, dozens of blades for the different saws, a .22 caliber Hilti gun that shot concrete pins, and an electric generator and gas-driven air compressor both frozen into the mud.

Nolan was jacked on caffeine and his own manic cycling as he turned their next thirty minutes into hell. He wished they had time to breakdown and clean the tools which, only halfway through the winter, desperately craved a wet rag and oil.

After sitting in these same spots since July, the tool chests, generator, and compressor were sealed into the ice as if welded by a torch. It took almost two hours to chip away the five-inch ice skirts surrounding each of the tool chests. At 3'x3'x5', they made for a brutal carry over the tortuously pitted landscape. Next up were the generator and compressor, and over the next hour their hatchets smashed the ice in sweat-filled curses. This level of activity made layered clothing a necessity. If the chilled air reached the moisture trapped beneath, hypothermia was a foregone conclusion.

The compressor was an old Roll-Air monster, and through the long months of continued abuse, it was covered in a splattering of oil and a permanent stench of gas. Like a wheelbarrow, it had a single wheel in front. The two horizontal air tanks resembled a scuba apparatus with a lawnmower engine mounted on top. Since wheeling it across this terrain was unthinkable, they hoisted the 200-pound beast and carefully ascended the icy trench. A hundred yards later, they deposited it into the bed of the pickup and both men walked it off, panting, trying to hide the actual toll this journey had just inflicted. Worse, the generator, all 250-pounds of it, was sitting out there waiting to be collected. Unlike the compressor, which was easily carried, the generator was a square block of ungainly engine.

Bending at the knees, Nolan asked, "Ready?"

"Yeah."

They lifted and this time it was Nolan's turn to walk uphill backwards. Progress was brutal, and by the end each was visibly squirming through the pain. Elias' hands shook on the cold steel frame, which felt as if it might slip from his grasp at any second. Nolan no longer even looked over his shoulder and instead just gambled with every step. At the last second, they reached the pickup and heaved the generator into the bed with one final gasp. Neither said a word. Two cigarettes were lit. Nolan said, "Let's get all of the shit into the boxes. Hoses, guns, and nails in one—saws, blades, and tools in the other."

Nolan jumped up into the pickup and played receiver as Elias ferried over the tools. It was nearing eleven o'clock when they finished, but because of the sun's low winter angle, the temperature stayed stuck at 8 degrees. Lathed in sweat, they stopped working and soon felt even colder.

Nolan collapsed into the Ford. Knowing that what had just been loaded would soon have to be unloaded all over again, he never gave it a second thought.

The basement foundation for the Gildman School had been poured just two weeks earlier and left to cure beneath a giant propane-heated tent. As part of a nationwide system of grants for the expansion of educational facilities for special needs children, the town of Spring Valley, as the county seat, was legally bound to have this fully accessible school operating by the start of classes in September. This meant a construction schedule that usually allotted nine months for a structure of comparable square footage would now be cut in half.

Ted Beckham, head of the Public Works Department, was serving as Project Manager for the entire build. He had to hire and schedule the excavators, the concrete contractor, carpenters, masons, roofers, electricians, plumbers, HVAC guys, drywallers, plasterers, painters, finish carpenters, tile and rug guys, and fielding any and all of their details, problems, questions and complaints. Beckham was originally a ski bum from Hartford, Connecticut. He had moved here twenty years ago to work and play with the big boys at 10,000 feet. But once the skiing ended and the Mudseason of April and May warmed into the seventy-degree high mountain summer, Beckham found himself the newest casualty of one of the town's oldest maxims—the winters might bring you here, but the summers made you stay. He spent a decade banging nails until surviving the six-month winters became too much with a wife and growing family.

As for this project, Beckham did not want to say it was cursed. But after the concrete guys hit a granite shelf, the demolition crew almost killed everyone with an overcharge. Then the company with the framing contract, New Home Builders, was torn apart when one of the lead guys drove a skillsaw through his hand and needed microsurgery to reattach three fingers. The other was re-arrested for nonpayment of child support. The owner of the company had called Beckham with this news on Friday night, just forty-eight hours before work was set to commence.

So when Nolan Harris randomly called Beckham's cellphone Saturday evening looking for work, it should have been a godsend. Considering that Beckham had spent the previous day feverishly searching for an adequate replacement, and had almost set off the warning bells of delay to an already irate boss, Nolan's call should have allowed Beckham an escape from this threatening, though not yet fully developed, disaster.

It did not.

Since no one's existence or reputation in a town this small could remain hidden, Nolan Harris was about as well-known as Al Capone. Before Beckham dropped his tool bags and moved into the office, he was once Nolan's crew boss and knew all of the stories firsthand. Like when the twenty-year-old southern Californian arrived in the valley and took a previously out of control taste for alcohol and cocaine to stratospheric extremes. Legendary, chaotic debauchery, like the night he and two friends drove a stolen police car off a switchback up near Forked Head Pass. Or the time a group of Texas Tech football players started a beef, and Nolan got blindsided by a punch before asking his assailant, "Does your husband hit as hard as you?" which then ignited a full-fledged riot.

An accomplished skier and fierce competitor, Nolan attacked the surrounding mountains and his own life with a brutal recklessness. In a place already known for its western tradition of providing safe haven to society's furthest fringe, Nolan fit right in. And since half of the town was from somewhere else, it seemed most still had a skeleton or two hanging in the crowded closets many thought they had left behind.

Nolan was no exception. He put Beckham through the ringer before quitting and heading for Las Vegas. He returned a year later with a soon to be ex-wife in tow since they were barely in love. Stacy was beautiful, and in a town where the adult male-to-female ratio was five-to-one, Nolan soon found himself beating his way through the onslaught of perverts trying to invade her pants. Sick of catching horny ski bums ogling his wife, he made Stacy quit her bartending job and things only got worse from there. He came home one Friday and saw her note saying she was out with friends, but after heading to the bar and lining up the first of fifteen rum and cokes, he inhaled an eight-ball of blow and staggered home to find their house still empty. Convinced of her treachery, he called around with threats but no one had seen her. After he showed up at the house of one of her jewelry store co-workers, a quiet but likeable guy named Eddy, Nolan committed his last mistake. Eddy, who was half Nolan's size and liked listening to The Smiths, had no clue where she was. But Nolan, already jealous of the friendship with his wife, drunkenly misconstrued reality and beat Eddy into a half-conscious rag dragged headfirst down the stairs. Nolan then returned to the house and smashed everything he could, including two of Eddy's likewise undersized roommates.

No longer protected under the banner of "boys will be boys" as cover for his shenanigans, Nolan was locked up and faced assault, battery, and mayhem charges. Once word leaked that the District Attorney was also considering felony attempted murder, it ensured this event would be a watershed for the accused.

Beckham, as Nolan's boss, fronted his bail. The assault charges landed Nolan six months in the old Salinas County Jail. Accommodations were suitable enough—cable TV and three-square meals contracted out to the Steakman Diner. But after his release, he had to complete 180 hours of community service and worked for free on a low-income apartment build during a string of weekends. He also had to pay off the medical bills and property damage wrought on that stupefying evening. His marriage, never a pillar of strength, promptly collapsed three months into his new sobriety.

Beckham was happy to hear Nolan had not touched a drop of alcohol in seven years. The blow and weed had also been jettisoned, leaving behind a stark reality with no release. Instead, fierce addictions to coffee, cigarettes, strippers, gambling, and high-speed downhill skiing had to suffice. Without the boozing and drugging, he now poured all this surplus energy into his already over the top work ethic and ground through rain, snow, and blizzards, blending into his work all of the pent-up aggression and perceived injustices the guilty always bear. He also solidified a new reputation on jobsites throughout the county. After teaming up with Rand Holmscomb, another master carpenter who had a penchant for mean streaks and chaos, a general contractor knew what to expect—mainly a professionally framed house or commercial structure in half the time it usually took others. Half. This, in a profession accustomed to expensive delays, deadbeats, and unforeseen events, was an incalculable bonus. The question was not whether Nolan Harris could frame your building—it was more a matter of surviving the project knowing that at any moment he or Rand might explode, a fact not lost on Ted Beckham, who at this point had little choice.

In his office that Monday morning, he thought of somehow manipulating the wording of the contract so as to reward the majority of money only upon completion, but knew Nolan would balk. The only other option was Pat Stills and his crew, but they were infamous slackers. Beckham could picture the eight-week frame taking four months and that was all the convincing he needed.

Reaching for the phone at a little before noon, Ted Beckham punched in Nolan's number like a gambler jonesing for a dose of luck.

"All right, here's the deal." The Ford was barely shifted into park before Nolan started issuing commands to Elias. "I'll help you get the generator and compressor out. Gas them up and run the leads from each to the left front corner of the foundation. Set me up a saw, a drill with a ¾-inch spade bit, a gun loaded with framers, and an impact wrench with a ¾-socket. Then, we'll get out the boxes and you'll load them up while I go over the plans with moron." Nolan consulted his cellphone for the hundredth time. "And he's already late, swell."

Elias popped in a stick of gum. "Sounds like fun."

"Oh, you're about to OD on fun, my friend, believe you me. And Thomas ...?"

"Yeah?"

"Don't forget to hurry up."

The Gildman school was at the end of a half-mile road that funneled into a large clearing chainsawed out of the woods. The site had been completely plowed out in anticipation of the as yet undelivered lumber.

Nolan paused a moment to visualize where everything should go. He opened his window and pointed twenty yards to the left. "That's where we're putting the job-boxes. Lumber gets stacked to the left of that." He reversed the truck, jumped out to help Elias unload, and then hastily answered his phone. Seconds later he told Elias, "That was your inebriated half-brother Fabio. After we're done, you're gonna take my truck and go pick his drunk ass up."

"Why?" Elias received an armload of saws from Nolan. "What's up with that guy? Doesn't he have a car?"

"No." Nolan shoved a stack of guns to the edge of the bed. "He doesn't even have a license."

"Jesus."

They offloaded the generator and compressor into a plowed-out hollow. It was obvious that the DPW crews had been hard at work, because the snow berms were fifteen-foot-high walls, giving the place a fortress-like demeanor.

Elias glumly nodded down the narrow road and said, "With only one way out it already feels like a prison."

"That's the spirit. I want this place to turn into your own personal hell."

"Mission accomplished." Elias grabbed more tools.

———————

Ted Beckham was anxious about the road conditions leading out to the Gildman build, so he switched the Cherokee from 4x4 High into Low for increased torque. It was almost one o'clock, and after a morning of trepidation, the sight of anyone—even Nolan Harris—hard at work out here provided a welcome relief. Nolan's tools were already rolled out even though no contract had yet been signed, and Beckham realized that no matter the history, Nolan was now Beckham's guy. Which meant Ted would play ball—would listen to the complaints when the blueprints were in error, or how the architect was a moron, or that the lumber drops were late or totally wrong. He would make sure payroll was on time and all design questions quickly answered so that Nolan would have no excuse. And if they made it through the next eight weeks, then maybe they could reminisce about the adventure they had just shared. Either way, pulling up and seeing Nolan in his Occidental tool bags standing in the middle of the plowed-out yard seemingly already pissed off that he was being held up, stretched a cautious smile across Ted Beckham's face. He grabbed his gloves and threw open the door. "Where's your truck?"

"I sent my new guy on an errand."

"Tell me how, in a town this small, I don't ever hardly see you."

"Wife keeps me on a short leash, Ted."

"Someone has to, right?" They shook hands and shared a brief hug. "How's things? I hear you and Rand been tearing it up."

"Absolutely. Just trying to ride this wave, you know? What about you? How's the kids?"

"Cindy's a senior and Teddy's a sophomore."

"Holy crap. That's incredible."

"I know. I've got some serious tuition payments coming up."

"Feels like a lifetime ago, doesn't it?"

"Me and you have been around the bend, my friend." Beckham nodded at their surroundings. "How do you like the site? I told the plow guys I wanted half a football field cleared out. Figured between the lumber drops and the semi-trucks turning around, that ought to be enough."

"Looks good." Nolan was sharpening both ends of his carpenter's pencil. "Can I see the plans?"

Beckham motioned to his truck. "I got the contract too, if you want to handle that now."

"If it includes the details we've already discussed, we can get legal after work. I'd really like a look at what you got going on before my guys return."

Beckham fished out the rolled-up prints from his Jeep. Sliding them across the hood, he said, "Wood drop was supposed to be at noon."

"What a shock. Who's handling lumber?"

"Dick at Après."

"Christ."

"They cut me the best deal. And they stock big timber."

Nolan rolled out the prints. The first page always showed a rendering of what the finished structure must resemble. Leeway was allowed in small matters of framing, but anything requiring a major design change had to pass the architect and engineer's approval.

The next page was the foundation and not his problem, but he did ask, "How'd it come out?"

"Pretty close." Beckham pointed to the far-right wall. "I think it might be a ¼-inch out, but other than that I remember Tony saying it was dead balls."

"Tony Bones." Nolan flipped ahead fifteen pages to the roof framing plan. "I remember back to when he and his old man used to go at it something awful."

"Like two wet cats in a bag. They might've hated working alongside each other, but that kid absolutely learned his shit."

"He sure did. He's almost better than his old man. Cuts the straightest line ever."

"Maybe."

Nolan glanced at the plans and scanned the skeletal structure of the roof. He saw the A-frame dormer extending off the front. "Carport?"

"Yes. Considering our winters, it's a must-have. We got kids in wheelchairs, crutches, with all kinds of disabilities. They're gonna need to get off those buses and put boots on dry ground."

"What about this beast?" Nolan tapped a sketch of the giant decorative logs comprising the exposed front of the A-frame carport. "Bust out the chainsaws."

"And twice more, too." Beckham pointed to both gable ends of the roof on the main building. "We're still waiting for spec, but figure two feet or more on the diameter for the logs."

"Wow. That's a lot of money for a non-structural decoration, right?" Nolan scanned the roof plan again, looking for bearing points. In most ways the roof dictated how the rest of the structure would be constructed. All point loads had to carry straight down through each floor and land squarely onto either the concrete walls of the foundation, or posted onto specific footers built into the basement floor. He found a dozen of them and then gradually worked his way back through the plans, floor by floor, and checked to make sure all twelve were accounted for.

"If you want to, Noll, we can call in Terry and his boys for the timber." But Beckham quickly realized by the immediate freeze in Nolan's expression that maybe this suggestion ought to be retracted. "Only if we're pressed for time of course."

Nolan fished out his Marlboro Lights. "How long were you thinking again?"

"Eight weeks." Beckham blew into his cupped hands.

Nolan lit a cigarette. No flinching. *All or nothing.* "We'll be gone in five."

"That ..." Beckham started to laugh until he saw that Nolan was not kidding, so he raised an eyebrow instead. "That would be most appreciated."

———————

Beckham left a half hour later, so Nolan got to work. He fired up the generator and, thanks to Elias, the tools were placed exactly at his feet.

At least he's not a total moron. Nolan pulled the five-sided plumb laser from its case. The size of a small hardcover book, the laser's nose shot five red dots—one from both sides, the front, top and bottom. A recent industry development, the laser was the new $600 toy that self-leveled before shooting perfect ninety-degree beams from center. It was love at first sight after Nolan saw one on a jobsite outside Vail, and he bought one the next day.

The left front corner of the foundation was designated as the control point for the entire rest of the job. From there the layout for everything—all floor joists, wall studs, and roof rafters—would emanate from this single spot. The box would grow out and up from here.

He marked 5½-inches with a crow's-foot (V) pencil mark, and then post-holed through two-feet of snow to the other side of the foundation. Cursing, he realized squaring a foundation in these conditions was not a one-man job. The tiny laser dot would be thirty feet away, and just as Nolan was about to freak out and start throwing things, he heard the clacking of his diesel engine.

"It's about time!"

Elias killed the engine. Rand Holmscomb dropped down from the cab looking bleary-eyed and wounded. He was still buttoning and gloving up as Nolan yelled, "Nice of you to join us."

"Believe me, the pleasure's all yours." Rand coughed and swayed.

"What took so long? You're getting old, Fabio."

"He was puking when I got there," Elias said, and Rand shushed him.

"Nothing like tonguing last night's dinner, huh?" Nolan cackled.

Rand pushed past toward the tool chests. "I don't want to talk about it."

"Damn right you don't."

Rand wrapped his Occidentals around his waist and cinched the leather belt until it sank into its familiar crease.

"I used to be like you," Nolan said. "Drinking like a pig, waking up to hell on earth and finding your pockets empty because you just spent a hundred bucks boozing on a Monday night."

"Yeah, well, it's not like we got the weekend off or anything."

Nolan smiled and nodded toward the plans. "If you think you're abused now, wait until you get a load of these."

Nolan unrolled the blueprints across one of the closed tool chests. He gave Rand a recap of his talk with Beckham. Rand pulled a tomato from his jacket and ate it like an apple, saying, "Should be a piece of cake. 2,000 square feet, four classrooms, a couple of closets and bathrooms, covered by a trussed roof. Eight weeks ain't a problem."

"Well ..." Nolan's right eyebrow guiltily arched. "Thing is, we only have five."

"Five what? Weeks? Who the hell said that?"

"I did."

"You *what*?" Rand pushed the sunglasses up his nose. "Now why would you go and do a thing like that?"

"Because our company's gonna need a kick-start here in the beginning. You'll see. I got it all figured out. We can bank that extra three weeks and hit our next job on the fly."

"What company? It's me and you."

"And Thomas."

"Whatever." Rand glanced at Elias. "No offense."

"None taken. I'm just the wood bitch."

Rand looked back at Nolan. "Are you trying to kill us?"

"Rand ..."

"Five weeks? Why would we do that to ourselves in the middle of freaking winter?"

"Because." Nolan corralled a growing agitation as he rolled up the plans. "I'm sick of it, you know? Just absolutely sick of it."

"What're you talking about?"

"Everything, okay? I'm sick of getting kicked in the face. Finally, this is our chance to blow the doors off this place. Make a name, get some momentum, maybe hire some more guys, and really turn this into a full-scale operation."

It might have been the lingering effects of the alcohol, or maybe Rand was truly distressed. "The only thing you and I are gonna get," he said, "is a couple of broken backs."

A tractor-trailer wailed an air horn but was not yet visible through the snowy trees.

"Thomas ..." Nolan pointed off to the right. "Land that guy over there."

"Yep."

There was an awkward pause until Rand finally shook his head, disgusted.

Nolan said, "Just roll with me on this one, okay? And then we'll make adjustments."

"Such as?"

"An extra cut at the end. For both of us if we hurry up."

"This isn't about the money."

"It could be."

"Well ..."

"See? Who said a few Benjamins can't buy love?"

"Amen."

"Let's square this bitch while Thomas plays lumber boy." Holding out the end of the chalkline, Nolan pointed across the frozen landscape. "Late guy takes the walk."

"Fuck me." Rand tried to stay dry by replicating Nolan's steps exactly. But since he was shorter, and their strides did not match, in places he sank thigh-deep.

Nolan listened to him curse, watched Elias guide the semi into place for offloading, and felt a small part of this new destiny unfolding.

Fifteen minutes later they had a 5½-inch chalkline snapped around the perimeter of the foundation.

"Thomas!"

"What?"

"Snap the bands on the pressure-treated 2x6s and start hauling that shit over."

"Huh?"

"Here." Rand pulled the hatchet from his belt and walked over to a stack of green-colored 2x6s. He swung the blade through the metal banding straps and said, "This shit is pressure-treated. It's the only wood that ever gets near concrete."

"Why?"

"It's moisture-resistant."

Elias frowned. "But why's it green?"

"From all the chemicals they pump into it."

"So it's like a pressure cooker filled with cancer and wood?"

"In essence."

"Hey!" Nolan popped his head up from where he was scanning the plans. "You two scientists done taking notes or what? It's fucking wood, man, haul that shit over."

"Spread them out around the foundation," Rand counseled. "We need enough to plate along the chalkline me and dumbass just snapped."

"And then what?"

"We'll drill out the holes—you see those bolts sticking out of the concrete?"

The ⅝-inch threaded bolts were spaced every four feet along the walls like tiny 3-inch posts.

Rand said, "We always start with a double sill plate. The pressure-treated will be drilled and laid down first. Then a second board of regular Doug fir 2x6 will be drilled and bolted on top."

Elias dragged and dropped all the wood. Rand unrolled the sill-seal, which was a moisture barrier of thin pink Styrofoam he punched over the bolts. Nolan, surveying the activity while studying the plans, gulped down the last of his thirty-two-ounce coffee. He saw that it was already two o'clock. With full dark by 4:30, and first light somewhere around seven, conditions would be tough for the ten-hour, six-day shifts he envisioned. These guys would hate him, but without those kinds of numbers, there was no chance they would make the five-week deadline.

"All right!" Nolan clapped his hands. "Game on."

Rand and Nolan cut and drilled while Elias followed behind with washers, nuts, and an impact wrench to tighten everything down. He also shoveled out the path forward and got more extension cords so they could snake around the foundation.

"Listen, girls, time for a family meeting." Nolan jammed a cigarette into his teeth. "Tomorrow we start at six-thirty instead of seven, okay?"

No one said a word.

"And we go until dark."

Again, nothing. Elias spit out a wad of phlegm.

"Figure six-day weeks until we're finished."

"Hurry up." Rand held the next 2x6 as Elias drilled the holes.

———————

Across town, the women met at a new French bistro downtown over-looking the frozen Blackstone River. The tall oaks were like sticks whose leaves winter had stolen months before. The back patio was snowed over and forgotten, abandoned till the warmth of spring.

Inside, mahogany mantels and crown molding were splashed in the fireplace light. Well-dressed people with free time on a Tuesday after-noon gathered on couches with coffee drinks and snifters.

She spotted her two friends and quickly joined them. A starched waiter approached Kara but Sarah Vaughn said, "She'll have a Bloody Mary and I'll take another."

"Just more coffee for me." Rebecca Johns was the Colorado out-reach officer for the National Ecological and Geographical Association. Originally part of the National Preservation Society, NEGA was now a strictly scientific organization whose only mission was to catalog plant life, animal patterns and migrations, endangered species, and the ecosys-tems in all fifty states.

Kara was a member of the Community Relations Committee for the local chapter of the Colorado Preservation Society. She worked closely with Sarah Vaughn, the CPS' chief legal counsel. Having risen to prom-inence as a hired gun for the oil and gas industry, Vaughn eventually switched teams in order to land her name on a Denver firm specializing in real estate law. From environmental legislation to land conservation and tax shelters, the partners of Fanning, Roberts, and Vaughn billed out at $500 an hour. Vaughn wore tailored business suits. Her open collar was a distraction of muscular definition and cleavage. Her shoul-der-length gold hair was streaked gray, her pretty features sharpened by an uncorrected nose.

"I hate to rush the party but ..." Rebecca Johns paused when the waiter delivered their drinks. Her auburn hair was cut too short to frame her face. Her only blemish, as the mother of two toddlers, was the hollow look of the permanently exhausted. "I've only got forty-five minutes. My meeting with the DSV is going to be a doozie."

"I don't mean to highlight my own ignorance," Kara said. "But what's a DSV?"

"Director of Science and Vegetation." Rebecca pulled a laptop from her briefcase. "We meet once a month updating open cases."

The CPS had been founded in 1972, but the original chapter, the Oregon Preservation Society, dated back to the early 1960s. Upset by the sale of prime coastline for development, and proposals to allow harvesting of the ancient Oregon forests, a grassroots movement toward responsible land management quickly coalesced. Momentum grew until people concerned about the direction and costs of unchecked expansion used Oregon's example to establish chapters in every state. These branches focused on local environmental and zoning laws, marketing the tax breaks that conservation easements afforded landowners, and fundraising.

Kara watched her friends juggle their laptops and Palm Pilots now that she was just a bank teller with a forfeited career.

Sarah Vaughn pegged Kara with a glance and said, "I've got nothing but bad news, so you better start us off."

As leader of the five-person Community Relations Committee, Kara served as liaison between the CPS and the citizens of Salinas County. "Well, we might as well start with McCombs."

Sarah Vaughn said, "I saw the public notice in last week's *Anchor*. It was in the classifieds, in the real estate section."

"Guess old T.K. is just raring to go," Rebecca drolly noted. "I just can't believe this is actually going to happen."

Plenty of folks were angered by the long-rumored sale of T.K. McCombs' Double RR Ranch. South of town on County Road 30, it was 750 acres and the largest privately-owned parcel in Salinas County. Spread across the valley floor, the scenic vistas stretched like postcards in every direction. The 15,000 square foot mansion was broken into five-star suites and was, at the height of the winter season, staffed by a crew of thirty. A dozen rental cabins also spared no luxury, dotting the landscape at 50-acre intervals.

The McCombs clan, as one of the original forty families halted by winter on their way to Utah 120 years before, had staked off 750 acres of prized land currently valued at over $20 million. According to Colorado state law, parcels of 35 acres or more could be bought and sold without the oversight, and outside the jurisdiction, of the local planning commissions and county zoning boards. But if that 35-acre lot was broken down into smaller parcels, the full force of the local subdivision laws automatically triggered. So what had formerly been a transaction of private property between two individuals now had to pass through the rigorous apparatus of both the town Planning Commission and City Council. Depending on differing variables, this journey could be short and sweet or, more predictably, filled with small town politics, petitions, class-action lawsuits, injunctions, and a general blood-letting on all sides.

By publishing his intentions, T.K. McCombs had finally fired the opening salvo in this long-feared land war. Soon after, rumors spread about other property owners enticed by this surging market. Henman and Cahill were two names that, like McCombs, were listed on the town's original charter.

After keeping 50 acres for himself, McCombs was about to create a pair of 350-acre developments split into ten lots of 35 acres each. Per requirement, all houses had to be a minimum of 13,000 square feet and no closer than a quarter-mile off the new road that would eventually connect them to County Road 30. Essentially, there would be twenty mansions on 35-acre grids heralding the town's arrival as more than just another winter destination.

Kara said, "Rebecca, why don't we start with the science."

"You can hold your breath, because this won't take long. There is no argument on ecological, biological, or environmental grounds. No endangered habitats or species will be impacted, and there's only twenty feet of wetlands ringing the circumference of Frost Pond. Two small streams on the property that feed into the Blackstone River will be, according to the proposed site plan, adequately outside the fifty-foot encroachment zone."

"What about the freaking hot springs?" Vaughn asked. "That property's laced with them."

"True enough. But the aquifers that feed them are deeper than code requires. And the above-surface and subsurface pools have already been independently mapped by us *and* Regional Diagnostics, who was hired by McCombs. They also submitted a complete land survey, perc and water tests, each of which reflected our own results." Rebecca clicked her pen in the silence before lowering the boom. "NEGA's position is that, so long as the proposed sites remain fixed with no wetlands encroach-ment, the property is entirely suitable for development."

Sarah Vaughn closed her eyes while massaging the bridge of her nose.

"That..." Kara stared blankly at the table. "Really sucks."

"Yes it does." Because of her official role, Rebecca tried to remain detached. "There's nothing else to report."

Vaughn reached for her Bloody Mary. "We better order another round, 'cause this meeting's getting shorter by the second."

Kara looked at her notepad, at the title she had scratched up top that read, "McCombs Planning Session." Underneath it was now written, "NEGA just finished us." And the rest of the page was blank.

"I guess it's up to you, Miss Vaughn," she said. "Regale us with your adjudicatory prowess."

Vaughn punched a button on her laptop and settled her gaze. "We'll do the bad news first. Basically, the thirty-five-acre exemption kills us on the spot. The law is very particular in this instance and reflects this state's long-held position on the curbing of governmental regulation of private property. The subdivision laws, as we've discussed, don't apply. Environmental concerns, as we've just heard, are negligible. And since the proposed homes will all have their own wells and septic systems, concerns about the town providing water and sewer lines are negated. And while we're on the topic of infrastructure impact, the developer's willing to bear the full cost of running electric and cable lines, con-structing all necessary roads, and will negotiate a flat fee for each home in regards to other infrastructure improvements, like schools, Fire and Police, and any other town services required by the new inhabitants. As for the usual causes cited to prevent development—noise, traffic, and/ or skyline regulations—"

"Refresh my memory," Kara interrupted. "The exact provisions of that ...?"

"It's a local ordinance which refers to visual impact—meaning no one's allowed to build on peaks or ridges or in any other way disturb the scenic vistas shared by all. Unfortunately, these units are low-lying along the valley floor and located ten miles from their nearest neighbors."

"Great."

"At this point, honestly, the only way to prevent construction is to either buy the land outright from McCombs, or somehow talk him into selling the development rights and placing the majority of his estate into a conservation easement."

Kara frowned. "I thought you said there was some good news?"

"There is. We'll have a much better shot at Cahill and Henman if they decide to sell their ranches. Since McCombs just sucked up the entire high-end market, these guys get the leftovers, the subdivisions and smaller lots. Any sale of their properties would be subject to the subdivision laws, public hearings, zoning approval, the Planning Commission, and a Town Council vote. We could put together a legal nightmare that could last years and cost them a fortune."

Kara said, "So our only chance is to bid on the property which, at twenty million dollars, means we're totally screwed anyway."

"What about the easement idea?" Rebecca asked.

"No chance," Kara said.

"He'll never go for it," Vaughn added.

Rebecca frowned. "It'd be highly unethical of me, a scientific representative of a nonpartisan organization, to instruct representatives from a more political entity on how best to prosecute their affairs, but as a resident of Salinas County, I would hope that an organization funded in part by my private donations would exhaust every possibility in order to prevent what will be, to put it bluntly, a seven hundred acre preserve for the rich."

"Now, now, you're starting to sound like a socialist," Vaughn said. "The issue is not judging someone's success, but the impact of their actions. This land is already privately owned, end of story."

Kara did not need to do the math. "He'd also be giving up millions to do the right thing ..."

Designed mainly for farmers and ranchers working vast tracts of land, conservation easements allowed the owner to keep his land while selling only the development rights. These easements provided one-time lump sum payments to ranchers who, if they owned 500-acres, might realize $500,000.

"Ladies ..." Rebecca had her computer stored and coffee drained. "I hate to drink and run, but the DSV awaits. How about two weeks from today for our next meeting?"

"Works for me," Vaughn said.

"As it is..." Rebecca glanced at them. "This whole thing's gone too far already."

"Cahill and Henman are next," Vaughn reassured them. "Believe me, this little town's not gonna be chopped up and served to the highest bidder, friends, on that you can rely."

CHAPTER SEVEN

They got lucky with the weather. No snow on Tuesday or Wednesday canceled the usual hour spent shoveling every morning. They had set two monster beams, triple-packed 30'x16"x1¾" gluelams, into the pre-notched slots in the foundation. Once the beams were shimmed up flush with the sill plates, the floor joists were run over the beams and nailed on "layout." The term itself seemed to hold significant importance, because Elias heard frequent cursing whenever "layout" was blown. Starting from the control corner, 15¼-inches was marked, the tape measure was reset there, and every subsequent 16-inches was crow's-footed (V) after that. Once the entire plate was marked, Rand went back with his square and penciled a line through every crow's foot. He then slashed a capital X on the right side of every line.

"I don't get it," Elias finally said. "What happens if you don't follow layout?"

"That's not an option." Rand pulled his knife to sharpen his pencil. "You've got to think of this entire building as a series of stacking points. The floor joists start at 15¼-inches, and the wall studs above them will start at the same. After we get to the second-floor, it's all repeated until everything is continuously in line, right?"

"Right."

"And the plywood sheets, remember, whether it's for the floor, walls, or roof, measure four feet by eight feet. Each of those sheets have to break on a floor joist, wall stud, or roof rafter, otherwise we got nothing to nail the edge too."

"So if a sheet doesn't break on a joist, you either have to add another joist ..."

"Or cut the sheet, which is gonna pull you off layout, which also means you'll be cutting unnecessary sheets instead of just slapping them down and nailing them."

"Huh." Elias grinned. "Layout's pretty important, huh?"

"Yup." Rand had sharpened a thousand pencils, but he dropped this one and the knife at the same time and said, "Fuck."

Then Elias saw the blood streaming off Rand's fingertips like an opened spigot. "Jesus, man, here." Elias handed him his glove. "Clamp it. How many fingers did you clip?"

"Just one." Rand held out his hand and Elias saw the side of Rand's index finger flapping like sushi.

"Whoa!"

"What's going on?" Nolan abruptly roared. "Why is no one hurrying up?"

Rand said, "Noll, grab the super glue."

"For who?" Nolan craned his neck, saw the blood, and then headed for his truck.

Elias stared at the wound, fascinated.

"Appreciate the gesture ..." Rand handed him back his glove as blood poured from the cut. "But never give away your gloves."

Nolan arrived and took Rand's hand, dabbing napkins at the cut. "You really filleted that thing." He gave Elias the super glue. "Open that."

"Jesus Christ, I thought you guys were kidding. Super glue in an open wound?"

Nolan snorted. "Listen, if it's good enough for the Vietnam guys, it's good enough for this dumbass. Go get some duct tape will ya?"

Rand winced as Nolan applied the glue, re-attached the inch-long skin flap, and then held the wound closed. It was dry and wiped off thirty seconds later. Elias arrived with the tape as Nolan wrapped a napkin around the finger. Soon after, Rand flexed his fingers. "Good to go."

The pace of construction, at least for Elias, was unbearable. It might have been twenty degrees, but he was hauling wood like a rat on a wheel and sweating profusely. After Nolan and Rand checked distances for each section of joist, Nolan headed out to the floor joists and ran a chainsaw through sometimes fifteen of them at once. Elias then dragged them all over to where his bosses waited on either side of the span, nail-guns at the ready. He quickly realized that they were usually happiest when they had something to nail or smash with a hammer. But leave them waiting for a requested item and their blood pressure rose as fast as the steam exiting their mouths.

Next, the bays along the beams had to be blocked, and even this was done at a breakneck pace. As Nolan whacked the blocks out of leftover floor joists, Elias heaved them out to Rand who placed and nailed them as quickly as Elias could reload.

The next morning, Rand and Nolan double-checked the completed floor system. Elias carried over and stacked forty sheets of ¾-inch tongue-and-groove sheeting. Unlike the disaster of the last jobsite, where the wood was stacked fifty yards away over treacherous footing, his new commute was down to thirty feet.

Elias was also quickly finding out the difference a ¼-inch could make. The wall sheets were ½-inch thick, the roof ⅝-inch—but to account for the bearing weight of the occupants and all of their belongings, building code held a ¾-inch minimum on sub-floor construction. Which also meant there was no way Elias was carrying more than one sheet until Rand, claiming to want to lend a hand, picked up a pair with ease. Not to be outdone, Elias followed suit, but after five round trips, once Rand finally peeled off to help Nolan with something else, Elias found cover for a wince-filled gasp.

At lunch, inside Nolan's truck, the heat blasted as they silently ate. A round of cigarettes leaked smoke from the cracked windows but the heat was too warm, the food just settling in.

"No way." Nolan lowered the windows and killed the engine. "I know where this is going."

"Are you kidding me?" Rand wrenched closed his coat. "It's twenty fucking degrees out there, man!"

"It's for your own good." Nolan held out his hand. "Gimme a light."

"Only if you close the windows."

"Gimme the light first and then I'll close the windows."

"No way."

"It's awful cold out there, son."

"All right!" Rand flung his lighter across the seat. "Let's go, dude, make this right."

"You know, it's a funny thing about life ..." Nolan lit another cigarette before pocketing Rand's lighter. "My dad once told me—"

"Gimme back my lighter."

"—that some things in life won't always be pleasant—"

"Gimme back my lighter and shut the windows."

"—and that no matter what, no matter how awful the experience—"

"Just knowing you has been an awful experience."

"—things could always get worse." Nolan exited the truck. "No more
slacking off, morons, hurry the fuck up."

"Unbelievable ..." Rand watched him trudge toward the deck.
"Fucker freezes us out and then steals my lighter ... again. Do you believe
this?"

From the backseat, Elias said, "Naw, man, I'm down with O.P.P.—
Other People's Pain."

"Then fuck you too."

"How long you been partners with this guy?"

But Rand was no longer listening. He stared out at the remaining
half of the floor they had yet to sheet.

———————

When Ted Beckham pulled down Gildman Road at 3:55 P.M. of that
second day, he had only intended to drop off a revised list of measure-
ments for the rough openings of the second-floor windows. But once
his Cherokee punched out of the woods and he saw the first wall already
standing, a rush of excitement swept away any remaining doubts.

Beckham zipped up his jacket. Ecstatic after months of speculation
and anxiety, he tried hoisting himself onto the first-floor deck but created an embarrassing spectacle by getting stuck halfway.

Nolan rushed over to lend a hand. "Sorry, Ted, I was meaning to get
a ramp built."

"Don't apologize for me being old and weak." Beckham brushed
himself off, adjusted his Stetson, and thumped his boots across the
freshly sheeted deck. "Looks great, Noll. How'd she come out?"

"Dead balls." Nolan pointed to the far-right corner. "You were right,
it was a quarter-inch out, but we adjusted."

"Incredible."

"Right? Imagine if every foundation was like this?"

"I can order the trusses?"

"Yep." Nolan pulled out a Marlboro Light. "We're exactly twenty-eight feet end to end."

Beckham reached inside his coat for a small notepad and pen. "That's great news. I also brought the finalized window schedule for the second-floor."

"Nice." Nolan exhaled as he watched Rand and Elias finishing up the next wall. "For old times' sake, feel like lending a hand?"

"Sure."

"Hey, Fabio!" Nolan shouted above the roaring generator and compressor. "We ready to go?"

Rand was bent over nailing and nodded his upside-down head.

"Thomas! Grab four twelve-foot 2x4s, the laser, the sledgehammer, and the six-foot ladder."

Elias retrieved the requested items as Rand, aiming to give their fingers some room, slammed wedges beneath the top-plate of the just assembled wall.

After spreading themselves equidistantly, they unbuckled their tool bags in preparation for the lift. Somewhat anxiously, Beckham cracked his knuckles. "Just like the old days."

"Twenty-eight feet of heaven." Nolan pointed at Elias. "Once we get it standing, you and Ted stay put while Rand and I brace it off."

Elias nodded. "Game on."

"All right, guys ..."

They all squatted.

Nolan made sure everything was set. "After it's off the deck, there ain't no going back, all right? That's how people die. On three ... One, two, three!"

There was a collective grunt on the dead lift, but momentum slowed once the weight increased along the arc. With the top of the wall on their chests at the halfway point, people began to gasp.

"Go! Go! Go!" Nolan screamed.

From the far-right corner, Rand's thrust carried through to the others.

"Go! Go! Hurry up!"

Once the wall crested the apex, the weight dispersed along the arc. Nolan, like the others, tried to catch his breath. "You guys got the wall."

He and Rand started at the corner. Nolan used the sledgehammer to tap the wall onto the chalkline, then Rand nailed the bottom-plate into the floor on both sides of every stud.

In order to level the wall in-and-out, they set the laser on the bottom-plate and split the dot on its edge. Then they pulled on the 2x4 brace until another dot split the top-plate above. Nolan yelled, "Nail it!"

Rand let fly four nails in quick succession.

"Jesus," Beckham said, "he can really work that thing."

Nolan said, "That's because we popped all the safeties."

Beckham winced. "As your GC, I never heard that."

Nolan and Rand repeated the process until all four braces were nailed off. They stepped back and admired their work while the sun died over the horizon.

Beckham said, "I can't believe it's only Wednesday. Guess I should order more wood."

"Have the second-floor here Monday if you could." Nolan lit a smoke. "We'll have the exterior and interior first-floor walls completed and stood by then."

"Monday? Seriously?"

"Actually, you might want to make it Saturday instead. All right, fellas, let's roll it up before we lose the light."

They detached the nailguns from the hoses in loud pops of pressurized air. After Elias hopped down and killed the generator and compressor, the ensuing silence was shocking. It took twenty minutes to gather up the tools, hoses, and cords, but with the loss of whatever meager heat the sun had supplied now gone, the temperature was in total freefall. They locked the tool chests and headed for their vehicles.

Beckham waved good-bye and stood in the gathering gloom. His imagination fast-forwarded to September when this finished structure would receive its students. He knew he was coming dangerously close to believing in Nolan's five-week declaration even though a million pitfalls might await. Then he realized he was freezing his ass off for no good reason and scurried toward the blissful reprieve his heated truck provided.

CHAPTER EIGHT

B orn in Brooklyn, New York, Elias was the middle son of three raised in a working-class section of Bay Ridge. His father was a line technician for Con Edison who did not believe in sick days and was never late for work. As the son of immigrants, he knew all too well the importance of a good job. It was an example not lost on his children.

With high school completed and no money for college, Elias led two friends into Manhattan where they crammed a one-bedroom Bowery apartment with three lifetimes' worth of crap. Long an aficionado of underground magazines, Elias ultimately wanted to start his own but right now needed a job. In a city of ten thousand restaurants, diversity was everywhere, and so was Elias. An aspiring cook, he learned different cuisines and slowly built himself a name. During a five-year span he completed stints at places like the Imperial Garden, a heralded five-star Chinese eatery specializing in southern mainland cuisine, and La Frité, the newest French establishment to cause a Midtown stir. Steak houses, Italian bistros, even sushi—Elias fought his way through the ethnic bias and closed-door policy that often left these kitchens stocked entirely with natives. Even if he was not the most talented practitioner of said cuisine, his dedication and effort earned him high regard among the people who mattered most—his co-workers. Since life in the kitchen could be a turbulent affair, Elias' obscenity-strewn tirades on whatever topic was being discussed inevitably offended someone's sensibilities. But by balancing out his opinions with a ridiculous work ethic, he made himself indispensable. Head chefs and kitchen managers were loath to fire a guy who did the work of two people, showed up every day on time, and either had them laughing hysterically or cursing the day they ever met him. He had been suspended more times than he cared to remember but never fired, and his presence behind the line, when the orders came streaming in, helped anchor the kitchen.

Elias, who averaged fifty hours a week in the restaurant, found his true calling after becoming a founding editor of *Insurrection Magazine.* A joint venture with two other like-minded people, the magazine covered cultural events, political trends, and grassroots reporting on their community. Designed specifically for those living below 14th Street, the magazine culled stories from the diverse fabric from which lower Manhattan had long been woven. His cofounders included Linda Paulson, a lifelong resident and feminist from Alphabet City, and Wayne Starks, an anarchist born in the Bronx. Linda wore calf-high black leather logging boots, a T-shirt that usually expressed some outrageous opinion, and a sense of humor even some men found disturbing. Starks, on the other hand, was educated at Columbia and known for his anti-establishment rhetoric. Retro to the 1970s, Starks sported a two-foot afro and wide bell-bottomed pants in tribute to what he said represented the last period before the death of the individualistic black man.

Insurrection, which started off as a monthly publication, eventually became a small-time sensation. With Starks covering politics and Linda scouring the community, Elias reviewed the arts and became known for lengthy unedited interviews with people the mainstream often missed. Whether it was the reductionist poet Ethan Franks, who lived in a converted pigeon coop overlooking Houston Street, or the brash trumpeting of Ernesto Cruz, the surrounding streets of lower Manhattan teemed with the pulse of a million dreamers.

Going from a first-run copy of a hundred magazines, *Insurrection* grew over three years into a bimonthly periodical averaging five thousand subscriptions. And instead of chasing stories or individuals, their phone now rang first. Whether it was with news of an Eastern European juggler who used live animals, or the genitally-pierced nude performance artist that had entire passages from the Book of Revelations tattooed across his body, as always, genius was in the eye of the beholder.

But supporting a secretary, graphic artist, and bookkeeper/accountant began to take its toll on *Insurrection's* already marginal profitability. All three editors still held other fulltime jobs. Linda worked at an abused women's shelter, and Starks proofread legal documents for a law firm specializing in housing discrimination. So when Sundry Publications, a subsidiary of the corporate monolith Global Media, came calling with promises of increased readership and financial stability, the cracks in their partnership expanded.

Long opposed to any outside influence or interference, Elias was stunned by his partners' relief after Sundry first approached. He tried changing their minds but discovered they had grown weary of stressing payroll, overhead, and non-existent personal lives. He was out voted two-to-one and, passing judgment on them, resigned at the same weekly editorial meeting they had held for the past three years.

With *Insurrection* gone, Elias began publishing under a new banner titled *Wreckage Magazine*. Authors contributed short fiction, nonfiction, essays, and poetry, but readership was scant. The black-and-white magazine arrived infrequently, as its owner/publisher was often low on funds, and outside of a few independent bookstores, coffeehouses, and whatever street corner Elias commandeered, the publication failed to sell.

The worst part was crossing paths with his baby. A year later, while shopping for used CDs on East 8th Street, he saw the latest copy of *Insurrection* and finally, more curious than angry, took a peek. He recognized two familiar names but the format had completely changed. *Insurrection* was now the product of polished personnel. New reporters contributed pieces about the garbage monopoly in Chinatown as well as a pigeon problem in Battery Park City. There was Linda's interview with the new chef at Le Cirque but her technique was stilted. The questions were topic-obvious, the answers sound-bite ready. After two pages of verbally jerking the guy off, she finally asked a real question about a controversial protégé which she promptly allowed him to dodge. Like running into an ex-girlfriend that had now grown even less appealing, Elias tossed the magazine back on the stack and left.

Three months and half a continent later, New York still cast a monstrous shadow. Despite everything northwest Colorado represented, he missed the city, missed the anonymity, since the difference between eight million people and seven thousand townsfolk tucked into a valley was immeasurable. The rules here were drastically different. He found this out after nearly mowing down a family in a crosswalk, which people here actually used. Then there was the sadness of the Taco Bell incident. In line at the drive-through forever, Elias finally shouted into the intercom, "This is supposed to be fast food, man, what the hell?" Afterward, he jerked to a stop at the window and found a fearful teenager warily awaiting.

Even at the supermarket, when he passed by a guy who simply asked how he was doing, Elias frowned at the intrusion before ignoring him completely. Seconds later, he turned back and saw a wounded expression on the guy's face.

"I'm okay," Elias belatedly replied. "How're you?"

That perfect strangers would inquire into the well-being of others, or just generally show respect for people in their community, was disconcerting. Elias used to walk down the street surrounded by a thousand people who pretended no one else existed. Now adjustments had to be made on the fly. Up was down, left was right. *Just don't be such a dick*, he often reminded himself.

Despite Spring Valley's middle of nowhere location, he was also still discovering improbable gems, like the Olympic-sized pool at the downtown health club. Instead of chlorine, the entire pool was sulfur water from the nearby hot springs. Because the town's residents included world-class cyclists, kayakers, skiers and snowboarders, many of these workout facilities rivaled others in much more heralded locations. Still true to his back rehab from years before, Elias pulled half a mile in the pool every day like an installment plan against the next disaster.

Now, parked in front of his condo, he could barely get out of the car. He eased open the sliding glass door and saw he was alone. His roommates, all restaurant workers, would often still be partying when Elias rose for work. Knowing they were doing what he was not—mainly skiing all day, punching the clock for a token number of hours, and then carousing into the dawn—did nothing to boost his already frozen morale.

Wedging off his boots, knowing there were still three more days to go before his only day off, Elias reached for the bong.

————

Since thirty to forty-five feet of snow fell through a six-month winter, Spring Valley averaged two feet every week. Some nights it was just an inch or two, other times it might snow for three days straight. The record was sixteen feet over four days back in 1974, coincidently the same year Mt. Lassiter doubled in size from twelve to twenty-four trails. That particular season was a seminal moment in the outdoor sport and skiing communities, for as word spread amongst the diehards, those craving fresh powder on a daily basis finally found their fix.

When Spring Valley awoke on Thursday morning, another foot had fallen with six more inches forecasted by lunch. Arriving at 6:55 A.M., Nolan and Rand found Elias stuck halfway down the as-yet unplowed Gildman Road. Already in a foul mood, Nolan stared blankly through the slapping wipers and said, "A fucking Skylark." He turned to Rand. "Can you believe somebody would actually drive a piece of shit like that all the way up here?"

Rand did not care, focused instead on the fruit cradled in his lap.

"Look who I'm talking to," Nolan said. "At least he has a license."

Rand rolled his eyes and said, "Fuck. You."

"No more talking." Nolan powered down his window as Elias approached. "Having a good morning, Thomas?"

"I don't even know what those are." Elias coughed into a glove. "It's fucking cold out here, man."

"Thanks for the update." Nolan nodded toward the Skylark. "Put that piece of shit into neutral and get your seatbelt on."

"Oh, great."

Closing the window, Nolan worked his grin into a caffeine-jerked twitch. "I say we break him today. I say we make this motherfucker hump so much wood, he'll wish he was back cooking at Burger King."

"That's a horrible idea." Rand bit into a peach. "Run off the only halfway decent laborer we've ever had. Every month we have to break in another fucking new guy."

"FNGs, baby." Nolan eased the F-250 forward until Elias' bumper disappeared from sight. "I was only kidding, by the way."

"I hope so." Rand chucked the peach pit from the window before peeling a banana. "Remember that black kid?"

"Oh God. So cheap he duct-taped the holes in his pants?"

"Yeah, but he was good, man. Showed up on time every day until you had him chasing your dog through the six-foot snowdrifts for half the day."

Nolan warmly laughed. "What a stupid dumb bastard that moron was."

"But he wasn't, man, what the hell?" Rand glommed down a mouthful of banana. "Am I just talking to myself or what?"

"Yes. As a matter of fact, no more talking at all." Nolan cranked a Ministry CD while gently nudging the Skylark forward. After Elias waved okay, Nolan pressed ahead.

"Watch this."

The two vehicles clumsily bumped along until Nolan punched the gas and transformed the Skylark into a plow blade spewing snow fifteen feet into the air. After Rand started laughing as well, Nolan became so distracted he nearly jerked both vehicles off the road. They punched out of the woods and slid to a stop at the base of the foundation.

Elias exited into the falling snow and said, "That was something special."

"Like that?" Nolan shrugged into his gear, his cigarette flopping as he said, "You need to rig up, man, before that shitbox kills you."

"Don't get my hopes up."

Rand laughed and tossed Elias an extra apple. Together, all three stood looking at the completely snowed-in jobsite and their smiles faded fast.

"Bust out the fucking shovels," Rand murmured, stepping through the knee-high mounds. "Weren't they over there?"

"By the boxes, man."

The tool chests looked like they had grown massive white afros overnight. Elias kicked through the snow until his boot helped exhume the shovels. Over the next hour, they became hunchbacked machines flinging snow off the first-floor deck, the pathways to the boxes and lumber piles, and finally even the lumber itself. By the time they finished, a fresh inch had already fallen in the places first cleared, but no one dared bitch. Pride alone would not allow that kind of morale-buster. At 8:30 A.M., it felt like five o'clock since the storm played hostage with the sun. The wind picked up, so they hid beneath hoods cinched tight in the gathering gloom.

They rolled out the hoses, cords, and only the necessary tools. The laser, save for brief moments, spent the day safely inside its case. The same, however, could not be said of the carpenters currently surrounding a recalcitrant generator that refused to start. Taking turns yanking the ignition string became monotonous after ten minutes, so Nolan, growing enraged, called a halt to this futility.

"Thomas," he said, "get the weed burner. It's in the back of my truck."

Slouched forward into the wind, Elias returned with a propane tank. It was connected by hose to a thin two-foot pipe with an end shaped like a soup can. Nolan took the wand and cursed the fact that he had to remove a glove to work the lighter. There was a knob on the pipe stem, so Nolan dialed the torch down to its weakest setting. After easing open the gas, he flicked the lighter near the soup-can head and a wafting orange flame ignited. He said, "Why don't you guys load the deck while I cook this motherfucker."

Since anything was better than standing still and freezing, Rand and Elias bitched over fifty 2x6 studs and a pair of sixteen-footers to plate the next wall.

Nolan blasted both the compressor and the generator for ten minutes until steam rose in mists off the machines. Killing the torch, he looked at Rand and said, "First thing we do is build these guys a doghouse."

"Yep."

Elias was already heading for the wood stacks as Nolan called out, "Six twelve-foot 2x4s and two sheets of half-inch plywood, Thomas."

"Yeah."

After lighting a cigarette, Nolan's expression turned aggressive, as if the nine o'clock start, continuing snowfall, frozen tools, and God Himself were determined to see him fail. Internalizing this misery sparked combustible conditions, and as he pulled on his glove with the cigarette between his teeth, he looked at Rand and said, "I'm thinking the rest of the first-floor exterior walls would be a good day's work."

Rand's blond goatee framed a wide grin. "Then you better hurry the fuck up."

"Hurry up," Nolan muttered. After a few quick yanks, both machines wound to life in a rattling haze of belching smoke.

Elias arrived with a saw and gun. Nolan and Rand belted into their

Occidental tool bags and hastily assembled a three-walled lean-to for the two screaming machines now raging inside.

"Jesus Christ!" Nolan dragged a piece of half-inch plywood across its opening. "Remind me to tell fuckface we need a temp pole put in out here for the electrical ASAP. I'm not spending a month and a half listening to this shitshow at close range."

"Fuck yeah." Rand grabbed the saw and gun and turned for the deck. As they trudged along the trench in single file, the snow continued falling.

They took lunch three hours later like frozen junkies jonesing for heat inside the idling truck. The windshield wipers slapped away the snow in a futile gesture since the storm had already dropped the promised six inches with no end in sight.

Their faces were bright red, their hands throbbing chunks of meat. In order to survive the afternoon, they jammed their wet gloves onto the dashboard defroster to dry out and subsequently steamed up the windshield.

"Let's see …" Nolan munched on a bag of Fritos. "The entire back, left, and right walls are up, and the plates for the front wall are already cut and ready for framing." He turned to Rand who was inhaling a cold-cut sandwich. "We're actually gonna be ready for that floor system tomorrow afternoon." After Nolan took out a pack of cigarettes, Rand and Elias were quick to mooch, fish-bowling the truck in the stifling heat.

"Who's got my lighter?" Rand asked.

"Not me," Elias answered from the backseat.

"Hey." Rand poked Nolan's shoulder. "Give it back."

"I don't know what you're talking about."

"Noll—"

"Seriously, dude, I don't have it."

"Thomas—" Rand looked back over the seat. "Let's have it."

"I'm not kidding, man. He lit up the last one."

"All right, lunch's over." Nolan rolled down all the windows and killed the engine. "Everybody out, hurry up."

"Jesus." Elias' scowl greeted the swirling blasts of frozen air.

"Out! Out! Out!" Nolan screamed, and once the truck was cleared, he secured it and then joined them for the coldest part of any winter day—the first half hour after lunch.

They shoveled off the deck for a third time and used up the last dry chalk-box to snap a line for the front wall. The studs were cut and placed between the top and bottom-plates, the window and door headers assembled. Elias, lacking any skill with the tools, ferried wood and cleared away cut-offs. He offered to build them a fire but Nolan was no fan of anything that allowed guys to stand around doing nothing.

An old beat-up radio appeared, and Prong's "Snap Your Fingers, Snap Your Neck" blasted across the jobsite like a horrible warning.

Because the front wall had four windows and two doors, the six headers of tripled up 2x10s made it even heavier. The mood intensified when the spacer blocks were placed beneath the top-plate in preparation for the upcoming lift. Elias was in the middle, Rand and Nolan on either side.

"I'm not gonna lie." Nolan dropped his bags. "With only three guys, this is gonna suck." He blew into his hands and said to Elias, "Once this thing's in the air, there ain't no going back."

"Noll, I got it."

Squatting into position, Nolan said, "All right, girls, here we go. Safety last."

"Safety last," they murmured, adjusting their grips.

"On three. One, two, three!"

They rose in unison. The weight sank in, compressing. With the top-plate waist high and resting in their palms, the real test had now arrived. They had to go up and spin their palms at the same time. Their breaths were explosive bursts of pressure until Rand screamed and lifted, praying Elias could transfer the momentum. In the middle, Elias heard the shout and heaved until he thought the wall might just be high enough, but it was not, and the weight came back and buckled his legs. With the top-plate practically across his throat, Elias' anger flashed over. He thrust and screamed and drove until his arms finally extended, pushing in relay toward Nolan as the wall slid perfectly into place.

"Boy," Rand said. "That was—"

"Some fucked up shit." Still holding the wall, Nolan pointed at Elias. "The second that wall lifts up off the deck, you drive like your life depends on it because guess what—it does."

"Noll—"

"Naw." Nolan hushed Rand. "I ain't having it. This is how people die."

"It's twenty-eight feet and loaded with headers." Rand's sunglasses reflected the falling snow. "Hell, it took four of us to lift the back wall, man, don't be such a fucking dick."

"He needs to learn."

"Just back the fuck off, is all."

Nolan swallowed his rebuttal, nailing off the corner and then working the bottom-plate in and out according to the chalk line. Elias, seemingly nonplussed, held the wall until it was nailed and braced.

"I gotta call dipshit about the lumber drops." Nolan hopped to the ground. "Rack that motherfucker, will ya?"

Rand's jaw was squared as Nolan departed for his truck. Elias had his hands in his jacket, chewing gum with a look of pure disgust.

"Don't pay him no mind," Rand said. "Some bitches never change."

"Whatever, man. All's I need is money to jet and this place will be a gone motherfucker." He turned toward Rand. "What was he talking about? What does *rack* mean?"

"Let's grab a bunch of eighteen-footers and I'll show you."

They hopped down and slid six long 2x4s onto the deck. Rand said, "We need to rack the square. We already have the walls leveled as far as in and out goes, right?"

"Yeah."

"So now we have to level them left to right." Rand climbed a ladder, held the 2x4 diagonally along the wall, and then nailed it into the top right corner. He handed the gun down to Elias and said, "Ever fire one of these?"

"Only once. At Butcher Block."

"There's no safety, so big-boy rules apply. Watch your trigger." Rand grabbed the six-foot level and placed it against the wall. "We gotta go out. Here. Jam this cat's paw behind the 2x4 and crank this fucker out."

Elias used Rand's hatchet to drive the cat's paw into the floor just behind the 2x4. Wrenching on this improvised lever, he was surprised to hear creaking as the entire wall visibly shifted right.

Rand eyed the level. "A little more. Get ready with the gun."

Elias increased pressure.

"A cunt hair more."

Elias cranked down harder.

"Nail it!"

Four shots rang out. Elias glanced up seeking confirmation. Rand double-checked the level one last time and said, "Dead balls, bro, nice. Let's do 'em all."

They racked the other two and were finishing the front as Nolan climbed back up on deck. "How'd we do?"

"Titties." Rand climbed down the ladder. "Was just getting ready for the second top-plate." He reached into his coat for a smoke, but even unzipping for ten seconds caused a body-wide shiver. "Got a light?"

"Yeah, here."

"Ha!" Rand swiped his lighter back and held it up. "You're a lying motherfucker."

"What's numb-nuts doing?"

"Scrapping out."

"Thomas!" Nolan called out. "Can you bitch over eight sixteen-foot 2x6s?"

With no dumpster yet on-site, Elias ferried the waste into a pile out front.

"How's he doing?" Nolan pulled out a cigarette and motioned for the lighter.

Rand shook his head. "Nope."

"Come on, man, have a heart."

Rand worked his lip into a frown. "I want it right back."

"Sure." Nolan took the lighter, lit his cigarette, and started walking away.

"Um ... excuse me. I think you forgot something."

"Hop on up there, Fabio," Nolan called out over a shoulder. "I'll get you the broom."

"Goddamnit." Rand pulled himself up onto the wall. 2x6 top-plate was one-inch wider than the balance beam in women's gymnastics. He found his equilibrium on the snow-covered top-plate and poked his foot to test the slippery conditions.

"Here." Nolan held up the broom. "Start sweeping while I drag the saw over."

"I want my lighter." With both hands in his pockets, Rand stared down at his tormentor. "Right now."

"It'll be safer down here with me. You might slip and fall to your death."

"Then you can take it off my dead body."

"I have too much respect for the dead."

"Who the fuck are you kidding?"

"You're right. Your presence is an offense to humanity." Nolan tapped Rand's boots with the broom. "Take it."

"No."

"Take it now."

"Noll ..."

"Hurry up."

"Goddamnit." Rand grabbed the broom. "This ain't over."

"Whatever you say."

Rand carefully cleared the snow so they could lay another 2x6 onto clean wood. In order to lock in the corners, this second top-plate would overlap the seams where each wall met. He swept off the whole perimeter and tossed the broom to the deck. He hooked his tape measure on the first corner and said, "Hey, thief, your first number is 184½."

Nolan whacked a 2x6 and handed it and the Hitachi up to Rand. Watching Rand work at height entranced those not used to it, like Elias, who just gazed up in awe. Rand held the nailgun in one hand and somehow maneuvered the fifteen-foot 2x6 into position. Like others that made everything dangerous look easy, Rand provided a horrible example. Placing the board along the top of the wall, he flushed it up at the corner and nailed it. Then he worked it in and out as needed, nailing as he went. In a windblown snowstorm, this already tricky balancing act became even sketchier walking a 5½ inch top-plate in reverse.

The Jeep Cherokee with Spring Valley Public Works on its side pulled in thirty minutes later. It was already getting dark, so Nolan abruptly shouted, "That's it, fellas, roll this fucker up."

Since the same Prong CD had been blasting for the past three hours, Elias killed the radio first. Rand, done nailing, rappelled the nailgun to the deck and then crashed down beside it.

———————

Seconds later, Ted Beckham's elation about the progress was plainly evident by his wide eyes and even bigger smile. He buttoned up in the still swirling storm and crunched stiffly through the snow.

"Boy oh boy," he said, and this time successfully pulled himself up onto the deck. "A foot last night, eight-inches today ..." Beckham shook Nolan's hand. "You fellas got any nerve endings left?"

"No." Nolan grinned. "How you doing, Teddy?"

"I'd be better if there was any chance in hell I could get that second-floor system here before Monday but I can't."

"No sweat. We'll have this thing sheeted by lunch, and then we'll throw up the interior walls and finish the hardware—drill out those hold-downs and epoxy in the rebar—tomorrow afternoon and Saturday."

"I better call for more 2x4 then."

"Already done. I sweet-talked my way onto the nine o'clock truck."

"Excellent. Any problems so far?"

"None." Nolan's face was a wind-whipped mask with gaping pores, his lips blistered like split worms. "We got plenty of half-inch sheeting for the walls."

"How we doing on nails?"

"No problem. Got a hundred pounds of each." Nolan wound up an extension cord. "No offense, man, but we're getting the fuck out of here ..."

"No worries." Beckham meandered around the first-floor as the others gathered tools, ferried waste, and tarped the lumber stacks out front. They called farewell to Beckham, who was still daydreaming the future school into existence.

Inside the pickup, Nolan immediately jacked the heat. Neither he nor Rand wanted to let out a gasp of exhaustion, so they silently settled back into their seats.

Reaching for a cigarette, Rand said, "I want my lighter."

"What lighter?"

"Noll ..."

"I already gave it back to you."

"You heard me."

"I'm sorry but the captain's turned on the No Talking sign." Nolan cranked Motorhead and launched the truck down Gildman Road.

CHAPTER NINE

After work, Lena Holmscomb was in the kitchen with her two children bouncing off the walls. Twelve-year-old Emily wore a new hair-style that straddled child and adulthood. Kenny was four years younger but already displaying the same recklessness that plagued his father. He was four weeks into an eight-week broken arm. It had become his favorite story, how he and two friends built a ramp to jump Fork Creek, a tiny tributary that Lena herself could broad-jump from a standing start. That he had spun this feat into a tale of man versus nature was as much amusing as it was concerning. Rand, who regularly hucked his Honda CR500R sixty feet through the air, was already clamoring for Kenny to have a dirt bike of his own. Lena, once again forced to be the disciplinarian, was beginning to resent her role as spoiler-in-chief. If Rand wanted to risk his own life, that was his business. But to show their young son homemade videos of himself and a few suicidal buddies ski jumping eight lanes of I-5 was not exactly the example Lena thought he should be providing.

It took years for her to realize that the same qualities which at first made Rand so attractive, now completely repelled her. But his accomplishments were not in doubt. By the time they met at that New Mexican state park, he had already been a skier on the national team, an oil-rigger, a master carpenter, a two-time defending champion kickboxer at 210 pounds, and listed in the Guinness Book of World Records after excavating the largest crystal in North America.

Because of his stoic, businesslike demeanor, word of these achievements was only sporadic and offhand—like when they were just driving up the coast and coincidentally passed the spot of his now infamous I-5 jump. She had glanced up the fifty-foot cliff and remembered shivering.

He also seemed to have a thousand hobbies, so as she collected up the bits of his past, his competitive drive seemed endemic, as if through sheer force alone he might overwhelm all obstacles. And largely unnoticed, too. If she had not spent so much effort prying loose this information, she was convinced no one would have ever known a single thing about him. He did not have any close friends and thought extraneous conversation pointless.

A transient, he had garbage bags of clothes and tools and a long list of possessions lost to uncollected storage units and pawn shops along the way. Despite making $7,000 a month in cash, he was penniless and had a credit rating that would make a delinquent teenager proud. In the last years of their marriage, she used to show up at his job every Friday before he could drink or snort away half a week's pay at the bar.

In the beginning, before the children, this cash allowed them to trek through a string of towns, following his job, the money, her whim, or sometimes all three. A year in, she remembered falling for him despite months convincing herself the attraction was mainly physical and manageable. But somewhere near Green River, Utah, she ultimately realized the scope of her growing commitment. And then she got pregnant with Emily by mistake and serious decisions became unavoidable. They bought a house in Camp Verde, Arizona, and Rand hired on as a lead carpenter at a motel near Sedona under construction. At first, he attacked fatherhood with the same vigor and force he applied to everything else, but as time wore on, and Kenny was born, and Emily began exhibiting the independent spirit genetically inlaid from both parents, he began to realize the magnitude of this task. These were not accomplishments he could manhandle into reality. Without control, with no trusted technique or long-rehearsed maneuver on which to rely, he got lost amid the various role's fatherhood demanded.

Neglecting his duties, as well as taking off with coworkers for weekends of mountain climbing, crystal digging, dirt biking, and skiing, became unacceptable to Lena. The binge drinking returned as their fights grew more complicated, since each now had years of ammunition from which to draw. She started kicking him out of the house so frequently that, after he finally got a place of his own, the end of their seven-year marriage began.

He came and went after that, vagabonding through the west until hooking up with Nolan, a man Lena respected and liked but whose reputation, at least among the locals, was nearly as bad as Rand's. They both handled simple disagreements and miscommunications in anger, always leaving violence within easy reach. And while Rand never struck her, there were a few times when she definitely thought that line might get crossed. The week she contacted a divorce attorney, she counted six gaping holes punched through various walls and figured maybe the kids had seen enough.

Now, at the sink, she washed raw chicken until Kenny shrieked, "Look, mom!"

She turned and saw a yardstick stuffed into his forearm cast. The look of glee on his face killed her reprimand, so she turned psychological instead. "Didn't Dr. Martin warn you about that? I don't think you'll be laughing if that arm gets infected."

The word paused him, ticking through his mind like the tumblers in a lock until the meaning finally opened.

Emily tried one of her new condescension-laced glances. "Typical."

"Both of you," Lena said. "Clear off that table. Dinner's almost ready."

Kenny swung the yardstick like a sword toward his sister's head until she screamed, "Stop attacking me!"

Lena snapped her fingers. "That's it. If you two can't stay busy on your own, I'll find something for you to do. Both of you get upstairs and clean those rooms."

Sullenly, after repeated rebuttals, they gathered their belongings and headed for the stairs.

Despite her and Rand's obvious faults, she was thankful the kids were resilient. If the divorce was the worst trauma they would face, she would be even more grateful. In the last three years, as the wounds from their separation healed and closed, she and Rand salvaged a basic friendship. Also, he could not be away from his kids. And while he played obvious favorites with Kenny, which irritated her, at least he was present in their lives, no small feat considering the gypsy streak Lena knew all too well.

As part of Lena's job in the town's municipal office, she was a caseworker for SSI and welfare recipients. But the benefits package was really why she stayed. Without the pension and health insurance, their family surely would have suffered. After all, as part of her job, she got to see how far people descended when left to freefall through the cracks.

She put the chicken into the oven. Headlights swept across the kitchen. She saw Rand emerge from Nolan's battered salt-streaked pickup.

Some nights, when Rand stayed late with the kids, she allowed him to sleep over. If things went well, he would push his luck and return the next night and the night after that. He had not, after all, grown any less physically attractive—it was mainly his immaturity and episodic rages that finally wedged her away. As for the occasional sexual encounter, at least he was still good for something. The periods of normalcy were nice, and the kids reveled in having their father to wrestle with and climb on, if only for an evening. Or two. Or three. Or sometimes even a week until the good times went bad and he either came home drunk, or some girlfriend called the house, or she, Lena, might have a date, or finally she just got sick of cleaning up after him while listening to him bitch. He was physically gifted, good-looking and healthy, but certainly found a lot to complain about. His job, Nolan, paying taxes, getting screwed by child support—the list was never ending.

Rand knocked once and came in. She was at the oven and glanced at his red face and saggy wet clothes. He untied his boots and slowly groaned. "If I have to bend over one more fucking time—"

"Daddy!" Kenny was beaming from the upstairs rail. "I learned a new wrestling move! I'll show ya—"

"Kenneth Holmscomb." Lena immediately stalked in from the kitchen. "Not before your room's clean, homework's done, and dinner's eaten. Besides, your arm's *broken*, remember?"

"Mom!" With his head stuck between the balustrade, Kenny looked like a prisoner pleading from his cell. "Can't we just wait—"

"Now, please." Her raised eyebrow shoe-horned him from the banister.

"Wrestling with a busted wing." Rand peeled two pairs of soaked wool socks from his frozen feet. "I think we need to get him on Ritalin or something."

"Hardly." Lena diced an onion with extra vigor. "His teacher called me at work this afternoon."

"Oh yeah?" Rand was unbuckling the shoulder straps of his Carhartt jumpsuit. "I'd be calling too if I had such a great kid in my class."

"He is a great kid ... just has a bad example."

"Excuse me?"

"'*Motherfucker*?'" Lena threw him a withering look over her shoulder. "That's what he called one of his classmates today."

"So immediately my—"

"Where do you think he learned that word?"

Rand pulled off two sweatshirts. "Sunday school?"

"That's not funny." Lena cocked a hand on her hip. "This house is not a jobsite. I want you to watch your mouth, Randall. Seriously. I'm not raising two animals."

"Because of a few—"

"Motherfucker is not *okay*." Lena quickly looked toward the staircase and lowered her voice. "Apparently, he was running around calling people motherfucker all day long."

Rand laughed before he could stop himself.

"Honestly." Lena hacked through a pair of carrots. "Sometimes I wonder exactly what your role here is."

"Excuse me?"

"You heard me. An eight-year-old boy no less."

"Seriously, what the f—" He caught himself. "I'm sorry."

"Sure you are. Wanna know the best part? I'm the one who gets the calls. You prance around here like their best friend, and I do all the screaming."

"Oh, here we go."

"Yes," she said matter-of-factly. "One more time, right honey?"

He was finally stripped down to his boxers. The goose bumps were like a rash across his skin. "I said I'm sorry, okay? Please, I don't want to fight now. I can't, babe, I'm beat, frozen, and starving."

"Fine."

He stood there staring at her back. "I promise I'll watch my mouth, okay?"

"Then stop saying it like you're doing me some stupid favor."

"All right."

"You better shower up," she said. "Dinner's almost ready."

Her bedroom was down the hall from the kitchen and more like a closet. Upstairs were the kids' bedrooms. While it was nothing like the custom homes Rand built, it was cozy and situated in a quiet subdivision far from the touristy chaos.

Elsewhere, especially near Mt. Lassiter and its western approaches, construction was booming. Be it bland condominiums or 13,000 square foot castles, she knew Spring Valley was in the middle of drastic change. Having lived here for nearly a decade, Lena now watched her beloved sleepy mountain town lurch beneath this growth. The schools were swelling and needed replacing. Sewer lines were being forced in because the over-crowded septic fields were polluting the town's water, so one word had sprung up as a label for all new arrivals—poachers. At the same time, while Lena knew the beauty of this place was being threatened, without the current boom, men like her husband would have trouble earning a living. As a former park ranger and fervent environmentalist, she figured marrying a tree-murdering carpenter was pretty high up on the list of life's great ironies.

She finished the salad and set the table. Stirring the corn, she felt his approach before his hands encircled her waist. He rested his chin on her shoulder and asked, "What's in the oven?"

"Chicken." The familiar scent of his shaving cream and shampoo crept beneath her nose.

"I was serious before." His voice was low in her right ear. "I'll watch the cussing around the little fellas."

She stirred the corn.

"What else is wrong?" he finally asked.

"I can't use this now, you know?" She gently peeled out of his embrace. "What we do when the lights are off is a different story."

"That sounds like something straight out of a bad talk show."

"Don't start with me."

"Sorry, okay? Sorry I hugged you. Sorry for trying to be nice."

"I don't mind that you're nice—"

"But I can't hug you? We can fuck each other like a couple of kids—"

She shushed him, but he carried on. "It's just not fair. What kind of bullshit head fuck is this?"

"Rand, please—"

"I mean what're we doing to each other, honey?"

"I don't know." A sudden gasp forced her hand across her mouth. "I wish I did."

"Lena ..."

"You have to go." The tears were streaming now. "I can't do this tonight, you know? And your fucking swearing has just got to stop."

She turned for the bathroom and quickly slammed the door. Rand stood there for a solid minute until the simmering corn and quiet sobs were the only sounds he heard. Stunned, he finally gathered up his things and called Elias for a ride before shouldering back into his soaked jacket and gloves.

"Dad?"

Rand froze, turned, and saw Kenny at the top of the stairs as Kenny asked, "Where ya going?"

Lying made it hard for Rand to smile. "I gotta go, kid, got some things to do that I forgot about."

"What? But you just got here."

"I know, bud. We'll wrestle tomorrow. I promise."

"Okay." Kenny hung his head. "I'll see you tomorrow, right?"

"Yeah." Rand paused as if unsure of knowing what was worse—once again letting his kids down, or acknowledging this whole mess was more or less entirely his own fault. "Right after work ..."

"I love you, daddy."

"Love you too, buddy." He watched Kenny turn and walk down the hall. It did not feel good to hear your ex-wife crying as your disappointed kid trailed away like someone had just killed his pet. Opening the door, Rand cast a look of pure hatred into the snow-doted pixilation the frozen night provided.

———

Elias found Rand on County Road 61, a lone black figure in the windblown dark. Through the headlights, snake-like wisps of snow eerily eddied just above the road. Because of the icy conditions, it took a while to stop and even longer to find a plowed-out spot to turn the Skylark around.

"What the hell?" Elias said, watching as Rand deposited a clump of wet clothing onto the floor. "Everything all right?"

"Naw, man."

Elias checked left before slowly gaining speed. The snow was tapering off, the clouds quietly moving east as if guilty about the two-day havoc just unleashed. In their place, the stars crowded around the face of a three-quarter moon. With the cloud cover absent, the temperature just kept dropping.

They drove in silence as Elias scanned the only four radio stations in a hundred-mile radius—watered down hip-hop out of Culvert City, a local Spring Valley station that played acoustic and folk, country music on another, and an alternative rock station that had its entire format on tape. If the tape got stuck, which it frequently did, the listener was subjected to an obnoxious hum for an indeterminate amount of time—usually however long it took someone to phone Buster, the station alcoholic and lone technician. After barely checking on the non-selections, Elias killed the tunes altogether.

"I really appreciate it," Rand said.

"No kidding. Fucking hicks. Radio out here might as well not even exist."

"I was talking about picking me up."

"Oh."

As they approached town, Elias asked, "Where am I taking you?"

Rand grunted, staring out at the frozen night. "You got anything going on tonight?"

"Other than smoking a fat joint and passing out?" Elias was painted green in the dashboard glow. "Naw, man, not really."

"Wanna get a beer? I mean, we haven't really hung out together, is all."

"Listen, I'd love to, but I'm seriously strapped."

"I'll buy." Rand pulled out a giant roll of twenties. "I got paid today."

"You sure did." Descending onto Main Street, Elias swung an arm like a game show host. "It's all you, brah, where we headed?"

"The Dresden."

"Oh man."

Parked around back, their boots stomped down a set of metal steps to a steel door behind which a giant goateed slab greeted them with a scowl.

"Hey, Casey." Rand stepped past. "How is it?"

"Sausage fest, man. And it's fucking lady's night."

"Not good."

"Who you got with ya?"

"This is Thomas."

Casey extended a hand. "I seen you around, haven't I?"

"That's right. You kicked me out of here just last week."

Rand chuckled. "Shocking."

Inside, a dented aluminum bar-top fit in perfectly with the décor, which hovered somewhere between industrial Goth and a prison waiting room. There was a huge stage and a state-of-the-art sound system. This was where punk and metal bands took advantage of Spring Valley being the most populated town on the seven-hour drive between Denver and Salt Lake City. Reeking of stale beer, the main room was a dank stinkhole hauntingly lit by purple candelabras. A hallway led to a separate bar where concrete walls, stainless steel chairs and stools, held all the ambience of a psych ward. Save for the bartender and a Mohawked drunk passed out in the corner, this bar was completely empty.

"Nice." Rand hung his jacket on the back of a metal stool, nodding toward the bartender. "Beam and a Bud."

"Make it a pair." Elias pulled up a seat just as Alice in Chains' "Dem Bones" ripped apart the bar. The drinks arrived and Rand lifted his shot. "Here's to it."

"Game on."

Rand pulled out a pack of Marlboros. "Where did you say you live at?"

"About seven fucking minutes from the gondola, man."

Rand handed Elias a smoke. "You sound bitter."

"Of course, I'm bitter. I just got my cast off last week and was hoping to crush some serious powder. Instead, I'm now working six freaking days a week."

"I can't believe you started working for us a day after getting your cast off. You a martyr or just plain crazy?"

"Well, it wasn't like I was sitting on a small fortune, you know? Originally the doctor told me to take eight weeks off and I was like, am I moving in with *you*, doc? I was back at work the next day." Elias made a fist a couple of times and the wrist grated as if filled with sand. "Yeah, it'll never be the same. I should've just stayed on skis. I bought a board and broke my arm the same day. I don't even know how the fuck I'm gonna pay for this either."

"Don't. Shit should be free anyhow. Those insurance cocksuckers are out of their blessed minds."

"Doctors, insurance companies ... they're like the mafia—they always get their money."

"I hear ya."

"So anyway, I got fired and now I'm bitching wood six days a week. I came out here to ski, bro."

"Who didn't? But not to worry. We'll squeeze in a few powder days. Got any roommates?"

"Yeah. Five of them."

"Any hotties?"

"No. What about you? Where you at?"

"I ... my old lady lives east of town."

"You married?"

"Used to be." Rand started picking at the beer label. "I lost my apartment last month. Been staying mostly in motels."

"Good thing you got a big fat roll of twenties."

"No shit."

They drank in silence.

"You want another shot?" Rand asked, and Elias quickly nodded. The refills arrived along with a commotion of shattering glass from the adjoining room.

Elias winced. "This place is some kind of shithole."

"You got that right. So what happened last week?"

"What?"

"When you got kicked out?"

"Please ... One of my roommates, this guy Beal, he's just a super nice guy, you know? One of the only normal dudes in our condo. Dude's all hippied out, tie-dye and everything. No one even knew him before James brought him home from a party one night. We all wanted cheaper rent, so we offered him the landing between the first and second floor."

"Sounds spacious."

"So anyway, some bully from Nebraska got all up in his grill one night and soon enough another idiot crowns Beal with a bottle and that was that. The hate was flying everywhere."

"Awesome."

"I'm twenty-eight, you know? How much challenge is there in stomping on a bunch of kids?"

"Not much."

"Rough lessons ..."

"Sometimes you got no choice."

"You're right. Except where I come from, the other guy might be pulling out a gun."

"We've been working together for a week and I don't even know where you're from."

"New York."

"City?"

"Yeah."

"What the hell made you come all the way out here?"

"Man ... I don't even know where to start."

But a moment later he did. He still seemed uneasy trusting a partial stranger with the worst six months of his life. Actually, it was more like the worst three years, but things never start out like that. He had met Lisa Gendreau at the premiere of a Sean Penn film in the East Village. There to cover the event for his fledgling magazine, Elias was immediately overwhelmed by her dark brown eyes and black hair. After enough cocktails, he summoned up the nerve, boldly timing the refill of his drink with the emptying of hers.

Never particularly suave, Elias was startled when she fully participated in his sordidly candid conversation. Originally from Burlington, Vermont, Lisa attended N.Y.U. before becoming a teacher. Majoring in special needs, she taught at PS 63, an elementary school in Alphabet City, and could barely pay the rent.

They eventually left the premiere and stopped at three other bars before ending up entangled on the floor of her miniscule kitchen. He awoke Saturday morning in her bed and before either one knew it Sunday turned into Monday before he was finally forced to leave for work. They had things in common, Gus Van Sant films and Cormac

McCarthy novels, but otherwise time was tight. She adapted to his grueling schedule of fifty-hour work weeks and his nightly magazine duties until all he had left to share were late nights inside his tiny apartment. This adjustment was rough, as neither one had ever been this committed. They were also both twenty-three and trying to jump-start their respective careers.

In addition to teaching, Lisa was in a master's program while working as a tutor for developmentally challenged children. Because of her job, she had a tremendous amount of patience which, fortunately for Elias, helped keep the peace between them. Whenever he got inflamed to the point of losing focus, she was usually able to disengage this downward spiral.

Despite these occasional lapses, he was surprisingly attentive. In bed, exhausted, he would ask about her day before listening to a full recounting. He also cooked and cleaned in a general way. While he only made fourteen dollars an hour, he always took her out on Friday night.

Two years later, after professional successes for each, they discussed upgrading their apartment since all of their belongings were stacked, layered, and stuffed into every available inch of his one-room place. There were even shelves and boxes in the bathroom, and Elias used to joke that they would have made excellent submariners even in this, a city full of people shoe-horned into their own lives.

They spent her twenty-fourth birthday in a quiet West Village bistro. He remembered she was wearing his favorite dress, a strapless black Dior.

For the occasion, Elias donned a suit, trimmed the goatee, and shaved his head. She liked the way he looked, simple and defined. His green eyes were intense but excited. The birthday cake was not a surprise but his awful singing was, and they laughed at his disgrace.

Later, walking down Thompson Street, they decided to find a new apartment even though this search would not be easy, not if they intended on remaining in Manhattan, which Elias more or less insisted upon. Born and raised in Brooklyn, he had finally put the East River between his past and this new life, so retreating was not an option. Nor would they consider Queens or Upper Manhattan or prolonged commutes alongside a few hundred thousand miserable co-combatants.

Elias had a deadline the next morning for *Insurrection's* bimonthly run, so he had to stop by the office. He made Lisa promise not to open her gift until he got back to the apartment. Later on, he would remember watching her cross the street and disappear into the crowd just like who they might have been.

———

"I gotta piss." Elias rose from the barstool battling the alcohol and fatigue. In the past hour they had consumed three shots, four beers and now, after running at the mouth for the better part of the last twenty minutes, Elias seemed embarrassed.

Rand watched his cigarette burn down to the filter. He found that listening to someone else's pain, after just experiencing his own installment barely an hour before, eased his mood. Besides, he had nothing better to do, nowhere else to go, and was drinking with probably the one person in town he did not know well enough to hate.

Elias returned from the bathroom, which was little more than a shit-smeared box near the kitchen. As a food industry lifer, he was thoroughly disgusted. "I can't believe this place has the gall to even serve food."

They were on their stools for a full minute before Rand finally said, "So ...?"

"There ain't nothing much else to add, man, you know? It just didn't work out."

"Yeah, okay. So you and her just broke up?"

"Something like that." Elias fidgeted uncomfortably. "It's a really horrible story, man. This guy, he was retarded, he almost killed her."

"What? What retard?"

"She never had a chance. Beat her bad, man. And after that we went down in flames. I just don't want to talk about it right now. No offense."

"None taken."

"I've been trying to forget about it for the last six months."

"I hear ya ..." Rand squashed out the cigarette and raised his beer. "Well, fuck it. Here's to your third week on board—"

"Second."

Rand laughed. "Really? It's so horrible it only feels like three, right?"

"Something like that. Most of my muscles are still screaming."

"We ought to be charging you a fee for getting you in shape."

Elias gave him the finger.

Rand said, "You really gonna split?"

"Who knows? I really thought I was but now ... now I'm not too sure if there's anything left to go back to, you know? And I'm not just talking about her." He appeared ready to elaborate but reached for the smokes instead. "I mean I'm a fucking cook ..."

"Not anymore. What you are is a laborer, about to become an apprentice, about to become a journeyman, about to become a lead guy."

"Oh yeah? That easy, huh?"

"If you put in the time and make this shit your own, someday you'll be making thirty bucks an hour."

"After twenty years of slaving?"

"Only if you're a moron. It took me three years."

"Huh."

"Seriously. You already got the work ethic, which is ninety percent of what this job demands. You wouldn't believe how many lazy, whiny fucks there are in this business."

"Ever work in a kitchen?"

"Nope."

"Believe me, the deadbeats are everywhere."

"People are weak."

They drank in silence until Elias lit a smoke. "Thirty bucks an hour, huh?"

"No lie."

"That's a shitload better than ten."

"Just stick out the next two weeks and I'll make sure you get a raise."

"Still off the books?"

"Yep."

"What about overtime?"

"Don't even bring it up with him." Rand envisioned that conversation and almost laughed. "That would not be in your best interest."

"Do other guys pay—"

"Listen ... This ain't no union and the other guys can do whatever the fuck they want. But no. There ain't no OT. Outside of working for a contractor on giant commercial jobs, there's no such thing as OT. Especially not for you, because you'd actually be losing money instead."

"Because ..."

"Because figure at ten bucks an hour, for a fifty-hour week, with overtime included, you're looking at six hundred fifty bucks before taxes. After taxes you might see four hundred."

"But under the table, with no OT, I'm looking at five hundred."

"Yep."

"But if I'm not on the books, that means I'm not officially part of the company."

"So?"

"So what if I get hurt?"

"We make one phone call, tell them you started the day before and boom—there you are."

"Boy, you dudes run it lean and mean, don't ya?"

"You wanna get ahead in this joke of a world, I don't know how you could think or live any other way."

"Amen." Elias drained out the Budweiser before motioning for another round. "How long you been swinging a hammer?"

"Off and on since I was in high school."

"And how old are you now?"

"Thirty-seven." Rand frowned. "Why you smiling?"

"I ..." Elias seemed amused. "That's not what I heard, is all."

"Don't you worry about what you think you may have heard." Rand finished his beer in a flourish. "As a matter of fact, no more thinking at all."

"I'll drink to that."

The bartender arrived with the next round as a group of ten guys in brand new ski gear filed in from the other room. They were young and loud and seemed to know enough not to situate themselves near the stoic pair observing them from the end of the bar.

At nine o'clock, the growing crowd could be heard clamoring for drinks.

"Boy," Elias said, as if suddenly shown a vision. "Tomorrow's gonna really suck."

"Don't be such a pussy." Rand drunkenly raised his shot. "To a couple of broken-backed sons of bitches."

"Amen." Raising his glass, relieved to have the alcohol playing defense against what ailed, Elias played nice and for once followed the leader.

———————

The half-mile road meandering through the woods to the Gildman School had been plowed before they arrived Friday morning. The snow was jammed up on either side into twin berms wedged ten-feet high. On the roadbed, patches of dirt shone through like scabs scraped open by the plow.

At 6:58 A.M., it was minus three degrees as Nolan's pickup barreled along this snow-choked channel like a bad idea headed for an even worse conclusion.

"Good God." Nolan lowered the passenger side window and then quickly locked it. "Is there any whiskey left in town or did you two boozebags drink the entire county dry?"

Beside him, Rand squirmed through the freezing wind while trying to close his window. "Unlock it, Nolan!"

"Ha-ha!"

"This ain't funny!"

The cold sliced Rand's face like a razor as he buried his head inside his jacket.

"At thirty miles an hour," Nolan gleefully informed him, "that puts the windchill at minus thirty-three degrees!"

They picked up speed, popping out like a missile from the tree line. Nolan locked up the brakes twenty feet behind Elias' car and skidded to a stop right beside it.

"All right, stinky, time to work off all that booze." Nolan hopped down and saw Elias clearing scraps off the deck. "What about you? You as hungover as your boyfriend here?"

"Totally. I'm a complete blank from ten o'clock on."

Cackling, Rand suddenly coughed in the icy air, and then continued laughing. "That was some epic shit all right."

"Hey, Noll." Elias wedged himself deeper within his hood. "Ask him how the ride home was."

"What happened?"

"Do you even remember her name?" Rand asked Elias, who in an effort to stay warm, dumped another load of scrap off the deck.

"Carrie?" Elias said. "Mary something?"

"How fucked up was that?"

"Goddamnit!" Nolan screamed. "What the hell happened?"

Elias said, "Well, as we were leaving the bar, this girl needed a ride home. She lives right up Timber Lane. Anyway, I stopped for gas, went inside to pay, and when I returned Mr. Foreplay here's in the backseat getting his pipe skulled by this little spinner."

"Fucker." Nolan was clearly jealous. "How cute was she?"

"I thought she was hot." Rand glanced up at Elias for confirmation.

"Smokeshow." Elias stomped his already frozen feet. "Tiny little thing, wasn't she?"

"Nice tits too." Rand banged his gloves together. "Goddamn, man, it's fucking freezing out here!"

"Thanks for the weather update, Fabio. Think of this as your punishment for defiling someone young enough to be your own daughter."

"Dude!"

"Shh, Señor Creepy, no more talking." Nolan squeezed a Marlboro Light into his pinched lips and headed for the tool chests. Unable to work the lighter with gloves, he and Rand cooked the locks while cursing their instantly frozen hands. As if awaiting this unguarded moment, the subzero winds gutted them against the boxes.

Elias worked the worm-burner over the generator and compressor. He glanced at their ice-covered surroundings. The crystal-coated trees creaked in the breeze, and with wind gusts approaching minus twenty-three degrees, Elias took a moment to ponder if anything in these conditions, even skiing, was worth the required trauma just surviving it entailed. On his face, though, he betrayed none of this. Over the last two weeks, he saw that his bosses' effort never wavered, even when common sense and good judgment screamed otherwise. As far as Elias was concerned, they would drag his dead body out of here before he gave in to the sound, rational urge to flee.

"How's it going?" Nolan hovered over his shoulder.

Elias swung the worm-burner back and forth. "I think they might be ready."

Nolan's face mask and hat made him look like an armed robber. The only exposed skin was around his eyes, which was already reddened from the searing cold. He said, "Minus thirty ain't nothing to fuck with. You need to put on a mask. Like right now."

"You're right."

"I'm gonna crank up the truck. Get an extra set of gloves and any other clothes into the frontseat to warm up."

"Okay."

All three retreated toward the vehicles for additional clothing against the assault. With the added layers, they looked like swollen clots waddling through the dawn.

"I never thought I'd say this," Rand said. "But I think it's even too cold to smoke."

"Don't be such a quitter."

Lips, eyeballs, nostrils—anything moist quickly ached. And then froze. Especially wet gloves, which the windchill ravaged until their fingers felt like calcified stumps pulsing in agony.

Nolan scooped out enough Vaseline to smear across his face, and handed the jar to Rand and then Elias, who inevitably stated, "Of all the uses ..."

"Tell the truth, dude." Nolan pulled his mask back into place. "You got excited for a second there, didn't ya?"

"A subzero circle jerk? You guys need some better hobbies."

Rand chuckled while trying to light a cigarette, but his grease-smeared hands fumbled the lighter into the snow.

"Fuck!" He stomped his feet like an enraged child. "Fuck! Fuck! Fuck!"

Nolan turned to Elias. "It's like I always said. You can take the idiot out of the moron, but you just can't take the moron—"

"Gimme your lighter," Rand demanded.

"Where's yours?"

"Nolan!"

"Did you hear that?" Nolan cupped his ear. "This voice just said, '*No More Talking.*'"

"I'm not kidding."

"Users lose." Nolan turned his back and started walking away. "Hurry up."

"Motherfucker!"

Elias gave him a light instead.

The generator and compressor finally roared to life as if enraged by this request. Nolan cursed, because in the time it had taken to get re-dressed and rolled out, both the gun and saw had already frozen.

"Put them by the heater," Nolan instructed Elias. "And get another set rolled out because these fuckers are going to be freezing up all day long."

On each end of the front wall, Nolan hooked the bottom sill plate and made a crow's foot eight-feet up. Then they snapped a chalk line for the first row of plywood sheets.

"My goddamn fucking fingers!" Rand drove his hatchet halfway through a wall stud. It was such a solid strike it even vibrated the floor.

"Marinate in the misery, simpleton," Nolan cracked, and then waddled over to retrieve the gun. "Thomas! Goddamnit, let's get some sheets over here!"

But Elias was already turning the corner with a pair across his shoulder.

"That's right, sheet-boy." Nolan loaded the gun with two clips of 8's. "We'll keep you warm, all right, running sheets like some immigrant bitch."

"Thanks for the pep talk."

If layout was correct, and the studs were sixteen-inches on center, the only sheet they would need to cut was the last one in the row. It took a few sheets to establish a rhythm, but once in sync, they geared into full production. Nolan ran the gun like an automatic weapon as Elias kept them fed with sheets while also switching out the hoses, gun, and saw, which were freezing up at twenty-minute intervals. If any part of this assembly line halted, the cold became a living presence preying on lack of movement.

"Need more sheets!" Nolan screamed half a dozen times, but Elias was moving fast. Trekking halfway around the building with every load left him winded. By 10:00 A.M., when the sun finally punched through the clouds, the first-floor was completely sheeted.

Nolan said, "Elias, the chainsaws are in my truck heating up. Hurry up."

Nolan and Rand stomped their feet in the blistering cold until Elias returned with a beat-up pair of Husqvarna 240s. Nolan and Rand toggled the chokes and fired them up in bursts of acrid smoke. In an effort to both increase structural stability and to save time, they had sheeted over the window and door openings. Now, with the chainsaws screaming, they sliced out the perimeter of each hole in a spray of splintering plywood.

"That," Elias said, "was fucking awesome."

"Let's keep going." Nolan pointed. "Elias, load the deck with 2x4 studs for interior walls. Rand, get another gun and saw rolled out."

Rand, apparently unhappy about being ordered around, paused a moment to clean his sunglasses. "And you?" he asked. "What're you gonna do?"

"Consult the plans, my friend." Nolan climbed into the heated cab of the still idling diesel. "All right, people, let's hurry up!"

"Hurry up and suck my nuts," Rand mumbled.

"What was that?"

"I said I'm all about the team." Rand looked over at Elias. "How about you?"

As he headed for the lumber stacks, Elias turned and said, "Teams are for weaklings, man, fuck the team."

"See?" Rand asked Nolan. "You're already ruining the new guy."

Just before he closed the door, Nolan said, "No one cares about your problems, Señor Creepy, hurry up."

Abandoned, Rand said, "Fuck it," and dug out his cigarettes. He aimed his masked face toward the sun while the cold and smoke tore into his lungs. Moments later, disgusted by even this lack of satisfaction, Rand went back to work.

The building inspector was due at their last job by one o'clock, so after lunch Nolan headed over to meet Mike Conyers at Butcher Block for the final walk-through. Telling himself to be rational and calm, if only to squeeze out the last check for $10,000, meant Nolan would have to spend the next hour greasing Conyers' ass. This was the part of the job Nolan hated—the painful small talk with morons who drove around in designer denim outfits and brand-new pickups worth more than he earned all year.

Sadly, the initial excitement of starting his own company was already waning into the stark reality that now, having established his independence, absolutely no one had his back. From here on out, he would have to carry liability insurance, worker's compensation, handle all of the billing, payroll, tools, repairs, taxes, and between all of that, line up work for what he hoped would be an ever-expanding company. Every night for the past week, he worked the math, angling for his slice. If he could find two more guys like Rand and Elias, they could split into two crews on different projects, and Nolan could step back, drop his bags, and focus on the business aspect of lining up new customers and maybe, if all went well, eventually building homes on spec.

Even though he was only thirty-four-years-old, time was already running short. The search to find the fifty-year-old carpenter broken down by thirty years of labor did not take long. As a matter of fact, most of the guys Nolan fired fit that bill exactly. Loafers, deadbeats—guys who could only make it to work three or four days a week—the work ethic of the modern American was slipping into disgrace. Was it really that difficult? Showing up on time and working hard at what could be, with just a little dedication, a well-paying trade?

He was sick of the bullshit and now, as owner, swore to look out for the guys who looked out for him. Pay them on time and in full. Christmas bonuses and maybe even a few paid days off. But he did not want any whiners or big talkers, guys who showed up on the job claiming outrageous knowledge and exorbitant salaries despite the fact that Nolan had forgotten more than they would ever know. Guys like that could head to IBC or Hemmings Incorporated, the two giant commercial construction firms in charge of employing some of the worst carpenters northwest Colorado had to offer. Each firm was currently building what were, at least for a town of Spring Valley's size, considerable resorts. This was also why, as the pace of new construction boomed, a showdown with the Planning Commission was only a matter of time. Fearing this, developers and builders had deluged the Building Department with a flood of new permit requests even as opposition to expansion gained momentum. To get his taste at the table, Nolan wanted to blow this project out, position himself in line for a nice new custom home, and hopefully frame out only high-end jobs from there. It might have been a stretch to think about custom homes this soon, but that was part of his DNA. Was it better to think about a slow progression, the same five dollars per square foot cookie-cutter bullshit he could nail off in his sleep? That was, he knew, how the timid existed. Having worked and crewed on his share of northern Californian mansions with old world precision to detail, Nolan knew that was where the big boys played. Those guys rolled out at ten grand a week and drove trucks more expensive than some small homes.

So here he was, thinking all these grand thoughts until the horror show of Butcher Block swung into view. "Oh my God. What a shithole."

The eight identical boxes were about as inspiring as sleeping pills stuck into the hillside, and this, coupled with the fact that Conyers' pickup was already there, almost caused Nolan to swing a U-turn.

Charlie Waters was one of only three building inspectors in Salinas County. Nolan recognized his old green Ford Ranger and considered this an unexpected bonus. Waters, born into a Wyoming ranching family, grew bored with raising cattle and left for Texas on his eighteenth birthday. He fell into carpentry by mistake, and because of his restless mind, earned electrical and plumbing licenses as well. Plainspoken to the point of offense, he was a favorite of Nolan's. When a person thought of Stetson hats, sun-cracked faces, and worn-out cowboy boots, a Hollywood casting agent could produce no better. Waters was not big on conversation, excuses for poor craftsmanship, or builders who got pedantic with explanations. Almost sixty, he had been involved with every aspect of home construction longer than half the framers in town had been alive, so questions as to his judgment usually caused the uninitiated a lot more harm than good.

Regarded by most as an obstinate stickler, it paid to know what Waters was looking for in his inspections—mainly proper nailing, bearing points, and beams. If all three were accounted for, and the signed and stamped set of blueprints submitted to the Building Department was exactly adhered to, Waters would sign off without hesitation.

As Nolan parked and zipped up, he saw the temperature was twenty-degrees warmer without the wind on this side of the mountain. He watched Waters' wiry frame and Stetson hat bobbing uphill from unit four. Nolan hopped down and called out, "Afternoon, Charlie."

"Now don't say it," Charlie Waters yelled back, stomping through the snow.

"Say what?"

"'Cold enough for ya?' I swear to God, the next sumbitch that says that simple shit is gonna have a meeting with my boot."

"Fair enough. But I can't believe you're not wearing some kind of winter hat."

"You looking to fail this inspection?" Waters feigned offense while grabbing the brim of his Stetson. "I'll just pretend you never said that." He held a clipboard in a gloved hand and stuck the other one out in greeting. "How you doing, Noll, it's been a while, son."

"Everything's good. I'd be a bitch if I complained." Nolan seemed humbled by the other man's presence. "You and Beth have a good Christmas?"

"Absolutely. As my father used to say, 'marriage is a relationship where one person is always right, and the other is the husband.'" Waters' thin mustache twitched in the nerve-grinding breeze. He cocked his head and squinted up at Nolan. "How 'bout you?"

"Kept it simple this year, Charlie, just me and the wife." Nolan glanced around at the houses. "Some kind of shit-dump, huh?"

"Conyers," Waters said, as if that were explanation enough. "Ask me, this kind of shackery ought to be kept off in the woods somewhere." He pinched ice from his mustache. "Heard a rumor, so I crept by your new location the other night after work." Waters gave him a wink. "You fellas are tearing the ass out of that place."

Nolan held up his hand and spread each finger wide. "Five weeks, may the big guy in the sky strike me dead if not."

Waters grinned. "Careful what you wish for."

"Right? So how'd we do?"

"Pretty good." Waters consulted his clipboard. "Found two hangers missing in number three, and unfilled blocklines in the basements of one through four."

"That's it?"

"The clipboard don't lie." Waters held it up.

"Sweet."

"Listen, long as we're talking about rumors, mind telling me what happened between you and Mike?"

"What's there to say? Tell me if I'm wrong, Charlie, but what kind of message does he think he's sending by slow paying, no paying, and nickel and diming me to death?"

Waters said nothing, so Nolan said, "I've had it, you know? I mean on a fucking Friday night, after busting my ass to get a nut all week long, this motherfucker's gonna make *me* chase *him*? Never again, man, never again."

"He offer you a bump after you walked?"

"Of course he did. So he gives me a raise and then what? I got to chase him down for that too?"

"I see what you mean."

"Of course you do, Charlie, because you're not a moron. Some of these guys think payday is an option or some kind of charitable donation."

Waters laughed. "Gonna have to remember that one."

"Hey fellas," a voice called out.

They swiveled their heads as Conyers and a woman waved from the front door of number six.

"Game on." Nolan lit his cigarette. "Keep that clipboard handy, will ya?"

"Not a problem." Waters wedged down his hat. "But let's get moving before my old boney ass freezes solid."

"I hear ya. But it's good to be on this side of the mountain today, man, because the wind is killing us at Gildman."

Inside number six, Conyers was still speaking with the woman before pointedly smiling at Nolan.

"Good to see you, Nolan." He rolled a shoulder against a wind gust. "Cold enough for ya?"

The ensuing silence was worse than the chill, so Waters held out the clipboard and pen. "If you don't mind, I just need you to sign page six. I'll do a final sign off when the punch-list is done."

"Otherwise, she all good?" Conyers asked with a tinge of incredulity. "I'll be damned."

Nolan said nothing, thankful his sunglasses hid his mounting fury.

The woman, noticeably offended by the lack of introduction, finally stuck her hand toward Nolan and said, "I'm Kathy Landis."

"Nolan Harris."

She had a firm grip and an equally determined look. She was wearing a full dress Carhartt winter jumpsuit, and her boots looked as trashed as his. This was no saleswoman or decorator. Her expression relayed a sense of regret, as if this place was now hers alone to bear.

"I'm Charlie." Waters nudged Nolan aside and peeled off his hat. "It's awful nice to make your acquaintance, Miss Landis."

"No offense, Nolan," Conyers said. "But she's a whole lot easier on the eyes than your grizzled mug."

"That right?" Nolan tried to hide the surprise, as she must have been tired of that. "Just another framer banging nails in the cold?"

"Yes. Just moved up from Durango."

"Well, welcome aboard," Waters said, and Nolan thought the old man might be laying it on a bit too thick.

Conyers handed back the clipboard. "Couple of hangers and blocklines." He looked at Nolan with a pinched smile. "When can I expect that to be done?"

"Tomorrow morning. You got my check?"

"I do. But given the present circumstances, I'd feel more comfortable if we split payment. Half today, half tomorrow."

"Come on, Mike. As if what I just said doesn't mean a thing?"

"I'm sure it'll be completed by tomorrow." Conyers perched an eyebrow. "It's only business, Noll."

Kathy Landis, as if content with sharing in another framer's pain, genially said, "It's too cold to stand around. Nice meeting you both." And then she headed for her truck.

"I've gotta be moving along as well." Waters wedged down his Stetson. "See you fellas later."

Not wanting to be alone in Conyers' presence for one second longer than necessary, Nolan took the check and jammed it into his jacket.

"I'll be here first thing," he said, "and expecting full payment by noon at the latest."

"No problem." Conyers stuck out a hand. "I'm glad it's ending like this, Noll, without all the petty gripes."

"You're delusional." Nolan gave him his back. "See you in the morning."

––––––––––––

While Nolan dealt with Butcher Block, Elias was feeding Rand a sixteen-foot 2x10 through the door when Rand, usually sure-handed, lost his grip. As the giant piece of lumber slid back at Elias, a bright pain seared his palm. He looked down and saw a two-inch splinter piercing his left glove.

"Fuck!" Elias examined his hand as if intrigued by the mini-flagpole impaling his palm. "Holy shit."

"That's a monster." Rand twitched his nose beneath his frosted mask. "Fuck, man, I'm sorry. Drop the board. We got to get that thing out immediately. One, two, three."

They dropped the huge 2x10 as Rand hopped down and took hold of Elias' wrist. The wind howled even louder. They both knew this unintentional stoppage had to be fast or the cold would eat them alive.

Rand propped his sunglasses onto his cap to better examine the two-inch splinter stuck straight into the meat beneath Elias' thumb. As if appraising one of his gems, Rand worked the hand into different angled views and then said, "Take a deep breath."

"Good to go."

But it broke off inside the glove.

"Fuck!" Rand carefully worked the glove off as he said, "You need to know this. Any splinter, I don't care how small it is, you've got to dig it out immediately or you might not find it again."

"And then ...?"

"If it's deep enough inside the muscle, you're talking about swelling, infection, fever ... there's a million bacteria riding in on every single one."

"What? One *million*?"

"Yes." Rand stopped what he was doing and rotated his blue eyes onto Elias. "Listen. I'm gonna switch out my blade and then it's game on, Tex. We got to cut that thing out."

"Great." Elias examined the wound as Rand pulled a utility knife out of his bags. He switched blades and used a lighter to cook it clean. The splinter had pierced straight down. Elias could actually feel it embedded like an h'dourves toothpick through the muscle. "You guys aren't big on doctors, are ya?"

Rand's smile creased his frozen mask as he worked the flame across the razor. "Five hundred bucks for a couple of stitches ain't no choice at all."

"Hurry up, man, it's freezing."

The blade was glowing orange.

"Here we go." Rand hooked and corralled the arm against his own side, his back to Elias as he said, "You don't need to see this."

"Fuck." Elias did not like being blinded. "Dude—"

"I'm gonna cut in at an angle. Going head-on will only push it further in."

Elias was resigned. "On three."

"One, two, three."

Elias cursed, flinched, and then shot straight up onto his toes. "Dude!" He winced, torqued his head the other way, and felt a scorching burn as the blade cut and probed. An instant slipperiness appeared.

"Stop moving and start breathing," Rand commanded.

Elias, who was biting down on both lips to digest the flood of pain, heeded this advice. He inhaled deeply and jerked every time the razor switched directions.

Stone-faced, Rand finally released the hand. He held up an inch long dagger pinched between his bloody thumbnail and the razor. "That was huge. One of the biggest I've ever seen."

"Considering how long you've been doing this, should I be proud or embarrassed?" Elias examined the ragged half-inch cut and decided it felt worse than it appeared. The palm was dribbling blood but already clotting, growing numb in the subzero gusts.

"I wish we had some disinfectant." Rand wiped the bloody blade on his pants and then slotted the knife back into his bags. "Hell, even alcohol—"

"I've got a bottle of Beam in my trunk. Super glue is in the glovebox."

"Nice." Rand headed to the Skylark.

"Here goes nothing." Elias gritted his teeth and then jammed his fist into a snowbank. He quickly sloughed off the runny blood-water and then wedged his frozen hand into his armpit. "This is fucking hateful."

"What's that?" Rand returned down the trench with a roll of duct tape, napkins, and whiskey.

"I said I should've been drinking the Beam before letting a certain Civil War butcher slash into my hand."

Rand took his wrist and then upended the bottle. The pain was brief but nothing in comparison. Rand used a napkin to wipe it dry and then sealed it with the glue. After it dried thirty seconds later, he applied another napkin over the cut. Unwinding a length of tape, he began wrapping this makeshift dressing.

"Some First Aid kit," Elias cracked, "a sooty knife and booze."

"Fall in love with the duct tape, bro, because out here Band-Aids are useless. If they're not soaked and immediately dislodged by sweat, then they're frictioned off from movement."

And so it was—punctures, cuts, smashed fingertips, gouged knuckles, sprained fingers and wrists—whiskey, napkins, and duct tape.

After work, Elias pulled into his condominium, stared at his taped-up fist, and smiled at the day's events. Earlier at lunch, as Nolan drove by job after job where no workers could be seen, Elias had to wonder about the sanity of actually having to *cook* your tools in order to keep working.

Yet it was still there, even now as he sat in the blasting heat, exactly what he had felt all day even as the radio declared temperature warnings and hazardous windchill conditions on this, the coldest day so far this season. While the other crews were inside losing a day's pay, Nolan and company ratcheted up the pace just to stay warm. It took a whole new level of masochism to make something barely survivable even worse. Even when Elias was a cook, it was only when the orders came flooding in at such a rate that the ticket machine rattled as if possessed, and the grill, sauté, fry, and salad stations were in an absolute deluge of panic, that Elias would take a second to glance into the stricken eyes of his co-workers and laugh at the sheer lunacy of what they were about to attempt. After all, the Manhattan dinner crush in a midtown hotspot on a Friday night offered the foolhardy a chance at basking in the true high pure suffering produced.

"Fuck it." He killed the engine, grabbed his gloves and gear, and then cursed because he was just starting to warm up. He punched open the door like a soldier greeted by hostile fire and ran up the embankment. Inside his condo, he followed his routine. Around a gas-fed cast iron stove, he propped his boots and fanned out his clothes and gloves. As if cooking a meal, he tended the garments every half hour, flipping or rotating accordingly. That awful lesson had been quick and painful—nothing ruined a day faster than putting on wet boots in the morning.

The house phone rang as he finished, so he ignored it since hardly anyone ever called for him. But after the answering machine kicked in, and the silence crackled loudly on the open line, he heard her say, "Hi, this message is for Thomas ..."

The dial tone clipped on as he stood there in his long-johns freezing, the silence roaring until the phone rang again.

"Hello?" He yanked some extra cord. "Lisa, is that you?"

"Yes ..."

He could hear her sniffling and still, even after everything, the sound of her crying hurt even worse than his torn hand.

In the three months since he left the city, the disastrous last year had shifted into clearer focus. Yet here he was again, exhausted, still trying to escape the one person he had never really wanted to leave in the first place.

He knew the violence of that night destroyed their relationship. After the attack, the flashbacks to other horrible moments became unleashed again. The once vivacious and sparkling woman was smashed to pieces, poorly reassembled, and now stared back with those hostile, searing eyes. It was jarring. Her withering contempt-filled expression, which had originally pushed him even further away, was exactly what he now felt pulsing through the phone.

"Honey ..."

He had tried everything. After getting her home from the hospital and disconnecting the phones, as she requested, he kept the drapes pulled twenty-four hours a day. He checked out every noise or hallway commotion at her panicked insistence until, finally at wit's end, he met with her counselors in hopes of gaining some new perspective, insight, tips, advice—anything that would help him help her, for the situation had become untenable. She was on leave from work and refused to exit the apartment for any reason. Without her income, Elias double-shifted and lost track of everything else. In his absence, his partners destroyed his magazine while his girlfriend bizarrely obsessed over the peephole in their door. In the few hours she was not perched in front of it, she layered it over with so much duct tape it looked like the door had grown an abscess. She also spoke about their neighbors like a crazed Peeping Tom aware of everyone's movements. She reported that the nice young Hispanic wife next door was having an affair while the husband was at work. The single mom across the hall was sometimes leaving her kids unattended, probably because she had a job and could not afford daycare or find a babysitter or whatever the problem was, it certainly was not Elias'. He did not want to hear about this petty nonsense or other people's negligence or their own looming disasters—he was just trying to survive his own.

Now Lisa said, "I thought it would be a good idea to call, that enough time had come and gone, but even hearing your voice ..."

He figured she was about to hang up. He loved her. He did not think even now that this had changed. Knowing what they had been was no longer his to hold onto, he was left to wonder how she was in that place he used to know.

———————

Predictably, it did not take long for one to call the other. Even though they had been out drinking the previous evening, and still had to work a full Saturday tomorrow, the bar stools were soon beneath their asses. Still thrown by Lisa's call, Elias just wanted to booze and hear someone else's problems, so he made sure Rand's shot glass stayed full.

The bar, El Rancherito, was filling up with a mid-twentyish crowd split between hippie wannabes and multiple-pierced snowboard rats from moneyed families back East.

"What is with this fucking town?" Elias finally asked. "There's like six chicks in here, man."

Rand winked. "Five-to-one, bro."

"Is that really the ratio? That's just ridiculous."

"Be thankful you ain't in Alaska. When I was working up there it was more like ten-to-one."

"Fuck. That." Elias emptied his glass and ordered another round.

"See the bartender? You could take a swipe at her. Her fiancé died last fall."

Elias gave her a second glance, which was not difficult since she was beautiful but emanating a distinct hostility, as if whatever pleasure she had originally derived from slinging drinks and being constantly hit on had worn thin long ago. "How'd he die?"

"He was a world class whitewater guy." Rand tapped the ash from his smoke. "Drowned in Devil's Gorge."

"Isn't that close to here?"

"Bout an hour and a half south."

"Huh." Elias looked at her with this new information and found her weariness now had clearer meaning. "Sucks for her."

"It's a wicked place. The cliffs rise up on either side for hundreds of feet and the water, it starts getting funneled in a couple miles back. It squeezes from a river down into this thin channel strewn with boulders and rocks and the force of it ... the water just explodes against the walls like cannon fire."

"How do you know?"

"Because I been through there."

"Really?"

"There's all kinds of cool kayaking around here. The Little Snake up in Craig, the San Miguel down south, the Colorado River, and Blanding's Pass, but that one ain't nothing nice." Rand paused as if reliving an unpleasant episode. "Yeah, fuck that place."

"Gimme a smoke, will ya?"

Rand passed the pack and said, "Idaho, Wyoming, hell, man, take your pick."

"I get the point." Elias lit up. "Do you still paddle?"

"Every now and then. What about you? Ever been?"

"Naw, man, I'm from Brooklyn. The only whitewater I've seen is in a flushing toilet."

"Speaking of gross, did you know I nearly made it my whole life without smoking?"

"What happened?"

"I started working with Nolan ... Biggest mistake I ever made."

"The partnership or the cigarettes?"

"Ha ..."

They did another shot as the jukebox belched out Motörhead and the place suddenly came alive.

"How's the hand?" Rand nodded at the duct-taped fist.

"You were right. I put a bag on it, showered, cooked, and did the dishes—it's still tight as a drum."

"Let it breathe overnight."

"I will."

"Unreal ..." Rand spotted a new arrival. Elias followed his gaze toward a thin man with greasy brown hair sidling through the crowd.

Elias asked, "Who's that?"

"Crackhead Joe." Rand squinted. "Kid smoked so much crack he had a stroke and he's only like twenty-five. He still owes me a hundred bucks, but that ain't why I'm clocking him. Rumor has it he just got popped with some serious weight."

"So?"

"With his record, there ain't no way he should be out this fast. One thing you need to remember is that there's four different police agencies watching Route 61. Idaho, Wyoming, Utah—all their drugs come through here. Speaking of cops and drugs, you ever hear the Hells Angels story?"

"Negative."

"Well, every year they have a national run. Last summer, they chose Spring Valley. Since it was summer and most of the hotels were empty, they basically took over the Iron Horse Inn. I mean there must've been four hundred fucking Angels in town—a hundred of them in that place alone. Turns out one of them, after tweaking on meth for days, decided his own brothers were going to whack him. Of course they weren't, but this guy was such a delusional mess it didn't matter. Anyway, he came out of the bathroom blasting and clipped a couple of his bros. The cops surrounded the place after the ambulances left but the Angels wouldn't let anybody in. So the cops called the staties and Feds and pretty soon it was an old west standoff. A day later the Angels had ripped the hotel room down to the studs, I'm talking about carpet, drywall—any evidence—they packed all of it up into a box truck, put the Angel who did the shooting inside of it too, and then caravanned right by the cops. No one was ever charged with anything."

"Holy shit."

"It's still the wild west out here, man. Any of your roommates do blow?"

"Yep." Elias finished his beer. "Manhattan ain't got nothing on this place, boy, and we're in the middle of nowhere."

"Just watch out is all." Rand lit up another smoke. "People up here have a nasty habit of throwing each other under the bus. Just ask Crackhead Joe ..."

More drinks arrived and the silence extended, so Elias asked, "Were you born in Colorado?"

"Yep."

"Where at?"

"Close by."

Elias chuckled until Rand said, "What?"

"Is this top-secret information or what?"

"Kind of. In this profession, guys are barely around long enough to learn each other's last names, nevermind personal histories." Rand took a drag. "That said, my folks had a place down near Salida, at the base of the DeCristo Mountains."

"Yeah?"

"I was born there, but I grew up in Wyoming."

Then he spoke of a town called Bondurant and a six-room house his father built by hand. It had no running water or toilets but that was fine with Rand's mother, a woman unfazed by hardship. Their property bordered Grand Teton National Forest, which made their backyard a 485 square-mile playground. The Holmscombs had four sons and two daughters raised old-fashioned in their beliefs.

The father, a large man named Evan, was a college graduate who enlisted in the Navy in the late 1950s. Recognized for his high motor and drive, he was already a frogman on the Underwater Demolition

Teams before earning a slot on one of the original SEAL teams created by the Vietnam War. His service left him with two Bronze Stars and a pair of Purple Hearts before he retired at twenty-nine. From there, he went on to play outside linebacker for the Kansas City Chiefs under a legendary coach named Stram before a Grade Three dislocation of the shoulder ended his modest five-year career.

Soon after, he met Rand's mom at the Kansas City airport while she waited for her flight back to Cheyenne. He told her he was headed to Wyoming to look for land and apply for a contractor's license, and then switched seats so he could sit next to her on the plane. She was a ceramics artist and commercial backwoods guide, and after that initial encounter, they became inseparable.

Rand's siblings shared their mother's penchant for long hikes, but Rand was usually beside his father humping eighty-pound packs in the opposite direction. Evan Holmscomb taught his son how to navigate by the stars and what not to eat. He instructed him on his surroundings, how to track and which footprint belonged to which animal, and how they ate and where they gathered, how to shit, sleep, cook, start fires, and most importantly, how to cover his tracks. The father then began lessons in basic self-defense before breaking out the real business of hand-to-hand combat and knife training and aspects of Wing Chun Kung Fu adapted by the SEALs. Lethal strikes and sentry disarmament and neck breaks no one should be taught, least of all an eighteen-year-old kid who, one night drunk at a party, smashed in another kid's windpipe.

His mother, of course, was not pleased by this development. But his father would not be deterred, and off they would go into the woods again. Rand spoke of those encounters, where his father and his old Navy buddies would stake Rand a six-hour lead before setting off to hunt him down. And while he kept the details to a minimum, it was not hard for Elias to piece together the kind of anxiety one might feel with four or five ex-SEALs trying to rundown, cut off, or otherwise prevent his progress toward a designated rally point a couple dozen miles away.

There were more lessons focused on survival as he progressed. Land navigation at high altitude on limited supplies while battling sleep deprivation, and mountaineering with a focus on cliff ascension and rappel, were not for beginners. And if Rand's father was not proficient with certain disciplines or maneuvers, then one of his friends surely was, and Rand would subsequently be sent off into the woods with him.

Much to the father's disappointment, Rand was the only child interested in this brutal taste of lifestyle by instinct. The others went on to college. Rand's oldest sister became a computer programmer, one brother chose medicine, another went to law school, the youngest sister directed a youth services center and Colton, the baby of the litter, earned a doctorate in child psychology. That meant Rand, socially stunted like his dad, eventually lost track of everyone. Especially after his father's death—or disappearance might be more accurate. But he would not speak of that.

Sitting there now, somewhat self-conscious in the moment, he was staring at his beer as if it were the last one left on earth. "You need to tell me to shut up when I start to babble."

Elias said, "If even half of what you just said is true, I think that's about some of the coolest shit I've ever heard."

"I hear ya."

"The best part is that you're still using it, which means it was probably worth every minute."

"Well, I appreciate that, Thomas."

"Can I ask you something? I mean with all that kick ass training, how come you didn't just join the military?"

"Because I don't take orders. Off anyone. Ever. You play pool?"

"Yeah, for about another twenty minutes. After that, the double vision might make it more of a challenge than it's worth."

They signed their name on a chalkboard, but there would be no game. A fight was breaking out between two country boys and three Marines.

"One more time, little man," the Marine warned. Like his buddies, the Marine's bulging muscles were encased in a shirt two sizes too small. He had thick black eyebrows that resembled a shelf above his eyes which were, like his demeanor, filling in with menace.

"What're you going to do about it?" Country shot back.

Like two dogs alerted to danger, Rand started looking for the exit as Elias grabbed an empty bottle just in case.

"We better finish our beers," Rand said once the shouting began.

Bystanders headed for the exits as others cat-called for the approaching brawl.

"I ain't worried about you! I ain't worried about you!" the Marine screamed. He and Country were inches away, nose to nose, and Elias could not believe their disproportionate sizes.

"Hope that hick's got a good health plan," he said.

The bartenders called for order but dialed 911 just in case.

"I ain't hanging around for the pigs." Rand grabbed his jacket. "You ready?"

"You sure? This is just gettin' good."

The Marine's right hook smashed Country instantly unconscious.

"Let's go." Rand led the way. They hit a fire exit as the sound of fists and utter violence mingled with the grunting of those being wounded.

CHAPTER TEN

Crosstown, Kara and Nolan had dinner at Aunt Bee's Barbecue Shack. The walls were filled with animal heads and paneled wood steeped brown from the smokehouse cooker.

On this Friday night at the height of the season, the place was packed. Kara knew Nolan was not good with crowds or tourists, and so distracted him by asking about his day.

"That Conyers ..." Nolan tore into the ribs. "You should've seen it today, sweetie, I mean what an absolute bag of shit that guy is."

"Splitting the final payment was just insulting and stupid."

"Right?" He paused in mid-rack, wiped the mess off his face and hands, and then reached for a slice of cornbread. "I would've had more respect for the guy if he had just said, 'Job's not done yet. See you tomorrow.' I been to hell and back with this guy, and even though I'm splitting off, you'd think he'd like to at least end things on halfway decent terms. Instead, he's out to ensure that we're enemies forever."

"Oh, I think he's already realized that." Kara reached across the table and used her napkin to wipe his chin. "Easy, killer, you might want to come up for air."

"So good."

His appetite was prolific. Some nights he could eat half a meatloaf and baked potatoes and an hour later chase it with a bag of cookies. And while she might not have won any cooking awards, there certainly was a small amount of pride in watching her meals utterly devoured.

He was babbling about something stupid Rand had done when he noticed her distraction. "What're you looking at?"

"Your hands. Those chapped cuticles must be killing you ... Nolan, they're split wide open."

He shrugged while chewing.

"It's kind of incredible," she said, but could not understand it. How he and Rand and the new guy Elias could endure whole days in conditions that made normal people dread even walking to their cars, was either a testament to their own personal fortitude, or a massive cry for help. Knowing her husband, it seemed a combination of both.

"How's Elias doing?" she asked. "Nolan, please, wipe your chin, honey, regular people don't need to see this. It's gross."

Reaching for his wasted napkin, Nolan said, "The little fella's doing all right. Me and Rand got him on our own personal workout program."

"It's a miracle he's lasted this long."

"Oh, he's not going anywhere. This guy is some piece of work, honey. He got fired off the mountain because he wouldn't stop cursing in the kitchen. Claims personal censorship is against his beliefs." Nolan smiled through the grease. "Who knew morons could have beliefs?"

"Sounds like he fits right in."

"Kid's tough, I'll give him that. In the beginning I wondered why he was always wincing until he tells me he'd already been working with a broken arm for a month and a half before hopping on with us."

"Oh my."

"Right? But I got a special treat in store for him tomorrow. He and Rigor Mortis are about to have a close encounter of the worst kind."

"Oh my God. You're gonna stick him with Riggy?"

Nolan only laughed. They finished the meal and Nolan helped her into her coat.

Outside, she hugged him and looked up. "I won't be long."

"Thanks for taking me out." He leaned down and kissed her. "Tell Sarah I said hey."

"Yep. Kiss me again. You taste like barbecue."

"I'll be waiting for you at home on the couch."

"Gee." She rolled her eyes. "What a surprise."

"Oh, I'll surprise you all right." His hands snaked down to her backside. "I'll put on my Stetson and assless chaps—"

"Nolan!" She giggled while trying to escape his molestations. "Keep it up and the only thing you'll be getting tonight is a giant case of blue-balls!"

"You wish."

She wrenched free and then smoothed out her rumpled jacket. "Behave yourself."

"Watch your driving."

With his truck and her Subaru parked side-by-side, the vehicles were as disproportionate in size as their respective owners.

———————

The 650-acre Henman Ranch was a vast property that abutted the Blackstone River, County Road 30, and the lower parts of Sleeping Horse Mountain. It had been in the family for 117 years.

Kara had spent weeks calling and begging Eugene Henman for a minute of his time. Alongside Sarah Vaughn, Kara hoped they could make Henman see the light and shelve his planned 150 house subdivision on 225 acres of land. Henman was a simple man with a thousand head of cattle. Together with Gloria, his wife of thirty years, they had married off two daughters while caring for a severely autistic son.

The chained-up tires of Kara's Subaru clawed the ice-covered road. The night was a black wall of blowing wind and drifting snow, so she studied the road intently. There were no streetlights or other houses. When Henman's glowing two-story box appeared around the bend, she squinted to find the driveway. Fortunately, Sarah Vaughn's SUV had already torn fresh tracks through the snow.

Other than general maintenance, the house was over a century old. It had a covered porch surrounding the entire first-floor. A giant barn the size of an airplane hangar and various sheds dotted the darkened landscape. Kara focused on the treacherous road and could see Vaughn's Jeep Cherokee parked on a cul-de-sac near the garage.

They met on the way to the front door. Sarah Vaughn was wearing a full-length leather jacket and a black knit cap. "My goodness. Seems like I spend half my life shivering."

"Been here long?"

"Just pulled in. And let's not make a night of it, either. I got a hot date."

"New one or a re-tread?"

"What's the difference?" Vaughn knocked on the door. "Lord knows I'm getting too old to care."

Kara knew this was a long shot. Eugene Henman's reputation for being as stubborn as the winter cold was deserved. Accordingly, he dodged Kara's calls for months until she finally just showed up at his ranch last week, hiked a half mile out to his cattle pen, and whether it was through pity or the sheer force of her determination, he ultimately acquiesced to her request for a meeting.

The front door opened. Henman's balding gray head held gray-green eyes tucked into the weathered wrinkles. He was tall and thin and carried the no-nonsense demeanor acquired by men who spent a lifetime working in Mother Nature's shadow. He was in jeans and a flannel shirt, hurrying them to enter.

"Evening, ladies." He closed the door. "Can I take your coats?"

"Thank you." Kara smiled obligingly. "Mr. Henman, this is Sarah Vaughn, CPS legal consultant."

"It's nice to meet you, Ms. Vaughn."

Kara's eyes swept the foyer and stairwell leading up to the second-floor. The place had a soothing smell of burning wood and lingering scents from dinner. She saw pictures of the family—the daughters, their husbands and children, and Eugene Jr.

"That won't be necessary," Henman said when they started to dislodge their boots. "Just knock the snow off and head into the kitchen. It's too drafty in here for socks."

They did as instructed while Kara tried flattering him on his home. Although remodeled, the kitchen had the same utilitarian shape and feel of its pioneer days. A fireplace the size of a small car, one of four in the house, threw a tremendous amount of heat.

"Have a seat." He ushered them toward the table. "You'll have to excuse my wife. She'll be along shortly. She's taking care of our son. Got a pot of hot coffee brewed though ..."

"That would be nice." Vaughn, like Kara, was cataloging their surroundings. "The smell of burning wood reminds me of home."

Henman poured out three cups at the stove. "You girls locals?"

"No, sir," Kara answered. "I'm from northern California and Sarah's a Kansas girl."

"Oh yeah?" Henman dropped off their coffees while seeming to appraise Vaughn in a different light. "Where from?"

"Modoc."

"Well, well." Henman fetched sugar and milk. "That's ranching country."

"Sure is. My daddy's still down there working himself to the bone."

"What do you do?"

"I'm a lawyer."

"And you? I already know you work for them CPS folks ..."

"I used to work in finance," Kara said, "but my husband's job ... I work at the bank now during the day."

"What's your husband do?"

"He's a contractor."

"What's his name?"

"Nolan Harris."

"My, my ..." Henman stretched a grin of yellow teeth. "And here I thought my wife had it rough ..."

Kara's smile froze. "You know him well?"

"Well enough." Henman sipped his black coffee. "When old Billy Leinart's house caught fire, me and a couple other guys got together to lend a hand, but we sure as heck weren't no carpenters. We scraped up enough to hire on Nolan and that other crazy bastard, pardon my French. What's his name?"

"You must be thinking of Neal. Neal Killea."

"That's not what they call him."

"Well, his nickname's Rigor Mortis."

"Yeah, *Rigor Mortis*." Henman smiled again. "May Jesus strike me dead, those boys could frame, but boy-oh-boy that Neal character ... what an absolute mess that guy was."

"He's not so bad when he's not at work." Kara knew Neal Killea better than most, and while certainly crazier than Nolan, he was at least respectful to her. "Sometimes he gets a bad rap."

"Well ..." Henman let it linger. "Not to change gears on y'all, but I've got an awfully early start tomorrow, so if you don't mind ..."

"Sure." Kara knew this would be their only shot. She opened a file while appraising him of the situation. She described the impact of selling 225 of his 650 acres for the planned 150 house subdivision, and the stress that would place on the town's already strained infrastructure.

Kara wished Henman's wife had been down here since polling indicated women were two-to-one against expansion. If Henman's deal went through, that would mean houses on Sleeping Horse Mountain and along the Blackstone River, two areas long considered communal possessions.

She did not want to bore him or beg him but thought she might have just done both. She watched for his reaction, and her heart sank after he yawned.

"Excuse me," he said, and covered his mouth. "It's just way past this old man's bedtime."

"Mr. Henman—"

"Now I know you ladies didn't travel all this way just to tell me not to sell." He looked at Kara expectantly. "What's the pitch?"

Kara spun around a sheet of numbers. "The pitch is this. If you decide to put those 225 acres into a conservation easement, which basically cedes all development rights, your heirs will be able to inherit your land without breaking it up in order to pay the estate tax and penalties accompanying, well, your untimely demise, shall we say? Since development rights are sometimes worth 90 percent of the acre price, the conservation easement will also significantly lower your property taxes, since the highest value rights of the land have already been relinquished. And considering that Sleeping Horse Mountain and the Blackstone River are in line to be affected, we're also prepared to offer you a one-time lump sum payment."

"How long's this easement thing last?"

"In perpetuity." Kara sipped her coffee, trying not to raise her hopes. "It runs with the land. This whole thing is designed so that ranchers and farmers can hang onto their land and still work it and afford the lower property taxes before passing the estate down to their heirs."

Henman smiled. "So how much are you offering?"

"Well." Kara consulted her paperwork. "We're prepared to offer you that one-time payment of half a million dollars. That works out to over two thousand an acre."

"Hmm." Henman leaned back and crossed his arms. "That's an awful lot of money."

"Yes, it is."

"Unfortunately, if I go with these other guys, I stand to make almost twenty thousand dollars an acre. That comes out to over five million dollars."

"I understand that."

"Both of you, take a look around." Henman nodded at his surroundings. "Tell me, who's gonna be ranching? My daughters are married and gone and my son ..." He worked his lips. "God forbid anything happens to me or Gloria, because that boy's gonna be on his own. I need to provide for him too ..."

"Yes, of course—"

"Now, I'm not a stupid man. We're simple people, but we ain't dumb. And I know if you have the power to make this offer, you'll also respond if it's not taken, am I right?"

"Well, I don't think we should talk about that now. Maybe after you and your wife have had time to think this through ...?"

"I'm sorry, missy, but I think my mind's made up. I hate to say it, but what other choice is there?"

"We could—"

"I want to know right now. It's the least bit of courtesy you could afford me."

Kara looped the hair around both ears, finally accepting defeat. "Sarah?"

"Mr. Henman." Sarah Vaughn leaned in. "We're not here to strong-arm you. Please understand that. But as representatives of an organization whose sole purpose is to protect the wide-open lands of this great country of ours, we do have certain legal means through which to protest these vast sales. First of all, T.K. McCombs beat you to the punch and swallowed up the whole high-end market, or you'd be building starter castles on thirty-five-acre grids as well, would you not?"

"Probably. If it would get me out of all this nonsense, I surely would."

"Unfortunately, timing is everything. So instead of straight property sales, you're going to have to create this subdivision. Each house on acre and a half lots. Again, unfortunately, this opens you up to a whole host of legal hurdles. Wetlands, visual impact, noise, traffic—the fact that there's not enough room for septic systems or clean water wells means you'll have to be directly connected into the town sewage and water systems. That's huge. New streets means more sewers. Impact fees to infrastructure, the fact that the town would have to install streetlights and deliver mail and pick up the garbage ..."

Kara watched the hard lines of Henman's face turn to stone. Originally, he might have been politely listening to Kara, but Sarah Vaughn now had his undivided attention. Vaughn said, "Add to that the needs of fire and police, electric and cable, and we're talking about a practically infinite set of variables, anyone of which could potentially derail your plans indefinitely. But the biggest obstacle for you is that, no matter how the Planning Commission rules, the Town Council would still have to vote on whether or not to annex your proposed subdivision into the town itself. And if the developer you've signed on doesn't assume responsibility for the protracted legal fees a battle this size might incur, you'd be on the hook for it instead. Which means you might not ever see a dime and actually lose a small fortune fighting this thing in court."

It was the kind of devastating delivery that Kara had been hoping to avoid. But that was Sarah. The bad cop. She was there to make you squirm. Henman, though, was not about to give an inch, especially not to a pair of women barely older than his own daughters. His face was flushed as he worked his hands, cracking all the knuckles. "I don't particularly like being threatened in my own kitchen."

Sarah countered, "These aren't threats. We're trying to come to a solution that benefits all of the parties involved."

"What business is this of you people? I thought this was America? My property ain't mine after all?"

"Of course it's yours—"

"Apparently not!" He frowned as if disappointed at himself for yelling. "No offense, but I can't listen to another sentence. This ain't communist Russia ..."

Sarah said, "Russia's not communist anymore."

"Now you're gonna play cute with me?"

"Sarah—" Kara placed a hand on her elbow. "Mr. Henman, I apologize if we've upset you. It's just that a large portion of the community feels strongly about these issues. Sleeping Horse and the Blackstone are part of what makes living up here so special, would you agree?"

He would not agree. He had difficulty looking at either one of them and finally just batted a hand. "I don't need this." He pegged Sarah with a hateful glance. "And shame on you. Your daddy's a rancher? If he could get his hands on this kind of money and finally enjoy life, would you tell him to take less instead?"

"My intention wasn't—"

"Your intentions can go to hell." Henman stood. "And so can you." He took their coffee cups and turned for the sink. "I'm sorry, but I think you two should see yourselves out."

Minutes later the door was shut behind them.

"That," Kara said, and shuddered in the cold, "was rather unpleasant."

Vaughn sighed as she fixed her hat. "He just called me a communist daddy-hater. I think I need a drink."

"He was just upset."

"Yeah, well, he's kind of right. We're fucking up his whole program ... did you know the son was autistic?"

"I did but ... it slipped my mind until we got here. I didn't even know Nolan knew him."

"Nice job on the homework."

"Hey, wait a second ..."

"That guy cleaned our clocks." Vaughn opened her door. "Please don't do this to me again."

CHAPTER ELEVEN

Saturday morning, Elias woke up to a screaming alarm clock. His hangover was so ferocious the vertigo from just sitting up almost caused him to puke. The horrible mix of bad breath, old booze, and stale cigarettes made an already volatile situation even more combustible. Punished by consciousness, he yanked the shrieking clock from the wall, covered his face with both hands, and groaned until the stink of his own breath became intolerable.

"Oh dear God ..."

Since there was only a small box of gray light spilling in through the tiny access window, his basement room was always a tomb. He wondered about his wallet, keys, phone and cash, but could not even remember coming home.

Stumbling into the bathroom, he washed his face, puked, and then washed his face again. His skewered palm seemed fine and scabbed over and barely hurt. He looked into the mirror. Bleary-eyed and sickened, he gathered his things for work.

Elias and Dennis Mitchell had basement bedrooms, so Elias had to pass by Dennis' rhythmic snoring. With Elias and Dennis both in their late twenties, they were the elder statesmen of the condo. They formed an instant friendship working in the ski lodge kitchen under the same chef both would eventually quit. While one was from New York and the other a Texan, the initial barrage of culturally obvious jokes at the other's expense had long since run its course.

A rockabilly hick with short spiked hair, lively blue eyes, and a righteous Texas drawl, Dennis was a born brawler like his father before his father became an ex-husband, and Dennis soon found his fists an invaluable equalizer against the long list of drunk losers his mother inevitably sought to rehab. While she found God, her only son acquired a lengthy rap sheet before quitting school altogether.

He told Elias about his street life through the Dallas punk rock scene. At eighteen, he landed roadie jobs for small bands like Romeo's Revolver and Six Inches to Death. By twenty-one, he had spent three years crisscrossing the country on tour buses that never stopped moving, and as his reputation and experience accrued, he finally became tour manager at the ripe old age of twenty-five. An already fervent supporter of alcohol and cocaine, and with the overpowering charisma born leaders command, his was a rising star until one day at the Canadian border destroyed his whole career.

At airports and border crossings especially, the dumping of all contraband was a duty he delegated to either Scary Mary, his head of security, or Tricky Dicky, his right-hand man and tour operations supervisor. Said tour had been pinballing around Canada for three weeks after just completing seven miserable months in America. The band, a quartet formed in some back alley El Paso shithole, had that rare mix of what made this business, at times, miraculous to behold. For despite doing everything they could to destroy their own career, the anguished screaming and staccato guitars had finally, after two unnoticed albums and subsequent tours halted by arrests, overdoses, and various disasters, crossed over into the mainstream with a single off their third album most stations still refused to play. The buzz grew, the concert halls sold out, and the crowd changed accordingly. Now, instead of bikers and skinheads, the audience became a blend of middle-class kids and students out for a degenerate joyride. Industry executives flew in for shows and agents started calling on behalf of sponsors who, though somewhat anxious about connecting themselves to this level of decadence, nonetheless wanted a slice of the next Big Thing. But all was not well. Disgusted by the rampant hedonism, the last tour manager quit on short notice, so Dennis got the job by default.

Now, after eight months of pillaging abuse, they staggered through the Toronto airport like a pack of zombies. The bassist was a drunk, the guitarist and drummer were heroin addicts, and the lead singer powered through enough cocaine to stay awake for days on end. Tricky Dicky had been put on high alert before their last show. Supposedly, he discarded everything except the small amounts needed to get to the airport before later hooking up with their Boston connection on the other side of the border. Despite these efforts, the usual after-show debauchery occurred fueled by the parasitic groupies and drug dealers rock tours acquire like STDs. In the morning, already late for the airport, people fumbled through the final drug check. Later, at the International Departures gate, after the customs officers found the first vial and called in backup to corral the developing fifteen-person riot, Dennis' world imploded. The drug bust was bad enough, but Dennis had also been sleeping with the bassist's wife since just after the tour began. Swept up in the moment, the camera had been *her* idea. One of these tapes, along with varying amounts of cocaine, heroin, marijuana, Valium, and Percocet were seized, effectively ending his career. As news of the drug bust and expanding depravity spread, their record sales and Caligula-like reputation as being sinners of the highest order exploded. But the sex tape—that was career suicide. There was no room for employees banging band members' wives on tour. No band wanted a buddy-fucker on board while they themselves fucked everything that moved. No, that was unjust treatment, a breaking of the *Code*.

Their third album went on to sell over five million copies right before the lead guitarist overdosed and died. The rest of the junkies, suddenly awash in cash, never played again. Dennis, already ruined and thrown out of his dream job, suffered a final humiliation when the bassist subpoenaed *him* to testify against *her* adultery.

Now, in the darkened basement, he abruptly came awake as Elias tried creeping past.

"You are unbelievable." The cigarette-graveled voice had a Texas drawl. "A got-damn martyr, that's what y'are."

"Sorry I woke you up, bro." Elias suddenly clutched his stomach. "Oh no ..."

The chewed-up voice chuckled in the dark. "Damn, killer, you closed the place out and I brought you home after m'shift."

"Oh man ... I can't remember anything."

"You? I served you more tequila than any of us."

"Dude, please, you're gonna make me hurl." Elias was bent over and sweating. "This is some horrible shit."

"Yeah, well, good luck with what you got going on there, good buddy. Keep on keeping on, Mr. Martyr Man."

Elias stepped out of the basement into the vaulted common room. He didn't think he could even drink coffee. Nolan called and said not to drive in, he would be right over, so Elias stood sweating at his door with a hangover that felt like a second person crammed inside his skull.

Just when he thought he could not feel any worse, Nolan's F-250 roared into the parking lot like a home-delivered nightmare. Elias pulled himself aboard, but Nolan quickly said, "Oh great. You girls went out boozing again, didn't ya?"

"We met up—"

"I don't want to hear your explanations." Nolan lowered and locked Elias' window. "Time to take your medicine, stinky."

Having seen it done to Rand enough times, Elias said, "Come on, dude, there ain't nothing funny about this."

"Says who?" Nolan punched the gas down Snowmass Road. It was a balmy twenty degrees compared to yesterday's subzero pain, but doing 40 MPH with a gaping window was more than rude enough.

"What the hell, man!" Elias rolled his shoulder, ducking beneath his jacket. "This is some kind of bullshit!"

"Ah-ha-ha!" As usual, Nolan was balancing a half-gallon jug of coffee, smoking, and dialing a cellphone while laughing at the writhing mess beside him. "This is for your own good, Thomas!"

"Shut the fucking window!"

More laughter as the pickup barreled through the dawn. Above each structure, smoke was rising in solid columns from vents, pipes, chimneys—from any heat source until, across the valley floor, it seemed as if an arsonist had run amok.

"Señor!" Nolan shouted into the phone as the wind whipped through the cab. "Yeah, we're on the way. I got your new buddy right here with me ... Ha-ha! See you soon."

He flipped closed the phone, saw Elias' hate-filled glance, and finally closed the window.

"It's about fucking—"

"Hey, stinky, no breathing." Nolan shoved a pack of gum at him. "I expect to see a piece of that in your mouth for the rest of the day."

"Can you just take me home?"

"Never."

"This hangover's killing me. I'll give you twenty bucks."

"Nope."

"Forty?"

"There is no amount of money that will prevent me from bathing in your pain. Speaking of which, you've got a special assignment today." Nolan hit the blinker and pushed his coffee jug toward Elias. "Hold that." He turned the wheel, smoked, and then dialed the phone. "What room's your dumbass half-brother in?"

"302."

"Yeah, hello? Room 302, please." Nolan flicked the cigarette butt out the window and lit another. "Oh my God, Fabio ... Dude, you sound totally destroyed ... I've got him right here and he stinks worse than you did yesterday ... Yeah, well, get ready. I'm dropping Thomas at Butcher Block with Rigor Mortis, then I'm picking your dead ass up." Nolan laughed before looking at Elias. "Yeah, new-meat's in for a special day alongside Señor Haywire ... Right? Ha-ha! ... All right, no more laughing. Get your pathetic ass up and please brush your teeth." Nolan flipped closed the phone and reached for his coffee.

Elias said, "Who's *Rigor Mortis*?"

"Dude, I don't even know where to start. He's one of my oldest bros, I mean going way back to Orange County ..."

So he told the story of Neal Killea, who was three years older than Nolan and fourth generation Irish from a long line of tradesmen distinguished, in part, by the brute force those accustomed to hard labor and short lives developed on instinct. His father was a legendary mason on the 1960s cinderblock gangs that literally laid the foundation for much of downtown Los Angeles' subsequent expansion.

"I met him at an intersection in some hippie town in north Cali," Nolan said. Elias could sense the nostalgia those times evoked, because Nolan was actually smiling and calm and almost like a buddy as he said, "It was the weekend of my twenty-first birthday. I'd been up for like three days. Me and a bunch of bros had a half-ounce of blow and just packed up the coolers and tents and tore ass for the hills, ya' know? Seventy-two hours of rockstar-quality partying at some cabin in the middle of nowhere. I mean that town had like one bar and we just overran it, man, laying waste. So anyway, like I said, we'd been up grinding for days and I just needed some juice, man, I was dying of thirst. It was like ten o'clock in the morning and I never saw the red light and just T-boned him dead on, dude. Then it was just on. He came flying out of that piece of shit Bronco, which already had half of its windshield smashed out, and we nearly beat each other to death in the middle of the street."

"Awesome. Can't wait to spend the day with him."

"Yeah, well, I ended up working for him back in Palos Verde, out near Long Beach. You ever been to Cali?"

"Naw."

"Well, whatever. That was my first carpentry job."

"Ever?"

"Yep. Believe it or not, I was just as stupid as yourself once upon a time."

"Wow," Elias dryly observed. "What an inspiration." As he watched his window start to descend, he quickly added, "I was only kidding!"

"That's more like it." Nolan ground his cigarette into the already overflowing ashtray. "So anyway, today you and him are gonna finish up the bullshit out at Butcher Block."

Hungover, Elias lit up a cigarette and instantly felt worse. "Whatever. Why's his name Señor Haywire?"

"Because he hates Mexicans. And he's also crazy. Take your pick—Señor Haywire, Black Death, Rigor Mortis ..."

"*Rigor Mortis?*"

"Yeah, because that's what you'd rather have than spending five minutes with the guy. But you can't call him any of that."

"Why not?"

"Because ..." Nolan seemed at odds at how best to describe it. "Listen, he's my best friend, and I love him like a bro, but still, after like a day or two working together, he and I are absolutely ready to kill each other."

"I thought you just said you were best friends?"

"We are ..." Nolan pulled off his hat and ran a hand through the bed-head turned hat-head. "It's just ... he's kind of psychotic."

"*What?*"

"Or maybe sociopath is a better way to put it."

"Are you shitting me?"

Nolan's smile enveloped his face. "It won't be bad for you, though. Just don't call him Rigor Mortis or anything else. Those are my names for him. And he won't touch me because I'll crush him. But you ... he doesn't know you from jack."

"Nice." Elias scoffed. "Sounds like it's gonna be a great fucking day."

Nolan laughed like that was just about the funniest thing he had ever heard and then tapped Elias' shoulder. "You'll be fine as long you remember to hurry the fuck up."

"Speaking of no talking."

They took a right on MacArthur Street and passed the new state-of-the-art high school funded by the town's current expansion. Whether for or against the construction boom, it was hard not to recognize the updates and improvements to many public facilities, especially the schools, which were rapidly filling up.

They passed the new football stadium and steadily climbed. Silver Mine Road had a dangerously wide bend above a 160-foot drop to the valley below, and as the curve peeled new scenery into view, Butcher Block sprang up like an abomination scarring these pristine surroundings. Elias had to agree. The aesthetics of the place were just blatantly offensive. On a hillside dream site which, if it had to be built upon at all, should have at least contained compelling structures, these eight boxes with gable to gable twelve pitch roofs inspired nothing but disdain.

"It's a good thing I'm dropping you off," Nolan said, "because I really hate this place."

"Is that why Neal's here?"

"Naw." Nolan hit the blinker. "This is a two-man gig at best. Me and Rand will get going at the school."

"What do you want me to do when I'm done here?"

"Have Riggy drop you off. What the hell ...?" Nolan squinted at a pair of approaching twenty-ton dumptrucks and instantly went from zero to rage. "Do you believe this? After six months of making us slog through the mud and snow on this fucking hillside, he waits till the pansies are due to put down gravel?"

"What pansies?"

Nolan was seething, staring ahead. "The shit-tubers and sparkle-heads."

"Who?"

"The plumbers and electricians!" Then he spotted Conyers' pickup at the rear of the caravan and almost had a stroke. "Oh no. Hop out, man, because if I have to talk to this fucking puke for even one second, I just might kill him."

"All right, all right, take it easy." Elias grabbed his gear, slammed the door, and watched Nolan peel away.

The dumptrucks stopped at the driveway. Inside the makeshift parking lot, Elias saw a smashed-up F-250 hooked to a sixteen-foot trailer with HIGH MOUNTAIN FRAMING sloganed on its side.

With all of Nolan's warnings still echoing through his mind, Elias swept the scene as if expecting to get jumped by a wild beast. Then he heard someone banging around inside the trailer just as Conyers' truck cut him off.

"Say," Conyers said through the window. "Better tell this fella we're getting ready to throw some stones. He's gotta move his rig."

"Yeah." Elias swung open the trailer door and his expression, after gazing at the wall-to-wall pornography and centerfolds, filled with awe. "Oh my God ..." He realized he should have been saying hello and introducing himself, but his inner pervert made him helpless.

"Good to see respect being shown." The voice came from the back of the trailer but Elias still could not look. He heard boots stomping toward him and then felt a tap on his shoulder. "Check this one out."

As Neal Killea directed his attention, Elias quickly appraised him and found the fearsome expectations sorely lacking. Killea was encased in as many layers as Elias, so it was hard to gauge the physique other than guessing Killea was about six feet tall, had startling blue-green eyes, short black hair, and dimples. *Pretty boy*, is what Elias instantly thought and almost laughed, since Nolan had him picturing a hand grenade on legs.

Rigor Mortis stuck out his hand. "Neal."

"Thomas."

"Right on, Thomas. Super-Framer left me a list." He dug into his pocket. "You got any idea about what's going on out here?"

"Me? Dude, I'm a wood monkey."

Rigor Mortis grinned at the self-mutilation and said, "Great. At least you know your place."

"What's first?"

"Let's get air and electric rolled out to number one."

Large hooks with cords and hoses hung in neat rows. Reaching for a perfectly rolled-up hose, Elias paused when Rigor Mortis said, "One more thing before we get after it. My tools, all this shit, I've spent years collecting. Don't learn from your boss. He's a sloppy fucking pig with a low IQ. If you don't know where something is, just ask. If you don't know where something goes, ask. Because if I come in here and see a bunch of shit cluster-fucked in the wrong place, I'm gonna fucking lose it."

"Okay." It was hard not to smile, because Rigor Mortis seemed so serious. Originally preoccupied with all the pornography, Elias now had a moment to scan the rest of the trailer. Shelves on each wall were loaded with every tool imaginable. Framing guns, roofing guns, finish guns, three drills, four skillsaws with hot-wired hundred-foot cords, Husqvarna chainsaws, two sawzalls, rows of C-clamps, half a dozen levels of different lengths, a table saw, a pair of gas driven Rolair compressors, a 1000-watt Craftsman generator, ladders, and two stainless steel tool chests loaded with everything else. Half of the stuff he had never seen before, and the remainder was barely familiar.

"Holy shit." He pulled off his sunglasses and squinted into the shadowy corner. "What the hell is *that* thing?"

"What?"

"That ... that giant freakshow thing."

"This?" Rigor Mortis hoisted the biggest saw Elias had ever seen. "It's a beam saw. Got a thirty-six-inch blade."

"Unreal."

"Here." Rigor Mortis held it out. "It ain't gonna bite. You won't believe how light it is."

It looked like a prehistoric ancestor of the sidewinder skillsaw. There was a horizontal bar for his left hand, while the right gripped the handle and trigger. Other than its motor, the rest of it was all blade. A spinning disk with dreadfully hooked teeth, it reminded Elias of a pizza tray turned vertically homicidal.

Looking up, paused by its potential ferocity, Elias said, "This is one of the sickest things I've ever seen."

"Yeah, well, I worked with a guy who cut off his own leg with it."

"What—you mean this actual saw?"

"Well how the fuck do you think I got it? These things are like thirteen hundred retail."

"Whatever."

"Give it here before you drop it."

Elias did and then grabbed some cords. "Before I forget, that moron Conyers wants you to move your rig. Says they're getting ready to lay some rock."

"Yeah, well, he can tongue *these* rocks, because I ain't moving shit until we're all rolled out. You know where the main power is?"

"Yeah. It's posted downhill."

Rigor Mortis grabbed a thick 240-watt cord and tossed it to Elias. "Make it happen."

Elias descended through the rutted ice and drifting snow. It was easy to wonder how the dumptrucks would ever be able to negotiate this hillside.

The main power was located on a 4x4 post sledge-hammered into the ground. Inside the breaker box was a single fuse with two outlets beneath it. Elias plugged in and payed out the cord as he ascended the hill. He saw Conyers arrive at the trailer, say something into its opened doors, and then recoil as if slapped.

"In the dead of fucking winter!" Rigor Mortis shouted. "What kind of moron throws rocks on top of six inches of ice? How ridiculous is this?"

"Nevertheless. The dumpers are here, the back-hoe's on the way, and in an hour we're gonna have this whole place rocked out—"

"Fantastic." Rigor Mortis rolled his eyes. He shoved tools at Elias and said, "Get this crap over to number one and then help me unload the compressor so I can move the trailer for these fucking idiots."

Conyers frowned beneath his Stetson. "I don't think—"

"Gee, no shit. Not thinking makes you stupid. As a matter of fact, it's a miracle your company even exists."

Elias, who had an armload of tools, watched as the words did funny things to Conyers' face—twitching his eyes and mustache as he seemed to be thinking the same thing Elias was, which was pretty much, *Holy Shit*.

"You know, you got a big mouth, son." Conyers frowned. "I can't wait to be done with this, this fucking bullshit, and send the whole lot of ya down the road!"

"Whatever, fake Tex. You're an ass-clown."

Conyers' right eyelid trembled as he searched for an appropriate rebuttal but none appeared. "Just get this thing moved!"

Rigor Mortis ignored him, lubing up a saw until he swung his gaze across Elias. "Well?" he said. "Show's over. Hurry the fuck up."

———————

Per building code, to prevent floor joists from rolling or leaning over time, 2x10 blocks were required in every bay along all beams. Four of the six units needed beams blocked, so Elias dragged the tools, hoses, and cords from house to house as Rigor Mortis carried the boom box. With the death metal cranking, the chorus screamed out—

Cut me off something!
Tie the knot!
Cut me off something!
GET SOME!

This last sentence apparently sent a bolt of ecstasy through Rigor Mortis, because he repeatedly shrieked '*Get Some!*' and replayed the same song half a dozen times until Elias begged for mercy.

In the last unit, as they forced their way through a three-foot crawl space under the first-floor, the serious pain began. The screaming boom box, alongside the nailgun's close-quarter thunder, assaulted the senses.

"Fucking hack," Rigor Mortis yelled. They crawled through the dirt in the frozen dark while Elias fed him blocks. "Your boss is a fucking hack!"

Because of the tunes and gunfire, Elias could not hear a thing. "*What?*"

"This shit should have been done before the joists were fucking sheeted! Uh-oh! Hear *that*, motherfucker?"

"Hear what—oh no ..." Elias winced as the opening riff re-commenced. Like an airplane roaring to life, the dreaded mantra started up:

It wasn't the first time
You lied to me ...
It wasn't the pain
Left inside of me ...
It wasn't the thought of letting go,
But you gotta admit I fucking hate you so!

Cut me off something!
I hate you so!
Cut me off something,
GET SOME!

"*Get some!*" Rigor Mortis shrieked, firing and ricocheting nails off the concrete walls around them.

After they finished, Elias handed the tools up through the floor. "I feel like I've just been assaulted."

"Balls deep, baby! Whoa. Look at this disaster."

Outside, one of the dumptrucks was fighting gravity, months of ice, and the general laws of physics. With the weight of its load now gone, the three rear axles clawed for traction. Every time the squirrel-faced driver punched the gas, the giant diesel belched black smoke from twin chrome stacks and slid even further downhill. Conyers shouted instructions, but the driver wore a look of doubtful trepidation.

Rigor Mortis' smile, though, could not have been any broader. "You think there's a Guinness record for stupidity?"

The two drivers and Conyers gathered in conference.

"Like a couple of monkeys trying to fuck a football," Elias said, and Rigor Mortis let off a peal of laughter.

"Come on," he said, and punched Elias' shoulder. "Time to show the lower half of the food chain what it's like to have a functioning brainstem."

They joined the conversation. After a brief argument, the drivers sided with Rigor Mortis, who dismissed all of Conyers' suggestions by saying, "That's the stupidest thing I've ever heard."

They backed the second dumptruck in and parked it on the crest of the hill. Rigor Mortis positioned his F-250 in front of that and then strung chain between all three trucks. The diesel engines loudly rattled.

"Okay," Rigor Mortis shouted from his window. "Ready? Punch it!"

The column roared but slid backwards until he leaned further out and screamed, "Punch it! Get some! *Get some!*"

The veins in his neck ballooned into ropes as he continuously bounced up and down and shrieked "*Get some!*" so many times Elias thought he might pass out behind the wheel. But as the snow and ice flew out from the chained-up tires, a meager momentum began to build.

"Get some!"

Both dumptruck drivers worked their gears. They watched the rear end of the pickup slide side-to-side until it began inching toward the street. With a final jerk, the last dumptruck topped the hill in a cloud of exhaust and burnt tire as Rigor Mortis shouted, "Who's the stupid fuck now!"

Conyers ducked behind the cover of his cellphone while the drivers high-fived one another. Rigor Mortis, though, was all business. He gathered up his chains and ignored the drivers whose fate, up until a minute ago, had been entirely in his hands. He noticed Elias' lack of participation and said, "Hey, halftime, wanna lend a fucking hand or what?"

As the looming Planning Commission vote drew near, Spring Valley found itself cleaved into rival factions. In addition to the pending sale of vast ranchlands for development, another bill, if passed, would allow a dilapidated section of downtown to be annexed, demolished, and re-zoned for commercial use through eminent domain statutes. Innocuously entitled 'Proposition 6,' no one doubted the effect this measure would wield if passed. In the last week, signs pleading "*Vote YES for the Town's Future*" or "*NO on 6*" were stapled, tacked, taped, and staked into every available square inch of partisan ground.

Rigor Mortis and Elias finished up at Butcher Block and drove downtown for lunch. Since it was Saturday, the protest against Proposition 6 was just getting underway. It was thirty degrees and sunny, so turnout was larger than expected.

Along Main Street, those opposed to Proposition 6 marched with signs as a leader with a bullhorn excoriated the "business elite in this devastating endeavor."

"Look at this mess," Rigor Mortis complained as traffic slowed to a crawl. "Fucking hippies."

As a new arrival, Elias was interested in these increasingly combustive events.

"What's up with them?" he asked, and pointed toward a group of Arapahoe Indians.

"Who cares?" Rigor Mortis scanned the crowd as it marched in the other lane. "Look at that hottie." He pointed at a young woman among a pack of friends. Leaning out the window, he gave her a salacious hello as the pickup crawled alongside. "Nice day for a parade, huh?"

She smiled but blushed from his attention. "This isn't a parade, it's a protest."

"Oh, my bad, I always get the two confused."

"Really?" She coyly smirked. "How come I don't have a hard time believing that?"

Her friends whispered back and forth as Rigor Mortis leaned further out and said, "Why don't you hop on in? We got plenty of room."

"Is that right?" she gamely asked. "But wouldn't that defeat the purpose of this march?"

"Not really." He shrugged. "With all of this walking, you must be hungry. We could make a sandwich."

"With what?"

"With you." He grinned. "Hungry?"

It might have been the blatant disregard for her humanity, or the fact that Rigor Mortis had just asked a perfect stranger for a three-way, that caused Elias to wince. The women, once a coquettish center of flattery, immediately transformed into a pack of rage. They booed and cursed, punching at the side-wall of the rapidly fleeing trailer. Elias watched them fade in the sideview mirror and said, "Jesus Christ, dude, what is *wrong* with you?"

On the outskirts of town, they parked in front of the 120-year-old Rocky Mountain Tavern. It was an old saloon with brass railings, a thirty-foot mahogany bar, and giant murals of the surrounding valley on every wall. It was also a national landmark because of a phone booth which, in 1926, became the final resting place of a Mr. William "Bad Bill" LeBean, a notorious rustler and bank robber shot dead by marshals pursuing a federal warrant. The six bullets that killed LeBean were still embedded in the phone booth walls, which also housed a functional public phone. But around the blasted holes was now written the detritus of a thousand moments—the phone numbers and names of people jotting down information on the fly, a smattering of lewd depictions of genitalia, and X-rated jokes amid ninety years of graffiti.

The place was only a quarter full because it was Saturday and people were either skiing or picking sides at the downtown ruckus.

"Sit at the bar," Rigor Mortis said. "I gotta call Super-Framer."

"He already told me to get dropped off."

"Hey, easy. We gotta eat lunch, right?"

Elias pulled himself a stool. His eyes were drawn to the three levels of crown molding around the fifteen-foot-high ceiling. Behind the bar, the giant mirror had an ornate frame that one might find in a church or museum. Even the stools had old-world ball and claw feet.

But the place was poorly kept, the tables strewn with dirty dishes, the mirrors smeared in smoke. The balding bartender, who was almost as wide as his five-foot height, glanced at Elias as if the energy required to wedge himself along the narrow space was not currently worth the effort.

"Help you?" the guy asked, his breath a labored wheeze.

"My buddy'll be back in a minute but I'll take a Coke."

Rigor Mortis reappeared and grabbed himself a stool. "What's he pouring? And don't tell me it's a Coke."

"It is."

"Pussy." He glanced at the bartender. "Dump that shit out. We'll take two shots of Makers and a pair of Buds."

"No, we won't." Elias pulled out his wallet. "I got two bucks for this soda and that's it."

"Two bucks? What the fuck's he paying you?"

"I'm trying to pay off some shit so I can—"

The bartender placed down the drinks and said, "You fellas gonna eat?"

"Maybe." Rigor Mortis shoved the shot at Elias before bottoming out his own. "We'll take another pair."

"Oh dear God." Elias stared at the whiskey but shuddered as he drank it. "So what'd he say?"

"Who?"

"Super-Framer."

"You like that name, don't ya? And it doesn't matter what he said, because he ain't my boss."

"Whatever." Even though Elias' hangover was abating, he knew drinking now was just plain stupid. Boozing heavy before spending the afternoon bitching wood and tools in a frozen hellhole while being screamed at by three psychos now instead of two? Staring at the shot glass, taking that exact scenario into account, he decided Rigor Mortis might just be onto something, so he downed another whiskey.

They pushed aside the empties and lit cigarettes. As Rigor Mortis scrolled through his phone, Elias gazed at the completely battered hands—the knuckles like boney ridges filled with scabs, the fingers cut, scraped, and swollen into sausage links from the cold, his cuticles split open and busted. Two fingernails had been blackened from hammer strikes and the right thumb had a three-inch cut. Knotted, calloused, and creased, the hands were even more frightening when compared to his own and their healthy shade of pink.

"So..." Rigor Mortis blew a stream of smoke through each nostril and put away his phone. "Let's see what I know so far. You've got two dollars in your pocket, weren't smart enough to pack a lunch, and now you're boozing again before your last hangover's even gone."

"The booze is your fault. The rest I have no comment on."

"How long you been working for Nolan?"

"Three weeks."

"And how long you been framing?"

"Exactly the same."

"Oh man. Are you totally fucked or what?"

"Jesus ..."

"What did you do before this?"

Elias hesitated. "I was a cook."

"A *what*?" Rigor Mortis laughed and shook his head at the same time. "Oh man, does he know how to pick them or what? This is some ripe-ass shit."

"Fuck you."

"Here." He pushed Elias another shot. "If anyone needs this, believe me, it's you."

Within fifteen minutes they had finished three shots and a beer. Rigor Mortis called for another round before turning to Elias. "We're gonna make this Oompa-Loompa earn his motherfucking tip, boy."

Elias was not sure if the bartender heard the comment above the labored wheeze even the smallest movement seemed to cause him, but it certainly had been loud enough.

Trying to change the subject, Elias said, "So S.F. said you guys are bros from way back."

"S.F.? Oh yeah, that's a nice one. That's his new handle, good buddy. Old S.F. Yeah, me and him have been down the road a mile, friend." Rigor Mortis swigged his beer, ashed the cigarette, and smiled so warmly it seemed some reminiscence might be forthcoming instead of what he then said next. "A piss-filled bucket's got more common sense than that hapless fucktard."

In mid-sip, Elias sprayed beer across the bar. He wiped his mouth. "Man, he was right on the money. You really are a total freaking mess."

"That what he said?"

"Pretty much."

"Thatta girl. Fucking A, you gotta love the pain."

A pair of shots arrived and before Elias could object, Rigor Mortis put a hand in his face and said, "I don't speak pussy, so just shut your hole and drink."

Minutes later the alcohol buzzed Elias' brain. Exhausted and drunk, he floated in and out of the conversation. It seemed Rigor Mortis was recalling some confrontation, because as Elias rejoined the train of thought, it ended with Rigor Mortis saying, "So I grabbed him like this ..." He palmed the back of Elias' skull. "And then went BLAM!" The fake headbutt ended at the last second, but Elias did not appreciate the abrupt intimacy which, incidentally, could have caved in his face. He shoved away the gnarled hands and said, "I bet you don't have many friends."

Rigor Mortis thought that was funny and pushed over another whiskey. "Should've seen it, man. The human skull is a bowling ball and at close range ..." He shook his head. "Egg yolk city."

"Sounds like fun."

"Yeah, well, I'm a people person."

"Obviously." Elias belched and waved a drunken hand. "What better way to show that than by smashing in someone's face?"

The door opened and a cluster of people entered. Finished with the march, they stacked their *VOTE NO* signs in the corner. The couples were chummy and exhilarated on this sunny afternoon, having participated in the bonds community and protest inspired. They pushed together two tables so the eight of them could sit.

"Might just be a bunch of moms," Rigor Mortis said, "but I'd hogtie two or three of them for sure."

"You're such a romantic."

"All right, let's roll out." Rigor Mortis parceled out the last two shots, peeked at the check, and dropped sixty dollars beside it. "You can thank me later."

He headed for the door before suddenly veering left. He stood at the foot of their table and said, "Excuse me."

At first, they all smiled. But Elias, having known him all of five hours, sensed a whiff of chaos in the air.

"Nice day for a march, huh?" Rigor Mortis asked, and one of the women excitedly recounted their entire morning.

When she was finished, he said, "It's going to be something, though, isn't it?"

Their smiles became confused. One of the men, a guy with glasses so big he resembled an owl, tentatively asked, "How do you mean?"

"I mean after we build out this entire valley. After the banks and big money pigs line up the developers and builders, and after they all slime each other and those zoning idiots with bribes and advertise like crazy, and every other small businessman in town gets a sniff at the big dollar potential real growth represents, do you actually think a bunch of middle-aged ex-hippies-turned-yuppies-turned-Saturday-afternoon-protestors are ever gonna stand a chance in fucking hell?"

Elias had never seen a group of people more horrified in unison. For a painful second, the ambush and mockery left them looking toward each other for cover—looking anywhere but at the green-eyed menace smirking at their increasing discomfort.

Someone said, "Well, that wasn't very nice."

But Rigor Mortis just stood there like a kid with a bug squirming beneath his thumb. "It's reality time, people. Fantasyland, Disneyland, you're about a thousand miles off." He belched and headed for the door. On the way out, he grabbed two of their signs and tossed one to Elias as they hit the street.

"That's right, motherfucker!" Rigor Mortis lunged at Elias, swung his handle like a sword, and then repeatedly smashed his sign into a building, screaming, "Get some! Get some!"

"Sanity," Elias called out in answer, but knew he was enthralled.

———————

Rigor Mortis' truck and trailer careened down County Road 40 at 80 MPH with the stereo cranked to dangerous levels. Riding shotgun, Elias had a moment between life-threatening skids to scan the interior, which, in direct contrast to the fastidious trailer and tools, was absolutely destroyed. The rearview mirror was gone, probably wrenched off in some spasm of violence, and trash was strewn across the floor. The ignition was hanging off the steering column like a spooned-out eyeball, and the engine was started by screwdriver since the owner, who had lost the key some time ago, chose to smash apart the housing instead of funding its replacement.

There was no conversation on the ten-minute drive mainly because Rigor Mortis was blasting death metal and Elias, with all that alcohol poured into an empty belly, was getting drunker by the second.

Even with the trailer attached, they took a hard left turn onto Gildman Road. Up ahead, as they punched through the tree line, Nolan and Rand could be seen standing another first-floor interior wall.

Rigor Mortis skidded to a stop and dialed down the music. "All right, little fella, out you go. Tell your master I said to suck it."

"What? You mean you're just dropping me off?"

"Boy, you don't miss a beat, do ya?"

"That's fucking great. You get me shitfaced and then run home like a little bitch."

"Have a great afternoon, sucka!"

"You son of a bitch." Elias almost fell out of the truck. "I don't have any fucking masters."

"We'll see about that." Rigor Mortis hit reverse and then, through his lowered window, shouted, "Hey, Nolan! Your boy here got all fucked up at lunch!" He revved the diesel. "I think you should fire his ass!"

With that, he cackled and tore down the trail.

Elias ascended the 2x10 ramp leading to the front door and saw Rand and Nolan's quizzical expressions.

Nolan asked, "What's that ass-clown babbling about?"

"Who knows." Elias jammed on his gloves. "What do you need me to do?"

"We need about a hundred 2x4 studs up here. So how'd it go? He finish up with Conyers?"

"Oh, I'd say so."

"Why'd you say it like that?"

"Well, let's see. First, he called him stupid. Then he said it was a miracle he even had a company at all." Elias finished recounting the story by adding, "—with him screaming *Get some! Get some!*"

Rand said, "Man, there ain't nothing right about that guy."

"You haven't heard the best part. Driving through town, your boy hangs out the window and asks this little honey if she'd like to hop into the backseat for a cock sandwich. Then he ordered twelve shots and four beers for lunch, man, who the hell does that? I mean half the time you don't know whether to laugh or just get ready to fight."

"Fuck, I've spent the last fifteen years doing that." Nolan checked his watch. "How drunk are you?"

"Not drunk enough for this."

"Well, that's good." Nolan rubbed his hands together. "By five o'clock, my goal is to have both of you booze-bags puking in the dark."

"Awesome." Rand reloaded the gun. "Once again, your motivational qualities are outstanding."

———————

When Rand awoke the next morning, he heard a steel door slam and a second later remembered where he was. He rolled over on his bed, which was a hard metal rectangle bolted into the cinderblock wall. The fluorescent lights never turned off and hummed a maddening white noise. Alongside this, the sounds and echoes of jail were the same as he unfortunately remembered.

He winced at the light because his brain was parched from too much booze and cocaine. To block the light, he slung an arm across his eyes, but his mind still replayed the events leading up to his current incarceration inside the Salinas County Jail.

He remembered heading downtown for cocktails with Elias after work. Though already drunk, Elias held tough until midnight and then he abruptly disappeared. In the bathroom, Rand found Todd Lynn, a carpenter with a reputation for no common sense and bad work, so he was promptly nicknamed Re-Todd. But he also happened to be holding. They horked up the cocaine in the stall before Rand foolishly decided to visit his kids and Lena Marie.

Had Elias still been with him, this ridiculous idea would have died on the spot. But the cocaine convinced him otherwise, and, just wanting a break from his awful motel, he set off for the home he used to own. He thumbed for a ride no one stopped to give. After the five mile walk through the cold night failed to sober him up, he finally stood at an unshoveled driveway, *his* unshoveled driveway, so turning back was not an option.

The details of what followed were, even now, sketchy. He remembered spotting an unfamiliar pickup parked next to hers before he pissed all over it. Then, after stumbling toward the front door, he recalled veering off to peek through the darkened living room windows like a total creeper.

Lying here now, he watched the various links of the evening reconnect themselves into a noose around his neck. Nevermind the previous arrests for beatings at bars across town. Or even the horrific night he was blind drunk and arrested for DWI, resisting arrest, and six counts of assault on peace officers. All of that was bad enough, but because of an earlier domestic incident, he knew this time consequences could be severe. After their initial separation years ago, Rand was watching the kids while Lena went out with friends. Rand's new girlfriend coincidentally appeared at the same bar and Lena, returning home drunk, came after him with a wine bottle. Her bruises were from him holding her wrists until the police arrived. It did not matter that she had attacked him. It did not even matter that she was completely hammered. Rand was judged a violent man with a violent past and handed six months on a domestic violence charge.

He had no idea what time it was now. Four o'clock in the morning? He rolled over on the shelf that was supposed to be a bed and sickly glanced at the wall. He recalled banging on the windows and scaring Lena and her loser boyfriend half to death. From an upstairs window, she begged him to leave, but he just stood there screaming until, with no other choice, she finally called the police.

Since he was arrested on a Saturday night, there was no bail until his Monday morning arraignment. Thirty-six more hours. He could not believe it, just could not believe how stupidly his mind sometimes worked. And fucking Elias. If he had not split out early and left him alone maybe none of this would have happened.

The good news was that he had not touched her. He recalled screaming at the guy to come out and take his beating like a man—tried to remember the guy's face but could not since he had already fled further into the house once Rand started losing it. It was just as well. Stomping that clown into the ground would have been satisfying, but even Rand realized this was unacceptable. The behavior of a moron. A drunken douchebag of a moron. After all, she had had at least half a dozen boyfriends in the seven years since their divorce. Reawakened by the cocaine still trailing through his system, and lying there in the misery of a hangover that would probably last all day, Rand Holmscomb cursed it all.

Across town that same Sunday morning, Kara Harris had her CPS case files spread before her. The reality was she and Sarah Vaughn had accomplished very little. T.K. McCombs was out of reach, Henman's lawyer was threatening legal action if the CPS moved against him, and the last of the big three ranchers readying to sell, William Cahill, would not return her calls.

When the phone rang, Lena Holmscomb's voice was filled with panic. "He just wouldn't leave. The kids woke up, Roger was scared out of his mind and Rand ..." Lena was blowing her nose. "There's always been a side to him that's just completely unreachable when he's drinking."

"Do you know if he made bail?"

"There's no bail till Monday ..."

Because the crew worked together six days a week, the wives turned to each other by default. Kara would often ski with Lena and Rigor Mortis' wife Tyra Killea. During summer, they and their kids kayaked and swam the Blackstone River. Before Lena's and Tyra's marriages imploded, the families also vacationed together at various National Parks to allow their husbands, and themselves, the privacy to blow off steam. Mountain biking, shooting guns, or wake-boarding—the women held their own while also guarding the children after the husbands broke out the whiskey and dirt bikes.

Kara admired Lena, admired anyone who worked a fulltime job while raising two children pretty much alone. Three kids, if you counted Rand, but that was apparently set to change.

"You've been down this road before." Kara refilled her coffee. She was wearing a pair of Nolan's boxers and his wife-beater that read HARRIS FRAMING across her breasts. "You both date other people, you sometimes sleep together ... I mean, no offense, but this whole thing is kind of a mess. And the closer you and Roger get, the harder it's gonna be for Rand if you don't stop—" She wanted to say fucking him, but chose her words with caution. "Maybe the extracurricular activities—and by that I mean doing his laundry, dinner when he's visiting the kids—should be shelved until you see what happens with Roger. He sounds like a nice enough guy."

"Well, he is. Stable, nice, sweet ... I think he really cares about me."

"What's wrong with that?"

"I'm in my forties, but that doesn't mean I'm ready to just ... I can't believe I'm about to say this, because you're absolutely right. He brings me flowers, takes me down to Denver, buys Emily and Kenny toys and videogames and I mean, he's really trying ..."

"But?"

"But I just don't get that *feeling* when I see him, you know? How stupid does that sound?"

"It's not stupid."

"I mean here's this intelligent guy with a stable job and a positive outlook on life, and the only thing I can find wrong with him is that I'm ... I just ... I feel like being with Roger is a settlement with myself. Like a way that I can make myself believe that this is the way I should be treated."

"Being treated right is not the problem. Besides, at this point, why not switch things up? I love Rand for who he is too, but ... I totally understand where you're coming from. Don't you think I want Nolan to walk through the door with a bouquet of flowers instead of laying around complaining all the time? I mean it's Sunday, his only day off, and where do you think he is? With the new guy, Elias, cleaning tools ... *again*."

"That poor guy ..." Lena sounded amused. "First, Nolan was Rand's chauffeur and now Elias ..."

"What do you think of him?"

"Who, Elias?"

"Yes."

Lena said, "We haven't talked all that much, but he seems courteous whenever he's over. Rand says he's the best laborer they've ever had which, incidentally, bodes well for no one."

"Right? With those two mad scientists imparting all of their glorious wisdom?"

"That poor guy's totally screwed, isn't he?"

"Even Frankenstein had better teachers."

"Listen, Kenny's calling me to help him with his homework. You gonna be around later on? I'm thinking about taking the kids to that new Disney movie."

"Oh yeah?" Kara scanned the empty apartment and then saw the paperwork of the dying Cahill proposal. "You know what? Count me in. Maybe we'll grab something to eat since Nolan will be treating."

"Awesome. I'll call you in a couple of hours."

———————

An hour later, the phone startled Kara again. "Hello?"

"Kara?"

She immediately recognized Rand's voice but he sounded sick.

He said, "Hey, no offense, but I don't have much time. Is Nolan around? I just tried his cell but there was no answer."

"No, he's out at the storage unit with Thomas."

"Fuck!"

"Excuse me?"

"I'm sorry. They only give you one call, and I'm already over my limit."

"Are you all right?" Realizing how ridiculous that sounded, she said, "What do you need me to do?"

She grabbed a pen, made note of the amount for tomorrow's arraignment, and could almost picture Nolan's reaction.

On Monday, the second-story floor system was offloaded by 8:00 A.M. The driver was a loquacious fellow from Wyoming unknowingly in the worst possible place for small talk. Nolan nodded and smiled once or twice at the nonsense about the weather and asshole bosses but Elias, whose job it was to place 2x4s beneath the load before it was forklifted to the ground, barely said hello.

"Let's rim this shit." Nolan fired up the screaming generator and compressor before asking Elias, "We all rolled out?"

"Gun and saw are on the deck."

"Then crack those bands and drag a bunch of that shit into the building."

Unlike Rand, who walked top-plate while nailing the rim at the same time, Nolan set up a pair of ladders to minimize the risk.

"Thomas! Get in here and get on this ladder."

Since the left front corner was the designated control point for the rest of the structure, the layout for the second-story floor joists was exactly the same as the first-floor below it. After marking 15¼ inches from the left corner on top of the front wall, Nolan set a nail, hooked his tape, and marked every 16 inches after that. Since the joists ran front to back, he then pulled layout along the top-plate of the rear wall as well.

Nolan called out, "You need to remember layout is exactly the same for all of this shit. It's a continuous line down to the foundation. Wall stud, floor joist, wall stud, floor joist—everything stacks in one line. If we don't fuck up layout, this line transfers the load directly down to the concrete, almost like a column."

"I think I'm getting it," Elias said.

"Listen. The less thinking you do, the safer all of us will be." But after Nolan continued doing all of the measuring, cutting, and nailing, he finally said, "This ain't gonna work. We need to get you up to speed."

"Oh yeah? You need me to think?"

"Whoa, easy, Stimpy. Let's not get crazy. Go grab Rand's bags so I can show you how to measure and cut." As much as Nolan wanted to kick ass through this fortunate spell of calm weather, he also knew instructing Elias on the fundamentals would, hopefully, make him more of an asset.

Elias returned buckling into Rand's leather Occidentals. There were three pouches on either hip, each one smaller than the last, and descending in size like narrowing steps. From there, individual customization occurred but the carpentry basics never varied—30-foot tape, pencils, chisel, knife, speed square, chalkline, cat's paw, and hammer. Some guys also carried additional chisels, nail sets, a calculator, a torpedo level, and metal snips, which were basically industrial-grade scissors. Together with the 28-ounce hatchet and two dozen racks of nails for the gun, Elias guessed the weight to be fifteen pounds at least.

Nolan screwed a cigarette into his lips and said, "Remember back in math class when you thought you'd never use fractions or geometry?"

"Oh no..."

"Yup. Triangles, squares, and rectangles, that's all we're building here." Nolan nodded at the uncut piece of rim-board. "Take out the tape, hook the board, and mark off 186⅜ inches exactly."

Elias did, kneeling down to better see the tape. He made a crow's foot (V) next to the number and then looked up at Nolan who said, "Now use the speed square to square off that line."

Elias centered the metal triangle directly through the crow's foot and then dragged a pencil down its length. Since the rim was twelve-inches wide, he had to flip the seven-inch speed-square to the other edge to complete the line.

Nolan grabbed the saw and nudged Elias aside. "Now watch how I cut this. We pin the guards because they're a nuisance, so make sure you don't amputate yourself." He pointed to the blade. "After you take your finger off the trigger, this thing's gonna be spinning for at least five more seconds. Rule number one—never take your hand off a saw that's still spinning. That blade catches something and it'll jerk itself into anything that's near it, mainly your legs."

"Okay."

"Take the board like this ..." Using his left calf and ankle as an improvised sawhorse, Nolan wrestled the sixteen-foot rim board until the cut line was six-inches to the right of his left calf. Bent at the waist, his left hand held the board while the right lined up the saw. "Always remember, the blade itself is an eighth of an inch wide. So you want the left side of the blade to leave the line. If you don't, if you cut it on the wrong side of the line, you're gonna be off an ⅛ inch every time."

Elias squeezed in for a closer look.

The saw sprang to life and chewed through one stroke later. Nolan, with the board still across his ankle, dangled the saw from his right fist until the blade stopped spinning. He said, "Remember, gravity's your friend. Just line up the blade, hit the trigger, and let Mother Nature drag it down."

"No sawhorses? So you guys don't cut off your own feet?"

"Rule number one—don't be a pussy. Now let's nail this bitch off so I can get you another number."

They climbed the ladders holding the long board between them. Nolan started nailing from the corner. Elias worked it in-and-out according to Nolan's instructions. Ideally, the rim would be toe-nailed perfectly flush with the outside edge of the top-plate, providing a nice straight line for the floor joists to later butt into.

At the end of the board, Nolan arced his tape nine feet out and hooked the edge of the wall. "Need one at 94⅝ inches to finish it out."

Elias was already poised, his tape hooked before the number was even called out. He marked and squared off the line seconds later, wrangling the sixteen-footer across his bony ankle. He reached for the saw while envisioning pulsating streams of blood, and tried to copy Nolan's previous example precisely.

"No offense," Nolan called out from the ladder. "But double-check that number before you hand it up."

Elias did not hear him because he had, despite the previous warning, put down the saw which had, as predicted, caught a piece of wood before spitting it across the deck.

"What the fuck did I just tell you?" Nolan frowned and turned away as if trying to keep himself in check. "This ain't no fucking kitchen, you know? Out here, a bad day means somebody shoots themselves with a gun, cuts off a finger, or falls to their death."

"I know—"

"No, you *don't* know. But you will. Believe me, no one gets out of this shit for free." He held out his hand. "Ready for the wood."

Elias handed up the board while silently digesting the reprimand. He climbed his ladder to help, but Nolan, because the board was so short, worked the piece alone. He placed it on the wall before saying, "Goddamnit." He tossed it back to the deck with a crash. "Are you listening to anything I'm saying?"

"Yes—"

"Really?"

"Fuck ..." Elias nodded. "I cut it on the wrongside of the line, didn't I?"

"You better start focusing, man, or you'll be a wood-bitch for life. Get ready to cut another."

Elias climbed down the ladder.

They had the entire exterior perimeter rimmed a half hour later. Nolan checked the time and said, "Guess we should go bail out dumbass."

Piling into the F-250, they cranked the heat and headed to town. After the debacle with the saw, the silence had barely been broken.

Nolan pulled into the parking lot of the Valley Savings Bank and shoved a check at Elias. "Go to Kara's window. She's already got assclown's bail money squared away."

Elias' black sunglasses were blank squares. "Wood-bitch *and* errand boy?"

"It's called multitasking, simpleton." Nolan smiled as he reached for his cigarettes. "I can't go in there today. She caught me with a hundred bucks in scratch tickets and flipped out. Now hurry the fuck up."

Elias hopped out and pulled up his hood. His logger boots crunched through the ice-strewn sidewalk. In the bank, he scanned for Kara's window.

Still tending to a customer, she smiled and waved him over.

He nodded awkwardly. Working for Nolan was one thing, but coming across as inappropriate in any way in front of his shapely wife was near the top of probable death offenses. Elias knew enough to handle her and Nolan's money the same way—at arm's length and with caution.

Still, from their brief encounters, Elias knew she was a lot like her husband. Unabashedly direct, she enjoyed her role as the boss' wife and had no problem going for the throat, not even the one belonging to the indefatigable Rigor Mortis.

Once Kara finished with her customer, he stepped up to her window. "Hey, Kara."

"Thomas ..." She wore no makeup, her olive eyes upon him. "I trust you're having a good day surrounded by warm companions ..."

"Oh, God." Elias handed her the check. "I don't even know where to start."

By the way she laughed, it was apparent even Nolan was fair game. Her hands flew across the keyboard as she said, "So I understand you and Rand were out on the town Saturday night?"

Completely straight-faced, Elias nodded and said, "If you consider caring for the elderly and reading to the blind, quote-unquote 'Out on the town,' then I guess I'm guilty as charged."

"So you're the charitable sort?"

"It's all that Nolan preaches."

She counted down a stack of twenties before sliding them through the window. "Tell him I said he left the bathroom a mess this morning."

"Stop shocking me." Elias pocketed the money and then tossed her a salute. "Talk to you later."

"Take it easy, Thomas."

He exited the bank.

Inside the truck, Nolan asked, "How'd it go?"

"Great." Elias handed him the money. "She said you totally bombed out the bathroom ... she also said you ought to give me a raise."

"Keep dreaming."

They arrived at the Salinas County Jail minutes later.

"Here." Nolan pushed a thousand dollars into Elias' chest. "I'm not exactly a sight for sore eyes around here."

"Seriously? What the hell ..." Elias started patting himself down, tossing a six-inch buck knife, a bag of weed, papers, and his phone into the glovebox. He glanced at the weed and then looked at Nolan. "Hope you ain't the kind to take a pinch while a brother's got his back turned."

"I already told you, I'm a drug-free motherfucker and actually don't appreciate you having that shit in my rig at all."

"Just checking." Elias zipped up his jacket and thumbed the roll of bills. "You got an extra something in here for me, considering what a hard worker I am?"

"Nope. Now go in there and bail that drunk-ass, punk-ass, lame-ass out, will you please? And bring me the receipt."

Elias shut the door and scowled because, as far as he was concerned, the police were human beings who suffered from what all human beings fell prey to eventually and that was themselves. Alcoholism, fanaticism, bad marriages, financial strain, drug abuse, and greed were not specific conditions relegated to only those outside law enforcement. Badge or not, Elias thought it just good common sense to keep a wary eye peeled toward anyone carrying a gun—whoever they might be.

Ten minutes later he hopped back into the truck. "He'll be out in a couple of minutes."

"How'd it go? You make some new friends?"

"How many people live in this town?"

"Five or six thousand year-rounders. Why?"

"I just think it's weird. The Spring Valley Police, the Salinas County Sheriff, the Colorado State Patrol—that's three different squads in one podunk town?"

"You forgot about the D.E.A. and the N-CAD Task Force."

"The what?"

"Northwest Colorado Anti-Drug Task Force. On top of the D.E.A., N-CAD is a group of local and county pigs for this whole part of the state since Sixty-One is one of the few continuous roads between Denver, Utah, Wyoming ... basically the whole northwest."

"Lots of blow and weed passing through, eh? No wonder this town's got a brand-new lock-up with a hundred and fifty beds in it. Who do you think they're gonna find to fill that place up?"

"Well, they've apparently started with drunken idiots who like harassing their ex-wives."

"Seriously."

"Oh, I can't wait." Nolan rubbed his hands together. "After being locked up for two days with a hangover and no cigarettes and yet another fucking court date, I'm planning on enjoying every last second of this moron's pain."

"Speak of the devil. Here comes Mr. Happy."

Rand jumped into the backseat.

"Enjoy your stay?" Nolan quipped.

Rand immediately reached for Nolan's cigarettes. "Get me the fuck out of here."

They headed toward town while the sun poked its face through the roiling gray clouds cloaking Mt. Lassiter's western edge.

"It's good to see you got popped wearing your work clothes," Nolan said into the rearview mirror. "Because guess where we're going next?"

"I don't give a fuck." Rand hungrily inhaled. He cracked the window and watched the eddying smoke. "None of this shit matters anymore any-fucking-way ..."

"What'd they say?"

"Who?"

"The judge, the pigs, what up, man?"

"Aw, man, fuck'em all, man, y'know? Fuck every last one of these cocksuckin' motherfuckers."

"Easy, killer. You hungry?"

"No."

"Let's get something to eat." Nolan checked his watch. "It's almost eleven anyway."

"Thomas," Rand said. "We need to smoke a joint. Like right now, man, what do you think?"

"I think that's a feasible request."

Nolan allowed it by saying nothing and then they pulled into the Snowpeak Diner. "I'll meet you stoners inside."

They smoked a joint in silence until Elias finally asked, "You okay?"

"Yeah ..." Rand sucked in and held a giant hit before handing back the joint. "It's just so useless, you know? This whole town ... I need to get out of here before they lock me up for good."

"What this place needs are some real criminals."

"Ha."

"Seriously. My neighbors, two of my roommates ... Everyone gets locked up."

Rand said nothing, but then remembered his grudge. "Maybe if you hadn't bugged out on me Saturday night, I wouldn't be in this goddamn mess."

"*What*? Really? Is that what you're thinking?"

"Where'd you go, anyway?"

"Fuck, I don't know." Elias handed back the joint. "I woke up in somebody's basement on Wharton Street."

Rand, deadened by the last forty-eight hours, chuckled nonetheless. "That's what you get for boozing at noon."

"So what happened?"

"Aw, man ... I went by my place—my *old* place, that is. Anyway ..." He recounted running from window to window like some deranged peeping Tom until the police swept down the block.

"Got charged with a drunk and disorderly and a disturbing the peace." He frowned, embarrassed by how stupid all of it sounded even now. "I really need a change of scenery, man."

"Tell me about it."

Rand punched the back of Elias' seat. "No chance, bro. You're not going anywhere."

"You just said the same—"

"You had your chance."

"And now?"

"Now you signed away your soul."

"What soul?"

They saw Nolan angrily stomp out of the diner. Hopping into the driver's seat, he said, "You girls had your chance."

"What?" Rand reached for his door. "We were just—"

"On your way to work? Is that what you were about to say?" Nolan locked the doors and fired up the F-250. "Users lose."

"Oh man ..."

"Thomas, put away the weed." Nolan lowered and locked the windows as his passengers dove for their jackets. They ripped down Main Street as Rand said, "Hey, man, I really do need something to eat."

"Riddle me this ..." Nolan spied him out in the rearview mirror. "If a moron speaks, and no one's there to hear it, does anyone really care?"

"What?"

"Exactly. Hurry up."

Nolan cranked the tunes.

They hit a stretch of good weather. By the second week of February, progress on the Gildman School proceeded at a breakneck pace. Their five week build plan seemed within reach, a fact highlighted by the physical bounce back of Elias whose first weeks of torn muscle, mind-numbing discomfort, and overall lack of conditioning had, by this point, given way to rebuilt muscles thirsting for more abuse. Another surprise came after he showered and spotted his physique springing to life in the mirror. He had dropped fifteen pounds, saw the outline of abdominals for the first time since high school, and felt an overall sense of calm not directly unrelated to the exhaustion sixty-five-hour work weeks created.

He went from eating no breakfast to needing three eggs and waffles just to wake up, and was still starving by lunch. Dinner was chicken or beef alongside a half pound of pasta, salad, a couple bowls of cereal, and all the dessert he desired. It was a testament to exactly how many calories he was burning that he could literally double his daily food intake and still lose weight. But while his body thrived, his mood faltered as the March 1st departure deadline approached. Once his debts were cleared, and he had enough money for the drive home, decisions had to be made. His roommates were already searching for his replacement, a fact that might cause him to be homeless even if he decided to stay. And while New York would always be home, it was getting harder to justify his return. He knew he could always find a job, maybe even restart his dreams of publishing his own magazine, but in the end those options seemed more like a retreat or surrender than truly serving his best interests anymore.

Then there was Lisa. The disaster of their last year together began that night on her birthday. After dinner, Elias had to return to the office because of *Insurrection's* morning deadline. Though he promised to be right home, he found Linda and Wayne swamped in last minute details and could not leave until after midnight.

Like many New Yorkers accustomed to chaos, he had, at first, thought nothing of the ambulance and police cruisers lined up along the block. In fact, he had even forgotten their presence altogether until the elevator opened and he turned right and saw a cluster of cops in front of his and Lisa's door. He remembered frowning, somewhat incredulous until fear exploded across his brain and down his legs which were already sprinting down the hall.

Hearing the commotion bearing down on them, two policemen corralled him at the door.

Sir.

What's happened?

Sir, please.

I fucking live here, man. Where is she? Is she all right?

They're bringing her out.

What happened? Let go of me!

Buddy. If you don't calm down, we're gonna escort you from the building.

Lisa!

Listen—

Goddamnit, get the fuck away from me!

Sir—

They slammed him into the wall when the EMTs rolled her out seconds later. Her face was beaten, her eyes puffed slits leaking blood. The nose was broken and crooked beneath the oxygen mask twisted around her head, which, somehow swiveled toward his voice. He yelled her name while her hand, the one with the IV stuck in it, blindly reached out toward him.

Sir, we need to get her to the hospital.

Sir, please calm down.

After the elevator disappeared, the cops let go of his arms. He said, *What's wrong with her eyes? Did she fall and hit her head?*

Sir, we need to ask you a few questions.

He looked at both policemen. *There's been some kind of mistake, right?* It was hours before he was allowed news of her condition. Hours more until the reality of what had occurred settled in like nausea.

Mr. Elias, these questions are just routine.

Could you please tell us where you were this evening?

Can you explain why there are no signs of forced entry?

Twenty-four hours later he was cleared as a suspect after someone else turned up at the 10th precinct to make a statement. He remembered her name was Magdaleña but, as was the case in this faceless city, neighbors rarely knew much more about one another than their first names revealed. Elias knew she lived on the floor below them, remembered seeing her down in the basement doing laundry with her—

He closed his eyes. After sitting at a detective's desk answering the same questions in differing order off and on for the last twelve hours, Margarita's appearance made him shiver. Then he stood up, which startled the detective, a square-faced man named Humboldt.

Since Lisa taught students with developmental and psychological disabilities, she often spoke with Magdaleña about her cousin, a twenty-year-old man with Down's Syndrome and an IQ below fifty. Institutionalized at various points for violent behavior, and with state funds slashed and mental hospitals closing, this cousin got bounced around his extended family until Magdaleña's turn came do. Though she willingly fulfilled this familial duty, she was also a single mom with two jobs who was not equipped to handle the needs of a six-foot man-child. He sometimes wandered through the building, which is how Lisa ran into him in the basement laundry room and accepted his offer to help carry up her heavy baskets.

Because of her head injuries, Lisa was in an induced coma for a week. Her parents were quiet people from Vermont, so her mother spent a month at their apartment while Lisa recuperated. Besides the head trauma and facial lacerations, there were no other injuries. There had been no rape. She was assigned a violent crimes counselor, booked for twice-weekly outpatient treatment, and released one week later.

But as she healed and the balloon-like distensions slowly drained away, and the black bruising around her eyes faded to a purplish-blue, Elias noticed her physical recovery did not address something ominously shifting within. Not that she had been a carefree dervish before the attack, but her dry sense of humor and sarcastic rejoinders had always kept him grounded. She enjoyed a good joke and occasional bottle of wine. She loved her job. Loved Elias, too. But that was set to change.

The Regis Camp for Gifted Students was near Lake Champlain, Vermont. The camp offered the usual outdoor activities but also maintained a summer curriculum staffed by graduate students and professors from the nearby University of Vermont. Lisa was twelve-years-old. She hung out with her teachers, sitting with them at meals or after class or even as the other kids built fires at night. Appreciative of her attention and intellectual thirst, the staff granted her leeways the other students did not receive. Determined to have the periodic chart of elements memorized by the end of camp, Lisa ran through her flashcards every night with one of her teachers.

As in most cases involving the trust of children, the ensuing sexual assaults were rationalized until she merely nodded yes. He pressed this advantage, talking her into things so abhorrent, outside of the events and memories of the participants, they might not have existed at all. These unreported incidents, however, had been waiting to explode in the aftermath of this newest assault.

She took a leave of absence from work. She attended the crisis sessions with her counselor before deciding the outside world posed too great a threat. She became paranoid and distrusting of people, men specifically, and Elias was made to suffer.

He double-shifted at work to make up for the loss of her income. This also diverted him from the magazine as his partners contemplated selling out. While Lisa spent long vigilant hours behind the peephole of their locked door, Elias sickly watched the deterioration of who she used to be.

After doing all he could, he finally visited her therapist who assured him his efforts would not be in vain. Be patient, he was told, and she will make it back because of it.

He completed most of the household chores even though she was home all day. He also found them a new apartment several blocks away, thinking a change in scenery might dislodge her from the peephole, their neighbors, and her now suffocating paranoia.

Yet even as he gave her the space she demanded, ignoring her belittling tone and endless character assaults finally became impossible. After nine months, she returned to work, but he still came home each day to her silence or sneering reproach, and he at last resolved to make demands of his own. Forget about the sex, which they had not had in so long that Elias now thought of jerking off in the quiet bathroom as an erotically enchanted evening. Forget about their future, which had been completely subsumed by this disaster. Inevitably, as she pushed him further away, he reached back toward what remained of their connection before cutting her loose for good.

It was in this last conversation that she finally reappeared. Her bitterness and callous disregard were finally breached by the conviction of his candor. Because of it, telling her of his impending departure was made easier since it was no longer a threat. But in that moment, as they faced each other on the couch, her hands were busy partners wrestling in her lap. At first, she began to cry at the recognition of what this meant, and then harder once she realized it could no longer be avoided. She apologized to him, trying to smile through her tears. She said she was sorry that she had forgotten who to be, and that was all Elias could take. He reached for her in a silent way bereft of any animus or malice, and they hugged like two people now destined for journeys that could no longer be made together.

———

In Manhattan, he had been cooking alongside a twenty-one-year-old transplant from Newport, R.I., named James LeCavalier. Although he liked the Grateful Dead and smoking pot, James was otherwise pretty clean-cut. Most women characterized him as sweet, but Elias just thought them easily duped by his play. Clever and witty, James was also self-deprecating and came across as a best friend until, after some heartfelt conversation, and possibly one too many chardonnays, the women found themselves separated from their clothing.

At work, he and Elias made a good pair behind the line. When the kitchen got busy and Elias blustered and cursed, James made cracks behind his back to keep the pressure in check.

It had been James' idea to move to Spring Valley. He painted a rugged vision of this place tucked inside the Rocky Mountains just as the rest of Elias' life imploded. He felt like a passenger on a doomed airliner until someone like James, with parachutes in hand, stood ready at the door.

James left three months before Elias to rent them a place. By then Elias had quit *Insurrection* to self-publish *Wreckage Magazine*, but found himself losing heart. Having come so far, he was now back to a four-page black and white pamphlet with smudged photographs. Worse, no one seemed to care. Going out of pocket for the expense, standing on street corners without even being able to *give* the thing away, he finally tossed the last stack into the trash and thought everyone could just fuck off.

Three days later, drunkenly licking his wounds in the tiny room he rented by the week, Elias finally got the call from James.

On Monday, the same morning Rand made bail, the roof trusses arrived. They were thirty-foot equilateral triangles banded together into a giant stack that slid from the hydraulically upraised tractor-trailer with an earth-shuddering thud.

Unlike the layout of the floor joists and studs, which were sixteen-inches to carry the vertical load of the building, the roof trusses were engineered for only the weight of the roof. Spaced two-feet apart, layout was pulled along the top-plates of the front and back exterior walls.

On Tuesday morning, as Elias rolled out the tools, and Rand and Nolan double-checked the blueprints, DEATH WISH CRANE OPERATIONS pulled on-site with a belch of blue smoke from its growling engine.

"Nice. O.D. is in the house." Nolan checked the time at 8:29 A.M. and looked at Rand. "Let's have this motherfucker gone by ten."

"I hear that."

"Hey, Thomas!" Nolan shouted. "Get down there and tell O.D. to set up directly out front!"

Since the staircase had not been cut in yet, Elias stepped out onto an extension ladder perched below a second-floor window. Using a new trick recently stolen from Rand, Elias wrapped his hands underneath each side of the ladder, splayed out his feet, and then dropped downward like an elevator descending. With alternating pressure from the arches of his feet and hands, the rate of descent could be specifically controlled. But still unaccustomed to managing the momentum, Elias rocketed to earth.

"You break a leg and it's on your bill!" Nolan shouted. Then he turned to Rand. "Seriously? Ain't this shit dangerous enough without you teaching him all your awful tricks?"

The crane driver smiled up at Nolan like an amused old friend. He was a former lieutenant in Murder Incorporated, an outlaw MC based in Sioux City, South Dakota. After swapping out his bike and gangland prestige for a ten-ton crane with a twenty-six-ton lift, he now went to work like everyone else. Because of his short stature, scorching red hair and beard, he resembled Yosemite Sam. His name was Chuck Trailor, but everyone knew him as O.D. Originally from the southside of Chicago, Trailor used to claim he was the only white guy mean enough to survive growing up in a drug-infested ghetto overrun by violence. O.D.'s mother had been a junkie and his father a recidivist thug who took turns beating them both when he was not locked up or running the streets. Imprisoned at eighteen for armed robbery, O.D. made some new friends inside Joliet, who had other friends out west, and upon his release, he decided a change of scenery might be best. Arriving in South Dakota, all of those years beneath his father's fists paid off as O.D. was put in charge of debt collection, turf enforcement, and anything else requiring threats and violence. Murder Incorporated had branches in seven western states and over a thousand patched-in members. They moved cocaine from Los Angeles to Chicago, heroin from Chicago to Denver, and in between dominated the white trash distribution circuit of home-cooked methamphetamine. Besides the Mongols and Hell's Angels, both of which had more members, Murder Incorporated made its living in the small towns and vast spaces that left law enforcement stretched too thin.

The nickname O.D. evolved after a pair of murders committed with laced heroin. It was further cemented by over-the-top beatings inflicted upon various rivals lucky to survive. The process usually began with the breaking of fingers, the initial screams working into a crescendo before the wrists and arms were shattered next. It became a signature move, because if someone abruptly appeared in twin arm casts with a horribly disfigured face, there was only one name wise people never mentioned.

He served nine more years in an Iowa prison for three counts of felony assault and a second-degree attempted murder charge, did another year and a half in Minnesota for various weapons violations, and six months in Kansas for threatening the lives of three D.E.A. agents who had gotten too close. All in all, he was a forty-two-year-old ex-con biker until, in one of those rare turning point moments, O.D. became transformed.

A daughter was born to a particularly unpleasant woman O.D. had been fucking on the side down in Denver. The woman, who was as mean as O.D. was violent, was a cocaine addict and continued using even through her pregnancy. But in her ninth month, after speedballing cocaine and heroin and having a heart attack in her dealer's basement, the doctors performed an emergency C-section in order to save the baby.

A day later, after O.D. got a call from the hospital in Denver, he drove down to bury the girlfriend before signing over custody of the infant. Though she was three weeks premature, dangerously under-weight, and in critical condition as she detoxed from the drugs, the baby had a pudgy face and fierce disposition discernible even through the plexiglass wall of the Natal ICU. To think for one second that he would assume custody of this baby would have been a farce had he not left that day completely consumed with guilt. And that, for someone who broke apart other people's appendages as they begged and pleaded for mercy, was completely unnerving.

Since he had not yet signed the papers, O.D. spent the next two days drinking and drugging in Denver while trying to forget the kid even existed. He buried the woman in a plot bought with cash, hooked up with some brothers looking to hit the road, and cruised I-25 in a straight line north to Boulder.

But she was there waiting, no matter how many shots, puffs, or lines he devoured. She was a tiny helpless bundle of arms and legs tagged with IV drips and wires leading to a bank of machines running constant sur-veillance. Seeking a source of inspiration, O.D. looked toward his own parents until realizing a wife-beating drunk and negligent junkie would not be example enough.

He walked into the hospital three days later, wringing his hands. He pulled a chair into the hallway, arranged it so it was in front of her crib right beyond the glass, and over the next eight hours only rose to urinate twice. He watched her fighting for everything—the miniscule breaths, the intake of sustenance, her very life—and somehow realized the enormity of what this meant.

With the child in ICU for three more weeks, his Social Services counselor, still doubtful as to the depths of his intentions, enrolled O.D. in a basic parenting class so he could see what exactly would be required. It was offered as part of the hospital's outreach program for first-time parents. He was there every night, the fiery biker in full regalia predominately surrounded by Latino and black women taken aback by this newest peer. After learning how to change diapers, feed, burp, and care for a baby—learning how to put them to sleep and all about SIDS, infections, and inoculations, he carried her out the front door of Denver Health five weeks later.

No one thought it would work. Not his friends, associates, or even the woman he had been seeing.

Did you hear about O.D.?

Ain't he somebody's daddy now?

Good Lord above, the apocalypse must be near.

Instead of the cramped trailer that stank of dog piss and spilt beer, O.D. brought the child home to a small apartment on the outskirts of town. The girlfriend, a wide-bottomed woman who had been a waitress for twenty years, thought this arrangement somewhat constraining. The way she figured it, she had made it through her entire adult life without children, so why start now? O.D. kicked her out the next day, checked on the $200,000 stored in two safety deposit boxes, and paid the retired grandmother next door to help him with the baby.

Taking care of his brothers, though, became the true dilemma. Syndicate members did not just walk in and say they were taking early retirement. Things had to be negotiated, matters resolved, because the alternative was not survivable. Blood in, blood out. But with O.D.'s tenure and record, motive was not an issue. Neither was the money or

thoughts of greener pastures elsewhere. So as he sat across from Donny
Teagues, longtime friend and president of Murder Incorporated, and
told him of his new plan, the mood was light. They were drinking Long
Island Iced Teas in a Sioux City strip club as O.D. formally resigned
control of operations in northwest Colorado and Utah. Teagues,
though annoyed at the loss, was not about to stand in the way of someone like O.D. Friends for twenty years, they had originally met in the
maximum-security Iowa State Penitentiary. But he did tell O.D. that
his one-percenter days were now over. He could wear no other patch.
Forever. Teagues assigned O.D. a replacement, told him to break him in
over the next three months, and then they would speak again.

O.D. saw the crane soon after, parked alongside County Road 39. It
had a FOR SALE sign beneath a spiderwebbed windshield and looked
like an oversized toy stuck amongst the weeds. The owner said it was
only five-years-old, had logged less than a thousand hours, but acknowledged the beating the winters had inflicted. So O.D. paid $37,000 before
spending another $10,000 on new tires and a complete engine overhaul.

In the vacant lot next door to his apartment, like any guy overcome
by unchecked power and little-boy awe, he played with his crane for
a solid month before acquiring a Class C operator's license, liability
insurance, and an OSHA certification after a week-long class in Denver.
Gathering up his nerve, he bought space for his first ad in the *Spring
Valley Anchor* which read:

> *Weak of heart for some heavy lifting? Call:*
> DEATH WISH CRANE OPERATIONS
> 1-908-555-4242

That had been almost three years ago, and by coincidence perfectly
timed with the beginning of Spring Valley's construction boom. Now
the proud owner of two cranes, Death Wish was also one of only three
companies in the entire county providing this service at a time when six
could easily compete.

"Fucking O.D." Nolan and Rand were lighting cigarettes in an
upstairs window as the crane's brakes moaned and hissed. Nolan, though
ten years younger, had known O.D. since before his transformation.

O.D.'s marathon cocaine blowouts were the stuff of legend. Rand, who was practically the same age and had once stepped in the same one-per-center circles O.D. ruled, shared an unacknowledged connection that two guys, possibly mellowed by age, might confuse as wisdom. Either way, it was almost like a class reunion once O.D. hopped down from the cab.

"Whatcha got here?" O.D.'s curly red hair poked out from beneath his knit cap in clustered bursts. His long orange beard was resting on his jacket like a napkin, and his eyes shared the smile he tossed up toward the window. "Heard a couple of psychopaths were out here framing in the woods ..." O.D. made a joke of looking around. "Seen anybody that fits that description?"

"I think I'll plead the fifth." Nolan grinned. "How's things, man, you having a good winter?"

"The best." O.D.'s teeth munched together before spitting out a slew of sunflower husks. "Lunatics like yourself kept me busy even through December."

"It was a cold one, huh?"

"The goddamn coldest December I can recall, anyways." O.D. looked about. "The grapevine told me that what I'm seeing actually took you two weeks. You fellas lookin' to see which one of you is gonna drop dead first?"

"Something like that." Nolan nodded toward Elias. "That's Thomas. Say hello to O.D."

They shook hands as Elias scanned the logo decaled across the door and said, "Nothing inspires trust like a company named Death Wish."

O.D.'s smile was shaded by his beard. "Let's them know where I'm coming from, is all."

"And where they should be standing whenever shit's flying overhead, right?"

"Absolutely." O.D. glanced up at Nolan. "At least this one can read, huh?"

"Barely." Nolan looked at Elias. "We need some sixteen-footers up here for bracing." He glanced back at O.D. "Basically, you got the two gable ends on top of the stack, and there should be eighteen commons beneath."

"Where we gonna start?"

"Right here." Nolan pointed to the left front corner. "Gable first and then we'll run the commons."

"Swell."

"How much stick you got?"

"Fully extended? A hundred and twenty feet."

"Nice."

"Yeah, I should be able to boom that whole stack without relocating at all."

"Nice." Nolan flicked away the butt. "How's your girl?"

"Josie? Aw, she's fine, Noll, coming up on four-years-old."

"It's a great age, ain't it? Mine's almost eleven and getting ready to tear the hell out of me and my ex-wife."

"Please, I do not want to hear about it. And you ..." O.D. pointed at Rand. "Ain't you even gonna say hello?"

"I was told never to interrupt my elders."

"Why, you son of a bitch. You calling me old, you son of a bitch?"

"Misery loves company, ain't that what they say?"

"Well, it certainly explains how you fellas have lasted this long, right?" O.D. chuckled. "How you doing, Randall?"

"I ain't dead yet, man."

"Amen." O.D. pointed at the crane. "Just let me get my feet down and we'll be good to go."

"Right on." Nolan nodded down at Elias as he walked by with a shoulder full of wood. "There's your rigger. Show him what you need and remember—he likes it rough."

O.D. threw down four wooden pallets and lowered the four outriggers which lifted the entire crane a foot and a half into the air. Then he climbed into the control seat directly behind the cab. The actual base of the boom was on his right, allowing the impression of a massive appendage shooting off-shoulder upwards for a hundred feet. Working the levers, he raised the boom and telescoped it into the sky. Like the collapsible antennae of an old-style walkie-talkie, the crane fit four different sections of itself inside the main boom arm. As it extended out, the diesel revved and roared blue-black smoke from the twin stacks like vomit into the air.

Swinging the boom toward the stack of trusses, O.D. cabled down the ball and hook. He hopped out and showed Elias how to rig each triangle by securing canvas straps on either side of the peak. Then O.D. attached a long thin rope to the bottom right corner of the truss and said, "This is a tagline. Once this bird's in the air, work the line, keeping enough pressure so the wind don't spin it."

"Okay."

"You don't seem too convinced."

"Yeah, well, these guys are a total mess. If it ain't done right and fast ..."

"They can suck it." O.D. handed him the rope. "Just pretend you're flying a thirty-foot kite made of wood."

"Hey, Thomas!" Nolan screamed from an upstairs window. "Once you hand off the tagline to Rand, get up the ladder to help us out!"

"Noll, you ready to rock?" O.D. shouted from his seat.

"Bring it!"

O.D. made eye contact with Elias before slowly cabling up. The truss rose, slid off the stack, and then hung vertically in the breeze. Like a rodeo hand trying to corral a lassoed steer, Elias worked the tagline as both the wind and the crane's movements battled in opposing force. He figured out how to let the rope pay out while keeping enough consistent pressure for control. The truss rose higher as O.D. boomed left in a graceful arc.

Elias walked it toward the building. Rand, smoking nonchalantly on top of the second-floor wall, reached for the tagline. O.D. slowed his movements, inching right until Nolan, waiting on the back wall, could grip the truss as well. Without any radios, and because distances sometimes played tricks with the operator's assessment, a specific system of universal hand signals functioned like a sign language from afar. Boom left, boom right, up, down, in, out—cable up or down—O.D. watched Rand's upraised hands while following their directions precisely. Crane operators, knowing the recipient's safety and lives were on the line, always allowed them full responsibility for their own fate.

As the gable end slid into position along the outside edge of the wall, Rand abruptly made a fist that ceased all movement. He checked with Nolan to make sure the truss was not hanging off his side before toe-nailing it into the wall.

It took another truss placement before they found a rough synchronization. Elias traveled up and down the ladder, strapping trusses and then, once upstairs, taking back the straps before firing up a pair of 2x4 blocks to Nolan and Rand. Two blocks were nailed in between each truss to provide spacing and support. But as Elias tossed them to his bosses, he quickly found out how hard it was to shoot a two-foot gap twenty-feet away from individuals perched inches away from their own death.

Of the first three blocks Elias tossed to Nolan, one went sideways while two others sailed over his head like misfires from an unsighted gun.

"Jesus Christ." Nolan was disgusted. "Are you a fucking moron or what?"

"Fuck, man, I'm trying—"

"Listen to me, zippy. That crane's costing me three hundred bucks an hour, so stop thinking and *just do it.*"

Infuriated by the reprimand, Elias launched the next block directly at Nolan's head.

"Thatta girl," Nolan said, plucking it from the air like a Seattle dock worker palming fish. "Now go toss one like that to your alcoholic sister over there."

Rand gave him the finger, Elias scurried up and down, and an hour later all twenty trusses were rolled.

"Fucking A," O.D. said somewhat unappreciatively. "Seems like I just got here."

Nolan was climbing down the ladder. "Sorry, bud, but every second you're on-site is one less dollar in my pocket."

On the ground, as O.D. pulled up the outriggers and readied for departure, Rand and Nolan stepped back to appraise their work. Lighting cigarettes, they glanced up at the skeletal structure of the roof like two victims who knew the worst was yet to come.

"Fucking A," Rand said, and exhaled smoke.

"Fucking A," Nolan repeated.

Together, buckling back into their bags, one led the other toward the ladder.

———

After they nailed on the sub-fascia and fascia boards, the plywood came next. They laid down a few courses before Nolan had to leave for the bank. Rand looked down at Elias and said, "Are you here to learn?"

"Excuse me?"

"It's hard to teach you anything with Freakshow losing his shit every fifty seconds, but I wanna show you how to walk roof without dying."

"Okay."

"Get on up here."

Elias climbed out a window. It was unnerving to be doing this thirty feet in the air. From the 2x10 staging, he carefully pulled himself up onto the roof. For a novice, it was easy to become disoriented. The faraway view collided with adrenaline and fear in a vertigo that was hard to control. The ground actually seemed to beckon for his body. Pulse pounding, he checked his footing. "Jesus Christ, it's crazy up here, right?"

"I love it." Rand lit a cigarette and stared at the mountains. "Mother Nature's penthouse, bro. But it has rules. Rule number one. Never step on a wet roof for any reason ever. Any questions?"

"Seems pretty straightforward."

"One slip and you'll be sailing for the edge. If that happens, spread out like a starfish. Try to create as much friction between you and the roof as possible. You might stop in time."

"Might?"

"Try to snag or splinter on something." Rand smiled. "You'll have about three seconds to figure it out. One time, I was lucky enough to drive my hatchet straight into the roof."

Elias looked appalled. "You mean there was more than one time?"

"Rule number two. Watch where your feet are at all times." Rand held up the nailgun and pointed at its attached hose. "One step on the hose and you're gonna go sailing."

"Okay. Um, one question. Don't they have ropes and shit, harnesses, to prevent all this?"

"They do." Rand dragged on the smoke. "We don't."

"Why is that?"

"Well, like the airhose, stringing ropes all over the place is actually more dangerous. The safety gear also gives a false security. You shouldn't be doing anything up here outside your skillset. That'll get you killed. Also, none of that shit goes along with hurry up. Ass-Face would blow a gasket."

"Jesus."

"If it makes you feel any better, I'll nail in a kicker. That's a long 2x4 along the edge. You can smash into that, little fella, to prevent yourself from dying."

"Gee, thanks."

"Rule three. Especially in winter. A thin layer of ice forms overnight every night. The sun will hit one side before the other. Never step on the backside of any roof until the sun bakes it dry. One step and you're a goner for sure, and even faster now because you're sliding on ice." Rand approached a stack of plywood. They had nailed beveled 2x6s into the roof to form a makeshift table. He picked up a 4x8 foot sheet like a giant playing card, walked up the roof to the next vacant spot, and dropped it across four trusses. He used a foot to guide it as it slid into place like Tetris. He picked up the gun and said, "Proper sheet nailing calls for six inches on the seams, eight inches in the field." He blasted off the seam, nailed down over the next two trusses, and then seam-nailed the fourth truss. He looked up at Elias. "Any questions?"

"No, but Jesus Christ, you're an animal with that gun."

"If you are on the ground while guys are working on the roof, and you hear someone scream out 'headache,' it means something has fallen off the roof. Could be anything. Tape measure, wood, whatever. You drop something up here and gravity's gonna bring it down in a hurry. You don't yell 'heads up' because you don't want to get your face smashed in. Remember, nothing falls straight down unless it's dropped straight down. Otherwise momentum sails shit out over the edge. You hear headache you dive for the wall. The overhang might save you."

"Okay. Yell headache if I drop something off the roof. Got it."

"Now walk the next sheet over here."

"It's a lot windier up here."

"Yes, it is. And it will try to rip it from your grasp. When it's really windy it can feel like walking across a boat deck in a storm. Don't panic, keep your balance, and try to keep the sheet pointed into the wind. Remember. Regardless of what Nolan says, nothing's worth dying for. If something goes wrong save yourself. But keep in mind whatever it is that leaves your hands could kill someone down below. That's the way you need to think up here. I'm being totally serious. You're responsible for the lives of the people down below."

"Great." Elias stepped to the stack. He checked his feet, checked the route he would take. Then he picked up the plywood sheet. At first it was ungainly. He repositioned his weight on the eight-pitch roof. Step by step it got easier. He approached the next vacant slot and dropped the sheet. Rand saved him because the sheet did not land fully on the trusses. If Rand had not shot his boot out, the sheet would have slid into Elias' ankles.

Rand grinned. "Don't do that again." He picked up the sheet. "It's okay to toss it. Get it out there on the trusses and let gravity do its thing." Rand flung the sheet and guided it into place with his boot.

Elias frowned. "You make everything look so easy." He went and got another sheet. This time there was no problem. By the sixth he was moving with confidence.

"See?" Rand said. "Even I can train a monkey."

"Out of the way, amigo." Elias dropped the next sheet. "You're standing in the way of progress."

CHAPTER TWELVE

Spring Valley, because of its size, was too small a place for anyone's actions to remain inconspicuous. Whether for achievement or disgrace, word traveled like a gunshot, especially inside the building community. Progress on projects or lack thereof was always a hot topic for discussion.

The SUVs started appearing midway through the third week of the Gildman School build. Some had tinted windows whose occupants remained unseen. Others disgorged developers and prospective owners eager for conversation. Nolan, who as a rule was generally not fond of idle chatter or strangers or certainly any combination of the two, now found himself glad-handing and bullshitting like a politician on the make. To him, the brand-new SUVs resembled their occupants, who usually climbed down with wide, showy smiles and a projected sense of power. They handed him rolls of blueprints and business cards and spoke about the epic implications of their proposals. Grand schemes of future developments and financial reward were often dangled like carrots. Nolan smiled when he could, laughed weakly at their jokes, but never allowed them the appearance of control. The owner and builder relationship was, at least in his mind, based on a simple assumption of roles—they wrote the checks, and he nailed the wood. Period. They were welcome to visit the site and ask fundamental questions, but soundly discouraged from offering opinion or meddling in any way with the course of construction. If the owner had a problem or change of heart in some aspect of the build, Nolan could redesign on the fly, but nothing came for free. Once the signed and stamped set of prints was in his hands, anything extra required a change-order billed at cost.

That the SUVs were appearing here this soon was something of a surprise. Originally, when Nolan had met with Harmon Andrews, the purchasing agent at one of the town's two lumber yards, and let slip word of his five-week goal for completion, Nolan knew this boast would be quickly spread. Placing orders for nearly sixty percent of the town's ongoing builds, Andrews was the hub for all gossip-related job activities, and for such a burly outdoorsman to be so chatty, was both amusing and somewhat disconcerting.

Four units in an apartment complex, a single-family ranch, duplex condominiums—the SUVs contained these offers and more but Nolan was not enticed. Besides, as the Gildman School neared completion, and word of its time-frame expanded, soon he would be able to exercise an even clearer command on price. So he collected proposals and stored the blueprints in his backseat, which as the weeks passed by, began to resemble an artillery battery of rolled-up tubes.

As for worker morale, they were approaching their sixth week of sixty hours per, and nerves were starting to fray. Elias and Rand could drink themselves into a coma but Nolan had only two avenues for escape—a horrible gambling problem and the occasional strip club blowout. To this end, on Friday of week three of the Gildman build, he gathered his crew as the snow began to fall.

"Gentlemen," he said, "it's time for a different kind of show."

Elias and Rand were standing side-by-side, hesitant, their expressions cast in doubt.

"I'm fucking beat," Rand said.

Elias frowned. "Doesn't this show already suck enough?"

But Nolan was already gathering up the tools. "It's almost three. If we leave by four, we can make Denver by seven o'clock."

Rand punched Elias' shoulder. "You're gonna love this."

"Love what? Getting snowed on in another part of this godforsaken state?"

An hour later, after they were showered and changed, the Ford headed south on County Road 61. The two-lane road snaked up Mt. Lassiter's western edge. Low-lying clouds and falling snow eclipsed its peak. Vast ranches bracketed the road until it began its ascent, and then individual homes were carved into the pines like outposts stuck cliffside for the view.

Equipped with studded snow tires and chains, the F-250 growled uphill. Elias, who had not left the valley since before the first November snows, watched it all fall away. At 9,000 feet, they started a tortuous six-mile climb along switchbacks that were, even in the summer months, traversed with extreme caution. They quickly approached 11,000 feet. In the dead of winter, when average conditions meant eighty to nine-ty-feet of snow and blistering windchills, the last three miles leading to and from Forked Head Pass was not for the faint of heart, or those lack-ing four-wheel drive, chains, and cellphones in case of trouble. Because it was National Forest land, the closest ambulance was back in Spring Valley, which meant the earliest one might see a hospital was an hour and a half after the crash.

"Jesus Christ." Elias watched a car speed downhill toward them. "Can't these hicks at least put up Jersey barriers between the lanes?"

"Getting nervous?" Nolan cracked.

"What was the rating again?" Rand asked Nolan.

"Sixteen."

"Hear that?" Rand called into the backseat. "You're currently riding on the sixteenth most dangerous stretch of road in the continental U.S."

"Awesome. Make sure they put that on my headstone."

Nolan turned to Rand and said, "The M.D.H. would kill him."

"Absolutely."

Elias said, "Okay, I'll bite. What's the M.D.H.?"

"Million Dollar Highway." Nolan glanced into the rearview mirror. "Only the most dangerous road in America. Story goes, one of its earli-est travelers said she would have to be paid a million dollars to ever go through it again. Official name is Red Mountain Pass. It connects Ouray and Silverton on US 550 straight through the San Juan mountains. In the winter, if it's even open, if you drive faster than ten miles an hour, you're gonna die."

"Great. Is there anything in this state that's not trying to kill us?"

Nolan smiled. "Ain't he pleasant?"

"Not exactly." Rand reached into a bag at his feet. "I've seen wet cats in better moods." He passed a flask of Jim Beam into the backseat. "Sip on that, little fella."

"Thank you, hoss." Elias took the bottle as the summit neared. "Holy shit, look at that ..."

Because the air was too thin past 11,000 feet, the vast sea of pine and spruce trees dead-ended like a hairline near the peak. Giant rock slopes replaced them covered in windblown drifts and cyclones of swirling snow. The road was still climbing but slowly straightening. In order to pass a highway over a mountain, construction crews had blown open a hundred-foot-wide gap through twenty feet of granite. The size of this opening may have seemed overkill for only a two-lane road connecting remote locations, but up here, at the highest point for over 150 square miles, where cold Canadian air collided with Pacific coast moisture to produce a region-wide snowmaking machine, there had to be somewhere to put all the snow. Road crews from the Department of Transportation manned the earth-moving equipment stored up top year-round. Giant ground scrapers, bucketloaders, and plows carved a tiny tunnel through the engulfing cliffs of snow. Incredibly, on each side of the road, white walls extended straight up for thirty feet. The DOT crews drove a special tractor equipped with a one-ton vertical arm that resembled a giant hedge trimmer. Cocked perpendicular to the ground, it clipped along the wall like a razor across a cheek.

The sign was barely visible through the blowing snow—

FORKED HEAD PASS
SUMMIT 12,868 FEET
MECKLENBURG 32 MILES
DENVER 192 MILES

"What's with the name?" Elias called out. "Did the guy who discovered this peak have a two-headed prick?"

Nolan squinted into the gloom. "We might not be able to see it, but it's coming up on the left."

The pickup slowed as twirling yellow lights cut through the sheets of snow. A bucketloader was filling two dumptrucks while one lone bundled up worker morosely watched the action.

"I think that's it," Nolan said and pointed across the road.

Elias scanned along the flatland of the summit. The claustrophobic ice-trench cut across the top of the mountain had now planed down into a wide-open snow prairie. Amongst the rocks, a dark granite figure

suddenly rose up. Its creepily distinct facial features were split in two as
if cleaved by an ax. How Mother Nature had managed this violent feat
remained unknowable.

"That," Elias said, "is pretty disturbing."

"Ain't it though?" Nolan fired up a smoke. "I always thought of it as
a warning to the first motherfuckers who tried making it through here."

"Imagine those people?" Rand asked. "Back then, if you hadn't
crossed over this bitch by September ..."

"Donner Party time. Grab your cousin and bust out the A-1 steak
sauce, bro."

"Gross." Elias rolled a joint and sparked it.

Rand passed back a wedge of paper with cocaine tucked into its
crease.

Nolan growled, "Look at you fucking junkies. How many drugs can
you do at once?"

"We'll see." Rand cackled and blew his hit out the window.

"Why'd you quit all this anyway?" Elias asked between snorts off the
paper. "I mean, what's the fucking point?"

"After you been there and back so many times ..." Nolan glanced into
the rearview mirror. "Like you just said, what's the point?"

The pickup gripped the snow-covered road as it fell away into another
series of dangerous switchbacks, but this time they were descending.
Drifts of snow cascaded down from above, the ridges blown clean by
the northwest wind. The road twisted, clinging to the mountainside for
another four miles. At 7,000 feet, they punched out into the North Fork
National Forest. From there, sporadic houses popped up like glowing
outposts in the failing light. But living in such complete isolation was
not without risk since practical options, if disaster struck, were virtually
nonexistent.

Thirty minutes later, the town of Mecklenburg emerged from the
dusk. Little more than a three-block strip of two-story brick buildings,
the town had spent eighty-five years feeding and re-supplying those just
passing through.

They stopped for a quick piss and a six-pack at the lone gas station. Nolan's gambling jones ignited when he saw the scratch tickets,
so he bought $50 worth for no reason. He also purchased a steaming

thirty-two-ounce bathtub of coffee and enough cigarettes to fumigate a small village. Paying for the gas, he left the station and saw them in the truck busily attending to their vices. Rand, whom Nolan had partnered with for longer than he cared to remember, was easily diagnosed. Usually tight-lipped and deliberate, the cocaine eased his intensity into what was, at least for Rand, a somewhat jovial mood. The normally deadened blue eyes switched out reproach for a borderline decency. Elias, though, was too new for assessment on any level except one—effort. He rarely spoke unless questioned or provoked, but seamlessly hauled, carried and obeyed like someone who intuitively understood that work, at least for some, was as much a cathartic release as a means to earn a check. If one had to be out there in the misery of a six-month Colorado winter, why not redirect this perceived injustice onto the work itself?

Nolan had only two rules—show up on time every day, and bust ass until dark. That he never had to mention either one of these directives to his newest employee even once meant something must be definitely wrong with Elias. Since he had already threatened a return to the East Coast, Nolan knew he might lose a valuable asset at the worst possible time. For starters, Nolan would raise him up from ten to twelve dollars an hour cash.

As he passed in front of the pickup, Nolan saw Rand and Elias cracking on him. While one pointed, the other broke out laughing. *That's all right, motherfuckers*, Nolan decided. *He who cashes the checks laughs best.*

Denver was located in the north-central part of the state. The surrounding suburbs of Aurora, Englewood, and Littleton gave the city a rolling sense of sprawl. Interstate 25, which began in Montana and dropped due south through five states until dead-ending at the Mexican border, also served as a main artery for every major city in the state. Fort Collins, Boulder, Denver, Colorado Springs, and even Pueblo, were all on a line drawn vertically north to south. East of this line were the biblical flatlands of Kansas, Nebraska, and Oklahoma. West of this line, the entire landscape exploded and heaved itself into the six different ranges comprising the Rocky Mountains. Over two dozen National Parks and

Forests consumed half the state. After cresting the Rockies, feral prairies gave way to the red rocks and heat of Utah and northern Arizona.

From Spring Valley, County Road 61 ran 130 miles southeast into the crossroads town of Silverthorne. With renowned resorts like Breckenridge, Copper Mountain, Loveland, Keystone, Beaver Creek, and Vail all within a twenty-mile radius, Silverthorne served as a vast strip mall of ski and snowboard equipment outlets, hotels, and eateries. It also provided cheap rent and housing for thousands of commuting resort employees.

Between beers, Rand and Elias smoked out the truck and hit the straw until Nolan, growing sick of their increasing stupidity, lowered and locked the windows.

As the high-pitched whir of the turbo-diesel kicked in, they rocketed uphill on I-70. At 11,013 feet, the Eisenhower Tunnel was the highest in the world and blasted straight through 1.7 miles of granite. It also highlighted Mother Nature's unpredictability, because a sunny day in Denver could turn into a raging blizzard on the other side of the tunnel.

After a hellish descent, the lights of Denver appeared like white dots popping through a black curtain. They passed suburbs founded by white-collar families on rolling hills that funneled down toward the city.

"This is gonna be good." Nolan cracked his knuckles. "Bust out the titties and thongs, bro."

In one of the city's hardest neighborhoods, The Brass Lady Gentleman's Club was located off Colfax Avenue. Devoured by every plague common to major urban centers, Colfax served as a clearing house for street sales of crack, blow, meth, X, and worse. Gangs, strip clubs, and prostitution were only part of the felonious distractions that doubled for everyday life in a place dominated by need, greed, and impulse.

After flipping on his blinker, Nolan said, "Round up your drugs, morons, I got to valet this bitch."

Elias bagged the empties while Rand secured the weed and coke in a Ziploc Elias then stuffed inside a rolled-up set of blueprints. Wallets were checked, cigarettes stored like ammo.

The anticipation this close to where half-naked women writhed and danced was growing increasingly primal. A trio of bouncers in worn tuxedo shirts and headsets waited to intercept them at a spectacularly-lit front door. They were tall and thick and exuded the promise of blunt force trauma. After a thorough pat-down, a twenty-dollar cover allowed access to the low-scale pandemonium raging inside. The lights were dim, the music loud, and it was already packed on a payday Friday night.

Nolan made a beeline for the cashier and walked away with five hundred dollars in singles. He pushed a hundred of it onto Elias who said, "I can't pay this—"

"It's not a loan." Nolan's right eyebrow lifted toward one of the six stages where a limber brunette held court over dumbfounded expressions. "Let's go."

Nolan wedged them through the crowd and secured seats as the DJ cut in and said, "That's right, fellas, be good to these lovely ladies. On stage one—it's the beautiful Monique with her dazzling pole tricks ..." A cheer went up as a sultry drumbeat pulsed through the speakers. "On stage two, say hello to Isabella, the Brazilian beauty straight from the clubs of Rio de Janeiro!" A louder cheer erupted because Isabella was even more gorgeous, her long black hair fanning out with every movement.

The DJ introduced the other dancers but Nolan was oblivious. Setting fifty dollars onto the bar was like throwing blood in the water. Isabella, already tending to one of the forty guys seated around her stage, seemed to sense the arrival of tastier prey nearby.

The opening riff to "Paradise City" tore through the bar as Rand arrived with their drinks.

Nolan stupidly smiled while feeding a handful of singles into Isabella's G-string. He said something into her ear and she immediately laughed, turned around, and bent over. Her long legs formed a perfect "A" up to where her genitals gently pulsed against her thong. She fed him her ass, brushing it across his nose as Nolan laughed and tossed more singles toward her upside-down face. She stood, turned, and then placed his head directly into her cleavage.

Their money did not go unnoticed. The women began circling in twos and threes to take a swipe at the close by action. The music got louder, the drinks flowed freely, and more strippers joined their private party at the edge of the stage. Elias had a woman on each knee while Rand played hide-and-seek with another's breasts. Nolan threw more money at Elias who became a rockstar when he just handed it over to the waitresses and strippers.

After her set, Isabella joined them and soon she and Nolan got their own table. Rand and Elias drank themselves into partial comas, laughing at the madness until the money dwindled and the strippers alighted for more prosperous targets elsewhere. They hit the bathroom for a quick session with the straw and then jumped right back into the fray.

Later, Nolan pulled Elias aside at the bar and bought him a shot of whiskey. "I'm starting to get things in order."

Elias squinted, confused, his teeth grinding beneath the cocaine's command. "What does that mean?"

"It means soon I'm gonna have to know where you stand for real." Nolan chain-smoked another Marlboro Light. "I don't want to count on you if you're still planning on blowing town before the next job starts."

Elias glanced away as if exposed. "Noll, a fucking monkey could do my job—"

"Seriously. There's some pretty big shit on the horizon." He pulled out his cash and peeled off a pair of hundreds. "Put this in your wallet, because it ain't for tonight. And starting Monday I'm bumping you up to twelve bucks an hour, cash."

"Noll—"

"Shhh, no talking." Taking a last drag on the cigarette, Nolan exhaled a giant cloud of smoke. "I need you here, Thomas." But he did not seem comfortable in saying it. "You get it, you know?"

"What's that?"

"The utter uselessness of the big picture." Nolan ground out the smoke, corralled his cigarettes, and left Elias sitting at the bar contemplating life which, as now, never felt even half this good.

Section Two

Late Winter, 1998—Still Year One

By the end of week four at the Gildman School build, Ted Beckham was impressed. It was late afternoon on a windswept Saturday, and the setting sun kaleidoscoped the sky. Though Nolan and his crew had been gone for an hour, the walls still seemed to kinetically echo from the furious motions that had, over the previous month, hammered this place into existence.

Thankfully, Beckham's initial misgivings about hiring Nolan had so far proven unfounded. When he took a six-foot level corner to corner seeking proof that the accelerated build schedule might have caused sloppy work or blatant mistakes, no such evidence surfaced.

He consulted the master blueprints and found all of the window and door rough openings were exact. As for the actual framing, Beckham was hard-pressed to find even a single deviation from the core principles that separated good builders from the hacks—all joints and cuts were tight, the nailing, including the plywood sheets on the floors, walls, and roof, was every six inches on the seams, and eight inches in the field as per code. Within the floor system, the beams for the stairwells, chimney, and HVAC openings were either hangered or supported by triple-packed 2x6 columns, and every single point-load from the roof down to the foundation was supported.

Even as he was running out of light, Beckham still fought against common sense and his own thirty years of experience which dictated the impossibility of two carpenters and a laborer maintaining this level of production, much less through these conditions. Fact was Nolan was on track to bring this project to a close even before his ludicrous five-week prediction.

The wind from the west ripped through the empty windows as the evening dark rapidly descended. Beckham, a former builder himself, was not too proud to acknowledge what his eyes confirmed. The successful roof inspection yesterday meant the roofers could start Monday, the same day as the framing inspection, which meant the electricians and plumbers could be unleashed as early as Monday afternoon. Windows would go in as soon as the roof was shingled, but taking into account the hard-partying and reckless lifestyle most roofers enjoyed, Wednesday was the best Beckham could hope for. At the lowest rung on the food chain, roofers got cooked by the sun, frozen by the winter, and paid poorly for what was widely assumed to be a simple trade. Yet if one could easily hump eighty-pound bundles of asphalt shingles back and forth and up and down roofs so steep that at times it felt like clinging to a cliff face, while at the same time dodging the unpleasant though frequent occurrence of flying feet, ass, or head first to the ground below, then yes, roofing was indeed quite easy.

Pressed for time, Beckham had settled on Wade Bigsby, an alcoholic who, when sober, completed work second to none in the valley. But every so often, usually after things inevitably went awry, so did Wade Bigsby. A member of the 1980 Olympic team at Lake Placid, Bigsby had subsequently blown out his knee, traded in his skis for a construction company and then, after his marriage dissolved, lost even that to the bottle. With his fame long gone, now he was just a local with a past that some made use against him.

Beckham chided himself since this was no time for second thoughts. His aging knees popped as he knelt down to pick up the fallen level. He stood and brushed the snow from his jeans. Taking one last look around, he considered himself lucky compared to those who would follow, because never again would someone get work like this, for a price like this, and Beckham surely knew it.

The kid's pulled off a miracle, he thought. *Thank the Lord above.*

At the same time Beckham was inspecting the Gildman School, Kara Harris and Sarah Vaughn approached the 500-acre Cahill Ranch. It was on the northern fringe of Spring Valley's city limits and served as part of the border between Salinas and Haywood Counties. CR 61 descended from Forked Head Pass, straight through town, and then shot 190 miles across the high plains toward Salt Lake City.

Unlike McCombs and Henman, Cahill seemed more open to the CPS proposals. After initially stonewalling, his pleasant, plainspoken demeanor now poured through the phone in such a genial way, Kara figured he either drank too much coffee or desperately needed a friend.

"I've got a good feeling about this," she declared.

"That's nice," Vaughn answered, "but please don't get your hopes up."

"Considering our abject failure so far, I'll take what I can get."

With the vast property approaching, Sarah Vaughn carefully braked the Cherokee Commander along the ice-covered road. Turning in, the chained-up tires rattled over the cattle grating. A quarter mile later they parked alongside a triple-decker farmhouse. The clapboard siding had been beaten gray by years of sun and snow, its three chimneys chugging out smoke in rolling columns that filled the sky.

Killing the engine, Vaughn sat and stared ahead. "Let's close on this." She looked at Kara, her blue eyes humorless chips. "We need this one bad."

"I know—"

"I don't like losing."

"Listen. We're both here for the same reason."

"I'm just saying." Vaughn reached for her briefcase. "Let's make sure we're having a celebratory round of drinks after this meeting's over."

"Oh yeah?" Kara hopped out and slammed the door. "And I know who will be buying."

They only needed one knock on the massive hand-carved oak front door before it swung open to reveal a small wiry man with a wide tooth-filled grin. His short gray hair was Brylcreemed perfectly across the horizon of his scalp. His ears, like opened car doors, reminded Kara of Ross Perot, especially after he spoke.

"Afternoon, ladies." He shook their hands. "I'm Bill Cahill. Hope you found the place all right," he said, and closed the door behind them. "I know some folks shoot clear on past before they stop and say, 'Hey, I must've missed old Bill's place.'"

His worn cowboy boots clacked across the hardwood floor. "Come on, lemme show you to the kitchen. My granddaddy built this place in 1906. Did you know that? He was one of Salinas County's first municipal judges before the first Great War ..."

Following him down the hallway, Kara turned back to smile at Vaughn because Cahill recounted the first twenty years of his grandfather's existence while seating them at the kitchen table.

"This here's my wife, Dot."

Dot was a plump grandmotherly woman. She stood in front of the stove as Cahill pointed at her like a product on display. "Ain't she something? Me and Dot have been married going on thirty-eight years, and every single one of them has been better than the last. Ain't that right, honey?"

"Praise be ..." Dot nodded while brewing tea. "The good Lord was looking out."

"Yes, He sure was." Cahill's mood turned reverent. Seated across from Kara and Vaughn, he clasped his hands and said, "We've been very lucky people."

"You have a very nice home," Vaughn tried interjecting, but Cahill would not be denied. He spoke of how they met, their wedding, and the three sons that quickly followed. "All three still work the ranch. The two oldest—Billy Jr. and Sanders—they're married and got houses over yonder, and Paulie, he's my youngest ... say, are you girls already spoken for? Because Paulie, he's one handsome devil. Good with his hands, too."

"Billy!"

"Now, Dot, you know what I mean." Cahill blushed. "We're here with proper people, the best kind of people there is ... God's people."

"Praise be." Dot, unlike her husband, was portly to the point where she waddled when she walked. Her house dress was not low enough to hide her bowling-pin calves and distended varicose veins, but her curly gray hair surrounded a cherubic face as plain as Cahill's shirt. She put a tray with a teapot and four mugs in the center of the table and then pulled herself a seat. She said, "Help yourself, girls, I hope you like Earl Gray."

"I like coffee," Cahill immediately informed them. "But Dot likes tea, so we drink tea." He poured out four mugs and then proffered the cream and sugar. "Now I know you two didn't drive all the way out here just to listen to a couple of old folks ramble on about coffee and tea."

Kara jumped into the breach before Cahill could reload. She spoke of the Cahill family's long presence in the valley, and the just-mentioned fact that all three of their sons currently worked the ranch. "I also know your property is already in the town's Master Plan for possible development, and I know you've been contacted by developers who want to lop off one hundred and seventy-five of your five hundred acres for a subdivision but ..."

Unlike McCombs, whose prized land was valued at almost $28,751 an acre, or even Henman, who was still looking at a $20,000 an acre price, Cahill had the misfortune of owning an unremarkable stretch of property completely blocked off by Sleeping Horse Mountain. There were no scenic vistas or lakes or underground hot springs, or mountain views save for Sleeping Horse, whose backside was more a mud-strewn mess of rock and boulders. All told, Cahill's best offer to date was just shy of $5,000 an acre for what would potentially contain 175 houses on single acre plots.

"That's $875,000." Kara looked at Bill and Dot Cahill. "For that, you'll be new neighbors with 175 perfect strangers and their families."

Cahill's hands were wrapped around his steaming mug. "Well, I guess you ladies know what's happening to our livelihood."

Dot patted his wrist because Cahill was suddenly somber as he said, "A way of life is dying out here, and the wellbeing of families that have lived on this land for a hundred years apparently don't mean nothing."

"Billy," Dot hushed him. "It's not anybody's fault." She threw Kara and Vaughn an apologetic expression. "He just gets all riled up when we talk like this."

Cahill awkwardly shrugged. "Well, it's true. Ranching, farming, hell, even fishing. This country wasn't founded on the backs of corporate hoodwinks. Before these industrial pig farms and dairy farms and strip mines, there were good folks united by a way of life." Cahill was close to tears. He looked at his wife's hand covering his own and then his lips began to tremble. "We're the last of a dying breed ..."

"Oh, Billy ..." She patted his hand again. "Drink some tea. It'll help settle you."

"But that's what we're here to offer you." Kara slid proposal sheets in front of them and explained the purpose of the conservation easement. "By signing away the development rights, you'll get the same amount we offered to Henman—half a million dollars. And, you'll keep all your land instead of shedding one hundred and seventy-five acres for a giant grid of box homes built in rows ... on your granddaddy's land, no less."

Cahill just shook his head. "Dear Lord above. See what we've been pushed to? I got mortgages and loans on property that's been ours for a hundred years just to stay afloat."

"That's exactly the purpose of our organization," Kara said, and Vaughn nodded in agreement. "The only reason we exist is to try and keep the people who tend to the land on the land, plain and simple. It's also going to substantially lower your annual property taxes. Over time, that alone will save you tens of thousands of dollars."

Cahill briefly examined the numbers on the paper Kara handed him, and then said, "I want my sons to still be here when I'm ... when we ... when our *time* comes due."

Dot squeezed his wrist. "Long time from now, praise be."

"Praise be." Cahill nodded. "Don't nobody get to buy and sell on that, now do they?"

They all shared a laugh.

Cahill looked at his wife. "Honey?"

Dot smiled as if he was just about the only reason for her to smile at all. "You know what my vote is."

"Yep, I guess I do." He looked at Kara and Vaughn. "Let me talk to m'boys. We'll all sit down and hash this one out."

Kara handed him her card. "Call me if you have any questions. If need be, we'll be happy to speak with your sons as well."

"I appreciate that, but I think we're all of a likewise mindset. This town ..." Cahill shook his head. "The devil's got ahold of it now. And with all them wrestling over money ... We, all of us, we're all gonna lose. The devil never plays fair..."

Afterwards, Kara and Vaughn had one too many margaritas at the Tequeros Café. They toasted each other on the day's success, and when

Kara got home at five o'clock, she was drunk enough to nearly trip on the curb and laughed.

Upstairs in their apartment, she found him lying on the couch in a pair of boxer shorts demolishing a bag of Cheetos.

"Hey, babe."

"Hey, you." Kara tried pulling her boots off one at a time but lost her balance.

"Uh-oh." Nolan's face was smeared from the orange snack. "Someone's been out cocktailing."

"That's right." With her boots popped free, she shed her jacket before pouncing on top of him. She put her chin against his chest and then licked his face. "Yum ..."

"Gross." Nolan turned his head from side-to-side. "That tickles."

"Cheeto-powder," she purred, and then she kept on licking.

Nolan rolled her over to escape and tossed a pillow at her. She laughed, because his boxer shorts revealed the beginning of something else. "Hey, Tex, why don't you bring that thing over here?"

"I won't be taken advantage of like this."

"Yeah, right."

From the kitchen, he called out, "You want anything from the fridge?"

"Honey, I'm drunk."

"I know."

She heard bottles clanging around the refrigerator. He said, "You've got a bottle of wine in here if you want some ..."

"I need to sober up," she said, "our reservations are for seven."

"Yep."

It was at times like this that she felt at odds with his perspective, since he had not taken a drink in years.

"How about a Diet Coke?" she suggested.

"Coming right up."

She grabbed the remote and clicked through the channels, laughing when he rounded the corner with his boxers still distended.

"That's nice," he said, "this is all your fault."

She took the glass from him and pat the seat beside her. As he stretched out, she curled up into his shoulder. "How was your day?"

"Good ... no surprises. What about you?"

"We closed on Cahill." She felt him twitch. She peeled her face off his shoulder and looked at his profile. "You're awfully quiet. Nolan?"

"What?"

She frowned. "What's wrong?"

"Nothing."

"What're you annoyed at?"

"I'm not annoyed. It's just getting harder to explain, is all."

"What does that mean?"

"Well ..." He tried hiding behind the sitcom he was watching. "I'm busting my ass to make something of myself, and you ... you just wiped out one hundred and seventy-five potential jobs for these guys. People are talking."

"What *guys*? The same guys you've sworn to crush?"

"You're my wife. How do you think this looks?"

She was taken aback. "How long have you felt like this?"

"Like what?"

"Nolan ..."

"I was trying to be supportive, all right?"

"So you just lied ..." She felt sick. "I knew you were never a fan but ... The one goddamn thing I have, and you just took a big steaming dump all over it—all over me."

"Honey, this is my fucking job."

"So what?"

"So this is how we eat! Is it really that hard for you to understand?"

"How long have you felt like this?"

His gaze retreated back to the television.

"Nolan!"

"Since you started this whole thing, all right? Is that what you wanted to hear? Fine, I've said it."

"So you just faked it all until we finally convinced one of them not to sell, and then the truth comes out. Pretty lame, Noll. That makes you a prick. A miserable fucking prick."

"You're drunk."

"And you're eating alone tonight." She got up and went into the bathroom. She was so angry, so ... what was that? She heard him moving about and cursing in mumbled tones. Zipping up, she washed her hands before opening the door.

He was in his jeans, lacing up his boots.

She said, "And apparently you're a pussy too."

"I'm leaving before we start throwing shit at each other."

"Then just go."

"You shouldn't come home drunk."

"Fuck you, Nolan, you know? Just fuck off."

"Nice." Standing up, he shouldered into his jacket. "That's real nice." He threw her one last look before heading for the kitchen.

The front door slammed closed.

Soon after, the F-250 growled up Snowmass Road. Nolan worked the wheel, a smoke, and dialed the phone before spilling coffee all over his thigh.

"Fuck!" He juggled the phone. "Naw, man, I just burnt my balls ... What're you doing ...? Yeah, well, not anymore. Grab your purse and get outside. I'm turning in as we speak."

He had driven around for ten minutes until his anger cooled. Never a fan of gossip or idle bullshit, he nonetheless knew Kara's role in the town's struggles was beginning to affect his reputation.

He slid to a stop in front of Elias' condo and barely waited two seconds before flashing the high beams and honking the horn.

Elias came out, scowling at having to shrug back into his cold weather gear. His black boots were untied and flapping through the snow. Nolan fired the high beams directly into his face and laughed at the look of pure hatred Elias passionately returned.

Elias hopped in and said, "Long time no see."

"Where's your gay half-brother tonight?" Nolan wheeled them toward the street. "Thought for sure you and him would be ass-deep in a vat of Jack Daniels by now."

"We're behind schedule. What's your deal? Thought you and the old lady were heading out for dinner?"

"Aww ... we had a change of plans." Swallowing the understatement,

Nolan took a right turn back onto Snowmass Road. "World War Three erupted ..." He was deciding on whether or not to declassify this information. For reasons Nolan had so far yet to determine, Elias, while putting forth the impression of an irascible beast of burden, also emanated a distinct loyalty and discretion that Nolan, after initial test runs, finally decided to exploit. Whether visiting Kara at the bank to make deposits, or handling Nolan's credit card on various errands, Elias was becoming the repository for much of Nolan's personal information. Whether or not he fucked that up before receiving the beating of a lifetime was still to be determined. Nolan said, "You know, it's not like I'm trying to make a living or anything, right? Getting this company up and running is like squeezing out a twenty-pound ball of shit."

There was silence in the cab until Elias, apparently unable to forestall that horrific image, slowly closed his eyes. "Jesus, that's so gross..."

"Tell me about it."

"Where are we going, anyway?"

"Don't you worry about that. First stop is for gas and smokes."

They turned onto CR 61 and stopped at a convenience store.

Nolan threw a hundred bucks at Elias and said, "Smokes, gas, and get me some scratchies with the rest."

"Anything else?" Elias stared at him incredulously.

"No, that'll do."

Afterward, Nolan scratched every ticket like a junkie before tossing them onto the floor. "Fuck."

"That's one vice I'm glad I don't have."

"No more talking."

They looped back up toward the mountain. Cigarettes were lit and L7 was cranked as traffic gathered for the six o'clock dinner rush. Seeing as how this was a resort town with a third of the populace on vacation, the impending binge meant tomorrow's payback for tonight's release was never considered.

They passed a new office plaza built for professionals. Gradually, Spring Valley was acquiring the technology and conveniences the recent influx of transplants demanded. Computer technicians, accountants, lawyers, doctors, and entrepreneurs arrived to prey on the growing frenzy.

Snowmass Road was actually an eight-mile U beginning and ending at different points off CR 61. They drove by the ski pavilion and towering hotels and took a right into Black Diamond Estates. They passed a pair of recently completed three-story duplex condominiums, with two more under construction. Nolan parked in front of a newly poured foundation, killed the engine, and high-beamed the site. "Here she is."

"Here what is?"

"The next job, numb-nuts."

Elias stared out to where the headlights eventually lost their power to liberate the night. "Great."

Nolan angrily puffed his smoke. "You know what? You fucking guys are unbelievable. You're like another pair of wives."

"What's that supposed to mean?"

"Nothing. Absolutely nothing. Which is exactly what I get from both of you."

"Aw, come on ..."

"Naw, forget it." Nolan swung open his door. "How can I expect anyone to understand anything when they're only out for their own!"

After the door slammed, Elias hissed out smoke. He watched Nolan hop up onto the two-foot concrete wall and walk the perimeter of the stone-filled pit.

Shaking his head, Elias replayed the entire exchange. Was he supposed to be thankful to have been shown the spot of his next enslavement? He was a cook, no, a wood bitch, no, he was exactly a bunch of nothing, in the middle of nowhere, while still being in love with someone who had basically told him to get lost.

Realizing there had never really been a decision left to make, Elias reached for the door.

Nolan's excitement rekindled once Elias' silhouette approached through the headlights. Nolan pointed at the two units currently under construction and said, "That's our competition. Big Swann's crew is framing the building on the left. They're about to start standing the third-floor walls. And the other is where Team Sweater's crew is stroking it something awful."

Elias walked the wall. "Who's *Sweater*?"

"The golden boy of framing. He showed up a couple of years ago swinging his resumé around like a true cockslapper." Nolan batted a hand. "So he's an engineer from Stanford who's done some custom monsters in Santa Barbara, so what? I fucking made my bones out there too—Monterey, Morro Bay—nailing up fifteen-thousand-square foot mansions. Trust me, Cali sucks. Twenty-five million morons suffering through three-hour commutes to work ... I grew up with the stink of L.A., the bullshit sideshow of San Fran and now, standing right here—" He swung his arm across the frozen night. "The big-money players are coming all the way up here to put us on the map."

"You think that Proposition 6's gonna pass?"

"Fuck yes I do."

"But isn't Kara fighting—"

"It's a free country, man." Nolan's smile was splashed by the head-lights. "She can fight whatever she wants, but in the end, nothing stops the dollar."

Elias jammed his hands into his pockets and nodded at Sweater's jobsite. "Why are you saying they're stroking it?"

"They've been over there working for four weeks and the sec-ond-floor is barely finished. Mark my words. Sweater's going down."

"Yeah?" Elias suddenly sounded inspired.

"He's got a four-week lead, Thomas, what do you think?"

"Well ..."

Standing side-by-side, they both stared across at the presented chal-lenge. Elias said, "I don't know enough to even take a guess, but I've seen you guys in action, man, fucking A."

"Oh yeah?" Nolan reached for another cigarette, unable to take it for granted. "You thinking you got some extra time on your hands to help drag down one of Spring Valley's finest rising stars?"

"Absolutely. By the way, why do you call him Sweater?"

"Because he wears one every day. With *pressed* Carhartt pants, no less. Seriously, what in the hell is this world coming too? Are you listen-ing to me? We got four more days out at Gildman, but come Friday, I'm gonna mush you and fuckface like a team of dogs—"

"Or a pair of slaves."

"Right, just like a pair of slaves, as a matter of fact. And we're gonna haul, cut, and nail together so much wood the two of you are gonna need a support group just to cope."

"Right."

"And, as if I'm not gonna enjoy the fuck out of that, I also get to set my sights on one of the biggest, most arrogant morons this valley's ever seen." Nolan shook his head as if no one deserved to be this lucky. "I'm telling you, hit the lights and start the cars, bro, because this party's totally over."

CHAPTER FOURTEEN

BLACK DIAMOND ESTATES
Spring 1998—Still Year One

"Well, well, well," Nolan said midway through the day. "Look at what the moron just dragged in."

Interrupted from work, Rand and Elias looked up, but only Rand recognized the new arrival.

"Goddamn," he said with a laugh. "If it isn't Shithouse Bunns the Third."

Indefatigable as he approached, the guy stuck out his hand toward Elias and said, "I'm Steven."

"Thomas." Elias appraised him. "Guess I'm the new guy again."

"We used to work together," Steven said, nodding toward Nolan and Rand. "Me and the Brothers Grimm."

"You have my condolences."

He and Elias were about the same age and size, but Steven seemed good-natured behind that perfect white-toothed smile. He had disheveled brown hair, canted eyebrows, and red lips beneath a wispy Fu Manchu. As with most people who spent large portions of the day outside, his eyes were raccooned from the tan lines created by his sunglasses.

Though a hard worker, it was Bunny's predilection for weed, mushrooms, and live music that earned him a party-boy reputation in a small town consumed with idle gossip. Originally from Connecticut, after a stint in rehab, Bunny became a carpenter mainly to piss off his father. The youngest of four sons who all graduated from Dartmouth, the same was expected of Bunny until he stole $30,000 from his college fund and headed for Colorado. After using the money to finance a four-month booze-filled ski party, he was broke and unwelcomed back home. He sold sandwiches at Phish shows and traveled the country, spent his early twenties in a penniless daze, and was generally a kind-hearted guy with no common sense. Generous, kind, but also rowdy, he stumbled across Nolan and Rand and then spent the next five years being fired and rehired, at times on a daily basis. He was a decent carpenter and basically competent until he got wasted or scored a great deal on an ounce of blow or mushrooms and thus violated Nolan's commandment number one—Never miss work for any reason ever.

Currently, Bunny seemed hesitant, as if still gauging the ramifications of his arrival. He said, "We were up in Teton hiking until I broke my leg. The money ran out after I couldn't work, so," he shrugged, "figured I'd come on back and get a nut saved up, because this summer's gonna be rocking."

"Oh yeah?" Nolan set a flame to his umpteenth cigarette of the day. "Who would've thought back-breaking labor could make you so excited?"

"I'm talking about the shows, man, there's—"

"Oh, there's gonna be a show all right." Nolan panned a hand across the concrete and frozen snow. "It's called the Fuckshow, simpleton, and I've already got your front row seats reserved."

"Noll—"

"Where's your saw and bags?"

"Back at—"

"Where're you staying?"

"Well, I was meaning to talk to you about that."

"Oh, here we go ... It never ends."

"I might just need you to co-sign with me."

"Jesus ..."

"And maybe ..." Like a little kid, Bunny pushed at the snow with his boot. "And maybe get a small advance—"

"Jesus *Christ*."

"Which I would immediately repay, Noll, I swear. You can even take it straight out of my check."

"Gee, thanks." Nolan motioned toward Rand. "I'm already playing his daddy too, man, what it this—*My Three Sons*?"

"Hey." Rand's features instantly crunched into a scowl. "What's that supposed to mean?"

"Well, let's see, I pay your child support, alimony, give you numerous loans for lawyers and bail, rampant hotel bills, various bill collectors, fines—"

"What?"

"And, since you're too incompetent to even get your license back, I get to drive you around like goddamn Miss fucking Daisy."

Elias burst out laughing until Rand threw him a murderous look. Then Rand glanced toward Nolan and said, "You can kiss my ass." He stomped off back to work.

Nolan, though, could not smile any broader. "Fucking A, Bunny, I knew you'd come back."

"Oh yeah?" Bunny sheepishly grinned. "How'd you know that?"

"Because the dumb ones have no choice." Nolan nodded at Elias. "This one used to be a cook."

"Hey—"

"I used to cook too," Bunny said.

And Nolan only laughed and laughed. "You just can't make this shit up."

Elias grabbed his crotch, gave Nolan the finger, and then headed to the back wall where Rand was marking layout. The double sill plates were already bolted down. The rim, floor joists, and beams of the first-floor system were set to follow.

"There're times," Rand said, marking crow's feet at sixteen-inch intervals, "That I truly hate that motherfucker."

"It's not hard. He just makes you feel so appreciated, right? Why's he called Bunny?"

A huge smile stretched across Rand's face. "His last name's Bunncamper."

"No it's not. You're fucking with me, right?"

"Can you imagine growing up with a name like that?"

"Bunncamper? You've got to be shitting me."

"I wish."

"Bunncamper ...?"

They were both laughing while trying not to, and glancing over to see if they had been noticed.

Rand quietly said, "So at first it starts off as Bunny and then, like all good nicknames, it gets dragged straight down into hell."

"Ass-camper?"

"Ass-camper, Outhouse, Bunn-dumpster ..."

"Shithouse Bunns the Third? My God, that is just freaking awful."

"It's the way of the world, man, there ain't no stopping that."

"Hey ladies!" Nolan called out. "Less gabbing, more work!"

"Oh yes, sir," Rand parroted. "Abso-fucking-lutely."

Under his breath, Elias said, "Commander Assface and Private Dumpster."

Rand threw back his head.

"Hey!" Nolan yelled, smoke seething from his nostrils. "What're you girls cackling about?"

"The world, man." Rand knocked each boot against the foundation to clear the treads. "And every sorry-ass motherfucker in it."

As far as reunions went, four days later it seemed like this one was headed for disaster. Elias white-knuckled the armrest while Nolan's mouth, like his whirring studded tires, would not be silenced.

"So let's recap, okay?" Nolan jammed another cigarette butt into the already porcupine-like ashtray. "Moron shows up broke on Friday. *I* rent him a place that same night, then buy him a hundred bucks worth of groceries and what's my thanks? A no-call no-show on Tuesday like I'm now *his* fucking bitch?"

Elias squirmed. "Noll—"

"I swear to God—"

"Noll, watch out!"

The pickup swerved around an elderly dog moseying along the shoulder. "Jesus Christ." Nolan brushed spilt coffee from his Carhartt jacket. "I am going to absolutely murder this motherfucker."

Already fatigued from the drama, Elias clocked the time at 7:26 A.M. His bleary eyes reflected the long night he had spent working in his basement bedroom. Intellectually idle since his arrival last November, Elias was now thinking about starting another magazine and had begun gathering information about the town's history. His desk was a half sheet of plywood with 2x4 legs pillaged from the job. In no way stable, it was shoved into the corner of his room.

Now, with all thought of last night's progress crushed beneath Nolan's growing wrath, Elias could not disagree. "You're right. This shit's totally unacceptable."

With a measure of stunned appreciation, Nolan said, "Fucking A right I'm right."

This was not the first time Nolan had ordered Elias into the truck for no other reason than to have someone else to bitch to, since Rand had by this point grown exhausted playing therapist. After torquing himself into a lather, Nolan's tunnel vision made rationalization impossible. Like a bull drawn to red, or a fist toward someone's face, every perceived slight or act of disrespect was met with a swift finality that left no room for misinterpretation. Nevermind that he was usually right—Nolan took no chances.

Which was something else Elias was beginning to appreciate. Inside the daily madness of Nolan's barely controlled insanity, existed the ethos and discipline those who succeeded at anything recognized as priority number one—the job came first. No matter the problem, no matter how late the party went or what errands needed to be completed—get to work and clear the mind, because the effort would fail if not collectively attacked. Elias had worked in enough kitchens over the years to loathe the strokers that pulled no weight. The losers who called out sick, the lame excuses for poor performance, and the guys who could milk a ten-minute task into a full half hour. They were morale busters. Work was work, and the less one did only made it that much harder on the person standing beside you.

Barely knowing Bunny, Elias was hesitant to pass judgment. Yet one would figure, especially after having previously worked with Nolan and Rand, conduct like this would be the last thing he attempted. Especially not right after Nolan had laid out a thousand bucks just to secure his housing. But it did make Rand's comments on yesterday's drive home seem almost prophetic.

"Bunny's a good guy, but kind of a space shot."

"With what, drugs?"

"Them too. He's like a little kid that sometimes doesn't think two steps in front of his own face."

Still, even now, as Nolan's veins distended from his continued screaming, Elias hoped for Bunny's sake that he was not at home.

They took a right onto Alpine Road and pulled into Chester Estates. A strip of one-room apartments stacked end to end like boxes, this two-story structure was one of Spring Valley's monthly efficiencies. Built onto a ridge, it caught the rising sun as it ricocheted off the snow-covered valley floor. The parking lot was a ghetto of vehicles barely hanging on—rusted, cracked, and disrepaired.

"He's in number six." Nolan's sudden calm was even more unnerving. He parked next to Bunny's dilapidated Subaru and stared straight ahead. "I can't get into this without killing him, so you better go instead."

Elias adjusted his sunglasses and stepped down from the truck. He felt like the messenger behind which stood a thousand pounds of hate. At the door, he knocked and quickly called out, "Bunny!"

The tumbling clack-clack of the pickup's diesel filled the pause. Another knock.

"Bunny!" Elias worried about waking the neighbors until Nolan jammed on the horn. For a full ten seconds, the world was filled with shouting and horn, knocking and nothing.

"Goddamnit, Bunny, open the fucking door!"

Elias heard a slam behind him before sensing Nolan's arrival.

"Move."

Nolan's size sixteen Wolverine landed near the knob and instantly buckled the jamb.

Inside, the sunlight poured across a mess. Barely rented for seventy-two hours, the empty food containers, heaps of fetid, unwashed clothes, and the sweetened stink of spilt beer were a further provocation as Nolan's shadow filled the door. Incredibly, Bunny remained asleep on the pull-out couch. The TV babbled near his head. On the nearby table, Nolan found a scorched soda can and handed it to Elias.

"He took the cash I gave him and smoked up a bunch of rock." Nolan looked at the still sleeping Bunny. "Didn't ya, fuckhead?"

Nolan swept aside the TV, grabbed Bunny's head, and jammed two fingers up his nostrils.

Bunny's eyes shot wide open.

Nolan slowly lifted his arm. "Rise and shine, Bunny, thought I'd give you a ride to work today."

"Jesus Christ, Noll—" Bunny's hands were lightly fluttering around the fist whose fingers were currently reaming out his face. Reflexive gagging brought tears to his eyes and snot into his throat, the pain just settling in. "Oh, please, man ..."

"Let's shower up." Nolan dragged him to the kitchen sink and, after leveraging Bunny's head beneath the faucet, allowed his fingers to slide free with a pair of loud wet pops.

Gasping, Bunny ran his face under the water. His stained boxer shorts and pale skin added to the overall repulsive situation. Unfazed, Bunny toweled off his head and said, "Huh." He shook out his wet brown hair like a dog. "That was certainly interesting."

"You need to get dressed." Nolan pushed him aside to wash off his hand. "And since you bought a bunch of crack—"

"Noll—"

"Shut up!" Nolan whirled on him. "Shut up and don't say anything else until you're in the fucking truck. And don't ask me for shit, because you're not gonna see another dime 'til payday."

"When's that?"

"For you?" Nolan scoffed. "Right after I get back my grand." He stepped toward the door, nodding at the mess. "After work, you're gonna clean this fucking place up, too."

"What the ..." Bunny lifted his foot off a chunk of snow. "Couldn't you guys at least take off your boots?"

Elias had to consider it a gift, to be assaulted in one's own apartment and minutes later seemingly forget it ever occurred. Either that, or Bunny had been made frighteningly immune to the violence.

"See you outside, B."

"Yeah, Thomas."

Elias stepped past the fractured door. Once inside the pickup, he could only say, "Incredible."

Nolan leaned on the horn for added pain. "It's just fucking amazing, you know? In three days, he's already trashed the place."

"At least he's got a good disposition."

Nolan cracked a smirk. "If that's a polite way of saying he's a complete moron who's also a total fucktard, then I wholeheartedly agree."

"I liked how he was pissed at us for tracking in snow."

"That's because he's a moron," Nolan said matter of factly, and then his voice became a sudden menace. "Just you watch. I'm gonna turn today into this loser's own personal *Crying Game*."

"I don't even want to know what that means."

"You're goddamn right you don't."

Together, they waited for Bunny.

During the last month, the mystery illness plaguing Nolan's daughter Emily worsened. Previously diagnosed with viral pneumonia, and treated with micon drugs that were initially effective, a new round of fevers had choked off her recovery. Nolan knew that the doctors were confident they would find a diagnosis. But with her eleventh birthday approaching, combined with his ex-wife's growing psychosis, Nolan bit the bullet and set his sights on California.

The F-250 was packed and gassed up for the eighteen-hour drive, but he needed one last council with the troops. It was the beginning of week two at Black Diamond Estates, and with the first-floor already stood, sheeted, and decked, the second-floor walls were ready to be framed.

Blasting the horn, Nolan watched the three of them waddle over like penguins in their jumpsuits and hoods. He lowered the window and said, "Cheer up, girls, you've only got another ten hours in this frozen hell." No stranger to hate-filled glances, Nolan basked in their pain. "Daddy's got to take a little trip, so I'm leaving your big sister Rand in charge."

Rand squashed out a cigarette with his boot. "Daddy my ass."

Elias said, "Beach-bumming motherfucker."

Bunny looked confused. "Um, Noll, are you paying up before you go?"

"What?" Nolan laughed in his face. "You've got to be joking."

"Actually—"

"That was a rhetorical statement, moron, in fact, no more talking at all." He glanced at Rand. "Keep these pukes in line, will ya?"

"Aye-aye, Cap'n." Rand tossed off a mocking salute while clearing a nostril into the snow. "The fuckshow rolls on."

"Oh no ..." Bunny craned his neck. "Speaking of fuckshows."

They turned in unison and caught sight of the pickup and trailer with High Mountain Framing stenciled on its side. It drew closer to where a laborer on Team Sweater's crew had been re-stacking wood, so a small pile of 2x4s lay strewn across the ice-covered road.

"Hey!" Rigor Mortis screamed. "Somebody move this shit!"

The laborer immediately broke off to clear the road, but it was already way too late.

As the sound of cracking wood exploded across the site, Nolan was unable to contain his laughter. "Ain't he something?"

"Señor Haywire." Rand mockingly clapped his hands. "Old Snapcase himself."

Bunny, though, did not appear even slightly amused. "You're sticking Rigor Mortis here with us?"

"That's right." Nolan winked. "A little extra insurance, just in case."

"Aw, fuck me ..."

"By the way, since you've been gone, he's finally embraced his own inner crazy, and has come to love his nickname."

"Is this a set up?"

Rigor Mortis gunned the engine, wailed the horn, and slid to a stop as the music pulsed—

Slashed my wrists
Cut my throat
Killed myself!

As he powered down, the silence was a relief until he hopped out of his truck.

"Well, well..." he said, rounding the front end, "I heard a rumor a certain transsexual had returned to town ..." He punched Bunny's shoulder. "So how'd the operation go?"

Bunny accepted the dare. "Real funny, Riggy."

"It sure is." Rigor Mortis' bright green eyes flashed across the gathered few. "First, old Super-Framer here gets replaced by a chick out at Butcher Block—"

"Hey!" Nolan angrily snapped.

"And then he re-hires one for his own crew."

"Ha-ha-ha." But Bunny was not laughing. "Only a drag queen like yourself—"

A sudden bang swiveled all five heads to the rear of Rigor Mortis' trailer. Two guys were standing behind a smaller guy with perfectly combed blond hair. He was wearing spotless Carhartts over a turtleneck and thick wool sweater. His smile was obsequious and beaming. "Morning, fellas."

Nolan grimaced, not wanting to further delay his departure for any reason, much less because of Team Sweater. Disgusted, he looked at Jamie Fallon, the late twenty-something, impeccably-dressed, educated know-it-all who now frowned at Nolan like an infant covered in his own shit. Confidence was one thing, but flagrant arrogance always bred disdain. Reverse familiarity was also at play, because once different crews worked the same site, confrontations became inevitable. Additionally, Fallon also called 10 A.M. and 3 P.M. coffee breaks for his guys, a practice Nolan found abhorrent. He was not paying anyone, not even himself, to sit around drinking coffee. But while Nolan and Fallon's relationship remained polite in a frigid, competitive sort of way, there was certainly no love lost between the crews. Just two days before, Elias had to restrain Rand from taking out a particular loudmouth talking smack from across the street.

But now, only one week in on an eight-week build, Nolan knew it was too early to start burning bridges, so he tiredly asked, "What's up, Jamie?"

"Well, we all know about Mr. Killea's infamous temper ..." Fallon's thick eyebrows had been perfectly plucked into apostrophes. "Exactly what was that display all about?"

"What're you talking about?"

"That pile of kindling this gentleman"—he nodded at Rigor Mortis—"was just kind enough to provide?"

"Who you calling a gentleman?" Elias cracked, but Rigor Mortis instantly stepped forward.

"This is a worksite," he said, and faced down Fallon and his men. "Not your own backyard."

Fallon might have been a neat dresser, but he was no newcomer. Especially not with his guys behind him, so he, too, took a step forward. "My crew was literally in the process of re-stacking those 2x4s before you rolled over them."

"You know what?" Rigor Mortis wickedly smirked. "This ain't Malibu, or wherever the fuck it is you strokers rolled in from. But if you were any good, you'd be cutting and nailing that shit up instead of reshuffling it just to keep the place looking pretty."

"Thanks for the lesson."

"Seriously. Answer me this ..." Riggy jerked a hand toward Fallon's jobsite. "How long did it take you milkmen to get even that far?"

"We're not milking anything—"

"How long?"

"It's the dead of winter—"

"Like I said ..." Rigor Mortis gave him his back. "Less stroking and more nailing and maybe even you pulse-stoppers might stay warm."

Fallon stepped after him. "That's totally uncalled for!"

"All right, all right." Nolan cracked his door and jumped between the action before Fallon got his ass kicked. "Bunny, Thomas, go pick that shit up."

"But he's the one—"

"Bunny!" Nolan snarled. "Get moving."

They headed for the pile as Nolan turned a blank face back to Fallon. "I don't have time for this, okay? Stop being such a cunt."

"Noll—"

But Nolan was already heading over to where Rand was rolling out the tools.

"Hey," he quietly said. He tugged Rand's jacket since Rand was bent at the waist and half-disappeared inside one of the giant tool chests. "You need to keep this shit in line until I get back."

"Oh really?" Rand straightened up, clearing a rack of 8's from the gun. "As if you give a fuck?"

"What?"

"Hey, man. He's your deal. He's barely here thirty seconds and almost causing a riot. You can deal with his mess."

"Oh, come on ..."

"The fuck we need him here for?" Rand was stuffing his bags with racks of 16's for the gun. "You trying to tell me something?"

"Is that what this is about? Come on, man, I just wanted to keep up with the schedule, give each of you a monkey to work with."

"Thomas ain't up to speed like that. He can barely cut."

"Well, let him haul all the shit and maybe you cut for Bunny and Riggy." Nolan shrugged. "I ain't trying to tell you nothing, man, you know that, right?"

"Doesn't seem so."

"Come on, man, this is the last fucking thing I needed before I hit the road."

"Whatever, dude. It's cool." Rand grabbed the gun and saw. "Have a good trip."

"Rand—"

But Rand did not stop.

Nolan called out, "Don't forget to—"

"Hurry up. Yeah, you should probably do the same."

"I'll be back by Saturday," Nolan answered, but no one was left to listen.

"Irrational psychosis? Or moronic psychotic?" Rand paused as if unsure which term best applied. But as the police hauled Rigor Mortis off to jail, and Rand and Elias had to set off on foot because Rigor Mortis' truck had just been impounded, Rand had plenty of time for reflection. His first conclusion—Riggy was a master carpenter. His lack of composure made him a hand grenade, but when it came to framing, he was the real deal. Second, it was a miracle no one had already killed the guy. His hair-trigger temper was dangerous enough, but he was also completely impervious to established norms or a basic sense of fear. Like the other morning when he had faced down Team Sweater, Rigor Mortis would have battled all three on his own without even blinking an eye. Previous precedent already existed. In Vail, Rand and Nolan had left a bar to find a group of bikers dangling Rigor Mortis upside down off a third-floor balcony. Unlike anyone else faced with this same situation, instead of begging for his life, Riggy actually tried swinging up to attack his attackers. In a Denver strip club, he grabbed a stripper's ass and was asked to leave. Instead, he smashed a bottle into the head of a bouncer nearly twice his size. Six more then converged on them, so Rand and Nolan had to fight their way to the door.

But that was nothing compared to what Rand and Elias had just witnessed. The behavior was textbook Rigor Mortis—provocation answered by an overwhelming response. The fact that no fists were involved meant nothing since he did not always need physical violence for his assaults.

Since there were few things more disgusting than buying lunch at 7-11, that's exactly where Riggy had taken them out of spite. The clerk, a tattooed kid in his late teens, was hungover and barely nodded when asked about the bathroom. So far, this had not been a good day for Rigor Mortis. Those who worked with him preferred his screaming and carrying on versus the pressurized silence of impending doom. That morning, he arrived at work without a word and acknowledged no other presence until they broke for lunch. Brooding, pacing, he mumbled incoherently, revolted. Locked inside this mounting fury, anything and anyone became fair game. Today, Bunny seemed to be the most likely target, but after surviving the morning and fleeing home for lunch, Elias and Rand got blindsided instead.

Rigor Mortis was getting a drink. After he depressed the lever and nothing came out, he yelled, "Hey, you guys got any iced tea?"

The kid, as if fed up with the stupidity of the human race, snidely asked, "Did you hit the lever?"

"Yeah." Riggy tapped it two more times with his cup. "Nothing."

"Well, I guess we're out then, huh? What do you think, pal?"

Reminiscent of old-style dueling, where two equal-sized assholes might cross one another's path, now, as then, only one was to be left standing.

"What do I think?" Rigor Mortis screamed, and then overhanded the Big Gulp. *"Get me some fucking tea!"*

The Big Gulp sailed end over end spewing cubes and lemonade, which had already been half-added. Pinned between the register and cigarette rack, the clerk had no time to move and, from twenty-feet out, the Big Gulp caught him in the chest and exploded.

"Goddamnit." Lemonade rolled off the kid's face. "You fucking suck, mister."

Aroused by the ruckus, the manager poked a fearful head around the corner, the phone already against his ear. "Jesus, Trent, you okay?"

Rand nudged Elias and quietly said, "Let's go."

"He did it!" The clerk pointed at Rigor Mortis. "This fucking guy's mental!"

"I didn't do anything."

While the manager called 911, the clerk kept pointing at Rigor Mortis. "Fuck you, mister!"

Rand and Elias were already heading for the truck.

"I don't know, man," Rand said, climbing in after Elias. "That's just not the way normal people act."

"You think?"

"Fuck." Rand punched the dashboard. "I already got two cases, I'm out on bail and probation ..."

Then Rigor Mortis exited the 7-11.

"Look at him," Rand said, "just sauntering out like he doesn't have a care in the whole wide world."

"Yeah, well, he's about to." Elias nodded at the approaching lights. "Here comes the One Time."

———————

"You've got to be joking." Upon hearing the news, Bunny smiled like a brand-new day had dawned. After lunch, he had happened upon Rand and Elias trudging through the cold. "They really impounded his truck?"

"Yep." Riding shotgun, Rand blasted the heat.

"But I don't get it." Bunny dialed down the music. His cassette deck, which hung from the dashboard like an eviscerated intestine, garbled up the Grateful Dead. "Who hit who first?"

"There was no hitting. Haven't you listened to a single thing I've said?"

"But how'd the cops get there so fast?"

"Turns out they were right around the corner."

"Now that's what I'm talking about." Bunny cackled loudly, a joint dangling from his lips. "Man, I would've paid a thousand dollars just to see them cuffing him."

From the backseat, Elias reached for the joint. "I mean we were on a lunch break, man, who does that?"

Rand hoisted up a wallet. "He gave me this. Said to come bail him out."

"Oh no you don't." Bunny exhaled a cloud of smoke, practically euphoric. "After working next to that heart attack all week? This afternoon's gonna be a vacation, bro, here ..." Bunny handed him the joint. "This is just the appetizer. Wait until you see the red-haired stickiness I'm gonna pack up next."

"Yeah, well, don't huff yourself into unconsciousness. You're already stupid enough as it is."

Elias coughed out the hit and laughed before coughing again. "Oh, Jesus. In the immortal words of Super-Framer, hurry the fuck up."

So Bunny passed the joint.

Section Three

Thirteen Months Later
April, 1999

Beginning in mid-March, with millions of gallons of water melting off the mountains, Spring Valley began the annual rite of passage known as Mudseason. One could step into their own backyard and either find solid ground, or quickly sink a foot deep into the fudge-like earth. Cars and pickup trucks, once coated in the salty brine of winter, now passed by covered in mud and slime. Local teenagers, celebrating this end to winter, partied behind the high school before firing up their parents' 4x4s and transforming the football field into a rodeo of flying turf.

For those who had to work in it, though, conditions were not ideal. Winter boots were sometimes switched out for the knee-high rubber waders fishermen and farmers wore. Meanwhile, for those whose footwear was not laced up tight enough, the viscous mud would often suck the boots right off peoples' feet. The tools, if dropped into the ooze, had to be stripped and cleaned before further use. And for guys like Elias, who primarily spent the day ferrying supplies, every step became a workout against the suction. Normal people had landscaped yards graded to help absorb the moisture. But out here in the churned mud of the jobsite, there were no trees, grass, or bushes to lend a hand, so the place was usually a slop-filled mess.

Elias was riding shotgun in Rigor Mortis' pickup. Despite the mud and slush, they barreled down the dirt road at over 80 MPH. Kid Rock's *"Devil Without Cause"* had finally summitted Mt. Lassiter during the winter, and for the next year, it could be heard blasting from every pickup truck and jobsite across the valley.

As with most things concerning Rigor Mortis, if danger in some form was not within immediate proximity, the day was not complete. He dialed down the music and said, "I already told this motherfucker. For the past two months I've been asking him to just *drop my shit off*..." Riggy looked sick. "That's what you get for helping people out, man, shame on me."

"Who is he anyway?"

"Some moron your stupefied half-brother knows."

Elias grunted at the backhanded slap toward Nolan and then said, "Hell, man, you and him are the ones who have known each other since forever, which makes him *your* moronic life mate. Man-love is a bitch, huh?"

As rare as it was, Riggy's smile was not short on teeth. His green eyes, formerly besieged by his furrowed brow, turned warmly onto Elias.

"You know what, Thomas?" he said, and slowed as a driveway approached. "There are some days when I think you're just about one of the stupidest motherfuckers I've ever met ..."

Elias smiled. "But ..."

"But then other days I just want to bend you over the bumper of my truck—"

"Oh God."

"And fist out your ass—"

"Oh Jesus."

"Just like some prison fucking rape scene."

Elias laughed until Rigor Mortis, apparently suffering from suicide withdrawal, swung a sudden right down the driveway and nearly rolled his truck. He pinned the accelerator while the rear end bucked wildly back and forth shooting gravel, stone, and mud from the spinning tires.

Ahead, a small yellow house was set back a quarter mile from the road. Two abandoned pickups were snowed over on the long front lawn. There was a rusty van by the garage which had Haven Brothers Construction sloganed on its side. Beyond that, at the end of the driveway, a pile of scaffold poked through the melting snow like bones from a partially revealed body.

"He didn't even tarp it!" Rigor Mortis screamed, and it was then that Elias finally reached for his seatbelt. Riggy slammed the brakes, spun the wheel, and sent a wave of stones hurtling into the van and house.

Elias, who was now staring out at the front yard, said, "I'll be damned. You almost made it the full one-eighty."

But Rigor Mortis was already on the move. Wasp-like in his black Carhartt jacket, bright yellow Smith sunglasses, and yellow knit cap, he grabbed a shovel out of the bed and headed directly for his scaffold. There were four twenty-eight-foot aluminum posts, two planks at sixteen feet, and four pump-jacks which rode up and down the posts to provide a movable platform for the planks.

Elias reached for a shovel as the garage door began to rise. A large man with blond bed-head and an enormous beer gut abruptly appeared. At six-foot-three, he must have weighed 350 pounds, and his swelled face, which rippled as he belched, did not warm in welcome.

"I saw the way you came tearing on down here," Dusty Haven said, his Louisiana accent one long slur. "Y'all got some nerve, Neal, showerin' m'house like 'at."

Rigor Mortis stopped shoveling and rose up. "This is five grand worth of scaffold, Tubbs. Now either you grab a shovel and drag your morbidly obese ass over here to help me dig it out, or go back inside and feed yourself another Twinkie."

"Fuck you! Ya got a lot of balls!" Haven lurched forward with his big right arm cocked, which proved to be his last mistake.

The plastic shovel made a brutal sound against Haven's skull. The big man swayed with a stunned expression just long enough to start bleeding from his ear, and then his knees gave way. He fell onto his back and could barely focus as Rigor Mortis berated him from above.

"Listen up, because you only get one more chance." He bent over and knocked on Haven's forehead as if it were a door. "This is it for you, Jabba, you know what I'm saying? If I even catch a glimpse of you out of the corner of my eye, I'm gonna rip off one of your bloated limbs and beat you to fucking death with it, okay? Shake one of your chins if you understand what it is I'm telling you."

Elias was ten-feet away and nervously scanning their surroundings as if looking for witnesses. His eyes returned to the van long enough to wonder how many brothers Haven Brothers employed. "Hey, man, let's load up and get the hell out of here."

"Yeah, this loser's barely conscious any damn way."

Their shovels were a blur. Minutes later, they lifted the planks onto the roof racks when Haven abruptly vomited.

Elias said, "Yo, he's not even on his side."

"So what?" Rigor Mortis shoved one of the posts up onto the racks. "You Mother Theresa now too or what?"

"He's gonna choke ..."

"Fuck'im ..."

But Elias walked over. With considerable effort, he pushed until Haven oozed over onto his side. He was making gurgling sounds but clearly breathing, so Elias stood back up.

"Don't be such a pussy," Rigor Mortis called out, but Elias left the bait untaken. Once all of the scaffold was loaded up and cinched tight with the hold-downs, they tossed the shovels into the bed, knocked the snow and mud from their boots, and then climbed aboard as if a beaten and bleeding man were not laying just fifteen-feet away.

CHAPTER FIFTEEN

During his first year of incorporated independence, things had gone more smoothly than Nolan ever hoped. Rand, and even Rigor Mortis, remained out of police custody as the money and jobs poured in. They currently had three ongoing builds with Nolan, Rand, and Rigor Mortis running as lead guy at each. To back them up, Nolan had been hiring and firing until culling a select core of dependable workers from the chaff. He stayed away from older guys, who were already set in their bad habits and poor skills, and instead focused on drafting and teaching the youth. Neil Abbot, a soft-spoken twenty-two-year-old kid from nearby Kimmit, had a pink face and boyish appearance that inspired Nolan's nickname of Baby New Year. A proper westerner, New Year always wore a Stetson hat and denim. He in turn brought in his twenty-six-year-old brother-in-law, James Wyatt, a wiry Texan who was partial to chewing tobacco and wife-beater T-shirts. Wyatt had barely introduced himself to Elias before Elias heard the Texas drawl and said, "Jesus, Cooter, slow your roll." The nickname instantly stuck. Cooter wore thick glasses that slipped down his nose a thousand times a day. Also included in the new hires was Brian Osmanski, who made the mistake of proclaiming an orgasmic prowess with the ladies. That mistake inspired the mocking call-sign "O-Zone" to be branded on him forever. He was from Minnesota, had straight white teeth, a trim black beard, and a sinewy strength born working the farms back home. The orgasm comment was out of character because he was otherwise a humble machine whose work ethic spoke for itself. His only rebellious streak was wearing a GMC baseball cap just to piss off all the Ford truck owners. He was the only son, raised by five older sisters, four aunts, and his mom, so he knew more about women than most of the crew combined. With the exception of Rand, O-Zone was also the most gifted athlete in the crew. Despite their diverse backgrounds from across the nation, all the new hires were basically the same guy—smart, strong, and competent, they took advice the first time without repeated instruction, did not bitch or bang out sick, and possessed a maniacal work ethic that made other crews look like they were standing still. Through horrible weather, at remote locations far from help, the impossible could not be attempted if the strengths and weaknesses of the man beside you were in question. At the top of the food chain without yet knowing it, their bond quickly formed.

Cooter and Baby New Year were with Rigor Mortis banging out a custom home, Rand was framing a duplex condominium with O-Zone, and Nolan kept Bunny and Elias for himself at the boathouse job along the Blackstone River. With the heavy boot of winter lessening its pressure as Mudseason took hold, Nolan looked forward to a jump in production which, even through the worst part of the season, had barely slacked at all. Because of the intense build schedule, they had framed fifteen structures in the last twelve months, totaling 59,000 square feet. A number like that was crushing, and other framers, who sometimes barely worked more than three days a week in the winter, could only watch in awe as Nolan's price soared from eight to sixteen dollars a square foot. He was currently at the point where he could practically name his price, and since he was already booked through the following year, often the negotiations became one-sided.

"We're turning onto Sixty-One as we speak," Nolan said into his phone. "Yeah, I got Elias and Bunny on board, so let's bang this out and call it done."

He flipped the phone closed as Elias, riding shotgun, asked, "What time's the crane coming?"

"Noon." Nolan looked at them both. "The only lunch you bitches are gonna see today is the hot dog I got stuffed in my pants."

"You mean that bite-sized weenie?" Bunny asked from the backseat. "I gave up meat for Lent, man."

"What for? There isn't going to be any afterlife for you, Bunny."

As they rounded the bend on County Road 61, Rigor Mortis' jobsite sprang into view like a feudal castle. Tucked into a fold at the base of Sleeping Horse Mountain, built on thirty-five acres along the picturesque valley floor, the 11,000 square foot behemoth mimicked the landscape. The house, like the mountain behind it, was shaped into a giant L. Considering the eight bedrooms, five bathrooms, and thirty-six-foot-high vaulted ceiling in the great room, this particular build would serve as Nolan's showpiece for a whole new level of clientele. And despite Rigor Mortis' system-wide failures with the human race, he was still a gifted carpenter whose work made other framers, when they were not being abused or flat-out running for their lives, generally admit as much.

Meanwhile, the architect, no stranger to constant worry and way too much caffeine, was driving Nolan crazy with his constant stressed-out voice mails. After the first few, Nolan ignored the guy completely for his own safety.

Because the crane billed out at $300 an hour, Nolan planned on throwing six of his guys at the job before this cost ate into his profit.

The driveway leading in was a mud-strewn canal banked on either side by fields of melting snow. As they approached, Rigor Mortis appeared in an upstairs window with both middle fingers extended.

"Oh God ..." Bunny shook his head. "I knew I should've smoked more weed."

But Nolan was positively beaming. "Ain't he something? Ain't he just the sickest goddamn thing you've ever seen?"

"You got that right." Elias lit a smoke. "If mental illness has a masterpiece, your boyfriend up there would be its Mona Lisa."

Rigor Mortis had a boombox in the bed of his pickup cranked to near-Messianic levels. It spewed out a rotating diet of speed metal and old-school punk, which was absolute torture for Baby New Year and Cooter's more country-western sensibilities. They, too, were in an upstairs window smiling as Riggy, fully pumped by the tunes, drove his hatchet into a wall stud while screaming along—

Cut my wrists till the cysts bleed empty,
Purge my soul through the pain—redemption
REDEMPTION!

"What a mess ..." Bunny winced. "I'm guessing this isn't going to be a very enjoyable experience."

Nolan killed the engine. "All right, ladies, let's show these morons how it's done."

They opened their doors and immediately dropped into the mud.

"Oh, fuck." Bunny cursed because the mud had just de-booted him. *"REDEMPTION!"*

Using a remote control, Rigor Mortis dialed down the volume from above as he called out, "Hey, Bunny! Since you're such a pathetic loser, you get to stay down there in the mud rigging up the trusses!"

"Awesome." Bunny was balancing on his left foot while trying to reclaim his boot. "And since you're such a goddamn psychopath—"

"What was that?"

Bunny looked up and said, "I said just being around you makes all of this worthwhile!"

Elias pulled Bunny's boot from the suctioning ooze. From here, where all of the trucks were parked, and around any high foot-traffic area, the April sun had churned the snow and earth into an eight-inch layer of brown slop.

Once inside, Nolan called out, "Riggy! How many guns you got rolled out?"

"Two!"

Nolan turned to Elias and said, "Grab another gun from the porno shack and a hundred feet of hose."

Elias handed him their tool bags and dropped back into the mud. He stepped up into Rigor Mortis' trailer. Purely Pavlovian—*Hustler, Penthouse, Swank*—anyone who entered became transfixed by a thousand fantasies.

For such a complete headcase to be so fanatically organized was still a source of amazement. Every wrench, cord, blade, and socket had its own place while Nolan, barely able to focus, tossed all his tools into the goulash of his boxes. Rigor Mortis refused on principle alone to spend a half hour sifting through Nolan's tools for something that might very well be already lost or broken. It was one of many subjects that angered Nolan, so of course Riggy made mention of it whenever he could.

Three blasts on the air horn signaled the arrival of Death Wish Crane Operations. O.D. scanned the jobsite, found the trusses, judged where it would be best to park, and stroked his long orange beard.

Nolan called down, "Welcome to the show!"

"You ain't kidding." O.D. hung out the window as he pointed at Rigor Mortis' trailer. "You telling me no one's killed that crazy son of a bitch yet?"

"Naw, he's too stupid to die." Nolan looked around the second-floor for Riggy. "Hey, sunshine, come say hello."

"That motherfucker can—"

Nolan quickly cut him off by yelling down, "Yeah, he's a moron all right."

"Hey, O.D., what's up?" Rigor Mortis nodded from the window. "Set that fucker up over near the L." He pointed to where the house bent 90 degrees. "You should be able to boom the whole stack from there."

"Well, Neal, I appreciate the advice ..." But the way O.D. smiled without letting any of it reach his eyes meant that was obviously not the case. "The ground ain't been leveled yet, and it's all sloping down toward that spot. At full boom, the mush might tilt me in."

"Okay." Riggy tossed a fraudulent salute. "Far be it—"

"*Hey*," Nolan hissed, but then he turned back to face O.D. "Don't mind the backseat driving, man, set up wherever the fuck you want."

O.D. nodded and threw it into reverse.

"Riggy!" Nolan closed in fast. "What's your problem?"

"Nothing. He just wants to tack on more time by having to break down and set up twice—"

"Who's writing the check? You looking to get a piece of O.D., you stupid fuck?"

"Whatever, man." Rigor Mortis walked away. "You're the boss."

"Listen to me. He comes and goes and there ain't gonna be a problem, understand? Don't fuck with my business, guy."

But Rigor Mortis was already making busy by a stack of blocks. "Cooter, goddamnit, we need like sixty blocks, man, what the fuck?"

Even though Cooter obediently grabbed the saw, dragged over more 2x4, and quickly began to cut, Rigor Mortis had been stirred.

"Each one of those had better be 22⅜ exactly or I'm gonna fucking lose it."

"I'm on it, boss." Cooter bravely smiled. He was thin but strong and had an impervious disposition. That, along with his Texas accent and

stern religious beliefs, made him somewhat of an oddity amongst the
general hostility of those employed by Harris Framing. Outside of a few
beers on Friday nights, Cooter enjoyed Slim Pickens records, spending
time with his budding family, and chewing an entire tin of Copenhagen tobacco every single day. He had small eyes and wore the incom-
plete mustache of a twenty-six-year-old man still acquiring his ways. He
was also a rising star on the crew and was able, despite Riggy's mayhem,
to absorb and retain the knowledge this master carpenter imparted.
Together, he and Baby New Year had so far been able to survive and
even thrive beneath his tutelage, for even though Rigor Mortis had his
moments of blinding rage, he could also be generous, funny, and selfless.
This juxtaposition, for all concerned, remained utterly irreconcilable.

"Bunny!" Nolan screamed out the window. "Stop holding your cock
and help O.D. get set up!"

As Bunny rolled his eyes, Nolan almost lost it. But since the jobsite
mood was already deteriorating, he turned away instead.

2x4s were needed to stabilize the trusses, so Baby New Year was on
the ground feeding sixteen-footers up to Elias as Nolan rhetorically
called out, "We got blocks, bracing, level, laser, guns, spikes ..." He
walked over to the window. "Ready when you are, O.D.!"

Elias quickly hopped up onto the wall. He adjusted his bags while
finding his balance. The 2x6 top-plate of the second-floor wall was
thirty feet in the air. It was something he was beginning to love, since
walking top-plate introduced the element of death into the day's otherwise excruciating routine. Six months ago, after long observing Rand's
high wire maneuvers, Elias finally climbed up onto the wall. Nolan had
already left for the day, so Rand took a minute for serious consultation.
He was standing above Elias, who was cautiously squatting on the 2x6
top-plate. Rand said, "When you're up here, first thing you've got to
remember is that if you're gonna fall, make sure it's into the house. Surviving a ten-foot drop to the deck is a whole lot prettier than falling
twenty-five feet to the ground."

"Okay."

"Also, OSHA says fifty percent of all falls over ten feet are fatal."

"Bullshit."

"I ain't lying."

"What?" Elias seemed amazed. "That is some kind of horrible number, boy."

As with most on the job situations, a twenty-year vet like Rand had more than a few horrible stories from which to draw—sudden wind gusts, hangovers, black ice on the plate beneath their feet—even Remote-Control Pete, a former protégé of Nolan's paralyzed after sliding off a roof in Montana. Something of a twisted bastard to begin with, old Pete had re-named himself Remote Control because his life was now entirely run by machines.

"Remember where your feet are at all times," Rand sternly warned. "You don't take a single step up here without looking first, okay?"

"Yeah."

"Then either stand the fuck up or climb down, man, because it's getting way too late for squatting."

Elias took a deep breath and used his quadriceps to slowly rise straight up. He held both arms out for balance as his eyes went wide with fear. "Safety last."

"Focus on my face. Good, now put down your fucking arms, man, you can't exist like that up here."

"Like what?"

"Like you're waiting to fall to your death, man, shit. Convince yourself you won't fall and it will never happen."

"Never happen?" Elias finally lowered his arms, but a half-inch to his right was a thirty-foot drop. "Holy shit, man, this is fucking crazy."

"You all right?"

"Yeah. What's next?"

"This." Rand rose up onto the balls of his feet. "Ever watch the way a cat walks when it's climbing across things up high? It keeps its weight on the forward part of each paw, focusing the energy directly into its toe pads to allow for better balance and a quicker reaction."

"Walk like a cat," Elias instructed himself. "Okay, what's next?"

"Well, do it." Rand lit up a cigarette. "Thomas, look at me. Stop wobbling around and just *be*."

"But I can't—"

"Focus on my eyes or get off this fucking wall."

"Fuck."

"I said my eyes, not my chest."

With a final wrench, Elias looked straight at him.

"Focus," Rand hissed. "Focus on my eyes. Does it look like I'm thinking about falling?"

"No."

"What's it look like?"

"It looks like you're disgusted by my fear."

"What else?"

"That you're not scared of falling."

"And why not?"

"Because if you don't think about falling you never will."

"Say it again, but this time tell yourself before you take a step."

"Jesus—"

"Take a step right now."

Elias inhaled and forced his right foot forward.

Rand said, "Take another."

Elias did and said, "I can't believe you're walking backwards."

"Am I thinking about falling?"

"Apparently not."

"That's why I'm not worried."

"But I thought you just said to look where every step is going?"

Rand grinned. "That's the rule for you, little fella, now take another step."

"Wait a minute, the ladder's way back there."

"Screw the ladder." Rand ashed his cigarette. "It'll be there on the other side."

"The other side of what?" Then Elias' eyes grew wide. "I ain't walking the whole perimeter, man, fuck that."

"Yes, as a matter of fact we are." Rand looked over his shoulder. "You got ten feet left until we turn the corner."

With each step, Elias' confidence grew. He exaggerated the balls of his feet maneuver until he almost looked like a petrified ballerina wearing toolbags.

Rand said, "Nice, keep moving like that, man, nice and smooth."

Since Elias was now finally striding with an open gait, Rand faced forward in order to set the pace. Once they reached the ladder, Elias proudly smiled. "That was fucking awesome."

"Squat down, I wanna show you something."

Elias obeyed as Rand said, "If anything goes wrong, and you're forced to fall outside the house, this is the only thing that's gonna save your life."

Rand abruptly stepped off the wall and, like an acrobat, somehow caught the top-plate before shooting through the window. Glancing up from the decking, Rand smiled and said, "What's the problem?"

"That ..." Elias could only shake his head. "That was fucking crazy. Almost as stupid as that two-story backflip you hucked last winter into that snowbank..."

"And?"

"And so stop making me look like such a pussy, man, fuck you."

Rand chuckled and said, "Come on down and let's roll this motherfucker up."

Lesson ended, they put away the tools and headed to the bar.

———————

The first truss was flown up minutes later, so Cooter and Elias walked the walls. Once the gable end was nailed off and braced to the floor, two blocks were shot into it perpendicularly along each side so the next truss could just lean against it.

Like a scurrying ball-boy, Baby New Year fired up a pair of blocks to Elias, ran to the other wall to heave up two more to Cooter, grabbed the tagline Elias detached after receiving the truss, and dropped it back down to Bunny for reuse.

After the rhythm became established, O.D. worked his deft touch and kept the crane in constant motion. Like a general surveying his troops, Nolan watched with mounting pride as the operation unfolded without a hitch. Below, Bunny had a copy of the truss plan but Nolan had little faith and no trust and so checked each one as it arrived. Things were rolling smoothly until he noticed Rigor Mortis on the phone. It was not that a lead guy could not make personal calls—only the apprentices and laborers got screamed at for jawing on company time. Even still, since Riggy had originally demanded autonomous control over this build, and Nolan had basically stepped aside to only sign and cash the checks, why was he, Nolan, the one now up here babysitting? In the last hour, they had rolled half of the roof and Nolan had not seen Rigor Mortis even once.

They were approaching the L bend in the house. This transition was where the great room's thirty-six-foot-high vaulted ceiling would be hand-cut out of massive log rafters. Elias and Cooter rappelled their nailguns to the deck before joining them with a crash. They re-routed to the far side over the garage, and worked from that gable end back toward the center. The truss plan called for a total of forty-six commons, two gable ends, and two monstrous girder trusses bordering the great room. Comprised of four trusses carriage-bolted together, the girder truss was engineered to hold roof loads almost like a beam. These two were designed to carry the weight of the transition from the eight-pitch commons into the twelve-pitch vault.

Progress was good, and O.D. began retracting the boom arm into itself even before the two-hour mark. Nolan called out for Elias and Cooter to start bracing off the trusses and then went down to pay O.D.

Descending the stairs, his annoyance flashed as he rounded the corner to see Rigor Mortis disappearing inside his trailer. Nolan had no idea what was going through Riggy's mind, but after nearly picking a fight with O.D. of all people, those present, himself included, had apparently been briefed on his current level of crazy.

Nolan grabbed his checkbook and caught up with O.D. as he raised the mud-covered outriggers.

"You know what?" O.D. asked. "A job this size usually bills out at around four hours minimum. Sometimes as long as six."

Nolan smiled as he wrote the check. "I'm sorry about that, bro, I had no idea I was even better than I thought."

O.D. chuckled as he pulled up the wooden pads beneath the outriggers. His knee-high waders were splashed in slime, and brown chunks had even worked into his red beard.

"I'll put this in the cab." Nolan detached the check. "Listen, about before—"

"Don't matter." O.D.'s blue eyes reflected zero misgivings. "That guy's an animal, Noll, plain and simple."

"He gets a bad rap—"

"Really?" O.D. bent over for the last pad and struggled to pull it free of the mud. "Seems like a bad rap is the shit that doubles as popular music these days, not beating old Pat Sisson half to death for no reason at all."

"Riggy said he got lippy."

"Seriously? He yanks a sixty-year-old man out of the cab of his own truck? The guy's a fucking Vietnam Vet."

"O.D., man, no offense, but you ain't exactly the one to be handing out lec—"

"You a history teacher now too, Noll?" O.D. heaved the wooden pad up onto the bed of the crane. "Besides that, wasn't anyone I ever visited that didn't have it coming. You can believe that."

"He's having a rough—"

"I don't give a fuck. I honestly don't. And if that crazy fucker ever steps near Pat again, he'll be walking alone."

"I ..." Nolan swallowed the rest of his reply. "I'll talk to him. Pat ain't got nothing to worry about."

"I know." O.D. opened the door and pulled himself up into the cab. "Tell your boy if he wants to play badass again to call me up instead. He'll come to love what's left of his life, son, bet you that."

"Thanks for coming out." Nolan swung the door closed, chafing beneath the threats and reprimand. Cleaning up his messes *again* ... As the crane belched and hissed along the driveway, Nolan suddenly needed to get out of there. He could feel his anger about to punch through. He stuck both fingers into his mouth and whistled before shouting, "Elias, Bunny, load up and let these bitches finish this. Hurry up!"

He did not want to see Rigor Mortis for even a single—

"Hey."

Nolan ignored the greeting while heading for his truck.

"Hey, wait up."

Closing his eyes, Nolan paused at the door of the pickup as he heard Rigor Mortis' boots slopping through the mud.

"Hey, Noll, you think I could squeeze that check off you before you go? I mean, the roof *is* rolled."

It was almost more than Nolan could handle. His hands twitched as he cut the check.

"Hey, wait a second ..." Rigor Mortis examined the amount. "This ain't right."

"What're you talking about?" Nolan looked like his pulse was squirting across his eyes.

"This is the third draw, man, and once the roof is on—"

"Take a look at that fucking roof!" Nolan abruptly screamed, and even Rigor Mortis was taken aback. "You've got another week at least before the fucking roof is anywhere near being finished!"

"That wasn't the deal. You're ripping me off—"

The words had barely left his lips before Nolan whirled on him, grabbed the check, and ripped it to pieces. "Roll up your shit and get the fuck out of my sight!"

"Noll—"

"Ripping you off?" Nolan was throttled by another paroxysm of rage. *"Are you out of your fucking mind?"*

"Stop, man, you're spitting on me—"

"Get your fucking porno trailer ass out of here now, man, I'm through playing wet nurse for your disasters!"

Rigor Mortis was so caught off guard he did not even put up a fight. Nolan was on his ass cursing, insulting, and berating as the others watched in awe while trying not to get caught looking.

Rigor Mortis was backing up his truck as Nolan paced close by.

"You got some fucking nerve, you know that? Without me, there isn't a moron stupid enough to even think about hiring you, so good luck trying to eat, motherfucker."

Riggy walled off the abuse as he hooked up his trailer and then gathered his tools. Nolan, however, was like a symphony of hate spewing out its greatest hits.

"Ripping you off!" Nolan could not remove the phrase from his blinded vision. "The only thing I'm gonna be ripping off is your fucking head if you don't get the hell off my job!"

After switching into 4x4 Low for more torque, Rigor Mortis eased through the mush. He did not pause or signal in any way, just stared straight ahead as if his next destination already awaited.

"Fuck!" Nolan stalked over to the garage and repeatedly punched the wall. He bent over and palmed his knees, knuckles bloody, trying to catch his breath. "Fuck!"

Save for the chugging of the gas compressor, there was not another sound for miles.

Nolan hopped into his truck and fired a hard U-turn. Those left behind found a window to watch the pickup disappear around Sleeping Horse Mountain.

Cooter shot a stream of brown juice between his teeth and said, "Didn't seem like the two of them was finished, did it? Good old Rigor Mortis."

"Whatever, man, he'll be rehired by the weekend," Elias said. "But he should know better. Fucking around with Nolan's money's just plain stupid."

Bunny laughed. "Sympathy for a psychopath." He pulled out a joint. "You guys are fucking lost."

Elias looked up into the maze of trusses. "I guess we should brace this bitch off."

"Inmates running the asylum?" Bunny passed the joint to Elias while nodding at the other two. "You dudes should really start smoking pot."

Cooter jerked his thumbs at his own chest. "Not this guy. I ain't weak like 'at."

"Didn't you call it the devil's lettuce?" Baby New Year's voice was soft but his smile made light of Cooter's self-righteous proclamations.

"You dang right I did. Cripples your mind while making you easy with temptation."

Elias blew a giant cloud of pot smoke directly into Cooter's face and said, "Tempt that, motherfucker."

"That's awright." Cooter shifted his cud of tobacco. "When it's my time to stand before the Lord, my life's work won't be leaving me lacking in His presence."

"Cooter, man ..." Elias passed the joint to Bunny while re-buckling into his tool bags. "Considering the utter disgrace of mankind, if smoking weed is God's biggest beef, than I've got some serious beefs of my own."

"Like what?"

"Well, how about the fact people have been killing each other in His name since forever? How vain is that?"

"Yikes." Bunny took a giant step to his left. "No more weed for you, man, there's a lightning bolt headed straight in your direction."

"There sure is," Cooter added. "Dang, Elias, I didn't even know you could think."

"No thinking. Only hating."

"Okay," Bunny said. "Wow. Way to creep everyone out ..."

"Hurry up," Cooter said and together, without a lead guy at the helm, the choiceless returned to work.

———————

Rigor Mortis lived in a subdivision of ranch homes on a plateau overlooking town. The fact that a person with his building skills and resumé only owned a single-story tract home showed just how bad his divorce had been. But at least he owned a house—Nolan rented a two-bedroom apartment and Rand, if not for local motels, was one step away from homeless.

Rigor Mortis' mud-covered pickup and trailer were in the short driveway when Elias wheeled in. After he pounded on the door, Riggy yelled out, "Who the fuck is that?"

"Bill Clinton. I heard you had some little girls in there."

"You're a sick bastard, Elias, you know that?"

The door opened and Elias held out a bottle of whiskey. "Needed some help killing this thing."

"Good, I'm almost out." Riggy swiped it from his grasp. "Maker's, too. Ain't you a gentleman."

Elias closed the door and pointed at his muddy boots. "You want these left outside?"

"Naw, right there's fine ..." Riggy gulped from the bottle. He was wearing sweats and sandals and a knit cap on his shaved head. The living room bordered the kitchen. A big screen TV flashed motocross highlights over a punk rock soundtrack.

Elias sat at the kitchen table next to an empty whiskey bottle, a bong, a pile of weed, and what looked to be pieces from a pair of disassembled revolvers. "Oh great, we playing Russian Roulette tonight?"

"What's that?" Focusing on the gun parts with an oily rag, Rigor Mortis did not even look up. "A little spring cleaning is all."

"Fantastic. What's better than mixing handguns, whiskey and drugs?"

"Listen, if you're just gonna sit there and babble like a moron, believe me, I got better things to do."

"Oh, I can see that. Apparently, Psychotics Anonymous has a weapons manual, and you're absolutely overwhelmed with shit to do." Elias reached for the whiskey. "Hell, I'm just glad you could squeeze me in."

"Yeah, that's right. Rest assured, I'll be squeezing one into you right after we finish that bottle, motherfucker."

"Oh my God."

"Put that in your pipe and smoke it."

"Speaking of which." Elias packed the bong while watching motocrossers huck backflips and hit hundred-foot jumps.

It might have been a small home, but Rigor Mortis had laid down the hardwood floors, blew out two interior walls to open it up, built and installed the oak cabinets, custom granite countertops, and built a wall-length cabinet for his television, DVD, VCR, stereo, and Xbox.

"I gotta hit the head." Elias headed down the hall. The remodeled bathroom had a steam shower and hot tub with space enough for six. After Elias closed the door, he found a photo-collage tacked to the back. Photographs of young Riggy with a purple Mohawk, working at assorted jobsites, and alongside people that might have once been friends. There was a shot of him and Nolan at least a decade before, drunkenly facing the camera. And below that, in a separate series, were the gray-haired parents, grandparents, and repeated shots of a gorgeous brunette—his wife, the three kids—the loss of which Rigor Mortis pathologically never spoke of. But Elias knew the story. How Riggy had won a date with his wife-to-be after outbidding everyone else at a charity auction. The fact that Rigor Mortis was at a charity event was amazing enough, but the courtship that followed defied the odds. Her name was Tyra and she was a dental technician vacationing from New Mexico. Before she knew any better, she was in love and six months later moved up from Santa Fe. She was a cool woman, which meant she had a large tolerance for her man's misbehaviors. They also had an attraction that was almost feral. He was a good-looking guy with a well-paying job, and his charisma worked its charm. And while violence destroyed Riggy's life in many ways, physically abusing his wife and kids was a line he never crossed.

Tyra was no stranger to Riggy's fierce disposition. That, combined with her equally unstable father-in-law, finally showed her she could not allow her three boys to soak up their dangerous examples. In an effort to keep her, Riggy agreed to counseling and even traded in the weed and booze for the medicine prescribed to lessen the rage. But it did not work, and for the last two and a half years, Tyra and the boys had sent their regards from Santa Fe. Nevertheless, the collage was undeniable—a guy nicknamed Rigor Mortis could also be a son, husband and father.

Stoned, Elias faced the mirror. He laughed when he saw the ornately folded hand towels. How a guy with such a horrible disposition could have this origami-like knowledge was almost as unnerving as it was stunning.

They did shots and bong hits until Rigor Mortis finally had the handguns reassembled. Then he wiped the table, cracked two beers, and said, "Let's shoot some stick."

After his family left him, Rigor Mortis turned the spare bedroom into a billiards parlor. He was racking the balls as he said, "Fuck him, man, what a bitch."

"Oh, come on ..." Elias grabbed a cue and chalked the end. "You know him a whole lot better than that."

"So what?" Riggy stretched out his arms before shrinking the gap to an inch. "See that? That's about how much I care."

"Who said anything about caring? Just don't sweat him is all."

"Whose fucking side are you on?"

"Whoever signs the checks."

"Pussy." Rigor Mortis nodded at the table. "You break."

As Elias lined up the shot, Riggy called him off at the last second. He calmly described how his feet should be set, and the positioning of his hands. He watched Elias prepare and said, "Just like work—straight lines and angles."

"I don't like it when you stand behind me."

Rigor Mortis chuckled. "Gives you a bad feeling, does it?"

"It's just creepy. Kind of like those hand towels in the bathroom, man, where'd you learn to fold like that?"

"Fuck you, Elias. Take the shot and hurry up."

Elias did and missed it.

Riggy grabbed his own cue and said, "Seven ball in the corner. By the way, that draw was mine."

"Not really. Technically speaking, the roof wasn't done at all."

"Hey, wood-monkey, what do you know about anything?"

"Enough not to tell Nolan he's ripping me off, boy, what did you think was gonna happen?"

"How—"

"Maybe that's it." Elias exaggerated the dawning of a sudden recognition. "We already know the two of you are in love—"

"Fucker."

"—a fifteen-year relationship where each man-lover knows exactly how to push the other's buttons—"

Rigor Mortis shot the ball and said, "You are so gonna die."

"—and before tonight's through, I wouldn't be surprised to see him at your door—"

"Stop."

"—with a bouquet in one hand—"

"No ..."

"—and a tube of KY in the other."

Riggy chuckled while dropping the nine ball. "You really are a stupid-dumb-bastard."

"I've had outstanding teachers."

"Yeah, well, get a load of this next lesson." Rigor Mortis pointed with the stick and drilled the seven into the corner. "What'd Super-Framer say after I left?"

"He just took off. I thought he was chasing you down. Came back an hour later and was all business."

Riggy missed the shot.

Elias said, "So what're you gonna do now? Grab a frame on your own?"

"Maybe. Whatever happens, believe me, I'm in no rush."

"Right on."

"I'm starving, man."

"Me too."

Elias followed up with another miss, so Riggy said, "You are one of the worst pool players I've ever seen."

"Don't be hurtful."

"You know what? It's rib night at that Hacienda shithole downtown."

"Nice. You're buying."

"There's even a slutty waitress down there that I'll let you have seconds on right after I drop one on her face."

Elias shuddered. "Just knowing you is like being in a car wreck every single day. At this point, I just show up to see how bad it's gonna be."

"Ain't that the truth."

"I call shotgun."

"You really want me to drive?"

"Yeah. I do. Hopefully we'll die in a fireball."

"Ha-ha! That's what it's come down to. Dying or framing for fuckface."

"Jesus ..." Elias grabbed his jacket, swigged from the bottle, and said, "Guess I'll see you in hell."

"Who you kidding?" Rigor Mortis stashed his guns in a cupboard. "Like there was anywhere else for you to go?"

CHAPTER SIXTEEN

In the year that had elapsed since William and Dot Cahill agreed to put 175 of their 500 acres into a conservation easement, Kara Harris and Sarah Vaughn had also been involved in the eventual settlement struck between Eugene Henman, the CPS, and the Spring Valley Town Planning Commission.

Henman was the rancher who had kicked Kara and Sarah Vaughn out of his house. He finally succumbed to his attorney's advice, knowing the town, the CPS, and other organizations could tie him up in court for years. The more controversial aspects of Henman's proposed subdivision, mainly the large tracts of land along the Blackstone River and Sleeping Horse Mountain, were instead put into an easement. Henman had not been happy about any of it. In lieu of 150 houses on 225 acres, he settled for 80 houses on 120 acres. The remaining 105 acres were put into the easement for which he was paid $750,000. That, combined with the $2.4 million for the 120 acres, meant he realized a profit of $3.1 million instead of the initial $5 million offered straight up for all 225 acres. He also saved himself from what could have been hundreds of thousands of dollars in legal fees and grief.

So out of the original big three ranchers, the CPS lost McCombs, split on Henman, and got Cahill into an easement. Instead of the 360 houses originally proposed in the town's five-year master-plan, only 115 would now be built.

But the land was a different issue. 1,100 acres had been put up for development and the CPS had only managed to save 280 from the auction block. McCombs' 700 acres had been the killer.

Currently, Kara and Sarah Vaughn were awaiting the latest court decision relating to the other land issue, Proposition 6. The referendum had so far been postponed three times as the Town Council and the affected homeowners slugged it out in court. At issue was the five-square-block section of downtown whose dilapidated houses and lean-tos looked like abandoned tombstones. Though an eyesore compared to the renovations sweeping along the rest of Main Street, these were still peoples' homes, and the right of the Downtown Development Authority, empowered by the Town Council, to condemn these structures with an eminent domain statute was, as expected, being fought in every public and legal venue. These five square blocks had come to symbolize the divide between the pro-business, pro-growth lobby, and those residents horrified at whose land would be seized next if this project was not stopped. Consequently, rational dialogue on either side was in short supply.

Since the land was already developed, the CPS' only concern was keeping all structures seventy feet from the Blackstone River. That was it. There was no other reason for them to meddle in the middle of what was largely becoming, as each day passed, a low-scale civil war.

As for the planned re-development, the winning proposal had been submitted by Denver-based Aegis Corporation. After the excavators and bulldozers tore everything down, the new Main Street would have a block-long three-story building with an old west brick and wood motif. The ground floor would be rented out to businesses, and the two floors above would house luxury condominiums and apartments. Sales taxes from the businesses would benefit the town, while the condominiums' prime location made them a developer's dream.

The remaining land was zoned for a pair of restaurants along the river, a block of shops across the street, and Victorian homes with wrap-around porches. *The Spring Valley Anchor* had published the building plan replete with artist renderings of the finished structures and, pro or con, most people, no matter their stance on Proposition 6, were largely impressed by these modest and tasteful designs.

But Kara was now under no illusions. Nolan was right. Once the smell of dollars was chummed into the water, the big-money players would tear Spring Valley apart.

Nolan had three ongoing builds—the boathouse, a duplex, and the custom monster Rigor Mortis had been framing. Now, without Riggy, it was all hands-on deck. Nolan ran the crews from dawn to dusk, savoring their pain when he told them that, as spring deepened into summer, the end of the workday might now coincide with the setting sun at nine o'clock. It was not a joke, and did not happen unless they were jammed up, but whenever guys heard him ordering pizzas at six o'clock, everyone shuddered.

With another two jobs starting in the next few weeks, Nolan's schedule was jamming up. Since frozen ground halted excavation through the winter, springtime in the valley was either feast or famine. If, like Nolan, a framer lined up jobs and had foundations poured before the November snows arrived, he avoided the crush of carpenters emerging into March like hungry bears from hibernation.

With time running out, and since he was not yet desperate enough to subcontract the upcoming jobs to the same local hacks he was now intent on crushing, Nolan called Cameron Rogers.

Ninety miles south of Spring Valley, Cam Rogers made a living off the vast reserves of wealth Aspen and Vail attracted. Custom homes, commercial buildings, hillside condominiums, summer vacation mansions built into the mountains—Cam Rogers had done it all. In his mid-forties, he had been building since his high school days in Midland, Texas. His mild manner did not affect the driven disposition demanded of both himself and his employees. And while Nolan, Rand, and Rigor Mortis flung themselves into their projects, Rogers approached his own with discipline and tactics in place. Not that he had any compunction against jobsite violence—in the end it was just counterproductive and fiscally unrewarding to have guys beating one another instead of attacking the stacks of wood.

His body, especially his lower back, had stiffened through the years. His long blond hair, leftover from the 1980s, was now thinning in the front. The rest was collected into a ponytail. He was thick but physically unremarkable save for his powerful hands, which resembled a pair of paint cans wrenched into his wrists. The small blue eyes were dispassionate and tucked into the deep creases created by the sun and wind. Having known Nolan and Rand since even before they knew each other, and having crewed alongside some of the legendary old-timers responsible for much of the Rocky Mountains' initial growth, Cam was connected to just about every peer building within a thousand miles. He employed six guys he treated like family but slightly underpaid, while Nolan's crew earned more for withstanding his breakneck pace and pain.

Cam Rogers' wife, Holly, was also his business partner. She had a sense of humor almost as raw as the men working for her husband, and was considered a formidable woman. Having been married for twenty years, they had one daughter named Clara left behind every time Cam went off to work. Because unlike most women, Holly had no problem taking jobs for him in Idaho, Utah, and Wyoming. Business was business. And if Cam had to fill his schedule by spending weeks away from home, so be it. She was setting up their future, driving Cam hard while plowing the profits into both established real estate and tracts of undeveloped land. The daughter of a contractor herself, she knew Cam could not grind this pace into his fifties, so Clara's college fund and their retirement became the primary considerations.

It was Tuesday evening when Cam got Nolan's call. Despite the fact that Cam was exhausted and the lower half of his body was caked in mud, once he recognized the number, he flipped open the phone and said, "So you made it through another winter. They ain't getting any easier, are they?"

"Old man winter can suck both my nuts." Nolan could be heard lighting a cigarette. "Ain't this some kind of mess, though?"

"Hell yeah." Cam's drawl, twenty years removed from Texas, was never far from the surface. "Mud's a foot deep down 'ere."

"The other day, you know what it reminded me of? That job we did up in Leadville."

"Oh God. That was some hell on earth."

"Am I lying? Didn't one or the other of us get stuck every single day?"

"You're bringing back some horrible memories, man, thanks a lot."

"No problem. Listen, I hate to keep it short, but I was wondering about your schedule. What you got coming up?"

"Hmmm." As Cam post-holed through the mud toward his truck, he cycloned an index finger at his workers in the universal gesture, so they began rolling up the tools. "I think I got some things I could juggle around, but I'll have to check with Holly. Why, you got a hole in the ground that needs filling?"

"Yeah ... actually, me and Señor Haywire had it out."

"Oh boy ..."

"Yeah. Anyway, I'm spinning three as we speak and got another deuce coming up."

"What are they?"

"One's a convenience store, the other's a 2,500 square foot gable-to-gable custom."

"Hmmm ... I imagine the convenience store's blow and go, right?"

"All the way. I'm talking four exterior walls, a crane for the trussed hip roof and done, period."

"Can't see why I couldn't at least help you out with that one." Cam did the math. "Our next gig's a condo, but that's still three weeks out. I got another week here at this dump but I could leave one or two monkeys behind to finish ... Lemme call Holly and I'll get back at ya."

Two days later the black F-350 and a white box truck crested Forked Head Pass. The massive pickup hauled a twenty-foot trailer with a tongue-in-cheek name and logo that Holly Rogers, in a fit of inspiration fifteen-years before, had sketched across her cocktail napkin. HUNGRY BEAVER FRAMING was stenciled above an anthropomorphized female beaver in high heels, bikini, and Occidental tool bags. The caption beneath read, A GRIN FROM RIM TO TRIM.

Descending into Spring Valley, they pulled into Treetop Condominiums and found Nolan already waiting in the parking lot. Since the winter tourists were long gone, condominium rentals and hotels were half-price, restaurants and bars ran nightly specials, ski and snowboard outlets gutted prices to clear inventory, and the whole town contracted after shedding the winter bloat. The shuttle bus and taxi-clogged streets were now quiet. Not wanting to operate at a loss, many shops and restaurants closed until the summer season, but the bars, as always, remained open.

"Cam!" Nolan yelled from his truck. "Before you girls get settled in, follow me out to the job first, will ya?"

The caravan departed. A half-mile down County Road 61, the jobsite was already teeming. Rand, Cooter, Baby New Year, O-Zone, Bunny and Elias could be seen squaring the foundation, drilling out the plates, and pre-positioning lumber for the upcoming assault.

Nolan exited his truck and began exchanging handshakes and hugs with the new arrivals. Since their two companies collaborated on builds and even traded employees when tempers inevitably flared, the scene was festive. Cam Rogers' right-hand man was James Spooner, but everyone knew him as Spoons. A former partner of Nolan's, once upon a time Spoons and Nolan had lived in Las Vegas for eighteen months of work and pure debauchery. Toward the end, in addition to addictions to gambling, partying, and strippers, the cocaine kept them up for five days straight before Nolan crashed their truck.

"Spoonie." Nolan warmly clapped him on the back. "How you living, bro?"

"Good, dude, how you been?" Spoons had square white teeth surrounded by a box-like jawline. At six-feet, he was lanky and carried a dozen years' experience. His expressive blue eyes and constant smile reflected the same sense of humor that had allowed him to survive extended duty as Nolan's co-pilot. But now, at thirty-one, Spoons was attached to a fiancée unimpressed by both his friends and former lifestyle.

Spoons forked his tongue and let fly a piercing whistle. "What's up, old man?" he yelled toward Rand who, as always, was bent at the waist with work.

Nolan threw a handshake to Rick Cadmus, a twenty-six-year-old Roman Catholic from Pennsylvania Amish country. He had curly brown hair, a sharp wit, and a predilection for good weed, live music, and philosophical discussions. However, after he made the mistake of telling everyone how he had lost a testicle jumping a fence as a kid, he was immediately re-named Uno. Unafraid of others sensibilities, he fired from the hip, but because of his book-smart condescension, Nolan was not a fan.

"Nolan, *como te va?*" Louis Soldano warmly hugged him. Alongside his younger brother Hector, who Nolan greeted next, the Soldano brothers were originally from Guadalajara and had become, like most émigrés eager to assimilate, almost too American. They spoke decent English, loved hip-hop and, if challenged, proudly stood their ground. Still in their early twenties, they went out of their way to prove they could compete at this level, a fact not lost on Cam or the others working beside them.

As the crews mingled, someone cranked the tunes and soon a pair of joints circled the crowd. Guys were laughing and reminiscing as Nolan and Cam detached from the group.

Nolan said, "So what's up, man? How's life down there amongst the rich and infamous?"

"What's this?" Cam abruptly stopped and pointed. His smile, framed by the wind-seared wrinkles, grew wider on approach. Swinging open the door to Nolan's trailer, he read,

Team Hate Rules:
1. No Talking
2. You Are Always Wrong
3. See Rule #1
4. No Laughing
5. No Singing
6. Self-Esteem is for Pussies
7. You Will Never Amount to Anything
8. No Questions
9. Beware of the Necrotic Black Death
10. Most important—No Thinking

"Oh my Gawd ..." Cam drawled in a graveled chuckle. "I love it, man, but why Team Hate?"

"Because we hate everything."

"Who did it?"

Nolan frowned. "Elias."

"Come on, brah, you don't like it?"

"Oh, I fucking love it. Every time I read what that moron did to my door with that permanent black Sharpie, I make sure I go and find him for a little extra one-on-one time with his master."

"Fucking priceless, man." Cam shoved the door away as they resumed their walk. "What did you ask me?"

"About the job. How's things?"

"Work's good. We got a couple of custom monsters coming up that ought to be very tasty."

"Nice. How's Holly? Still kicking your ass?"

"Every day, son, every day."

"Kara wants you over for dinner this weekend. She says I need to start hanging around with a better class of people."

"Poor girl. I got her fooled good, don't I?"

"So far."

They were walking the perimeter of the foundation until Cam said, "So how'd she come out?"

"Pretty much dead-nuts except for the back left corner. We just got out here an hour ago."

"Awful nice of you to square this fucker off. You ain't getting soft on me, right?"

"Naw, just showing the love, man. You're really helping me out."

"So what do we got?"

They stood at the two-foot concrete wall of the rectangular foundation as Nolan said, "A hundred feet by thirty for the walls ..."

Cam softly whistled. "That's a big fucking convenience store."

"Half will be a laundromat. But that's it." Nolan nodded at the gravel fill. "After we're done, they're gonna pour a concrete slab, stuff this place with an acre of the worst junk food on the planet, stick a dozen gas pumps out front and call it good."

"How high are the walls?"

"Twelve feet."

"Wow."

"Yeah, it's gonna be a pig."

"Can you think of anything even remotely like this?"

"Me? Hell, me and Rand thought you'd be the one to ask."

"Longest continuous wall I ever built was sixty feet. And that was only 2x4."

Nolan grinned sadistically. "A hundred-foot 2x6 exterior wall loaded up with window and door headers? Wipe your balls from the walls, bro, because no one's surviving this."

"Guess we could section it, but what would be the fun in that?"

"Right? Safety last."

"Listen, I hate to change the subject ..." Cam's small eyes were blue chips surrounded by weather-burst capillaries. "But it's too bad about your boy."

"It's just never-ending, you know? Rigor Mortis is almost forty, and I've still got to run around town cleaning up his messes. Do you know he almost killed the Aprés Lumber guy?"

Cam, who had once been boss to Nolan, Rand, and Riggy, started to smile. "He is something else."

"This is no shit. The guy didn't have a pen for Rigor Mortis to sign the receipt. He gets lippy with the guy, the guy tells him to go fuck himself, so Ye Old Snapcase drags him down from out of the semi—"

"This was the *delivery* guy?"

"Yeah, and Riggy's straddling the guy's chest pounding his head into the mud while telling him next time he ain't gonna get off so easy. Couple of weeks later we're rolling a roof and the crane guy, O.D.—"

"I know O.D."

"Right? The guy's a former assassin for the M.I.M.C., and he's out here pretty much throwing Rigor Mortis on the line. After that I just snapped. Everything turns into a fucking headache with that guy. But you know what? I'll hire him back again because I'm the biggest moron of all."

Cam laughed. "It's kind of like having a pet alligator, right? Sounds cool until it kills you."

"Thomas made up a sign and stuck it near his trailer."

"What'd it say?"

"Same as the door says—Beware of the Black Death."

"Jesus ... You gotta love it."

"Yes, you do."

"How's Bunny been working out for you?"

"Speaking of morons. He told me you and him got into it over money."

"You know? He's just the worst." Cam still could not believe it. "After everything you do for the guy, he either wants to be paid early or comes up with these phantom hours."

"Six months with you, six months with me ..."

"Right? I'm starting to feel like a goddamn government program with this guy."

"Yeah. He's a train wreck."

Cam said, "And the best part is that a couple months ago we're driving around and he's ragging on all these framers that are in their late forties and can't hardly walk, and have nothing, and that are still living week to week, and I was like, 'Bunny, you're thirty-two. You're just a couple of years away from being one of those guys, man, wake the fuck up.'"

"It's true."

"I mean he's like an infant."

"Most of them are. Fucking Rand's blowing through almost two grand a week in cash."

"It's just incredible is all."

Nolan flicked away the butt. "Let's get financial. I got a ten-grand down payment for you plus a third up front. How long are you figuring?"

"A week and a half. If it takes a second longer for four walls and a roof, I should sell my bags in disgrace."

"Stay the remaining half-week for fascia and soffit?" Nolan almost begged.

"We'll see. Actually, I'll gauge where we are by the weekend. If I have to show up down there a few days late, so be it."

"That's a beautiful thing."

"I'll just have to hurry up, is all."

"Music to my ears."

They started walking back toward the trucks.

"You know," Cam said, "It's good to see you tearing the ass out of this place."

"It could be yours too, bro, just waiting to be had." Nolan swung an arm across the valley. "If I got you up here for six months, we could run gangster over this whole town. The place is just filled with hacks. I barely have to wake up and I'm already half a day ahead. You know Bill Reynolds?"

"Big Talk Bill?"

"Yeah, well, he rolled a whole roof, braced the trusses off with a single 2x4 that was nailed halfway down the gable, *halfway*, and the whole fucking thing dominoed during the night. Twenty grand in trusses special-ordered from Canada, a day's labor, crane costs, and the next day the shit's lying on the ground like kindling."

"Unreal."

"Best part is, the GC fires him, he takes his crew over to those condos near Eagle Road, and they got him rolled out working barely an hour later."

"People are fucking desperate, huh? If things weren't going so good down in Vail, I'd be right up here beside you."

"And this Proposition 6 thing, if that passes, Aegis Corp out of Denver is going to level a five-by-five square block area of downtown, bro, and then let the real frenzy begin. Did you hear about this?"

"Sure did. Also heard you got about a hundred houses going out to bid over the next five years..."

"It's just incredible, isn't it? I tell ya, once this ball starts rolling ..."

"Game over, brah."

As they neared the group, Nolan said, "Jesus Christ, look at these thugs. If we lit a trash barrel and stuck it in the middle it'd look like the corner stoop in the projects." He called out, "All right, girls, enough of your fucking chattery."

The crew circled up around the bosses.

Nolan said, "Here's the deal. Cam's guys work here. Rand, Bunny, and Elias got the boathouse. Myself, Cooter, New Year, and O-Zone are taking over Riggy's custom. These guys—" Nolan motioned toward Cam. "They're gonna call up when they're ready to lift these God-awful walls, and then we'll all gather over here for a good old-fashioned intestinal blowout. Any questions?"

No one said a thing.

"Good." Nolan pointed at his crew. "Roll this motherfucker up, boys, and let's get after it tomorrow. Oh, and one more thing. I know how teary-eyed you girls get at these reunions, so mind your manners tonight and keep the drinking down to a low-key riot, will ya please? I'm not getting out of bed to bail anyone out, and if you show up late tomorrow morning, your hungover ass is mine. Any questions?"

Silence again.

"Zero-seven-hundred in the morning, bitches, and don't forget to hurry up."

Bunny rolled his eyes. "Boy, he can really rally the troops."

"Kind of like Patton," Cooter said.

"Awesome comparison." Elias grabbed a skillsaw. "Sociopaths get shit done."

Cooter frowned. "You need to put down the hippie lettuce, Elias, because that shit's rotting out your brain."

"Amen to that, brother." Elias shouldered into bandoliers of rolled up hoses and cords. "The faster I can forget this nightmare is my existence, the happier I'll be."

"You'll never be happy." Nolan was stalking behind them like a wraith. "And listening to your pain only adds to my enjoyment." He looked from Elias to Cooter and said, "You guys are like the Dukes of Dumbass. Bo and Luke Dumbass."

Bunny grinned. "So I guess that makes you Boss Hog."

"No joke cracking, simpleton, you need your remaining brain cells for work."

Nolan peeled off toward his truck as Elias smiled.

"I think I love that fucking guy," he said, and might have even meant it.

The boathouse build was on the Blackstone River. A kayak company had, in exchange for tax breaks, agreed to provide public restrooms and a dock/staging area for boaters.

Rand, Bunny, and Elias had been there framing for the last two days. Elias turned the corner with a monstrous stack of 2x4's balanced on his shoulder. He suddenly stopped. Rand was kneeling motionless on the top-plate of the first-floor wall. Rand's right knee was on the top-plate, his left boot a step ahead.

Elias dropped the wood with a tremendous crash and said, "You striking a pose up there or what?"

"Sort of." Rand stared ahead, calmly breathing. "You need to promise that you're not gonna tell anybody."

"Uh-oh ..." Elias looked around for Bunny. "You didn't kill him, did you?"

"This ..." Rand pointed to a dimple in his right quadriceps three inches above the knee. "It's a 16, man."

"Aw, bullshit." Squinting up from below, Elias thought he was being played. "Do you think this is my first day—"

Rand squeezed his thigh with both hands until a red stream spilled eight feet to the deck.

"Okay, enough. I believe you."

"Fuck."

"What happened?"

"I was toe-nailing in the rim and—" Rand winced because any movement hurt. "My bootlace got caught. I guess I tripped ... I just can't believe it."

Morbidly curious, Elias approached. "Let me see it."

"Fuck, man, get me down from here."

"How many times have we been through this? Fuckface has got all the ladders." Elias stood beneath him. "Put a boot on my shoulder and I'll lower you down from there."

Rand started awkwardly maneuvering himself. "Jesus Christ, who's ever heard of having no ladders on a jobsite?"

Since the nail was shot through layers of muscle, Rand took pains to keep his right leg immobile lest he shred more muscle around the spike. Once on deck, he rolled onto his back while clutching the still bent leg.

"Let me see it." Elias corralled the thigh. "Wow, that's a good one."

"Use your pick-axe, man, the cat's paw didn't have enough leverage."

The thigh was clearly indented around the nail, the muscles sunken inward.

Rand exhaled slowly through the pain. "Pull it."

"Dude—"

"Please, man, pull that fucking thing out!"

"All right!" Elias frantically glanced around. "I need something to pry it against." He found a chunk of 2x4 and placed it on the leg. Carefully levering the nail head into a special slot cut into the blade of the pick-axe, he then slid the wood beneath it. "You know it's in the bone, right?"

"I'm gonna fucking kill you if you don't—"

Elias made him scream after wrenching the nail out in one motion.

Rand gasped, gulping pain. A minute elapsed before he could say, "Thanks, man. That was awful."

"I bet."

"Where's Bunny?"

"Probably out by the car getting high. Here, hold this." Elias handed him the bloody nail and then grabbed both sides of Rand's leg, squeezing out more blood. "We need to get this flushed out immediately."

"No way." Rand tossed aside the nail and made as if to stand.

Elias blinked. "That thing was in your femur."

"You don't know that."

"Do the math. 16's are 3½-inches long. Squeeze your quad. All that soft tissue and tendons—"

"Who cares?"

Elias stood up. "Fine, fuck it."

"Gimme a hand."

"Nope."

"Thomas!"

"What the hell are you bitches doing?" Bunny stumbled in with a lopsided smile. "Get a fucking room, man."

"Bunny, c'mere and help me up."

"You okay? Did you fall, grandpa?"

"No."

"What happened?"

Standing, Rand could not take the weight. He hopped until a minimum of movement reappeared, but the blood was seeping through.

Bunny squinted at the deck. "Is that fucking blood, man?"

"No."

"Jesus!" Bunny turned toward Elias who had already returned to work. "Did you see this?"

"See what?" Elias did not even turn around. "We got shit to do, man, hurry up."

Bunny stared between the blood-smeared floor, to Rand hopping about, and then to the bloody nailgun. "Oh my God."

"Bunny," Rand sternly warned.

"You shot yourself, didn't you?"

"I didn't shoot—"

"You owe me a hundred bucks!"

"Nobody saw a thing—"

"Elias did."

"No, he didn't."

"Elias!"

But Elias had left the room.

"You motherfucker." Bunny mockingly wagged his finger. "How

many times have you laughed your ass off at other people? This sound familiar? *You'd have to be a total moron to shoot yourself.*"

"Well, it's true." Rand stopped backing up, seemingly defeated. His right leg hung out in front of him as if winged by an errant bullet. "Twenty-five years, man ..."

"I thought you said you were thirty-seven?"

"I am."

"So you've been framing since you were twelve?"

"Bunny..." Leaning against the wall, fighting to light a cigarette with his blood-smeared hands, Rand said, "I now have about half a dozen reasons to kill you."

"It's okay. You're kind of like the Cal Ripken of jobsite injuries. Or at least you were."

"Speaking of injuries ..." He made as if to throttle Bunny but Bunny scampered away.

"Hey." Elias reappeared, holding his cellphone out toward Rand. "It's fuckface. He says it's time to play human crane over at Cam's disaster."

They joined the others at the convenience store job ten minutes later. Off of CR 61, it was set back twenty yards from the road and surrounded by mud. Both thirty-foot sidewalls had been framed and stood the day before. Now the massive back wall awaited.

The rest of the crew was occupied with final preparations. The foundation was two feet above ground, so the bottom-plate of the wall rested on the concrete. But in order to keep it level horizontally as it was being built, the top-plate was nailed into makeshift posts stuck out in the gravel fill.

Elias parked his Skylark next to all the pickups and killed the engine.

Rand stared out at the monstrous wall and said, "Anyone in a betting mood?"

Elias said, "What's the point? You might not even be alive to claim it."

"They could've just sectioned this thing, you know?" Bunny was disgusted. "Fucking heroes, man, they're out of their minds. 'Let's build the biggest wall ever and cripple everybody.' Who cares!"

"Right?" Rand looked at the wall. "You could land an airplane on this fucking thing."

They stepped out into the late afternoon's settling chill as Nolan screamed, "I sure wish you ladies had brought your husbands to help us lift this thing!"

"Blah, blah, blah."

Levels, guns, sledgehammer, bracing—everything was ready. The mood was jovial but cornered by the stakes. As they joined the others, Elias said, "Safety last, baby, good-bye righteous widows."

"All right." Nolan began motioning. "Cam, myself, and Rand are gonna be at quarter intervals along the wall. Cooter and Spoons are taller, so they'll be in the middle. The rest of you dwarves fan out down the line."

They stepped into position. Guys took practice squats until Nolan said, "There's twelve of us, which means nine feet of wall per moron. Rule number one—once this thing's in the air, there ain't no going back. There is no rule number two, and rule three states that any moron who abandons the lift to save his own ass will in fact wish he had been crushed by the wall instead."

No one was laughing.

"On three."

Everybody squatted and adjusted.

"Ready?" Nolan scanned in both directions. "One, two, three!"

They hissed and grunted through the initial lift, but the wall was barely at their waists.

"UP! UP! UP!"

In unison, the men heaved and pivoted their hands beneath it. At shoulder height, the point of no return was passed, so the screams went down the line.

"Up!"

"Drive!"

"C'mon, you weak-ass *motherfuckers!*"

With one last surge, the wall passed the fulcrum and clanged roughly into position. They took a minute to recuperate, red-faced and distended.

"That," Cam finally said, "was some rude-ass shit."

"Fucking A." Nolan coughed. "Nobody move or this fucker's gonna fall. Me and Rand will nail it off."

Rand detached from the wall and limped over to retrieve a gun.

"What's the matter with ..." Nolan squinted. "Is that *blood*?"

"Nope." Rand checked the 16's in the slide and then headed for the corner.

"He shot himself!" Bunny called out with glee.

Nolan immediately said, "Hey, come here."

"I'm fine."

"Is Bunny lying? I don't think I've ever seen you limp like that."

"It's nothing." Rand tried to shield himself with the six-foot level, but backed into the corner, he had nowhere else to turn. "Fuck me ..."

"My goodness ..." Nolan was truly amazed. "The king is finally dead, huh?"

Rand pursed his lips. "I had a good run though, didn't I?"

"Man, I would've paid a thousand dollars just to see your face the second that thing shot into your leg."

"It was in the bone," Bunny added.

Nolan looked at Elias. "That true?"

"Yes. Not sure how deep it was but it was definitely in there."

Nolan took the gun away from Rand. "That's it for you, let's go."

"I'm fine."

"Not for long. Not with about a billion bacteria shot inside your marrow." Nolan glanced at Cam. "You got this? I've got to take Sally here to get her shots."

Rand limped toward the trucks. "I hate you all to death."

"What else is new?" Nolan followed him out. "And I'll definitely be docking this from your next check."

"Oh really?"

Even Nolan could not keep a straight face and burst out laughing. "Listen, if it's any consolation, just don't forget to—"

"Hurry up. Yeah, man, believe me I fucking got it."

———

The Horseneck Saloon was tucked into a branch-clogged bend along the Blackstone River. It had a sagging roof, a rotted front porch, and toilets that barely worked. For any other bar, these structural and aesthetic deficiencies might have been attributed to financial restraints or the unavailability of contractor assistance. But since the Horseneck catered almost exclusively to the trades, and on any given night usually served enough carpenters, plumbers, and electricians to equal a thousand years experience, the dilapidation was accredited to character, and in this way the tourists were shed as well.

Inside, the old timber frame skeleton and ceiling-high mirrors were stained from the smoke of a million cigarettes. The lights were wall lamps that broadcast forlornly through the yellowed haze. Animal heads were stuffed and hung like dead ghosts on cast iron hooks. A black bear stood in the corner frozen in rage.

As they had since Team Beaver's arrival four days earlier, the nightly reunion tour continued around three tables near the windows. A growing flotilla of empty beers, shot glasses, and pints ominously accrued. Bunny and Uno arrived with a dozen more reinforcements. The juke-box, seemingly stuck on a never-ending loop of Lynyrd Skynyrd, blasted *Sweet Home Alabama* as the surrounding drunks horribly sang along. The Soldano brothers, Cam Rogers, Spoons, Rand, Uno, Elias, Bunny, O-Zone and even Cooter were in attendance. Cam, though long past the point of pointless inebriation, was not averse to weed or having the occasional night out with the boys. Spoons and Rand were sharing jokes while the Soldano brothers and Bunny hosted a discussion on bong hits versus blunts.

In the center of the table, Uno sat across from Elias and said, "I totally disagree."

"How?" Elias frowned. "Political parties, corporations, religious affiliations ... individual identity in America is dying."

"I'm religious." Uno pointed toward Cooter. "Cooter's at church every Sunday and me—" he motioned toward his own long curly hair and earring. "Am I not an individual?"

"If your church tells you to do something, do you do it?"

"Like what, pray?"

"No, like get down on your knees and beg for forgiveness. If mankind is created in God's image, then what the hell is any man doing on his knees in front of any other man, if not handing over the very right to do otherwise?"

"If God is the father of us all, do you not show your father respect?"

"How? By being a slave, some beaten-down loser afraid of life and sin? What the hell are any of us doing here then?"

"We're alive, we make choices. And sometimes those choices are wrong. In order to clear them away, the individual must be held accountable."

"So who does God confess His sins to?"

"God doesn't sin."

"So I guess we're not created in His image after all."

"Do you believe in God?"

"No." But Elias' tone seemed unconvinced. "I can't."

"Why not?"

"Because it defies logic."

"How?"

"Women were created from a rib bone? Some guy lives in the belly of a whale while another scours the earth for two of every species before a worldwide flood kills everything else?"

"Well, a literal translation is different from—"

"From what? Blind belief? Unquestioned allegiance?"

"No." Uno frowned. "They're parables and stories meant to guide us, all of us, on how to lead good lives."

"So it's a fantasy then, right? Like Disneyland for adults. You've got good versus evil, heaven versus hell. Sorcerers in robes divide the sea and walk on water, and a dwarf throws a stone that kills a giant. You've got armies and plagues and damsels in distress. And if that isn't bad enough, each of these weird groups then gathers up all this nonsense into its own book of hate—"

"Book of *what*?" Cam Rogers was eavesdropping and smiling while Elias torqued himself into a lather.

"The Bible, the Torah, the Koran—the Books of Hate. Love another who believes as you, but hate and kill every other motherfucker that doesn't. Hell, they've been trying to kill the Jews for ten thousand years. Jews hate Muslims, Muslims hate Jews, and Christians hate everybody."

"Holy shit." Cam was laughing and shaking his head. "You are one hell of a mess, Elias."

"Not really." Rand glanced at Elias with a small measure of pride. "At least he ain't like the rest of these brainwashed imbeciles."

"You don't believe in God either?" Cam asked.

"I believe in myself." Rand swigged his beer. "God, no God, I'm not spending whatever time I got left on this planet being afraid of nothing."

"But why does God equal fear?" Uno asked. "That's completely opposite the intention."

"Not really." Rand cocked an eyebrow. "The guys who wrote this shit down weren't stupid. They knew the power of a good threat. You don't do what you're told you're going straight to hell."

"So God's a gangster? This is unbelievable."

"Why else would there be a hell?" Elias reached for another beer. "Threats and violence to keep billions of sheep in line."

"Dang, Elias," Cooter drawled. "I been trying to ignore the stream of bullshit flowing out your mouth, but it's like a blasphemous flood now, man, shut your fucking hole."

"See that?" Elias nodded toward Cooter. "That's how they defeat logic. After they're done inbreeding with their cousins, they issue threats of their own."

"America's a Christian country," Cooter proudly stated. "It don't take no degrees to figure that one out."

Elias lit a cigarette. "The founding fathers came here fleeing religious persecution—"

"George Washington wasn't a Christian?" Cooter asked. "Lincoln, Jefferson, ain't none of them Christians neither?"

"They might have been Christians, Cooter, but they were also politicians."

"So what?"

"So the only thing worse than a politician is a priest, man, wake the fuck up."

"All right, all right." Cam put out his hands to separate the factions. "Cooter's right—America's predominately Christian, and Elias is right about organized religion and brainwashed sheep and politicians being prostitutes."

"Can we please talk about something else?" Spoons motioned toward his empty beer. "Like who's going up to buy the next round?"

"What time is it?" Cam checked his watch. "Fellas, this old man's heading home."

"Hell, man, it's only ten o'clock. One more for the road, boss-man, what do you say?"

"Well ..."

"Count me out." Cooter rose and fit his Stetson on his head. "I got to get home to my loving wife while Elias and the rest of you test your Maker's resolve."

"Maker's?" Elias perked up. "Good idea, man, let's do some shots." He winked at Cooter. "I got nothing but love for you, hoss."

"And I got nothing but an overall distaste for everything you represent. I hope you know what you're doing, Elias, because I don't think He's gonna put up with a whole lot more of your nonsense."

"I guess we'll see." Elias stood up. "All right, fellas, this round's on me."

"It's about time." Spoons rolled his eyes. "We've been here since like five o'clock."

"Yeah, well, better late than never. Who wants a shot?"

As the jukebox cranked out Don Henley's *American Pie,* the sing-along began in earnest.

So bye-bye Miss American Pie.
Drove my Chevy to the levee but the levee was dry ...

Elias returned with the drinks as the chorus rewound itself. The drunken patrons united around the lyrics. They raised shots, knocked beers together, and when the final stanza arrived, chanted in unison,

And them good old boys were drinking whiskey and rye,
Singin' this'll be the day that I die ..."

Over the next week and a half, the two companies morphed into differing crews assembled by skillsets according to the day's agenda. Since New Year, O-Zone, and Cooter excelled at fascia and soffit, they were sent to the condominium job on Mt. Lassiter. Nolan and Bunny were installing windows at Rigor Mortis' custom, Cam Rogers and the

Soldano brothers were finishing the rafters at the boathouse, and Rand, Spoons, Elias, and Uno were at the convenience store flying trusses.

Because of the open floor-plan, the trusses had to run unsupported thirty feet from wall-to-wall. They were monstrous triangles made from 2x6, and the old crane lifting them wilted against the weight. After one of its bolt heads sheared off and shot a one-inch hole through the wall, no one said a word—they just wanted this deathtrap gone ASAP.

After lunch, they were readying to sheet the roof until Uno said, "Time for a safety meeting."

They scaled into the trusses. From this vantage point they could keep an eye on all avenues of approach. Elias fired up a joint while Uno cut four monster lines of cocaine on a 2x4 block.

After hitting the block, Spoons' perfect white teeth were in a line from ear to ear. "Man, I love safety meetings."

Rand said, "Bust out some more of that shit, you one-nutted freak."

"You don't have to be so hurtful." Uno cut more lines.

"Wow." Elias' foot was already drumming. "This shit's for real."

"I was in Denver for those Primal shows last weekend." Uno used the razor from his utility knife to square off another round. "The tunes were flowing, the bitches were fine, and the pharmacy was definitely open."

"Nice." Rand sniffed up his share before angling the straw again.

"Hey, sniffy—" Elias reached for the block. "No grabbsies."

"I can't believe how fast it's gone." In typical Spooner fashion, he was completely off topic as he hit the joint. "It seems like we just got here."

"When're you guys rolling south?" Rand puffed the joint before passing it to Elias.

"Friday night supposedly."

"It's too bad." Uno put away the cocaine. "The Valley's where it's at come summertime. Kayaking, biking, sitting around the fire at night with big-titted Betties ..."

"Ain't that the truth." Rand made the mistake of pulling out a pack of cigarettes and lost four of them instantaneously. "I love this place, man, but I wish summer would just hurry the fuck up."

The April breeze swirled through the trusses as they balanced like birds on a power line. For normal people, standing on the vertical 1½-inch edge of a 2x6 fifteen-feet in the air would be challenging enough, and that was before the weed and blow. The cigarettes tasted good after the drugs, but the cocaine made standing still impossible.

"What do you guys think?" Incredibly, Rand did a pull-up through the gap, swung his legs up, and then stood balanced on top of the trusses. "We got two stacks of plywood on either side ..."

"Oh yeah?" Stoned and tweaked, Spoons smiled crazily at this challenge. "Think you got that, old-timer?"

"Careful up there, Pops," Elias added. "Wouldn't want you to fall and break a hip."

"Not likely, little fella." Rand dropped back down and straddled the bottom cord of two trusses, shuffling off toward the wall. "Elias, you cut for me. Uno, you run the blade for Spoons."

They dropped in one by one and followed Rand.

Elias said, "Did I hear him right? He thinks four guys can sheet a football fields' worth of roof in a single afternoon?"

"Why not?" Uno cracked from behind. "We'll take another safety meeting in an hour to keep our RPMs at full throttle."

Bringing up the rear, Spoons called out, "Love the safety meeting."

"¡Ándele!" Uno said, "That's cocaine for hurry up."

"Ándele," they chanted and, at differing intervals, dropped ten feet to the gravel below.

Section Four

During summer it did not get dark until nine o'clock, so they were able to waterski after work. Temperatures rarely broke eighty degrees, and the wide blue sky, dotted by the occasional cloud, was otherwise as clear as the bone-dry air. From the waist-high hay fields along the valley floor, to the rockiest reaches of the surrounding mountains, summer was in full effect. Guys showed up for work in boots and shorts and eventually passed around the sunblock after the initial weeks of tanning. And while irresponsible when it came to bringing enough money, food, drugs, or cigarettes to remote jobsites, no one ever forgot their water. Since caring and sharing were not attributes in close proximity, survival became an individual responsibility.

"Riggy! You're gonna kill the guy!"

"Don't be such a pussy." Rigor Mortis had his Evinrude 375 barely open to a quarter-throttle, and the fiberglass hull shot like an arrow across Lake Chance. Located on the western edge of town, Lake Chance was an eight-mile-wide freshwater respite for an otherwise landlocked public.

Nolan, connected by a tow-rope, worked the wakeboard side-to-side. He straightened out long enough to mouth something while pointing to the surrounding vista, but Riggy evilly smirked.

"Look at him," he said to Rand and Elias. "Fucking hippie-boy's loving nature."

By this point, prolonged exposure to Rigor Mortis had created a sixth sense, so they quickly grabbed hold of the boat after it rose up like a missile planing the surface. Nearly jolted from the tow-rope, Nolan fought against this sudden velocity and churned wake that forced the wakeboard, and subsequently his attached legs, to undulate like furious pistons.

"Let's see if Super-Loser can handle this." Rigor Mortis swung the wheel and dove the boat into a vicious, digging turn. The engines growled as if choked, the bow driven under. Elias and Rand clung to their seats while out back, canted forty-five degrees, Nolan shot far left before catching an edge and splattering across the surface.

Nolan treaded water as the boat approached. The sun glare made him squint as Riggy called out, "Hell yeah, Hollywood, you were really carving it up out there!"

"Fuck. You." Nolan pulled himself aboard, facing the expectant grins with a menacing one of his own. "And fuck you guys too."

"What?" Rand pointed at Rigor Mortis. "Blame your girlfriend over there."

"I will." Nolan was suddenly beside Rigor Mortis. "Ready for a swim?"

"Hey, wait, I got my phone—"

Nolan shoved him backwards over the rail, and since Elias was sitting right there, Nolan tossed him from the boat as well.

"Motherfucker!" Rigor Mortis screamed, holding up his drenched wallet and phone.

Nolan turned to bounce Rand but then could only smile. "You're allowed to stay."

"Gee, thanks."

Nolan fired up the engine as Rigor Mortis cursed and tried to make it back to the boat, but it was already long gone.

The past two summers, whenever Nolan gave them more than 24 hours off, Rand and Elias threw backpacks into the Skylark and hit the road. Upon arrival wherever, Rand, with almost canine precision, would lead the way on foot. Vegetation, landscape changes, differing grades of soil—years of experience and instinct allowed him to bloodhound the land. Usually, they traversed the hills and mountains of Colorado, Arizona, or Utah as if merely strolling through a portion of Rand's backyard. Elias, shouldering his own eighty-pound pack as well, became amazed at Rand's ability to translate the sun and sky into a map of readable coordinates. Oftentimes, after hiking and digging for days, Rand would just lead them straight out of the wilderness and find their car as if connected by a rope.

For Elias, a lifelong city-boy, these forays were workshops where he learned how to use a compass, basic navigation and terrain appraisal, how to cook and shit and live while leaving his surroundings basically untouched. Because while Rand observed few laws, hated authority, and considered himself a separate entity stuck inside society's regulation, out here he lived in deference to nature. The mating ritual of the bighorn sheep or the impact of the brown beaver damming up the straits of the Taylor River provided him more fascination than anything other than seeing his kids. These trips were also one of a dozen reasons that made it impossible for Elias to leave. He was making serious money and being taught a trade by some of the best framers in the country. They were also teaching him how to waterski, jetski, motocross, and snowmobile to remote back country locations with pristine powder conditions. And while he was originally supposed to stay only long enough to fund the car ride home, now he was not sure if he was even leaving at all.

Depending on the specific gem Rand might be seeking, a location was charted and Elias' Skylark dutifully responded. On this particular Friday night, they pulled into Leadville, which was four hours south of Spring Valley. At 10,152 feet, it was also the highest incorporated city in the United States. In 1890s Colorado, during the silver and gold boom, Leadville's population of 40,000 was second only to Denver. Currently, even though only 2,000 people remained after all the mines closed, it still contained the original architecture and atmosphere made legendary by the old west. As a former hub for the vast mines that reached 14,000 feet up into Lake County, Leadville prospered until all the years of digging contaminated the ground and water. The Environmental Protection Agency had to step in to supply clean water and the hundreds of millions of dollars it would take to decontaminate the entire region. Subsequently, jobs up here were scarce, and other than the extreme altitude, a few saloons, curio shops, and the Mining Museum, tourists had little, if any, reason to stay.

They checked into an old hotel with a bar which had polished wood-work like a cathedral. The bartender, a girl named Dot from Durango who was covered in tattoos and intimate piercings, served drinks and lively banter to the new arrivals. After the one o'clock closing time, she even joined them upstairs for a nightcap and other impromptu actions that lasted until dawn.

After they said good-bye to Dot and descended south on US 24, they passed Mt. Elbert which, at 14,433 feet, was the highest peak in Colorado. An hour later, as they neared the town of Buena Vista, Elias was in awe. The Collegiate Mountains—Mt. Harvard, Mt. Yale, and Mt. Princeton, alongside Mt. Antero and Shavano Peak, were stacked side-by-side like giant triangles climbing 14,000 feet into the sky. Buena Vista, a tiny nondescript town, was virtually at the feet of one of Mother Nature's most spectacular achievements in a state already spoiled by her furious workings. Hence the town's name, which literally translated meant Good View.

By 10:00 A.M., they passed through Salida, in Freemont County, after which Rand abruptly said, "Take a left up here."

He pointed at a dirt trail and Elias hit the brakes.

They forced the Skylark over the uneven terrain and rock-choked trail before finally abandoning it off to the side. They swallowed what was left of their hangovers, donned their massive backpacks, and eventually followed the still-rising eastern sun. Occasionally, Rand would pause to examine soil, poke around the vegetation, and then suddenly veer off in another direction. He pointed out different striations in the soil and certain mineral veins that were telltale markers for the gems beneath. Now a veteran of numerous expeditions, Elias knew they could dig for days and find nothing, or else stumble across a pocket of smoky crystals, clear crystals, or turquoise hidden in bunkers beneath the earth.

They hiked east through the sage brush and across dusty hilltops. With backs bent beneath the sun's relentless pressure, they each carried two gallons of water, along with a portable filtration system and chlorine tablets to purify anything else culled from nearby streams. At noon, Rand thought he had found a vein, but after three hours of fruitless digging, they re-packed their gear and turned once more to the interior guidance system Rand's instincts provided.

Weekends like this, together with the job and workouts alongside

Rand, continued transforming Elias' body. Compared to when he arrived, he was basically unrecognizable. For a regular person to carry eighty pounds for twenty feet would be a big deal. But hewn and tanned, his conditioning had improved to the point where humping that kind of weight for miles was no longer a test.

They marched single file past four o'clock. Dropping their packs, each tried not to show the strain from lack of sleep and last night's party, but the alcohol and sun had lathered them in sweat. The mountain breeze was chilly despite the seventy-five-degree day. The view, which stretched in every direction for a hundred miles, was a cautious reminder of true peril's exact proximity. The absolute silence, save for the wind, isolated them even further.

They drank water and smoked cigarettes and then re-shouldered their packs. Because of the sun, Rand pulled on a ballcap while Elias wrapped a bandana around his shaved head.

"What do you think?" Rand, whose abdominals flexed into a grid, pointed at his watch. "Eight o'clock sound good to you?"

"To camp? Sure whatever, man, but let's get ourselves a hit here, digger, what say you?"

"Fucking A." Rand stepped forward, inspected the ground, and together they climbed onward.

He found a spot by a stream and after three more hours of digging, sifting, and finding nothing, they decided to camp right there. Near the interspersed boxelder and cottonwood trees, they gathered kindling and a fire sprang to life. But the night was far from ended. The sunset, which spilled blue, yellow, and purple across the sky, held both of their attentions. Seated against the rocks, they shared cans of tuna and bread and fruit before the Jim Beam appeared.

"Ain't that beautiful?" Rand asked, because only a sliver of sun remained like a crown across the curve of the earth. "Shit like this makes what we do and who we are the biggest joke of all."

"What do you mean?" Elias swigged off the whiskey, rolling a joint.

"I mean us, all of us. I think this country's in a state of devolution. Everywhere you turn, we've reverted into a bunch of spoiled whiny pussies."

"No argument there."

"The saddest part is that most people spend every opportunity trying to get ahead, and at the end they turn around and realize they missed the best part instead."

"Well, I'm sure they're saying you're the one who's crazy. You don't save a single penny, you've got no retirement plan or health insurance, you're a drunk, divorced, in your forties—"

"Hey."

"Oh sorry. What's it this week? Thirty-six? Thirty-seven?"

Rand punched his arm but Elias only laughed. "Whatever, man, you know? You're like a chick with this age thing."

"Fuck. You."

"Ha-ha." Elias licked the paper, sealing the joint. "Depends on perspective, right?"

"What does?"

"I mean people are a mess. One dumbass goes to college, another dumbass drives a truck, everyone's got opinions and baggage and thinks they know what's best ..." Elias lit the joint. "My whole thing is, this is America. Believe whatever you want, just leave the rest of us alone."

"That's deep."

"I'm serious. View everything the same, right? Go out of your way to view everything the same. When I meet somebody, anybody, it doesn't matter—they all get the same fifteen seconds."

"For what?"

"To crumble. Sometimes I'm wrong, but people are usually too stupid to hide who they really are, even if it's only for a quarter of a minute."

"So if the fifteen seconds goes by and they're a douchebag ...?"

"Then we might as well have never met at all."

The joint pinballed between them until Rand said, "So you're telling me that you have no prejudices?"

"I can't, man, or I'd have to hate myself."

"What does that mean?" Rand paused. "Are you ... are you part black?" he carefully asked, and Elias, who had just taken a hit from the joint, started coughing and laughing simultaneously.

He said, "No, man. But that was some funny shit." He bugged out his eyes. "*Dude, are you black?*"

"You suck."

And Elias only laughed and laughed. They shared the whiskey as full dark crept in. The fire crackled.

Rand said, "I don't know about the job. I mean, when we started this whole thing, it was a partnership ..."

Elias groaned. "Not this again."

"Seriously. I'm being serious. Why isn't my name on that goddamn trailer too? Holmscomb and Harris, man, that's how it should read."

"Somebody's got to be the bullshitter, right? You telling me you'd rather be shaking hands and kissing ass and stressing all this nonsense, or do you just want to show up and bang some nails?"

Rand said nothing.

Elias frowned. "Can you imagine dealing with all those idiots? The owners, the GC's, other subs ...? No thanks, Frank."

"Yeah, well, I want access to the books. I want to know what the hell's going on with this company, man, or I'm quitting."

"Have you even asked to see the books?"

"What is he, my fucking dad?" Rand spit into the fire. "As a partner, I shouldn't have to ask for shit."

"Have you asked him or not?"

"Ahhh." Rand batted a hand. "He always comes up with some bullshit excuse. The accountant's got the books, the bookkeeper's got the books, my dog ate the fucking books ..." Rand grimaced, disgusted. "I think he's playing me, man."

"C'mon, now."

"Serious, dude. It's getting to the point where I'm just gonna have to lose it."

"Here, man, take a swig before your head explodes."

They smoked and drank in silence. Elias rolled a second joint as the chill night forced them into sweatshirts. The fire was fed, the joint was smoked, and soon Elias asked, "What's out here to worry about at night?"

"Other than rattlesnakes, scorpions, and hyenas? Nothing at all, little fella. Which reminds me—did I ever tell you about that time with the Mojave rattlesnake?"

"Please do. I'm sure it'll help me sleep tonight."

"I knew about a spot for smoky purples out near Socorro, New Mexico. I'd been up there digging for days until I saw a vein running up this ravine to a ridge. It ended at a ledge near the top of this huge hill. It took me four hours to climb the face, hacking through brush and up slopes with half my gear, which was still a good forty pounds. Anyway, I finally made it up to the ledge and saw that it was actually a little cave, you know, carved right into the top of the peak. I followed the sediment lines and I'm in this little—it couldn't have been more than six-feet deep— this tiny cave bent and digging at the wall when I felt this—" Rand's hand fluttered near his own left ear. "I felt this disturbance behind me and as I turned, there was this beautiful Mojave right beside my ear. I mean it was right fucking here. They like to seek out shelter in the daytime, stay out of the sun, so it had its body wrapped around a tree root punched through the earth ceiling. That's also why I never saw it until it was too late."

"Jesus Christ."

"Yeah. They also pack ten times the venom of a Western Rattlesnake, and those things are already among the deadliest in the hemisphere. Once the Mojave's neurotoxin goes to work way out in the middle of nowhere all alone, peace out. So anyway, I turned and saw that goddamn head not four inches away from my own, and as I jumped back in shock—"

"Oh no."

"Yep. Right down the hill, asshole over elbows. It was fucking brutal. I was lucky I didn't crack my head open or bust an arm, but after I slid to the bottom, I was pissed boy, lemme tell you. I mean my gear was still up there, it was like four o'clock, and another four-hour climb wouldn't put me back up in that cave until eight o'clock. That meant I would probably have to stay the night—but I was gonna kill that fucking snake."

Elias slowly chuckled. "Thatta boy."

"So I started climbing and climbing and once I finally got back up there, he was still coiled around that root. I yanked out one of my .22s and drew down on his head but he didn't even flinch, you know, he just flicked out that tongue a couple more times toward the barrel, and my pulse was banging and we're literally eye-to-eye with each other and staring and then ... I don't want to sound like I lost my mind, but the snake and I ... something passed between us. Like—"

"Did you guys make out?"

"—things were understood, you know? And since he'd had a chance at killing me and didn't, I ... I couldn't take the shot. I just lowered the .22, broke eye contact, and went back downhill with my gear."

"Are you kidding me? That's insane."

"Tell me about it. Pass that bottle, will ya?"

They lit another round of cigarettes.

"I like you, Elias, because you don't pretend to know everything."

They took turns on the whiskey and then Rand yawned out loud.

"Boy," he said. "Last night was some kind of fun, wasn't it?"

"Hell yeah. Kind of felt like too much of a porno, though, but it was cool."

"Good old Dot."

"Right?"

"Too bad we didn't bring her along."

"Uh-oh. Do I have to sleep on my back tonight?"

"Hah."

They unrolled thin rubber mats on either side of the fire, and without a tent, found shelter inside their sleeping bags. Lying down, they passed the whiskey, talked more shit, and after they smoked a final cigarette, Elias yawned. "So what's the plan for tomorrow?"

"We're gonna keep to this ridge. I saw something earlier when I went to take a piss."

"Yep." Elias yawned. "Don't forget to hurry up."

"Hurry up," Rand said, and after a knot from a log exploded inside the fire, each of them, on their backs, watched the blasted embers rise.

———————

They awoke early enough on Sunday morning to greet the dawn over a saucepan of black coffee. They sheared off chunks of cheese and bread and ate more fruit, but were otherwise on the move. Considering they had to be at work in the morning after a six-hour ride home, they decided dinnertime was their drop-dead time for departure.

The path rode the ridgeline like a ribbon as they continued their ascent. The surrounding flatlands were a vast ocean of tan dirt punctuated by hilly islands and individual mountains moored in isolation.

Rand, kneeling down, sifted the soil. He looked up and blinked into the sun, then he stood and continued on.

The rock-strewn trail rounded a corner to reveal a fifty-foot wall on their immediate right. To the left, a gentle slope slid off the path. Ponderosa pines were interspersed and scaly from the sun, and the dust kicked up by their boots was instantly blown away.

"Well, well," Rand said.

"Is that …?" Elias squinted. "Is that a hole?"

"It certainly appears to be." Rand stepped down the slope and Elias quickly followed.

Once they pulled away the sawed-off trees and sage brush, they stood in front of a five-foot trench descending into the ground.

"Wow." Rand shed his pack. "Can't say they didn't try like hell to hide it."

"I thought you said it was against the code to poach on someone else's hole?"

"It is." Rand guiltily grinned. "So shut the fuck up and lend a hand."

They cleared the mouth and revealed mounds of excavated dirt.

"See this?" Rand knelt to investigate these tailings. He picked out a purple crystal which was six-inches long and as thick as a dill pickle. "If they left shit like this behind, you can only imagine what they really found."

"Look, they're everywhere."

In small piles on the mounds of excavated dirt were crystals of varying sizes.

Rand said, "It's ten miles to the nearest trailhead."

"And ten miles back." Elias did the math. "Fully loaded, could take them four hours at least."

"You keep an eye out." Rand dropped into the hole. "Some of these fuckers carry shotguns."

"Great. Hope he's a good shot, because I don't want to feel a thing."

"Yeah, well, you better duck, because I ain't carrying all this shit back alone." Rand stepped into the darkened entrance where, within seconds, he exclaimed, "Holy sweet Jesus."

"What?" Elias almost jumped in as well but then returned his gaze to the designated surveillance. "What's going on down there?"

"You wouldn't believe me if I told you."

"Fuck this." Elias dropped into the trench before stepping into a tiny hand-dug 5'x5'x6' box. Rand's flashlight played across the walls, which were loaded with so many crystals there did not appear to be any room for dirt. They were bursting in pairs and chunks and clusters that looked like porcupines stuck on the wall. Because of the sheer amount, picking a spot to commence excavation took longer than expected.

Rand aimed the light at Elias' face and said, "I'm gonna toss this shit out to you so you can stack it up above."

"Sweet. What about the shotguns?"

"Thirty minutes, man." Rand pulled out his chisels and grips. "I'll accept that risk for a shot at one of the sweetest pockets I've ever seen."

Elias stepped outside as Rand rifled the walls and hauled out various pieces. Like two thieves in a vault, they hurriedly secured the loot. Both were covered in sweat. Nervously scanning the perimeter, Elias was in awe at the growing pile before him.

"All right, that's it." Rand reappeared with one last armload. "We could spend the next day and a half just shelling this place out."

"We'll come back next weekend. Who knows? Maybe they've had their fill."

"Maybe." Rand frowned, gazing forlornly back into the hole. "But fuck me, man, it sure hurts to leave this ..."

"C'mon, man, we should DD."

Rand hopped up to help Elias load the packs. Once finished, they rearranged the branches and brush to re-camouflage the hole. Passing a jug of water back and forth, they shouldered into their packs as Elias said, "Oh my God."

"Yeah." Even Rand was off balance. "We just added another forty pounds to each of us."

"A hundred and twenty pounds? Call the Marines."

"Fuck that jarhead shit." Rand pointed at the path that had led them in. "We got thirteen miles to go, little fella, so zip up your man suit."

"Time to ratchet up the hate," Elias concurred, and together their boots formed a cadence.

———

They spent the next three hours cursing through the heat until the Skylark finally appeared. It was just past noon when they dropped their packs and collapsed against the car, panting like a pair of worn out dogs.

"That," Elias gasped, "was some horrible shit."

"Gimme that." Rand upended a water jug over his head. "I need a smoke."

"Yeah." After Elias produced a smashed pack from his shorts, they smoked cigarettes bent into the letter L. "By mile ten, the hallucinations almost made this death march worthwhile."

"Wanna know the best part?"

"Of course."

The crippled cigarette drooped from the corner of Rand's mouth as he said, "Tomorrow you get to relax by showing up for work."

"No kidding. Way to rest up on the weekend, right?"

Rand held up one of the crystals which, like the others, was covered in a layer of tan grime. "Where we gonna scrub these off?"

"Up the road, bro." Elias, with considerable effort, slowly gained his feet. "Saddle up, old man."

They heaved the packs into the trunk like dead bodies. In the front-seat, which was awash in CD's, empty cigarette packs, sawdust, and dirt, they kicked off their boots and headed home.

Rand's story unfolded sometime after the Collegiate Mountains faded into the rearview mirror. They smoked a joint as Johnny Cash relayed the myriad sufferings all people take to heart. Rand put away the weed and said, "I ever tell you about that time in the Cascade Mountains, in north Cali?"

"Is this when you and your nut-bag ski bros jumped I-5?"

"No. I had heard from a friend about a spot he hit on in the Shasta-Trinity National Forest. I'm talking way up there, like an hour south of the Oregon border. Anyway, I saw a vein and tracked it for over a mile, digging here and there but I didn't find anything. I kept tracking on it up this hillside and finally, beneath a half-dozen monster Sequoias, I found the biggest crystal I've ever seen."

"Seriously?"

"The top of it was barely two feet below the surface, and you could tell by its posture that within another millennium eventually the earth was going to work it free." Rand looked out the window. "Of course at first I couldn't believe it. I mean I saw the shaft, I had excavated two sides, but never in my life did I think the tip would be intact."

"Holy shit."

"No lie. A perfect five-point cone. A one in a billion find. I was literally shaking."

"Jesus."

"After I excavated the tip, I just dropped my shovel and sat there next to it. What was the point? If it was a ton, approximately, how in the fuck was I going to get it out of there? Chopper? Horses? And without knowing whose land it was on, I sure as fuck wasn't about to keep digging."

"Yep."

"So I covered it back up and headed to the nearest town, a place called McCloud, which was still a ten-mile hike. I found this Mexican who had a pair of horses and a converted manure spreader for a trailer, but I had no idea how I was gonna lift the crystal into its bed. And then, after I nosed around one of the bars, I found out the land wasn't part of the National Forest at all, and was in fact owned by a man named Jarrett, and that pretty much killed me in my tracks."

"What's the difference?"

"Well, if it was public land, no one except the government could put up a fight, and even then they would have to catch me in the act. But with private property involved, tell me, what landowner would even cut me in on half of what could be a five- or ten-million-dollar discovery?"

"You don't think you could even get half?"

"If I showed up at your door, told you I found ten million dollars in your backyard without your permission, why wouldn't you just tell me to fuck off and hire a company to pull it out for twenty-grand instead?"

"Huh."

But the old memory seemed to leave a foul taste. "It's still in the ground up there. I check in on it every couple of years and I swear, before what's left of me rots away into old age, I'm going to find a way to dig that fucker out and never work again."

"Sounds good. Me and you can split it fifty-fifty."

"Not in a million years, little friend."

They were passing back through Leadville by three o'clock, and after flirting with the idea of round two with the amorous Dot, they for once listened to common sense and kept driving.

US 24 North dead-ended into I-70 West, which ten miles later dropped them at the beginning of CR 61. The Topongas River paralleled the road, and since they also needed a place to rinse the crystals, after three hours behind the wheel, Elias eased the Skylark down the embankment.

They stretched sore muscles in the bright sun and dumped their packs on the pebbled beach. Disgusted by their own condition, they washed themselves before grabbing rags and brushes and furiously scrubbing at the stacks before them. Eventually, the crystals, which had been tan-slimed objects, revealed the particular azure beauty created by the crushing weight of timeless pressure. The startling array of shapes, sizes, color, and overall condition were not lost on Elias, who said, "What's the biggest pocket you ever found?"

Seated in the stream, toothbrushing the crevices of a baseball-sized cluster sprouting a dozen crystals, Rand said, "I remember one time I pulled out a hundred pounds of turquoise ..."

"Where at?"

"We just passed it. It was in a shelving I found along Mt. Yale."

"You're a freak. You know that, right?"

"Yeah ..."

For the next two hours they continued converting the slimed shapes into purple mounds and shot the shit as the afternoon rolled by. Coalmining and different sources of power came up, so Rand said, "Every living thing contains energy, right?"

"Well ... human beings have electrical impulses, but a plant or tree ... they're alive but ..."

"But they'll die and dissolve and turn into coal or carbon or natural gas ..." Rand held up the crystal he had been washing to better inspect it. "One day our bloated carcasses will do the same. All of this ..." He motioned toward the valley. "Strip away the so-called progress and we're merely bags of meat waiting for the great decay."

"Amen." Elias seemed relieved. "I couldn't have said it any better. Life is totally pointless."

"Wait a minute, I never said—"

"It's really fucking horrible. Man starts off as a helpless infant, spends his whole life learning from the same mistakes every other man since ape-kind experienced, and then, just when he's at the apex of his knowledge and wisdom and power, he degenerates into a pile of goo and shits himself while waiting for death in a wheelchair."

"*What?*" But Rand was smiling.

"Seriously. That's why collectively we'll never amount to a goddamn thing. Imagine if Einstein or da Vinci kept amassing knowledge?"

"So just because one day down the line I'll be dead, that makes my existence pointless?"

"Exactly."

Rand shook his head. "That's about the most cynical, self-destructive, self-loathing thing I've ever heard."

"Whatever."

"So why even live? Why don't you just kill yourself instead?"

"Because I like the pain. And because I'm fueling myself on spite alone."

"Man, what happened to you? Don't you have anything else to think about?"

"No thinking." Elias stood up, and the streaming water broke around his ankles. "Time for another bone." He rolled a joint while watching Rand's diligent care with the stones. "This shit really gets to you. I mean you're using your own freaking toothbrush, man ..."

Rand looked up with a squint. "They're symbolic, you know? A result of flukes and coincidence and ... and that sometimes out of a million tons of regularity ..."

Elias took a hit. "Deep down, despite all your hate, you're just a hippie after all."

"If that means I believe in the human spirit, then I guess I am. There isn't anything anyone with enough heart can't achieve, no matter how negative they might be."

"Touché. Here, smoke some pot instead of getting high on life."

Rand flicked water up at Elias before taking the joint. "You're a real downer, you know that?"

"No kidding." Elias sat back down alongside his pile of crystals, scrubbing. "After another forty years of this, I get to die broke and alone."

"You sound just like Nolan. The two of you ought to just have a murder-suicide and end it."

"Look at you. At the height of your physical power and awareness, and we can trek all over the place without you consulting a map, and even you, after all the years crush away your abilities, even you will end up—"

"—in a diaper shitting myself to death, yeah, I get it." Rand shoved the joint at Elias, disgusted. "Nice try, but I'm not gonna crack."

They repacked their rucks as dinnertime approached. Back in the car, Elias said, "Maybe one day before you're fifty you'll have a license so I don't have to do all the goddamn driving."

"Maybe." Rand grinned. "And then again maybe not."

Nosing up to the lip of the parking area, Elias checked both ways. Ninety miles later they crested Forked Head Pass and plunged back inside the valley.

Nolan dropped his bags and said, "I can't take it."

"Noll ..." Rand was staring down at him from the top-plate of the wall. "He's gonna show. He said he'd be here."

Nolan threw out his arms. "Take a look around, man, you seeing something I'm not?"

"We need him."

"Who, *Bunny*? Are you kidding me? He pulls a no-call no-show yesterday and now—" Nolan looked at his watch. "It's almost noon?"

"Dude—"

"Naw, man, fuck that. He ain't running this show." Nolan turned for his truck. He yanked open the door and glanced up at Rand. "I'll be back."

"Bring me something to eat."

"Nope."

He drove through town with eyes peeled above a chiseled grimace. Because of the glorious weather, Bunny could have been kayaking, camping, or somewhere sleeping one off. But the best and worst part about small-towns meant there were only so many places a person could hide their car. So like a cop scouring side streets for a wanted fugitive, Nolan was on the prowl for Bunny's rusted out '89 Subaru.

"Please God ..." Nolan pulled back onto Main Street. "Just let me find this stupid-dumb-bastard and I promise he won't die slowly."

Bunny loved breakfast, so Nolan cruised restaurant-row but could find no trace. He drove up toward the mountain and, behind a row of shops filled with knickknacks for tourists, finally spotted the Subaru tucked in next to a dumpster.

The Powder Trail Bar, unlike the older, original saloons downtown, was cheesily adorned to attract a younger crowd. Nolan wanted to keep his arrival secret, so he walked in through a kitchen entrance, ignored the lone cook who did not want to be a hero, then pushed through a door that led directly behind the bar. Because it was off-season and barely noon, the place was empty save for three guys drinking at the bar. The closest one, speaking with his two companions, had his back toward Nolan.

One of the guys, thinking Nolan must be another bartender, tapped his glass for a refill. Instead, Nolan snuck up behind Bunny and said, "Nice try hiding your car, dumbass." He grabbed his hair and cranked back until he was looking upside down into Bunny's frightened face. "Did you actually think you were gonna no-call no-show again, motherfucker?"

"Noll—"

Nolan wrenched down harder. "Don't even bother."

"I was just—"

"Boozing." Nolan glanced at Bunny's two companions. "And who are these idiots?"

"This is Billy and Todd—"

"I was only kidding." Nolan looked down into Bunny's face. "You're dead to me now, understand?"

"Noll—"

"Shh!" Nolan could not pull Bunny's head back any further without breaking his neck, so he used his other hand to pull out a prearranged wad of twenties. "Consider yourself paid in full. Then call Cam. Maybe he'll put up with this nonsense again, but I'm about ready to fucking kill you."

"Hey." The bartender reappeared from the basement carrying two cases of beer. "You can't be back here, man, what the hell? Leave that guy alone."

"Relax." Nolan shoved the money into Bunny's shirt pocket and then released his head. "I'm just passing through."

"Still—"

"I said, relax." Nolan stared at all four of them as if warning them for the last time. Then he glanced at Bunny. "For this? You blew off lead guy pay to pal around smoking rock with these fucking morons?"

No one said a word. Bunny rubbed his aching neck, but the words and treatment seemed more hurtful.

"Please, Noll ..."

But Nolan was already walking out the door.

———

Cutthroat as it was, month to month the crew continued to expand. Nolan had six frames going simultaneously and was finally forced into subcontracting two of them out to locals. Like stray dogs wary of their turf, Nolan's guys demanded segregation, so the intermingling of crews was not allowed. Also, by currently having four jobs within which to distribute personnel, Nolan curtailed any damage from inevitable events, like an architect's mistake, or delays in the delivery of material, each of which could dead-stop a job. And because of payroll, taxes, invoices, insurance, and managing all six builds, Nolan finally caved—he brought a bookkeeper and accountant on board.

But the addition of a seventh frame forced him to subcontract it out to a crew he knew nothing about. When they pulled up, Nolan overlooked the obvious because the van they were in, like its ghastly occupants, stank of various disorders. Rail-thin, dirty, and nervous, they claimed outrageous accomplishments and were said to hail from Denver. Their leader, a guy named Ross who had sweaty palms and shaky hands, greased Nolan like a pro. Ross, who was as tall as Nolan but half his size, had matted brown hair and that certain sour milk stink those who have not showered in weeks exude. "*It's a simple two-floor box with a truss roof, Nolan, me and my guys can handle it.*"

Rumors on the local building circuit carried news of questionable crews arriving from out of state. California, Arizona, Texas, Wyoming—the smell of blood was in the water, because the giant pickups cruising CR 61 were not filled with tourists. Local tradesmen, always wary of the unknown, tolerated this invasion because there was currently more than enough work to go around. But after the boom ended—as they always did—guys either packed up and blew town, or the real ugliness ensued. Nolan remembered a situation near the Utah border, when the jobs ran out and guys, with no way to earn, cut each other's throats. One day it got so bad, Nolan returned from lunch to find another framer actually trying to undercut Nolan's bid and steal his job, but the guy took a beating instead.

No stranger to abusive addictions, Nolan knew he should have exercised better judgment when Team Ross appeared. But blinded by the money and bragging rights of kicking ass simultaneously on seven different jobs, Nolan ignored the obvious. Goggle-eyed and stunned, the four corpses spent the next ten days screwing up everything they touched. And even though Nolan checked in like a babysitter, it seemed Team Ross even lacked the basic knowledge and core principles that separated posers from real framers. Window-jacks were the wrong height, headers were barely nailed together, and the whole place was out of level. Between hits of methamphetamine, they had rolled a floor and stood four walls and taken *eight* working days to do it. Even with the harshest of conditions, it should have been finished in three at the most. Since payment was for the job and not how long it took them, Nolan had no idea how these guys could even eat.

But food did not seem to be a problem, since the only thing getting cooked was chunks of meth in a soot-smeared pipe. On the eighth day, after Nolan showed up and discovered the window rough openings for the rear wall were totally wrong, he finally snapped. He fired Ross and told him to have his gear packed up by the morning. Proud of his self-restraint, Nolan thought he had taken the high road until Ross called later that night to babble on about his cut.

"Listen," Nolan responded. "You're lucky to be getting paid at all. I've got to cut down nearly half of what you did."

"That wasn't necessarily what—"

"Goodnight, crackhead."

The next morning, after the general contractor called Nolan and told him Team Ross was nonetheless back at work, Nolan gathered up Rand, O-Zone, and Elias. There was no music or small talk as the F-250 roared through town. They took a left on Breakman Drive and continued on until the jobsite sprang into view.

Nolan turned to Rand. "Do you believe this? Are these morons testing the sound barrier of true stupidity?"

"Apparently so." Rand chuckled. "Team Skeeter's really on the go."

Rand's joke was aimed at the fact that after Ross and company saw Nolan's truck turn the corner, they burst into blatant activity.

"Wow." Elias snapped his gum. "You can see the back wall leaning out from here."

Nolan grimaced. "Fuck me, man, fixing their mistakes might end up costing more than just ripping the whole place down. Mark my words, because in the next thirty seconds these hackers are gonna be absolutely fleeing this disaster."

The truck was barely shifted into Park before Nolan hopped down and started shouting, "Get your tweaked-out asses off my job!"

Ross, standing somewhat askew, seemed unaware of what truly approached. His eyes were twitching, his brown teeth ground into nubs. "In order for us to clear a little more cash, I thought we'd—"

Nolan snatched the saw from Ross' hand and slung it twenty feet over a wall. He then pulled out a check for a thousand dollars and jammed it into Ross' tool bags.

"I'm no thief." Nolan tried to corral a mounting rage. "I shouldn't be giving you shit but I'm paying you off only because I don't want you liening my job. We're even, you're gone, have a nice day."

"But—"

"Listen ..." Nolan pegged a finger at his face and said, "Since you're practically stealing from me, the only reason you're not taking a beating as well is because I can't afford the drama or the case. Not anymore. Now take that money and your crew and get the fuck back to wherever it is you all crawled out of."

"You can't hustle—"

Nolan slapped him, grabbed him by the cheeks, and twisted his head until it was beneath his own. "You've got five fucking minutes."

Ross' crew received the message. They heaved the tools, hoses, and cords into their van as if the place was readying to explode. Ross, recovering from the bitch-slap, blinked through a stunned expression.

"We did the best we could," he said, and actually seemed to mean it.

On every level, whether it be lead guy, apprentice, or laborer, the first day was a wake-up call for all new hires. Some guys never showed up for day two, or maybe it was at four or five where they decided something— anything—would be better than volunteering for this assault. For those with years accrued in the trades, this high-speed slaughterhouse ran in direct opposition to every previous experience they had known. The guns had no safeties, the saw guards were pinned, and instead of using sawhorses, they slung the wood across their ankles. Without multiple coffee breaks and lunches that ended whenever, here you showed up at seven o'clock exactly, got thirty minutes at noon, and had no idea when you would be leaving. Sometimes it was 5 P.M., 7 P.M., but by no means before 4:30. And never ask either, because extra hours would be tacked on if only to prove a point. And surely do not make any plans for Saturday because Sunday was the only day off. There were no paid vacations, overtime, sick days, health insurance or excuses for missing work, and once the beautiful summers ended, there was extended an obligation to share in winter's maw. Whether it was the withering verbal abuse, or the expectation that guys be in constant motion and never caught standing around for even a single second, the herd was continually culled. Unconditioned, overweight, incompetent—the pace of the day showed no mercy for the exposed, and quite a few thought the Harris regulars were exploited idiots for tolerating such abuse. The idea that this hell could be therapeutic was not a thought rational people entertained. And then of course there was always the initial introduction to the inestimable Rigor Mortis.

Elias had been a walk-on, O-Zone was recruited by Rand, New Year brought along Cooter, and in between dozens of workers came and went. Some guys fit in perfectly but for whatever reason could not put down their roots. Like Smiley, a burly framer who had removable front teeth to replace the originals smashed out by a hockey puck years before. He wore his red hair in a giant afro that made him look like a demented lollipop. On his way to Costa Rica, Smiley was actually a violent hippie who instantly fed off the team dysfunction. He was also from Alaska, which made him the one guy no one else could bitch to about how awful the winters here were.

Then there was Herb, a fifty-year-old finish carpenter who had thirty-years' experience. After this crew had opened a portal onto his youth, Herb became revived. Because of his feathered gray hair, soft-spoken demeanor, killer smile, and reputation amongst the ladies, he was promptly nicknamed the Silver Fox, and usually consulted on issues concerning the fairer sex. Doing his best to hang on despite the pace, Herb lasted six months before returning to the lesser stresses finish carpentry presented.

But some did stay. Like "Showtime" Dan Delaney, a New Orleans native with degrees from Vanderbilt and Tulane. Loudly gregarious, Double D was at times hilarious, annoying, and possessed by a manic drive and gallon of coffee per day habit even Nolan could not top. With Brad Pitt's face on a portly body, and all inhibitions removed, Showtime's charisma was like a firehose to the face. When it came to jobsite personalities, no one—from the lowliest laborer to the GC of the entire job—no one held the stage like Showtime.

His partner was Robert Campbell, who everyone just called Soup. In his late thirties, Soup had a bad back but his intelligence, ponytail, and Western-style fedora quickly became trademarks. His dry wit counterbalanced Dave's explications, so they made a great team. Specializing in siding and interior finish work, their tight cuts and attention to detail were second to none, so Nolan brought them on as his own personal siding team.

With three crews, two subcontractors, and even Rigor Mortis back on board, Nolan had the company running like a buzzsaw through almost 10,000 square feet a month. Word was out. His ambition was ruthless. He wanted to own this valley, this county, this entire corner of northwest Colorado until every build site had a HARRIS FRAMING sign staked into the ground. Seven jobs? Why not seventeen going at the same time with guys puking from exhaustion? If it was out there for the taking, then why not indeed?

In late August, he called a meeting at his apartment. Rand, Rigor Mortis, Elias, and O-Zone arrived at eight o'clock.

"I don't usually like to do this," Nolan said, "but I guess I have to offer you pukes something to drink."

"What, Pepsi?" Rigor Mortis scoffed. "Teetotaling motherfucker."

"Hey," Kara Harris called out from the couch. She was curled up with a book and threw a look in his direction. "There's a lady present."

"I know." Riggy nodded at Elias. "She's standing right here."

After the laughter died down, Nolan told everyone to shut the fuck up and then apologized to his wife.

They stood around the kitchen table as a few impatiently checked the time. Nolan held up a roll of blueprints and said, "Since it's Friday night, I know you girls probably have hot dates, so I'll keep it brief. September arrives in one week, so guess what? We're gonna celebrate Labor Day by laboring. No one gets the day off so don't even ask."

A round of groans ran the table.

"September also means we've got less than eight weeks until it snows. But daddy's been looking out for you simpletons … check this out."

He unrolled the plans as everyone immediately leaned in for a glimpse.

"Wow."

"Holy shit."

"Is this a joke?"

Nolan, palming the table, looked up at them and said, "This is Cascade Peak. This is going to be our magnum opus, our Mona Lisa, our grand announcement to all of these bitches." He pointed at the two massive rectangles on the plans and said, "Say hello to the next eight months of your lives. This unit is 48,000 square feet. It's four floors and has thirty 1600 square foot condos." Nolan pointed at the other rectangle and said, "This sister unit is exactly the same and will be built right after."

There was silence as they devoured the images. Rand took charge and started at the foundation page as everyone leaned in for a closer inspection.

Nolan said, "A-Unit is slated to begin December 1st. And the best part for you ungrateful bastards is that the whole foundation, which is as big as a football field, will be covered by a heated tent. How does framing in shorts and T-shirts in the middle of December sound?"

By the cautious looks that were revealed, no one wanted to be the first, and thus the biggest pussy, to comment on this good fortune.

"A tent?" O-Zone reflected the collective skepticism. "With the snow loads—"

"And wind." Rand tapped the page. "But still, that's a great bonus."

"Here's what I'm thinking." Nolan pointed to a spot on the far-right corner of the table. "Out here on 61, there's a yard behind old Charlie's pathetic trailer park. Guess what? We're gonna build ourselves a plat-form and frame every single wall out there."

About to turn the page, Rand blinked. "We're gonna do *what?*"

"Every single motherfucking wall," Nolan repeated. "We're gonna build them, we're gonna stack them, and then we're gonna truck them over to the site and vomit this place into existence."

"That," Rigor Mortis said, "is absolutely crazy."

"Which is why you, out of anyone, should be immediately on board." Nolan glanced at the rest of them. "Trust me, daddy's got it all figured out."

Rand flipped from the second-floor to the third and fourth and said, "What's the roof height?"

"Fifty-five feet."

The truss plan seemed to humble the assembled group. Two massive dormers on each side of the roof would be hand-cut out of 2x10s, but all the rest were trusses.

"Obviously, we're getting into a whole different ballgame here." Nolan flipped the plans back to the foundation page and said, "Hold-downs are gonna have to be drilled five feet into the concrete and the holes loaded with epoxy."

"What kind of hold-down?" O-Zone asked.

"They're engineered for earthquakes. A ¾-inch rebar that will be drilled and bolted through the bottom wall plates. I can't lie, it's gonna suck ass, because the design schedule calls for one every six feet along the exterior walls and at every corner."

"Holy shit."

"Believe me ..." Nolan held up a thick binder. "There's so much hardware in this place the engineers gave me this just to keep track of it all."

"What about the height?" Rigor Mortis had his arms crossed. "There ain't a crane in the valley with enough stick for this."

"Which is why our friends in Germany have been contracted to lend a hand." Nolan pointed to a spot equidistant from each unit. "They're bringing in a fixed platform crane. I've seen a video on this thing and it's absolutely badass. It self-erects until it's 160 feet in the air. Any questions?"

"96,000 square feet in eight months?" Rand's chuckle built into a laugh, triggering the others.

"I quit," O-Zone said, and everyone rolled again.

"It won't be that bad," Nolan promised, but could not keep from smiling. "Seriously, you morons should take heart in the fact that you're gonna be a part of the build that breaks the county record for a continuous wood structure by almost 10,000 square feet."

"Make sure you tell that to the coroner," O-Zone cracked.

"Oh, there won't be any dying. You might at times be wishing you were dead, but no such good fortune awaits you."

"What about the crew?" Elias asked. "We're good, but we ain't that good."

"You're exactly right, Elias, way to admit your own inadequacies. Our friends on Team Beaver will be in town, and we'll also be hiring on another ten to fifteen local losers. Which is why I brought you guys here tonight. This—" Nolan's hand panned across the table. "This is the core of operations. I'm talking about a lot of responsibilities and even more work, so you're all just gonna have to hurry the fuck up."

"Hurry up," they echoed together.

Nolan proudly grinned. "You morons are something special, you really are."

"Right back at you." Rigor Mortis cracked his knuckles. "Okay. Unlike your little friends here, I don't need the pep talk."

"No, but you could always use a good beating." Nolan rolled up the blueprints. "All right, everyone out of my house. My wife and I have big plans."

From the couch, Kara rolled her eyes. "Yeah, right. Lemme guess. We're gonna watch SportsCenter for the next three hours."

The guys hooted as Kara enjoyed her burn.

"After they leave ..." Nolan held a mock fist aloft before shouting at the others, "All right, get the fuck out of here, meeting over, *adios*, goodnight."

He shuffled them out and closed the door.

"Do you think they were into it?" he asked, leaning against the fridge.

"Honey, those guys ..." Kara shook her head. "They'd follow you off a cliff."

"I'm not asking—"

"Seriously," she said. "It's practically unnerving."

During one of those rare occasions when Nolan considered the importance of team morale instead of the six-day work week, he gathered the crew at his storage unit at noon on a Friday. The trailer was emptied of tools and reloaded with tents, motorcycles, kayaks, and canoes. The women, who had filled a dozen coolers with food, beer, and ice, were already assembled at Nolan and Kara's apartment.

Cooter's wife, Jane, was a pleasant but talkative woman given over to scripture and proselytization. Her fourteen-month-old Elsie was within arm's reach at all times. Clayton, her three-year-old son, had Jane's brown eyes and Cooter's chin while also displaying an early knack for imitating his father's look of squint-eyed disapproval.

New Year's wife, Audrey, was Jane's younger sister, and while Jane was overly demonstrative, Audrey kept her own council outside the fringes of conversation. She had curly blond hair and blue eyes that positively beamed at her six-month-old son Evan. And that was it. After finding motherhood, even though they were both in their early twenties, each sister seemed fulfilled by what this destiny provided—mainly a bountiful family that adhered to God's word.

Also present was O-Zone's longtime girlfriend Beth. She managed a local ski equipment outlet, but was always wary around people she did not know. Beth had short brown hair and never wore makeup. But her athletic, toned body and pretty face were ruined by the intensity of her gaze. Originally from Centuria, Wisconsin, she had been in town for five years, dated O-Zone for the last three, and at twenty-nine impatiently awaited O-Zone's commitment to a more substantial arrangement. As always, Spring Valley accorded new arrivals an escape from their skeleton-filled closets, and Beth was no exception. Judged a local girl gone bad, she woke up one day to find her reputation for partying and ill repute was a branding no small town ever forgot. So she followed a friend to Colorado, visited Spring Valley by mistake, and reinvented herself. Astute and standoffish, she seemed constantly on guard against the breaching of her secrets.

Lena Holmscomb, despite her relationship with accountant Roger, was also in attendance. As things grew more complicated between her and Rand, Lena kept the focus on the kids. It was the only reason this dysfunctional family vacation was even possible.

Lena and her kids, Emily and Kenny, carried the supplies down from Kara's apartment. At just past one o'clock, the pickup trucks came careening around the corner in a swirl of dust and honking horns.

"Let the games begin …" Kara inventoried bottles of sunscreen, insect repellent, and the contents of a first aid kit.

Nolan and O-Zone sought out their women. Rand, Cooter, and New Year kissed their families. But Rigor Mortis and Elias remained in the truck. Riggy said, "Look at this fuckfest. What the hell are we doing here with all these speds? A weekend with other peoples' wives and kids?"

"Easy, big fella, take a deep breath, because this show's just begun."

"Here …" Rigor Mortis handed him a bowl and giant bag of weed. "It's your job to keep us constantly stoned."

"Don't forget about the boat. Didn't you want to check the oil?"

"Ahh …" Disgusted, Riggy threw open his door. Around back, the eighteen-foot Streamliner had a 375 Evinrude engine. Elias puffed on the bowl and watched him in the sideview mirror. He knew this was going to be a dangerous mission, seeing as how Riggy's own wife and kids were hundreds of miles away. He also knew hanging out with Rigor Mortis was a lot like playing with a snake—it might be exotic and dangerous, but it could also kill you.

Elias looked to where the couples coalesced around the excited children, but their mood was not contagious. Since arriving in the Valley,

Elias had scored with the occasional tourist, but quality local women, due to the skewed male-to-female ratio, usually meant suitors were lined up before the body of the last boyfriend was even cold. Backstabbing one another, screwing each other's girlfriends and wives, the males of the town were beholden to a million years of evolution and weak resolve while also wrecking every relationship in their path.

"Elias!" Rigor Mortis shouted. "Can you grab me that oil?"

Elias tapped out the bowl and reached for the quart bottles on the floor. Around back, Riggy worked a set of wrenches inside the guts of the Evinrude. He tapped his own wrist as if it was a watch and said, "It's beer-thirty, bro, grab us a couple of cold ones."

In the bed of the pickup, the Coleman cooler was more like a coffin-sized tomb stuffed with Coors and Maker's Mark.

"Señor!" Nolan yelled. "You gonna give us a hand with all this crap or what?"

"I'm busy!" Riggy nodded at Elias. "Go help that simple motherfucker, will ya?"

Climbing down, Elias said, "Both of you slave masters can kiss my ass."

"Everybody is somebody else's bitch, friend, welcome to the world."

"Hey!" Nolan yelled again. "Hurry up!"

Elias joined the group and said hello to the women.

"Thomas ..." Kara shoved some backpacks in his direction. "Are you ready for a weekend with the extended family?"

"You know me ..." He shouldered the gear and headed for Nolan's pickup. "Nothing says a good time like taking orders off the boss' wife."

"Which one?" Lena kicked in as well.

"Oh great." Elias rolled his eyes. "It's in stereo, too."

"Thomas, here!" Kenny chucked a football, but since Elias' hands were already full, it thumped off his shoulder instead.

"That's great, Kenny, you're a chip off the old block, all right. Always kick a man when he's down."

Kenny doubled over with laughter.

They heaved the gear into the trucks. Nolan double-checked the trailer stuffed with motorcycles and kayaks, and then told O-Zone and Beth to climb aboard.

Cooter and New Year packed their families into Cooter's rusted out Suburban.

Rand road shotgun in Lena's 4x4 Subaru.

Stuck with each other by default, Rigor Mortis turned to Elias and said, "Grab us some road sodas and pack that bowl, because this is going to be the worst weekend ever."

"Amen."

The caravan departed and they headed northwest on County Road 61 for a hundred miles. Unlike the treacherous ascent to Forked Head Pass in the opposite direction, the road lay flat upon a high plateau of scattered towns strung like dots along a line. The vast ranches that stretched in every direction had an eighty-to-one ratio of cattle versus humans.

Their destination, Flaming Gorge National Recreation Area, was shared by Wyoming and Utah 20 miles from Colorado's northwest border. The lake created by the completion of Flaming Gorge Dam in 1964, was 91 miles long and surrounded by 200,000 acres of land. In 1869, John Powell, a one-armed explorer who led a team from Green River, Wyoming, south along the Green and Colorado Rivers, called it Flaming Gorge because of the reflected sun blasting off the red rock cliffs.

The influx of tourists created five full-service marinas scattered along the southern and eastern shores. Boating, fishing, camping, jet skiing, and rock climbing were just a few of the activities alongside world-class stocks of lake trout, kokanee salmon, and smallmouth bass. On land, antelope, rabbits, lizards, western rattlesnakes, and assorted scorpions roamed the grounds.

Since the crew craved isolation, they headed for the more desolate western shore. WY 530 ran north to south, and unlike the steep cliffs and mountains ringing the southern and eastern coasts, the western edge of the reservoir bordered a high desert of scrub-covered hills rolling down toward the shore.

Nearing the end of the three-hour ride, Riggy shouted into his phone, "Nolan! Why are we the caboose? The King of Hurry Up is suddenly driving like a ninety-year-old bitch!"

Elias ignored him. Born and raised in a concrete box, he was, as always, awed by the passing landscape. The wide clear sky held the high sun like a stationary comet burning above where the road stretched on forever. Pebbled desert sprouted tufts of brush as the wind kicked up the dust.

"Fine!" Rigor Mortis ended the call and tossed his phone to Elias. "Watch this."

Out of all the phrases utilized by Rigor Mortis, none struck fear like this one. He punched the gas and rocketed the turbo-diesel into the opposite lane.

"Oh great." Elias could see a pair of approaching cars. "This is a great idea."

Rigor Mortis hooted as they passed Cooter's Suburban, but when Elias glanced in the sideview mirror, he saw their boat trailer ominously swaying side-to-side. "Hey, the fucking boat—"

"No more talking."

They pulled even with Nolan as Nolan pointed to their approaching death, but Riggy just gunned it harder.

"Suck it, grandpa!"

"Riggy! Jesus Christ!"

Their screams ended only after they swung in ahead of Nolan. Elias slowly blinked. Reaching for his cigarettes, he said, "That was awesome. Really, I mean that. Plowing into someone head-on at eighty miles an hour would really make this experience so much more enjoyable."

"Shut yer hole and pack a bowl."

"You're gonna lose them if you don't slow down."

"Fuck 'em." Rigor Mortis smiled. "They got a map."

From WY 530, it was a few miles over dirt roads until they reached the beach. With no one else around for miles, they set up camp mere feet from where the perfect blue water lapped ashore.

Kenny and Rand set off to collect firewood.

O-Zone and Elias helped Nolan erect the tents.

The women cataloged the coolers and secured the children.

And Rigor Mortis, as always, busied himself inside Cooter and New Year's affairs. Almost a crew within the crew, Riggy took a shine toward the wellbeing of "his boys" and their growing families. Otherwise not known for overt sentimentality, Rigor Mortis bought toys for their kids on Christmas and, when warranted, new boots and gear for their fathers. Currently, the three of them were seated in a circle cleaning and oiling their bolt-action .22s in the hopes of blasting some rabbit for dinner.

"How much ice do we have?" Kara wound her brown hair into a ponytail. The jean shorts framed out her summer tan.

The red-headed Lena, however, was layered under sunblock, ballcap, and sunglasses. A forty-three-year-old ex-athlete, her tank top revealed the hard work of old habits at the gym in the rare off-hours single moms cherished.

"There should be two Colemans loaded only with ice." Lena scanned for her daughter but she was already in the water. "Emmy! Come back and get some sunscreen!"

Rigor Mortis worked the action on his reassembled rifle. "That stuff causes cancer, you know."

"Paging Doctor Riggy? Seriously?" Lena threw him a look. "Why don't you just concentrate on making sure you don't kill anybody with that thing."

"Lady, I fire guns all day—"

"*Nail*guns, honey, nailguns. Try not to confuse the two."

Kara smirked. "Yeah, Rambo."

"Hey. My status is classified."

"It sure is, Mr. Hyde."

"Very funny."

New Year and Cooter chuckled until Nolan, who was swamped inside a tent and rapidly losing patience, screamed out, "O-Zone! Get me the fuck out of here!"

"Watch the language!" all five women yelled in unison, so no one rose to his defense.

By five o'clock, the tents were in a ring around the rock-lined fire pit. Even though it was eighty degrees, summer nights in the clear high desert sometimes dropped into the forties.

Rand and Kenny returned dragging a load of wood in a makeshift sling. The kindling was stacked amidst talk of dinner, but playtime was still at hand. Save for the women, everyone else was now splashing into the water.

With the camp organized, Kara, Lena, and Beth sat and cracked beers by the shore.

Kara watched the guys diving for footballs in the waist deep water and said, "Can't say they're not having fun. Somehow, they were at work five hours ago."

"On a Friday, too." Lena shook her head. "How they do it I'll never know."

Beth said, "The way O-Zone describes it, without this job, half these guys would be in prison."

"Ha-ha!"

Kara said, "That's not too far from the truth."

"Audrey, Jane!" Lena Holmscomb waved to where the sisters had corralled their infants. "If you need a hand with anything, just let us know."

The return looks were cool enough to wrinkle Lena's pride.

"Uppity little things, aren't they?" she whispered. "Babies having babies ..."

Kara said, "They're not that young."

"Maybe not physically." Lena took a swig off the beer and pointed toward the water. "Look at them out there. It's like recess at the zoo."

For the ladies, the sight was not altogether unpleasant. While the guys decked each other, their tanned bodies provided evidence on how they made their living. From the sheer number of calories burnt six days a week, excess body fat was nonexistent. Forearms and biceps were strung with veins connected to chests that varied in both hairiness and proportion. Nolan was as tall and wide as an oak door in a twelve-foot wall. Rand, however, had a body of near anatomical perfection. The women, behind their sunglasses, made ample note of this.

In the water, Nolan and Rand launched Kenny back and forth like a missile. Laughing hysterically, Kenny soared and crashed with a glee that made his father proud. On shore, fourteen-year-old Emily was too old to play with the kids but too young to hang with everyone else, so O-Zone took her aside to toss a Frisbee back and forth.

"Snap the wrist," he told her. "Let your arm follow through."

"Like this?" Her concentration paid off after it sailed into his gut.

"Nice. A couple more throws and we'll start working on your catches."

Watching the scene, Kara said to Lena, "It's amazing how big they're getting. Especially Emily."

"When we went shopping for new bras the other day, I told Rand she was already being asked out on dates and I thought he was going to be sick."

"I'd hate to be the first kid showing up for a date with her. Imagine dealing with that daddy?"

"Think Christine will have it any different?" Lena asked, referring to Nolan's daughter. "California or not, pain travels fast."

Kara sipped her beer. "Who knows, right? You never know."

Beth lit a cigarette and said, "You two thinking about that?"

"I dunno if that's a good idea. A part of me ... I just wonder if we could even pull that off, you know? And if not, how much longer we'd have together."

"You don't know that," Lena said. "How could you possibly know that?"

"Kids need stability. Our marriage ... it's hard. At some point the sixty-hour work weeks plus having a kid might just blow this whole thing apart ..."

"Lena's right," Beth said. "You never know. Hell, I can't even get O-Zone to buy me a ring."

"He's good with kids." Lena watched him and Emily toss a Frisbee. "He's really kind-hearted. And you can tell that he absolutely adores you."

"He does. It's not him, it's his parents. They went through such a bad divorce when he was a kid, he won't even talk about it."

"Has he ever spoken to anybody else?" Kara asked.

"Therapy?" Beth rolled her eyes. "Do you think any of these guys could ever open up like that? All I know is that I can't wait around forever."

Elias emerged from the water. He opened a cooler and started lobbing beers into the hands waving from the lake. "Incoming!"

"What about us?" Lena called out, so Elias lobbed three more toward the ladies.

On his way back with a bottle of whiskey, he said, "You girlies want to do some shots, or are you all just gonna sit there pretending to represent?"

Kara yelled, "Speaking of representing, we were just talking about you, Thomas. With a cute rear end like that, you'd almost make a beautiful woman."

"Better looking than you three hags!"

"Hey!" The three of them booed and hissed while Beth flicked her cigarette in his direction.

"Elias," Kara said, "is one hot mess."

"I never thought I'd meet anyone more depressing than Rand," Lena concurred.

"What about Riggy?" Beth asked. "Who could be worse off than that guy?"

Lena said, "Riggy's just crazy and sad. But Elias ... he once told me that even another billion years wouldn't fix the worst of who we are. I mean, who says stuff like that and actually means it?"

Kara swigged her beer. "I will never understand how they all found each other. It's like a fucking support group for the insane just popped up in the middle of the mountains ..."

"Is that a good thing for them or a bad thing for us?" Lena asked.

"I think it's good on both accounts. Without each other, like Beth said, they'd be in jail. And without us, they'd probably end up fucking one another since no one else can stand them."

"Oh my God." Beth laughed. "What have I gotten myself into?"

———————————

The kids were fed dinner before the adults popped more beers. Drug use was forbidden in front of the younger crowd, so the guys allowed themselves the occasional stroll along the coast.

Since the sun was still high at 7:00 P.M., everyone piled back into the water. Rigor Mortis and Cooter, in preparation for tomorrow's list of spectacles, backed the dirt bikes out of the trailer before inflating a pair of Zodiac boats.

While Cooter corralled his young son, wife, and daughter into one, complete mayhem broke out for seats on the remaining boat. Since Nolan was the only sober sailor, he called out immediately ignored commands as Rand, Rigor Mortis, and Elias sang illicit songs like drunken pirates. Completely out of sync, their paddle strokes torqued the boat in circles until Nolan, standing in the rear, used his oar to soak them all. Scrambling for cover, trying to return fire, the drunken crew lost their beers and then the fight, before turning on each other.

An hour later, the kids held impaled marshmallows over the fire. Above, the perfect black curtain was pinholed by a thousand dots. The pale moon glowed like a shadowy plate. As the temperature continued to drop, sweatshirts and hats were donned against the breeze.

While the adults and kids congealed around the bonfire, Rigor Mortis and Elias detached from the group. A deck of cards was broken out between shots of whiskey, and soon most of the crew had peeled away from their families.

"Hit me." Without drugs or alcohol, Nolan was fiending on the action.

"Gimme the ace," Elias pleaded. "Blackjack, baby!"

"Come on, Riggy," Rand threw down a twenty-dollar bill. "Cash me in."

Shouts of triumph and defeat rang across the site. Kenny, alerted by what young boys' thirst to know, quickly settled in next to his father.

"The dealer's showing a deuce," Rand whispered in his ear. "So I'm sticking with sixteen."

Kenny whispered back, "Why?"

"Because the two means even if he has a face card, he's gonna have to hit it. His chances of bustin' go up. Remember, he can't go over twenty-one."

"All right, girls, moment of truth." Rigor Mortis flipped his card to reveal a jack.

"Nice!" Nolan loved the juice. "Here comes the bust of the century."

"I second that..." O-Zone drunkenly smirked. "*Adios*, Señor Mortis."

Kenny whispered, "Why do they call him Rigor Mortis?"

"Because hanging out with him is worse than death."

"I heard that." Riggy dealt himself a card, paused for added drama, and then flipped it over as the crowd cheered and high-fived each other.

"Another face card," Rand told Kenny before reaching for his winnings. "Like clockwork."

Over by the fire, the women completely ignored them.

The following morning, Rigor Mortis played alarm clock by smashing the horn of his F-250. "Rise and shine, campers!"

Groans erupted.

"It's seven o'clock, people!" Beep-beep! "Hurry up!"

Inside Cooter and New Year's tents, babies started wailing.

"Dang it, Riggy!" Cooter's sleep-tossed head popped out of his tent like an angry ball from the unzipped seam. Fumbling with his glasses, he squinted and said, "Ain't you got even a shred of basic decency?"

"No." Riggy hit the horn again. "Elias! Let's go! We're already late!"

"Goddamn psycho ..." Elias shivered in the cold, sliding into his sweats and boots while wiping away the sleep. "Surprised you're not already boozing."

"Good point." Rigor Mortis foraged around the coolers like a deranged bear. He then hoisted a massive Bloody Mary in a mason jar and pointed at Elias. "You're driving."

"What the fuck, man, how about some coffee?"

"Oh sure thing, sweetie, lemme just brew you up a big hot cup of blow me."

"Both of you morons!" Nolan abruptly roared from inside his tent. "Get the hell out of here!"

Elias grinned as he jammed a screwdriver into Riggy's long since destroyed ignition switch. "Your stepdad sounds pissed."

"Fuck him." Rigor Mortis reached for the CD player. "Time for a lullaby."

He cranked Skinlab across the sleeping campers until Nolan's tent spasmed like a sickened stomach before vomiting him out in a pair of boxer shorts. He was so enraged he promptly tripped and sailed face first into the sand.

"Punch it!" Rigor Mortis screamed. "Here he comes, man, hurry up!"

Elias quickly wheeled the truck and boat down the path.

Watching Nolan recede into the background, Riggy cackled loudly. "Oh my God, what a stupid-dumb-bastard."

"Dude, that was some horrible shit."

"No kidding. Poor Kara. Did you *see* that motherfucker …?"

The trailhead dead-ended on WY 530. Since the beach at the campsite was too shallow to launch the boat, a marina thirty miles away on the northeast shore was their closest option. With his right boot cocked on the glovebox, Rigor Mortis watched the dawning scenery while nodding to the music. He packed a bowl, lit it for Elias, and then settled back into his seat.

Twenty minutes later, they found the Five Star Yacht Club was actually a concrete box stuck into the shore. Since it was one of the last Saturdays of the season, a line of pickups with boats were waiting to launch.

For a guy like Rigor Mortis, backing up with trailers of any kind had become second nature. But for those unaccustomed to the intricacies of these maneuvers, the spotlight could prove disastrous. Like a jury poised above the launch chute, occupants in the idling pickups passed judgment on those below that crumpled.

"Look at this fucking idiot." Riggy pointed at a jack-knifed trailer. "This is his sixth time trying to make it." He pulled himself out the window and screamed, "Hey, moron! Why don't you let your wife have a try!"

But Elias' turn was coming.

"You all set?" Rigor Mortis asked. "I would rather you be a total pussy and hand over the wheel now instead of making me look like one of those …" He nodded at the last guy with disgust.

"Just sit tight, superhero. You need a pen?"

"For what?"

"To take notes on the free lesson I'm about to give you." Elias swung into position and then geared it into reverse.

"Thatta girl." Riggy watched the concrete siding of the launch-chute sliding perilously close to his truck. "Remember what I told you. Submerge the trailer, release the wench, and then pull back up slowly. I got brand new slicks on this thing and don't want you burning up a thousand dollars on this slime-covered deck."

"I got it, dude, this ain't my first rodeo." Completely backed in, Elias levered the emergency brake. "Grab your rubber ducky, sailor boy …"

"Lock this shit up and I'll pick you up on the dock." Riggy climbed aboard and throttled the engine while Elias manned the wench.

"All right ..." Rigor Mortis scanned his surroundings, ignoring the jury above. "Ease her in."

As Elias cranked the wench-arm, the cable released, and the boat slowly slid into the water.

"Keep going." Riggy waited until the boat was floating freely and then raised a fist. He leaned over the bow and disconnected the cable. "Wind it in."

Elias did and then climbed back into the truck. The next pickup was already being signaled downhill, so he slipped into first gear and yanked the brake.

Nothing. The tires just spun as the pickup actually slid backward.

"I said take it slow!"

Elias eased off the gas but it made no difference. The mirrors showed the rear wheels slipping six inches beneath the water.

"*Slowly!*" Rigor Mortis bellowed.

"I can't go any fucking slower! Fuck this!" Elias switched the 4x4 from High into Low for added torque and punched it.

"*Goddamnit Elias!*"

"Get some!"

The tires spit out jets of water and green moss until skinning themselves on the cement. The smokeshow continued until the pickup shot forward onto drier pavement. The crowd hooted at the freebie, but Riggy was apoplectic.

———————

Coffee steeped inside a saucepan as the campsite awakened in fits and starts.

Still yawning, Lena Holmscomb cracked two dozen eggs into a bowl. Beside her, Cooter's wife, Jane, stabbed sausages onto metal skewers. Her blond hair, still tangled from sleep, was covered by a John Deere ballcap.

Lena said, "I love Clayton's outfit."

They both looked to where the three-year-old was clad head to toe in denim.

Jane smiled warmly. "Ain't he just the cutest thing ever?"

"Those little cowboy boots ..." Lena chuckled. "He looks just like his daddy."

"Sometimes James takes him out on the tractor ..." Jane watched him playing with his matchbox cars. "It just gives me such a warm feeling. I wish more people could be as lucky as us."

"Amen. These days, if you don't have a second home or a diversified portfolio, most of us might as well not exist."

Jane smiled politely. "I was speaking more about the Lord, and how wonderful it is to have Him right beside us, in our homes, and in our lives. James says it every night—we are a blessed family."

"Religion's nice ..." Lena cracked more eggs. "Anything that can help you gain perspective, right? Like education, for instance."

"Do you homeschool too?"

"Me?" Lena laughed. "I have a fulltime job, sweetie—actually three jobs if you count taking care of the kids and still doing Rand's laundry."

"Huh. Funny, I just don't think of it as a burden."

"What's that?"

"Motherhood." Jane's look said she was trying to be pleasant. She skewered another sausage and said, "I'm looking forward to homeschooling Clayton. The public schools these days ... it just flat out scares me to think about what might be going on."

"Honey, look at my kids."

They watched Kenny chase a squirrel with a stick.

Lena wiped her hands. "All right, take Emily. Academically she's in the top five percent of her class. She's funny, she's smart, and she knows how to be around other kids."

"Are you saying homeschooled kids can't socialize?"

"No, I'm not. I just think people lead better lives if they're trying to find the middle. Of anything—whether it be their politics, education or even ... or even their religion."

Now Jane's smile pulled into a tight line. She jammed the sausage down the skewer and said, "Well, if raising children is such a burden, I can see how maintaining an active spiritual life could also be considered 'fanatical.'"

"Excuse me? I love my children—"

"By calling them a job?"

"At least I'm not reckless. This neurotic nonsense about immunizations is absolutely appalling. Your kids are in jeopardy every second of every day."

"Yes, well at least they still have their daddy around. The Lord said the path would never be easy, so abandoning one another after pledging otherwise would surely seem to be in flagrant disregard of His wishes."

"You little bitch—"

"Okay, okay ..." Kara came flying between them. "Let's not do this here."

"Stop pushing me." Lena tried to escape from Kara. "Why're you coming after me? She's the one—"

"Please." Kara nodded at the gathering audience, which included most of the kids. With her hand on Lena's back, Kara steered her toward the beach. "Let's just take a walk, all right?"

"This is bullshit, Harris."

The reservoir stretched before them like a vast blue tabletop.

Lena said, "I don't know what it is about that girl that gets me so unglued. Did I make a mess? Was it a scene?"

"Lady Mortis?"

"Awesome. I told you I wasn't a morning person."

"She touch a nerve with that Rand comment? I heard the tail end of that blast as I approached."

"That little ... We slept last night with the kids between us but ..."

"It must be tough. Maybe this thing with Roger is more serious than you thought."

"I ..." Lena seemed more resigned than startled. "I guess it is. We—me and Rand—haven't slept together in over a year but still ... I never felt awkward about just *being* with him, you know?"

"You're walking a pretty tight rope there, sister."

"You got that right."

"Still, it's nice to see you all together again."

"It's like a time warp, right?"

They walked along the beach until something darted into view. It looked like a toppled triangle rocketing across the water.

Kara said, "Wow, that guy's flying."

"Is that ...?" Lena squinted.

The boat arced wide before re-setting its sights directly at them.

"Unbelievable," Kara said in awe. "Riggy's playing chicken against the earth."

———————

By 9:30 A.M., Rigor Mortis shuttled the adults out four at a time to either wakeboard or water ski. Here was the softer side of Rigor Mortis, giving instructions, checking the lines, and laughing like one of the boys.

Cooter buckled his wife and kids into lifejackets. Because he wore jeans at work even in summer, Cooter's pale legs glowed like incandescent sticks. His bottom lip was packed with Copenhagen. He held onto the canoe in waist deep water while trying to instruct his son.

"Grab it like this ..." Cooter gripped the toy-sized oar as example before handing it back to Clayton. "Nice smooth strokes, son."

Clayton's tiny fists brought the oar down with a splash. Liking the way it soaked his dad, he reloaded again and again until making himself hysterical.

"All right, that's enough." Cooter confiscated the weapon as he saw his wife smiling from the stern. He pushed up his soaked eyeglasses and squinted to gain a clearer focus. "I saw that, Miss Jane."

"As always," she said, "I am only laughing with you."

"I highly doubt that. And how's Miss Elsie handling her first day at sea?"

Clutched in Jane's arms, Elsie's wide blue eyes rotated in the way infants oddly wonder.

Jane said, "Don't let us get too far from shore."

"Baby, I'm only hip deep out here. Besides," Cooter nodded out toward Riggy's traveling circus. "We need to keep those yahoos on our scope."

As if cued, Rigor Mortis swung a gentle arc across the horizon. One-arming the toe-rope, O-Zone cut a picture-perfect arc on the wakeboard's edge. On par with Rand's level of expertise, O-Zone was pure instinct. And while Nolan and Riggy were mercilessly competitive, blunt force and big balls played no part in the deft touch required for a spinning backflip, which O-Zone now threw, ramping off the engine's chop.

For a city boy, Elias held his own. But New Year and Cooter, wildly thrashed into spectacular crashes, earned their stripes in pain.

———————

Rigor Mortis' mood of relative normalcy had, throughout the afternoon, markedly declined. While the others played volleyball and dirt-biked, he packed his boat with beer and roared off into the fjord alone. Made immune to these tectonic mood swings long ago, none of the campers gave it a second thought.

Dinner came and went in a splashed sunset across the desert. A raging fire was surrounded by sixteen faces, while off in the gathering shadows creatures embraced the night, creatures like Rigor Mortis, who suddenly reappeared with his searchlight blasting along the coast. The boat was on slow approach, its engine a chugging gurgle until an anchor crashed the surface. He killed the lights and engine before slipping over the edge and swimming to shore.

In his absence, the jovial mood had been bolstered by alcohol and a pair of acoustic guitars. Rand went solo until Beth, after O-Zone's prodding, answered him one-for-one. Trading riffs, Beth's awkwardness disappeared into the supportive cheers and clapping hands.

Nolan and Elias were seated outside the firelight. Elias chased whiskey while Nolan chain-smoked.

Nolan nudged him. "Hey ..."

They clocked Rigor Mortis emerging like a specter from the water before heading directly into his tent.

Nolan said, "He's been out there for hours."

"Yeah ..."

Nolan looked back to where Rand and Beth led a rousing rendition of the Beatles' "Paperback Writer."

Elias scanned the animated faces in the dancing flames, cataloging the singing and laughter. He seemed fearful of what lay in store for them after Rigor Mortis emerged from his tent and skulked by the coolers. Outside the firelight, he then disappeared into the shadows.

The song ended amid applause and scattered greetings to the new arrival, but Riggy ignored them while devouring a sandwich. At his boot stood a half-full bottle of Maker's.

The fire was reloaded and poked until a flotilla of embers soared into the sky. The guitars charged through Jane's Addiction's "Jane Says" as people sang and people drank.

An hour later full dark descended amid a smatter of conversation. A segue from local events and issues led to a discussion on the land and vast ranches up for bid.

"So out of 360 houses originally proposed," Jane said, "you stopped 245 from being built?"

"Yes."

"That's right," Lena proudly said. "That's our Kara. It's quite an accomplishment."

"According to who?" As Rigor Mortis' voice lurched out of the dark, heads swiveled to pinpoint his face. "Far as I can tell, the only thing she did was take money out of our pockets—" Riggy nodded at the circle. "Out of *all* our pockets."

"Oh, here we go ..." Nolan was suddenly alerted. "It was coming sooner or later."

"245 houses ..." Riggy scoffed, his body a drunken sway. "You must be fucking kidding me."

"Hey!" Lena motioned toward her kids. "Ease up on the wording, will ya?"

"No, I won't. The rest of you can sit here like a bunch of hippies saluting socialism, or you can stand up for what's right."

"They want to cut and pave the entire valley," Beth countered. "Some of us have a problem with that."

"And some of us like to *eat*." Rigor Mortis slowly paced, his face splashed by the flickering flames. "The only thing these idiotic hippies did was steal about three years' worth of work from a place that already doesn't have shit all else to offer."

"Exactly who are you calling idiotic?" Nolan was still seated but losing patience. "I know you're not talking about my wife like that ..."

"You?" Riggy laughed. "After all the shit you talk behind her back, now you're going to defend her?"

"I never—"

"All three of you cunts," Riggy drunkenly accused. "You're out of your fucking minds."

In the second it took for a collective gasp, Nolan and Rand gave chase. Once they became lost into the darkness, the crowd heard a crash of bodies and a shout before the sudden violence. By the time O-Zone, Elias, and Cooter found them, Riggy was beneath both Nolan and Rand.

"You just never learn, do ya?" Nolan's hand was a smashing piston. "Calling my wife a cunt? Are you out of your fucking mind?"

Rand twisted Riggy's head after he tried spitting into their faces.

"Nolan, what the fuck ..."

"Get the fuck back, Elias." Nolan gave him a hateful glance. "If anything, you should be helping ..."

Riggy's teeth were smeared in blood as he drunkenly cackled. "You fucking morons."

Kara leaned over his face and said, "Apology accepted."

Rigor Mortis tried to re-focus despite the booze and beating. "I never apologized."

"You will now, though."

He took two more blows before his cheek split open. He gasped and wheezed, drooling blood. "Enough, all right, I'm sorry."

"We're finished with you tonight." Nolan glanced at Elias. "Start packing up his shit. You're driving him home."

"What? What about the boat?"

"Take my truck." Nolan slung him the keys. "I'll get his fucking boat in the morning."

Sets of hands pulled a dazed and bloodied Rigor Mortis to his feet. Like a scarecrow, they threw his arms around their necks and half-dragged him toward the truck. "He'll just never get it..." Lena's face held the shock-like residue. "It will never be any different ..."

"You know what?" Kara said. "I think I'm over it."

She took Nolan by the arm and led him up the shore.

Riggy was passed out cold and leaning against the passenger side window. The others stood in the headlights of Nolan's idling pickup.

"I'm sorry about this." Nolan clenched his jaw. "You all right to drive?"

Elias said, "Sure."

They both knew it was a lie.

"I tried not to break his nose." Nolan peeled off a pair of hundreds. "In case you need gas or a motel."

"Yep."

"Hey ..."

Elias turned back as Nolan said, "I'll have my cell on if anything happens."

"Stop sweating this. See you back in the valley, bro."

The taillights faded like red eyes into the dark.

After drinking all day, and the three-hour drive home, Elias passed out on Rigor Mortis' couch. In the morning, raked by dry mouth and a pulsing headache, he heard what he thought could only be part of a dream.

"Wake up, fuckface."

It was not a dream. Elias cracked a squint to see Rigor Mortis hovering above him with two black eyes and a blood-smeared face. "Morning, sunshine. Mind telling me what the fuck is going on?"

"Dude ..." Elias was still reconstituting his state of mind. "What time is it?"

"Nine-thirty." When Riggy smiled, his split lips oozed blood. He was wearing sweatpants and a bloodstained T-shirt. "What the hell happened to me?"

"Are you saying you don't remember anything?"

"Moron, where's my fucking truck and boat? Why is fuckface's vomit green shitwagon parked in my driveway? And why the fuck does my face look like a pizza?"

"Oh my God," Elias groaned, pulling the pillow over his head. "Sometimes just knowing you is worse than having internal bleeding ..."

"Dude!"

"All right!" Elias swung himself upright on the couch. "You took your own private booze-cruise, called the chicks cunts, and Nolan lost a nut ... him and Rand. But you don't look half as bad as I thought you would."

"Oh, so you think this is all right?"

"Considering? Hey, where you going?"

"To shower," Rigor Mortis called out. "And get the fuck out of my place."

The camping trip was over. Elias went back to sleep.

CHAPTER SEVENTEEN

After the proposed land development concerning the big three ranchers and the CPS was settled, the other major issue, Proposition 6, was finally readdressed by the beleaguered town. Once it was included on the upcoming November ballot, people realized that their primary angst—the vast ranch sales—had now been largely cauterized. Like the relief found after pulling a rotten tooth, the citizens had a chance to exhale and reevaluate exactly what was in the town's best interests. No one really wanted to annex anything, but most agreed that the dilapidated area of downtown targeted by the eminent domain statutes was an eyesore compared to the remodel Main Street was currently undergoing. Besides, since most of the affected homeowners had all but signed off on the generous offers for their land and homes anyway, momentum in favor was steadily gaining.

As word continued to spread, and builders poured into the valley, guys like thirty-three-year-old Chris Carmichael began arriving. Originally from Leadville, he was an unathletic six-foot carpenter who now specialized in siding and trim. He had his own tools, scaffold, and trailer, and had hired on a friend rudely nicknamed Spud because of a particularly oversized endowment. Competent but always stoned, Spud was thin and bearded, simple in his tastes.

As if to prove that a man and his beast could personify one another, Carmichael, who wore an unruly mop of red hair and baggy flannels, treated his giant black Newfoundland named Tucker like a shaggy drooling brother. The dog was massive but unaggressive, and had a bark like a cannon. Slowed by age, he still adhered to every command and, whether Chris was at work or running errands, Tucker either roamed the jobsite or waited patiently in the shotgun side of the truck. Team

Hate was not big on loose affections, but Tucker was always treated like one of the boys.

Though gregarious, Chris enjoyed living in the middle of nowhere twenty miles up Fortitude Pass. In his garage, he tinkered with stand-alone tools collected from a different era. Three lathes of varying size, a thickness planer, drill press, a joint planer, and bandsaw were just a few of the cast iron monsters dating back to the 1930s. More importantly, they still worked better than anything made in the seventy years since. And while he could have made more money crafting old world tables, chairs, and balusters, his love for the outdoors finally made working in a dust-filled shop impossible. He seemed good-natured until he hit the jobsite, and then all bets were off. Nolan nicknamed him Red Riggy two seconds after meeting him that fateful day. By chance, Nolan had stopped by a job to bid on a potential frame. Dismounting from his truck, he heard Carmichael completely losing his mind on the project manager. Cost overruns, slow pay, delayed build schedule—Carmichael listed his litany of complaints, said he was losing money, and then loudly wondered if the guy was partially mentally incapacitated. They almost came to blows, but Carmichael got fired instead. Nolan, observing the entire exchange from twenty-feet away, took heed of Carmichael's criticisms and got back into his truck without bidding on anything.

On the drive back, he thought of his own siding team and decided there was nothing wrong with a little competition. Showtime and Soup were kicking ass, but Nolan liked Carmichael's demeanor. He called him up and the next day they met for coffee and smokes in a vacant lot.

As it was with every eventual longtime employee, Nolan knew from the first handshake that a similar thought process and work ethic were shared by each. Nolan did not mind snapcases like Rigor Mortis, Rand, and Red Riggy—guys who would abruptly lose their shit and start tossing tools and wood and cursing. Hell, they could show up high on PCP and light themselves on fire for all he cared, just so long as the work got done. Hurry up.

During their conversation, Carmichael revealed that he had dabbled with many careers through the years, but turning into an LSD chemist who would eventually supply northern California and much of the Northwest, meant his name started traveling in all the wrong circles.

Production increased too rapidly, and potential customers were no longer properly vetted. After a longtime courier got popped at Denver International Airport carrying a book of paintings that also happened to be sheets of acid, Carmichael's name got squeezed out as part of the courier's deal. When the F.B.I. showed up with a warrant twenty-four hours later, Chris lit a cigarette and watched the destruction of his whole life. He was looking at federal conspiracy, distribution, and possession charges carrying fifteen to twenty-five years. His lawyer was nervous because if it went to trial, with the courier's testimony and the size of the seized lab, half his life could be lost. As part of Chris' deal, he kept those who had been loyal out of trouble but handed over two violent deadbeats as payback for past transgressions. After pleading out, he was sentenced to six years and flown to a high security federal prison in California where, as luck would have it, he was assigned a notorious cellmate. Aguilar Desoto was six-foot-three and had the large barrels of his arms and chest covered in the stained purple ink of serious convict paint. Desoto was also a founding member of the Oakland chapter of Los Soldanos serving ten years on a second-degree manslaughter charge. The California Attorney General was busy trying to charge him with fourteen other murders in a pending RICO case. Carmichael, as they led him down the cellblock, only hoped he would die a quick and painless death. Soon, though, he felt pretty foolish, because while Desoto's credentials were not in doubt, and Carmichael imagined all of the horrific fates every convict fears, not a single one of them ever materialized. There was no stabbing, beatings, or rape, as happened to some of the less fortunate prisoners incarcerated without allegiances to save them. Instead, Desoto, who took pride in his small living space and the peace within its confines, also took a vested interest in the wellbeing of his cellmate. Sure, he could have turned Carmichael into his own personal toilet, but Desoto was not a robot—at some point even he would have to close his eyes, and that's when all the toughness and fear in the world meant nothing with his throat cut ear to ear. In consequence, they became friends and eventually shared meals and the other necessities guys doing serious time traded and bartered beneath the prison's notice. Because of Desoto's influence, Carmichael got the easiest jobs, partook in the contraband loot other prisoners paid Desoto as protection, and not once, in the ensuing six years, did he ever again fear for his life. That luxury alone was worth more than any small mission Desoto requested. With the eleven gang captains under constant surveillance, communication and orders were issued through others. And while people might have gotten hurt as a consequence of the messages Carmichael delivered, this was still prison, and surviving it in one piece brought no shame.

As Carmichael told the story, Nolan was transfixed. They were chain-smoking Marlboro Lights in the falling snow until Nolan said, "That's some of the craziest shit I've ever heard."

"Right?" Carmichael had a graveled voice and, like his dog, was at times over-supplied with saliva. "I got out fourteen months ago and headed to the top of the closest mountain."

"I'll bet you yodeled your fucking balls off."

"Damn straight. I had some cash the feds never found, so I was able to get up and running pretty quick."

They smoked in silence.

"You should know ..." Carmichael seemed loath to admit it. "You should know that I got time left on parole ... this little bastard named Sykes has his head stuck halfway up my ass twenty-four hours a day."

"I know Sykes. And you're right, he's a tremendous douche. But I ain't worried about that. Believe me, half my guys are on probation and the other half probably should be."

Carmichael smiled. "Sounds like a good crew."

"The best. And with you being new in town with no references, and all that fucked up history ... Come on board and I'll put you on the books as a sub. 1099. You'll bid me job to job."

"That would be great, man." Carmichael exhaled through both nostrils, glancing along the valley floor. "How much longer do you figure?"

"For what?"

"This boom. There's some real fucking hackshows pulling into town."

"After November's vote, they'll keep on building until the money runs out, bro, you can bet on that."

"Nice."

"Yeah." Nolan stuck out his hand. "We got a deal or what?"

"Fuckin' A, we do." Carmichael gripped it and said, "You won't be sorry, man, I really appreciate it."

"Don't thank me yet. Winter's on the way. Pack a lunch ..."

"Ha."

They lit another pair of smokes as the daylight began to wane.

———————

One month later it was October and the townsfolk, aware of winter's imminent arrival, took last rides on their bikes and boats before the first snows arrived.

The town was also bracing for the impending influx of 4,000 workers and second-home owners, in addition to the thousands of tourists arriving and departing weekly on vacation. By November, most businesses hired fulltime staffs and took a loss until Thanksgiving weekend, the unofficial opening to the season. The ski and snowboard stores were already running last year's stock at a fifty percent discount and, like every other business, re-stocking fresh inventory off tractor-trailers arriving daily from Denver and Salt Lake City.

As for the building community, chaos was at hand. While a third of the crews shut down for the winter, the die-hards fought to get enough concrete foundations dug and poured to last until spring. Favors were called in, and tempers easily flared.

When summer and fall collided head-on, the weather created monsters like this morning's windstorm. All night, Nolan listened to it whipping and rattling until finally, at 3:00 A.M., he grabbed a flashlight and hit the road. He made two loops past all seven ongoing jobs which, despite his fears, remained upright and intact. The same, however, could not be said of a handful of other sites he passed. Three jobs had their roof trusses toppled like dominoes, and six more had walls blown over onto the ground.

Unable to sleep, he left again at 6:00 A.M. to make another loop before meeting the crew at 7:00. He, Rand, and Elias were working on one of four duplex condominiums alongside three other crews at a job called Cliffside Park. As its title implied, the condos were literally stanchioned into a granite ledge along Mt. Lassiter's western face. The wind, which blew northeast over the mountain and downhill toward town, smashed through their jobsite before any other obstacle broke its path. Gale-force warnings had been in effect since midnight, and a line of severe thunderstorms was already assaulting Moffat and Rio Blanco Counties. The sky was a swollen mass of roiling clouds as Nolan heard the radio pegging wind speeds at 98 MPH. Trees, bent forty-five degrees and spraying needles and leaves, were almost ready to snap.

As the pickup rocked amid the windblasts and flying debris, Nolan feared his windshield might crack. Up ahead, he saw the jobsite and the trees which, because of the sheer velocity this high up the mountain, were flattened into layered steps.

He parked on the paved road behind a Dodge Ram full of guys from a different crew. As he forced open his door, the wind caught it and nearly smashed it into his left front tire. He saw something in the bed of their pickup, a trio of levels that poked out from beneath a tarp and looked oddly familiar, but he could not see if they were painted. With the ominous sound of creaking wood heard from fifty-feet away, Nolan grabbed his bags and made a mad dash uphill.

There were four units under construction. Nolan's was on the far right. The first-floor walls had been completed, the floor rolled and sheeted, but the exposed second-floor walls now groaned beneath the onslaught. It was eight hours work stood and braced off with 2x4s which, to Nolan's horror, could be seen clearly vibrating through the hurricane-force winds. Just standing on the second-floor deck proved challenging as leaves, dust, stones, and grit sliced through the air. Then he saw one of his tool chests fly open because the locks had been cut and were laying on the deck. Had someone stolen his shit? There was no time for that now. He feared the back wall would smash in and kill him first, so he added three more 2x4s while behind him, with a sudden crack, the entire left side wall sheared its bracing and toppled from the deck. Enraged, he cursed and squinted and at one point hung onto a brace just to remain upright. The gales were so relentless that the right-side wall, tired of this fight, exploded from its bracing. All around him, he could hear the smashing of walls at surrounding jobs but would not leave the deck. He saw the truckload of guys down there pointing up at him and ... and were they *laughing*?

The loss of the side wall forced him into action as the front wall trembled with ominous moans. Squatting just to maintain balance, he pulled four 2x4s across the deck and was attempting to nail them in when he saw the Skylark screech to a stop below. Rand and Elias, having spotted him, grabbed their bags and immediately sprinted uphill against the whipping shrapnel. Clattering up the ladders, they were nearly blown flat on deck and had to quickly readjust to these conditions. Nolan hung onto a 2x4 as if he might, by sheer will alone, hold the wall in place.

"Look at that!" Rand screamed, pointing at the bellying back wall. "If that thing goes we're dead!"

"I already reinforced it! Help Elias, man, that whole front wall's getting ready to go!"

The groaning had turned into a horrible creaking of wood slowly splitting. Nolan could see the nails on the brace he was holding gradually working free as around him, blasting across his face, it seemed the entire place might soon blow apart.

Rand and Elias nailed in six more braces on both the front and back walls before Nolan shouted, "Enough! We're outta here."

They headed for the ladders. Down below in the sheltered carport, they huddled and lit up smokes.

"Jesus Christ." Nolan's eyes were saucers. "This whole place might go."

"I never would've agreed with that," Rand said, "but I've never, in twenty years of this misery, I have never seen a 2x4 pulled apart by the grain."

"Never. I thought the blocks would pull up off the floor and some did. But that—to have the actual 2x4 pull apart in the middle—I don't ever want to see that again."

Elias said, "We better check on the other jobs."

"Not yet." Nolan's boot squashed his smoke. He pointed at the cut locks and open tool chests. "We gotta make a quick stop first. Think I caught these fucks stealing our shit."

"*What?*"

Rand said, "Noll, they're working right next to us. They couldn't use that shit without us seeing—"

"The pawnshop pays cash money, bro. Who knows? Maybe they just have a death wish."

Bent into the blasting wind, Nolan led them around back and

further downhill so their approach would remain unseen. They crossed the street and behind the cover of bushes, paralleled the road. They remained hidden as they neared the vehicles.

Nolan dropped his bags and whispered, "Lemme check the gear in the back. If they jacked us, I'm going for the driver."

Nolan slipped between the bushes. The wind had blown back part of the tied-off tarp, so Nolan saw the green and red stripes that he had spray-painted on the levels himself. Since jobsite larceny was a high crime, Rand and Elias waited for Nolan to make the first move before they exploded through the bushes. In the truck, pot smoke clouded the better judgment of the occupants who, without locking their doors in time, now found themselves under attack.

Of the five guys in the truck, after the first three were yanked out and thrashed, the remaining two sprinted away. Nolan paid special attention to the lead guy named Phipps, who was from out of town, annoying, and had been a know-it-all braggart since his arrival from Grand Junction. The fact that this piece of shit, a twenty-year guy, would rip Nolan off and then laugh as he almost got killed on deck, meant this morning would turn into Phipps' own private lesson. On the ground, as Nolan close-fisted Phipps' face back and forth like a bleeding piñata, it seemed that the lines of communication were definitely opened up between them. On the other side of the car, Nolan could hear Rand slamming something against the hood and guessed it was the head of Phipps' buddy.

"No! Please, my nose!"

Through the car windows, Nolan saw Elias' elbow smashing into someone's face. The music of violence was filled with grunts and gurgling sounds until Rand pulled back and shouted, "Let's go!"

"You fucking thief." Nolan reared back and punched Phipps' head into the ground for the dozenth time. "Who's laughing now, you thieving puke?"

"Fuck, man, he can't even hear you." Rand shoved Nolan off the guy's chest. "For Christ's sake!"

Breathing hard, Nolan spit into Phipps' destroyed face before standing into the raging wind.

"Elias!" Rand screamed, "what the fuck, man, what the fuck!"

Elias stopped, his eyes filled with a swirling malevolence.

Standing over what they had done, all around them the wind now filled with rain.

"Let's go!" Rand grabbed the tools and then strong-armed them toward the truck.

"Naw, man, my car." Elias scanned for witnesses, holding out his bloody hands as if they were suddenly covered in shit. "Let's roll."

The rain was now a full assault as Nolan said, "Meet back at my place."

Inside the F-250, Rand took the keys from Nolan and said, "What do you think?"

They inched forward past the slow crab-like movements of the bodies as Nolan said, "I think that since this is the first time you've driven a vehicle in over a decade, you better not fuck up my truck."

"Three years isn't a decade."

"As if it matters. You won't be getting your license back because you're not too fucking bright ..."

"Funny you should say that." Rand sped up toward the corner. "Tell me, since those idiots we just smoked are working right next to us, how you think this little massacre's gonna shake itself out?"

"Are you kidding me?" Nolan pulled off his shirt and wiped his soaked face and lacerated knuckles. "If those pukes have any manhood left they'll just keep their mouths shut, stop stealing other people's shit, and try not to piss us off again."

"Yeah, I guess their other approach didn't work out too good."

"Naw, man, I wouldn't say so."

They took a right down Snowmass Road and saw, out along County Road 30, a line of black clouds rolling in like a soot-smeared wall.

Nolan knew the beaten crew would remain silent, because if word got out that they were thieves, their reputation was finished. Period. There was no worse offense than stealing someone else's tools, not amongst guys who made a living pinching every nickel and dime just to buy them. Nonetheless, Nolan switched out personnel just in case. Rand and Elias were sent back to the boathouse job and Rigor Mortis took their place. Pulling on-site, Riggy further punished Team Phipps who, despite their gruesome welts, cuts, and discolorations, stalwartly shouldered their disgrace. Even as Rigor Mortis called them pussies and shit on their work and asked why they allowed their boyfriends to beat on them so badly, and while he shouted out the phone number for a domestic abuse hotline and told them it was okay that they liked it up the ass, the other crew refused the bait and instead redoubled their efforts, if only to escape the pain.

In mid-October, Nolan and Elias were snapping lines on the foundation of the newest job when a strange caravan approached. Three white guys got out of the lead Chevy pickup, and in the rear two vans, after the doors slid open, eight Mexicans abruptly appeared.

"Huh," Nolan said, winding up the chalkline. "What do you think this is?"

"The beginning of the next nightmare," Elias quipped, and Nolan could not disagree.

"Afternoon," one of the white guys called out. His freckles were dots on a sun-creased face, his red hair parted and unruly. "We just got into town. I'm Wade. Wade Shannon."

They shook hands.

"Nolan." Behind his sunglasses, Nolan gave away nothing.

"Nice spot out here, huh?" Wade Shannon made a point of scanning their surroundings. "Yeah, you guys sure are lucky to be up here."

"Can I help you with something?" Nolan dispatched Elias to the other side of the foundation with the chalkline.

"Well, we just got in from Washington state. I saw your sign at a couple of different jobs and they said I might find you here."

"What do you do?" Nolan pulled the chalkline tight through the crow's foot, looked over at Elias who nodded that he was ready, and then snapped it in a huff of red dust.

"Computer programming," Shannon said, but the joke lamely failed. "Naw, we're framers. This is Buck—" he pointed to a bald guy shaped like a bowling pin. "And this is Richie—" he nodded toward a smaller man with black hair worn high and tight like a Marine. "We're looking for work."

"What made you guys come all the way out here?" Nolan reeled in the line as he walked to the next corner trailing these new companions. "Washington's a long way off."

"Change of scenery." Shannon nodded at the Mexicans. "With eleven guys on board, we need to keep things rolling."

"Uh-huh." Nolan sent Elias ahead with the chalkline one last time to complete the box. "You planning on staying through the winter, because lemme tell you, this ain't no rainy season."

"Shit, man, we're ready."

"What about them?" Nolan nodded toward the vans. "Any guys with skills?"

"Oh yeah, hang on." Shannon stuck two fingers into his mouth and whistled.

A pair of Mexicans detached and booted through the mud.

Shannon said, "This is Alonzo and Perfidio. They're brothers and lead guys that really know their shit. The others have varying skills, speak some English, but all of them work like hell."

"Nice." Nolan shook hands with Perfidio and Alonzo, sizing them up like a rancher viewing cattle. "*Hola, vatos, ¿como te va?*"

They grinned, and while smaller than Nolan would have liked, he could tell by their calloused grips that this was not their first day on the job. They held his gaze as Perfidio, who wore a thick black mustache and seemed the spokesman for the pair, thickly said, "Things are good, sir, how for you?"

"Oh man, he's the only one that has to call me sir." Nolan nodded at Elias who instantly frowned. Nolan turned back to Shannon. "Eleven guys, huh? My number's on my truck. Gimme a call after dinner and I'll see what we can do."

"That's awesome, man, thanks." Shannon shook his hand, and having not been introduced to Elias, nodded at him awkwardly. "Okay great, I'll look forward to speaking with you later."

"Yep."

Nolan and Elias returned to work, waiting until the caravan faded from view.

"What do you think?" Nolan finally asked.

"Well, that Shannon guy looks like Danny Bonaduce, man, what the fuck?"

Nolan laughed.

"Seriously," Elias said. "What about his partners, Uncle Fester and the Clean Marine?"

Nolan was now cackling and said, "Team Bonaduce."

"Total posers, man, you better hope those Mexicans can pick up their slack."

"White guy disease?"

"You saw them. Pimping all the way."

Nolan lit up a smoke. "But eleven guys doubles our workforce with another ten on sub."

"Don't overdose on the dollar signs, Mr. Trump, because you don't know a fucking thing about them."

"We'll give them this." Nolan nodded at the hole in the ground. "A two-story box with gable ends? Hell, even a half-conscious moron like yourself could frame this joke."

"Don't do me any favors." Elias dug out a cigarette of his own. "Can you take me back to work, or do I have to stand here like you stroking it for the rest of the day?"

"There will be no tandem strokings." Nolan stored the chalkline in his bags and then pointed at his truck. "Princess, your carriage to the fuckshow awaits you."

———————

While the scenery might change, the actual routine of building never varied. A task commenced, a rhythm became established, and the individual pieces inside the machine coalesced into an established groove. The accompanying conversation, however, usually went from bad to worse.

Rigor Mortis, O-Zone, Cooter, New Year, and Elias were dropping plywood sheets over a maze of floor joists. New Year used a caulk gun to apply beads of adhesive to the joists before O-Zone dropped down a 4'x8' sheet. Cooter then used a sledgehammer to tap the tongue-and-groove sheeting tightly together before Rigor Mortis blasted it off with the nailgun. Elias, ferrying the sheets across the yard, kept the machine fed with wood.

"—that's not what I was saying," O-Zone said. "Titties are nice but they aren't everything."

"Bullshit." Rigor Mortis pushed him aside before bending over to nail off the four floor joists beneath the sheet. "Titties are the engine of the world, bro, we spend our whole lives sucking on them. Just ask Cooter."

"Y'all can leave me out of this one." Cooter was wearing his obligatory wife beater T-shirt with a Copenhagen-filled grin. "After I got married, questions like 'at were put to rest."

"Your wife's got a huge rack," Rigor Mortis said, "so stop being hypocritical."

Cooter winced, adjusting his glasses. "Just because I don't want to talk about my wife's ... her ... *titties*, don't make me a hypocrite."

"It does if you're saying that's not one of the reasons you married her."

Cooter shook his head as if dismayed, and then used the sledgehammer to tap the next sheet tight. "I didn't marry my wife's tits, I married her. The titties were just part of the overall package."

"We both got lucky," New Year bashfully said. His ubiquitous Stetson was stained with a ring of sweat. "Guess it runs in the family because both sisters ..."

O-Zone laughed. "New Year's blushing."

"Maybe I am." Plainspoken, Neil Abbot's bright cheeks were now completely flushed. "I love my wife, but that don't mean I can change the obvious."

Flustered by this betrayal, Cooter looked at his brother-in-law and said, "But that ain't why you married her, Neil, c'mon, man, you're killing me here ..."

As Elias approached and dumped another sheet onto the deck, O-Zone asked, "What about you?"

"I'm an ass man." Elias wiped his brow. "Titties, no titties, a woman with no ass is like a country without a flag."

O-Zone nodded. "Same here."

"And a shaved beaver." Elias smiled because Cooter rolled his eyes. "What about you, Coot? Do you like your beach nice and clean, or are you one of those guys who likes to hit his ball into the rough?"

Rigor Mortis loudly laughed. "A big old man-eater of a bush."

"Fur burger." O-Zone slapped down the next sheet. "Damn that's nasty."

"Damn right it is." Elias left to get more wood. "Who wants a face filled with urine-soaked pubes?"

"Dude!" O-Zone winced while even New Year chuckled.

"Elias," Cooter said, "that's one of the most disgusting things I've ever heard."

"Cooter!" Rigor Mortis yelled while pointing at the sheet. "Tap it in, man, hurry up."

The machine rolled on. Glue, sheet, tap, nail. Glue, sheet, tap, nail.

"Hey, Guinea!" Rigor Mortis yelled out. "How many sheets we got left?"

Out at the wood stacks, Elias yelled back, "Twelve more! And I'm not Italian, you dumb ass!"

"Not Italian?" O-Zone dropped the next sheet into place. "Huh."

"What are you?" Cooter tapped the sheet tight with the sledgehammer.

O-Zone said, "Hungarian. I hope you don't hate Jews, Cooter, because you're standing right next to one."

"No kidding?" New Year looked up from where he was busily gluing the joists. "A Hungarian Jew from Minnesota?"

"That's right." O-Zone shouldered over another sheet. "Cooter?"

"Me?" Cooter shot a tight stream of tobacco juice through his teeth. "I'm Scotch-Irish. My family's been in this country for over two hundred years."

"Who gives a fuck?" Riggy had retrieved more nails and now rejoined the group. "Stop babbling like a pack of twats, man, hurry up."

Elias arrived with another sheet as New Year asked, "If you're not Italian, what are you?"

"You'll never guess."

"Tell me."

"He looks ethnic," Cooter called out. "I'm guessing Greek."

"Nope."

"Turkish."

"Nope. I'll give any one of you fifty bucks if you even guess it."

"He's part monkey!" Rigor Mortis abruptly roared. "Everyone hurry up!"

Glue, sheet, tap, nail.

Glue, sheet, tap, nail.

As a small business owner dealing with myriad setbacks per day, when the opportunity to run fast and save money appeared, Nolan drove his best dogs and pocketed the change. That's why Rigor Mortis and Rand walked top-plate rolling trusses as Elias fed them blocks.

The crane operator, a new guy from a company out of Craig, was quickly overwhelmed and flustered by the pace.

"One hour!" Rigor Mortis kept screaming down at him every time the flow became disrupted. "You reading me, twinkle-tits? If we're not done here in one hour it's on *your* fucking dime!"

Elias, trying not to laugh, increased his assistance to the operator out of sheer pity alone.

"Elias! More blocks! Hurry up!"

"I heard you the first time!"

He frowned up at Rigor Mortis, who was on the wall pretending to slowly dry hump an imaginary buttocks held between his hands. "Come on up here and make me smile!"

"Oh dear God." Elias climbed the ladder. "Every day with you is like one long sex crime."

Fifty-five minutes later, the roof was rolled. The crane operator, not entirely pleased by this experience, made record time breaking down and fleeing.

Back on deck, Rand said, "Lookee here."

Off the main road leading in, Nolan's truck was followed closely by a white van.

"Oh great." Rigor Mortis dropped down from the wall with a floor shuddering crash. "Faster than a speeding moron, here comes Super-Framer ... and it looks like he's got the Scooby-Doo mobile in tow."

Elias got the 2x6 ready for sub-fascia. Rand dropped down off his wall, reloaded the nailgun, and watched the vehicles skid to a stop.

Nolan was on the phone and pointed at something, so the Mexicans scurried off.

"No way," Rigor Mortis hawked up mucus. "How the fuck do you say hurry up in Spanish?"

"*Ándele*," Elias answered and immediately regretted it.

"What's that make you? Their retarded half-brother?"

Nolan trudged upstairs, closed the phone, and looked at their collective expressions. "What?"

Rigor Mortis nodded. "What's with the beans?"

"Fuck me," Nolan spit. "You should see what those fucking hacks are doing out there."

"Then why would you bring—"

"Not the beans." Nolan checked to make sure they could not hear him, and then seemed embarrassed by the upcoming admittance. "Turns out Team Bonaduce is a goddamn hot mess."

"Gee, what a shock—"

"I'm talking about the gringos. Perfidio and Alonzo? I got a good feeling about these guys. I also got a feeling that hack fuck is ripping them off hard."

"How do you know and why would you care?"

"Because Alonzo told me they haven't been paid in four weeks. If they're good, and I kick them a fairer slice, stand the fuck back."

"So you're gonna gank the guy's whole crew?" Rand looked concerned about this proposal. "That's an act of war."

"Stone cold," Rigor Mortis concurred.

"Fuck 'im." Nolan shrugged. "Capitalism's a bitch, man, deal."

"They better bust ass, man," Elias said.

"We're about to find out. I got them rolling out to sub-fascia and sheet this bitch. Without Bonaduce around to fuck things up, we'll know if my hunch is right before the afternoon's over."

"Yeah, well, good luck with that, professor." Rigor Mortis detached his gun from the hose with a compressed pop. "Keep me posted on your little experiment."

"Load up and all three of you head out to the condo." Nolan stepped to the window as he watched the hurried activity below. "Let the fuck-show begin."

———

Within a day, Nolan had seen enough. He parked his truck and readied his thoughts. He stepped down into the mud, looked up at the distant faces on the roof, and shouted, "Alonzo, Perfidio, can you come down here for a second!"

They issued instructions so work could continue in their absence, and then climbed down through the second-story windows.

They met Nolan by the trucks and shook his hand. As siblings, they shared the same polite sense of humor and soft-spoken demeanor, but were otherwise physically unalike. Perfidio was five-foot-ten and slightly taller than his older brother. He always wore a Stetson. He was also cautious among people he did not know. But Alonzo, who wore braces on a wide smile, was markedly easier to know. Both had thick black mustaches that were meticulously groomed, and both were married, but only Alonzo's wife and children had made the journey north.

"Fellas, let's take a walk." Nolan steered them down the mud-choked driveway. "Listen, I'm not big on messing around with other people's businesses or how they make their living, but I can tell you this—I started this company because the shithead I was working for didn't respect me or what I did enough for him to show up every Friday with my paycheck in his hand. What guys like us do is pretty simple. We don't ask for much. Just drop off the wood and nails and keep us paid. That's it. That's what all this bullshit really amounts to, isn't it?"

On either side of Nolan, both Perfidio and Alonzo nodded.

"Now I know guys like yourselves probably have some pretty big considerations, either here or back home, and when the money ain't coming in, things must get uncomfortable. Plus, what's worse than showing up and faking it in front of the same asshole that ain't paying you?"

They solemnly nodded.

Nolan said, "After I saw how bad Shannon actually was, I made some phone calls back to where it is he said you all came from, and lemme tell you, the news I got back wasn't good. The District Attorney out there is planning on filing felony larceny charges on behalf of three builders who claim this guy took deposits on jobs he never did, which is why he ran off and ended up here. His soon to be ex-wife is getting ready to nail what's left of his nuts to the wall and take half his company which, after watching him work, ain't worth shit to begin with."

When they did not respond, Nolan thought he might have pushed too far. He stopped walking and said, "Look, I'm extending a hand. Come on board and I'll make all this vagabond bullshit disappear. In the next year, I've got over a hundred thousand square feet of work that you"—he pointed toward the roof—"and your bros can definitely grab a piece of."

The brothers looked at each other, eyes alive, communicating in silence. Nolan stood there and watched but wanted to continue the seduction.

"I'll start you guys at twenty-five bucks an hour. Gustavo and Jaime will get fifteen, Luís and Jose twelve, and ten for Angel and that big motherfucker—"

"Oscar," Alonzo said with a brace-filled grin. Both brothers seemed self-conscious of their accents, but their English was not in doubt.

"Yeah, Oscar." Nolan smiled. "He looks like a salty S.O.B."

"*Es mi tio,*" Alonzo answered. "He used to be … how you say? Treeman?"

"Logger?"

"Yes, log-ger." Alonzo nodded. "He is from Costa Rica."

"Yeah, well, any fifty-year-old who can carry a ton of wood can be from outer space for all I care. That dude definitely knows how to hurry the fuck up." Nolan reached into his jacket for a cigarette. "I wanted to tell you guys all of this because after I leave here, I'm driving over to inform your boss that he's a fucking hack loser who's costing me money before I shed his ass for good." He lit up. "Think about it. Because by tomorrow you're either working for me or following that other train wreck down the road."

"Okay." Perfidio's face was plain, but his mind was definitely in motion. "Is very generous of you, *gracias.*"

"Yes, Mr. Nolan."

Perfidio cleared his throat. "One last thing, please, Mr. Nolan. If we do agree to this, Gustavo and Jaime, they are worth more than *quince.* From one *jefe* to another, I must tell you that."

Nolan stared off into the distance. When he turned back, his sunglasses were so black Alonzo and Perfidio could see their own reflections staring back.

Nolan said, "You must be a good boss." It was hard to put the men first, but then again, once they knew that, they would walk through hell to help you. "They start at sixteen and we go from there." He handed Alonzo his business card and then turned back toward the trucks. "Gimme a call when you know what you guys are planning on doing, all right?"

"*Si*. Okay, Mr. Nolan."

"Just Nolan."

"Okay, Nolan."

Up on the roof, six curious faces watched the conference break apart.

Afterward, not wanting to take any chances, Nolan drove from job to job and collected up Rand, Rigor Mortis, O-Zone, Elias and Red Riggy, who was fresh off parole. The CD player cranked Spineshank at near-death levels, so no one bothered to speak.

Outside, the sun's path was already lower than its summertime arc. And while the crew was still tanned and wearing jeans and T-shirts, November's long shadow was knocking at the door.

They turned off County Road 61 and quickly approached the job.

Nolan dialed down the tunes. "Look at this. A fucking week and these strokers barely got the first-floor up."

The pickup skidded to a stop in a spray of pebbles and mud. All four doors opened. Boots hit the ground.

The three guys working inside turned their heads in unison.

"Hey, Nolan." Wade Shannon waved from a window before his green eyes slid across the five other guys fanning out like phantoms.

Nolan stepped up the 2x10 plank that led into the front door. "Hey, man. Got to speak to you for a second."

Knowing there was never an easy way to cut someone off at the knees, Nolan decided to be as professional as the situation, however it developed, demanded. But there was no need to dance, so Nolan said, "Listen, I like you guys, but I don't think this is gonna work out."

Shannon's red eyebrows furrowed together as he said, "*What?*"

Nolan tried steering him toward a corner for more privacy, but Wade side-stepped and said, "How do you mean?"

Nolan's smile was tight, as if wary of turning into something worse. "Look, it's just my opinion. I'll pay you off for what you've done and give a reference if needed, but really, my hands are tied."

"I don't get it." Wade looked around the structure. "What don't you like?"

"Wade—"

"Seriously. I mean what the fuck?"

"Please ..." Nolan was rubbing his forehead. "Don't make me do this."

"Do what? Fuck, man, I'm getting fired here and I don't even know why."

"Okay fine." Nolan shot an arm at the surrounding frame. "First off, I was here last night checking shit out and what should have taken three days took you a week. On top of that"—Nolan pulled Shannon's tape measure from his bags and turned for the nearest window— "every window height is wrong."

"What're you—"

"And all the plumbing head-outs are wrong. Now I gotta go back and cut them in." Nolan extended the tape measure like a pointer. "I mean the numbers are right on the goddamn plans."

"So I'll fix—"

"But see, that's not what I'm looking for. Not now. For the monster shit I got coming up, the way this company's gonna need to run, going backwards ain't an option."

"I'll do it on my own nickel!" Wade was almost pleading. "Come on, man, it's just a little fuck-up."

"Every window and door needs changing. On top of that, it's sheet-nailed to death, bro."

"I said I'd fix it for free, man, Christ—ain't you ever fucked up?"

"Yeah." Nolan tried not to smile but was not successful. "I hired you, didn't I?"

"You son of—"

As Shannon drew back, Nolan's right hand snapped closed around Shannon's windpipe before he even had his fist cocked.

"Don't do this." Nolan backed him against the wall. Nolan's guys quickly intercepted Shannon's crew before they could reach him. Nolan hissed, "Make this stop right now before no one walks away."

Guys were shouting and shoving until Nolan squeezed harder and Shannon finally sputtered, "Okay!"

Nolan lessened the pressure just enough to allow Shannon to call out, "It's all right! I'm all right, everybody just cool out!"

The action paused as Shannon's men found themselves encircled by this hostile posse of unnerving eagerness.

"Just pack up your shit," Nolan quietly told him, "and we'll all be friends again, all right? Let's not play hate and I'll cut you a check."

Shannon slowly nodded and coughed once his throat was free. "Buck, Richie, roll it up. We're outta here."

He turned and helped his men gather up the tools and cords. Nolan motioned his crew to exit.

Not even out of earshot, Rigor Mortis said, "Dick, Buck and Moron—sounds like a top-rate law firm."

Snickers erupted until Nolan hushed them. He cut a check and left it on Shannon's frontseat before herding his own crew back into the pickup.

"You really think it's gonna end like this?" Rand asked.

"Probably not." Nolan reversed the truck. "But I'm done thinking about it."

"Losing a job's one thing, but after he finds out his crew's gone too ...?"

"It's his life," Nolan said matter of factly. "And he can end it anyway he likes." At the end of the driveway, he swung left back out onto CR 61. "We can play nice or we can play hate ... and we're a whole lot better at one than we are at the other."

Since Riggy's truck was getting serviced, Nolan gave him a ride home.

"Wait here a sec." Rigor Mortis disappeared into his garage before re-emerging with a rolled-up towel. "Until you figure out what's going on with this moron ..."

Nolan unrolled the towel and found a 9mm Beretta.

"Um ..." Since it was Riggy's distorted way of showing concern, Nolan said, "I appreciate that ..."

"But?"

"But I ain't killing this stupid fucker over a goddamn job."

"That's funny. Assuming the choice is even yours, right?"

"Riggy—"

"You saw his face." Rigor Mortis snorted. "The second you cut his balls off, all of it—the busted jobs back home, the coming mutiny from his unpaid guys, and on top of a divorce? Seriously, the guy's drowning, and you just fucked him in the ass and stole his whole crew."

"*I* fucked him in the ass? His work should be in the hacker's hall of fame, and this is somehow my fault?"

"You stole his whole crew. Is this your first day or what?

"Are you—"

"Outside of taking someone's job or banging their wife, you gank the entire crew?"

"I didn't *steal* anything. I just offered them a job."

"And you think Bonaduce is just gonna be okay with that?" Rigor Mortis was almost laughing. "You hire him on and a week later he's fired and all his guys are gone?"

"Riggy—"

"All right, fine." Rigor Mortis rolled up the gun and pointed a finger at Nolan's head. "Better keep that thing on a swivel."

"I will."

"You're a good bro, Noll, but don't be stupid. That guy even so much as calls you, I better hear about it. I will rectify that motherfucker like you read about."

"I got it ..."

"I will break bones he doesn't even know he has."

"Okay, alright, Jesus Christ. I think we're a long way off from torture."

"Says who?" Rigor Mortis hopped out and Nolan drove away.

"Fucking Rigor Mortis." But it did feel tainted. Nolan was loath to recognize his own breaching of the code, but he also understood that Bonaduce was like a mortally wounded animal not long for this world. Nolan had seen it enough times over the years to not recognize the final flailings of a framer going down. Overextended on jobs and payroll, with unpaid taxes and in a constant mad scramble for cash, the ending always involved dodging lawyers and ex-wives while begging employees and creditors to just hang on ... Hell, he had almost done Bonaduce a favor. With his suicidal tailspin finally over, he might even find a chance to regroup.

Nolan pitied the poor bastard. He really did, but thankfully he had so far only known the burdens of making payroll which, on a weekly basis, was now surging past $22,000. Back in the day, that was exactly what he and Rand would have split on an eight-week frame. But now, with a dozen full-timers, the siding crews, and two outside crews under contract, Nolan felt like putting a gun to his temple every Thursday night. And that was just payroll, before taxes, workers compensation insurance, tools, repairs, accountant, bookkeeper, insurance for every jobsite ... He went to sleep worried about money and woke up doing the same. He knew the trap Bonaduce had fallen into was also waiting for himself and any other contractor who fell behind and then used the next job to pay for the last, and the one before that, until finally the entire house of cards came crashing down in a wave of liens, bankruptcy declarations, auctions, and lawsuits as far the eye could see.

He stopped thinking about it until he realized the Mexicans would now most likely be coming on board, which meant eight more mouths to feed.

CHAPTER EIGHTEEN

Brush Creek was one of a million small towns dotting the back roads of Colorado. Twenty-five miles west of Spring Valley, it had five stores, a bar, and a gas station. "Downtown" was six streets of triple-decker housing. 600 people were left over from the gold rush, when outposts sprang to life around mines now long dead. Current locals either commuted to work or did not work at all. Some lived in mobile homes with carefully tended yards. Others turned their property into a permanent flea market gone awry. Beyond close-knit, the locals knew too much about one another after generations in isolation.

After Bonaduce's dismissal, this was where Nolan rented apartments for the Mexicans. The four with families got their own apartments, the four single guys split a pair of two-bedroom apartments in the same building. Knowing they were trying to be careful with their money, Nolan originally thought the low rents of Brush Creek would save them thousands. Barely three weeks later this plan was totally destroyed.

For their own protection, Nolan kept Rigor Mortis away from the Mexicans. They either worked on their own or with O-Zone, Elias, Rand or himself. After gauging their skills, his fears subsided enough to pay them the highest compliment of all—he left them alone. And despite their half-hour commute, the Mexicans were always on time and worked hard and even volunteered for Sunday shifts as well. They did not call out sick or have ridiculous excuses or ask for money ahead of payday, or need to be taught the stiff discipline half the gringos he fired would never even know.

Nolan, wanting to know what the crew was saying behind his back, abducted Elias two weeks after the Mexicans started and pointed the truck toward town.

"So what's the word?" Nolan asked. "Any problem with Team Bean?"

"Not really." Elias lit a smoke. "I got no problem with them at all. Actually, last night me and Rand were out there playing pool with them."

"In lovely Brush Creek?"

"No kidding. What a fucking shit-dump."

"Ha-ha! Who knows, you might just find yourself a nice girl and settle down."

"Either that or suicide, right? I mean besides that bar, where it seems half the town shows up every night, there isn't a single thing about that place that doesn't smack of failure."

"How're the Mexies when you're working with them? Any bitches?"

"Naw, man. Alonzo and Perfidio run their own crews. Gustavo and Jaime are good apprentices, Luís and Jose will have those skills soon, but Angel and that big motherfucker ..."

Nolan grinned. "Oscar."

"Yeah, Oscar. That guy looks like he could wrestle a Mack truck."

"You know he's in his fifties?"

"I just love that he wears a cowboy hat and sings Shania Twain. And he couldn't give two fucks neither. Have you ever heard "Whose Bed Have Your Boots Been Under" sung by a fifty-year-old drunk Mexican?"

Nolan laughed.

Elias ashed his smoke out the window and said, "As for the rest, Gustavo loves hip-hop. Dude macks up on any chick he can find—white, fat, or otherwise, and Jaime thinks he's from the ghetto. But that Luís guy, I wish I could understand more of what he's saying, because whenever he opens his mouth, every one of those motherfuckers starts rolling."

"They're probably laughing at your gringo ass."

"Yeah, either that or the fact that I work for a total loser."

"Hey!"

"You know what they call Rigor Mortis?"

"What?"

"*Ángel de la Muerte.*"

"Nice. What about me? They have any nicknames for me?"

"Yeah, *El Grande Douchebag.*"

"Dude!"

"They love you. And the money. They also think you're fucking crazy."

"Nice."

"It's pretty miraculous, isn't it? I mean I know it's only been a couple of weeks, but most of them are married and go to church and so far, no one's even had to be bailed out. They might have a couple of beers now and then, but only Gustavo and Luís smoke weed. Is it just me, or are they better citizens than half the scumbags we hire?"

"Right? Except for the core group, I'd trade every last gringo for one of these motherfuckers instead."

"The work ethic in this country's gone to shit."

"Amen." Nolan lit up a smoke of his own. "What else?"

"You need to think about Rand, man. It's still the same old same old but now, with all these new guys especially, he thinks you're getting one over."

"*What?*"

"No shit."

"Unreal. Is he out of his—"

"Listen, just hold up. I tell him the same thing. You need to look at it from the other guy's perspective."

"Meaning?"

"Show him something ... anything really, even if it's fake. He just wants to know, man, that's all."

"He can look at whatever he wants. I got nothing to hide."

"Just placate him, will ya? What's the big deal?"

Nolan gnawed the cigarette as if it might have been Rand's face. "What else?"

"Cooter was making noise about a raise, especially with his next kid due in December."

"Yeah, well, tell him to wear a rubber next time. Santa's tapped out this year."

"10-4, good buddy."

Yet within a week of this discussion, conditions in Brush Creek exploded.

For the Mexicans without wives and families, the hours after work were interminable. Because TV was too hard to understand, they took to playing pool in the bar until the locals grew annoyed. With the sudden influx of immigrant labor this far north of the Mexican border, the mixing of cultures in the mountain towns was still a relatively new occurrence. Locals were used to a certain order of their ways, and this did not include the wellbeing of strangers brought this far away from home. Tempers flared, things came to blows, and soon enough Nolan got the call from Brush Creek at just past 1 A.M. He arrived to bail out seven of the eight Mexicans while the sheriff buttered him up. A portly man with three chins and deep bags beneath his eyes, the sheriff seemed to take a down-home approach to matters of this kind.

"Now, the locals can be ornery," he said. "Boys will be boys and all that, so keep that in mind."

"What're you talking about?"

But after Nolan was taken inside to their cells, and saw how badly the Mexicans had been beaten, his anger was quick. "You didn't arrest *anybody* else?"

"Well ..." The sheriff hooked two thumbs onto his gun belt. "Witnesses said these guys started it."

"Oh, is that what your brilliant detective work came up with?"

The sheriff squinted, failing to suppress a facial tic as he said, "Only three of these guys got valid IDs." He pointed toward the cells. "You want me to run the other four through INS, or do you want them back at work in the morning?"

Nolan sickly absorbed the threat. "I paid the bail, now can I take these guys home or what?"

The sheriff unlocked their cells. "They's all yours now, big boss-man."

Perfidio opened his mouth but then seemed too ashamed to speak. Both of his eyes were pounded into slits and his lips were split and leaking.

Alonzo sported a torn left eyebrow and had one lip shredded from being smashed into his braces. He swallowed twice before saying, "They came after Gustavo."

Nolan, stunned by all the beaten faces, had not heard a word.

"What the fuck," he said. "What the fucking *fuck*?"

The town was so small their apartments were only a block away, and on the walk back Nolan found out that the Mexicans had been playing pool. Gustavo, flirting with one of the local girls, was warned to stay away but did not listen. Even worse, Wade Shannon and his two white guys had also moved to Brush Creek due to lack of funds. Shannon had been at the bar drinking and clocking his former employees the whole night. Intoxicated, he egged on the crowd until the first fist flew. During the beating, Jaime escaped to their apartment to alert the others.

"I am very sorry." Alonzo blotted his mouth with a paper towel. His pride, even standing beaten in his own kitchen, was not in doubt. "We did not want for this to happen ..."

"Listen, this town's filled with a bunch of inbred redneck hicks." Nolan seemed humbled by this admission. "I should've known better."

"Is okay, no?"

"With you guys? Fuck yeah. I just don't want you to quit, is all."

"Maybe we could move back to Spring Valley?"

"No problem, man, no problem. I'm sorry. Please tell the others that too."

On the ride home, Nolan was seething while not caring about racial issues or socio-economic concerns, or Mexicans in general or even the mixing of two cultures—he only knew that guys who showed up and sacrificed and busted ass on his behalf had been stomped—it did not matter by whom or why. And to allow this indiscretion to stand without an immediate response was just not in his nature.

———

At ten o'clock the next night, the F-250 left Spring Valley heading west on County Road 30. The high-beams carved through the blowing leaves before reflecting off the eyes of deer caught motionless in the roadside shadows. Save for Cooter and New Year, who were family men and locals with no great love of Mexicans to begin with, the usual suspects were in the truck.

Nolan knew Brush Creek's only bar on a Friday night would be packed. He turned to Perfidio, who was squeezed between him and Rand, and told him, "You ain't involved in this. You just point them out."

Perfidio, whose face was a complete mess from the previous night's beating, obliquely nodded. "*Sí.*"

"Everyone else watches the crowd." Nolan eased off the gas in case the sheriff and his notorious radar gun were on the outskirts of town.

At the bend where the long-rusted train tracks paralleled Main Street, Nolan rode the brakes even harder. He took a right on Carson Street and crept passed the Iron Fork Bar. It was packed and surrounded in a halo of road-worn vehicles. Around back, Nolan killed the engine and made sure the empty beers were tossed into a dumpster.

He and Rand were first in followed by O-Zone, Rigor Mortis, Elias and the ex-con Red Riggy. They surrounded Perfidio like a phalanx. As the jukebox wailed country western, the new arrivals caught appraising glances which Nolan returned like a blowtorch. They headed for the bar which had license plates from all fifty states tacked into the wall. Further back, in a rear room, were two pool tables and video games left over from the previous decade.

"Can I help you?" The bartender had a pockmarked face around a pleasing grin.

Nolan said, "Only if you're the owner."

"He's in the back."

"Yeah? Then go fucking get him."

The bartender recoiled, his grin frozen. He turned and disappeared through a door and a minute later returned with a man who had Bryl-creamed hair and a beer gut drooping out over his belt like a rotten melon. He slowly approached while evaluating what or who awaited and said, "I'm Donny. I own this place. How can I help you?"

"Were you here last night?"

"Who are you?"

Nolan blinked. "It's a simple yes or no question."

Around them, people noticed the changing disposition of the men at the bar. Inquisitive glances filled with concern, but the blasting juke-box made eavesdropping impossible.

The owner was not new to this business, and so evenly countered Nolan's expression with an equal hostility.

"Perfidio ..." Nolan waved him forward and watched the owner's instant reaction. After a day of swelling, Perfidio's eyes were creased, dis-tended slits. His lips were swollen and scabbed as he nodded and said, "*Sí*. He was *aquí*."

Nolan looked at the owner. "Well, shit. There goes the benefit of the doubt. So I guess this is just the beginning."

The owner regained his footing and said, "I've never seen that guy before in my life."

"Yeah, well, he's seen you. And that means seven of his buddies have seen you too, and they all say the same thing. You wanna guess what it is they told me?"

"I don't have the first clue."

"Stop shocking me. They say you locked the door before these other redneck skanks stomped them into the ground."

"That's a goddamn lie."

"See, you're not getting it. This ain't no court of law, and I certainly don't give a fuck about your side of the story because you don't have one. Now here's the deal. You and—"

"I told you I ain't never seen this guy before in my life!"

With a look of pure amazement, Nolan turned to Rigor Mortis and said, "Do you believe this? I just don't think I'm getting through to this guy."

The place came to a dead stop after Rigor Mortis bounced the owner's head off the bar like a basketball. The broken nose splattered blood before he started to mewl. The other bartender flicked a switch which killed the jukebox. Then he fetched the owner a towel as chairs were pushed back and threats issued. Nolan grabbed the owner by the hair and jerked his head back until the blood ran down his neck like red paint. The owner gagged and sputtered as Nolan pushed him forward like a human shield and said, "Call them off before we wreck this place and every motherfucker in it."

"It's okay," the owner called out, arms flailing, gagging on the blood. "It's okay, folks, just us fellas talking things through, is all."

Nolan released him and smiled and said, "See? Was that so hard? I really wish you had done that to begin with." He turned toward the crowd and shouted, "Evening, folks. Me and Donny here have been talking and it looks like he's closing down early for a private party. Right, Don?"

The owner, whose busted nose now looked like a smashed beehive stapled into the center of his face, somberly said, "Yeah, it's closing time."

"But some of you will be staying. My friend here was partying with y'all last night, and if he recognizes you, you're cordially invited for some after-hours excitement."

There was mass movement toward the door but Rand and Elias were already there. Suddenly, Nolan saw Wade Shannon dart out of the back room and could not believe his luck. He grabbed Shannon from behind and spun him into a right-cross that instantly dropped him to the floor. "Tough guy, huh? Hey, wake the fuck up." Nolan kicked him with a boot. "You ain't sleeping through this."

Perfidio joined Rand and Elias, and after thirty-nine people were ejected, six were left pushed against the wall.

"This is it?" Nolan asked Perfidio. "You didn't recognize anyone else?"

Perfidio shrugged. "It was very fast, Nolan, maybe the rest no here."

"You six morons head over to the bar." Nolan locked the door and handed his phone to Perfidio. "Call them down."

"I ain't thirsty," one of the guys said, so Rigor Mortis immediately grabbed him by the earlobe and twisted until the man was walking on his toes. The other prisoners warily sat at the bar. Cars outside started up and some people watched while others pounded on the windows. Minutes later, Alonzo, Gustavo, Angel, Oscar, Jaime, Luís, and Jose were banging on the door. They looked fearful of all the patrons hatefully yelling. Once inside, they saw Wade Shannon sitting in a chair with a black eye, saw the bleeding bar owner as well, and almost panicked until Nolan said, "Relax. After the sheriff comes, we'll all have a couple of beers. The owner said you guys are welcome to play as much pool as you want. Right, Don?"

"Yeah, help yourself." Don had a towel tentatively clamped to his crushed nose. He tried to throw a reassuring look to the six locals seated at the bar but stopped when Rigor Mortis made a slicing motion across his own neck.

"Give everyone beers," Rand said, so the bartender reached inside the cooler.

"Where is that bloated pig?" Nolan waited for the cop, tapping the bar impatiently while scanning his hostages. "Fucking goddamn *Deliverance*-loving inbred scumbags."

Rand said, "I'll take two shots of whiskey."

"Me too," Rigor Mortis said.

So Red Riggy just reached over the bar and took the bottle. Beers were passed out as the Mexicans shot pool.

Nolan glanced at the locals and said, "Put your licenses on the bar." He gathered up their IDs. "The sheriff's gonna come and you boys are gonna say we're all having a real good time, and then the sheriff's gonna leave. Anyone says a goddamn thing otherwise ..." Nolan held up the licenses. "We will be back for you."

He heard a noise and turned to see Wade Shannon slumped over and crying softly, his smashed eye already swelling closed.

Nolan said, "Jesus, Wade, pull yourself together."

"Fuck you! Those are *my* guys!"

"Use your fucking head and stay the hell away from them or you'll be the sorriest motherfucker of them all."

"You're a thief, man, a fucking Judas!"

"Capitalism's a bitch, man. It really is. But you—you almost got people killed."

One of the prisoners, who was wearing lambchop sideburns and a flannel shirt, said, "Mister, I have no idea what this is about."

Nolan took a step toward him and said, "You see what happened to the last guy that thought I was stupid?"

The swirling red and blue lights finally appeared. The sheriff, with considerable effort, hoisted himself out of the car before easing through the door.

"Evening, Don." The sheriff looked closer at the owner's face. "What happened there?"

"Llewellyn hit me with the cooler door." Don nodded at the other bartender. "Sometimes the kid don't know no better."

"What about him?" The sheriff pointed at Wade Shannon. "He get hit by a door too?"

"Umm ..."

"Boy, I sure do see a lot of familiar faces." The sheriff said something into his walkie-talkie while casually strolling through the bar. "Got a couple of calls from people who said they was asked to leave in the middle of their drinks." The sheriff nodded at the abandoned glasses on the empty tables. "Any reason for that?"

"Me and Don got to talking," Nolan said. "And he was awful depressed about what happened last night. So he kindly offered to have the fellas back down as a way of mending fences. Ain't that right, Don?"

"It was the least I could do." Don looked at the sheriff hesitantly. "Don't want no bad blood is all."

"Really." The sheriff smirked as if he was not buying a single word of it. "So nobody's been assaulted here?"

"Assault?" Nolan looked incredulous. "That wouldn't be very nice, now would it? People shouldn't go around beating on other people." Nolan looked at his hostages. "Right, guys?"

"Violence don't solve nothing," one of them said.

"So it's just a bunch of good ol' boys playing pool on a Friday night." The sheriff openly smiled. "Okay. Mind if I stay on then, catch a little break from that cruiser?"

"Not at all." Nolan pulled him out a chair. "Get you some coffee?"

"Please."

"Hey, Don? The sheriff could use a cup of joe."

This charade continued for another half hour as the Mexicans played pool. Nolan's guys drank, the six prisoners morosely stared ahead, and Nolan sat with the sheriff and Don, who had his head tilted back the entire time to stop the bleeding.

"I should probably be getting back to it." The sheriff looked at Don. "You sure you don't want me to call you a rescue?"

"I'm fine, sheriff, a busted beak never kilt no one."

"Well, I'm gonna set up across the street, just in case."

"There ain't no problem here, sheriff." Nolan seemed offended. "As soon as Don wants us gone, we'll be history."

"We're gonna be okay," Don said and nodded as if to reassure himself.

The sheriff took one last perusal of the bar and then got back into his car. Parked directly across the street, he angled a radar gun out the window while keeping the place under full surveillance.

Nolan stood up and took the beers from the six at the bar and dumped them out. "You fucking pussies are gonna have to sit here until one o'clock and watch us drink. Second—your Spring Valley privileges have been revoked. Permanently. For those of you too stupid to understand what I just said, that means you're banned forever. If I see any of you anywhere at any time with no pigs around, I'm gonna beat you to death myself. Now smile at that bloated sow across the street and act like I just told a joke."

The six weakly laughed and high-fived one another for no reason. Nolan smiled and said, "That's right, morons, keep on being stupid."

———————

After the bar closed at 1 A.M., Nolan made sure the Mexicans returned home safely. Tomorrow was Saturday and moving day, so only one more night remained.

Loading up his gringos, Nolan noticed all of them were wasted. Elias, Rigor Mortis, O-Zone and Red Riggy had turned the backseat into a drunken brawl. They did not get far before the red and blue lights washed across the truck.

Nolan told everyone to shut up and said, "I told you fuckers not to bring anything, so if this pig finds even a single pot seed, the beatings will be severe."

He lowered the window as the sheriff's flashlight blinded him.

"Well," the sheriff said. "We meet again."

"Just heading home, sheriff."

"You mind stepping out of the truck?"

"What for?"

"You been drinking tonight?"

"No, sir, haven't had a drop in years."

"What about dope? You or anyone else carrying any contraband?"

"Nope."

"Well," the sheriff said, "then I guess you wouldn't mind if I checked?"

"Pig!" Rigor Mortis screamed.

But Nolan only shrugged. "I think he must be talking about his ex-wife, sheriff, he gets really lonely when he's drunk."

"Y'all need to get out of that truck right now. And you better pray to God that I don't find a thing, or you're gonna be about the sorriest motherfuckers Salinas County's ever seen."

"No problem, sheriff." Nolan held up his hands. "Some of us folks are behind you all the way ..."

———————

Three weeks later it was Thanksgiving, and since Elias' roommates either worked in restaurants or on the mountain, he was home alone. He had already phoned Brooklyn and spoken with family, but everyone was yelling in the background. His mom was mad he would not be home for the holidays again, so the call was thick with guilt.

Now, to celebrate the rare day off, his plans called for maximum couch time, football and cocktails, but his cellphone rang instead.

"What're you doing?" Nolan asked.

As Elias took his first sip of a freshly made Jack and Coke, he made the mistake of saying, "Nothing."

"Good. I'll be at your condo in thirty seconds."

Hanging up, Elias said, "Fuck."

Like a firefighter, he stepped into his prearranged gear and boots.

Outside, it was sunny and thirty degrees. The snow was already over two-feet high. When the F-250 rolled in, Elias grabbed the whiskey and Coke bottles.

Nolan shook his head. "I don't think so, Stimpy, no open containers in the rig."

Elias shrugged. "Then I ain't getting in."

"Goddamnit ..."

"It's fucking Thanksgiving, dude ..."

"Again, not my problem."

"Fair enough." Elias faked closing the door.

"All right! Fine! You are sad and gross. Bring the booze to drown your pathetic life."

"Right? I can't believe I've got forty more years of this shit."

"Till you retire or until you're dead?"

"What's the difference?"

"There isn't one for you. You're working until you die." Nolan hit the blinker and took a right down Snowmass Road. "You got any plans today?"

"Naw. Everyone's working. And without family, what's the point?"

"I hear ya."

"What about Kara?"

"She's cooking up a storm."

"Nice."

"You wanna roll by later for some grub? Riggy's coming by."

"That's not really a selling point."

"But just think of the pain ..."

"What're we doing today?"

"Well." Nolan found a cigarette and said, "Gimme a light."

"Aw, man ..."

"No whining. Gimme your lighter right now."

"Goddamnit ..." Elias handed over his lighter and then watched it disappear. "You suck."

"Since today's Thanksgiving, we're gonna spend it giving thanks to me, your lord and master, by cleaning all my tools. The condo gig starts December first, and that's right around the corner, simpleton."

"I think you're missing the meaning of Thanksgiving—"

"No thinking."

Nolan had spent the morning collecting his nailguns and saws. Now, at his storage space, there was a pile of rags and buckets as Elias said, "Great day for having wet hands, huh?"

"It just gets better and better, doesn't it?" In the bed of the pickup, Nolan shoved over the tools so Elias could reach them. "Unload this shit while I get us some buckets of warm water."

"10-4. Where's your girl Rand?"

Nolan hopped down. "He was smart enough not to answer his phone."

"Douche. You're enjoying the fuck out of this, aren't you?"

Nolan pat his shoulder and then grabbed the empty buckets. "Happy Thanksgiving, buddy."

An hour later the noontime sun took over the clear blue sky. Even with the surrounding snow, it was still forty degrees and hot enough for them to trade jackets for flannels.

Elias cleaned and oiled the fifteen Hitachi framing guns. Nolan wiped and greased all sixteen skillsaws, checked their oil, and then replaced a pair of worn-out triggers. Progress was smooth until a faint rumbling approached.

"What's that?" Nolan reached for a smoke.

"Don't know, but it's getting closer."

Thump, thump, thump went the cadence until there was a sudden screeching and Rigor Mortis wheeled around the corner in his salt-slimed pickup. The thumping was actually his stereo's bass reverberating out the windows.

Don't fear the blade—
it slices deep!
Can't save yourself
die, pigs, die!

The Ford gunned straight at them but stopped with only feet to spare. Riggy killed the engine and hopped down, saying, "Look at this fucking scene. A couple of homeless guys circle-jerking on milk crates ..."

"You're just in time." Nolan nodded. "Pick up a rag and wipe."

"Sounds like a tampon commercial. Speaking of tampons, what's up, Elias?"

"Fuck you."

"Thatta girl." Riggy peered further into Nolan's jam-packed mess of a storage unit. "My God, how are you not ashamed of this disgraceful disaster?"

Nolan frowned. "Flap, flap, moron, lend a hand or peace the fuck out."

"Nice work, Elias." Riggy swigged from the Jack Daniels. "At least you're good for something."

"Yeah. Happy Thanksgiving, fuckface."

Nolan laughed so loud that even Rigor Mortis smiled. He loaded the guns Elias had finished cleaning into Nolan's truck. Then he walked over to the saws which, because they each sat on 100 feet of coiled cord, looked like mechanized snakes. "I remember back to when you and your boyfriend Rand first started out ..." Riggy took on a wistful air. "Just a couple of crackheads with a pair of saws and one gun and then this moron"—Riggy nodded at Elias—"stumbled in, and together you three glory-holes have really shined!"

Nolan said, "I got something you can shine."

Elias said, "The Black Death is getting sentimental. But he's right. Look at all these tools three years later. Yo, Riggy, where's the bone, dude?"

"Right here." Rigor Mortis leaned into his truck and fired up a joint.

As he and Elias huffed it, Nolan shook his head. "How many vices can you burnouts squeeze in before noon?"

"Got any blow?"

Nolan frowned, tightening the last screws on a saw grip before stiffly standing up. "Listen, let's roll to the condo and check it out before we eat some bird."

Nolan took the backroads because it was the opening week of ski season. Hotel vans, condominium shuttles, and free bus service clogged the streets. Patriotic bunting adorned the downtown strip, and every lamppost a mile in either direction wore Christmas wreaths in welcome. The ski and snowboard shops were packed, the restaurants all staffed and trained, and eighteen of the twenty-six trails were already deep enough to open.

Nearing the mountain, the traffic worsened which, for Spring Valley, meant a two-dozen vehicle traffic jam at the liftbase pavilion.

"Holy shit." Elias gazed in awe. "When did that thing go up?"

"Two days ago."

A gigantic rectangular tent soared fifty feet in the air. It was located near the main gondola line and surrounded by two hotels. Nolan turned down the access road shared with one of the hotels. He parked by a portable office trailer in the back right corner that had BLM Construction written on its side.

Elias nodded toward the sign. "That your new master?"

"Absolutely, Stimpy, let's check it out."

Once they got to the tent, they pulled a Velcro flap back and got blasted by hot air. Six-foot long heaters, one in each corner, spit blue flame. Because of their size, they looked like rockets tipped onto their sides. Thick hoses ran propane to each from thousand-gallon tanks outside. The foundation itself was 150x90 feet and one foot higher than the graveled floor.

Elias stepped onto a sea of stones. "Unbelievable. It's like a domed stadium."

"Ain't it something?" Nolan asked. "It's roped off outside. The hot air keeps this thing afloat."

"Incredible. It's like eighty degrees in here."

"Didn't daddy say he would take care of you girls?"

Riggy approached while swigging whiskey. "I was up the mountain for a couple of turns this morning and from above it looks like a giant titty."

"Nice."

Elias took back the bottle. "This is gonna be a trip, huh?"

"Christ." Nolan started walking back. "Let's go eat some bird."

CHAPTER NINETEEN

THE CASCADE PEAK BUILD
Winter, 1999—Spring, Summer 2000

On December 1st, the mandatory meeting began at 8:00 A.M. Milling about outside the BLM trailer were Nolan's entire crew, Cam Rogers and Team Beaver, the Mexicans, and ten jobsite laborers employed by BLM.

"Bunny!" Elias high-fived Bunny. "Welcome back to the valley, motherfucker."

"Hell yeah, bitches." Bunny playfully shoved Rand. "I knew you'd miss me."

It had the feel of the first day of school as both the Director of Operations and Project Manager joined Nolan in the center of the group. Around them, forty guys stood clearing their throats and busting balls while chain-smoking in the freezing air.

"Welcome, gentlemen, on behalf of Buchanan, Laughlin, and Meyer, my name is Dennis Lambie." The Director of Operations smiled beneath a rope-thick mustache. His small frame and sloped shoulders made his head seem oversized. He had an alligator-like grin filled with too many teeth, and even though he was forty-five-years-old, his brown hair was thick and full with no gray beneath the red hardhat. Like most residents, Lambie was a ski bum transplant who climbed the ladder until reaching D.O. The tiny red ruby stud, long pierced through his left ear, was now the only marker from that previous life. His baritone voice, despite his small stature, emanated command. "Now I know you fellas are watching that gondola line wishing it could be you heading up to take a couple of turns, but unfortunately it's not ..." The obligatory laughter from the crowd. "So we're gonna talk about Phase One instead. For the record—and bear with me because some of you already know all this—the first-floor will be built on-site to account for any discrepancies with the foundation, but the rest of the walls, exterior and interior, will be built off-site."

There were a few looping whistles of appreciation as Lambie nodded and said, "It is ambitious. Prefabrication off-site entails a whole host of potential nightmares. But that, thankfully, belongs in the laps of these fellas." He nodded at Nolan and Brian Tresky, the Project Manager, and then said, "Seriously, guys, I've been in this business a long time, and my track record speaks for itself. I was a Project Manager for ten years, and in that time, I only had two serious injuries on my watch—and by that I don't mean stepping on nails or infected splinters. I'm talking about amputations and fatal falls." Now Lambie had their attention. "We've got this unit and then the next. That's 96,000 square feet of wood and roofs and cranes and costs, human and otherwise, so let's have a safe build, guys, that has to be priority number one."

"Safety?" Elias whispered to Cam Rogers. "That sure don't rhyme with hurry up."

Nolan, even from a distance, shot Elias a look of pure death just as Lambie said, "Nolan, the floor is yours."

"Thanks, Dennis." Nolan paused while staring at the troops. "My guys already know what to expect. As the first-floor's being built here, another crew will be out at the yard framing the next three. The pace is gonna be awful, no doubt, but none of us are getting paid to make excuses. The BLM guys are in charge of snow removal, offloading the lumber trucks, inventorying the wood, and forklifting material where it's needed. We'll also set up a chain of command so that a dozen carpenters aren't trying to run the show." Nolan shrugged. "That's all I got, Brian, floor's yours."

A third man stepped forward and said, "Good morning, fellas. I'm Brian Tresky, the Project Manager." He gave everyone a smile. Broad-shouldered and plain-faced, he had a Pennsylvania accent and, since this was his debut as P.M., a businesslike demeanor. He wore a hardhat and spotless denim Carhartt's as he said, "Dennis and Nolan have already covered the priorities, so let me just say the communication aspect Nolan spoke of is paramount. We're gonna have two CAT-9 forklifts running around, a crane slinging loads of multiple tons, a pair of S185 Bobcat mini-loaders, and a couple dozen humans scurrying in between it all." He paused as if searching for the right words before he said, "Now I know you guys have a certain reputation, but like Dennis said, safety is the number one priority. On-site, everyone has to wear a hardhat—"

"A *what*?" Spoons said.

"No way," O-Zone added.

Tresky looked at Nolan. "I guess you haven't told them."

Nolan smiled at his guys. "Surprise."

Boos and hisses erupted until Nolan growled, "No more talking."

Tresky continued, "Okay, we covered hardhats. Also, no one's allowed to walk exterior wall top-plate."

"What the fuck." Rand winced. "Are you kidding me?"

"In addition," Tresky stalwartly continued, "all ladders between floors have to be tied off, all saw-guards must be unpinned, and all guns must have working safeties."

Loud groans accompanied the murmurs and more boos.

"Hey." Nolan grimaced. "What's with you guys? Rules are rules."

"Also," Tresky said, "anyone working on the roof has to be harnessed and roped in at all times."

Disgusted, people were openly shaking their heads, but Tresky seemed amazed. "Look, fellas, it's for your own good. We're not trying to slow you down, believe me, but the Wild West show ain't gonna fly with OSHA. And don't think those guys never leave Denver, because just last week they hit us with a $10,000 fine at the Lakemont job for an unsecured ladder after an accident." Tresky consulted his clipboard and said, "All injuries need to be immediately reported, no drugs or alcohol are allowed on-site for any reason, and we've been asked by managers of both hotels to keep their guests in mind as far as expletives and the such." Realizing he was losing their attention, Tresky tried on a smile and said, "I'm looking forward to this experience, guys, and I think we're all gonna be really proud of what it is we've been gathered here to accomplish."

"Okay." Nolan pointed. "We're gonna back in Cam and Riggy's trailers, unload the boxes and tools, and for God's sake hurry the fuck up."

The crowd broke apart as Rigor Mortis turned to O-Zone and Elias and said, "So let me get this straight. We need to slow down, stay sober, and not swear."

"Don't forget the brain buckets." Elias frowned. "Turn on your suck lights, man, 'cause here comes a thousand watts of pain."

Knowing who the insurrectionists were, Nolan was instantly over their shoulders. "Keep yapping and you two bitches are gonna be wearing hardhats *and* tu-tus before I'm through."

Elias snorted. "You sold us out."

"The fucking thing might just save your life."

"That's exactly the point."

Rigor Mortis laughed and said, "*I'll* kill you, Elias."

"I know you would, buddy." They were walking uphill toward the trucks. "And that's why you're a total freaking mess."

Exasperated, Nolan lit a smoke as Cam Rogers corralled him away from where the forklifts moved wood and the workers rolled out tools.

"You excited?" Cam popped in a stick of gum and offered Nolan the pack. "Let the fuckfest begin, right?"

"Jesus. Drop your pants and grab your knees, because this is gonna hurt."

"Ha."

"Shit, man, I just realized I should've let you say something at that meeting. On-site here, this is your show."

"Well, that's kind of what I wanted to talk to you about." Cam took on a conciliatory posture, because even though he outranked Nolan as far as tenure, age, and experience, the job belonged to Nolan. Cam wanted to build instead of worry, swing a hammer instead of paperwork, so all liability was shifted off his shoulders. He said, "You're a big boy, Noll, and I'm not about to interfere with your operation. But I been doing this too long not to know that you can't ignore a gut feeling. I know you're planning on running other jobs at the same time we're building this, and I think that's a real mistake."

"Why? It's not gonna be a question of manpower, because I'll be subcontracting all of it out. I sign the contract, hire some local morons to frame it, and then cash the checks."

"I understand how it works." Cam was not hiding the sarcasm. "I'm saying it's a bad idea. 96,000 square feet ...? Just think about what I'm saying."

"Jesus Christ, dude, we can handle this ..." Nolan let his grin linger. "Are you getting cold feet on me?"

"That ain't it, Noll. The more plates you have in the air, the more you can expect one or all of them to come crashing down ..."

Nolan knocked on his hardhat. "That's why I'm wearing one of these."

"All right." Cam held up his hands. "I get it."

"It's gonna be okay." Nolan seemed amused by his concern. "Come on, big cat, let's go frame some walls."

They walked back into the tent.

The promised nirvana of the heated tent and its seventy-degree climate lasted barely three days. Though one could wear short-sleeves and actually break a sweat, this did not offset the propane rockets roaring twenty-four hours a day, or the diesel exhaust from the forklifts and mini-Bobcats maneuvering material. In fact, by the end of day two, people were growing agitated by the continued dizziness and headaches. Rand, for one, had the necessary tenure to finally proclaim what only a few others had begun to openly say.

"I feel like a gassed rodent," he told Nolan, because Nolan had so far dismissed their complaints as standard-issue bitching. But now, after spending an entire day with them inside the tent, even Nolan was nauseous.

"I think we have a problem," he told Dennis Lambie, but Mother Nature intervened instead. Over the next two nights, four feet of snow and constant wind rendered the tent into a precarious state of collapse. The engineers, who had originally required that the concrete foundation cure two weeks inside the heated enclosure, instead signed off on its demise.

"So it's either freeze to death or get the gas ..." Spoons shook his head. "I knew I should have gone to college."

CHAPTER TWENTY

B efore County Road 61 ascended Forked Head Pass, a smatter of dilapidated mobile homes were huddled behind a sign which ironically read, Happy Days Trailer Park. Behind a chain-link fence was also a dock and storage lot for boats along the Blackstone River.

This was where they built a sprawling makeshift deck. It was a 16x40-foot rectangle made out of 2x10s and plywood. The Mexicans, Rand, O-Zone, and Elias spent the week building walls and placing them into prearranged stacks in the plowed-out yard. Two-man cut teams sawed studs, jacks, and sills. Others assembled 2x10 headers, and the remaining guys framed walls. The assembly line was fluid and well-stocked with wood since surrounding the deck were triple-stacked bunks of 2x4, 2x6, 2x10, and ½-inch plywood for the exterior walls. Assembled on deck, the exterior walls were squared by tacking the bottom-plate along a snapped line, pulling tape measures from each bottom corner diagonally across to each top corner, and shoving the wall left or right until both tapes read the same. The plywood was then applied to hold it perfectly square. The interior walls, made only of 2x4s, went markedly faster.

They commandeered an eighteen-wheeler's trailer and stuffed it with their gear, tools, portable heaters, and a giant table where Nolan, Rand, Cam, and Riggy pored over the plans with rulers and calculators, checked each other's numbers, rechecked and checked again until they had every wall and all rough openings scaled, labeled, and broken down by each condominium unit. It was tedious work filled with specific details and horrific outcomes if even one set of numbers was wrong. The good news was that while the units on a particular floor might differ in size, the next three floors stacked above it would be exactly the same. So once the first-floor numbers had been broken down and collected, the next three floors above each unit were identical replications. Every wall was on long lists tacked inside the trailer, and a huge laminated blow-up of the blueprints provided a visual as to where each individual wall would stand. Cut lists for studs, jacks, sills, and headers were the final preparation before the skillsaws shattered the silence.

On a Thursday afternoon two weeks before Christmas, a swirling storm blew in as the temperature dove. Layered in gear, the workers out at the yard numbly proceeded until Nolan's pickup stopped at the opened gate. They watched him hop out into the headlights and put a bullhorn to his lips.

"Attention inmates. This is your master speaking. You need to hurry up. You will always need to hurry up. Suffering is for the common good."

"Oh my God." Elias shared a look with Rand as they worked. Beside them on the giant deck, Perfidio and Alonzo each ran their own crews, so three walls were being built at the same time.

From the truck, Nolan swept a floodlight across the site. *"That's right. You are always under constant surveillance. Repeat after me—I love authority."*

"What a douche," Elias said, and the Mexicans laughed.

"I can't hear you!"

Rand, who had been bent at the waist nailing off the wall, stood up and gave him the finger. "Can you hear that?"

"No back-talk, Fabio. Repeat after me—I am worthless and weak."

O-Zone laughed. "What a dick."

The floodlight instantly pegged O-Zone. *"You are in violation of the No Stroking Ordinance, O-Zone, back to work."*

"Yes, sir!"

"That's more like it. Your girlfriend Rand could learn a lot from your subservient nature."

They kept working as Nolan then said, *"And now for your listening pleasure ..."*

O-Zone winced. "Oh God. Is that ...?"

"Air Supply?" Rand asked.

"It's the fucking Carpenters, man." Elias blinked. "I think I'm gonna be sick."

"That's right, morons, pay homage to your namesake. Sing it with me ... Close to you!"

"I don't know what's worse." Rand reloaded his gun. "The actual music, or the fact that this loser owns it on CD."

"*La-lalala-la … close to you!...*"

"Yeah, really." Elias shoved more studs on deck and then turned and shouted, "You're killing my soul!"

"*Of course I am. Now let us ponder. To hurry up, or not to hurry up?*"

"Hurry up," they echoed through the storm, and Nolan only laughed and laughed.

———————

Back at the site, Cam Rogers and Rigor Mortis led the assault on the first-floor framing with Spoons, Uno, the Soldano brothers, Bunny, Cooter and New Year. Nolan bounced Elias and Rand between the framing yard and jobsite as needed, but since the Mexicans had found their niche, they were left to spit out walls at a machine-like pace.

After three weeks, the 12,000 square foot ground-floor was framed, stood, and sheeted. Because of the vast space and many rooms, as well as the second-story next to come, screaming out for each other or the whereabouts of certain tools was no longer efficient. To this end, Nolan dropped a thousand dollars on a dozen walkie-talkies and the madness ensued from there.

"Iceman, this is Maverick, do you copy?"

"That's a big 10-4, nut-lover, what's your 20?"

"I'm at your mom's house, moron, suck on that."

"Shut up!" Nolan or Cam would eventually scream, but the warnings were barely heeded.

"Spoons, where you at, there's a hottie at twelve o'clock."

"Nice. I see her. She's definitely worth a load."

Nolan would be in a meeting with Dennis Lambie and hear Bunny say, "Hey, Cooter, think that forklift could pick up your wife?"

Or after Rigor Mortis left early for lunch, and Elias hailed him on the open air by saying, "Riggy, where you at?"

"Waiting to order inside McDonald's, man, leave me alone."

"I can't. I don't care if there are people around you—"

"Elias—"

"I don't know why you keep denying what we have between us. I mean, is it so wrong to want to feel the touch of another man?"

"Elias!"

Loud laughter could be heard erupting from different rooms around the job as Elias said, "Don't forget, the Mac might be Big, but nothing beats a cockburger sliding between your golden arches."

"Elias," Rigor Mortis evenly said. "After I'm done raping you, I'm going to cut you into a thousand tiny pieces."

"Clear the air!" Nolan screamed, but it was already way too late.

———

At 6:45 a.m. the next morning, Elias was on his way to work when the flashing blue lights appeared in his rearview mirror.

"Ah, fuck me." There was no one else on the road, so Elias just pulled over. If it was a speeding ticket, he wanted to get it over with quick so he didn't have to listen to Nolan bitch about him being late.

Elias watched the cop approach, the cop all cop even though it was barely dawn. At the window, he said, "Good morning, sir. In a hurry today?"

"Morning, officer, just on my way to work. Cold one today, huh?"

"Sure is. I hate to say it but I got you on radar doing fifty-eight in a forty-five zone. I'm gonna need to see your license and registration."

"No problem." Elias handed out the documents.

"Sir, can I ask you something?" The cop's nametag read Alalatoa, a Samoan far from home. "Have you been drinking?"

Elias grinned. "I wish. Might help with this hangover."

"So you admit you've been drinking?"

Elias stopped smiling. "I had some beers last night, officer, is that against the law?"

"No," the cop answered. "But driving drunk is. Please step out of the car."

"Are you kidding me?"

"Sir, does it look like I'm kidding?"

Elias scoffed but then remained silent. The cop put him through the roadside test, which Elias passed.

The cop said, "Alright, sir, just blow through this tube in one long continuous breath."

"I can't believe this is happening." Elias did as instructed.

The cop waited until the machine beeped, and then he swung the gauge toward Elias and said, ".056."

"See, I told you—"

"Sir, turn around and put your hands on the car. You're under arrest—"

"I blew a .056! The limit's .08!"

"Not in Colorado, sir, .05 to .08 is a misdemeanor."

"Are you fucking kidding me?"

"Again, does it look like I'm joking? Do you have any weapons on you?"

"Holy shit. You guys need some real criminals out here. Arresting people on their way to work must be so rewarding."

The cop snapped the bracelet until it was too tight. "Let me know if that hurts."

"Just get this over with."

Elias went to jail.

———

The next morning, three tractor-trailers with spinning yellow lights and signs reading Wide Load carried the crane all the way up from Denver. But backing them down the narrow access road to the job proved harder than the six-hour journey. A crane and two Caterpillar forklifts unloaded and ferried the monstrous sections into position. Since it was self-erecting, the vertical column and horizontal boom arm would unfold from within like an old-style walkie-talkie antenna.

The engineers wore yellow hardhats that read Bachnau Lift Operations. They wore severe expressions and yellow down jackets while yelling at their men in German.

It took most of the morning to assemble the base, which was a tripod of thirty-foot steel beams. The center shaft was then hoisted on top and bolted into place. Next, the boom arm was lifted on top and bolted into the shaft.

"*Attention,*" a voice rang out from the central intercom. "*All personnel clear the site. Repeat, all personnel clear the site.*"

"Drop the guns," Nolan said. "They're getting ready to raise this pig."

Three dozen workers exited the structure and lit cigarettes beneath the Sheraton's carport. A siren rang out as the yellow lights washed across the falling snow and then the siren stopped. A huge intake of air roared once the generator fired up, and the vertical column, shuddering as the chain-fed cables engaged, began climbing into the sky. Progress was slow, but thirty minutes later the fully extended column was bolted into place by workers on ropes repelling down the sides.

"What's it topping out at?" Rand asked.

Nolan lit a cigarette. "A hundred-and-twenty-feet."

"That's like twelve-stories," Bunny said, "this is some cool shit."

"Enjoy it, Bunny, 'cause for every minute you strokers are standing around, I'm docking you twice as much."

Bunny laughed until he thought Nolan was serious. "Wait a sec. You can't do that."

"Moron, don't be stupid."

In addition to the regular everyday misery, the hardhats enabled the creation of a painful new game which involved sneaking up behind an unsuspecting victim and slamming a fist down onto their heads. Because the hardhats had a cheap plastic interior webbing, the exposed plastic nubs got driven into people's scalps. The pain left a searing, sick throb. Riggy lit the fuse. Starting in the rear, he quickly wedged through the crowd slamming heads as people yelped and screamed. The shoving started and soon twenty-five guys panicked while trying to smash each other's hats. Elias, no stranger to random outbreaks of stupidity, simply removed his hat and stood there watching the chaos and pain.

"What the fuck!" Nolan screamed, and grabbed the first person he could. "Spoons, cut it out!"

"Me?" Spooner was laughing. "Fuck, man, he's *your* girl."

"Rigor Mortis! Goddamnit!"

But no one listened. Bodies were dropping as others fled, yet everyone was laughing. The BLM guys, a loose-knit bunch of locals employed by this nationwide conglomerate, exalted in this anarchy like natives suddenly shown the way.

The Germans, visibly unimpressed, returned to work as no one, at least not anyone near anyone else, dared put on their hat.

———————

"Holy shit!" Rigor Mortis jumped from the wall before a bundle of floor joists swung through the exact spot where he had just been standing. "Rand, look out!"

"Jump!" Rand screamed to Elias as they both crashed to the deck.

"What the fuck!" Enraged, Rand drove his hatchet into the closest 2x4 wall.

"You guys all right?" Riggy poked his head into the room. "I'm going to kill this motherfucker."

"What's going on?" Nolan's voice crackled through the walkie-talkies. "Riggy, why's the crane guy running toward the trailer?"

"Because he knows we're coming for him!" Rigor Mortis, Rand, and Elias, sprinted down the hall and outside just as the BLM trailer door snapped closed.

"Hey!" Nolan was running to intercept them. "Don't you dare go in there!"

"That fucker almost killed us!"

"Wait!" Nolan got there first. He blocked the stairs leading up to the trailer. He held a hand against Rigor Mortis' chest, but turned to Rand instead. "What happened?"

"It's like he said. After all their safety bullshit, that little fucker with the remote wasn't even looking."

Nolan glanced at Elias, who only nodded.

"Fuck." Nolan gritted his teeth. "Goddamnit."

The door behind him opened and Dennis Lambie filled the space. "I understand we just had a near-miss."

"Bring your boy out here—" Rigor Mortis demanded, but Nolan shoved him back.

"I'll handle this."

"Noll—"

"Turn around and take a walk, like right fucking now."

Rigor Mortis glared at everyone, hocked up a ball of phlegm, and then sauntered back to work.

Nolan, pausing to readjust his composure, pointed to the bundle of thirty-foot floor joists still twisting in the wind. "I can't have that, Dennis, you know? I just can't. It's rule number one. The operator has to maintain visual contact with the load, or he can't fly it. Period."

"You're absolutely right and I apologize. He'd tell you himself but he's a little nervous."

"He almost killed three people, man, I'd be nervous too."

"I'm sorry, Noll," a voice called out from behind Lambie. "Seriously, man, I'm sorry."

The guy's name was Dave Owens. He was stocky, in his mid-twenties, and had worked for BLM since his arrival in Spring Valley two years before. "I lost sight of it and just ... I didn't think anyone was there."

Nolan said, "Well, at least no one got clipped."

Rand looked at Elias. "Disappointed?"

Elias snapped his fingers. "I knew I should have stayed on that wall."

"You know what?" Lambie said. "We were gonna have the weekly safety meeting tomorrow but we'll call it now instead. Give everyone a chance to calm down."

Nolan frowned after Lambie disappeared inside the trailer, saying, "Looks like you girls just weaseled yourself a break."

Rand scoffed. "Yeah, almost dying is some trade-off for ten minutes of bureaucratic bullshit."

"*Attention all employees,*" Lambie's voice echoed across the job. "*Safety meeting in front of the trailer ASAP.*"

Uno arrived and said, "My safety meetings are way more fun."

The crowd gathered as word spread about the near-miss. Lambie stood on the steps with the crane's portable controller in his hands. No bigger than a small box, it had four toggles and various switches. He held it up and said, "Fellas, like we've been stressing from the start, safety is job one. And we just had a perfect example of what can happen when people get careless." He spoke of ice-covered ladders and top-plate and said, "Now I know the framers and I have agreed that no one is allowed to walk exterior top-plate, but in light of today's events, I'm thinking about banning interior walls as well."

A round of groans erupted until Nolan said, "Dennis, man, that would stop us dead in our tracks. We can't roll floor off ladders."

"Yes, well, I can't have people heaving themselves off walls now either, can I?"

Rigor Mortis shouted, "Get someone with a brain on that box and maybe we can get this thing built!"

Nolan yelled, "No more quacking from the peanut gallery!"

"Issue two." Lambie tapped himself on the head. He pointed at Nolan, Cooter and New Year. "Other than those three gentlemen and my own BLM employees, not one of you is wearing your hardhat."

More groans spilled out as Lambie said, "Guys, I can't have this, all right? As of today, everyone has to have a hat on at all times or you're going to be sent home. OSHA will absolutely drill me to the wall."

"Mine's lost," Spoons said.

"Mine too," Bunny echoed.

"I hate them," Elias said. "They're for dorks."

But Lambie just held up his hand. "Whatever the reason, we have new hats inside but then that's it. You lose, you buy. And to increase your appreciation, the next ones I'm buying are all pink, so you best hang on to what you got."

Disgruntled whispers rustled the crowd.

Lambie turned to Nolan and asked, "Anything else?"

"Only one thing." Nolan glanced across the crew before zeroing in on Elias. "You fuckers get those brain buckets on and staple them to your goddamn heads if need be. This ain't no democracy, got it?" He nodded toward Dennis. "That's it."

"All right, guys, meeting adjourned."

––––––––––––

The first shot in the hardhat war rang out the following afternoon. In one of the ground-floor rooms where the massive tool chests resided, an informal break-room had taken shape. There was a table, a microwave oven, and a portable heater. Guys would drop their bags and hats and either fetch lunch off-site or in their cars, creating time for mischief.

The fact that Rigor Mortis returned from lunch and found that someone had used a permanent black marker to inscribe COCKLOVER across the front of his helmet, meant that by the end of the week nearly every hat had been subsequently disgraced. POLE-MASTER, MAN-LOVER, ASSBAG, FUCKFACE, SHE-MALE, NUT-WARMER, NUT-REST, HERMAPHRODITE, NAMBLA, GONAD, MAN-SACK, and WHORE-DADDY were only a few of the less offensive expressions. Still, it was hard to take people seriously when their helmet, like Spooner's, had a giant boner and scrotum on its side, or Bunny would approach with a hat that said, INSERT COCK HERE, with an arrow pointed at his ear.

The word HERMAPHRODITE was scrawled like graffiti across Elias' helmet, and he quickly experienced the joy this new nickname could produce—Hermaphrodite, Hermpf, Aphrodite—the crew's creative juices flowed through the walkie-talkies.

But of more concern than obscene hardhats was the fact that Nolan still needed additional personnel for a host of mundane positions. Of utmost importance was the hiring of more laborers to ferry supplies and gophers for miscellaneous requests. He could not afford to have guys making twenty dollars an hour walking room-to-room and floor-to-floor looking for tools, hangers, nails, hardware, and other equipment. So to this end, Robert Haddock was hired. At barely five-foot-two, he resembled a hobbit in a hard hat. Haddock had spent the better part of his sixty years either inside a coal mine or ranching in Wyoming. Recently laid off from the mines, and with ranching a dying way of life, he was now forced into this strange new world where Hurry Up ruled the day. Completely unskilled in carpentry, and despite making only ten dollars an hour, he nevertheless became indispensable and beloved due to his old-school work ethic. His two-pack-a-day habit, combined with the sun and dreary mines, had turned his face into a withered prune on a stick-like body. Unfailingly upbeat, he stood in stark contrast to the morose characters stalking about.

"Bob, I need 16's."

"Bob, I need a dozen 2x10 joist hangers."

"Bob, where's the fucking impact wrench?"

As the radio became a Bob hotline of endless requests, he dutifully responded. Scurrying about, unloading his parcels as even more requests spilled in, and often times talking to himself as he tried to remember the location of a thousand items, Haddock was paid the highest tribute of all once he was worked into the group vernacular.

"I need a Bob."

"Can somebody Bob me racks of 8's?"
"Get on your knees and Bob."

———————

On December 21, Nolan showed up driving this year's hottest status symbol. The bone white F-350 Turbo Diesel King Crew Cab had a long bed and dual rear tires that, combined with the truck's overall size, was nothing short of imposing. On both doors was painted:

HARRIS FRAMING
SPRING VALLEY, COLORADO
1-908-555-6262

Like children drawn to the newest toy, the guys gathered in awe and circled the Herculean vehicle while Nolan stood and smoked. There was talk of torque and horsepower beneath the lifted hood while others peeked inside.

"One hundred percent leather, man, even the dash."

"Look at the size of these seats."

Only Rand remained at work. Staring at the gawk-fest across the yard, his gaze slowly simmered.

———————

At the end of the day, Nolan and Cam gathered up the crew.

Nolan said, "A lot of you girls have been whining and crying about Christmas which, for you unfortunate bastards, falls on Sunday this year. Now, as an example of my good nature, we'll only work until noon on Christmas Eve."

"Jesus ..." someone uttered.

"What about Monday?" Uno asked.

"What about it?" Nolan shrugged. "See you at seven o'clock, simpleton."

"How come Cooter gets Thursday and Friday off?" Bunny yelled.

"Because he's not a moron. And his dad's sick back in Texas, so mind your own fucking business, Bunny." Nolan looked out over the crowd.

"Any other questions, because after this I don't want to hear another goddamn word about fucking Christmas."

"Hey, Riggy," Bunny said, "are you going caroling again this year?"

Rigor Mortis smiled sadly and said, "Well, actually your mom's coming over to deck the halls with my balls ..."

Nolan pointed at his watch. "Roll it up. See you morons in the morning. And don't forget to hurry up."

"Hurry up."

———

Elias had left work early to meet with his attorney. Actually, it was Rand's attorney on referral, so the attorney was already accustomed to complete nonsense. On the office walls hung various diplomas from distant schools. The attorney was balding but had tufts of hair like a clown around both ears. He flipped through the file and then glanced at Elias from over the rim of his glasses. "Okay, so I've been in touch with the district attorney. If we plead guilty, he'll deal on this. He'll go light."

"What's that mean?"

"Ninety-six hours of community service."

"No way."

"Excuse me? The alternative could be much worse."

"Really? I only get one day off a week, and I'm supposed to spend that one day doing what—picking up garbage on the side of the road just to freeze my ass off some more? I'd rather go to jail."

"*What*?" The attorney looked up from the file. "You're joking, right?"

"Nope." Elias did the math. "Ninety-six hours means one of two things. Either I spend the next twelve Sundays picking up garbage and freezing, or I get four days off in a row."

"But it's in *jail*."

"So what? At least I'll be able to rest."

The attorney could not hide his horror. "*Rest*? What is wrong with you people?"

"It—"

"Please don't do this. It will set a horrible precedent."

Elias shook his head. "Not my problem."

"Boy...in twenty years I've never had anyone ask to be imprisoned."

CHAPTER TWENTY-ONE

With the framing contract for the first building valued at $1.2 million, Nolan was flush with cash. He bought a new car for Kara, new ski equipment for both of them and Nolan's daughter, who, depending on the weather, was due to arrive down in Denver four o'clock Christmas Eve. He was hoping to spend the entire week skiing with her, since this would probably be his only chance all season. Things were good, which meant he had not wanted to blow his brains out for the last three weeks at least.

At work, the 12,000 square foot ground-floor was standing, sheeted, and floored by the end of the fourth week. That was also Christmas weekend. If this pace could be maintained for the next three floors, they might be at the roof by March. And if he could get the second 48,000 square foot monster started while some guys finished the roof...

He did not want to get greedy—but he was. He wanted this entire monstrosity wrapped up by July with his guys framing like machine guns every single day. Allowing a half-day holiday on Christmas Eve? It almost made him sick.

Before going home, he pulled his new truck into the framing yard, clicked on the high beams, and then slowly whistled. Stacks of walls had formed into walls of their own and were sometimes fifteen-feet high. Starting Monday, the entire second-floor would be trucked over to the site. Nolan wondered how fast it could be assembled. A week? Two weeks? And with these guys already framing the third-floor? He was positively salivating when his cellphone abruptly rang.

"Hey, babe."

"Where are you?" Kara sounded like she was at the sink. "Dinner's gonna be ready by six."

"I'm out at the yard." Nolan lit up a cigarette while dreamily scanning the darkened site. "You should see how many walls are out here, babe." He started to laugh. "I hope we got our numbers right."

"They're talking about snow tomorrow." Kara's voice was anxious. "I hope her flight doesn't get canceled."

"Yeah. Merry Christmas, right?"

"Come home."

"I am." Nolan slipped it into reverse. "I'll be there in a minute."

The walls started arriving on the flatbed tractor-trailers Monday morning. The forklifts unloaded stacks of them before the crane flew them into place. Up on deck, Cam Rogers consulted a master list and spoke by radio with Uno, who was on the ground darting in and out of this sudden maze.

"12BR4 through 20BR4, and then I need 16IR4, 18IR4, and six 34DR3s."

The demarcations were by unit and either interior or exterior. Uno was like a monkey jumping between the stacks. An avid back-country snowboarder, he maximized this exposure since who knew when he would next get a chance to taste the real thing.

As the walls were stood and nailed off, Rand and Elias pulled layout for the coming floor system. The plumbing and electrical head-outs also needed to be accounted for. Walking exterior wall 2x6 top-plate was sketchy enough, but walking interior wall 2x4 top-plate meant walking a board as wide as a smartphone ten feet in the air. In boots in the dead of winter, it made for tricky business.

"Ah, fuck," Rand said.

"What?" Elias lit up a smoke.

Rand held up the blueprints. "I grabbed the wrong floor."

"That blows. They're way the fuck over there. Want me to climb down and get them?"

They were standing on one side of the long hallway that would eventually extend the length of the entire building. They either had to walk all the way down the hallway to cross over, or climb down and cut through the maze of walls.

"Safety last." Rand lifted onto his toes.

"What're you doing?" Then Elias saw him staring across the hallway. "You're fucking with me, right?"

Rand did not even pause. Like a cat, he sprang four-feet across and stuck a landing on the 2x4 wall.

"That ..." Elias was stunned. "Don't ever do that again, dude. I'm totally serious. You wanna end up in a freaking wheelchair?"

It was 1 P.M. when a bullhorn blasted across the yard. "*Attention pukes. This is your master speaking. Always remember to hurry up.*"

Heads scanned the parking lot below, but no one could find Nolan's truck.

"*That's right. You cannot find me because I am omniscient. For you morons that are extra stupid, that means I am your God.*"

"There he is." Bunny pointed up at the scrawling gondola as Nolan said, "*Have shame, since the stupidest of all was the first to find me. Hurry up.*"

"He's going fucking skiing?" Rand was looking up at the bullhorn in the gondola car window as Nolan's daughter said, in a sweet voice that only added to the pain, "*My daddy says to hurry up.*"

Fourteen guys removed their gloves and pointed middle fingers at the sky. Bunny, never bashful, bared his ass instead.

"I just can't believe it." Rand stared at Elias. "I really think I'm gonna quit."

"Man—"

"Fuck this." Rand dropped the gun. "The guy buys a seventy-thousand-dollar truck, new K-12 gear, takes the week off to ski with his kid ... Hell, I got kids too, man, you know?"

"I don't know ... Maybe it's time to talk to him about a vacation."

"A what?" Rand cackled. "Fuck, man, around here you need to go to jail or die for that."

"I just said that to the attorney ..."

"Since you've been with us in the past three years, have either one of us even had a single fucking week off?"

"No."

"How about more than three days in a row?"

"Never."

"Man, this ain't fucking *Roots* ..." Rand unbuckled his bags and slung them over his shoulder. "I ain't working here with that motherfucker sailing over our heads all day long, man, fuck that." He glanced at Elias. "Let's roll, man, fuck this motherfucker."

"I can't." Elias looked at the deck.

"So you're just gonna let me walk out alone?"

"It ain't that ... I just ..." Elias tried to verbalize it. "This is all I got, you know? I'm not going back into the kitchen, man, fuck that."

"So you don't think you could get another job?"

"At eighteen bucks an hour? With barely three years beneath my belt?" Elias did not have to wait for an answer. "I helped build this fucking company."

"So what? The way this clown acts, we could be bankrupt tomorrow. As a matter of fact, he just bought a bone down in Grand Junction."

"A what?"

"A front-end loader. Guess how much?"

"No clue."

"$80,000. They're trucking it up here this week." Rand turned to leave and then turned back. "Do you own any stock?"

"What?"

"You heard me. Because the last time I checked, neither one of our names were printed on that brand new truck neither one of us owns."

"Rand—"

"Naw ..." Rand started walking toward the ladder. "I ain't trying to hear it."

"Why don't we go work with the Mexicans?"

"I got a better idea. Why don't *you* go work with the Mexicans while I go downtown and start drinking." Rand saluted as he descended the ladder. "Good luck with your company."

Elias watched him go.

———————

Later that day, out at the framing yard, Elias worked alongside Alonzo, Perfidio, and their crew. They all wore sunglasses and cinched hoods against the blowing snow as the generators and compressors wailed out the calamitous back song to the day. Above, the sun teased them through a crack in the surrounding blue-gray clouds.

"What the hell ...?" Elias squinted toward the gate.

Rand was booting through the drifting snow. His jumpsuit had been traded in for jeans and a leather jacket.

"I can't stand to see this." Rand stepped up onto the deck and unslung a backpack. "Three-thirty is close enough, man, roll it up."

"How'd you get here?" Elias asked, pounding his gloves together against the chill.

"Mountain taxi." Rand pulled out a twelve-pack from the backpack and the Mexicans clapped. "That's right, *vatos*, step right up."

They all shared a cold one until Rand tugged Elias' shoulder. "They got this shit under control, man, we gotta go."

"Where?"

"I know somebody who knows somebody ..."

Five minutes later they were in the Skylark.

The Reverend Ronolo Burby had Don King-like blond hair and eerily gray eyes that fueled an ethereal appearance. Also known as the High Heat and Sinister Minister, Burby was an emaciated stick in his late twenties who was addicted to his Pentecostal faith, other religions, reincarnation, and cocaine and heroin. The coke he dealt, the heroin he abused, but his condominium was always spotless. Since there were long lines of would-be servants for various tasks, he traded blow for maid service, meals, errands, sex, and protection provided by the local chapter of the Black Brigades. He was kind and courteous and loved to challenge people in conversation. But today, not having time for the usual banter, Rand said, "Rev, man, what's up?"

With the door cracked, the Reverend Burby smiled warmly and uncocked a 9mm Beretta. He was wearing a bathrobe and hugged Rand before inviting him and Elias inside. "I understand the two of you are in a bit of a rush."

"Yeah, sorry about that." Rand nodded at Elias. "After last time, I was afraid to even bring him back over."

"Nonsense." Burby bared a grin of unwashed teeth and hugged Elias as well. "My greatest challenge yet ... Thomas, how are you?"

"Good, Rev, staying warm, you know?"

"I hear that." Burby triple-locked the front door and steered them toward his couches. "What can I help you fellas with today?"

"Eight-ball city." Rand dropped a stack of twenties onto the coffee table. "I hate to blow and go, Rev, but like I said, we got a couple of ladies waiting on us back in town."

"Really now?" Burby disappeared into a back room and then returned with a stainless-steel briefcase. "Sounds like intrigue is afoot to me ..."

He produced a large sack of white and a triple-beam scale. Because he always tried to be a gracious host, the Reverend cut them some lines as they waited. He spooned out their request and then deposited it into a Ziploc. They cleaned their faces, snorted back the draining narcotic, and profusely thanked the Reverend.

Outside, they did more blow in the Skylark before wheeling toward town.

"I think he likes you," Rand said. "And I ain't talking about as a friend neither."

"Wow." Elias was in full deadpan. "A gay priest who's also a drug-dealing disaster ... you just can't make this shit up, can you?"

Downtown, it was nearing five o'clock. Rand directed them to El Rancherito. Once inside, he said, "Look, there's something I should tell you. I got Cheryl and you got Rita."

"What kind of name is that?"

"What, Rita?"

"Why'd you say it like that?"

"Like what?"

"Like she weighs three hundred pounds?"

Rand pulled him into an alcove and whispered, "She's not a pig, she's married."

"Great—"

"Just shut up for one second, okay? She's not in it for anything other than a good time, and she says her husband's totally down with it."

"Oh, I'm sure he is. Dudes love it when their women sling ass—"

"Listen." Rand held up an index finger. "Here's what's gonna happen. We're gonna have some drinks, we're gonna do some lines, and then we're gonna ball these chicks, okay? You don't have any morals, so don't even pretend that you care."

Elias shrugged. "True story."

They stepped back into the hallway. Past the dining area were two pool tables and a bar. A pair of brunettes on stools marked their approach with warm smiles and waves.

"Who's who?" Elias urgently whispered.

"Rita's on the right."

After the introductions, the guys shed their jackets and ordered drinks. Cheryl was tall and thin and had perfect red lips. Rita, whose smile put people instantly at ease, was shorter but had a curvy body. There was definite chemistry between Rand and Cheryl because they quickly resumed grinding against each other at the bar.

Elias and Rita promptly headed for the pool table.

"They sure didn't waste any time," Elias said.

"So, you're the wingman." Rita's hazel eyes shared in the joke. "Let's just say I'm glad you got here." She chalked up her cue. "It was starting to get unbearable."

"I can see that." He punched the release and the balls clattered into the trough. "Lag for break?"

She won, so Elias racked them up. He said, "I got a bad feeling I'm about to get rolled."

"What would make you say a thing like that?" But her break was loud enough to echo, exploding balls in all directions. "I'll be lows."

Then she ran the table.

"Beginner's luck, right?" Elias rolled his eyes. "Happens every time."

"Care to put down a friendly wager on the next game? Big, strong construction worker like yourself?"

"That's it." Elias feigned injustice. "Just for that, I'm gonna get my ass kicked again, just you watch."

He racked up the balls and then saluted her with his Beam and coke. "Table's yours, miss."

Her explosive break made him flinch again. He took a peek at the bar and then wished he had not.

"They're gonna get arrested," he said, and Rita glanced over as well.

"I hope you like playing pool," she said, "because it looks like it's just you and me tonight."

"What's the wager? How about if you win, we go out to my car and do a little ..." He twitched his nose like a mouse. "And if I win, we go out to my car and do a little ..."

Her eyes brightened at this revelation. "I would love to"—she twitched her nose in answer—"with you in your car right now."

"Good girl." Elias chucked his stick onto the table. "Screw these perverts. Let's roll."

They grabbed their jackets and headed for the Skylark.

"Listen," he said. "I hope you're not into appearances, because my car's a total mess."

"I've got the same problem."

"Nice."

In the frontseat, they huddled over the cocaine. He found out that Rita was a thirty-two-year-old transplant from South Boston, Indiana. She had married a man fourteen years her senior, but, between their two young kids and his fulltime job, he had subsequently lost interest in the physical aspect of their relationship. By granting her this freedom, he was also relinquished from this duty. Beneath her warm smile and easygoing nature, though, might have lurked the shapes of her regrets.

To reinvigorate the mood, he cut more lines on the CD case.

"I'm pretty jacked," she said.

"Me too."

Rand and Cheryl banged on the locked back doors, so Elias let them in.

"I see how it is." Rand immediately reached for the CD. "Rock-n-roll, my friends, rock and fucking roll."

The party rolled through a tour of bars, but certain appetites remained paramount. They stopped by the Reverend's for another eightball and popped some Vicodin to dull the edge. They spoke of vast ideas inside the enthralled buffeting of their own brains. More bars, more lines, and then it was 1 A.M. They headed back to Elias' condo where, down in the basement, Cheryl made her move. Seated on Rand's lap in an easy chair, she worked the button and zipper until he filled her hand.

She groaned and kissed him before nibbling on his nose. "I want to try out your friend," she said, and abruptly walked over to where Elias and Rita were making out.

They took breaks for blow and more drinks as both girls tried to do lines off Rand's chest but could not keep from laughing. Late night turned into early morning and no one slept at all. By 6 A.M., after dropping the girls off at Cheryl's, Rand and Elias finished off the third eight-ball. It was a brutal realization as all the booze and exhaustion crashed in. They pounded orange juice and aspirin before the Skylark pulled into the jobsite.

"Hurry up," Rand said.

"Hurry up," Elias echoed.

But neither one could.

An hour later Nolan found them on the second-floor. With the exterior walls already in place, the crane was now dropping packages of interior walls as fast as they could stand them. "Well, well, well. I heard you girls walked off the job yesterday."

Elias and Rand were not in the mood. Their hangovers prevented most forms of human contact, so they focused on the work instead.

"Hey, morons ..." Once Nolan stepped into their path, they dropped the walls they were carrying.

"Look." Rand lit a cigarette. He took off his sunglasses to clean them, so his bloodshot eyes stared back. "I was unhappy yesterday, all right?"

"So you two booze bags decided to get all lit up while your bros were over here busting ass?"

"You know what?" Rand dragged on his smoke. "I'm fucking here now, aren't I?"

"What about you?" Nolan turned his disgust onto Elias. "You as hungover as your girlfriend here?"

"Yes." But Elias was not amused. "And for the record, I was out with the Mexicans—"

"Blah, blah, blah ..." Nolan glanced at them both. "We're the lead gig at this show, guys, you can't fucking do this."

"I can do whatever I want." Rand exhaled smoke. "And right now, what I want to do is keep working, all right?"

"So if I go up the hill with my kid again today, you girls gonna run back to the bar?"

"I just think it's fucked up is all. I mean Emily and Kenny are at home on Christmas break too, you know? Seriously, this whole world ain't just about you."

Nolan could be seen searching for a hostile response, but then said, "All right." His mind was still turning. "I guess that's fair enough."

"I'm not trying—"

"It's still kind of early. If you head home now you could be up there pulling turns with the kids in an hour."

"Oh gee, thanks. What a fucking hero."

"I—"

"Just stop, man. I get it. No one else exists but you."

Nolan flinched. "Are you fucking kidding me? After everything I've done for you?"

"Oh, here we go."

"You ungrateful fuck—"

"Whoa." Elias quickly stepped between them. "You two girls need to kiss and make up. Like now."

"He—"

"Seriously. This is embarrassing."

Nolan stewed, unable to look at Rand. "Take tomorrow off instead. That cool?"

Rand said nothing.

"What about me?" Elias asked. "Can I have tomorrow off too? I mean I love my kids just as much, man, what the fuck?"

"You?" Nolan scoffed. "Somebody's dad? That's too horrific to even contemplate."

Into February, both crews were at peak production. Out at the yard, the Mexicans averaged sixty walls a day. The white guys at the site steamrolled through the dozens of arriving stacks. Nolan, who had recently purchased a Caterpillar front-end loader referred to as a "bone," tooled around the framing yard like a kid with a new toy. The bone had two different attachments—six-foot forks used for lifting bunks of wood or stacks of walls, or a platform so that guys could be telescoped to work at higher elevations.

"This thing's your own personal Abe Lincoln." Nolan shouted at O-Zone and Cooter. He passed by them with two bunks of 2x4 weighing 3000 pounds. "Bow down in praise, simpletons, because this machine just freed you slave-like bitches."

So far, only a few sets of interior walls had been wrongly transcribed from the plans. The real nightmare turned out to be the floor system and the incredible maze of joists. But once the floor was sheeted, the resulting deck looked like a football field made of plywood. After the crane started slinging walls, an astonishing pace of eight working days was all it took to assemble the walls for every floor. By February, eight weeks after they began, they were already a month ahead of schedule.

Nolan, Rand, and Rigor Mortis were on the fourth-floor deck waiting for the crane to sling them more walls. They walked to the edge and stood above a forty-foot drop to the ice-covered concrete. Their attention was focused on the unfinished foundation across the way. With framing slated to begin on this sister unit within the next month, the concrete company had hit a serious hurdle.

"There's a granite shelf in that back corner." Nolan pointed to where the sixteen-foot concrete forms snaked around the perimeter before abruptly stopping in the northeast corner. "They're bringing in demolition guys from Grand Junction to blow it clean."

"What a joke." Rand turned to Nolan. "Was it you who told me the concrete guys are getting paid to drive four hours back and forth from Silverthorne every single day?"

Nolan nodded.

"Unbelievable." Rand grunted. "Stroke'em if you got'em."

"What a fuckshow," Rigor Mortis added.

Their radios crackled out a heads-up warning, so they turned in unison as the first batch of exterior walls dangled from the swinging crane.

Ten minutes later, as part of moving gear up to the new floor, the crane flew the portajohn through the sky as the radios exploded with comments and laughter.

"Here comes the lunch truck."

"Talk about flying deuces."

"Watch out, Bunny," Spoons said, "your life is flashing before our eyes."

On the floors below them, teams of electricians and plumbers followed closely in the framer's wake. The building was alive with workers nailing, drilling, and welding. Then the drywall crews, with their screwguns constantly whirring, stalked about on two-foot stilts applying sheetrock and plaster to the ceilings and walls like creatures loosed from a nearby circus.

But disaster struck on a chilly Wednesday morning. Dennis Lambie had previously instructed his BLM workers to enforce the Controlled Access Zones, which meant that unless the floor was completely framed, no one except the carpenters was allowed access for any reason. The purpose of this rule was made brutally evident after one of the plumbers, who as a trade rarely dealt with exterior ladders, stepped on the top rung of a fully extended forty-foot extension ladder. This caused the ladder to cantilever against its perch, and the bottom footers dislodged. The plumber, with only one foot on the deck, plummeted three-stories to the ground where he luckily hit a snowbank. But he landed on all fours, shattering both knees, femurs, and wrists before his face smashed into the snow. In the immediate aftermath, guys ripped off their clothes for rags to staunch the blood from the compound fractures. Some of the other plumbers broke into tears after the helicopter arrived for the flight to Denver. Work for the day was halted. Near the spot where the blood had already frozen black into the ice, Dennis Lambie gathered up the electricians, plumbers, framers, and drywallers to say, "This should never have happened."

Sixty guys stood in silence. Lambie, usually good-natured, was now totally freed from that constraint. "The choice is up to you, guys. You can either come to work and follow the rules and go home to your families at the end of the day, or we can bring in more spatulas to scrape the rest of you off the ground."

Angered, the plumbers rallied around their leader, who pointed at the framers and yelled, "That fucking ladder should have been tied off!"

"That guy should never have been up there," Nolan shot back.

But Lambie had had enough. "OSHA will set the blame, man, we're all to fucking blame." He glanced across the group with equal measures of disgust. "I want my guys to remove every single piece of ice from around the base of every single ladder, starting with this one. I want this blood gone now. I want the goddamn carpenters to tie off every single ladder that spans between floors. I want all access points barred off with 2x4, and I want the rest of you—that means everyone—electricians, plumbers, drywallers, whoever—to stay the fuck out of any and all CAZ zones period. If you need to get up top, get a framer to lead the way." Lambie seemed at a loss, so he ended back where he began. "This should never have happened."

And then he walked away.

Two days later a bailiff yelled, "All rise!"

Elias and his attorney stood up. Elias was wearing a tie so new he had removed its store tag on the way into court. His head was cleanly shaven, the Fu-Manchu trimmed accordingly.

The judge was a pinch-faced man with little sense of humor. The courtroom was sparse save for the portraits of other pinch-faced forefathers hung in dire reverence. Afterall, it was a room made for justice.

The judge had gray hair and blue eyes that inquisitively settled onto Elias.

"Mr. Elias," the judge said. He read the charges matter of factly before asking, "How do you plead?"

"Guilty, your honor."

"I understand there's already a deal in place with the district attorney?"

"There is, your honor." The district attorney was a thrice-elected firebrand when it came to law and order. "We asked for ninety-six hours of community service, but the defendant has requested jail instead."

The judge swung his gaze back to Elias, incredulous. "It's usually the reverse, you know."

"Yes, your honor."

"I've been a judge for thirty-one years, Mr. Elias, so unprecedented things pique my curiosity."

"Okay."

"Do you have a problem with serving your community? That's what community service means."

"I understand that, your honor. It's just hard to explain."

"Try me."

"Well..." Elias knew he had to be careful. "I work outside six days a week. I haven't had more than two days off in a row in two years. Ninety-six hours means twelve Sundays freezing some more. My boss is already freaking crazy, so if he knew I was even telling you this he'd probably make me work seven days a week out of spite alone."

The crowd was made up of defendants and lawyers waiting their turn. Everyone laughed.

"Just to make sure we have this right," the judge said. "Ninety-six hours with good time, meaning you don't get into any trouble, actually means sixty hours of confinement."

"We'll see how it goes."

"Please, Mr. Elias." The judge was busy with the paperwork. "Please don't threaten to commit future crimes at your own sentencing hearing."

Elias' attorney was not laughing. He hissed at Elias until Elias sat back down.

The judge smashed his gavel. "Court is adjourned for ten minutes."

"All rise!" The bailiff escorted the judge to his chambers.

———————————

The next morning Elias reported to the Salinas County Jail. New and state of the art, it housed up to 150 prisoners either serving local time or waiting transfer into the statewide D.O.C.

Elias arrived at eight and by ten o'clock was showered and in a jumpsuit. They gave him a pillow, two sheets, a blanket, and a bag of toiletries.

There were fifteen ten-man pods inside the jail. Each pod had a bathroom, bunk beds, and a common room. Elias entered his pod and found an empty top bunk. He introduced himself and, as the others sized him up, told them why he was there. He soon found most of them were locked up for similar nonsense as well.

10 P.M. was lights out. 6 A.M. was lights on. They cleaned the pod daily and completed other facility chores. Elias kept to himself and slept

as much as possible. His body was so desperate to mend it was already stitching itself back together by day two. Meals were provided by the Steakman Diner, so he ate everything he could.

As luck would have it, Elias' roommate, Billy, the tall stork-like cook with the screaming demon skull tattoo, was three pods over. He was doing six months after his cocaine habit ran amok. Once thousands of dollars went missing from the liquor store he worked at part-time, Billy's party was over. Elias knew Billy was doing blow but had no idea how far-gone Billy was. They worked opposite sides of the clock, so sometimes Elias did not even see most of his roommates until the weekend.

There were a couple of heavy hitters locked in isolation waiting transfer to the maximum-security Colorado State Penitentiary at Cañon City. One was an accountant who became obsessed with his fiancé's best friend. He showed up at her apartment one night, cut both of her Achilles and raped her before stabbing her to death. Another was a framer Elias actually knew in passing. This guy and his buddy had been out drinking and got into an argument on the ride home. The framer told his buddy he was going to shoot him once they got home. The buddy thought he was kidding. After the framer shot him in the shoulder, he was kind enough to call 911, telling them, "I told him I was going to shoot him, not kill him."

Joker, one of the guys in Elias' pod, had a bunch of interesting stories. He looked like Ted Nugent and seemed just as crazy. He was originally wanted for strong-armed robbery, but was arrested for car theft, possession of methamphetamine and weapons. He told a story that was too crazy to believe. In Colorado, everyone had to warm up their vehicles. There was no such thing as a cold start. One morning, Joker, already on the run, threw a bunch of guns and meth into the trunk of someone's idling car and took off. Most of the charges were being dismissed, however, because in Colorado taking someone's running vehicle was not auto theft, it was joyriding. In addition, the traffic stop was judged illegal, which meant the search of the car was illegal, so the guns and meth were getting tossed as evidence.

Somehow, Joker had weed smuggled inside, and how it got there Elias never asked. So they spent a couple of afternoons getting high near an out-take vent in the bathroom and telling stories. Overall, it was easy time, so Elias walked out the door on day three feeling like a new man.

Rand picked him up in Elias' Skylark even though he did not have a license or insurance. They went to Elias' place so he could shower and change. Waiting, Rand grew bored. He grabbed a bottle of tequila and journeyed into the basement. Looking through Elias' CDs, he found something on the rickety plywood desk tucked into the corner of the room.

Realizing it was only the second time he had actually been in here, Rand scanned across the posters of an old white man in a wig and a black man in glasses. There were dozens of books stacked like bricks against the wall. Rand sat at the desk and began thumbing through a legal pad.

"Excuse me?" Elias was standing in the doorway with a towel around his waist. "You got a warrant or something?"

Rand held up the pad. "What's this?"

"Nothing." Elias kicked aside dirty clothes until he reached his closet.

"What is this?"

"Do you mind?" Elias held up a pair of boxers.

Rand used the pad to shield his eyes. He flipped through a dozen pages until he said, "Holy shit."

"You know what?" Elias was pulling on his jeans. "Why don't you put that down, man, this ain't no show and tell."

But Rand was not listening. He saw fifty crumpled balls of paper behind the door and finally asked, "How long is this thing?"

"I don't know."

"How long have you been working on it?"

"Since about four months after I got here."

"Three *years* ago?" Rand arched an eyebrow as he whistled. "And all this time I thought you were just staying home jerking off to gay porn."

"I was. That shit in your hand is for my man-wife to be."

Rand chuckled, returning his gaze to the pad before Elias abruptly ripped it from his grasp.

Rand said, "Listen, I don't have a very big brain, so tell me what's that about?"

"I was bored. Started working on a history of the valley. And you know what? It's a pretty interesting place. But it's kind of turned into a history of violence. Man versus nature. Man against man. White, black, red—it doesn't matter. We're a pretty useless species."

"Ha."

"I'm not kidding. There isn't a single positive thing we contribute to this planet."

Rand thought for a minute and said, "I ... we are ..."

"See?"

"That can't be right." But for every action, Rand saw the reaction.

Elias said, "We build, we fuck, we destroy, we pollute, we kill, hell, even our own shit is toxic. Did you know outside of ants and chimpanzees, humans are the only species that commits inter-species homicide for no reason?"

"Oh my God." Rand leaned back to stare at the ceiling. "Sometimes hanging out with you is even more depressing than actually being alive."

"I'll take that as a compliment." Elias pulled on a sweatshirt and socks and said, "Ready to go?"

"Yeah." Rand pointed at the poster of the white man. "Who's that?"

"Thomas Jefferson."

"And the guy with the glasses?"

"Malcolm X."

"What's *he* doing up there next to Jefferson?"

"Because they talked about the same thing. They believed in the rights of man. Government should serve the people or the people should tear it down."

"You know, dude, you're an absolute buzzkill."

"Let's go."

Together, they headed into the night.

They arrived at Bear Lake Condominiums and found Elias' welcome home party already in full swing. Between Team Beaver and the Mexicans, the entire right half of the building was almost exclusively under the control of Harris Framing. Currently, two of the eight condos had guys milling through them, and lucky for them, in an adjoining unit, the four wives of the Mexicans were preparing a feast. PlayStations ruled the televisions, stereos were cranked, and tables for blackjack and five-card stud appeared.

"Yeah, here they are!" Spoons shouted.

"Right on, bitches." Bunny tossed Rand and Elias beers after they shed their jackets.

"Right on, beeches," Gustavo roughly mimicked.

Bunny cracked a smile. "*Bitches*, man, *bitches*."

"*Beeches*, mang, *beeches*."

Bunny howled and clapped him on the back. "I told you I'd teach you English!"

Someone sparked a joint while someone else passed a bowl. The refrigerators were fully loaded with so many beers they looked like munitions for a coming war.

"Bow down, peons." Uno appeared in the doorway with a three-foot glass bong shaped like a genie bottle. "The hookah is open for business."

Cheers erupted as someone else passed the whiskey.

The next afternoon, Nolan was at his kitchen table surrounded by open ledgers, black coffee, and a calculator filled with numbers. His bookkeeper was on a month-long honeymoon to Costa Rica, and while she was a pleasant woman, Nolan currently could find no love for her. He was drowning in figures. Billing, intake, payroll, taxes, fuel, expenses, worker's compensation—the ledgers were a dizzying display of graphs and columns in precise arrangement. Or at least they had been. Now, amid a sea of paperwork and bills, he was guzzling coffee and chain-smoking with an annoyance akin to rage.

With forty guys either directly employed by him or subcontracting in some capacity, the tipping point toward insanity was rapidly approaching. On top of the two monster condominiums still in progress, he now had a pair of siding teams to feed and two other framing crews working a ranch-style apartment building on the west side of town. And while his employees had the luxury of leaving work at five o'clock, Nolan was either scheduling lumber drops, attending meetings, or scouring blueprints sometimes until midnight. Then he would barely sleep in a haze-like stupor filled with worry, and seem to wake up even more exhausted than before he went to bed. Just in case that was not stressful enough,

Kara was growing weary of her solitary existence, a situation that Nolan had originally tried to placate until realizing that where women were concerned, appeasement and evasion were not tactics prone to high rates of success.

It was noon when Nolan's cellphone rang. He was still seated at the kitchen table and found it buried beneath the paper and bills.

"Hey, Cam," he said in greeting.

"Hey, man ..." Behind Cam's voice could be heard the screaming of saws and sporadic nailgun fire. "We got a situation out here with the Black Death."

"What now?"

"Well, he beat a BLM dude and then threatened to kill one of the electricians. I don't know what to tell you, man, but Lambie and Tresky have pretty much had enough. They call you yet?"

"No ..." Nolan rubbed each temple, wincing. "Motherfucker, there goes my call waiting. I'll call you back."

An hour later, Rigor Mortis was banned from all BLM jobsites. Nolan was in Lambie's office and Lambie was not happy.

"Over a goddamn airhose." Lambie shook his head as if nothing this stupid should be wasting his time. "My guy Kenny's getting stitched up at the hospital. I'm telling you, Noll, BLM policy dictates termination and prosecution."

Seated across from him, Nolan said, "Jesus ..."

"Don't get pissed at me."

"Believe me, it ain't you I'm cussing out."

Lambie's office was small, crammed with a single desk, computer, and a bookshelf filled with building codes and company protocols.

Nolan said, "I'm sorry about your guy. I can't do nothing about that now, so whatever has to happen, happens." Nolan made sure he had eye contact. "Of course, we both have a stake in this."

Lambie's expression, amused by the insinuation, nonetheless gave them room to maneuver. They both knew their relationship was too important to be tripped up by one event.

"I'll take that into consideration." Lambie then called Brian Tresky into the office to review the progress of both ongoing builds.

Nolan said, "A-Unit, save for the roof, is done. That includes all interior walls and hardware."

Tresky nodded and told Lambie, "Nolan and I did a walk-through yesterday. We're signed off on all four floors."

"Excellent." Lambie tapped his fingertips together. "What's the status with B-Unit?"

Nolan said, "Ground-floor will be completed by today."

Lambie smiled for the first time since Nolan's arrival. "Would it be unrealistic to expect the same time frame for B-Unit?"

"Hell yeah, unless somebody burns it down."

"Where are we on the roof for A-Unit? We get word on engineering yet?"

"Yeah, Tri-Build called ..." Tresky consulted his clipboard. "Final approval for the redesigned truss system should pass engineering by tomorrow latest. Their dispatch seems to think they can have the first trusses on-site by the end of the week."

"All right." Lambie glanced at Nolan. "I'm guessing this delay means your fellas will be primarily framing B-Unit."

"Yes. Go, go, go. I got two guys on call for any back-out the drywallers might need in A-unit, but otherwise, even as we speak, I got half my gringos out at the yard with the Mexicans so we can really bang this fucker out.'

"How far along are they?"

"By this morning they had most of the second-floor walls already completed." Nolan could not believe it himself. "It's not my fault that I'm this good."

"It's a burden, eh?" Tresky smiled. "Seriously, I been in this business for twenty-three years, and through the dead of winter—I got to admit, at first I thought the prefab idea was suicide."

"Mark my words, because we're gonna have all 96,000 square feet finished by July."

"Eight months? Imagine that."

"What about your guys?" Tresky referenced the growing tensions between the crews. More pointedly, the carpenters thought the BLM guys were strokers and basic laborers at best. And while Tresky kept his loyalties in order, the tightrope he walked meant certain transgressions had to be sorted and then forgotten. The math was simple. Even though his own employees were harassed, the suffering of few would benefit the many in light of this blistering pace. It was the difference between he and Nolan, since if it had been one of Nolan's guys who had taken that beating, retribution would have been swift. Tresky said, "So far, this winter's been a bruiser. Your guys holding up okay beneath the strain?"

"I got a great crew, man. I'm sure they're aware of some discomfort, but true morons can't feel actual pain."

Lambie and Tresky smiled as Nolan stood.

"You're breaking all kinds of records, Noll." Lambie pursed his lips. "But you look exhausted." He held up a sheaf of papers. "Payroll has most guys at sixty-five hours per week since this whole thing began."

"Listen, this ain't nothing." But Nolan knew why he was asking. "They're aware of what they're doing, Dennis. Ain't nobody gonna get hurt because of a little hard work. Besides, the harder you work them, the less trouble they get into after work."

"Your friend Rigor Mortis might have a thing or two to say about that."

"Not anymore, he won't." Nolan grabbed his jacket and shook their hands. "If you need me, I'll be out at the yard today, mushing the dogs till dark."

"The window representative is gonna be here after lunch. Think you could make some time?"

Nolan held up his cellphone. "It'll be on me all day."

"Thanks, Noll."

"See you, Nolan."

Nolan walked out, already seething. In his truck he muttered, "It was just bound to happen." Rigor Mortis' relative three months of calm was now blown apart. Still, considering every other bullshit problem crowding his plate, Nolan was having a hard time staying angry. In fact, on his way out to the yard, he thought of an even better punishment for Rigor Mortis—pimping his ass out on a different job so Nolan could still turn a profit. *Hurry up.*

He pulled into the framing yard and made a few calls in the blasting heat. It was late February and still twenty-eight degrees, but Nolan cracked a smile as he watched his frozen employees work the deck. According to the dashboard thermometer, inside the truck it was a balmy sixty-eight degrees.

He dialed a number, got the voicemail, and said, "Hey psycho. Where are you? I got something for you, and it's not common sense, so don't worry. Your mess with BLM is your problem, but I got a line on something else to keep you fed. Late." Nolan triggered down his window and screamed out, "Hermaphrodite! Hurry up!"

In his hood and glasses, Elias looked toward the pickup with a mixture of hostility and disgust that was so distinct, Nolan loudly cackled.

Elias arrived through the swirling wind gusts and said, "What's up?"

"Cold out there?" Nolan made a show of adjusting the heating vents onto his own face. "It's kind of chilly in here with the window open."

Elias, who enjoyed other's people pain as much as his own, could not help but smile. "You are such a douchebag."

"That's *Mister* Douchebag to you." Nolan nodded at the others. "You girls keeping warm when I'm not here?"

"Did you call me over here for a reason, or is this just a way to watch me stand here and freeze?"

"Well, both, actually. It seems your psychotic half-sister lost her shit this morning."

"I heard. Bunny called over here and said he tossed one of those BLM dudes through a wall."

Nolan lit a cigarette. "Yeah, he's not too bright. Which is why I've got a special assignment for you. I just got off the phone with Fat Phil, the G.C. of a condo unit up on Snowmass Road. I'm gonna put the Black Death up there ..."

"So what?"

"So ..." Nolan braced himself against the upcoming reaction. "So he's gonna need some help."

"Count me in."

"Count ... what?" Nolan puffed on his smoke, confused. "Seriously?"

"Hell yeah. Anything to break up the monotony of these BLM dipshits and all these fucking walls."

"You're making this very difficult for me. Is this reverse psychology?"

"Your head's ready to explode, isn't it?'

"Well, I certainly don't want to make you happy ... maybe I'll just leave you here."

"Okay."

"Hermaphrodite!"

"What? Jesus Christ, just tell me what you want me to do and I'll do it."

"What would make you happier?"

"Flip a coin."

"Elias!"

"Dude! I've been with you for three fucking years, man. A trained monkey can frame walls. This job is for morons who love getting ripped off and physically destroyed and being unappreciated and ignored."

Nolan nodded. "Pretty much." He chewed on his bottom lip. "You are right. You are a moron with no hope or other means with which to support yourself. I am your Alpha and your Omega. You are a worthless, hapless, derogatory moron, so by the powers vested in me, I hereby wed you to the festering Black Death."

"Awesome. Let the games begin."

"Figure tomorrow morning. I got to firm up the paperwork with fatty this afternoon."

"Whatever." Elias turned his back against the breeze. "You done paying me to stand here and stroke, or can I get back to work?"

"By all means, cease stroking and resume working ..." As Nolan triggered up the window, he said, "Hermaphrodite, don't forget—"

"To hurry up, man, believe me I fucking got it."

Rand was at the bar alone by five o'clock. Cheryl, who had become something of a fixture in his life, was out with friends. Because of her good looks and party-like demeanor, it turned out that she could stay unemployed by relying on a rotation of local men to provide her with shelter, food, drugs, and money. And in Spring Valley, where the male-to-female ratio was five-to-one, a woman like that was treated like a queen. Since the sex was great and Rand made good money, she had made him the primary focus of her attentions.

He ordered another whiskey. This bar was near the mountain, so most of the patrons wore recreational winter gear. For once, their distraction was welcomed. Rand's ex-wife, having grown annoyed by his recent behavior and absences, had formerly filed for sole custody. Nevermind that Rand could not stand her new boyfriend, did not like being replaced, he now could not even approach *his* old home without raging against the other man's increasing presence.

That was just one mess on top of other pending court dates. One involved a fight two months back that might violate his probation. So as one lawyer fought the criminal charges, the other fended off Lena's pending litigation. In addition, his girlfriend was either at his hotel room sleeping all day or out freely spending his money while the relationship with his partner, a guy with whom he had worked with for over a decade, was now so bad it felt like it could split apart at any second. Through all the years and disagreements, Rand had never abandoned dislike for actual hatred. But he was getting close. Stewing over the company name, his lack of inclusion in decisions, his overall vital contribution and non-recognition—if it were not for the court dates and kids, he might have jettisoned both the whore and Nolan before shedding this place for good.

Just let me square away the court dates, he promised himself, and then pounded down the whiskey.

Two counts of assault and battery were filed against Rigor Mortis within days of his BLM throw-down. His lawyer, a permanent fixture in Riggy's life, planned a defense based on evasion and delay while hoping the prosecution's witnesses might leave town or lose heart. He warned Rigor Mortis that his long record threw serious jail time squarely on the table.

His wife, Tyra, had also skipped past the hopes of reconciliation and in subsequent conversations raised the prospect of formally divorcing. Elias, horrifically familiar with Riggy's Jekyll-and-Hyde aspect, lately found it was mostly Mr. Hyde showing up for work. Rigor Mortis' staggering gross consumption of alcohol, weed, and blow provided Elias a front row seat for one of the greatest downward spirals of all-time. A month after his dismissal from the BLM job, Riggy was drinking every night and on the verge of beating someone, anyone, half to death. Elias, who should have been the closest target, instead made sure his boss did not smash on any of the other three crews working alongside them at the Snowmass condo job. Like a great white surrounded by baby seals, Riggy had trouble obeying Nolan's directive against feeding of any kind. Instead, he threw tantrums and wood and his hatchet into walls, flew off the handle at imaginary transgressions, and slowly withdrew as his hopes of reuniting with his ex-wife and kids grew weaker by the day.

Springtime gave way to Mudseason and the exchanging of winter gear for jeans and hoodies. It was May before Nolan, worried about Rigor Mortis and Elias' sanity after their two months in isolation, gave Riggy the day off.

Riding shotgun, Elias wore a miserable expression even after he had gotten high.

"I don't know what to do ..." Nolan punched in the dashboard lighter as the mud-slathered F-350 growled through town. "Between you and me, with all of the nightmares I got going on, a part of me, the part that runs the business, knows what has to happen."

"But on his own ..."

"Exactly. Out of all the times I've fired him, it never felt like this."

"How do you mean?"

"Like at this point I'm genuinely concerned, even though I have plenty of reasons to flush his ass for good."

"I hear ya. He's a deranged mess. He showed up the other morning in jeans and a bathrobe, totally wasted. I love the guy but without you, man, he's got nothing. Seriously, if this thing with Tyra goes through..."

"He's been known to pull some horrible shit before."

"When he's cool, we have a blast. He buys me lunch every day."

"Unheard of, by the way." Nolan dragged on his smoke. "It is what it is. Eventually, dealing with Rigor Mortis 24/7 just sucks. Cooter and New Year took a pass on this current job because I went to them first ..."

"Like I said, he's a good dude when he's not totally fucked in the head."

"What's going on between you two? Is your man-love growing into a sequel of the *Crying Game*?"

"Oh God ..."

The usual banter of back-and-forth insults was lacking. The stifling weight of employing forty guys and babysitting psychotic bosses had flattened the mood for each.

Elias lit a cigarette. "Where's Rand?"

Nolan looked like he suddenly wanted to vomit. "No call, no show."

"Seriously? *Again*?"

"Twice in two weeks, man, and I'm beginning to lose my sense of humor."

"It's that coke whore ... She's a goddamn skank, dude."

"He asked me for a thousand-dollar advance last night."

"What? Payday's a day away."

"I told him I could give him a couple hundred but he thought I was full of shit. Guess that's why he pulled the no show."

Elias said, "It's more than that. She's feeding him a line of crap, too. Which ain't helping his sense of being fucked over. Get this. She's been telling him he should start his own business."

"His own *what*? Can you imagine that?"

"No. No no no. That guy could build the Sistine Chapel out of wood, but he has no address, phone, car, license, bank account, tools, people skills, or business sense."

"Oh, man. Amen, brother, amen."

"No kidding."

"You know Rand's lawyer calls my phone just to find out where he is? I mean who hires a lawyer and then avoids them? Seriously. I tell him his lawyer called and he just bats his hand. He's getting *billed* for this shit, his freedom's hanging in the balance, and he couldn't give a flying fuck." When Nolan turned to Elias, his mouth was a tight thin line. "Keep an eye on the coke whore. I want to know what else she's feeding him. That giant roll of twenties just sits in that hotel room with her all day long, too. Who does that?"

"No shit. And the guy's almost fifty? He's gotta get rid of this chick."

Nolan pulled in for gas and then nodded at Elias. "Well, what're you waiting for?"

"Oh, I'm sorry, *masah*," Elias affected a southern inflection. "I'll done hurry up now, masah, just don't whip me."

"I won't have to." Nolan handed him his credit card. "Apparently your Necrotic girlfriend already beat me to the punch."

———————

On his one day off, Rigor Mortis crashed his Honda XR400R. He was an accomplished motocrosser that even Nolan, in vain, always tried to best.

An hour west on County Road 61 was the town of Slidell, population 2600, and home to Dirt Hog Raceway. It was here that every gearhead within 500 miles had a chance to thrash themselves on either a quarter-mile racetrack or a full-mile loop loaded with jumps and moguls. There was also a jump ramp from which Riggy had once soared 113 feet. While he would never be confused with professional X-Games contestants, for a thirty-six-year-old, he more than held his own.

Except for yesterday. Misjudging his departure speed, he overshot the landing and bottomed out his bike. Thrown over the handlebars, his left foot twisted beneath him on impact. X-rays were negative, but the third-degree high-ankle sprain was horribly swollen into a purple/black bruise reaching halfway up his calf. Elias was sickly staring at it right now in Riggy's trailer as they readied for the day.

"That is totally awesome." Elias leaned in for a closer look. "I wish I had been there to see it. It looks like someone transplanted a rotten melon into your ankle."

"Ain't it something ...?" Rigor Mortis grimaced. "You got to help me get my sock on."

"What!"

"Dude, please, have a fucking heart, man, I can hardly bend my knee."

"Have a what?" Disgusted, Elias stretched the sock and carefully slid it over the distension as Riggy hissed and squirmed. Elias said, "That sock looks like a fat snake after it's eaten a rat."

"Hey, moron, don't forget the boot."

"Jesus Christ, this *is* the *Crying Game*."

"What?"

"Nothing." Elias took the mud-crusted Timberland and stretched it wide open. "Hurry up, man, this smells so bad."

"Oh my God, that hurts!"

The duplex was almost finished, so they started on the carport dormer over the double-wide front door. Rigor Mortis, with every step on his injured left foot, emitted a high-pitched squeal that was both comic and unnerving.

Elias said, "Dude, if you're gonna be making that noise all day, I don't think I'm gonna have to get high even once."

"Ah!" Riggy yelped as he stepped. "Ah! Get up on that fucking beam—Ah!"

Elias buckled into his bags and pulled himself up onto one of the two beams shooting out from the house. He took a number from the 2x10 ridge to the beam he was standing on, so Riggy could cut the rafter.

But with every step, every bend, every time Rigor Mortis moved, the sound was by now purely reflex. "So did—Ah!—you and Super—Ah!—Framer talk a bunch of—Ah!—shit behind my back?"

"Dude, man ..." Elias slowly chuckled. "Don't talk unless you're sitting down, okay?"

Riggy, who had been using the framing square to trace the rafter's seat-cut, now aimed it like a weapon. "Once you get down here, Hermaphrodite, I am going to beat you half to death."

"Only half?"

"What's the rush? First, I'm gonna take this saw and cut off your arms—Ah!"

"You ain't gonna do shit, hop-along."

By lunchtime the dormer rafters were rolled, sub-fasciaed, and sheeted. Rigor Mortis drove them to Taco Bell, and with various entrees in their laps, carefully steered them out.

"You know what's fascinating?" Elias wedged a burrito into his mouth. "Working all day on that ankle is only gonna make it worse, and yet for some reason, even though you know this, your own stupidity defeats reason."

"And you know what I find fascinating? You are a horribly stupid-dumb-bastard that I am going to beat—"

"—to death, yeah, believe me, the first thing I would do is jump up and down on that ankle until the blood exploded from it like a jelly donut."

Rigor Mortis wickedly smirked. "Touché."

As June dawned across the valley, Cooter and New Year were over-heard discussing the possibility of moving their budding families back to Texas, and O-Zone, who now had seven years' experience, was look-ing for lead-guy pay. Worst of all, as the jobs started to snowball, Nolan strong-armed Rand for a bag of weed, his first in nine years.

Initially, of course, he would only puff at night in order to relax. Then he got high at lunch for a special occasion and soon after he was burning morning, noon, and night.

The root cause of his growing financial crisis was a simple fact—Cam had been right. After scoring the BLM build, Nolan should never have taken on any additional outside projects. Most costly of all was a 9,000 square foot custom colonial that Nolan had subcontracted to Pierce and Son Builders. Hailing from Rifle, Colorado, Pierce was a thirty-year vet-eran with a beer gut and sense of humor. After his references checked out, Nolan, already besieged by various disasters at his other three jobs, gave Bob Pierce the autonomy someone of his accrued years expected and usually demanded.

Since the job was forty minutes up Alpine Pass, after the first few days, Nolan did not have time for the two-hour round-trip ride. Besides, the old-timer's salty disposition and vast experience had garnered a sense of trust until a Saturday two weeks later. Nolan, having made the run up Alpine, was at first mildly impressed. The first-floor exterior and interior walls were standing, the second floor-system was rolled and sheeted, the second-floor exterior walls were standing, and the two enormous gable walls on either side soared thirty-feet into the air. The site was clean, the wood was stacked, but something felt amiss. Digging through the back-seat, Nolan found the blueprints and unrolled them across the steering wheel. He glanced up, then down, then up, then down. He carried the plans and a tape measure up a 2x10 plank. Inside, he scanned the beams, the corners—the basics—and then his stomach sickly sank.

The first-floor walls were not ten-foot high like the plans called out—instead Pierce had mistakenly used eight-foot studs. Eight-foot fucking studs. Nolan was in such a rage, that after speaking by phone

with Pierce, old Bob literally packed up his gear and fled. It was Saturday, the day *after* payday, so Pierce was totally in the clear.

The entire house would have to be put into a dumpster. All of it. The
only thing old Bob had gotten right was the floor system, but even that
was now ruined. The gable ends were the wrong height, the stairs ... With
material and labor it was a $50,000 mistake, plus another $10,000 for
the wrecker and trucks to haul away the demo. Plus another $50,000 to
replace what had just been destroyed and the total was somewhere near
$110,000. Old Bob's worker's compensation insurance had checked out,
but after the clearance of that and his references, Nolan, occupied with
a million other details and disasters, had simply forgotten to check on
Pierce's liability insurance and bond. Now Nolan's insurance company,
after taking his money for years, thought they had found a loophole in
the state's subcontractor laws. There would be a costly fight with attorneys and drama, and if Nolan could just find old Bob Pierce right now ...

Nolan was potentially on the hook for the entire bill, in addition
to any legal fees. Old Bob Pierce was not back in Rifle either, because
Nolan later discovered he had sold his home before moving to Spring
Valley to cash in on the boom. Pierce had now fled town instead and
could have been one county over, or all the way to Florida.

In addition, at a condominium project that Nolan had subcontracted
to a local guy named John Bosco, one of his apprentices had driven a
skillsaw through his palm and would need microsurgery to reattach his
fingers. Bosco was on Nolan's worker's compensation which, at an exist-
ing rate of $3,000 per man, was already costing almost $120,000 a year.
Now, with the injury, Nolan was looking at another increase of nearly
$2,000 a month.

Everywhere he turned, the bad news kept pouring in. After being
ahead of schedule with the BLM job, a series of setbacks were so bad
that out of the $2,400,000 bid, $200,000 of which Nolan hoped to
clear in profit, he now might not earn a thing. Add to that Rigor Mortis'
downward spiral and Rand's recent flake-outs and every other conceivable catastrophe, and smoking pot became the least of his problems.

But that was soon to change.

CHAPTER TWENTY-TWO

B y August, Nolan and Rigor Mortis were like two planes falling out of the sky for different reasons. They showed up at their respective jobsites each day in horrible moods that only worsened by the hour. But on this particular morning, necessity had them at the same job rolling floor. By nine o'clock they were verbally assaulting each other as if looking for a fight. Rigor Mortis said, "Jesus Christ, would you hurry the fuck up? A blind monkey could nail those blocks faster."

Nolan swallowed his venom, not wanting to disrupt their progress since, once the floor was rolled, they could start the second-floor exterior walls—

"Did you hear me?" Rigor Mortis said. "I'm like a dollar bill waiting on a dime."

"Fuck you." Nolan reloaded the gun with 16's. "I could tie a hand behind my back and still do this shit faster than you."

"Yeah, right. All the time you now waste driving around acting like a fucking bigshot has eroded your skills. And your speed. You're turning into a tool."

"You know what? I'm not taking the bait—"

"On top of ripping everyone off, you're a fucking fraud—"

"Riggy!" Rand screamed. "What the fuck, dude?"

"Suck it, Fabio, you're not much better."

"Enough!" Nolan yelled. "It's awesome to get life advice from a guy who's such an incredible fuck-up his own wife and kids left him."

After Rigor Mortis launched on Nolan, they fell onto the joists and then, as they tried to choke each other out, fell through the gap between joists and dropped eight feet to the first-floor with a sickening thud. Nolan, dazed, clawed his way on top of a catatonic Rigor Mortis and started beating in his face until Rigor Mortis ripped his utility knife through Nolan's forearm. That was when everyone converged and dragged them apart before someone got killed.

Nolan strained against those who held him back. "You pull a knife on me, you bitch!"

"Cheap shot, motherfucker! Beatin' on me when I'm knocked out?" Rigor Mortis spit out a wad of blood and taunted Nolan by waving him forward. "Let him go, boys, and he'll get his!"

"It's over." Rand pushed Nolan toward the driveway. "Before one of you ends up in prison and the other gets a casket, it's over."

Elias drove Nolan and Rand to the hardware store to buy super-glue to seal up Nolan's arm. Then, at Nolan's request, they headed directly for La Cantina. There, beneath the late summer emptiness of the bar, all three sipped margaritas for the first time ever. Then Nolan went to the men's room.

"I don't know ..." Rand licked the salt from his lips. "This could be a real problem."

Elias sighed and lit two cigarettes, one of which he handed to Rand. "Kara finds out he's boozing again, she'll carve his nuts off for good."

Nolan returned soon after. He did not look well. His forearm was bandaged but seeping blood, and his eyes were puffed red from exhaustion. He said, "One of you pukes gimme a smoke."

Rand tossed over his crumpled pack.

Nolan lit up and then hefted the giant margarita. "Hurry up."

"Hurry up," they said and collided in the middle.

Four hours later they were wasted. Even after all this time, Rand and Nolan did not skip a beat. They played pool, hustled out-of-towners, and had Elias refilling their drinks every time he turned around. Nolan's phone repeatedly rang, but there was no way he could answer. She was probably worried sick.

———————

Inside Nolan's darkened apartment, despite all attempts at silence, he dropped his keys, smashed a knee into a counter, and then stepped on the tail of a sleeping cat. He stifled a laugh, felt his way toward their room, and stripped down to his boxers. In bed, staring up at the ceiling, he pulled the sheet up to his chin.

"God, you fucking reek." She was curled into a ball that faced the opposite direction.

Drunk, he stared at her back, fearfully, because this would not be easy.

"I'm sorry." His voice was a deep croak from all the alcohol and smokes. "I ... we went to the Cantina and ..."

"Why'd you do it?" She sounded more curious than angry. "Isn't this bad enough?"

"What?"

"Everything." She could be heard sniffing. "The jobs, the money ... us."

"There's nothing wrong with us." He sounded convinced. "It's just one night ..."

"The weed I can tolerate ..." She broke into a sob, and Nolan could not remove his eyes from her forbidding form. Blankness. A wall with no face and no way for him to climb. She said, "You can't just do this ..." And then she sobbed again.

"Baby ..." He tried to put an arm around her but she immediately tensed. "I promise, it was just a onetime thing ... I really needed—"

"To get shit-faced! After all your hard work and everything we went through, you just go down to the Cantina and throw it all away?"

"Baby, I didn't throw—"

"Stop calling me baby."

"Kara, please ..." He rubbed his forehead. "This ain't the end of the world."

"You're right. It's only the beginning of something worse."

"Baby—"

"I don't think you should sleep in here tonight." She pulled the sheet up over her shoulder, the wall now completely covered. "You stink of tequila and cigarettes."

"Fine." He threw off the sheet and stood up. "You wanna play games, play games."

"Don't even think about blaming me!"

He slammed the door, chased the cat from the couch and, feeling the room begin to shift, lurched into the bathroom.

The next morning at the BLM build, four tractor-trailers wide-loaded with roof trusses arrived escorted by the police. On the ground, Team Beaver and Nolan's white guys rapidly geared up.

"All right, people," Nolan began, but his hangover was his first in almost a decade. He had been drinking juice and chewing gum, but the tequila still hovered like a stench. "You see those pigs with the trac-tor-trailers? They're costing me sixty bucks an hour each, so four guys are staying down here to help the BLM morons get these trucks emp-tied and gone. Now Cam's guys rolled the other roof, so they're already familiar with the roof harnesses. But we got some new guys and other guys who have only been out at the framing yard, so just bear with me." Nolan held up a thin harness. It had shoulder straps and two step-through loops encircling the crotch. In the center of its back was a steel hoop where a tagline would attach. "Anyone working above wall height needs to be roped in."

"Just to roll trusses?" one of the new guys asked.

"It's fifty feet to the ground." Nolan shot a finger toward the BLM offices. "That's where the bosses are gonna be perched staring all day long, because if OSHA pulls in and sees no ropes, it's five grand per man. Hermaphrodite has tagged each harness so we don't get ours con-fused with BLM's. These things are ninety bucks a pop, so you're on the hook as of now." The harness had Team Hate in black lettering down each side. "If you've never worn one of these, you get into it like this ..." Nolan stepped into the loops and pulled them up into his crotch. He then slipped his shoulders into the straps. "Pull these tight ..." He cinched both sides of his crotch. "And connect these ..." There were two horizontal clasps across the chest to hold the shoulder straps in place. "Your tagline gets connected to the hoop in back, but remember, keep your shit tight, because if you go for a ride, you got a twenty-foot drop until the jolt of a lifetime racks your brains."

"And then you get slammed into the wall," Cam added, and everyone laughed at that.

As Nolan looked at the twenty-five gathered faces, he realized there were some so new he could barely name. "You guys need to hurry the fuck up. Seriously. Don't laugh. This fuckshow is now two months in arrears because I promised these idiots we'd be finished by July."

"Jesus..." Rand looked amazed. "100,000 square feet in eight months ... that is just fucking crazy."

"Nevertheless..." Nolan paced in front of the troops. "It's going to be eighty degrees today. The sun's not setting until nine o'clock, so get ready for the nightmare of a lifetime. Check your batteries and keep your radios on—Spoons, you work the truss list on the ground and crane up. The Soldano brothers, O-Zone, and you—what's your name?"

A new guy said, "Danny."

"Sorry, Danny—you four help BLM unload. We got twelve harnesses for the high-flyers and the rest of you deck monkeys keep their taglines clear, feed them blocks and nails ... you know the deal. Now please, each and every one of you, hurry the fuck up."

"Hurry up," they choroused.

Guys began to scatter.

Cam Rogers approached, adjusting his hardhat. "True what I heard?"

"Boy ..." Nolan lit a cigarette. "These bitches can't keep quiet about nothing."

"That surprise you?" Cam was not making idle chatter. "Anything I can do to help?"

"Naw, man, but you were right. I just thought ... I gambled for the whole enchilada, man, and now it's gonna be a dogfight just to get back to zero."

"I ain't worried about that." Cam clapped him on the shoulder. "Work is work. But if the stress is already this bad, we need to come up with a better plan. This other shit ain't gonna cut it. Just tell me what you need, all right?"

"Yeah ..."

"Don't let it snowball, Noll." Cam checked his harness and then buckled into his bags. "I seen it too many times. Once those dominoes get started ..."

"I hear ya." Nolan sickly grinned, but Cam was already angling toward the building. Overhead, the crane was arcing through the clear blue sky while below, on the ground, its shadow came racing toward him.

CHAPTER TWENTY-THREE

In mid-September, O-Zone was squatting on top-plate like a gargoyle when he noticed approaching clouds of dust. Himself, Cooter, and Rand were out at the rebuilt 9,000 square foot debacle Pierce and Son had fled.

"Hey." O-Zone pointed. "Looks like a whole bunch of pigs are headed this way."

Rand put down the skillsaw. At the window he saw the police cruisers coming hard, so he unslung his bags, ran to the stairwell opening, and dropped himself through to the first-floor deck. The cruisers were sliding to a stop as he bolted through the door, but then he heard one of them shout, "Don't even think about it, Randall!"

After they had him searched and cuffed, one cop asked, "How come you been blowing off your court dates?"

"How long's the warrant been out?"

"Eighteen hours." The cop sucked at his teeth as if dislodging a piece of food. "Almost a record in a town this small."

Before they put him in the cruiser, Rand shouted, "O-Zone! Square away my gear and then call fuckface, tell him to bail me out."

The deputy sadly shook his head. "Oh no, you ain't getting out before you see the judge. Not after repeated no-shows. You're a flight risk now, buddy, watch your head."

The deputy tucked him into the backseat as O-Zone and Cooter, in an upstairs window, flipped a coin to decide who would call Nolan.

Spring Valley, as the local seat for Salinas County, had four different police agencies feeding an unflinching criminal justice system. Locals, tourists, even other lawyers and cops—once inside the web struggling only made everything worse.

As part of the plea deal for misdemeanor assault, Rand got thirty days in the Salinas County jail. It was easy time and mostly filled with ski bums, East Coast kids gone awry, local white trash, and a few heavy hitters waiting transport into the statewide DOC.

As luck would have it, Rigor Mortis arrived soon after. The judge, no stranger to his exploits, denied his legal maneuverings. Within a month of his August arraignment, Rigor Mortis cut a deal since BLM's attorneys had a dozen eyewitnesses.

"As for counts one and two of assault and battery, how does the defendant plead?"

Rigor Mortis was standing and straightening his tie. "Guilty, your honor."

"In light of past offenses, you're lucky the prosecutor was in a good mood, Mr. Killea." The judge looked down at the paperwork through his bifocals. "I hereby sentence you to one-hundred-and-ninety-two days, with one third—sixty-four—to serve with good behavior, and the remaining one-hundred-and-twenty-eight to be suspended until the three-year term of probation has been completed. I'm also ordering another round of anger management counseling, but instead of thirty-six hours, we will now try one-hundred-and-twenty-six. Failure to comply or complete this course of counseling will automatically trigger the remainder of your sentence." He slammed the gavel. "We are adjourned."

It was a late October evening when the two pickup trucks parked facing each other, their driver's side-by-side.

Windows descended.

"Fuck, man, it's been years, dog."

"I know ..." Through the window, Nolan passed the other man money. "How you been?"

"Fearless. You know ..." The guy shrugged and then handed back a small tinfoil package. "Good to go, bro, good to go."

"Say hi to your old lady."

"I will, Noll, be in touch."

The other pickup pulled ahead as Nolan closed his window.

———————

The next morning, the inside of the truck felt like an undetonated bomb. Ever the good sport when it came to babysitting either Rigor Mortis, Rand, or Nolan, Elias nevertheless wore a haggard expression that reflected his third straight month of eleven-hour days.

Nolan said, "Bust up some more of that shit."

On a CD case, Elias cut the cocaine with a razor.

Nolan said, "Grab the wheel."

Elias steered the truck as Nolan pinched a nostril, inhaled, and said, "Good girl. Now pack us up a bowl."

"Sick fuck. It's not even ten o'clock."

"No more talking. Pack that bowl right now, hurry up."

Elias switched out the coke for the weed and emptily stared ahead.

Nolan sparked it up and said, "What's on your mind?"

"Nothing."

"Daddy can tell when you're lying."

But the usual taunts brought no rejoinder.

Elias said, "I guess I just wish it could be more like the old days, you know?"

"Oh yeah?" Nolan took his eyes from the road long enough to rest them on Elias. "What part do you miss? Me and Rand chasing people for money, you making ten bucks an hour, or all of us getting shit on by the G.C.s?"

"Half these fuckers I don't know and the other half I don't like."

"You like the Mexicans ... You like the Beaver."

"You know what I'm talking about."

"No ..." Nolan put down the bowl and lit a smoke. "I don't."

Elias' expression, when he turned, held no pretense. "We're going down, aren't we?"

"What ...? Why would you say—"

"Fuck me, man, you can't even keep a straight face."

"I can't do *what*? You don't think I got enough going on without *you* sitting here telling *me* we're going down?"

"The guys—"

"Fuck the guys." Nolan was distracted and swerved across the road. "And fuck you too. Rand and Rigor Mortis are in jail, I got fuckers quitting on me left and right, bills out the ass, three jobs hanging on life support, and now you're gonna brighten my day by telling me this company's heading into the shitter?"

"What's with this?" Elias held up the baggie of cocaine. "It's the end of the line, bro."

"You're one to talk." Nolan abruptly jerked the pickup onto the shoulder. "As a matter of fact, you know what? Just get out of my truck, motherfucker."

"Really?" Elias grabbed his tool bags off the floor. "Fine."

"You're a fucking traitor," Nolan said, and then he pulled away.

———————

Twenty minutes later, as Elias hiked alongside a pristine ocean of hundred-foot fir trees, he saw the pickup returning. It was autumn and still hot enough for shorts, so his boots clicked a cadence through the gravel. The pickup U-turned and swooped up beside him.

Nolan said, "Get in."

"No."

"I said get in here."

"Really?" Elias looked up into the opened window. "I'd rather walk."

"Did I hurt your feelings? Huh? Did daddy make you cry?"

"Get fucked."

"I see you're smiling."

"It's a sneer."

Exasperated by the slow pace, Nolan blurted, "Would you please just get back in here? I'm *sorry*, okay?"

"Pussy." Elias pulled himself aboard. "You should've known by now that I don't have any feelings."

"Or brains, common sense, or friends, neither."

"Amen."

Nolan grinned. "Let's do some more lines."

But the mood did not improve.

"Look." Nolan lit a cigarette. "Rand'll be out in a week, Riggy's got another month or so, the Mexicans are finishing up the BLM massacre ..."

"So now the glass is half full?"

"Jesus, what's with this attitude?"

"Noll ..." Elias was given pause by what Nolan could not see. "There's a horrible rumor going around that you're thinking about running on Sundays too."

"So what if I am?" Nolan angrily huffed smoke. "It wouldn't be for long, but so what? Are you on the team or what? Are we gonna save ourselves, or just roll over and die?"

"For guys like me and Rand, that's fine. But Cooter, New Year, Cam, the Mexicans—these guys have families, man. We're already maxing out at sixty-five hours a week."

"They can give me another month of pain, all right? Jesus Christ, when times are good and I'm pouring money across these motherfuckers like water, no one complains about a thing. But wait until I need a little bit of get-back and everyone's pussy starts itching at once." Nolan took another drag. "Maybe it's time we all sat down and had a chat. I'll buy a ten-gallon bucket of Vagisil and you bitches can squat in it one by one."

"They have a stake in this company too."

"What does that mean?" Nolan glanced over. "Is that what they're saying? That I'm squandering their fucking interest—"

"They talk about the new dirt bike."

"What? What else are these bitches fiending on ... my truck? New ski equipment, the bone?"

"Yeah."

"Well, I built this fucking company!" Nolan screamed. "And I'll buy whatever the fuck I want!"

"Jesus, dude, easy—"

"Get out of my truck." The sudden braking caused the pickup to fishtail across the shoulder. "You are a disgraceful bag of shit ... out of my truck—OUT, OUT, OUT!"

"You're a fucking snap case." Elias grabbed his gear and slammed the door.

Nolan drove away.

He did not return.

———————

That same night she never came home from work, which was probably for the best. Nolan had not slept in two days. His teeth were Jokered into a permanent grin. He had not eaten since breakfast, but fed from the Ziploc bag instead.

———————

Two days later he found her at their apartment packing clothes. Kara was businesslike and perfunctory. He was sober but sweaty from work. There was a chair in the corner of their bedroom, so he sat and watched her pack.

He said, "I don't think you should do this."

She had a stack of T-shirts in her hand and blinked as if the statement was absurd. "You can think whatever you want." She neatly placed the stack inside the suitcase. "You make all of our decisions now anyway, don't you, honey?"

"You know that's not true."

"Nice try." She had her hands on her hips, her brown eyes brightened by the same indignation that currently filled her voice as she said, "Shame on me. Hell, I might as well not even exist. I see you for two hours a night, which was hard enough before you started boozing but now ... now the fucking *cocaine* is back again." The tears shot into her eyes as she defiantly knuckled them away. "Fuck you!" She grabbed a pile of socks and rapid-fired them at his head. "You know who the stupid-dumb-bastard is? Fuck you, Nolan, fuck you." She was sobbing, and as he stood, she fired off another round of socks to force him back into his seat. "You're a worthless piece of shit!"

"Please, just let me—"

"Don't!" She turned for the chest of drawers and hurriedly gathered more clothes. "I'm such a fool!"

"I'm sorry ..."

"Oh, just shut up, will you please? I can't take any more of your bull-shit." She rapidly packed her panties, jeans, and tops, and then zipped closed the suitcase. She blew her nose and avoided eye contact before grabbing more clothes from the closet. "There's $40,000 in our savings account. I took half of it out this morning."

"What!"

"I have a job too you know!" She grabbed the suitcase and held up her cellphone. "I'll be at Cindy's."

"I know I fucked up, okay?"

"You don't give a shit. What possible difference could this make to you?"

"What?" He frowned. "But I fucking love you."

"Oh my God." She took a step toward the door and apparently thought he might do the same because she said, "Don't even think about it or I'll call the cops."

"Excuse me?" He was suddenly scornful. "I'm not gonna stop you!"

"I'll be back for my cat!"

"Fine." Nolan followed her as she stomped toward the kitchen. "I don't need you either."

"Prick."

"Take your shit and get the fuck out of here!" Nolan exploded a lamp against the wall. "You fucking traitor—you bitch!"

The door slammed back in answer.

After work, Elias was on his porch watching the mid-October sun bleed the sky. The mountains looked to be on fire. The fact that he could walk out his back door into a postcard of unimaginable beauty was still, even three years later, something he never took for granted.

He heard a motorcycle and turned to see Bunny screaming up Snowmass Road. Swooping into Elias' parking lot, Bunny howled as he smoked the back tire into a shrieking figure eight.

"Nice work, idiot," Elias called out after Bunny killed the engine. "My neighbors love that shit."

"Hell yeah, man, what's more American than the V-Twin Indian kicking some serious ass?"

"Dude, you have no license, insurance, or even tags, man, Bunny ... are you fucking insane or what?"

"I just bought it for five hundred bucks!" Up on the patio, Bunny pulled himself a seat next to Elias. "What're you, my dad?"

"Don't make me shudder."

Bunny grinned and looked around. "What's up, man, where's the bar?"

Elias cocked a thumb over his shoulder. "Coke and Beam are inside the door. Glasses are in the kitchen."

Bunny dropped a bag of weed and papers into Elias' lap. "Roll it up, motherfucka."

"And you're carrying weed to boot. What a moron."

They sipped drinks and passed the joint as the sun began to set.

"You don't look so good." Bunny inhaled swiftly, passed the joint, and then exhaled smoke. "As a matter of fact, you look like ass."

"Everything's just so fucked up, you know? I got a bad feeling, man ..."

"Cam was saying the same shit the other day."

"Uh-oh." Elias passed him the joint. "You guys aren't jumping ship, are you, because that would finish us for good."

"Cam would never do that to a bro. He might be thinking it, but he could never do Nolan like that."

"Thank God."

"I thought you didn't believe in God?"

"Well, I'm starting to. Wasn't it the Jews that had to build the ancient pyramids like slaves?"

"The Jews ...?"

"That's what I feel like. I feel like the Jews."

Bunny sang, "Ain't no news, but I feel like the Jews!"

"What?"

"I slave like the Jews!"

"Dude, shut up, I think our neighbor might be Jewish."

Bunny sang, "Hey, dude, I think my neighbor's a Jew!"

"Bunny!"

"Ha-ha! This is some good green, ain't it?"

They refilled their drinks and Bunny cracked jokes until he said, "Boy, you're a real dud tonight."

"Yeah ..." Elias stared drunkenly into the dusk. "I'm gonna miss this shit."

"What shit?"

"You think Rand's coming back?"

"Why wouldn't he—"

"And Rigor Mortis?"

"Riggy's hate and love, man, you know those two will never be quit of each other."

"And what about Nolan? He's coming apart like a hand grenade, man, what the fuck ..."

"Didn't you eat anything? Hey, Elias, you don't look so good."

"Whatever."

"Stop drinking that." Bunny stood and took his glass. "I'm gonna make us some pasta."

"Nice. Good luck. Break a leg."

Once Bunny disappeared inside, Elias took back his glass.

On October 17, Rand was released from the Salinas County Jail. With Nolan besieged at work, Elias picked him up instead.

In shorts and boots, Rand wore his customary scowl as he hopped aboard.

"Welcome back." Elias held out a palm which Rand slapped. "Did you make some new friends?"

"Oh yeah." Rand immediately reached for the cigarettes. "Thirty in the hole, bro. I feel like a new man. Seriously, my body feels fantastic. Three years' worth of nagging injuries and muscle strains are totally gone."

Elias steered them out. "How was Riggy?"

"Cool, man, no problems." Rand savored the cigarette. "Jail brought out the softer, gentler side of the Black Death."

"He still has another thirty to go, doesn't he?"

"Thirty-two. But this was the best thing for him. Gave him a chance to pull back—to at least clear his head from all this other shit with the wife."

"Yeah? Well, then Nolan might need thirty as well." Elias informed him of Nolan's narcotic backslide and current state of wifelessness.

Rand blinked. "Jesus Christ, that's horrible news, man."

"Just brace yourself is all. We're running twelve-hour days and started rolling out the last two Sundays as well."

"*What?*"

"Serious." Approaching town, Elias said, "You hungry? Because it's now or never. Daddy's waiting."

"Yeah, well, I been doing some thinking."

"Uh-oh."

"I don't think I'm long for this."

Elias' smile froze. "What're you talking about?"

"Well, Cheryl and me been trying to get a plan together ..."

"You and who?" Elias nearly spat. "Dude, she has no job, no money, no purpose, and oh yeah, she's been on top of half the guys in town."

"What's gotten up your ass?"

"I just hate watching a brother go down is all." Elias slowed to 25 MPH through town which, as another ski season approached, was filled with trucks re-stocking shops and businesses. "And I wasn't gonna say anything ..."

"But?"

"Since you just told me about you and her splitting town ... I saw her out while you were gone."

"So what? What was she supposed to do? Lock herself away?"

"I'm not talking about socializing with friends." Elias frowned. "You know what, fuck it. Forget I said anything."

"She ain't Yoko Ono, dude."

"Naw, man, she's way worse."

"I don't want to hear this. Where's the weed at?"

"He's got like two ounces under the backseat."

"Jesus *Christ* ..." Rand fished out the Tupperware container.

"Last call on food."

"I can't believe you're taking me straight to work."

Elias grinned. "From one jail to the next, homie."

"Speaking of which—the Beans quit yet?"

"Nope. They're wrapping up the BLM job."

"Still?" Rand lit the bowl and exhaled seconds later. "Haven't we been wrapping that job up since July?"

They passed the bowl back and forth as the wind blew waves of colorful leaves across the desolate road.

Elias said, "Can you believe in two weeks it's going to be winter?"

"I hope I'm not here to see it. But you didn't hear that from me."

"You're not going anywhere."

"You should start thinking about it, too..."

"I can't."

"Seven days a week? I can't believe people aren't quitting left and right."

"They are. The local pussies are coming and going but Cooter ... him and New Year are definitely planning something."

"What about Cam?"

"Who knows? Bunny says he's in it to win it but Cam ain't no dummy. He'll help bail a brother out, but if Nolan's disease jumps companies ..." Elias frowned. "Business is business, yo."

"You're going down with the ship, aren't you?"

"Yeah. I figure I was stupid enough to help him start this whole thing ..."

"And so now we'll all go down together." Rand faced front. "I kind of like the sound of that."

"Right? Why not enjoy the ride down too?"

"Huh."

"Just remember one thing."

"What's that?"

"As zero-hour approaches..." Elias glanced from the road to Rand and said, "keep your parachute handy."

———

On November 2, winter came to Northwest Colorado in a flood of wind and snow. The day before it had been forty degrees and sunny.

Now autumn was officially dead. Tempers were short and attitudes, never cheery to begin with, plummeted accordingly.

They caravanned from job-to-job, cleaning up all the cut-offs and waste. They stacked and tarped the unused lumber, and policed the grounds one last time since anything missed now would be lost until spring.

"Fuck! Fuck me, fucking fuck!" Elias punched the dashboard since the defroster was not working. "I swear to God ... "

"Easy, Hermpf." O-Zone, in the backseat, handed him the joint. "You're turning into Rigor Mortis."

"I think the heater's finally busted." Elias worked a hand near the windshield. Then he punched the dashboard again and again until the radio display finally cracked. The vent knob shot across the car. "Fuck!"

"Jesus Christ." Rand took the joint. "This is some kind of afternoon."

Ahead of them, Nolan took a right onto County Road 30. He had recently installed a one-hundred-gallon diesel tank in the pickup's bed to fill the bone, and also attached a brand new eight-foot Fisher plow to the front end. Like something out of a *Mad Max* movie, the F-350 was now a completely self-contained beast capable of traveling a thousand miles in any direction without fear of road conditions or fuel.

Rand morbidly stared at the gigantic flakes descending across the valley. "I really have to get out of here."

"Too late." O-Zone choked back a hit. "You already sold your soul, bro, hurry up."

"Six months of this shit," Elias blurted to no one in particular. "I honestly feel sick."

They watched Nolan turn off the main road and lower the plow blade. It scraped down to the dirt as they started to climb. After another mile they ascended Alpine Pass toward the rebuilt custom that Pierce and Son, nearly a lifetime before, had ruined and then abandoned.

O-Zone asked, "Think Cooter and New Year are enjoying the ride with Super-Framer?"

Elias smiled for the first time all morning. "Tee-totaling mother-fuckers. Hopefully Nolan's making Cooter take the wheel as he blasts through lines of blow."

Rand chuckled. Then, because of the calluses, he extinguished the roach between his thumb and index finger without even flinching. "I wouldn't count on it. He's so desperate to keep them on board he's probably tongue-washing their balls."

Elias looked into the rearview mirror. "O-Z, man, we need another joint."

"Fuck, dude, we're already here."

Up ahead, as the switchback leveled off, the 9,000-square-foot behemoth lurked inside the tree line like a medieval fortress.

Rand started zipping up his jacket. "God, this place is freaking huge."

They geared up and exited as Nolan emerged from the F-350 screaming into his phone.

"Is that what I'm paying for?" He had trouble securing his jacket one-handed, so he just ripped it off and stood in short-sleeves in the falling snow. "Really? You're supposed to be fighting on my behalf, not burying me with these cocksucking insurance motherfuckers!"

"Who's he talking to?" Elias asked Cooter and New Year after they fled the pickup like hostages on the run.

"His lawyer." Cooter wedged a giant pinch of Copenhagen into his bottom lip. "Fucker's telling Noll to cut a deal on this ..." Cooter nodded at the house. "Sounds like those insurance guys ain't gonna pay."

"Unbelievable. Hey—" Elias motioned toward the tin. "Gimme a pinch, hoss."

"Oh yeah?" Cooter's smile was a brown smear of tobacco particles. "Well, lookee here. You slumming with us country boys, Elias?"

"Fuck yeah, man, I love having sex with my cousins, too."

Rand also took a pinch.

"Dang, fellas." Cooter frowned. "Y'all are killing my tin."

"Guys," New Year quietly said and nodded toward Nolan's hateful glance.

"C'mon." Cooter looked fearful. "Let's scrap this bitch out before he has an aneurysm."

They pulled a wheelbarrow and two twenty-gallon garbage cans from the pickup and fanned out to gather up the scraps of wood. Chunks of 2x4, 2x6, plywood sheets—they corralled all of it into a giant pile and, with the assistance of the diesel tank in Nolan's truck, set the entire mound ablaze.

Twenty minutes later, Elias and Rand turned the front corner in time to hear Nolan scream, "Goddamnit, Kara, this is such bullshit. You can't just hide and send threatening letters ...: Well then just say that. Ten fucking years of marriage—oh sorry, nine years. Fine. Nine years and now this is how it's gonna end? ... Yeah, well, fuck you too!"

Elias flinched when Nolan's phone exploded against the wall. Then Nolan leveled a look of pure malevolence onto Elias and Rand before stalking down the driveway in his T-shirt.

"Jesus Christ." Rand stuck a Marlboro into his mouth. "I don't think I can take much more of this."

"You and me both." Elias watched Nolan disappear downhill into the snow. "He's coming apart at the fucking seams."

Nolan was so drunk he had trouble pulling himself out of Elias' Skylark. Cackling madly, he slipped and hit the ice-covered pavement.

"Nolan!" Elias nearly capsized beneath Nolan's weight. "Jesus Christ, guy, you gotta help me. Stand up, man."

"Hermpf!" he yelled, slurring his words. "Stop dropping me."

"Seriously?" Elias' breath steamed through the midnight air. After he had answered Nolan's drunken plea for a ride home, Elias showed up at the bar in time for Nolan to vomit beneath the table. Then he began force-feeding Elias shots which, normally, would have been more than welcomed. But now, in the middle of the parking lot outside Nolan's apartment, Elias had to somehow get him up two flights of stairs and inside so that he did not freeze to death.

"Come on, man." Elias squatted and threw Nolan's arm around his neck. "We got to stand up, all right? On three."

"I can't believe you're still driving this piece of shit."

"Nolan, Jesus Christ, man, pull yourself together ..." Elias crouched down for more leverage. "On three. One, two, three."

They rose shakily, with considerable effort, and Nolan chuckled. "You're getting stronger, little fella."

"Oh my God." Elias kicked the car door closed with his boot. "Don't make me drop you."

"Seriously, dude, I just can't believe you've survived three years up here in this fucking sled without any snow tires."

"That's because I'm not a moron. Speaking of which, left, right, left, big guy, all right? Here we go."

They limped toward the staircase which was covered in a fresh six-inches. "Left, right, left," Nolan drunkenly repeated as if counting off a Marine Corps cadence. "Hur-ry-up. Hur-ry-up."

They made it to the landing as Nolan said, "I need a smoke."

"No way. One more flight, man, here we go."

Elias then guided him down the outside hallway to Nolan's door and said, "Gimme the keys."

As Nolan searched his pockets, he fell on his ass and laughed and said, "I think I locked them in my truck."

"Fucking A." Elias considered the possible options. Realizing there were none, he pulled his coat sleeve over his glove, punched out one of the small rectangular panes of glass near the doorknob, and opened the door from the inside. "Let's go, booze bag. Hurry up."

"Hurry up ..." Nolan crawled through the broken glass. "You just broke my window, dude."

Elias shut the door, jammed his hat into the punctured opening to keep out the wind, and then threw on the lights.

"What the fuck ..." He was in awe of the disaster. Plates of old food and fast-food trash fueled a swarm of flies dive-bombing the sink. "You taking housekeeping lessons from Bunny now or what?"

"Whoa, that ain't right." Nolan crawled to the kitchen table and pulled himself up into a chair. "That was hurtful."

"Yeah, well, this place is a shithole."

"She was ..." But he did not finish the thought. He pulled out a crumpled pack of cigarettes and found them all broken. He swung his bloodshot eyes onto Elias and said, "Got one?"

"Yeah, man." Elias lit them a pair. "Got any brews?"

"Fridge."

Elias grabbed two beers and a bottle of Jack Daniels and joined Nolan at the table. He raised his can and said, "Here's to it."

Nolan clicked cans and smiled somewhat sadly. "Where's Rand?"

"He's at home, bro."

"Are you gonna quit too?"

The question was so unexpected Elias could only blink. "What?"

"When're you quitting?"

"I'm not going anywhere. And fuck you for even asking."

"You don't think I know what's going on?"

"Obviously not." Elias took a swig from the bottle. "These other fuckers can do whatever they want but me ... I'd race you to hell with a can of gasoline on my back."

Nolan blinked as if working drunken emotions. "You're all right, Thomas, you know that?"

"Don't ash on your own carpet, man, use this can."

"Did you hear what I said?"

"Yeah. Here." Elias shoved the whiskey at him. "Put yourself out of your misery."

"I won't forget what we did here."

"Neither will I, bro."

Nolan took a giant pull off the whiskey and then accidentally knocked over his beer. "Fuck it."

"We're not done, Noll."

"I know."

"We'll just strip it back, you know, like the old days. Get us some time to regroup ... It ain't over."

"No. It's not. You're right about that. Fuck all these motherfuckers."

"No shit." Elias took the bottle. "Fuck'em all, bro. And snapcase'll be out soon too."

"Rigor Mortis ..." Nolan's eyes almost misted over. "How I love that stupid-dumb-bastard."

"Yeah, it's gross." Elias raised his beer. "Here's to one of the worst human beings ever."

"Gimme another beer."

"You've had enough." Elias took Nolan's cigarette and dropped it into the soda can. Then he nodded at the couch. "Let's go, man, bedtime for Bonzo."

"Oh yeah?" Nolan heavily sighed. "I'm fucking wasted."

"We'll get your truck in the morning."

Nolan could barely stand. "Fuck everything, man."

Elias watched him stumble over and fall face first onto the couch. Then he finished his cigarette and found a blanket in the bedroom Nolan refused to sleep in.

Draping it over his passed-out boss, Elias stood and stared, wondering if they would make it or not or either way just survive the winter.

Section Five

———————

The Peak Four Build
November, 2000

During the second week of November, a wave of storms left behind seven feet of snow. It was a record amount that forced the crew into spending two hours each morning just shoveling out the jobs and stacks of wood while even more snow continued to fall.

The massive BLM job was finally wrapped up, so Nolan had the Mexicans framing a single-story row of ten apartments off CR 30 on the western edge of town. The custom that Nolan rebuilt after Pierce and Son fled was almost finished, and save for the two jobs subcontracted out to local framers, Nolan's docket was mercifully clearing up. Dumping all of the gophers and deadweight from the BLM gig certainly helped, especially with his worker's compensation cost. Not that he had any problem helping out injured workers. It was more from the fact that some guys thought of it as an easy way to get paid. They would step on a nail and be out for two weeks or whine about splinters and need surgery and time off while the insurance companies stuck Nolan to the wall. Weak, pathetic workers and barely functioning bureaucracies that stole his money—welcome to the new American work ethic.

Currently, he was out at the former Pierce job with Rand, O-Zone, and Elias. Cooter and New Year slummed with Team Beaver finishing the duplex condos left behind when Rigor Mortis went to jail.

They were sheeting the roof when Rand called out, "Hey, Noll!"

Nolan was standing on the ridge, still on the phone, and answered him by raising both eyebrows.

Rand motioned over the side and said, "Someone's coming."

From their perch, the entire two-mile climb from CR 30 was clearly visible. Through the snowy trees, Nolan saw a pair of black Ford Excursions claw up the frozen road. He ended the call and carefully walked the ridge to the gable end. Being on a roof hungover was not for the faint of heart. Forty-feet below, the monstrous SUVs parked behind his truck. They were clean and shiny and probably rentals since they did not have company logos stenciled on their doors. He saw a group of men in brand-new Carhartt outfits and Stetsons mill about before one of them squinted up at the roof and shouted, "Excuse me! You know where I might find Nolan Harris?"

"Fucking wannabes," Nolan growled beneath his breath, but then yelled down, "Who's asking?"

The man seemed taken aback and looked at his companions as if garnering support.

"My name's Ted Wright," he shouted. "I work for Danforth Construction."

"So what?"

"You Nolan?"

"What do you want?"

Despite his exasperation, Ted Wright said, "I just want to talk to Nolan Harris about a job I got. If now's not a good time, I could come back later. But this is sort of a time sensitive situation."

Rand joined Nolan at the edge and said, "What's up?"

"I don't know." Nolan lit a cigarette. "Some dickhead from Danforth is down there with his girlfriends trying to waste my time."

"Danforth? That's a pretty high-end outfit. Ain't they headquartered out of Vegas?"

"Who knows." Nolan sickly looked at all the work they had left to do before losing daylight. "Hang on!" he shouted and then turned to Rand. "I'll be back in a sec. Just lemme get rid of these clowns."

He climbed down onto the staging and jumped in through a second-story window. Down below, he came face-to-face with six guys who looked completely out of place—Danforth's money men. As Nolan was introduced, he tried to figure out why they needed $150,000 worth of SUVs to transport six people up a hill to talk to him in his ripped Carhartt's and cracked boots, but said instead, "No offense, guys, but I'm running out of daylight."

"This won't take long," Ted Wright was a few inches shorter than Nolan but pumped with the kind of swollen muscle mass the serious lifters acquired. His plain face had two brown eyes spaced too far apart, like a hammerhead shark, and a thick nose wedged between them. "I'm a Project Manager for Danforth Construction."

Nolan lit up another cigarette. "What can I do for you, Mr. Wright?"

"Are you familiar with the Vail area?"

Nolan's face froze. "Holy shit. You're the Peak 4 guys."

"Yes." Wright's brown eyes hardened at this recognition. "As you might imagine, we're in one hell of a spot."

"Is it true what they said on the news? Did the hippies really burn that place to the ground?"

"To the very foundation, yes."

Nolan spit. "Fucking hippies."

"Actually, it was a group—allegedly of course, because the investigation is still ongoing—a group called Listen to Mother Earth. Anyway, construction was completed on October 22 and six days later ... they ... they burnt the place to the goddamn ground." The cursing must have been out of character, because Wright quickly checked for his companions' reaction. "As you can tell ..." He motioned toward the falling snow. "This year's going to be a monster, and it's just around the corner, and now we're ..."

"Totally fucked."

"Well, yes. And in worse ways than you can imagine."

"Okay. I'm no brain surgeon, but I'm guessing you're looking for a builder ..."

"Yes."

"But it's already November. What am I missing?"

"We need to salvage part of the upcoming season. Because of various financial concerns, the owners can't take a zero for the year. We're talking about 20-30 million in revenue down the drain." Wright flipped to a glossy picture and handed a clipboard to Nolan. "This is what got burnt down."

"Nice." Nolan examined it closer. "You guys do good work."

"Not really. We're mainly an industrial outfit—steel, concrete, bridges, high-rises—we're commercial builders. We have finish carpenters and siders on staff, but no real framers to speak of. And the guys we originally hired to build this don't want any part of this new time frame or the conditions."

"Backbreaker."

"What you're looking at is a 30,000 square foot compound containing a cafeteria, a maintenance and First Aid facility, a ski patrol and gondola housing, a four-star restaurant, and six luxury condominiums."

"I'm listening."

"Now, obviously we don't have time to do a full re-build with winter bearing down."

"But ..."

"But we want to at least provide a functioning structure to partially recoup what can only be described as a tremendous financial setback."

"And then what? You'll start full-scale renovations next spring?"

"Exactly."

"What're we talking about?"

Ted Wright took back the clipboard and flipped to another page which contained a blueprint.

"This," he said, "is an exact replication of the bottom 2,500 square feet of the original structure. Our hope is to have a functioning facility containing only the gondola machinery, the ski patrol, and a bare-bones cafeteria operational by Christmas."

"You guys are crazy." Nolan's smile stretched wide as he looked at each of them. "I like that."

"So we've spent the last ten days making phone calls and most of the builders, to put it mildly, don't want any part of this."

"Why not? You low-balling them?"

"We're in no position to low-ball anyone. The conditions ..." He looked Nolan square in the eye. "At this time of year, at 14,300 feet, we're talking about blizzard-like whiteouts and gale force winds."

Nolan chuckled. "Sounds peachy."

"To be honest, we kept coming across one name. It's a pretty small list of crews capable of pulling something like this off at altitude. True high-mountain framers. Since we have collaborative projects with BLM, I made some calls and Dennis Lambie, he tells me you and your crew threw up a 48,000 square foot condo in three months in the dead of winter."

"That's true. But its sister unit nearly killed us in the summertime. Go figure, right?"

"Your guys are already acclimated, too. If we brought someone up from the front range, we'd lose two weeks off the jump."

"You're kind of screwing yourself by telling me all this."

"Because I don't have time for games. I'm talking about 2,500 square feet in three weeks at a price that I'm sure will be enticing."

"Oh yeah?"

"So what do you think?"

Nolan looked out over the valley. He shuffled his thoughts and said, "I take it you want to start immediately."

"Within the next five days. Materials are already enroute."

"Huh." Nolan pushed a pile of snow with his boot. "Let me do some math and get back to you."

"I ..." Wright seemed to search for words. "I hate to press you but obviously, we're already out of time. And the next guy on our list lives in Utah."

Nolan blinked. "I need to get a price together."

"Dennis told me you guys agreed on twenty bucks a square foot."

"But that wasn't at 14,000 feet under the gun, dodging blizzards, and throwing all this other shit"—Nolan nodded at the house—"on hold indefinitely."

"You didn't let me finish. I was going to say we'll double that price."

"It's not enough. No offense, I ain't trying to hold you guys up, but that leaves me three days to get geared up and transport all these morons and equipment four hours south—"

"Sixty dollars a square foot."

"Listen—"

"Seventy."

"Seventy?"

"That's a $140,000," Wright countered. "But I don't want to keep haggling. I'm authorized to go to $200,000, and time's already running out."

Nolan blinked again, shocked. He tried to wipe it from his face and said, "Huh."

"$200,000 for twenty-one days of misery. Minus workers salary, the rest is straight profit."

He did not even want to open his mouth out of fear it might somehow cause him ruin. "I ..." He stuck out his hand. "Consider it done."

A look of relief flooded across Ted Wright's face. "Awesome."

Both sides ran the circle of handshakes to seal the deal.

"This is wonderful news." Ted Wright handed him a business card. "We're staying at the Sheraton. Call my cell after work and we'll get official with the contracts and paperwork."

"Absolutely." Nolan examined the business card. "Thanks for coming out."

"Sorry we held you up."

"No problem."

The six guys from Danforth Construction piled into their SUVs and honked their horns before reversing down the driveway.

When he got back up on the roof, his expression was so goofy Rand asked, "One of those guys give you a blowjob or what?"

"Yep." Nolan started laughing. "You girls aren't gonna believe this one. In the immortal words of Bill Paxton, stop your grinning and drop your linen, because we're on our way to Vail."

A day later he was in his apartment packing clothes. The place was a shambles. The landlord, a small scurrilous man in his late fifties, had previously approached Nolan with complaints of unpleasant odors—to no avail.

Nolan held out a garbage bag and backhanded the empty beer bottles and fast-food trash off the counter. This made room for his backpack. He checked the cash in his wallet when he heard a knock at the door.

"Yeah, come in."

The door opened and Kara immediately crinkled her nose. "Jesus, Noll, how can you stand this?"

"It's a lot easier after you stop caring." The joke fell flat as he sorted through a pile of mail and pushed a stack of it toward her. "That's all yours."

She was at the sink and seemed to catch herself wanting to clean up, but common sense prevailed. He saw her double-check the counter before setting down her purse, hat, and gloves.

"I got your message," she said.

Even though she was only dressed in a turtleneck and jeans, and was even wearing one of his old work jackets through the storm, he realized she could have walked through the door in a brown bag and still looked hot. He felt that love was probably one of the worst tricks ever played on human beings and said, "I'm glad you came."

She took off her coat and laid it on her purse. "When're you leaving?"

"I'm gonna start picking up the fellas in an hour." He lit a cigarette and she did the same since she only smoked when stressed. He held the lighter as she thanked him and they stood at the sink and smoked. He said, "It's only three weeks."

"So you said." She exhaled in a long gray line. "So it's true what they said on the news? The whole place is gone?"

"Yeah. It's a shame, too. I saw some pictures. It was pretty sweet."

"I can't believe they're actually opening up Peak 4." She and Nolan had skied Vail many times. "It's dangerous enough just to ski up there, but to build ..." She pushed some hair around her ear. "Why did you take the job?"

"Remember that Pierce fiasco?"

"The custom that got butchered?"

"Yeah." He smiled when she said 'butchered' and did not know why. "It looks like I'm gonna be in court with these insurance fuckers forever, but if I lose ..." Nolan took a drag on the cigarette. "This job's paying $200,000."

"Oh my God. No kidding?"

"Yeah."

"$200,000 for three weeks?" She was dismayed and then quickly sickened by what this meant. "It's that bad up there?"

"Probably not." He shrugged. "It's just a job. It's more for the pain and suffering."

"Who are you taking?"

"All my guys and the Beaver. I'm leaving Red Riggy, Diamond Dave, and the Mexicans up here to keep things running, but they're on cruise control anyway."

"What about Riggy?"

"He gets out later tonight. Cam's in charge of that."

"Huh."

"I ..." he began but then felt foolish. He put a small key on the counter and said, "That's for a safety deposit box I got a week ago. Since you handled most of this stuff, after you left, I needed somewhere safe to put all this shit. It's got my will, the life insurance policy, the titles for my truck and the bone and the business account information, and the records for Christine's college fund."

She seemed startled.

"It's just in case," he said. "Hell, the drive down there is dangerous enough, right? The joint checking and savings accounts you already have, and you're still the named executor for what's left of my so-called estate."

"Noll—"

"I'm sorry," he said, and looked away. "I really thought I was gonna make this shit work."

"Are you talking about us or your company?"

"That's not funny."

"You sound like a quitter."

"Excuse me?"

"Is this you giving up? Is that what you're telling me? One job is gonna wreck your whole company?"

"Let me put it to you this way. I'm so overrun with bills and debts, that if this Pierce disaster hits the shitter and I can't make up the short-fall, it's Chapter 11 time. It's that simple."

"So this is it?" She pointed at one of the empty beer cans. "This is going to be your response? To just rollover and surrender?"

"I'm off the blow—"

"So what? How long's that gonna last?" She extinguished her cig-arette in the crowded, reeking sink. "Instead of fleeing to the top of a mountain, you should be staying here and getting some help." She looked him in the eye. "Doesn't any of this mean anything to you?"

"Kara, I love you."

"But?"

"But I've made some horrible decisions. Both with the business and ..."

"So you're just gonna let me go. That's how much I mean to you."

"The business—"

"Fuck the business," she hissed and grabbed her coat.

He stood in silence before making it worse by saying, "We'll talk when I get back."

But she was already on the move.

Pulling on her gloves and hat, she grabbed the safety deposit key so she could hold it in his face. "After nine years, this is who I am? The keeper of a quitter's estate?"

He could not look her in the eye.

"You're a fucking coward," she said, then the door slammed closed behind her.

—————

Elias dropped Rand off after work and then went home to pack. Rand stood in his old driveway awash in self-consciousness before mustering the courage to proceed. He was relieved to see only one car in the driveway. At the front door, where he used to walk right in, new locks now barred his entrance. He knocked and waited, stunned at his own discomfort.

"Right on time," Lena said, and swung the door open. She was wearing slacks and a tan sweater and an expression that was friendly but in no way overly familiar.

He stood on the doormat and knocked his boots together as she quickly returned to the stove.

"Can't let the veggies burn," she said, and worked a spatula across the pan.

He closed the door and sniffed around as if hunting for the interloper's scent.

"Sorry about the short notice," he said, pissed at his own unease. Since each had hired attorneys to gain full custody, every encounter was now a guarded hostility.

He said, "Where're the kids?"

"Upstairs doing homework." She threw him a polite smile that was worse than not smiling at all. "I don't mean to be rude, but I'll be finished here in a minute."

"Take your time." He shed his jacket and hat and hung them on the door. At the refrigerator he pulled out a can of Diet Coke and said, "So I told you on the phone that I'm heading to Vail, right?"

"Yes, you did."

"Remember a few weeks back, in the news—"

"That's what this is about?" She was suddenly attentive. "You know, when you mentioned Vail, in the back of my mind I remembered hearing something about that fire, but I didn't make the connection."

"Yeah, it's a shame. I kind of agree with what those hippies did, because Peak 4 is absolutely beautiful in the summertime, but ..."

"But what?"

"But something's gone wrong with this country. It seems that the minute people disagree nowadays they reach for a gun or a knife."

"Or apparently a book of matches."

"Yeah."

"I thought you would be impressed by that."

He sipped the Coke and watched her back and the long red hair that was draped across it. She half-turned from the stove and said, "I didn't mean—"

"I know what you meant. I didn't come over here for that, okay? I'm gonna say good-bye to the kids and then I'm gone."

Before she turned back, she said, "Sorry about that."

"Whatever. What're you cooking? Smells great."

"Just sautéed veggies to go alongside the pot roast I got in the oven." There was silence. "I'd invite you to stay but Roger ..."

"I got plans anyway. Nolan's picking me up here in ten minutes. Then we're ..." He felt like he had been suddenly punched in the gut. "Is that ..."

"What's the matter?"

"I ..." He did not want to say it. "Is that an engagement ring?"

"Rand—"

He held up a hand to stop her. "That's all right. Just wasn't prepared is all."

But it felt like a cheap shot, not telling him beforehand. He stared at his soda can to try and regain some composure since he was sure, on some level, that his reaction had pleased her. He said, "We're both adults, right?"

"So far …" She extinguished the burner and dumped the veggies onto a plate. The pan hissed in the sink and then she wiped her hands. Their eyes met in a way that seventeen years could not avoid, and then they both looked away.

"I brought something," he said, and reached into a pocket.

When she turned back from checking the roast, she was staring at a pile of cash. "What're you doing?"

"I been talking with Nolan." He pushed the cash across the counter. "It's for their accounts. The college ones you started years ago. You gotta promise me that's where it's going. Five grand in each."

"Do you want my lawyer to—"

"I don't want any more lawyers doing nothing. Those are my god-damn kids, and you're their mother, and I don't need a lawyer to tell me that, Roger or no fucking Roger."

"But we can't just do this. There's child support—"

"But no alimony, right?" He smiled at the ring on her finger. "The child support is mine, no doubt, but I want this money put away. Are you going to promise me that or what?"

She searched his expression, seemingly unsure of his motives or the consequences if she did as he said and just took the money. "How much is it?"

"I just told you. Ten grand. I don't have a bank account and I sure as hell can't leave it with that—" He did not want to say 'jock-riding coke whore,' although that was exactly what she was. "If I hold on to it it's as good as gone, we both know that." He pushed the money closer. "C'mon, take it. This ain't no scam. Jesus Christ, I'm trying to do the right thing here and in a minute I'm just gonna take all that scratch down to Denver and blow it."

"Just like the old days, right?" It was her turn to look about self-consciously. "I promise. I'll even get you a bank receipt. But I don't know what to say."

"They're your kids too, Lena, there ain't nothing you need to say. Just promise me that loser Roger isn't gonna touch any of it and that's all the peace of mind I need."

"He's not a loser."

"Whatever." He felt the old ugliness coming back and knew it was time to go. "Kenny! Emily! Come down here and say good-bye to your old man!"

"Daddy!"

Kenny straddled the banister and then slid ass-first down from the second-floor.

"Kenneth!" Lena shouted. "That's enough of that! You looking to give me a heart attack?"

Kenny was oblivious and flung himself at Rand.

"Yeah, big fella, how ya been?" Rand hugged him. At the top of the stairs, he saw Emily descending and noted how she was developing into the same beauty her mother had yet to lose. "Hey, angel."

She smiled warmly and hugged him. She sighed and stayed there as if nothing had ever changed, and it was strange to feel blessed, and even stranger to know that somehow, through all of his fuck-ups and failures, his kids had so far been stronger than both of their parents combined.

CHAPTER TWENTY-FOUR

Inclement weather delayed their departure for Vail until 4 AM. The Colorado State Patrol, in an unusual move this early in November, had closed high mountain passes and Interstate 70 from Glenwood Springs ninety-miles east to the Eisenhower Tunnel. Not wanting any further delays once Forked Head Pass reopened the following morning, Nolan dragged O-Zone, Cooter, Rand, New Year and Elias into his fetid apartment. They were handed a piece of floor and instructed to sleep, which they eventually did after boozing and a hundred bong hits and taking turns on the PlayStation until well past midnight.

"Goodnight, John Boy."

"Goodnight, fuckface."

"Goodnight, moron."

After his alarm went off at 3:30 A.M., Nolan emerged from his bedroom and shouted, "Rise and shine, sweeties, Operation Nightmare is a go."

He put in a quick call to Cam Rogers, who was already dumping coffee down the throats of his crew. He even had Rigor Mortis, just released from jail the previous evening, awake and accounted for. Uno, Spoons, Bunny, and the Soldano brothers were bitching about the early start, but Cam had stopped listening years ago.

Attached to each of the F-350s, their trailers were loaded with tools, supplies, the workers' gear and backpacks. Inside the cab of each truck, the crews were ornery and already exhausted.

Nolan called the State Patrol hotline to make sure Forked Head Pass was open before the caravan departed. It was pitch black and a fresh ten-inches had fallen since yesterday. The National Weather Service said an even worse storm was approaching, so Nolan wanted to get to Vail by eight o'clock. He flipped open his Nextel to ensure his voice echoed through both trucks.

"Attention all simpletons. This is your captain speaking. The worst three weeks of your life has just arrived. The No Talking sign has been permanently turned on, so please remain silent for the remainder of our journey."

"Jesus." Elias was aghast.

But Nolan only laughed and laughed. "Ain't that awful?"

For some reason, after weeks of depression amid the slow-speed collapse of his life, Nolan's mood improved with each mile they ascended. Now, instead of drowning in the valley as his company and marriage floundered, this escape buoyed his spirits entirely by mistake.

The steel-knobbed tires were belted with chains. Each F-350 weighed three tons, had a six-ton payload capacity, and could tow ten tons, all of which were currently maxed out. They slogged up Mt. Lassiter as the wind howled and the icy switchbacks tried to use their momentum to skid them off the side of the mountain. No one else was on the road. The snow was blowing sideways. Nolan squinted into the complete darkness beyond which the headlights could not pierce.

In the backseat, O-Zone, Cooter, and New Year were nervously gauging their ascent. Up front, Elias did the same, peering into the stubborn gloom torn foot-by-foot from the night black tomb. It did not take much imagination to picture their violent end in a series of rollovers and rag-dolled bodies flung to the valley floor below.

"Pack us up a bowl," Nolan instructed and then leaned forward to follow the disappearing road.

"Incredible ..." Rand shook his head. "It ain't even Thanksgiving yet."

The stink of pot washed through the cab followed by a round of cigarettes. Cooter and New Year did not object. At a recent sit-down with Nolan, they had agreed this would be their last winter before the two of them headed home to Texas.

"Get me some weather," Nolan ordered Elias.

"*From 1610 AM, this is the National Weather Service...*" The scratchy voice sounded far away. "*Severe weather conditions that have so far entered their second day show no sign of abating until late tomorrow afternoon. Residents of Grand, Routt, Tabor, Vail, Buckhorn, Lisbon,*

Salinas, Summit, and Carey counties are being advised by the State Patrol to remain off the roads except for emergencies. All government agencies, schools, and all non-vital social programs have been postponed or canceled. By storm's end accumulations of two to four feet are expected in the low country. Six to eight feet, blizzard-like winds, and white out conditions are expected at higher elevations. All winter driving laws are in effect. Motorists attempting and failing to negotiate mountain passes without four-wheel drive and chains are subject to double fines plus taxpayer reimbursement for their extraction ..."

"Shit." Nolan gunned the pickup. "If they close that pass we won't see Vail until the day after tomorrow."

"Whoa ..." Bracing against the door, even Rand became unnerved. "Ain't none of that gonna matter if we're all dead."

"Elias?" Nolan asked.

"Fuck it, man, gun it."

"Good Gawd," Cooter drawled from the backseat. "Y'all's about to get us all kilt!"

The Nextel radio clicked and Nolan said, "Yeah, Cam?"

"What's up, man, why you suddenly flying?"

"I think they're gonna close the pass. Tune in 1610 AM and get a listen."

The perilous switchbacks ended as the final push toward Forked Head Pass straightened out the road. The fir trees ran out of air at 11,000 feet and yielded to a lunar landscape of boulders and granite slabs already buried beneath twenty feet of snow.

"Jesus, look at this," Rand said.

Up ahead, giant earthmoving equipment and dumptrucks splashed their blinking yellow lights across the tunneled walls. As bad as these conditions were at 11,000 feet, Nolan could not imagine what Peak 4, at nearly three miles above sea level, had waiting for them. The wind outside was screaming as Nolan saw the temperature gauge on his rearview mirror hover at minus five degrees.

"Oh my God," O-Zone said from the backseat. "Look at that poor bastard."

A lone worker, layered and hooded, was barely able to remain upright under the gusting assault. Since CR 61 was the only road connecting

Denver to western Wyoming, northern Utah, and Salt Lake City, DOT crews up here were on call twenty-four hours a day.

"That's a miracle," Nolan said as they barreled through the frozen moonscape. "These DOT fuckers are like kids on a beach trying to spoon back the ocean."

"Now that Forked Head's behind us," Cooter commented, "think you could slow down a little before we slip off the other side of this godforsaken mountain?"

"Cooter," Nolan said, "anything for you, buddy."

Nolan was relieved. He had seen his $200,000 going up the skirts of Mother Nature's ass and now it was literally all downhill from here. But ahead, the dawn was still miles away.

They pulled into Silverthorne two hours later. Nolan allowed them a quick piss and coffee break but then forced everyone back inside the trucks. The radio was warning of an imminent closure of Interstate 70 from the Utah border, and they still had thirty miles to go before they reached it.

At 6:30 A.M., the darkness lifted into a gray morning of roiling clouds and stiff winds. Since I-70 was now reduced to a one-lane mess of stalled and abandoned vehicles, Nolan swerved around them and punched the gas. He saw troopers closing the snow-gates to the on-ramps and knew no one else was getting on the highway. The Nextel radio clicked, so Nolan pulled it off the visor and said, "Yeah, Cam."

From the truck behind, Cam ominously said, "Listen, your boy is losing his shit."

"What the fuck ..." Nolan looked at Elias. "Pack us a bowl right now." He glanced into the sideview mirror and then cued the mike. "Put that psychotic douche on the line."

There was a pause until the Nextel crackled in the now silent cab. "Yeah, Noll."

"Riggy ..." Nolan paused as if trying to summon a more ballistic threat. "Listen to me. If you don't stop fucking with those guys, you're walking the last thirty miles back to Silverthorne."

Nothingness. Dead silence. Nolan waited for the response like a grenade in the dark. He said, "You reading me, good buddy?"

A shorter pause and then, "Yup."

The tone of the monosyllabic response rang out like an insult, so Nolan yelled, "This is the last thing I needed on the worst fucking day for you to even think about pulling this shit! You got me? I got a migraine so big from taking care of all you whining pussies that it literally feels like my head's going to explode."

Because of the two-way walkie-talkie feature, there was not a single person in either vehicle that had not shared a piece in that blast. "Attention, morons! This is the last fucking warning!"

The access road to the Peak 4 liftbase was nearly impassable due to ice chunks and deep, drifting snow. With their plows lowered, the caravan wedged through a series of tight turns and angled switchbacks until reaching a leveled off plateau inside the White River National Forrest. Ten minutes later, Mt. Pershing swung into view like a warhead pushed to the top of the world. The liftbase itself was little more than a row of pickup trucks, a gondola line, and two small buildings used for operations and storage. As the trucks ground to a halt, the doors sprang open like a doomed jailbreak since there was nowhere else to flee to.

A sign listed the current elevation at 10,341 feet, but since both Harris Framing and Team Beaver had hometowns above 7,000 feet, the effects of altitude were so far negligible. Even still, the air was thin, a fact not lost on those who immediately lit up cigarettes.

Nolan and Cam set off to find the Project Manager. The workers cinched their hoods against the freezing wind. They shot the shit until Nolan shouted and waved them over to where he and Cam spoke with two men in brand-new Carhartt's and red hard hats. As the group joined the bosses, a blast of snow-filled wind made everyone instantly invisible.

"All right, listen up." Nolan pointed and said, "This is Ted Wright, Project Manager, and Evan Ledo, the owner. They want a few words."

Ted Wright stepped forward with a smile that was not returned. His hammerhead eyes searched the crowd. The faces staring back seemed to cause him to rethink what he was about to say next, because he abruptly consulted a clipboard that was already wrecked by falling snow.

"Good morning, fellas. First of all, on behalf of Skyview Resorts and Mr. Ledo, Danforth Construction and myself, I would like to welcome and thank you all for your participation in what we hope will be a brief but successful venture." He cataloged the unamused and disinterested glances and hoped he was not already losing them—not with his entire career hanging by a thread. Rising through Danforth's ranks for the past fifteen years meant that now, after all the hard work, his promotion to Project Manager should have heralded the start of an even more rapid career ascendance. As was the case with other PMs before him, a string of successful projects would put him in line for an executive's slot as Vice-President of Operations—

But the arsonists had killed all of that. Even after bringing his first assignment in on time and under budget, the fact remained that one of their clients had just lost millions of dollars, and without recouping some of those losses from this upcoming ski season, tens of millions more would follow. Looking at their faces, he prayed no one could discern his growing panic. As if in answer, the bitter wind swung the gondola cars in a dire rhythm as it blasted across the liftbase. Wright pulled a confident smile across his face just in time and said, "The short story is, on October 28th, after a year and a half of construction, our three-floor 30,000-square-foot compound was completely burnt to the ground by members of a group called Listen to Mother Earth. Members of LME had been threatening resort ownership for months, especially since this mountain and ski trails are on National Forest land rented from the federal government. But it's also claimed by an Indian tribe that has fought this project from the start. Anyway, today is November 13th. By Christmas, which is when the ski season really takes off, we are hoping to have this bare bones facility operational for hungry skiers."

The group shifted, bored. Wright sensed it and asked, "Any questions so far?"

"Yeah." Rand pointed uphill. "What's left up there?"

"Not much. The sprinkler system was still being tested when the fire broke out. Structurally it's a total loss down to the foundation. To be honest, we didn't even know the place was on fire until the next morning, when work crews arriving up top found it totally destroyed."

"What about conditions?" Spoons asked.

Wright sadly smiled, crossing his arms over his ruined clipboard. "Fellas, I won't lie. Peak 4, on this side of Mt. Pershing, was never opened because its westward face absorbs the initial impact of nearly every storm system that hits this valley. Also, the altitude is high enough to ensure inclement weather almost year-round. In the winter we're talking gale-force winds, subzero temperatures, and an average of sixty feet of snow. But given the changing dynamics of the ski industry, where extreme conditions are currently the rage, places like Peak 4 now have economic viability."

Silence crept across the group until New Year raised a hand and timidly asked, "Uh, sir? Exactly how are we getting up there?"

Wright hooked a thumb over his shoulder. "Behind this building are four Ohara Caliber Snowcats with trailers. For those of you who aren't skiers, and considering where you guys are from I won't insult you, the Snowcat is basically a box truck with tank treads instead of wheels. We should be able to get all of you and your gear up top in a handful of trips. They're going to be on call for the duration of the build, primarily ferrying supplies. We've also contracted a lift company out of Grand Junction that has two Sikorsky S-64 Skycranes. With 25,000-pound lift capacities—over twelve tons—they're capable of flying up just about anything else the Snowcats can't handle."

"Well, that's good news for Spoons," Bunny said. "Looks like your old lady will be able to visit after all."

"Bunny!" Nolan was not amused. "Unless you want to walk up the side of this mountain, I'd suggest you shut your mouth."

"Mr. Wright?" O-Zone asked. "I understand we're staying up there?"

"O-Zone." Nolan cut him off. "We've been through this. They've got arctic rated tents—"

"Excuse me, Nolan?" Wright's smile immediately dissolved. "Regrettably, our guys spent the last two nights trying to secure the rigging but as you can see these winds ... Those tents we initially spoke of were impossible to maintain."

"Really."

"Not to worry though." Wright tried to sell it. "We've got two semi-trailers already up there."

"Yeah, but I thought those were for storage? For our boxes and gear?"

"They are. But we're getting two more trailers lifted up this afternoon."

"This afternoon ..." Nolan did not want to do the math. "So we're gonna offload all this"—he pointed at the F-350s and trailers—"into the two rigs you got up there, and sleep in two others flown up in the middle of this blizzard?"

"Yes. We're expecting them by three o'clock."

"Well, then three o'clock it is." He turned to his employees. "The owner, Mr. Ledo, wants to say a few words, and then we're gonna pull the rigs around back and pack the Snowcats. It's eight-thirty right now. Expect to be climbing that mountain within the hour. Mr. Ledo, the floor is yours."

Evan Ledo was so tanned he looked like he had just left the beach. His smile settled the weathered wrinkles into their grooves. His silver hair was combed straight back beneath his red hardhat and hood. The perfect teeth were bleached white, his eyebrows meticulously groomed. Starting off as an oil field engineer twenty years before, he eventually designed and patented an O-ring for a transfer casing that promptly turned him into an independent financier with a taste for projects other developers shied away from. The small money, after all, usually came with low risk and low return, neither of which existed at 14,000 feet.

Ledo stepped forward and his charisma was instantaneous. "Gentlemen, on behalf of myself and my family, we thank you all in advance for your upcoming contributions. The sacrifices and hardship that await you up top will not be forgotten once the history of this place has been recorded." As he spoke, he made eye contact with every worker. "Regardless of what the environmentalists will have you believe, there will be no impact to the area other than a few felled trees and a bare assortment of unpaved roads to maintain this facility. By design, other than the gondola line, we have left the landscape completely undisturbed.

"As a small token of our appreciation, all workers involved with these emergency renovations will be granted free season passes upon completion. As Ted already stated, we're hoping the seventeen-day work schedule will be enough for your crew, after which the electricians, plumbers etc. will have roughly twenty-four days in which to make the place

temporarily presentable. Full-scale renovations, of course, will commence next spring." Ledo squinted into the wind. "Once again, on behalf
of Skyview Resorts and Danforth Construction, guys, Godspeed."

"All right." Nolan stepped forward. "Let's get these trucks pulled
around back and unloaded. Cooter, since you're the tool bitch, I sincerely hope there isn't one thing left behind or you'll be walking back
down to get it."

"Awesome. Thanks, boss."

"I'm not your boss, but I am your master. The rest of you morons
better get active or you'll be sleeping in the snow."

As Nolan and Cam turned for their trucks, and the others headed
for the Snowcats, Rand nudged Elias with an elbow and said, "How'd
you like that part about our 'upcoming contributions?'"

Elias snorted, trudging through the fresh six-inches fallen in the last
two hours. "I think it pretty much means pull down your pants and grab
the KY, man, because here comes the biggest nightmare ever."

"Fuck me ..." Rand quietly chuckled, adjusted his hood against the
shifting wind, and stepped toward what could no longer be avoided.

───────────

The liftbase office had two desks that lacked any personal effects.
A water cooler and a coffee machine stood near the door, and the
wood-paneled walls were crowded with chalkboards and clipboards
hung on nails.

The door swung closed. Ledo and Wright stomped their boots, shedding their jackets and gloves.

Ledo, rubbing his frozen hands, approached the window.

"Coffee?" Ted Wright nervously consulted the pot. "Is it warm
enough in here, Mr. Ledo? I can crank it up if not."

"Yes to the coffee, black, and no to the heat." Ledo looked back over
a shoulder. "We've been working together for over a year, Ted, and I
must've told you a thousand times to call me Evan."

Wright anxiously carried the two steaming cups over to where Ledo
stood transfixed by the view. Together they sipped and watched the
scurrying activity after the pickups pulled around back. The Snowcats

were idling, their flashing yellow lights pulsing like beacons through the snow.

"The weather isn't cutting us a break, is it?" Ledo glanced at Wright. "You seem tense."

"Just a little anxious is all. Truth be told Mr.—uh, Evan, from the planning process right on through the entire build, this project's taken up over two years of my life. And now all semblance of control is gone. And by that I mean, even if every single stage of this process goes off without a hitch, and every subcontractor we've signed on has thought far enough ahead to plan for the little things that usually stop a job dead in its tracks, we would still need a minor miracle to even flirt with making this deadline."

"Then I guess that would be the difference between you and I. I'm fifty-six-years-old, Ted. I've been blessed with good fortune, fine health, and even better looks—" He ribbed Wright for effect. "Of course I'm kidding, but by the way you're grinding your teeth, it would seem that you were the owner instead."

"The responsibility is still mine—"

"For what? The only responsibility you have is to do your job. I mean just think of it!" Ledo's blue eyes were lit up by this sudden possibility. "Five weeks to complete a harrowing build 14,000 feet up in the sky. The incredible stress and pressure as each tradesman gets his turn inside the cauldron ..." Ledo's eyes lit up. "I guess you have to be a little sick to appreciate it, but I've certainly been called worse."

They watched the men transfer equipment into the hulking Snow-cats. In the center of the action, Nolan Harris could be seen shouting and pointing at a thousand tasks.

Wright frowned and said, "That's a strange way to motivate, don't you think?"

"With threats and insults?" Ledo smirked. "In the middle of this storm, with all of his employees whirling about, he reminds me of Captain Ahab."

From behind the glass in the nice warm office, the scene was surreal. The workers, in their multiple layers with hoods pulled tight, looked like astronauts forsaken to this place. And while they proceeded with ant-like uniformity, the thoughts of both men watching seemed to be in sync.

"Honestly," Ledo said. "Do you think these guys can really pull this off?"

"On behalf of Danforth Construction," Wright candidly replied, "I sincerely hope so."

Outside, the storm remained relentless.

———————

Two of the four Ohara Snowcats looked like box trucks welded onto tank treads. The interior was diamond-plate and had two bench seats with a ten-person capacity. Hooked to the rear of each were flatbed trailers with a 3,000-pound limit. The other two Snowcats had the same two-man driver's cab, but instead of a rear-mounted shelter for humans, a stainless-steel deck was stacked with supplies. Total weight of the vehicles with their maxed-out 3,000-pound cargo limit was 11,580 pounds each.

They pulled the pickups and trailers close enough to the Snowcats so that an assembly line of swivel-hipped men could more easily transfer the gear and tools. It was miserable work in the blowing winds, and tempers were tight. Lastly, they grabbed their backpacks and coolers of food and shoved themselves into the Snowcats. The convoy readied for departure. As Ledo and Wright appeared to bid them farewell, the crew gave them blank faces while the tank treads shuddered to life.

The lead Snowcat was piloted by Reno Morello. For the next seventeen days, he and his team would be in charge of transporting materials, food, lumber, and anything else needed uphill. Reno was a patched-in Mongol MC and originally from the upper peninsula of Michigan. When he was not on his bike, he ran heavy equipment before hiring on at Peak 4. He was a giant man who wore a long Fu-Manchu mustache and a mischievous grin. His aviator sunglasses bracketed his skull-and-bones bandana. A sign above the dashboard said, YOUR MOM'S A WHORE. With Nolan riding shotgun beside him, and in the way strangers' bond when stumbling across those of a likewise mindset, Reno was quickly in step with the pulse of the crew around him. He cranked Fugazi as the windshield wipers slapped away the driving snow to reveal the outside gloom. Through a headset, he spoke with the three drivers behind him. Then he turned a slanted grin onto Nolan.

"You guys ain't gonna need seatbelts, man. Our load is maxed out. Once we start climbing and switch-backing, we might make eight miles an hour."

Nolan did not even ask, he just pulled out a bowl and soon they were stoned and listening to Ian McKay scream about social injustice and corporate prostitutes and the unrepentant.

Elias was crouched into the window-sized opening between the cargo unit and the driver's cab. He stared over their shoulders into the storm. "How long's this gonna take?"

Reno choked back a hit and then exhaled. "We got three-quarters of a mile before starting the real ascent. Fully loaded, figure at least forty minutes."

"Great." Elias turned back to Rand, O-Zone, Cooter, and New Year. "Who's got the beers, man, what up, yo?"

Only the wind outside howled back in answer.

It was late morning when the Snowcats finally clawed up the spine and summitted on Mt. Pershing's western ridge. The air was already thin at liftbase, but as they climbed, their chests ached from all the extra breaths. It was work just to stay oxygenated. O-Zone commented on the fact that if they had come up from sea level they would have been wheezing like beached fish, but no one took any solace in that.

"It ain't nothing," Reno called out over his shoulder. "You guys ski at 10,000 feet, so it'll only take a day or two to get acclimated." Then he spoke into his headset and informed liftbase of their arrival.

Because of the storm, visibility was down to thirty feet. The snow and wind screamed past. The windshield wipers continued their futile movements until the remains of the firebombed building crept into view.

"Holy shit." Rand got up from the bench and joined Elias by the hatch. They peeked over Reno's shoulder as the decimated lodge crept into view. Anything not covered by drifting snow had been completely torched. Like charred teeth, only a ring of first-floor walls remained.

"Jesus Christ," Nolan said in awe. "Those are some naughty fucking hippies."

The gondola line was intact but comically out of place since it stood at the end of nothing.

"Does it still work?" Cooter asked.

"The gondola?" Reno throttled back. "They think so. But the uphill motor's roasted. They got a team coming in from Sweden to rehab it next week. After you guys are done building, right?"

"Next week ..." Nolan clapped him on the back. "That's a good one, Reno."

Nolan's Nextel clicked before Cam's voice came through. "We haven't made the ridge yet, what's it look like?"

"Fucking Dresden, man, call Hitler."

Two semi-trailers could be seen at the top of the ridge to the left of the burnt-out structure and gondola line.

Reno arced them around toward the trailers and said, "It's too bad the weather's so fucked up, because on a nice day you can see all the way to Utah."

Rand zipped up. He motioned toward the chaotic conditions. "This what we can expect?"

"Not every day. But I gotta say, you guys must seriously hate your lives."

Nolan laughed. Then he turned to the cluster of faces in the hatch. "All right, ladies, gear up, it's time to DD."

Reno parked alongside the trailers.

Nolan crawled through the hatch into the cargo compartment. He tore through his bag and put on an extra thermal layer. "New Year ..." Nolan looked concerned. "You all right?"

Neil's smile weakened through the strain. "Can't catch my breath is all."

"It'll get easier. I can't breathe either, man, no worries."

"All this talk about breathing makes me want to have a smoke," Elias said, and Rand cackled hard at that one.

"Elias ..." Nolan was shaking his head as he yanked on his gloves. "You're one of the absolute stupidest bastards of all time."

"Safety last." Elias stepped to the rear hatch. "You girls ready?"

"Open that thing."

The wind caught the door and whatever heat that had been inside the Snowcat instantly disappeared. Snow poured through instead.

"Holy fuck!" Elias hopped out, followed by Rand, who had to lean into the wind just to stay upright. They held each other up through the onslaught, and Elias could not stop laughing. "Quick, somebody get me my tool bags!"

Rand shouted, "Seventeen days my ass!"

More hysterical laughter.

"Jesus Christ," O-Zone said to Nolan. "I don't think I've ever been this scared."

"Welcome home, O-Z." Nolan jumped out next and was nearly blown off his feet. The snow was up to their thighs as they post-holed toward the snowed-in trailers.

From the Snowcat behind, Team Beaver disembarked, and soon it looked like thirteen inmates had been transported to a burned down prison on the North Pole.

It took an hour to unload the four Snowcats. Trenches needed to be dug everywhere, and every step through the snow and altitude took quadruple the time and effort. Oxygen deprivation caused tiny bubbles to explode across their vision, and the labored breathing left some guys palming their knees. Because of the jagged cold, those first deep inhales were searing.

Having decided that Danforth was in no way going to be able to fly up the additional trailers through the storm, they cluster-fucked all the tools into one trailer and left the other empty for a place to sleep. There was a fully stocked fridge, a grill with a vent punched through a wall, and a microwave next to a makeshift sink. They tossed in their backpacks, coolers, and sleeping bags before locating the main power panel out back. Extension cords were hooked in to run the sawzalls and saws just as a tremendous roar chewed through the storm.

Like a maniac unleashed, Rigor Mortis hefted a thirty-six-inch Husqvarna chainsaw and screamed, "Stack out, bitches!" He revved it and then dropped it through the charred plywood bays between every other 2x6 stud. Spoons and Uno followed with sawzalls, cutting the studs at the plate so the sectioned walls could fall.

"Get some!" Rigor Mortis screamed, and his psychosis helped warm the others. As the day faded, the wind whipped sheets of snow across the site. The walls were cut down and dragged off to the right and piled up and soaked in gas before another bonfire atop the mountain roared again. They used impact wrenches to unscrew the bolts so the black-ened bottom-plates could be removed and added to the flames hungrily stretching into the sky.

It was nearing four o'clock when Nolan ordered New Year and Bunny inside to organize the gear and food. The gray day was already fading, and they needed the trailer powered up and squared away before the long cold night ahead.

They stacked thirteen backpacks and sleeping bags against the wall. A hole was drilled through the floor to hook in a power cord and a pair of twelve-way adapters to run the lights, space heaters, stereo, phone chargers, microwave, toaster, and exhaust fan for the stand-alone grill.

As they finished and looked down the length of the trailer, a horrific realization caused Bunny to say, "Seventeen days."

New Year hooked his thumbs into the belt loops of one of the two pairs of jeans he wore over multiple long-johns. "Those ain't good odds."

"Fuckin' A." Bunny headed for the door. "Like rats in a box, man, just you watch."

Outside, night fell early. The snow had lessened, but the wind showed no sign of surrender. Nolan had the guys digging out the bunks of wood so they could tarp them and then dig them out again in the morning.

They piled into the trailer as full dark fell by five o'clock. Soaked clothing was hung like laundry in front of the blasting heaters. Slowly, gradually, the fact that they would all be spending the next twelve hours inside this drafty rectangle before stepping back out into a still-raging tempest, settled into them like ice beneath the skin. The floor was soaked because of the snow tracked in by everyone's boots, so there was now no place dry to sit. The lone piece of furniture was a card table Nolan had already commandeered so that he and Cam could go over the plans.

"Hey!" Nolan called out. "Drag your whiney frozen asses over here so we can go over what's about to happen."

Cold and tired, they circled the table. Nolan pointed to the blue-prints and said, "Think of it as a T-bone steak. This is what gets built right now"—Nolan pointed to the horizontal part of the T—"and this longer, triple-decker part of the structure gets built next summer." Nolan pointed again. "We got four exterior walls, a carport roof shooting out over the gondola line, and get this ..." He flipped to the interior layout. "There's a grand total of twenty-four interior walls on the first-floor and"—he flipped it again—"because the upstairs is a wide-open cafeteria, we've got sixteen walls up there to frame."

"Tits and gravy," Uno said.

Nolan nodded. "Fellas, this thing's a fucking box with a trussed roof ... seventeen days?"

"Right on." Spoons liked the sound of that.

"But we gotta keep guys constantly shoveling." Nolan rolled up the prints. "We fall behind on that and we're totally screwed. Everyone takes a turn, myself included."

"Trenches ..." Rand sounded disgusted. "Brings back memories of Butcher Block."

Nolan grinned. "Remember that, Elias? That's where we popped your cherry."

"Yeah, thanks for the memories."

But people were already bored.

"What the fuck," Rigor Mortis growled. "Somebody pack a bowl."

"We'll keep busy," Nolan said optimistically. "Let's get three guys grilling burgers and getting dinner ready, and I brought a couple decks of cards ..."

"Yeah, well, I brought this." Rand hauled his backpack into the ring of despondent faces, unzipped both side pockets, and pulled out six bottles of Jim Beam.

"Thank God." Elias grabbed one and cracked the seal.

"Seventeen days," Cooter said with some regret. "We're liable to just about kill each other."

"Way ahead of you," Rigor Mortis said. "Ever play Pussy?"

"Naw, is that a card game?"

"Sure. Except there's no cards. And one guy punches the other"— Riggy squared off a shot to Cooter's bicep that sent him reeling backwards—"and the first guy who quits is the pussy."

Elias laughed until Riggy turned and punched him and then all hell broke loose. Guys wailed on each other before collapsing to the ground in a writhing ball of hate.

"Morons!" Nolan screamed.

But there were only cries of pain in answer. Nolan moved to break up the melee, but Cam stopped him by saying, "It might be quieter once they're all unconscious."

Uno shook his head and stepped around the thrashing appendages. He joined Cooter and New Year by the sink preparing dinner.

Eventually, the scrum ended and everyone scattered to catch their breath. They rubbed their aching arms and passed around a pair of bottles and then chuckled at what they had done.

"Is anyone gonna pack a fucking bowl?" Rigor Mortis asked, but no one could even raise their arms to do it.

———

Cam and Nolan were studying the plans when the burgers hit the grill and the fan, for whatever reason, did not vent the smoke.

"What's going on?" Cam asked.

Uno said, "Hell if I know. The power's fine but the vent's blocked."

"What the fuck?" Rigor Mortis was seated on the floor where he, Spoons, Rand and Elias were continuously doing shots. The smoke rolled off the grill, hit the ceiling, and had nowhere else to go but down.

"Uno!" Spoons yelled.

"Fuck, man, I'm trying!"

"If we have to open those doors ..." Nolan stopped before growing further annoyed. "Hermaphrodite, what the fuck is so funny?"

"Nothing, man, except that I'm stuck inside this meat tube with you yam-bags and even the burgers are trying to kill us."

"Oh, man," O-Zone laughed while passing him the bottle. "Here, dude, put yourself away."

Nolan joined Cooter and Uno at the vent until the frustration overwhelmed him. "Goddamnit!" He punched the wall as the grill spewed smoke and guys started coughing. "Open the fucking doors!"

Rand and Elias pulled on their gear and kicked open both doors. The wind instantly ran in and stabbed everyone. They dove for their jackets and hats but there was nowhere to hide. Outside it was pitch black and, while the snow had momentarily slowed, the falling temperature and wind continued attacking. Elias dropped to the ground in the bone-searing chill. Rand followed him out. They gathered a flashlight and a six-foot ladder from the other trailer and then leaned it against the wall to access the vent. Climbing up, Elias could see the inch-thick ice layered over the vent and punched it.

"I need a hammer!" he yelled through the wind, and Rand went and quickly returned with his hatchet. After beating it clear, the smoke immediately started spewing into Elias' face.

"Come on!" Rand yelled. "It's gotta be minus ten out here!"

"Embrace the suck!" Elias, once he climbed inside, turned to help Rand as well. "Tomorrow we build a ramp."

After dinner, the first day of altitude had left everyone with headaches, dehydration, and exhaustion. Guys were on the floor playing cards and shooting the shit as Nolan phoned Ted Wright and said, "It's me again."

"Yeah, Noll, I just got off the phone with Jack Trion from Skylift. He says if the storm blows through by tomorrow afternoon, we should be able to get the first-floor system—including all the joists and plywood—flown up in one shot."

"We're not gonna be ready for it anyway." Nolan turned away to shield his voice from the others. "If the weather stays this bad we'll be lucky to have the exterior walls done by the day after tomorrow."

"We're not gonna have any luck on that front, I'm afraid." Wright could be heard shuffling papers. "National Weather Service says most of the storm should blow by but the temperature ... they're talking zero degrees, and with the wind up there, it could hit minus thirty."

Nolan looked up at the ceiling before closing his eyes.

"Noll, are you there?"

"Yeah. Listen. This trailer business is a total disaster."

"What can I do to help?"

"At the least, we need another one. And more heaters, man, the wind is ripping right through this tin can."

"Maybe I'll have them lift the trailer up tomorrow instead."

"We're also gonna need some extra facemasks. And gloves, the neoprene ones like the divers wear?"

"What else?"

"Chairs. We're lying on the floor like inmates."

"No problem. I'm making a list right now. What else?"

"Booze. We've got whiskey, but we need more. And at least six cases of beer. There's nothing to do up here at night, man, so I need to keep these guys drunk."

"Not during work though, right?"

"Nope. That's what the weed's for."

"I didn't hear that."

Nolan smiled. He was starting to think Ted Wright might be an all-right guy after all.

"Anything else?"

"Yes. A shitload of baby wipes. These pukes are gonna need some way to half-ass shower."

"I'll send everything up with Reno. Facemasks, gloves, beers, chairs, baby wipes and heaters."

"Ten-four."

"Talk to you tomorrow, Noll. Stay warm."

"Later, man."

Nolan closed the phone.

———————

After consuming all that alcohol, even the act of urination was a nightmare. One had to carefully step over all the sleeping bodies, gear up, crack the doors, listen to everyone bitch as they were instantly awakened by the freezing blast, piss somewhere outside, and then listen to more bitching after opening the doors again. If someone needed an actual toilet, the portajohn was a short distance away and about as comfortable as shitting in a freezer. Nevermind the mountain of frozen turds—dropping trousers and sitting on the ice-cold rim was worse than knowing that the pile of turds below belonged to some of your best friends and ascending shit-by-shit closer to your own ass. By day three there would be thirty-nine of them and there were still two more weeks to go.

———————

From experience, working in the snow was more a nuisance than an outright show-stopper. That distinction belonged to the bitter cold, which assassinated strength and spirit. Anything moist—lips, noses, eyeballs—was instantly attacked, chapped, and quickly ached. Since there were only so many layers one could apply before walking top-plate or handling power tools became dangerous, fingers and toes were next on the list of nearly indefensible targets.

The morning after, when they stumbled out into the falling snow and the clouds, because of the altitude, swirled like fog around them, the only thing anyone knew for sure was that pain and misery would be walking with them hand in hand.

Exposed skin was non-existent. Faces were smeared with Vaseline and then covered in masks. The standing temperature was ten degrees, but the wind, despite every precaution and protection, quickly razored through them.

"Let's go! Let's go!" Nolan yelled. "Everyone out of the trailer! Bunny, Cooter, New Year, get the compressors fired up. Uno, get an extra set of hoses, guns, and saws in front of the heaters so we can switch them out once everything freezes up. Elias, O-Zone, and the Soldanos, start shoveling, man, let's get the foundation cleared off and de-fuck the bunks of wood. Rand, Cam, and Riggy, get the drills and saws and get ready to plate this bitch."

Everyone scattered, if only because movement created heat. The shovel teams worked from the trailer to the foundation and then cleared another trench to the bunks of wood. Fortunately, the snow was fluffy and easily tossed, but the sheer volume that needed removal meant they were also getting a serious workout.

Cam found Nolan and they shared a moment as the crew whirled about them. The wind had driven them deep into their hoods. As always, everyone either wore ski goggles or sunglasses to prevent going snow-blind.

Cam said, "We're at minus twenty-five with wind. My phone's already frozen."

"Jesus, man, I don't know." Nolan did not even want to stand there talking. "Another ten degrees might finish us off."

"Minus forty and the hoses will explode." Cam shuddered in the wind. "That's the coldest I've ever seen."

"I don't ..."

"Noll, what's on your mind?"

"I think I fucked us." He looked at the shovel teams just struggling to breathe. "This time I think I really fucked us."

CHAPTER TWENTY-FIVE

At eleven o'clock they heard growling through the snow-filled wind. Flashing yellow lights appeared just before a pair of Snowcats climbed into view. Reno blasted his airhorn in greeting and rolled right up to the trailers.

Nolan met them there as Danforth workers disembarked to quickly unload the heaters, chairs, and booze.

Reno, lacking enough proper clothing, found his teeth instantly chattering. "Jesus Christ, this is fucking insane!"

"Thanks for the morale boost."

"Goddamnit!" Reno punched his gloves together. "Seriously, you guys are out of your blessed minds."

"Listen ... I need a favor."

"What's up?" Reno looked forlornly into his heated Snowcat.

"Actually, it's two favors. The first—we need another layer of egg-crating to sleep on. We gotta get off the floor more. And our sleeping bags blow. One of our guys is a serious climber and he's saying we need, like, military spec shit." Nolan consulted a piece of paper. "30 ounces of 800 fill down, if possible. Whatever that means. He says any proper climbing store will have them, and we're gonna need thirteen of them. Here." Nolan handed him the paper. "Favor number two—please, for the love of God, get us more weed. I brought an ounce and a half but that was wishful thinking."

"Whatever you want." Reno yanked his hat down so far it covered his neck. "I'll have the egg crating and bags by tomorrow, but I'll need a day or two for the other."

"No problem. Here. That's five hundred bucks for the weed. Get whatever you can. The sleeping bags go on Danforth's tab."

"You heard about the lift, right? They're hoping to fly that trailer up here by three o'clock."

"That's their problem. Jesus, you okay?"

"Naw, man, I'm about eighty fucking degrees away from okay." Reno climbed back into the Snowcat and honked the horn to rally up his guys.

They made horrible progress into the afternoon because three guys were constantly shoveling. A fourth was tending to the tools like a chef and heating and switching out the frozen hoses and guns and saws almost every fifteen minutes. Hoses exploded and twisted like headless, hissing snakes. The snow fell into the wind as it screamed up the mountain and smacked them at the top.

"What's that?" Spoons swung his snow-covered head like an alerted rabbit.

"Must be the chopper." Rand surveyed the peak, but the cloud cover only revealed a hundred-yard perimeter. "Noll! Sounds like the bird's on the way!"

Nolan was helping Team Beaver wrestle plywood sheets onto one of the walls and shouted, "Who cares? Hurry up!"

The thumping grew louder until it felt like a second pulse inside their chests.

"Feels like it's on top of us already," Elias said, and seconds later the Sikorsky S-64 suddenly roared overhead. Snow and wind exploded across everyone's faces as the pilot, barely visible in the cockpit, looked to the ground for direction. Nolan jogged down the trench through this instant blizzard and repeatedly pointed to the far side of the furthest trailer. The pilot flicked him a thumbs-up before carefully working the chopper into position. His movements were slow and precise, the craft a hovering oddity since it was nothing more than a two-man fuselage connected to a bare spine and massive rotor. Its mid-section was totally eviscerated for cargo. The tractor-trailer, which had been firmly fastened inside this hollow belly, began descending on a cabled winch.

"That's cool as hell." O-Zone shielded his face from the ricocheting snow and ice.

"Jesus Christ, now it's like minus sixty!" Rand screamed.

The trailer dropped straight down until it was either caught by the ripping wind or rotor wash or both. It began to twirl.

"Huh." Spoons held a hand like a shelf over his eyes. "That can't be good."

The trailer was still thirty feet off the ground when its rate of spin increased. The pilot and co-pilot struggled inside the cockpit. Alarmed, Nolan backed away.

"What the fuck is going on?" Rigor Mortis screamed. "Do these chopper monkeys need a beating?"

"Something's wrong." Rand dropped the gun. "Nolan! Get out of there!"

Cam turned to everyone else. "Back up! Everybody get the fuck back!"

The workers fled the cycling trailer. The chopper rose up and down but nothing stopped the spin.

"Holy shit ..." O-Zone tripped and fell in full reverse as the trailer became an opposing propeller that dragged the helicopter around the sky. Reaching critical mass, the pilot finally detonated the cable and the trailer crashed into the other trailer filled with all their tools.

"Fuck!" Nolan roared. "You stupid motherfuckers!" He picked up the nailgun and started firing at the chopper. "Goddamnit! Goddamnit!"

The pilot shrugged helplessly and then pulled back as the nails sailed off into space.

"Get the fuck out of here! You fucking pukes! You goddamn fucking fucks!"

"Nolan!"

"Fuck!"

The chopper banked away.

The trailer with the tools was smashed in half. The trailer that had fallen was semi-flattened from the impact.

They all stood there, dazed.

Nolan got on the phone. With only an hour before full dark at five o'clock, the destroyed trailer had to be removed and the tools salvaged from the one beneath, or the wind and snow would bury whatever remained.

"All right," Nolan said. "O-Zone, Spoons, Elias, and Rand—get some metal cutting blades into the sawzalls and start cutting. Riggy and Uno, gather up whatever tools aren't crushed. Los Soldanos and Bunny, roll up the tools we were using before they freeze. Cooter and New Year, tarp the bunks of wood and the two walls we got built laying down." Nolan paused, looking nauseous. "Two fucking walls, man, unbelievable."

"Everybody move," Cam called out. "Clock's ticking." As the crowd broke apart on their various tasks, he pulled Nolan aside and said, "So what'd they say?"

"Nothing new." Nolan's expression was covered by his mask and glasses. "They're gonna fly up two more trailers tomorrow. Can't wait for that fucking show."

"What about the tools?"

"I gotta get a list together. They'll motor up replacements in the morning."

"Incredible."

They both turned toward the rattling sound of the sawzalls slicing through the trailer's aluminum skin.

Cam asked, "Do they know what happened with the chopper?"

"The pilot said the trailer was pulling them into a spin. I told them next time to put tag lines on the fucking thing."

"Right? What the hell were they thinking?"

"You know what? It doesn't even matter. Things were going way too smoothly to begin with."

"Looks like we got front-row seats."

"You're right." Nolan's mood seemed to ease. "Grab the popcorn and drinks, bro, because here comes the greatest fuckshow of them all."

———

The two trailers were in the shape of a cross smashed into the ground. The one that had fallen from the chopper was the first to be removed. O-Zone and Spoons sawed through its walls in three-foot verticals. Elias and Rand, beginning on either end of its now warped roof, cut it down the middle. Without sure footing, they held on with one hand while wedging their toes for a better grip.

"This thing's getting ready to go!" Rand shouted, backing up toward Elias.

Elias nodded and said, "I got six more inches to cut and then we bail."

"Roger that." Rand peeked down over the edge. "O-Zone, Spoons, heads up!" He looked back at Elias. "There ain't no more room for two, bro."

"No worries, Fabio. See you on the ground."

"Oh yeah? You think you got this, little fella?"

"Yes, sir."

Rand was not smiling anymore. "Don't be late, bro, or you're gonna ride this bitch into the ground."

"Understood."

"And make sure you clear eight feet or it'll come down on your head."

"Dad, I got it."

Rand whistled and then tossed his sawzall down to Spoons. Then he jumped into a snowbank.

Elias took one more look at his chosen landing zone because now Rand had totally freaked him out. Six inches of roof was the only thing holding the trailer together. Elias called out, "Here we go! On three. One, two, three!"

The sawzall wailed for five seconds before Elias launched himself off the side. Then the fallen walls were cut and dragged away. This allowed access to the crushed mid-section of the original tool trailer. Nolan and Cam shouldered over 2x6s and plywood and soon replaced its destroyed middle with wood walls and a ceiling. The tools were inventoried and anything damaged was tossed onto the stack of hacked-apart walls. Two heaters were pulled in to keep the surviving tools functional until the morning, then everyone retreated into the lone remaining trailer.

After yesterday's debacle, all boots and outer garments were now left by the door so the floor would not be drenched in melted snow. Once locked in, thirteen tense faces stared at each other in the gloom before Nolan, knowing he needed to boost morale after today's disaster, instead turned and said, "Get drunk and stoned, idiots, because this nightmare's far from over."

Someone snickered.

Cam glanced at Nolan for the first time with utter disdain. He then turned to the others and said, "Cooter, Uno, and New Year, start the meal. Bunny, pack the bong." Cam reached for one of the Heineken twelve-packs and started handing out beers. "Elias, get something on that radio so we can at least pretend to be human beings. Spoonie, get those heaters cranking and everybody dry your gloves."

"Anyone up for a game of Pussy?" Rigor Mortis asked, but everyone quickly moved away. "Pussies."

A poker game broke out as music played and the crew partied. Dysfunction at the top would benefit no one, so Cam pulled Nolan aside and tried to be discreet. Cam grabbed them two chairs and quietly said, "You need to pull yourself together."

"That fucking chopper and the wind—"

"*What?*" Cam's small blue eyes flashed in his reddened, wind-seared face. "Are you kidding me?"

"I ..." Nolan lost the words, seemingly embarrassed. He looked to make sure no one was eavesdropping before glancing back at Cam. "I just ... I got a bad feeling, man."

"So what? What are the options?" Cam hissed. "Do you wanna *quit*? I can't believe we're actually having this conversation."

"Fifteen days left?"

"So what? We're already in it up to our necks. Do you have any idea what that would do to our reputations? To our companies?" He raised his beer and drank half of it before lowering his voice and leaning in. "I've spent the last nine months battling with you side-by-side as you made some unilaterally horrible decisions. I've backed you when every other motherfucker with a brain and common sense would have jacked you and left you for dead." He pointed a finger at Nolan and amazingly, with every word he then said, poked him in the chest. "We're not going anywhere, got it?"

"Cam—"

"You leave this fucking hill and you're bankrupt. Me? I'll take a hit to my name, but I'll still have a company to run. You?" Cam scoffed. "You're as good as dead."

Nolan could not argue with the truth. He squared his chin, finished his beer in three gulps, and then crushed the empty can. "You're right," he said and then stood up. He turned to where the crew was playing cards and partying hard and shouted, "Spoons, where's that list of tools? I've got to call down to Team Tampon and give them a slice of hell."

———

The blasting windchill and sheets of snow departed by day three. From their mountaintop vantage point, the entire western plain leading up to the Rocky Mountains was one long white blanket rolled out beneath the cloudless blue sky that stretched two hundred miles to the Utah border. In awe of the view, they slogged as a group through the mid-thigh snow and stared out until Rigor Mortis yelled, "Why don't you losers take a picture! Let's go, hurry up."

"Hurry up," they chorused and returned to work. The high sun and five-degree heat wave allowed them to shed their masks. Also, without the wind, one man could carry plywood sheets without getting blown over onto his face.

By mid-afternoon, the Snowcats arrived with replacement tools, more heaters and supplies, as well as Evan Ledo and Ted Wright. They hopped down like tourists refreshed by the scenery and bright sunshine and quickly buttoned up their coats. Nolan met them at the first trench and shook hands as they surveyed the wreckage.

"Boy, I can't even catch my breath up here." Ledo's knee-high boots post-holed toward the destroyed trailers. "You weren't kidding, Nolan, it certainly is a mess."

Wright followed along and said, "I like what you guys did, sectioning in the wood walls and ceiling between the destroyed halves of that trailer."

Bringing up the rear, Nolan said, "Necessity's a bitch."

Ledo seemed intoxicated by his surroundings and in awe of what remained of the trailers. "Good Lord, it's a miracle no one got injured."

"Or worse," Wright glumly added.

After glancing over at the crew's ongoing work—itching to rejoin their efforts—Nolan stuffed a cigarette into the corner of his mouth. "So I understand the chopper's coming back today for round two?"

"This afternoon." Wright nodded and then squinted into the sun. "The pilot said ... well, let's just say he was not pleased by your response."

"He can suck my ass."

Ledo flinched.

Nolan pointed across the clearing and said, "He could have dumped that trailer twenty feet in any direction and never hit a thing."

"It's not part of their protocol," Wright carefully said. "Once the load puts the chopper in jeopardy, they're instructed to immediately detonate the cable. No exceptions."

"Protocol? He took out $40,000 in trailers, at least ten grand in tools, and cost me half a day's work." Nolan shrugged as he exhaled smoke. "He's an incompetent moron, plain and simple. As a matter of fact, he saved his own life by not killing any of my guys."

"Well ..." Ted Wright had nowhere else to turn, and certainly did not want to appear disloyal. "I understand your frustration."

But Ledo gamely winked. "It's just one more chapter in the eventual writing of this place, isn't it?" He pointed over to where the crew was finishing up the final first-floor wall. "It is absolutely fantastic to see those walls proudly standing!"

Nolan smiled because Ledo's enthusiasm was either annoying or contagious or both. "I totally agree."

Wright snapped his fingers. "The floor system. You'll be ready by tomorrow?"

"We sure will."

"Okay." Wright pulled a walkie-talkie from his jacket and hailed the base.

Standing next to Nolan, Ledo was half his size. He looked up at Nolan and asked, "How bad is it up here at night?"

"Ever sleep in a freezer?"

"If sharing a bed next to my ex-wife counts, then yes. Seriously, how're your guys holding up? Can we provide anything else? Perhaps some warm beds or whiskey snifters by the fireplace?"

Nolan laughed and flicked away the cigarette. "We're doing fine, Mr. Ledo, but thanks all the same."

"I heard the weather was a monster yesterday."

"Just the wind, really. As grown-ass men, they can handle it."

"Better than me. I'm still trying to catch my breath."

"Yes, sir." Nolan figured it might have been a decade since he had last called anyone sir.

"I want your honest opinion, Noll. You got fourteen days to go. Are you feeling confident?"

"As confident as a buck-toothed hooker in a room full of blind men."

"Hey, Nolan." Ted Wright rejoined them. "Chopper's on the way in from Grand Junction. They're gonna fly up the floor system and then the trailers."

"Nice. I'll be sure to be standing way the fuck over there."

———————

That night, after the crew split up inside the newly arrived trailers, Nolan found a quiet corner to huddle with his phone. Kara answered on the fourth ring and sounded half-asleep.

"So how is it up there?" she asked.

"It's all right. We're sleeping on the floor like rats, but the heaters are running day and night."

"How's Riggy doing? He kill anybody yet?"

"No ... he's actually been well-behaved. Must be the altitude."

"Huh."

The silence extended until it became a third presence on the phone.

"I miss you," he said. "I really do."

She was not about to bite. "We'll talk when you get home. Isn't that what you told me?"

"I don't want to wait for that."

"Well, I'm done living by your choices."

"What's that supposed to mean?"

"Don't patronize me, Nolan." She was now fully awake.

"I'm not patronizing—"

"Yes, you are. Stop whining. You made these decisions and now you have to fix them."

"Fuck ..."

"Is there anything else?"

"Excuse me? Can't you even talk to me?"

"What do you want to talk about? How about this? The landlord's put an eviction notice on *our* apartment. I've already taken all of my things out of there because it smells like a third-world bathroom."

"Jesus Christ. Don't be flip with me."

Kara sighed into the phone. "I have to go."

"Kara, I love you."

"We'll have to talk about that later."

The previous months of six and seven-day work weeks, combined with the altitude and brutal cold, left the crew exhausted by the end of day four. The eleven-hour shifts and constant partying made falling asleep, even on the hard freezing floor, a welcome reprieve from their existence.

With both the first-floor exterior and interior walls finished, Nolan tried not to think about how long this had taken. The clock was already ticking like a bomb inside his head.

On the dawn of day five, the big-boy weather returned. Ripping northwest winds filled with snow until the flurries became a suffocating white-out. The hooded, layered crew waddled about beneath the fist of Nolan's relentlessness. One group rimmed the exterior walls, another constantly shoveled out the site, and the remainder lined up the floor joists like giant piano keys waiting to be cut.

"Bunny!" Rigor Mortis, balanced on the icy top-plate, tossed away a ten-foot piece of rim. "You blew the number, dumbass, 116⅝!"

Bewildered, Bunny said, "That's what I cut ... at least I thought—"

"No thinking!" Rigor Mortis screamed. "Jesus Christ, you should drop your bags, because you sure as fuck ain't no framer!"

"Well, now you're just being hurtful." Unflappable, Bunny readied a fresh piece of rim, but the overall mood was ugly. Guys were cursing and grumbling as the weather worsened and the valley below faded into dots of distant light.

"Spoons, Rand, Elias!" Nolan shouted. "Let's get numbers for the floor joists. Uno and Cooter, get ready to cut!"

The wind whipped through as Rand and Elias climbed the ladder.

"Watch your step, ladies," Rigor Mortis chided. "It's slippery as fuck up here." A second later Elias' boot skidded off the wall before he caught himself at the last possible second.

Rand gave him a grin. "Do you need a change of underwear?"

"Yes." Elias took the end of Rand's tape measure and toe-heeled down the wall.

"Hey, Elias," Spoons added. "Just think, another forty years of walking icy top-plate in blizzard-filled wind storms and then you can retire."

"Oh my God."

While Rand and Elias precariously pulled numbers, Spoons wrote them down on a block of wood, which he then tossed out the window to Uno.

"Let's go, hurry up!" Nolan screamed through the blowing snow. "We need this floor rolled by lunch—"

A wave of sudden piercing screams rolled across the site. Those who saw it immediately ran over, while those who did not sensed the instant panic.

The guys on the wall said, "What the fuck was that?"

"What happened?"

Cooter was on the ground. Beside him, Uno, desperately trying to lend assistance, vomited instead.

Nolan and Cam got there first. Cooter writhed in pain.

Nolan said, "Cooter, goddamnit, stop fighting me!"

"I don't want to see it!" Blood was splashed across Cooter's glasses. "I'm sorry, Noll, I'm so sorry, man."

Cam forced him onto his back as Nolan grabbed the arm and said, "Jesus Christ, his fingers are gone!"

"Oh my God," Cooter wailed and then he retched as well. The blood was shooting rhythmic jets into the air like a fountain until Nolan squeezed with both hands but, like an uncapped well, it just spurted between his grip.

Cam was shot red across the face as he screamed, "Tourniquet that fucking thing!"

Rigor Mortis ripped off his tool bags, slung the bags off the wide leather belt, and joined Nolan in the growing pool of gore. Cooter's layers of clothing made the tourniquet impossible, so Riggy quickly knifed open his sleeves.

"Keep him on his back," Cam instructed. "And keep that arm in the air."

"Hold that arm, Nolan." Rigor Mortis was all business with the belt, wrapping the top of the forearm as Cooter screamed and screamed. Since there was no buckle-hole this far in, Riggy doubled the belt back on itself and then shouted for a roll of duct tape. Guys were tossing in sweatshirts to help with the blood, which by now only trickled through Nolan's hands.

"Cooter ..." Nolan blinked back tears. "It's all right, man, we got the blood stopped, okay?"

"Oh sweet Jesus." Cooter's spattered face twitched from adrenaline and fear as his eyes filled with pleading. "What's it look like, man? Tell me this didn't just happen."

"It ain't nothing, Coot." Miraculously, Nolan found it easier to look him in the eye. "We're gonna get you to a doctor, all right?" He rear-ranged his slippery hands on the stump, the blood now barely a trickle. He savored this small measure of relief until Elias, staying just beyond Cooter's line of sight, showed him a palm full of sawed-off fingers.

"Somebody get my truck," Nolan sickly said.

And then they remembered where they were.

———

Lifeflight helicopters were unavailable due to a fifteen-car pileup on I-70, so instead of an hour wait for a Snowcat, it was decided that two medics on a snowmobile would be dispatched for a mad-dash round-trip ride. Against every EMS protocol, Cooter would be raced downhill sandwiched between the medics. Even with a 4x4 mountain ambulance waiting, and reports of clear roads below, the soonest Cooter would see an emergency room was still an hour and a half away at best.

Rigor Mortis held the stump while Cam cast it in duct tape. They clamped sweatshirts around the freezing arm and rolled Cooter onto a sheet of plywood. Four guys grabbed a corner and loaded this makeshift stretcher into the trailer.

Rigor Mortis ordered him wrapped in blankets, overtly menacing with his concern. "Outta my way. You need to keep his feet up!" He crammed two sleeping bags under Cooter's feet and then tucked him in again.

Cam knelt down next to Cooter's shoulder. He immobilized Cooter's twitching arm by clamping it upright against his own chest. He said, "Cooter, look at me. Everything's squared away, all right? I just want you to slow down your breathing. Like this ..." Cam inhaled deeply and then prodded Cooter to join in. They inhaled together but Cooter sputtered through the pain. A single tear slipped beneath the corner of his blood-smeared glasses before streaming toward his ear. He said, "I'm only twenty-eight-years-old, man."

"You can't think like that." Cam found the utter meaninglessness of his own statement stupefying. "We got them on ice—"

"But my hand," Cooter pleaded. "This belt is at my wrist."

"So what—oh shit." Cam looked up at Rigor Mortis as Rigor Mortis called out, "What?"

"Yo, we got to move this belt."

Totally incredulous. "*What?*"

"C'mere. Help me unwrap this thing."

Nolan, whose entire upper body was splashed in Cooter's blood, had just finished screaming into his phone. "Sled's ten minutes out." He frowned at the again exposed stump and angrily said, "What the fuck are you guys doing?"

"We need to do something with his hand." Cam nodded at the purple swelling. "If it doesn't get blood they're gonna have to cut him off at the wrist."

"Jesus Christ." Nolan hit redial and seconds later was speaking to a paramedic downhill. Relaying the conversation, Nolan told Cam, "He says to ease off the tourniquet and find the brachial artery. It's up on the medial humerus ..." Nolan frowned and asked the paramedic, "What the fuck does that mean ...? Oh." He turned back to Cam. "Mid-bicep, on the side facing the body."

Cam handed the still-raised arm to Rigor Mortis and then grabbed Cooter's bicep. After a momentary struggle to find the pulse, Cam said, "Got it."

"He says to push on it, get rid of the tourniquet, use layers of gauze to cap off his stumps, and use direct pressure."

"No tourniquet?"

"No, fuck no. Not yet." Nolan hung up the phone. "He says keep the arm raised, feet up, gauze the hell out of the stumps and apply pressure. He says to call back if he doesn't stop bleeding. Tourniquet's the last resort."

While Cam and Rigor Mortis began treatment, Nolan stared at the amputation, at the perfect line the saw had taken. From the first knuckle on the index finger, it had traveled diagonally across all four digits until clipping the pinky clean off. The exposed bone ends and shredded muscle, however, almost caused Nolan to retch.

Bunny and Spoons pulled heaters over. O-Zone and Uno, who still had vomit in his beard, corralled New Year away from his brother-in-law's painful struggles. Nolan spotted Elias' macabre work by the sink and warily approached.

The reason Rand was blocking Cooter's view was because Elias held a Ziploc bag filled with Cooter's fingers. At their feet, as per instruction, a cooler had been emptied and refilled with snow. Elias wrapped the Ziploc in a dishtowel and then buried it, closing the lid. The three of them stood there for a while without having the heart to ask the ugliest question of all.

Was there enough blood left for Cooter to survive the trip?

———

"Did I ever tell you guys about Carlton Debolt?" Rand lobbed the question into the silence. After Cooter's departure, they burned all their bloody clothes and blankets. They took the saw covered in blood and tossed it into the flames. Then they returned to work like robots. Now, despite the additional quarters, they were all crammed inside a single trailer.

Seated or spread across the floor, the remaining twelve drank away the shock. Rand saw how shaken the younger guys appeared. Re-enactments were playing through everyone's brains. Lying prone, Rand said, "Carlton Debolt was a friend of my father's, and I was lucky enough to apprentice with him before I was even halfway quit of high school." He waited for the chuckles to stop and then continued. "Cam and Riggy are the only guys here besides me who came up hand-banging sixteen-penny nails—the rest of you pukes just grabbed a nailgun and started framing. Well, for us it was two hits. That's all Carlton gave you. One to set the nail and the other to drive it home. If he saw three hits to a nail he'd like as not plant the next one inside your skull."

"Hand-banging an entire house ..." Spoons shook his head in mock dismay. "You dinosaurs were really something else."

"Left and right-handed," Cam interjected, and then held up his book-sized hands. "You couldn't swing all day with one hand or you'd end up with a claw."

"Fucking A." Rand rose up into a seated position. "If there were enough missed swings, Debolt would set up a board with a row of nails just barely tapped in. There was an inch between them. You'd have to send them all home with alternating hands."

Bunny kept a straight face. "So what you're saying is that you guys are good at two-handing your hammers?"

"One time through ..." O-Zone raised his beer in honor.

Elias asked, "What other tortures were there?"

"I got one ..." Cam smiled at the reminiscence and said, "Like Fabio over there, I apprenticed under this crazy old-timer who was just about the most miserable motherfucker I've ever had the misfortune to know. No offense, Riggy ..." More laughter. "Anyway, he used to have this obsession with straight cuts. Didn't matter if it was rough-framing or the finest finish work, if the cut sucked, he would let you have it. Hated people who took no pride, right? He used to take his square and knife and square off a line that was literally razor-thin. Then he told you to pick a side. After that, he would etch more lines and make you keep cutting until he either lost interest or grew disgusted, because only a few guys ever concentrated enough to make a cut like that."

"Present company included?" Nolan asked.

"Shit, son, who do you think taught you?"

"Look how good that turned out." Rigor Mortis detached himself from the wall, the Jim Beam dangling at a noticeable angle. He worked his gaze like a shadow across their improving dispositions and said, "Our fearless leader hasn't even addressed what went down this afternoon."

"Riggy ..." Rand seemed fearful of where this might be going. "We weren't talking nothing about that. Not now."

"Tell me, Uno ..." Rigor Mortis stood in front of Uno and leaned into his face. "You were over there helping Cooter cut. After you were done puking like a pussy, and Cooter's fucking fingers were hacked off like sausages, did you think that was an okay environment to be working in?"

Nolan slowly stood.

Cam was already there. "Riggy, are you out of your mind, crying about the fucking weather?"

"What about the rest of you?" Rigor Mortis whirled on the group. "Did anyone think about how many dollars it would take to get us all up this fucking hill? To get snowed on, blown down and hurt?"

"Riggy ..." Rand left the threat unfinished while trying to cut off Nolan.

"It ain't $200,000, it's $260,000!" Rigor Mortis screamed. "And how much of that do you think Cooter's gonna see?"

Nolan attacked him. They crashed into a wall and exchanged blows before it was quickly broken up.

"Get him out of here!"

"Let me go!"

"Riggy, goddamnit ..." Spoons wrestled Rigor Mortis into a headlock, but Cam and Rand barely kept hold of Nolan.

"You'll never be dead enough!" Nolan surged forward while twisting in their grip. "We're through, you sick fuck, you hear me? Pack your shit and get walking!"

"You won't be satisfied until one of us is dead!"

"Riggy!" Elias helped Spoons drag him toward the doors. "This is fucking crazy!"

Rigor Mortis screamed, "Anyone who doesn't want to make a bunch of millionaires even richer, come with me!"

Rand yelled, "Get him out of here before he gets himself killed!"

Six guys later, Rigor Mortis was ejected from the trailer.

———

After Rigor Mortis was exiled to the trailer next door awaiting transport downhill, an unknown fracture abruptly appeared. For those who just wanted to go home, like the Soldano brothers, or those scared for their own safety, like Uno and New Year, a leader was now provided with which to formally lodge this protest. Awkwardly gathering up their things, they quietly voted with their feet.

"Can you fucking believe this?" Nolan was seated at the card table with Bunny, Rand, Elias, O-Zone, Cam, and Spoons. They cracked fresh beers while Bunny lit a joint.

Nolan said, "Who would have thought Rigor Mortis would be the Pied Piper to lead away all the pussies and the ungrateful?"

There were a few chuckles but Cam was not amused. "I think we have a serious problem."

"With who—Riggy?" Nolan almost laughed. "Once they sleep it off, they'll all come back—"

"I wasn't talking about them. When were you gonna tell me?"

"Cam—"

"Don't bullshit me." Cam leaned forward until both elbows hit the table. "$260,000 and I was what—just part of the same old deal?"

"That's not ..." Nolan shook his head at this confusion. "He's got it all wrong, man, that's not ..."

"You're pathetic." Cam stood up, his face mottled from holding back the rage. "After everything I—we've—done to rescue your goddamn pathetic ass, this is how you do me?"

"Fucking A, Noll." Spoons stood up as well. "That's about as ice-covered as it gets, bro."

They were gathering up their things until Nolan, after receiving a withering look from Rand, finally cleared his throat. "Okay, Riggy was right about the money. But what he doesn't know is that it all hinges on the contract. I promised you the money I did because it was all that I could afford in case we didn't make it."

Cam frowned. "Make what?"

"Because of the money, any idiot would have signed that contract if they didn't have to worry about ... what happens if they don't finish."

"What? Stop talking in circles."

Nolan blinked. "If this place isn't sheeted, sided, and roofed in seventeen days, we don't get paid a thing."

"*What* ...?" Cam shuddered. "What did you just say?"

"Holy shit." Spoons was frozen. "That's about the craziest fucking thing I've ever heard. Ever."

"Are you out of your mind?" Cam started packing his things. "You must be. I'll just tell them I didn't know anything about this."

"Cam—"

"This is insane!" Cam chucked his pack against the wall. "What? Was this some new bet you and Ledo dreamed up? That fucking corporate rat flapping his suck-hole about how this is all going to be some grand new fucking chapter—blah, blah, blah."

"That's not—"

"I'm so pissed right now, I don't know which way to vomit." He rubbed his forehead. "I didn't sign up for a suicide mission, Nolan."

"Listen. The guy that was gonna roof and side it backed out last second. Ledo all but dared me and I couldn't resist. $60,000 more?"

"You knew I would never agree to this. All or nothing. $260,000 for three weeks in hell, or three weeks in hell for free." Cam stalked back and forth. "No wonder no one else took this job. Spoons is right. This is the craziest, stupidest idea in the history of the world."

"Well, then help me make it." Nolan held out both arms, practically begging. "We hit that seventeen-day deadline and it'll be all of ours to share."

"Oh gee, thanks, now that you've been busted?"

"I wasn't going to say anything until—"

"It all makes perfect sense now. The whining, the worry ... and here I thought you might just be losing heart, which was gross enough, believe me. But no, instead, you knew you'd made a bad deal and an even worse bet that was going to finish us for good. And I sat there trying to cheer you up—"

"Cam—"

"Spoons, you ready?"

"Aces high, boss man."

"I'm gonna bill you for the last five days," Cam said, and then he and Spoons were gone.

It had not been a good day. Nolan and Rand were seated on the floor, their backs propped against the frozen aluminum wall.

"This is some kind of mess." Nolan stared at the beer can clutched between his heels. "I never thought this would be the way it ends."

Distracted by Bunny and Elias, who were at the card table doing shots, Rand said, "We gave it a good run, bro."

"A helluva run. We blew the doors off that entire valley."

"Here's to it."

They clinked their cans together. The silence extended.

Rand said, "Maybe this will be good. Dialing shit back to the way it used to be."

"It wasn't so bad."

"It really wasn't. I mean, before all of the tremendous fuckshows and multiple crews and whiny bitches and horrible subs, it was just a couple of bros getting together to bang some nails."

"Uh-huh."

Bunny called out, "Don't forget about Jesus."

"Are you eavesdropping on us?"

"Dude, we're in a fucking trailer."

"Well?" Nolan asked. "What do you maggots think about what I just said?"

Elias played with his empty shot glass. "Personally, I don't want to think about it at all. I've been up here for three years, and outside of that fiasco as a cook on the mountain, this is the only job I've had. And even though working for you two was a daily bloodbath, I wouldn't have traded any of that for any of this, man, not by a long shot. Those were some fun fucking days, bro."

"Is this ..." Bunny seemed to re-think his words. "Is it Chapter 11, Noll?"

"Fuck, man, who knows? But if this job falls through and the insurance company won't pay off that Pierce debacle, I'm as good as dead."

"You know ..." Elias refilled his and Bunny's glasses. "I understand why some of these guys want to go home, and why some of them are getting bitchy about the money. But what I don't get is, why now? Are things just blowing apart after three years with no vacations or time off or even an entire fucking weekend—"

"Hey!" Nolan yelled.

"Or is it because they're honestly tweaked about their safety?" Elias' expression filled with doubt. "The Black Death worried about safety? That's like getting a lecture on child abuse from a pedophile. Frankly, I didn't come up this mountain looking for anything. Time off, fighting over money ... I came up here because it was here and you said it was our next job. Period. End of story. If you turned around tomorrow and said our next job was a duplex on Everest, I'd say, 'See you in Kathmandu.' Personally, this shithole's already clipped off one of our bros and might've finished the company for good, so I'm hoping we stay out of spite alone."

"Who said anything about a vote?" Rand finished his beer and crushed it with his heel. "Elias' right. We're not going anywhere."

Nolan's eyes dotted about as if formulating a plan. "I'm going next door to talk to those pussies."

"Nice." Bunny clapped his hands. "Here's to the joys of carpentry."

Elias high-fived him. "After whoring, it's gotta be the second oldest profession."

"Whores." Bunny nodded. "Nice."

Rand slipped into his jacket. "Anybody want a beer for the ten-foot walk next door?"

"I'll take one," Nolan said, and then he squarely faced the door.

The strangest part of standing in front of them was that this time, instead of shouting orders or abuse, Nolan was there to make the peace. Shelving his pride was one thing, but the loss of respect from his guys tasted worse than failure.

The disinterested faces staring back were wind-chapped and exhausted. They drank beers looking openly annoyed. Cam and Spoons, seated in the rear, had not looked at him even once.

"You know what?" Nolan began, "I understand everyone's tired. I understand that Cooter's injury felt like the final nail in our coffin. And

I know you guys just want to get the fuck off this mountain. So do I. But do you really want to leave it like this?" He paused. "As far as the money, the only person in either trailer who should have a bitch with me is Cam. The rest of you are paid a salary that never stops. There hasn't been a single day in the last three years where I didn't have something lined up. You never came to work wondering about the future, because I was in charge of that. As far as I was concerned, the only thing I wanted you all thinking about was how fast you could nail one piece of wood to another. Sure, we've worked Saturdays and eleven-hour days, but your pay was where I made compensation. Fucking Elias showed up with no skills or brains and now he's making eighteen bucks an hour. Same for the rest of you. The only thing I've ever asked is that you hurry up. That's it. No thinking, no laughing, no bitching, but always hurry up. And you did. And I'm grateful for that. Seriously. We accomplished things in that valley that will keep people talking ten years after we're gone. We've put up almost 350,000 square feet in three years. We framed a 48,000 square foot condo in a matter of months. And now we're gonna build, side, and roof a 2,000 square foot box in seventeen days when it should really take three months. In a constant blizzard. And at 14,000 feet." Nolan started to pace. "Now I don't know how Riggy found out about the bet, and honestly, at this point, I don't even care. But he's gone. I should have been clean with Cam about the math and I wasn't. That's my fault and I apologize. As for everyone else, you were all going to be paid your regular rate plus a small bonus as a thank you for grinding through these conditions. But I don't like being called a liar or a thief. And I don't know how else to salvage the remaining twelve days without an all-star effort from every single one of you. So here it is. We make the deadline and divvy up the cash. With the siding and roofing added in, the new number is $260,000. Guessing both companies split $50,000 for taxes, that leaves $210,000. After the twenty-five percent payroll tax, that comes out to roughly $12,200 dollars per guy. That's a third of what some of you will make this entire year and you'll be doing it in under a month." Nolan stopped pacing and looked at each of them, even Cam and Spoons. "This job's already taken out Cooter and probably my company, but I'll be damned if I'm leaving this hill without a fight. No Cooter, no Rigor Mortis, so that leaves eleven guys. If you won't do it for me, then do it for yourselves or Cooter or the money, but let's not leave like this." Nolan stopped at the doors but did not look back. "Snowcats are coming up in the morning with supplies. There won't be any hard feelings against those who choose to leave."

———————

The following morning was day six. Nolan was the first one outside working at 5:45 A.M. He used the worm-burner to cook the compressors, saws, and guns before rolling out the cords. Without knowing what to expect, he kept himself from doing a head-count until he finally broke down and tallied ten—New Year was the only one who had not left the trailer.

Looking to break the ice from yesterday's confrontation, Nolan shouldered over a dozen 2x6s to where Cam was pulling them up from Bunny onto the second-floor deck. Once the last of Bunny's boards was hauled up, he headed off to retrieve another load.

Nolan looked up at Cam. "Ready?"

"Yeah." Leaning over, Cam clapped his hands together and then held them like a target.

Nolan shoved up four studs at once and Cam immediately reeled them in. When Cam's head reappeared over the edge, he said, "How we gonna do this?"

"Can I give you a kiss later?"

Cam slowly smiled, clapped his hands once, and caught the next four boards.

Nolan said, "I fucked up. I should've told you. I was just afraid that if you knew about the roof and siding you would've balked."

"You're right. I would've." Cam disappeared to stack the lumber and then leaned back over the edge. "So how'd that taste?"

"Awful, but that's on me, man."

Cam took the next load of wood and paused. "What's the plan for today?"

"You feel like handling the exterior walls while I steal some guys for the interiors?"

"Not a problem."

"Hey, Cam."

Cam got the wood onto his shoulder and looked back.

Nolan said, "Welcome to day six, man, thanks for staying."

———————

Soon after, the Snowcats arrived with more supplies. Nolan oversaw their unloading and then walked up the ramp into the trailer. He saw that New Year, like any proper traveling westerner, wore clean denim over multiple thermal layers. He was also fully packed and positively unnerved by this upcoming encounter.

"Nolan ..." New Year choked up. "I'm just so sorry I have to do this."

"It's all right, bro."

New Year was crying.

Nolan said, "He's your brother-in-law, man, you need to tend to family."

New Year embraced him. Nolan clapped him on the back. "You're one of the best workers I've got, man, you and Cooter both."

New Year's drawl softened. "He loved working with you guys."

"No past tense, bro, he'll be back. And believe me, he's a breath of fresh air compared to Rand and Rigor Mortis and the rest of these totally horrific morons."

New Year laughed and ended the hug. He backhanded away snot and tears.

Nolan counted out five hundred dollars and said, "They already got you a room at the Motel 6. It's three blocks from the hospital. If you need more cash, get in touch with Kara. She's at the bank and can wire whatever you need."

"Okay."

"Once you're at liftbase, they're gonna drive you straight to Denver."

"Have you heard ..."

"Nothing's changed since we last spoke." Nolan frowned. "Spoons heard from the Black Death. He's already at the hospital posting updates."

New Year abruptly grinned while wiping his eyes. "Can you picture that? Him hollering 'Get some!' at all them doctors and nurses?"

"Stop, man, you're scaring me."

"Poor Cooter."

"Right? Imagine sawing off your own fingers and then waking up to see that God-awful psychopath leaning over your bed?"

New Year laughed and then felt immediately guilty that it came at Cooter's expense. He put the money in a calfskin billfold. His wide-open expression, as always, made him seem in a state of constant wonderment. "They think he'll be awake today?"

"I'm sure. The second operation ended hours ago."

There was a loud knock before the trailer door swung open. Reno peered in and yelled, "I heard I'm taking some Neil guy downhill?"

"Who?"

"Nolan." New Year smiled. "That's me."

Nolan was indignant. "Your name's New Year. Baby fucking New Year." He looked at Reno. "Neil ain't here, man, but New Year's cocked and locked."

"Well, let's ride, brother."

They hustled his gear out to the waiting Snowcat. Guys on deck tossed scattered waves and salutes. New Year tearfully returned the gesture before grabbing the shotgun seat. He shouted to Nolan over the idling engine, "I'll be in Denver waiting till y'all get finished."

"Damn right you will. Now that fuckface just sawed off his own hand, you two bitches are mine indefinitely."

Reno and New Year were still laughing when Nolan slammed the door.

———

Without wind and weather, a startling fury became unleashed. The two teams swarmed across the exterior and interior walls, finishing the second-floor by dark.

On the phone Ted Wright was ecstatic and said they would fly up the trusses in the morning. "Do you want me to see if the choppers can stay on station? Help you roll the roof?"

"Are you fucking kidding me? Those ass-clowns couldn't even fly up a trailer. They're not coming anywhere near my guys ever again."

After dinner, most everyone was passed out by eight o'clock. At the card table in the corner, where Nolan force-fed Cam another beer, a lone lamp provided shadows for their whispers.

"Can you believe that time?" Cam quietly asked. "Ten hours, every single wall completed. That was a Hall of Fame day."

"It almost hurts to be this good."

Cam chuckled. "Is that how it is?"

"I'm being serious. At this point, every guy here has done the same thing so many times, it's like having eleven lead guys at once." Nolan leaned both elbows onto the table. "I've been following the weather obsessively. Liftbase says tomorrow should be as nice as today. Who knew ten degrees could feel so good?"

"And no wind." Cam sipped his beer. "It'd be nice, especially since we're hand-lifting trusses."

"Try not to think about it," Nolan quietly advised, but pondered nonetheless. "I was thinking it might be rodeo time."

"Oh yeah?" Cam's smile creviced every wrinkle in his face. "You gonna grab your lasso, Tex?"

"That's what I was thinking." Nolan used his hands to diagram the table. "Here's the building. We leave six guys on the ground. Put two high-flyers on the wall, and two guys inside on the second-floor pulling on the rope. The ground team carries over the truss, we rope one end, haul it up the wall with the ground guys shoving, then we yank the truss up and over on the flat to the other wall and stand it."

"Sounds easy."

"We did it with three guys at Butcher Block. Me, Fabio, and Stimpy shoved it up the wall." Nolan saw one of the sleeping bodies shift, so he lowered his voice. "We'll see how well everybody keeps their shit together."

"Boy, yesterday was rough," Cam whispered. "Worst injury I ever saw before that happened to these two electric company workers. They were in a pit eight-feet deep accessing a main line and boom! All you heard was screaming from a third guy standing above. The dudes in the pit were still frying when we ran outside. I mean they were totally *blackened* and their buddy, the guy that watched them die, I can still hear the sounds that guy was making ... it was fucking horrible."

"Sounds brutal. Like when Spoons and I were working in Vegas, we'd been up all night—"

"There's a shock."

"Right? We were going through blow like it was a second fucking job, dude. Anyway, we were framing in a subdivision in the middle of the desert. There was a concrete crew out front cutting into the brand-new street because one of the Public Works engineers had monkey-fucked a sewer line placement. So they set up that saw—" Nolan could only partially approximate the thirteen-foot diameter of what was essentially a giant wheel with industrial-grade diamond teeth. "They start to cut into the street. I mean you could hear this fucking thing from a block away. Spoons and I were heading for our van to do some more lines just as one of the guys running the saw, he had turned to yell at one of the others, got too close. One second he was standing there and the next he was cleaved in half from his head to his balls. Seriously, half of him was smashed into the street and spewed out the top of the wheel."

Cam winced. "Jesus Christ ..."

"One fucking second."

"Lucky for him."

"Right?" Nolan swigged his beer. "This Cooter thing though ... at least his doctors have been pretty positive."

"How're the fingers doing?"

"They're getting blood, man, so far so good. Thank God."

"What about Rigor Mortis? They ban him from the hospital yet?"

"Oh man ..."

"So you and him are back in love already? Honestly, this might be the most abusive relationship on earth."

"It's a definite sickness."

"I guess we don't get to choose the ones we love, right?"

Nolan slowly chuckled. "He was leaving me Cooter updates on my voicemail almost immediately."

"Of course he was. How cute."

"Fuck. You."

"Maybe Elias is right. After fifteen years together, maybe it's time you two kids just made it official."

"Elias ... now there's a stupid-dumb-bastard."

"Amen."

"Riggy says they have a metal halo screwed in around Coot's hand to even keep it from twitching."

"That's nasty."

"Not as nasty as Señor Haywire providing bedside comfort."

"Poor Cooter." Cam belched softly into a fist. "We got eleven days."

"Two days for rolling trusses, sheet the roof, sub-fascia, fascia, and shingle."

"No way."

"Why not?" Nolan double-checked the math. "Figure it's just a straight run gable to gable."

"Yeah, but only half these guys have ever roofed before."

"So *they* can run the guns while the rest of the monkeys feed them shingles. I mean what the fuck are we talking about here? It's shingles, man, blow and go."

"Never happen. Not up here. Three days is best case for the whole roof and even that's insane. Which leaves you eight to finish."

"Windows, doors, all the hardware and hold-downs ..."

"Six."

"Figure three, maybe four days for cornerboards, soffit, and siding."

"Two days remaining."

"Staircases, plumbing and electricity back-outs, and ferring strips on all the ceilings for drywall."

"One day left."

"What did we forget?" Nolan ran through the list in his mind. "The only other thing is that the gondola guys might need some carpenters once they start tackling that fried-out motor."

"We also need to finish out that roof over the gondola line."

"Fuck. Okay, that's the last day. So basically I'm telling Ted that the plumbers and electricians can start up end of next week."

Cam nodded. "Roof on, windows in."

"He'll love to hear it." Nolan dry-washed his face with his hand. "Goddamn, I'm fucking tired."

"Let's call it a night."

"We're still gonna need a miracle, aren't we?"

But Cam was already headed for his bedroll.

On day seven, a pair of Sikorsky helicopters roared up the mountainside with the giant triangular trusses dangling from their bellies. With low winds and light snow, they got lucky with the weather.

"All right!" Nolan screamed after the choppers departed. "Let's leave Uno, the Soldanos, O-Zone, Bunny, and myself on the ground. Rand and Elias, you take the wall. Cam and Spoons work the rope upstairs. Any questions?"

Nolan and five others carried over the gable end.

Rand balanced on top of the second-floor wall and dropped a rope.

Nolan tied it to a corner of the truss and then yelled, "We're gonna work this thing up the wall as far as we can, so tell those guys inside not to pull too early!"

Rand relayed the message and said, "Fuck me."

Nolan looked up. "What's the problem?"

"What's wrong with this picture?"

"Way ahead of you, homes," Nolan said. "They're flying up a man-basket tonight so we can do the siding. We'll sheet both gables from the basket."

"Perfect."

Nolan turned to the forces gathered behind him. "Ready? Drive!"

The corner of the truss slammed into the wall before sliding up the plywood in fits and starts.

"Drive!"

"Five more feet!" Rand screamed.

Inside, on the second-floor, Cam and Spoons hauled on the rope every time Rand screamed, "Up!"

"Drive!" Nolan screamed again, and this time it reached the top.

"Hold the line!" Rand screamed.

Cam and Spoons froze and took the weight. Rand looked at Elias. "We pull together. Let me do most of the work, because you're gonna have to back up along the hypotenuse."

"Let's get hateful. Ready?"

"Yeah. Safety last." Rand looked below. "Drive it!"

The ground guys could only provide a few more feet of thrust until the truss was taken from their grasps. Rand and Elias, ejecting breaths in steam like gasps, worked the truss hand-over-hand into the sky. Once it reached its midpoint, the truss cantilevered on the wall. They laid it flat, limbs quaking, as Rand glanced inside at Cam. "It's all yours."

Cam and Spoons dragged it across to the opposite wall and then handed up the nailguns.

Rand and Elias loaded racks of 16's into the guns as Rand said, "Just think, twenty more of these and then we get to sheet the roof."

"Awesome. Wake me up when it's over, will ya?"

They staged planking out the second-floor windows and nailed off the sub-fascia and fascia after lunch. Then they combined into a high-speed assembly line of tasks they had done a thousand times before. Some braced off the trusses, others carried in and handed up sixty pieces of ⅝ plywood for the roof, while another crew rolled the 2x10 outriggers that ran along both gables. Demands were everywhere.

"I need a 1x6 at 126¼!"

"Which idiot took the last rack of finish nails and didn't replace them?"

"Spread those roof sheets out so we don't collapse the floor, morons!"

Above, the sun shined on.

It was late afternoon when Rand turned to O-Zone and said, "Did you hear something?"

"Yeah," O-Zone scoffed as they sheeted the roof. "How about ten idiots running around screaming and yelling?"

"What about you?" Rand peered down into the trusses where Elias balanced. There were four parts to this machine—Uno shoved sheets up to Elias, who handed them up and out to O-Zone, who placed them down before Rand ran them over with the gun.

"Sounds like singing."

O-Zone frowned. "I think it's getting louder."

"Bloodhound Gang," Uno called out. "The roof is on fire!"

Once stimulated, O-Zone and Elias were like Pavlov's dogs, loudly singing along until Nolan screamed, "No singing! What the hell's the matter with you morons?"

But by now Spoons and Uno had joined in as well.

"Yeah I'm hung like planet Pluto, hard to see with the naked eye
But if I crashed into your Uranus, I would stick it where the sun
    don't shine.
Cause I'm kind of like Han Solo, always stroking my own Wookie
I'm the root of all that's evil yeah but you can call me cookie ..."

"I'll be damned." Cam watched from the window as Rigor Mortis post-holed uphill through the falling snow. "He's like Freddy Krueger, man, there just ain't no killing this guy."

"Hey, Noll, do you see this?" Rand called down through the section of unsheeted roof. "Your boyfriend's come to win you back."

"Yeah," Spoons added. "He's climbed mountains just to be with you again."

More laughter.

Cam looked directly at Nolan and said, "Man-loving ain't easy."

"Oh, here we go ..."

"Sometimes there's fights—"

"You guys suck." Nolan dropped his bags and headed for the ladder.

"Relationships are hard, man."

Down below, the Black Death approached while removing his headphones.

"Riggy!" O-Zone bellowed from the roof.

"Well, well, well." Elias poked his head out of the unsheeted gable. "If it isn't Ms. Necro-Nightingale herself."

Rigor Mortis' index finger shot up like a weapon. "I'm gonna climb up there and rape you, hermaphrodite—"

"Hey!" Nolan rounded the doorway. "We need to talk."

"Okay." Rigor Mortis panted as he unslung his backpack. He followed Nolan into the building.

Nolan watched him fight for air and said, "Did you have a nice walk?"

"I'm fucking frozen." Rigor Mortis was bent over with his hands on his knees. "I must've had sixty pounds on me, man, I can't even feel my legs."

"Are you in pain?"

More gasps. "Yeah."

"That's the best news I've heard all day."

"Just for the record. If I had called first, would you have let them bring me back uphill?"

"Probably not." Nolan smirked. "But you'll never know."

"You suck." Rigor Mortis pulled off the ski mask, his face beaten red by the cold. "You know I'm not gonna beg."

"And you know I can't have this. We're fighting for our lives up here. Fighting for our jobs, fighting for our future, fighting for Cooter ... I just don't have the energy to add you to the list anymore."

"I was cocked— "

"So what?"

"It was—"

"Not good enough. You know what? Maybe you are going to have to beg."

"Okay! Fine! I was out of line. You happy now, you fucking bitch?"

But Nolan was not buying it. "You talked to New Year, didn't you?"

"What? At the hospital? Of course I—"

"And he told you about the money."

"He might've mentioned—"

"You fucking snake. You heard it was now twelve grand per man and so you just decided to what—help out your bros, right?"

"Fuck you, man, these guys *are* my bros. You are some kind of ass-hole, you know that?"

"I want to know how you found out about the bet."

"Noll—"

"It's not a request. And you're gone this second if you don't tell me."

Rigor Mortis, having finally caught his breath, sighed. "I overheard them, Ledo and Hammerhead. They were in the building. Guess they didn't think anyone was around."

"Great. Awesome. Next time mind your own fucking business."

"You know what? I was actually on my way back to the Valley."

"So what ...?"

"Well ..." Despite the chill, Rigor Mortis wiped the sweat from his brow. "I figured since I had just lost my job, I now had some free time to help you fellas out."

"That's not funny. And I don't think this is a good idea at all."

"You need me." Rigor Mortis backed off a little. "I told you I wasn't gonna beg."

"You don't tell me anything! You were quit of this place. You could've already been home by now."

"Yeah, well, Cooter ... He's gonna need this money as much as everyone else. Including me."

"After everything we've been through, me and you, after always looking out for you and weathering the blunt force of your stupidity, now, when it was me who needed help, you were the first motherfucker to flake out."

"You threw me out of here! Besides, I already apologized. I was fucked up, okay? I was out of line, I'm a douche, I get it. Now stop being such a drama queen and let's bang some goddamn nails."

"Only if you stop fucking with my program." Nolan pointed a finger at him. "I've never been more serious. We got ten days left. You either get on board and kick some ass, or it's a phone call and you're gone again—this time for good."

"You don't need to threaten me."

"Threats are the only thing you've ever understood." Nolan was surprised by how good that felt to say. "Well? What's it gonna be?"

"I'm in, but only if you stop menstruating. Jesus, where did all these feelings come from?"

"Rack your pack and grab your bags." Nolan headed for the door. "We still got a half hour of daylight left."

On day nine, the Snowcats arrived with supplies, as well as Evan Ledo and Ted Wright.

In an upstairs window, Nolan's lighter flared inside the gloomy shadows as he told himself, *I don't have time for this.*

The entire building was alive with swinging hammers, crashing wood, and the sounds of indecent men.

Outside, Nolan met the bosses in a trench between the trailers and the stacks of wood.

"Nolan!" Ledo's bright white teeth disappeared into the surrounding snows. "Everything looks fantastic!"

They shook hands as Nolan marveled at his enthusiasm. "I'm glad you like it."

But Ted Wright, compared to Ledo's excitement, was markedly restrained. "Just talked to the hospital. Latest word on your guy is that they moved him out of ICU this morning."

"*Guy?*" Ledo sniffed, offended. "He has a name, doesn't he?"

"I just ..." Wright squirmed beneath the layers. He had wide dark bags beneath his eyes, and had developed what looked to be hives from stress across his neck. "I have a hard time calling him Cooter, okay?"

"Cooter." Ledo pronounced it as if savoring an exotic fruit. "Cooter." He looked at Nolan. "As I told you the other day, I can't stress enough how deeply saddened we are about this unfortunate accident. To both this young man and his family. I heard he has two children?"

"Yeah." Nolan winced. He had purposefully forgotten about that. "They were planning on moving back to Texas next spring."

"Absolutely horrific. Tragic. If there's anything more we can do ..."

"I appreciate that."

"Your company's been very fortunate. I heard this was your first major accident. Must be hard to swallow."

"None of it's easy." Nolan was not sure where this was going. "Running a power saw through ice-covered wood during a blizzard doesn't exactly help the odds."

"Hmmm ..." Ledo grew contemplative, staring at the building.

Wright changed the subject. "It's thirty degrees up here today. Your guys must think it's Miami beach."

"You know what's killing us?" Nolan pointed at the three pallets of buried roof shingles. "Can't roof without a dry day."

"Damn." Wright shared this frustration. "No roof means ..."

"No windows, siding, trim, electricians or plumbers."

"Damn."

"We finished sheeting the roof yesterday and today we're at a dead stop. I got my guys inside having a hardware party with all the hold-downs. But if it snows again tomorrow, the next day ... we could be seriously screwed. I've got enough inside work for today and then it's crisis-time."

"Daddy doesn't like the sound of that." Ledo crossed his arms. "My God, just look at all of this snow."

"Your future customers are gonna get their money's worth," Wright said, but it sounded too obsequious.

Nolan provided him a way out by asking, "What's the stock situation down below? I'm specifically hoping the siding, trim boards, and windows are ready to go."

Wright consulted his clipboard. "Siding is in. Windows arrive today. But the trim ..." He flipped through the pages. "The 1x6, 1x8, 1x10 are all here but additional 1x4 is coming tomorrow. They screwed up the order."

"Because that's the progression here. Roof, windows, trim boards and siding."

"I'll get the trim and siding up here today. At least you can put up your corner boards, right?"

"Yep. And paper. We need house wrap."

Wright nodded. "Two rolls of Tyvek are coming up today."

"Nice."

"How do we stand on nails?"

"Fine. No problem."

"Saw blades?"

"You know, I'd like a new twelve-inch for the chopbox to keep the siding and trim cuts nice-nice."

"You got it."

"What about Thanksgiving?" Ledo inquired from out of the blue. "It is only three days away."

"Not up here it isn't." Nolan saw Ledo's reaction and tried to make amends. "No offense, but there just isn't any time."

Wright equanimously said, "Evan was thinking about loading turkey and mashed potato into the Snowcats for an impromptu celebration."

"That's awful nice." Nolan tried to find a better way to say it. "But these guys haven't showered in over a week, they're eating slop out of cans, and shitting in a frozen box. Believe me, they'll be giving thanks the day we pack up our gear and head home."

"Not even a tiny celebration?" Ledo pleaded. "We show up with the food. They eat. We leave. Is that morosely quick enough for you?"

"Maybe."

"Or perhaps we should make them eat it while they're still working and getting snowed on and screamed at?"

Nolan chuckled. "That sounds more like it."

"Unreal. You are one of the most punishing experiences I've ever known."

"Stop flattering me."

"You have a lot riding on this wager ..." Ledo nodded toward the building. "Seventeen days ..."

Wright let out a tired sigh while watching the giant falling flakes. "We need it to stop snowing," he said, and no one disagreed.

———————

They were finishing breakfast on day ten when Nolan looked out over their faces and saw complete exhaustion. Some were still half-asleep, others scowled in annoyance, but there was no mistaking the evidence displayed before him. He did some quick math and knew snow was forecast throughout the day, so he said, "Forget it guys, let's get some rest today."

Wiping the sleep from their bleary eyes, the hooded workers huddled over their coffee mugs, suspicious of this statement.

"Seriously." Nolan pointed toward the world beyond the door behind them. "It's gonna snow all day. Which means no roof."

"So what?" Spoons asked.

"Yeah," Bunny added.

"So ... so I was gonna say that we should split up the day—have five guys sleep while five guys work. Make a bunch of meals and save our energy for this final push."

O-Zone said, "I don't like that idea at all."

"Neither do I." Rand squashed a stick of gum into his mouth.

"Nolan's right." Cam refilled his coffee. "We don't need anyone getting sick. Not up here. And certainly not living on top of one another like this. One sickee can take down the whole crew."

"Fuck that." Rigor Mortis stood up. "I ain't missing out on twelve bills just because a couple of old men are tired."

"Riggy!" Nolan could not believe it. "Sometimes I just want to drown you in your own blood!"

"I say we vote," Bunny said.

"No, fuck it." Nolan waved a hand as if shooing cattle. "You all want to be heroes, go be heroes. We'll work until we're dead."

Cam said, "Who's calling the shots—them or you?"

"You know what? They're right. Who gives a fuck?" Nolan watched his guys gear up while lighting cigarettes and busting balls. "Yo, everybody listen up. Uno's gonna be in here cooking all day—"

As O-Zone buckled into his bags, he turned to Elias and said, "Do bong hits count as cooking?"

Elias filled his bags with racks of 16's, a cigarette dangling as he said, "Hell yeah, brah, veggies."

"Hey!" Nolan was not amused. "I'm talking about real food. Soups and shit, right, Rick?"

"Sure." Uno grinned. "You fuckers are gonna love this."

"Uno sucks," Rigor Mortis complained. "Didn't Hermaphrodite used to be a cook?"

"No way," Elias instantly said, buckling into his bags. "The only thing I'm cooking you ballbags is a giant pot of blow me."

"Everybody shut up." Nolan's anger flashed. "This is an order—four meals today and all eight gallons of O.J. consumed. Half of you were so exhausted last night you couldn't even eat. No more talking, a lot more eating and working. Hurry up."

"Hurry up," they all said, and filed towards the door.

But as predicted, they hit a wall, and by three o'clock Nolan had seen enough. He did not ask questions, did not call a vote. Instead, he just killed the compressors, yanked out all of the electrical cords, and yelled into the sudden silence, "Roll it up!"

"Roll it up!" The word passed like a lit fuse, so guys gathered tools and tarped the wood.

Inside the trailers, the initial days of post work bedevilment were long gone. With quitting time at three o'clock today, their boredom now equaled their exhaustion. Stinky boots were piled by the door before they tucked their unwashed bodies into dirty sweatsuits. All of the magazines had been read, so a stack of Stephen King books made the rounds like a virus.

"There isn't even a decent place to jerk off," Bunny complained.

But Rigor Mortis was always close at hand. "I've got plenty of room inside my sleeping bag, Bun-Bun."

Elias burst out laughing. "Yeah, *Bun-Bun*, why don't you make the rounds?"

"We could cut a glory-hole into his sleeping bag," O-Zone suggested.

"Fuck you, man, this ain't prison."

The Black Death said, "Hey, Bunny?"

"What."

"Knock-knock."

"Who's there?"

"My giant penis ..."

Resigned. "My giant penis who?"

"My-giant-penis-is-gonna-be-jammed-down-your-throat-you-stupid-goddamn-bastard."

Throughout the afternoon, guys took turns unloading the arriving Snowcats, and by the end of the day all of the trim and siding was stacked inside the building.

"You fellas need tanning lotion?" Reno asked Nolan. "Whoever thought thirty degrees could feel this good, right?"

Their hands met, exchanged.

"Nice." Nolan inspected the bag of weed.

Reno shivered inside his cracked leather jacket. "Like Popeye's spinach, bro, green, purple, and tasty."

Nolan saw him staring and asked, "What?"

"Nothing." Reno screwed a cigarette into his grizzled face. "It's just like I told you before. I used to run heavy equipment with all kinds of kick-ass crews. But this ... it's 2,500 square feet, right?"

"Yeah."

"I just can't believe it," he said, "and neither will anyone else."

On day eleven, the sun beamed down across the vast frozen expanse like a heatless light bulb. The snow had ended but was replaced by a temperature of minus five degrees. After fifteen hours inside the heated trailers, they cursed their own existence.

"Listen up!" Nolan shouted. "Some of you morons have never roofed before, so don't make yourself any stupider by trying to think. We've got approximately 1,600 square feet of roof, which means all forty-eight bundles of shingles have to go to the peak. Guys, these things weigh eighty pounds each, so watch your step. Uno, O-Zone, take the four roofing guns, nails, a stapler, staples, drip-edge, bitch, and all the rolls of felt up to the second-floor. The rest of you dig out those shingles and start humping them up the ladders."

But a problem quickly arose. The shingles—snowed on during both transport and while stored at liftbase—were frozen into giant blocks. They used prybars and soon guys were cursing and loading the eighty-pound rectangles onto their frozen shoulders. The first trip was an exhilarating excursion up the ladder. The third trip was not as fun, and by the eighth, falling from the ladder became a better option than bearing anymore pain. Their quadriceps, glutes, and shoulders ached, but at the first sign of possible whining, Nolan shouted, "There're guys who do this all day long every day, ladies, so stop your fucking crying."

"Roofing," Rand scoffed. "There's a reason all those guys are one step away from prison."

"They're also in good enough shape to carry all you ungrateful bitches up and down these ladders as easy as monkeys doing tricks at the circus."

"I like monkeys," Bunny said.

On the roof, Spoons and Cam took the bundles from those climbing the ladders. Then they stepped up a row of 2x4 blocks nailed into the roof like a makeshift ladder. Parallel to the ridge on either side, long 2x4s had been nailed in so that the shingles could be stacked in a specific method.

"Careful, old man," Spoons called out as Cam stumbled and almost went sailing off the ridge. "If you fall you might break a hip."

"Hell, even with a broken hip I could still smoke your ass." Cam picked up the pace.

"Oh yeah?"

Now they both scampered up and down the roof.

"Jesus Christ." Climbing down, Rand said, "Is anyone besides me trying to leave this place alive?"

Drip-edge, which was an eight-inch-wide strip of aluminum, was nailed down around the entire perimeter of the roof. A roll of bitch, which was an ⅛-inch thick asphalt paper and super sticky, was unrolled along the drip-edge as an added protection against the biggest roof threat of all—water.

Once they rolled out four guns and loaded the second-floor staging with shingles, the gunfire soon rang out. For the uninitiated the lesson was simple. Since water rolled downhill, everything—whether it be drip-edge, step-flashing, paper, or shingle—everything must overlap on the upslope.

The shingles, one foot wide by three feet long, were only a ¼-inch thick and still weighed four pounds each. They, too, were overlapped halfway and nailed five times in equidistant spacing.

Cam, Nolan, Rand, and Rigor Mortis ran the guns, which were Hitachi NV45AB2's that ran on belt-fed nails from a coiled magazine. One guy was at each of their sides feeding them shingles, gun nails, razor blades and absorbing enough abuse to be registered as public toilets.

"Shingle shingle shingle!"

"Ammo, dumbass! I need more ammo!"

"How many more times are you going to fuck up my rhythm?"

Bam—one nail to set the corner.

Bam—one nail to set the other corner.

Bam-bam-bam—through the middle.

Bam. Bam. Bam-bam-bam.

From four guns the cadence varied but at times seemed to synchronize into a symphony of gunfire.

"More shingles!"

"Get that paper down!"

"Elias," Rigor Mortis said. "If you keep bending over like that, I'm going to mount you—"

"Oh dear God."

"Unsling my meat pipe—"

"I feel sick."

"And hang my balls from your ass like a Christmas decoration."

"Ugh." Elias shuddered. "I'd get you back, though. I'd shove a pineapple up your ass, light your balls on fire, and then make you eat your own shit."

Rigor Mortis chuckled. "I thought you just said you jammed a pineapple up my ass?"

"I did. But after your colon exploded, I spoon-fed you your own feces."

"That's it." Spoons, who had been ferrying them shingles and supplies, scampered up to the ridge. "I've never wanted to take a shower more than I do right now."

"What's going on?" Nolan called up from the other side.

"Rigor Mortis and Hermaphrodite are ... I think they're re-enacting a gay snuff film with each other."

"Fucking man-lovers!" Nolan shouted. "I don't hear any nailing! Back to work! Hurry up!"

"Hear that?" Rigor Mortis asked. "I think your dad could use a pineapple up *his* ass."

Bam. Bam. Bam-bam-bam.

———

Two hours later it was ten o'clock and they had shingled half of each side. Roof jacks held a plank that held the workers and supplies. Every six feet, the roof jacks were popped free and nailed in further up as the entire operation then ascended.

But that was before the snow arrived. Now they were in direct conflict with the number one cardinal sin of framing—never step foot on a wet plywood roof for any reason ever. The snow fell for barely two minutes before Cam slipped, and Spoons almost lost his footing at the ridge. That was enough for Nolan. "That's it. Police up all the staplers, nails, guns, and rolls of paper. We'll start siding this bitch instead."

They organized a careful retreat to the staging. The tools were then handed down and in through the second-floor windows. Inside, Nolan answered his phone as Rand lit them a pair of cigarettes.

"Yeah, Ted," Nolan said. "Now that you mention it"—Nolan peeked outside—"Okay, will do."

Rand asked, "What is it?"

"Apparently, there's one hell of a storm coming."

Rand's mask twitched. "Is that the bad news or the worse news?"

"Right?" Through the window, Nolan watched the increasing winds blow the snow sideways. He puffed while watching the workers regroup to start the siding and yelled, "Hey! Everybody listen up! Liftbase just called and said we're gonna be hit by a little storm here. It's five degrees right now, but winds are expected between twenty and thirty miles an hour."

"Great!" Rigor Mortis yelled back. "Who gives a fuck?"

"Just everybody layer up!" Nolan screamed back, glowering until he made sure Riggy was the first to turn away.

Rand said, "He's a piece of work."

"Right?" But Nolan found his usual anti-Rigor Mortis venom dampened by a greater problem. "We need to get this fucking roof on."

Ten minutes later, conditions were a virtual white-out.

"What's that?" Rigor Mortis screamed, nearly invisible. "Did you hear that?"

"Yeah!" Even though he was only five feet away, O-Zone's voice was swallowed by the raging wind. "Dude, I can't even feel my face!"

"Fuck this." Elias passed by with his jacket around his head. "It's minus fifty!"

"This ain't *Roots*." Rand detached the nailgun from the hose just as it exploded and air gushed from the burst opening like blood from a wound. "Kill the compressors!"

"Get all the tools!" Nolan screamed. "And then round up the two hoses we just ruptured. We'll fix them in the trailers!"

Even with the heaters cranked, the wind poured an icy chill through the thin metal walls. The crew was still in their gear and huddled beneath blankets on the floor like mushroom heads.

"Jesus Christ." Spoons nodded toward the door. "It's really rocking out there."

The trailers shook amid the gusts.

"What was that?" Nolan asked, perching his head as if angling for better reception. He looked at Rand. "Didn't that sound like something falling?"

"There it goes again." Rand stood up.

"No, dude," Bunny said. "Please, don't do it."

Rand stepped over the bodies to get to the door. "Sorry, bros." Once he cracked the door, it was instantly torn open and slammed against the side.

"Fuck!"

The wind howled through, kicked up loose papers and grit, and deposited bursts of snow. Rand dropped down to pull the door closed. As Nolan reached for it, he saw the answer to his earlier question—the eighty-pound packs of shingles were sliding off the roof.

"Harder, Fabio!" Nolan screamed, but Rand was losing traction. O-Zone and Spoons dropped down to help out and, as all four breathed in agony, they finally closed the door.

They ate lunch like hungry wolves. Since the coffeepot was broken, Rand boiled two gallons of water and dumped in a can of coffee. Eventually the grains settled and mugs were dipped and handed down the line.

"They call this cowboy coffee," Rand told them. "Back in the old days, fellas would be out in the middle of nowhere and—"

"Hey, Lone Ranger ..." Rigor Mortis nodded toward the milk. "How about helping a brother out?"

"Everybody shut up." Nolan turned up the radio as the National Weather Service relayed the forecast. "Who's got the time?"

"It's one o'clock," O-Zone called out.

"All right, listen up. They just said the wind will be done in thirty minutes. Then we're gonna re-dig our trenches, get those shingles back up to the roof, and finish the day with siding."

"Hurry up," Cam said.

They fueled up on coffee and granola bars to recommence the assault.

———————

On day twelve, the Snowcats growled uphill towing trailers loaded with every window in the building. The first-floor, which housed a mechanical room, administrative offices, and a First-Aid/Ski Patrol station, had a grand total of six windows. In comparison, the upstairs cafeteria was a fishbowl. Each wall had three sets of 4'x6' double-hung windows to showcase Mother Nature's mayhem.

As the workers unloaded the cargo, Nolan consulted his master list to direct each window into its proper hole.

Ted Wright emerged from one of the Snowcats, scowling into the snow. He zipped up his parka until his oversized hood resembled an aardvark's proboscis.

"What the hell are you wearing?" Nolan asked. "Is that your wife's coat?"

"What's that supposed to mean?" Wright's face looked tiny and far away inside the hooded nozzle.

"It means you look like a freaking Euro-weenie." Nolan shook his hand. "Happy Thanksgiving."

"Yeah, thanks for spreading your good cheer. Same to you. Hope everyone's ready for tonight's feast."

"As long as we get all of our shit done ..." Nolan did not want to reveal his disdain for this unwanted diversion, so he buried himself inside his jacket to light a cigarette. "Talk to me about Cooter. His wife says he's making good progress."

"He is. They moved him out of the ICU yesterday and put him in a room. Did you know between the surgery, and what he lost up here, it took four transfusions just to keep him going?"

Nolan shook his head, not wanting to relive it. "All I know is that he lost a lot of fucking blood, man."

"I'm glad you're handling the wife now ... she sounded scared to death."

"I talked to her this morning. And I need a favor. New Year's with her and I need you to get them some money for hotels and shit. I could write you a check ..."

"We'll wire it. How much?"

"A thousand bucks will cover them for a while."

"No problem." Wright dug inside his jacket for a pen. "Any message?"

"Yeah. If they need more, call."

"Anything for Cooter?"

"Tell him Rigor Mortis sends his love."

"*Rigor Mortis*?"

"He'll understand."

Wright made a notation on the clipboard. "The place looks fantastic, Nolan, no kidding. God bless you guys. Yesterday must've been a nightmare."

"I'll tell ya, that wind was strong enough to toss shingle bundles off the roof."

Wright was in awe. "Whole *bundles*? Those things are like eighty pounds."

"Yup. Never ever heard of that. Ten packs off the ridge ... gone."

"Incredible."

"Listen. Half the roof on each side is shingled. That means I can throw in the windows on the front and back, trim them out and then it's siding time."

"But it's supposed to be—"

"Completely shingled, right. I know. Water-tight. Fuck." Nolan kicked a hole into the three-foot high snow trench. "I got the siding run partway up all four sides, man, but I'm dying without these windows in."

Wright glanced at the wall where the siding currently ended just below the first-floor window openings. "You know what? The reason they want you water-tight is because of—"

"—rain blowing in through the peak and the spaces between the roof sheets, rolling down inside to the wall and dropping on top of the window, warping it ..." Nolan saw where this was going. "But who cares, right? Because it's snowing, not raining, and the only thing rolling down that roof will be the bodies of a couple of morons."

"Well—"

"You're beautiful." Nolan was as close to ecstatic as exhaustion allowed. He panned across the site before yelling, "Cam! We're a go on the windows!"

Cam nodded and then redirected the furious activity enveloping the job.

Nolan finished the cigarette and asked Wright, "What's on your mind?"

"Nothing. Day twelve, you know?"

"So? You don't think we're gonna make it?"

"Oh, you'll make it." Wright chuckled. "It's … I just watch these guys out here and wonder how any of this is even possible."

"Listen, they'll sign autographs later. I gotta get back to work."

"Hang on, Noll, gimme a second. Need to come clean about something."

Nolan paused. "I'm listening."

"I was never on board with this contract nonsense … Ledo's wager? That was between him and you—"

"*What*? What is that supposed to mean? You covering your own ass already?"

Wright did not like that and said, "One guy's in the hospital and this …?" He nodded at the scurrying workers. "We're just getting to the high stuff. I just—I don't want to have to send more checks to anyone else's wife is all."

"I don't want anyone else Life-Flighting out of here either, Ted, but then again you're the one that came to find me, right? Exactly how the fuck did you think this place was gonna get built?"

"I understand—"

"Where do you get off pulling this shit now? Is Ledo afraid of paying up, so he sends you up here whining about fucking safety? I thought you guys had my back?"

"We do."

"Listen, after Cooter went down, all of us, the whole crew, we had a long talk. I spelled out exactly what the new deal was and what was required, and that if anyone wanted to walk, they were free to leave."

"Nolan—"

"I've never had anyone ask me to slow down ever."

"I just don't want winning a wager to be the reason someone—"

"I can't believe we're having this conversation. Now is not the time to grow a fucking conscience, Teddy-boy."

"You're taking my concern the wrong way." Wright frowned. "Honestly, I just don't want anything to happen that somebody doesn't walk away from. I really don't think I could live with that."

"Me neither." Nolan gave him his back and walked inside the building.

They halted work at dark. The radio was blasting AC/DC as guys played cards, chain-smoked, and retold the same stories for the hundredth time. Morale was good, but as they awaited Ledo's Thanksgiving feast, various thirsts were on the rise. They broke out a bottle of whiskey and passed the bong.

Nolan was already on his fourth beer and exhausted from the constant worry. He went to bed anxious, woke up nauseous, and then spent the rest of the day gauging his progress toward insanity.

He was keeping everyone under surveillance when Cam pulled over a chair. He raised a beer and said, "Here's to eleven of the stinkiest motherfuckers in all of Colorado."

"No shit, huh?" Nolan sniffed his pits and winced. "The worst part is that you somehow grow immune to the stench."

"Twelve days, brah."

"On it goes."

Cam took a long draught, smacking his lips. "Did you call Kara?"

"Oh God. Blah blah blah, Happy Thanksgiving. It's like talking to a wall."

"You guys will patch things up."

A sudden gust of wind buffeted the trailer.

"Look at these morons," Nolan said, "playing poker and blackjack and losing their money faster than they can earn it."

"You're just jealous."

"You're right. My head's too fucked up to even play cards."

"What's the word out of Denver? How's Cooter?"

There was no other way to say it. "You know they still might end up chopping them off?"

"He's a tough kid, Noll. Texas always represents."

"Oh, is that right? Really?"

"We sure ain't like you California boys. Bunch of bag-tickling wannabes, from what I've seen."

Nolan chuckled, too tired to even fight back. "I need to get drunk."

"Twenty-one!" Rigor Mortis suddenly screamed. "Again, bitches, who's your daddy?" He stood and slapped high-fives.

Cam said, "Good to see Riggy's almost totally wasted."

"Right? They better get that meal up here soon. These Sallys can't take much more on an empty stomach."

"Seventeen days, thirteen framers, and one mountain."

"Sounds like the premise for the worst horror flick ever."

"Who else would've said yes to this?"

"Prostitutes, man. That's all we are."

"Easy ... You're starting to sound like Elias."

"Oh God."

Cam went to get fresh beers as the action around the tables ratcheted up. Spoons laid out a full house as guys threw down their cards and groaned. Cam returned with a lit joint dangling from his lips.

Nolan hit it and then hit it again. He opened the beer, passed the joint, and said, "Lemme ask you something."

"Yeah?"

"Do you think I should've ... I mean New Year's with him now at least, but no one else has shown up down there."

"Noll ..." To ease his chronic back, Cam leaned forward so that his elbows were on his knees. He looked at Nolan and said, "He would be more pissed if you didn't stay up here to make this deadline. Besides, after all your tough talk, you actually care about these sons of bitches?"

"If that rumor ever gets out," Nolan said, "you will never be dead enough."

Screams broke out after Bunny opened an accidentally shaken beer and drenched the table. Guys were reaching for beers of their own to return fire until Nolan's scream literally froze them in the act.

"Nobody move! Nobody even breathe!"

Rigor Mortis pointed at Bunny. "He must die."

"You know who's gonna die? The next moron that drenches the same spot where we have to sleep." He looked at Bunny. "Get up, get some towels, and clean up that mess."

Outside, the Snowcats arrived in a clatter of tank treads. Then there was a pounding at the doors. "Chow's here!"

Guys were instantly on their feet. The opened doors revealed Reno and a handful of Danforth workers silhouetted in the Snowcats' swirling lights.

"Gentlemen ..." Evan Ledo stepped forward with a case of red wine. He wore a Pilgrim hat despite the chill. "As reward for your hard work, Happy Thanksgiving!"

The Danforth workers handed up steam tables, a turkey, trays of mashed potato and stuffing, and cases of beer. The card tables were turned into a buffet line and soon everyone had a plate.

Without champagne for a toast, Reno passed around Dixie cups filled with whiskey.

"Your attention!" Ledo raised his own. "On behalf of myself, my family, Danforth Construction, and to the carpenters and the Danforth workers who have so graciously sacrificed this holiday, and to our good friend Cooter and his healing digits, I say to one and all, thank you. From the bottom of my heart, Godspeed and good luck."

"*Salud.*"

The crowd then broke up along class lines—workers on one end, bosses on the other. Without enough chairs, Ledo, Cam, and Nolan were seated Indian-style on the floor. Ledo's inquisitive blue eyes catalogued the trailer as he said, "No offense, but it's just hard to imagine."

"What's that?" Nolan asked.

"How you all have managed this." Ledo knocked on the wood floor. "That can't be too comfortable to sleep on."

"We got egg crating, sleeping bags, blankets ..." Nolan tried not to be too much of a pig as he inhaled the food. "Goddamn, this tastes good."

"That's why we were late. We brought it up from our resort."

The workers loudly cheered as the sound of beers cracked open. Cam Rogers told Ledo, "Careful. The citizenry has had a head start. And thanks again for bringing this food, Evan. We got a couple of guys cooking eggs and burgers and soups but this ... this is a life-altering experience."

Ledo seemed humbled. "It was the least I could do."

Nolan, recalling their acrimonious conversation, wondered about Ted Wright's absence. "Where's Ted?"

"He has family in from out of town but sends his regards." Ledo filled his fork. "I have noticed a slight change in his disposition."

Nolan silently chewed.

Ledo said, "His stress level is through the roof but he won't listen. I've repeatedly told him, after the first time you and I spoke, Noll, I was immediately put at ease. I've got a bullshit detector that's second to none."

"I appreciate that," Nolan said.

Cam added. "For any P.M., a build like this, under this kind of pressure, it takes its toll."

"Excuse me, gentlemen." Elias stood above them and passed out four more Dixie cups.

"Uh-oh." Ledo looked chagrined but did not shy away.

Elias held his up. "To the death of common sense."

"Here, here."

Ledo spilled some down his chin and guiltily smiled. "Let's see, I've been here exactly forty minutes and have consumed more alcohol than I normally would in a week."

Cam's grin was filled with stuffing. "Happy Thanksgiving."

"Oh my." Ledo watched Nolan refill their coffee mugs with wine. "I don't think I was prepared for this."

Nolan looked at Cam. "I think that should be our new company motto."

"You might be right. Or how about 'How the hell did I get into this?'"

An hour later the music was cranked as guys fought for seats at the crowded card tables. Ledo and Nolan led the charge, peeling off twenties as fast as they lost them. Empty beer cans filled every horizontal surface, and even with the stove's exhaust vent on high, the trailer was a smoke-filled box.

Ledo sneezed, drunkenly sipping his wine. "They'll be talking for years about what you all have done here. The pain, the suffering—"

"Sounds like a hemorrhoid commercial," Cam said.

Ledo swung his mug through the air. "I say let's drink! To sacrifice! To honor!"

"And to women that have none!" Bunny exclaimed, jumping into their circle. "Come on, old men, time to meet your Maker!" He held out a bottle of Maker's Mark as the guys behind him chanted, "Shot-shot-shot!"

"Oh dear." Ledo lost half of his just trying to hit his mouth, but the crowd hooted and clapped.

"Le-do! Le-do! Le-do!"

"I love you all!" Ledo nearly fell over. "Who's better than the King!"

"Who-zah!" they yelled.

"To all my friends!" Ledo swung his mug. "Who knew carpenters could be such fun?"

Cam said, "You need to get the lingo down."

"All right! Do instruct me!"

"If something looks good, you say 'titties.' If something is perfectly level, you say 'dead balls.' And if you see a woman that looks desperate, you call her a carpenter's dream."

"Why's that?"

"Because she's probably flat as a board and easy to nail."

"That's fantastic!"

Behind them, amid the shouting and music, Rigor Mortis and Bunny were getting into it.

"Well, look at that bully," Ledo said, zeroing in on the Black Death. "I don't think I care for him at all."

Cam snorted. "You and just about everyone else who meets him."

"Rigor Mortis!" Nolan shouted.

Ledo turned to Cam. "Did he just call him *Rigor Mortis?*"

"It's a long story."

"Riggy!" Nolan made a move but it was already too late. Rigor Mortis took Bunny by the back of the head and smashed a plate of mashed potato into his face. Then, in slow-motion, everyone dove for the remaining food. Nolan got blasted with sweet potatoes before jamming a pile of stuffing into Spoons' face. Rand ducked a shower of mixed vegetables before slamming an entire turkey carcass down onto O-Zone's head.

Behind them, Ledo was at the steam table lobbing candied yams like rounds from a distant mortar.

The clean-up took hours.

———————

On day fourteen, the worst idea in the world arrived by helicopter. They had been siding the building off adjustable ladder jacks and planks. But since the ladders did not extend high enough to access the gable walls, and because the gondola repair team would also need a way to reach certain components, it was assumed both crews could split the use of an AB-9 Extendable Basket.

The man-basket was essentially four giant tires bolted onto a rectangular frame the size of a pickup truck. The boom arm telescoped a 2'x4'x8' wire mesh basket forty feet into the air. It could be controlled from either the vehicle's main control panel down below, or inside the basket itself. Meant to provide manpower access to heights and a smooth ride around normal jobsites, it was in no way equipped to operate in these conditions. Side-to-side the base was six-feet wide, so an even bigger snow trench had to be dredged out and floored with plywood.

"Fuck this fucking thing!" Rigor Mortis screamed, kicking its tires. "Why the fuck don't we have pump-scaff, man, we could scale right up the side!"

"Riggy!" Without enough coffee or eggs, Nolan was already on edge. "Cap the psychosis, grab a fucking shovel, and dig out that tire, man, can't you see there's no wood under there?"

"Fuck!"

Nolan took the trench leading toward the building's double-wide front doors. He passed Rand, who was on an extension ladder trimming out the last second-floor window.

"Three days left, ladies! Hurry hurry hurry!" Inside, he found Cam and Spoons drilling through the bottom plates of the exterior walls. Behind them, Bunny and Uno inserted hammer-drills into these holes. After the concrete was drilled out, they epoxied three-foot pieces of rebar into the foundation.

Nolan tugged Cam's sleeve. "Got a sec?"

"Yeah." Cam gave Spoons the list and then turned back to Nolan. "What's up?"

"Let's review. We need to finish the trim, siding, and windows of both gable walls, we have half a roof more to shingle, some hardware left to do, and we have to finish out the small roof over the gondola line."

Cam did not want to reiterate what they had both said over the past four days, but in the end had no choice. "We need it to stop snowing."

"Wright called and said we might get a break after lunch. If that's the case, we finish that roof and then it's game on."

"Yes, sir."

"How do we stand in here?"

"Good." Cam pointed to where Bunny and Uno drove their hammer-drills into the foundation. "So far, ten minutes a hole."

"Listen, Fabio is finishing the front right now. After he trims that window, he's got eight small boards of siding before the front's completely done. You mind taking Spoons and O-Zone out back? I think we only have a couple of trim boards up high, right? After that the back will be done as well."

"Jesus, we just might make it."

"I'm glad you and Rand already cut in the staircase. That's a huge bonus." Nolan's phone rang but he ignored it. "The lead plumber and electrician are on their way up to scope things out. I told them roof—no roof—they can at least get their guys up here to drill their holes."

"That ain't our problem."

"Right?" Nolan, incredulous, then answered his phone. "This is Nolan ... Yeah, well, send them up." He flicked away the cigarette as the hammer-drills shattered the silence again.

———————

The Snowcat ground to a stop. Reno rolled down his window and saluted Nolan. "Hey, big dawg, how they hanging?"

"Frozen, brah." Nolan leaned against the door. "Heard you brought me some company."

Reno pulled his hair into a ponytail and then rewound the red bandana. He nodded over his shoulder. "They're in the back gearing up."

"You staying?"

"Yeah ..." Reno did not sound happy about it. "We gotta load up the bags of trash from the Thanksgiving fiasco. Man, did we get towed-up or what?"

"Fucking A. Watching Ledo barf in the corner was priceless."

"Wright said the little fella didn't even get out of bed yesterday."

"Oh man."

A voice asked, "You Nolan?"

Nolan turned and saw a ball-shaped man struggling to breathe. As the man leaned against the Snowcat for support, he looked like he might collapse. His winter clothes were too tight and barely zipped as he jammed an asthma inhaler into his mouth. "Goddamn air," he wheezed. "What the fuck was I thinking?"

"I'm Nolan." Nolan stared at his outstretched, unshaken hand and started to get pissed. "Who are you?"

"Oh, I'm sorry, Billy Chance. Lead plumber."

"'Take No Chance With Chance,'" Nolan quipped. "Teddy already gave me one of your cards."

"That was awful nice of him." Billy Chance had a wide face and brown bulbous eyes. His breath, though, sounded like mucus being sucked through a bag. "Heard you and your crew were from the Valley?"

"Yup."

"Beautiful place. Summertime's past me and the wife used to hike all over that place." Chance patted his giant gut. "But my back country days are long gone."

"Did the electrician come with you?"

"Oh yeah." Chance snorted as if Nolan was in for a treat. "He's still back there buttoning up."

"I can't remember. Where are you out of?"

"Glenwood Springs. Had my worst year ever last year and now it's come to this—" He nodded at the structure. "They told me down below but I really didn't believe it. This only took you fifteen goddamn days?"

"Billy, don't rush it, brother, this is day fourteen."

"Even worse." Chance grunted. "You must be one helluva piece of work."

"Hey, where you going?"

"You can wait for numb-nuts." Chance wobbled down the trench on his monstrous legs. "My fat ass needs a head start anyway."

Minutes later Frank Debusher climbed out of the rear hatch. Exactly Chance's opposite, Debusher was taller than Nolan and thin and nearly albino in complexion. As he shook Nolan's hand, he seemed unable to make eye contact. Nolan also noted he started most sentences with "Hmm …" and ended them with "you see?" and was already irritated enough to walk ahead of Debusher.

Inside, Nolan walked them around each floor, saying, "The main electric is buried out near our trailers. Same with the plumbing …" Nolan slowed down to wait for Chance again. "We got a line welded in for tap water at the well-head."

"Great." Chance's enthusiasm was flagging by the second. Both he and Debusher were taking notes and examining every single inch of wall as if already running their pipes and wires.

Nolan said, "They're saying good weather after lunch, which means the roof will be done by tonight."

"I'm planning on moving in by tomorrow morning," Billy Chance said. "I got six guys getting paid to sit on their ass down at liftbase."

"Hmm, I'm not entirely happy either." Debusher's thin pink lips worked into a frown. "Besides myself, there are two other master electricians and three apprentices down there collecting dust."

Not sure if he was being skewered, Nolan tactfully said, "You don't need a roof on to drill holes through studs, fellas."

"Oh, it's not you," Debusher quickly added, nodding at Chance as well. "They switched up our schematics. Made changes to account for next summer, when the full-scale renovations begin. The engineering came in last night and it gets stamped today. Otherwise, well, no stamp …"

"No go." Chance had seen enough. "Place looks great, Nolan, everything stacks up real nice."

"Yes, it does." Debusher brought up the rear as they headed toward the stairs. "The head-outs in the floor joists are dead-on, and the bays are free of nails so we can drill through without destroying our bits."

"Just trying to show the love, fellas."

Chance paused to look around before glancing up at Debusher. "He's handing this disaster off to us."

And Debusher said, "Hmm …" in answer.

———————

The weather broke after lunch, so they attacked the roof. Rand, from the tip of the ladder, reached with a broom to clear as much snow as he could, but a dangerous ten feet remained between there and the staging.

"Goddamnit." He knew he could not take a single step onto the shingles without a line. "Elias!"

Twenty-feet below, Elias swiveled.

"Get me some rope!" Rand yelled. "Hurry up!"

"What the fuck are you doing?" Nolan called up from the ground.

"Well, unless you're Spiderman and can shoot me a web up to that staging, we're gonna need a rope to even think about scaling this roof."

Frustrated, Nolan kicked a clump of ice that did not move. "Fuck! That really hurt."

"Our fearless leader …" Elias was in full deadpan as he returned with the rope. He took out his hatchet and chopped the block of ice Nolan had just assaulted, tied the rope around it, and then broke all the rules by putting two men on the same ladder.

"Nice work." Rand took the block and scaled up higher. Gauging the distance, he tossed the ice-block up and over the staging to allow it to roll back downhill. He yanked on the rope until the block wedged itself inside the roof jack. He tested the line. "Safety last."

Directly below him on the ladder, Elias shook his head.

Rand said, "You got any better ideas?"

"I was told never to think."

"Exactly." Rand stepped up to the top rung. "No pressure or anything, but you need to backstop my feet as far up as you can reach in case the block blows out."

"Great. Nice plan. I got news for you, Fabio—hey, cut it out!"

"What?" But Rand could not keep a straight face.

"Stop kicking snow on my head!"

"Hey, morons!" Nolan screamed. "I would rather you fall to your deaths than stand on that ladder not hurrying up!"

"You're gonna give the guy a fucking embolism," Elias said, trying not to laugh.

Rand knelt on the roof and waited to feel Elias' hands on his boots.

Then he heard Cam calling out from the other side, "Hey! We can't get to our staging!"

"We're working on it!" Rand yelled back. He then looked down at Nolan's tiny shape. "Get me another rope. I'll anchor in a line on our roof jacks and toss it over to them so they can avoid this trauma."

"Whatever the fuck," Nolan pleaded. "I got eight guys on the second-floor just waiting to climb up on that fucking roof—"

"I'm going right now! You know what? Fuck it. I hope this rock blows out and I fall right on your goddamn head!"

"Me too!"

"Hey!" Rigor Mortis finally screamed out the window. "We don't have time for this!"

Nolan left to get more rope.

Elias looked up at Rand. "When Snapcase's the voice of reason ..."

Rand scoffed. "We're fucking fucked," he said, and then he scaled into the void.

———————

That night things were noticeably less stressful inside the trailers, mainly because whenever the plumbers and electricians showed up, the end of any job was near. This instance was no exception. With three days left, and while no one wanted to jinx it, they were right on target.

Lying on his sleeping mat, Nolan propped his head on a pillow. The food was not sitting right inside his belly, so he feared a trip to the shitbox might be looming.

He felt someone approach and turned just as Rand sat down peeling an orange.

"Hey." Rand placed a wedge of it onto Nolan's stomach. "What are you all morose about?"

"Nothing, man, I just feel gross."

"We got a lot done today."

"I know. We're almost there."

Rand wiped the juice from his chin. "Electricians and plumbers tomorrow?"

"Yep. And then the Swedes."

"The gondola guys are in town already?"

"Yes."

"You know what I've been meaning to ask?" Rand handed him another wedge. "I know we came up here trying to shed some debt ..."

"Yeah?" Nolan was too nauseous to bristle.

"Well, it's just, what's this profit-sharing going to do to the company?"

Nolan did not know how to answer that. "What do you think?"

"I don't think it's gonna help one bit. You didn't say anything, but Cam and I know ..."

"Know what?"

"You're actually going to lose money on this job."

"Does it even matter anymore?"

"Well ..."

"We were staring into the abyss. If I hadn't plopped down the pot of gold this job was over. Which meant no one, including Cooter, was going to see a single penny. And you know what? I don't even care about what happens after this. I used to. Lawsuit, Chapter 11 and, if you really want to make yourself taste a bullet, just throw in a marriage that's about to blow apart."

"We'll work out of the Chapter 11. Fucking government pukes."

"I wish I could blame them. It's the goddamn insurance companies, man, taking my money for years and then ruining my life with their fucking technicalities."

"Whatever." Rand ate the rest of the orange in silence. Then he cracked a smile. "Remember how we used to argue about me being your partner or not?"

"You suck."

"How'd that taste?"

"Like a giant chunk of ass, man, fuck you very much."

———————

On day fifteen, the Snowcats dragged a whole new cast of victims 14,000 feet up into the sky. For the carpenters, their exclusive mountaintop retreat was now a thing of the past.

Like monkeys perched across the structure, the carpenters peered down at the new arrivals as they shuddered and struggled for breath.

"Fresh meat," Spoons said.

"Newbies!" Bunny yelled.

But their taunts went unreturned. Six plumbers and six electricians tightened their hoods against the blowing cold. Still adjusting to this horrible new world, their wide-eyed glances were already fading fast.

Elias and Nolan were smoking a bowl in an upstairs window until Elias said, "Jesus, is that Jabba the Hutt?"

"Elias!" Nolan watched Billy Chance waddling down the trench toward the building, and so opened the window. "Hey, Billy!"

"Howdy, Noll." Chance's breathing could not keep pace. "Is it okay"—he breathed—"if we unload"—another breath—"our tools into the building?"

"Yeah. We're pretty much done in here."

"What about our gear"—breath—"the sleeping bags and shit."

"Fuck if I know. You better call up Teddy. Last I heard they were planning on flying up another trailer."

"That man's dumb as my dick." Chance pivoted and took the trench to the building.

Elias was in awe. "What the hell is that poor bastard doing up here?"

"The same thing we all are." Nolan closed the window. "Fighting for our lives." Nolan finished smoking the bowl and said, "Let's go. No more stroking. Back to work."

Since plumbers and electricians predominately worked inside, both trades were unaccustomed to wearing this much gear. The electricians unloaded tool boxes, huge spools of different gauge wire, and crates filled with the small plastic boxes used for all outlets and switches. The plumbers ferried in stand-alone pipe cutters, copper piping, torches, and bins of connectors and end caps.

Rigor Mortis was shingling the carport over the gondola and looked down at the proceedings with disdain. "Slow, dumb, weak, and pathetic." He glanced over at Bunny. "Kind of like a family reunion for you, isn't it?"

"Fuck you, psycho."

"After dinner, my friend," Rigor Mortis said, "your wish is my command."

Cam and Spoons were standing on a plank jacked between two ladders twenty-five feet in the air. At that height, they were getting slaughtered by the wind. Bent at the waist, gloves jammed inside their jackets, the wind smashed them into the gable end like toys against a wall.

"Hey!" Nolan called up. "The wind ain't so bad down here!"

Mumbled curses were followed by Cam shouting, "Elias! Get that board up here!"

Elias dropped the blade on the chopbox and then tossed up the twelve-foot piece. Spoons, working the middle of the scaffold, slid the board to Cam. "You good?"

"Titties."

Their guns responded.

The next piece was already waiting.

"Nice work, Elias."

"Yeah," Spoons said. "Every moron gets lucky sometimes."

"Fuck you, Spoonie!"

"Hurry up, Elias." Nolan nodded at the stack of siding. "You're too dumb to talk and cut at the same time."

———————

After lunch the plumbers and electricians were still inventorying their gear and supplies. Nolan held a quick meeting with both Billy Chance and Debusher, and afterward overheard their employees unwisely speaking.

"About what?" Rand now asked, leaning into the corner as he and Nolan shared a pipe.

"About how cold it is, how hard it is to breathe—"

"Well ..." Rand expelled his hit. "We did that the first day too."

"Dude, they asked if they could take our heaters, the ones inside our *trailers*, and bring them in here so they can work inside a heated building."

"No way."

Nolan nodded as he took a hit. "They're out of their blessed minds."

"I'd like to see them outside for just one day. Imagine that? Besides, if they think it's cold now, wait till tonight ..."

"That's another looming disaster. Wright called. Those chopper douchebags are having trouble with their bird, and the other one's in Cheyenne. If we don't get that trailer lifted up by dusk ..."

"Are you kidding? There ain't room for that. They can go back down in the Cats."

"Right?" Nolan lit a cigarette and then heard a distant growling. "Speaking of which, I think they're here."

"Who?"

"The Swedes." He turned for the stairwell. "Wright said one o'clock." Nolan, trying to be hospitable, but also worried that they might unload their gear in the wrong spot, met the Snowcats at the end of the trench. The doors popped open. Guys in red jumpsuits with LAARSON ENGI- NEERING stenciled across their backs dropped down into the snow. Like perfect stereotypes, all seven had blond hair and blue eyes.

"Hi, Noo-land?"

Nolan smiled at the butchering of his name through the thick accent. The speaker had an average build, a face creased from the sun and wind, and a handshake forged from a lifetime gripping wrenches.

"I am Johann."

"Nice to meet you." Stoned, Nolan found the lilting tones of the Swedish brogue entertaining. "Hope you guys are ready for this."

"We? Us?" Johann was not idle with his pride. "We are the ones who installed this—" he pointed at the gondola. "Your concern though is, ah, cute? Yes?"

"Cute?" Nolan was not amused anymore. "Let me know if you need anything else."

He knew he must be getting older, and lamer, because even five years ago Johann's smug condescension would have been a death sentence.

"Hi, excuse me, Noo-land?"

Nolan turned back around. "What?"

"Where for our tools, no? And gear ... where for us to sleep?"

"These trailers are ours. You can put your tools under the carport or in the building. But as far as where you're gonna sleep, I think you better call Ted."

"And why is that?"

"Because I already have a job." Nolan did not let his glance waver.

"But what about the snow?" Johann angrily gesticulated toward the heaped and frozen landscape beneath the gondola's roof. "They said you would have it dug out, no?"

"*Me?*" Nolan batted a hand and then continued down the trench. "That's a good one, Sven, you're a real comedian. Shovels are over there."

———

"We need more trim!" Rigor Mortis screamed.

Even with dusk falling the level of activity remained consistent. Rigor Mortis, Bunny, and O-Zone were trimming the 6x6 posts holding up the gondola roof. Time was ticking away, so O-Zone hustled to get more wood. Bunny was cutting their last board when the saw abruptly lost power in mid-cut, splitting the board in two.

"Goddamnit." Rigor Mortis, from his perch on the ladder, tracked the cord to the wall where he saw the unplugged end. The men from Laarson Engineering had just carried over a large panel cover for the gondola's engine and unknowingly kicked it loose.

"Hey meatballs!" Rigor Mortis yelled out. "Somebody wanna plug us back in?"

"Riggy," Bunny quietly cautioned.

"No, fuck that. I don't have time for this nonsense."

"What is problem?" One of the workers approached. Broad-shouldered and red-faced, the guy's blue eyes had a malevolent shine guys like Rigor Mortis expertly perfected. "What is this"—he struggled with the pronunciation—"*meatball?*"

"Just plug in my fucking cord, all right?"

"Riggy—"

"Shut up, Bunny."

The Swede stepped forward again. "I think it is you that is meatball."

"Really. Have you seen these?"

The man's face wrinkled, unsure of the question. "These what?"

"These nuts, bitch, get down on your fucking knees!"

O-Zone turned the corner with a shoulder load of trim just as Rigor Mortis took flight from the ladder.

"Nolan! Get over here!" O-Zone dumped the trim and, joined by another Laarson employee, pulled apart the free-swinging twosome. More shouts erupted until reinforcements arrived and ended the brawl.

"That's enough!" Nolan bellowed.

With arms pinned by his co-workers, the Swede screamed, "You is dead man!"

"Learn English, bitch!" Rigor Mortis writhed and spasmed but could not wrench free from Cam and Spoons. "Swedish chef motherfucker!"

Nolan took a step in his direction. "I said that's it!"

"Yes." Johann motioned with his arms. "Is back to work time now. For everyone."

The factions split apart.

By nightfall it was apparent that the helicopter would not be arriving. After conversations between the four crew bosses up top, and Wright down at liftbase, it was agreed that only Nolan's guys would bunk in the trailer with the makeshift kitchen. The remaining nineteen workers would be squeezed into the other trailer after all the tools were transferred into the building. Food would be driven up for everyone in the hopes that within the next two days, after the carpenters' departure, the strain on infrastructure would be alleviated.

"Jesus, Riggy, I can smell your feet from here." O-Zone, like everyone else, was lying on his bedroll waiting for the food. Guys were either listening to headphones, napping or, like O-Zone, just staring at the ceiling while marinating in the pain. "Fifteen days without a shower."

"Greasy everything." Uno sniffed his own curly hair with a scowl and passed the bowl. "Greasy hair, face—"

"And the *stink*." Spoons winced. "It's God-awful, man, especially Rigor Mortis' feet. Like two moldy cheeseburgers wrapped in rotten leather."

"Oh yeah?" Provoked, Rigor Mortis rolled onto his side and said, "If you think my feet are bad ..."

"No! Dude!"

The impressive sound of Rigor Mortis' ass exploding brought both praise and condemnation from all quarters.

Spoons flinched. "I think my nose just died."

But an abrupt pounding on the trailer door swung their heads in unison.

"Open up, convicts!" Reno shouted through the howling wind. "I got chow and beer out here!"

———————

The following morning it was totally black inside the trailer. Spoons was the first to wake. He rubbed his face, noticed the silence, and then realized he was freezing to death. He sat up with a sleep-withered expression and stared at where the heaters should have been glowing.

"Fuck me." He laid back down and pulled the sleeping bag up to his shoulders. "Why should it be any different?"

Next to him, Nolan stirred and groggily asked, "Who's talking?"

"Me. I think we blew the power."

Nolan groaned into his pillow. "Are you fucking kidding me?"

"Dude, I'm no detective, but the heaters are dead and the lights are out."

"Fuck!"

Now everyone was awake.

The previous day the electricians had worked on the mainline into the building. Afterwards, the access hatch had not been properly re-secured. Snow had blown in and shorted the panel.

It was five degrees inside the trailers at 5:15 A.M. They had no way to make coffee or breakfast. And since it was pitch-black and freezing inside, work became a necessity.

Also, twenty-nine guys needed to use the shitter.

———————

Nolan suddenly remembered the generator in the tool trailer and rallied the troops. Jubilant, they hauled the beast out and filled it from the portable gas cans. But no one knew until it was too late that the unleaded generator had just been filled with diesel.

"They gave us diesel in cans labeled unleaded." Nolan was standing

alone with Rand, who tried his best to assuage him. "Diesel in the motherfucking cans."

"Here." Rand handed him a smoke. "Dude, you're gonna have a
stroke and it's not even six o'clock."

"Dude, my whole life's a stroke. The electricians shorted out the
whole mountain, fer Christ's sake, and these other morons gave us
diesel ..." He looked at Rand for confirmation. "Why does God hate
me?"

"Oh man."

"We're at a dead-stop without power, bro, goddamnit."

"That could be a reason right there. Ain't that one of the command-
ments? Thou shalt not take the Lord's name in vain?"

"If I don't get some goddamn coffee—"

"Nolan!" Spoons shouted from an upstairs window. "We can hand-
bang the siding!"

"Yeah, but we can't cut!"

Spoons thrust one of the battery-powered mini-skillsaws out the
window. "Trim saws will work!"

Nolan looked at Rand. "It is clapboard siding."

"Batteries are fully charged too."

Nolan liked the sound of that. "In this cold, we'll at least get an hour."
He turned back to Spoons and yelled, "Roll it out! Let's get the man-basket around to the gable you and your dad didn't finish yesterday!"

"Hurry up!" Spoons closed the window.

Nolan pulled off the glove to work his phone and his hand instantly
froze. "Time to get old Teddy boy on the case. It's two days before the
end and this definitely wasn't part of the deal."

"Fuck him and his deal." Rand yawned. "You're right about the
coffee, though. Someone's gonna die."

———

It was finally determined that the blown circuit had fried a switching
station downhill. Electricity was restored by 9:00 A.M., but no one had
been idle. Those not involved with siding the gable were either scrapping out or prepping for the day ahead. Once the power returned, the

onslaught continued. Wood was flying up and being nailed off as fast as they could cut it.

Otherwise, the one-day transformation was startling. The plumbers and electricians drilled through wall studs and floor joists with auger bits and hole-hogs like angry termites. The Swedish engineers, turning more wrenches than a NASCAR pit crew, had most of the gondola motor disassembled. Everyone was hurrying up.

"O-Zone! Elias!" Nolan yelled, "get in here and finish the bracing we forgot!"

On the second-floor, O-Zone shoved a saw, gun, and wood up to Elias. Precariously balanced in the trusses, Elias carefully stacked these supplies. O-Zone climbed up and together they nailed perpendicular 2x4s across the truss' vertical supports. They also squatted to avoid the thousand roofing nails poking through the plywood like an upside-down bed of nails.

Below them, a plumber holding a drill with a two-foot auger bit entered and glanced up into the shadows.

"Howdy, fellas." His voice had a clear Wyoming twang. "Dang if it ain't colder than a well-digger's ass at fly-time."

O-Zone laughed. "A what?"

"Yeah, ain't this something?" The plumber pulled more cord into the room and set down the drill. He was rail thin and dirty, his beard unkempt and scraggy. "I'd like as not to be home with my wife, but this scenery ... it sure is like God's window up here, ain't it?"

"You got that right," Elias answered as he and O-Zone scrambled through the trusses. The plumber left the room and Elias said, "Seems like a nice enough guy."

"We got plenty of wood—ow, fuck!" O-Zone had turned his head into a dozen roofing nails.

"I saw the whole thing." Elias sickly grinned. "That was freaking awesome."

"Am I bleeding?"

"Not enough."

The plumber returned. "My name's Lawrence, but the fellas just call me Jokey."

"Jokey?"

"Yes, sir. What kind of jokes do you fellas like?"

"Don't answer," Elias whispered to O-Zone who, of course, promptly called out, "Whatever kind you like."

"Oh yeah?" Jokey was lining out and marking the studs that he needed to drill. "A spic, a wop, and a nigger are in this bar, see ..."

In the shadows above, Elias threw O-Zone a look so hateful O-Zone tried not to laugh. He held up the next 2x4 as Elias ran the gun. Bam-bam! Bam-bam!

"—and so God looks down at the nigger and says, 'I told you you was stupid.'" When the plumber looked up, he seemed perturbed at their silence. "Get it? All right, I got another one. There was a whore, a priest, and two midgets in a row boat ..."

As they maneuvered through the trusses, O-Zone almost exploded in laughter after Elias whispered, "I am going to fucking *kill* you."

"—and so the whore says, 'Pick another hole, moron.'"

"Nice."

"Hey ..." Jokey looked up, determined to get a laugh. "I also like to shoot cans."

"Oh yeah?" O-Zone grabbed another 2x4. "You got a range where you set up cans?"

"Naw. Afri-cans. Mexi-cans. Puerto Ri-cans ..."

"Jesus Christ." Elias could not take it anymore. "None of this is funny."

But Jokey was undeterred. Reaching for his drill, he said, "How come you fellas ain't laughing at my jokes?"

"Because." Elias pointed at O-Zone and then himself. "You're talking to a Jew from Minnesota and an Arab from the East Coast, man, shit like that don't work."

"If that don't beat all," Lawrence the plumber said. "A fucking desert nigger way out here?"

Elias blinked, stunned. He tried not to work a response.

O-Zone pleaded. "Dude, don't—"

Elias stepped off the bottom cord of the truss, fell through the gap, grabbed the same truss he had just been standing on, and crashed boots first onto the decking.

Now it was Jokey's turn for revelation. He barely dodged a flying chunk of LVL aimed at his head before Elias hissed, "Say that shit to me again ..."

Jokey grabbed his drill and fled as O-Zone tagged him with a wad of spit. "Joke that, motherfucker!"

Everyone was coming apart.

———————

"So ..." Back up in the trusses, O-Zone would not let it lie. "You're one of the tribe, eh?"

"Yup." As Elias fired the gun this close beneath the roof, their heads got slammed in echo. "Me and you, buddy, a couple of tribesmen far from home."

"I remember you once offered fifty bucks if anyone could guess." O-Zone held up another 2x4 as Elias reloaded the gun. Bam-bam!

"People always think I'm either Italian, Jewish, Greek ..." Elias shrugged, "I'm proud, man, but anything's better than being known for that."

"For what?"

Bam-bam! Bam-bam! Elias had the gun in motion. "Fucking stand up for yourself, you know? Royal families, military dictators, oil companies ... the Middle East is a sewer hole of bad ideas, colonial hatreds, and the religions ... My whole family's Christian, so they chased my grandfathers out like dogs."

O-Zone grinned. "Tell me about it."

"Oh, you know about that too, don't you, Jew-boy?" Bam-bam! Bam-bam! Bam-bam! "The Christians, the Muslims, the Jews ... I say fuck'em all, man."

And O-Zone said, "Hurry up."

———————

Though usually despised, the sound of the alarm clocks on the final day was cause for celebration. Whether it was because of the prized payday or the hot shower and warm bed awaiting them tonight, their beleaguered spirits were buoyed by thoughts of the downhill ride.

Because of yesterday's electrical delay, an extension was offered but ultimately refused since another day would only prolong their sentence. After all, having worked 192 hours in the span of sixteen days was the equivalent of five normal weeks of work.

They stood and yawned, stretching off the night while downing coffee. Due to lack of sleep, altitude, and all the cigarettes, Nolan's eyes were distended and frog-like. In his long johns, he drank coffee from a saucepan while spinning the AM dial.

"—*from the National Weather Service, this is the morning update.*"Bunny staggered by holding his lower back and said, "I think my whole body's numb."

"No thinking." Nolan wiped crust from his eyes and blinked. The forecast was calling for a nice morning with afternoon snow. "Hey," he called out. "It's gonna be twenty degrees today."

"Like it even matters." Cam was shoveling a mountain of egg and potatoes into his face. "Come on, Noll, grab a plate. It's time to rock'n'roll."

By 6:00 A.M. the nailguns were banging as Nolan mushed his dogs.

"Let's go! Bunny, get that trim over to the gondola. Elias, more siding, more siding! We're running out of time!"

Nolan was on them like a second jacket. He clocked his phone for the time every couple minutes. His pulse, long emptied of adrenaline, was now powered by a sick flutter of caffeine and looming dread. Knowing he could not push himself or them any harder, he did just that.

"We got this last gable and the carport and then we're home free!" he yelled. "Hurry up!"

The pace remained relentless.

———

In an effort to save time, lunch was cheese sandwiches and baked beans chased by gallons of orange juice and milk. They sat against walls in the heated trailer and lit cigarettes.

"I think we're actually gonna make it," Nolan said.

But he had yet to look outside.

"Developing snow my ass!"

"Bunny!" Nolan yelled. "Shut your mouth and get up on that staging!"

Amid the blowing snow, Nolan was disheartened by the virtual white-out.

"Fire up the hate!" Elias yelled, and the onslaught was rejoined.

They pulled down the ladder jacks while others shoveled a path for the hulking, ice-covered man-basket. Additional siding was carried out from the building, the chopbox wiped clean of snow.

There was a loud gnashing of grinding teeth cloaked inside the white curtain before the Snowcats abruptly appeared.

"Good afternoon, gentlemen!" Evan Ledo's voice boomed through the handheld bullhorn. "The place looks absolutely fantastic!"

Nolan barked a list of orders and then met the bosses.

Ledo's eyes beamed excitedly as he clapped Nolan on the back. "Congratulations are in order. Brilliant performance, Nolan."

"It ain't over yet. Balls to the wall, man."

"Even with the delay, it's a tour-de-force and a wager that I'm happy to lose ... that's if indeed you make it."

"Don't kid yourself." Nolan looked at Wright. "Teddy, we're gunning to be out of here by nightfall. Think you can book us a ride?"

Not exactly the picture of health, Wright looked relatively relieved. And somewhat jealous. With Nolan's part in this bloodbath ending, Wright, in charge of both the remainder of this build and the upcoming summer renovations, had another nine months left on his sentence.

"Sure," Wright coughed into a fist. "I like your confidence, though. It bodes well for this ..." He held up a clipboard. "Guess what we forgot?"

"Oh shit. The framing inspection, fuck me."

Ledo shook his head as if admonishing a child. "You and Teddy almost blew it."

"He's here now," Wright said, and nodded toward the Snowcat. "But I mean what're we talking about, a day or two?"

Ledo perched an elbow on his crossed arm and tapped a finger against his lip. "I'm still not sure I fully understand the meaning of this transgression."

Nolan did not have time for this. "Plumbers and electricians can't proceed without a framing inspection. They can make you yank all the wires and pipes out of spite alone."

Moments later he was introduced to one of three building inspectors responsible for the entirety of Eagle County.

Nolan dodged the walk-through with the inspector and Wright, but failed to scrape free of Ledo. "And here are the intrepid Swedes!" Ledo cried through the bullhorn. "Bustling amid the grease!"

"Let me show you how it's done." Nolan took the bullhorn and turned to where his guys were finishing the gable. "Attention morons! Your very existence is an insult to humanity. Your efforts are pathetic and slow ... hurry up."

While Ledo laughed, Nolan sweat the clock.

The sun had started descending. The final task was siding the giant carport over the gondola machinery.

"Let's go, let's go, let's go!" Nolan and Spoons, not wanting any part in gathering up all the tools scattered everywhere, quickly climbed into the man-basket. "Riggy, you cut for us. The rest of you haul ass because the Snowcats are on the way up. Hurry hurry hurry!"

Nolan held onto the waist-high rail as Spoons worked the controls. The man-basket crept around the corner and crunched over the plywood Bunny hurriedly laid down.

Rigor Mortis gathered a saw and enough siding to finish the oversized carport.

"Twenty minutes," Nolan said, and Spoons nodded as he shot them into the sky. Against the triangular gable, they worked the tape measure together and gathered numbers.

"Riggy!" Nolan screamed. "These are all long points! 116⅝, 100¼, 84⅝! Hurry up!"

As Spoons lowered them through the complete white-out, he drolly said, "I seriously wanna thank you for one of the worst experiences of my life."

"Ha-ha! Hell yeah, buddy. Isn't this the worst thing ever?"

Rigor Mortis, in overdrive, had their three boards already cut and waiting. They climbed back up into the sky as Nolan caught Rigor Mortis predatorily glancing in at the Swedes and said, "Easy, little fella, just mind your manners for a few more minutes."

Rigor Mortis put on a "Who, me?" expression and then screamed at Bunny to get more wood.

Nolan yelled out, "82¾, 76¼, and 64⅝!"

Below them Rigor Mortis started cutting.

As they nailed up the boards, Nolan caught Spoons' glance and said, "What?"

"Nothing, man, I was thinking about what I'm gonna do with this money. I can't believe we're actually gonna make it."

Nolan finished nailing his side and handed the gun to Spoons. "Doesn't this remind you of Vegas?"

"Yup." Spoons fired two nails in rows into each board. "Just a couple of hateful bitches busting ass 24/7, bro, rock'n'roll."

"You got that right."

Spoons lowered them to retrieve the next three pieces of siding.

Back up top, Nolan yelled, "56½, 42⅛, 24¾ and then we're done!"

"Dumbass' getting more siding!" Rigor Mortis shouted back. "Let's case out this last beam instead!"

Spoons lowered them and steered the man-basket around the corner. He worked the end of Nolan's tape until Nolan yelled, "A 1x10 at 136¾!"

"Hang on," Spoons said, "I'm gonna move a little closer to the beam."

"Watch your head." Nolan ducked because they were right next to the six-inch-thick reinforced steel cable. Under incredible tension, it stretched a mile downhill and held over 200 gondola cars. The cable passed over his head and settled between them.

As they waited for Rigor Mortis, Spoons said, "That cold beer is gonna taste great on the ride down."

"You got that right."

There was a sudden roaring that sounded like an airplane under the roof. The cable jarred and then abruptly started rolling.

"They must be testing the motor," Spoons said but Nolan screamed, "Stop!"

"Oh shit!"

The closest gondola car was ten feet away. Nine feet, eight feet ...

Nolan yelled, "Riggy!"

Six feet, five feet.

Spoons, totally freaking out—"Swing us out, Noll!"

Nolan lunged for the toggle on the control panel. "Riggy, tell them to stop!"

Rigor Mortis screamed and flailed his arms at the Swedes but, as chance would have it, he instead caught the attention of yesterday's combatant.

The gondola crashed into the man-basket while the Swede, unable to see what was transpiring just out of view, thought Rigor Mortis was again insulting him.

"No!" Rigor Mortis screamed over the roaring engine. "The power! Cut the power!"

Nolan slammed both palms into the gondola's window, desperately trying to dislodge it. "Spoonie!"

Spoons shrieked, "We're going over!"

With the right-side tires in the air, the man-basket was stretched almost to forty-five degrees. They screamed and clawed at the gondola that was smashing into their faces. After descending far enough down-hill, the gondola car released them like a catapult into the air. Because of all the snow, it was easy to think of soft landings.

———————

As word of the accident and the extent of the injuries got relayed to liftbase, Life-Flight was called in for direct evacuation to Denver. With both men unconscious, and medics still en route by snowmobile, those up top were shaken but providing basic assistance. Luckily, one of the plumbers had been a combat medic in Vietnam, so cooler heads prevailed.

Spoons at least landed on the roof covering the gondola machinery before sliding off the other side.

Nolan had not been as fortunate.

After the helicopter departed, the abrupt silence was even more unnerving than what had just occurred. Small snowflakes drifted down. The framers were stunned and exhausted, but also starving. The Swedes, with their blonde hair and condescension, started to look tasty. They milled about near their things, waiting to see which way this might go.

Johann, their leader, stepped forward. Unfortunately, he stopped in front of Rand and Rigor Mortis.

"Is tragic, yes?" Johann asked. He had no idea his math was all wrong. His men might have been physically superior, but that was only a fact. "Accidents is tragic, always tragic."

"Is that your story?" Even Rand was on edge. "The fuck it is. Why would you start that thing up without even checking to see if anyone was around it?"

Rigor Mortis couldn't even bother to bother. "Ain't none of you immigrant cunts speak English, huh? No one heard us screaming at the top of our lungs, right? Is that what we're supposed to believe?" He stepped right into Johann's face. "Fuck you, you master race motherfucker!"

And that was it. Staggered by the loss, the framers engaged Team Swede in an assault so one-sided, the electricians and plumbers finally waded in to stop the carnage. With everything from the last year on the table, the Swedes were unprepared for the skill-set suddenly unleashed upon them. Fighting was one thing, but taking out the boss of Team Hate after seventeen days of torture meant their hell had no bottom.

———————

At 2:00 A.M. in Denver, the pair of F-350s with accompanying trailers seemed out of place in the back parking lot of the Rocky Mountain Regional Level One Trauma Center. The nine guys who entered the building had not showered in weeks and were, after the last five hours of drinking, bitterly exhausted.

At this late hour, their bootheels echoed down the empty hallways. After the helicopter's departure, the downhill descent, and two-hour ride to Denver, the gravity of what lay ahead seemed to dwarf what they had just accomplished. In an effort to thwart this horrible numbness, alcohol got poured into the void.

They pushed through double-doors with red letters screaming
EMERGENCY and found a lobby filled with bleary-eyed people awaiting
bad news in various states of desperation.

Behind a giant circular desk, a dozen doctors and nurses were in
motion until a nurse took notice. "Can I help you?"

Cam noted her appraisal of their overall condition and told her why
they were there.

"Oh yes," she said and calmly pointed to an adjoining room. "If you
guys wait in there, I'll get the doctor."

"Can you tell us how they're—"

She smiled politely. "The doctor's in a much better position to do
that than I am."

Cam turned and saw a handful of his guys pervertedly eyeballing the
nurses and said, "Let's go, everybody get in that room."

Last to file in, Rand sidled up next to Cam and quietly asked, "What
about their wives?"

"Supposedly Lizzie is en route but Kara ..." Cam shook his head. "She's
got a new cell. I don't think they've been able to get in touch with her yet."

"After we get this briefing, I'll call Lena. She's gotta have it."

"We need to find his phone ..."

The room was barely large enough to hold a conference table and
a small refrigerator with bottled water. They took seats and shed a few
layers, dropping their clothes to the floor. The stink of booze and body
odor stifled the air but they did not even notice. Minutes passed. Fatigue
and fear worked inside their stomachs.

"Gimme some water." Rand wagged a finger at Elias.

"Suck it."

"Hey." Cam pierced Elias with a glance.

No one said anything else until the door opened. A woman and two
men entered in white lab coats.

"I'm Dr. Cavanaugh," the woman said, and her nose immediately
flinched. She might have been accustomed to horrible trauma, but
nothing cut to the quick like stink. Her salt-and-pepper hair was long
and ponytailed. She looked to be in her mid-forties, but the late hour
and exhaustion could have swung years in either direction. The men
behind her politely smiled while also trying not to wince at the stench.

Dr. Cavanaugh said, "These are Doctors Hancock and Sinj."

"Cam Rogers." Cam shook their hands and said, "This is Randall Holmscomb and the rest of the crew."

Rand shook hands as well. He said to the doctors, "As you may have noticed, we've been in the hills for weeks."

"Not just any hill ..." Dr. Cavanaugh took a seat at the head of the table with her subordinates standing behind her. She opened two files and said, "I understand you're building on Peak 4?"

"We finished it today." Cam glanced awkwardly at the table. "We were actually just getting ready to leave when this ... this disaster happened."

Dr. Cavanaugh nodded while scanning her notes. Then she looked up at the anxious faces and said, "Why don't we start off with Mr. James Spooner. From descriptions of the accident, both men were apparently jettisoned from something called a man-basket. Mr. Spooner landed on a roof and rolled off the other side. His injuries are severe. X-rays revealed considerable damage to the right side of his body—six ribs, a double fracture of the tibia-fibula, and a badly broken shoulder. He also sustained a severe blow to the head, but CT scans have so far shown no signs of TBI, bleeding, or swelling. As of right now we're calling it a severe Grade Three concussion ..." She looked up from her notes. "Prognosis, outside of the head injury, is rather good. Mostly orthopedic, with a pair of surgeries to reconstruct the lower leg and shoulder."

"Is he awake?" Rand asked.

"No." Dr. Cavanaugh chose her words. "Neither one has regained consciousness before or after their arrival. Mr. Spooner was placed in a medically induced coma. Which brings me to your other friend, a Mr. Nolan Harris. He, unlike Mr. Spooner, landed on the ground. As you all undoubtedly saw, he did not leave that mountain in good shape. He sustained compound fractures to his left femur, right tibia, and also suffered bilateral fractures to both wrists. Internally, he ruptured one kidney, his spleen, and crushed the L2 through L5 vertebrae in his lower back. But most troubling of all was the head injury. The epidural hematoma was significant and required an emergency craniotomy, but the pressure buildup inside his skull ... I'm sorry, I really am. We tried everything and just could not stop the swelling. You have our sincere condolences."

"Your what?" Rand winced. "What did you just say?"

Bunny blinked. "Nolan's fucking *dead*?"

Cam said, "Bunny—"

"How can this be?" Elias abruptly shouted. "We just called them from the fucking highway!"

"Elias!" Rand shouted back. "Shut your mouth."

The doctors fidgeted behind Dr. Cavanaugh whose smile was now hard-pressed into her face. Fielding their anger and dismay, she said, "This is the worst part of our jobs. I can only tell you that chances are very good that Mr. Spooner, with the appropriate rehabilitation, will make a full recovery."

"Fucking butchers." Rigor Mortis stood up. "I'm not listening to anymore of this bullshit."

"Goddamnit, Riggy ..." Cam massaged his temples. "It should have been you inside that basket."

"Fuck you!"

"Everybody shut up!" Rand stood up. "Riggy, get out."

Rigor Mortis grabbed his clothes and slammed the door.

The rest stayed quiet until the doctors quickly evacuated the room.

The back parking lot was empty beneath the wide black western night. Stars faintly pulsed above the small gathering quietly drinking between the trucks. There had been brief testimonials interspersed amongst the vast pauses, but mostly only silence. They needed to shower, eat, sleep, and drive, but so far could barely sit and drink and blink their eyes. A few mumbled fierce invectives while others remained stunned. Collectively, there was no mistaking the sound of spirits crushing.

Ten minutes later Lena Holmscomb called Elias' cellphone, so he immediately handed it to Rand.

"Fuck ..." Rand stood up and detached from the group. As she spoke of finding Kara, and how they were both now readying to leave, Rand tried out a half dozen explanations before finally cutting her off. "I need to tell you something."

"What?" It was 3:30 in the morning and she sounded dazed and frazzled. After their nearly two-decade acquaintance, he had given her many calls in the dead of night, but never with news like this.

He lit a cigarette and inhaled deeply.

"Rand?"

He exhaled, working his lips, but could not say it.

She said, "We've got a three-hour ride ahead of us—"

"You don't have to bother now," he said.

And then she heard him crying.

Lizzie Braner, Spoons' fiancée, arrived at the hospital an hour later. Small, diminutive, and introspective, she was his exact opposite until it came to their future and approaching wedding. Tear-stained and haggard, she hugged each of them before her mother and sister tentatively ushered her down the hall as if unsure of what nightmare lay in wait.

Wednesday, the next morning, Team Beaver headed back to Vail to wrap up the loose ends and grab the money from Danforth. Then they would head north for the wake and funeral being arranged by Kara and Nolan's family.

Catatonic, Rand, O-Zone, and Elias drove Nolan's pickup and trailer home in silence. They stopped for beer and whiskey, refilled the diesel tanks, and then hit the road with this disaster locked inside their brains.

Forked Head Pass and the descending switchbacks were an icy mess they handled with extreme caution. Below it, Spring Valley glowed like a tiny village tucked inside the belly of the mountains.

Elias wheeled them into Nolan's complex and killed the engine. He looked up at the apartment with dread before saying, "I just can't believe this is happening."

They exited into the snow. Rand glanced at the pickup and trailer emblazoned with Harris Framing and company contact information, and then he slowly closed his eyes.

"Come on." O-Zone grabbed his arm.

The three of them climbed the stairs. At the door, they checked their courage before Rand slowly knocked. He said, "I hope she's not here."

They heard her approach. "Who is it?"

"Kara?" Rand had trouble working his suddenly thickened voice.

The door opened and she managed a smile until seeing their crumpled expressions.

Rand looked at his feet, angrily fighting back the tears as he said, "I just can't tell you how—"

She gasped. Her arms popped opened and suddenly wrapped around him. They both held on in mutual desperation until she buried her head into his jacket and the wind howled through behind them.

O-Zone wetly blinked and Elias, back to the wall, slowly turned the other way.

———

That night they told her many things. About the build, about Cooter, and even the episodes of hilarity, like Nolan firing a nailgun at the chopper, the horrible food, the frozen shitter, the Thanksgiving food fight, and Rigor Mortis hiking four hours uphill just to spite them all. A twelve-pack was brought up from the truck as they made her laugh and eventually ordered out for dinner.

"Thank God you cleaned this place up," Elias said, and then she smiled sadly. They were seated at the kitchen table with cold beers and empty plates.

Kara's black hair was pulled into a ponytail, her eyes streaked and puffy. Her T-shirt and sweatpants were dirtied from her efforts as she said, "Our landlord had posted an eviction notice while you guys were gone but ... for the last two days I've been cleaning so we can ... so we could have ..." She was crying and now seemingly ashamed. "I'm sorry ..."

"Don't apologize." Awkwardly, Rand put a hand over hers, but the sobbing only worsened.

"He really loved you guys," she said.

They stared at nothing and listened to her cry.

———

Early on Thursday morning, Kara heard the knock and rounded the corner to see Elias hunched against the blowing snow. She opened the door as he held out two coffees and a bag of donuts. "Breakfast?"

"Come in." She hugged herself and stepped aside. "Geez, it's freezing out there."

"Those sweats look awful comfy."

"Yeah, sorry, I was just lying in bed." She shut the door behind him. She wore the same ponytail but her eyes, swollen from exhaustion, framed a beleaguered smile. "Couldn't sleep either?"

"Nope." Elias set down his parcels. Pulling off his hood and cap, he blew into his frozen hands. "Haven't had a decent night's sleep in three weeks and now ... I wonder how this will ever get better."

His bitterness broke apart her composure. Tears squirted into the corner of her eyes.

He said, "I'm sorry."

She smiled but it cracked and then the tears spilled over. She accepted his embrace, her face turned onto his shoulder.

He said, "Aren't you glad I stopped by?"

She laughed as she cried and then abruptly disengaged. She used her sleeve to wipe her eyes. "Thanks for the coffee."

"No problem." He took off his jacket and slung it onto the counter. "Place opens at seven but I was there by six-thirty."

"I know the feeling." She sipped the coffee. "It feels like somebody cut off a piece of my body ..."

"Right? It's in my head, replaying twenty-four hours a day."

"I don't want to hear—"

"No, I know." He looked into his cup forlornly. "I just wish it would stop is all."

"Let's go inside." She was shaking. She grabbed the donuts and lead him into the living room. On the couch, she tucked her feet beneath her. But Elias could not sit in Nolan's recliner, so he snagged a kitchen chair instead. He lit them a pair of cigarettes while asking if she needed help with any of the arrangements.

"Thanks, but it's all set. Our families ... they're handling all of that."

"I'm just so sorry ..."

"Me too."

Elias glanced out the snow-filled window. "This is not how it was supposed to end."

Her face was a pinched misery around the swirling smoke. "It feels like I've been left behind."

They sat in silence and smoked.

Elias said, "You should know ... his using at the end, he was snow-balling by then. It had nothing to do with you."

"How can you say that? You don't know anything about that."

"He fucking loved you—"

"One has nothing to do with the other. It was the most self-destruc-tive crap I've ever seen. And knowing it would just push me further away, he couldn't hit it any harder. We were finished."

"It was the business, not you."

"You're smarter than that, Thomas. And so was he. He knew exactly what he was doing."

"He was going down in flames."

"Doesn't make it right. He wanted me away from what was happen-ing but I ... I should've known better. I shouldn't have left him here." She blew her nose and then suddenly everything collapsed. "You know before he left I actually called him a quitter and a coward?"

"Hey." Elias saw her crying again but was in no shape to lend a hand. Nolan's ghost was hanging in the air like a toxin.

Elias cooked them a giant breakfast. The last two days off were his first in weeks, so he actually felt his battered body knitting itself back together.

Kara was at the kitchen table staring at the falling snow until he dropped off a heaping plate. She said, "Oh my. Eggs, homefries, sausage ..."

"Don't forget the bagel."

"I won't, but I'm not going to be able to eat all this."

"Don't worry. I'll finish whatever's left."

So they set upon the food, and with each other to lean on, their appetites returned.

"Have you thought about ..." There was no easy way to say it, so Elias just said, "What happens now?"

"Not sure." She loaded another fork. "I've always thought about get-ting another master's degree. In English. I think I want to be a teacher."

"You'd be a good one."

"What about you? Have you and the others been able to talk?"

"No. But it's not looking good. I think a major exodus is about to happen."

"You too?" Kara crunched into her bagel. "Don't I remember Lena saying something about a project you were working on? What's it about?"

"The utter uselessness of the human race."

Kara smiled, chewing. "You know, it wouldn't kill you to lighten up a little bit. Oh, I forgot—your soul is dead. But you're luckier than you know."

They ate in silence until Elias finally cleared their plates.

"You don't have to clean," she said, but he was already at the sink.

Later, they had two more cigarettes back inside the living room.

"Will you stay here?" he asked.

"Probably not. Too many ... he's everywhere here, you know?" She blinked into the gray morning light. "Besides, I think I'm gonna need my family."

"A new beginning."

"Yes. We'll see."

But something worse was happening. As much as neither one wanted to be alone, neither could they mourn in small talk.

"I have to go." Elias finished his cigarette. "I'll check in with you later, but if you need anything, call me."

"I will." She hugged him. "Thank you for coming over. Breakfast hit the spot."

"No problem." Elias released from the embrace. "I wasn't kidding. If you need anything ..."

"I will."

He was at the door but paused when she called his name.

"He ..." Kara tried to fight the suddenly reemerging sorrow. "He couldn't have done any of this without you. Rand, Riggy, you, O-Zone ... he really loved working with you guys, Elias, try not to forget that."

"I won't." He opened the door. "You know, I thought about this last night. He gave me a job and a trade in a place that had nothing else to offer. I really loved him for that."

———————

The cemetery was called Rockland Gardens for a reason. It was located on the eastern edge of town where the mountains finished and County Road 61 blasted straight across the high plains all the way to Utah. The meager topsoil barely covered a billion years of landslides, rocks, and rubble. Unbeknownst to the original pioneers, their current descendants, out of duty and respect, had struggled with every burial since.

The sun was a bright dot over the group of people that stood in black. Turnout was larger than expected. Half the contractors in town paid the ultimate respect by halting work to attend. Alonzo and Perfidio and the rest of the Mexicans had also shown up at Kara's apartment with meals and heavy hearts for the departed *El Grande Jefe*. Kara and Nolan's families were in from out of state, as well as Nolan's ex-wife and daughter.

The other fifty people present had at one point either lived with him, laughed with him, drank with him, fought with him, or ran from him, but their loyalty remained unyielding.

Trench coats flapped in the crisp breeze behind the words of the hired minister. Because of the snow, there was no seating, so those in back saw nothing. Repeating after the minister, they said last rites and lowered the box into the frozen ground.

After the service, a meal was offered at Oatley's Restaurant, but only close friends and family attended. The crew met Nolan's surprisingly pleasant and undersized parents. His father was an engineer. He had a rotund body and a shock of white hair combed straight back. His mother was an old-school housewife who wore a cherubic expression despite the anguish. She also had a penchant for calling everyone 'dear.' Kara was seated next to them and pointed out certain people their son had known.

The men of Team Hate, for their part, itched inside their new black suits. They took turns discreetly fetching whiskey and Cokes nearly as fast as they arrived. While minding their manners, and fending off the screaming need to tend to other vices, they politely nodded amid the waves of small talk that swept across the tables.

Afterward, they met at Nolan's storage unit which Rand, Elias, and

O-Zone had cleaned out the day before. A space heater was cranked up as the Soldano brothers rolled down the steel door after Cam's belated arrival. Like the rest of them, his black tie was slacked around an opened collar. After so long in the restaurant, and a worse morning before that, guys passed each other bottles and bowls while cigarettes fumed the air.

"We're doing this now so no one accuses me of getting too comfortable with the money. All at once and then it's your problem." Cam put a black briefcase on the concrete floor as everyone circled round. He worked the locks to reveal rows of precise green stacks.

On one knee, Cam reached into the case for a piece of paper and said, "The contract was worth $260,000. And while I know most of you would like cash payments, this whole deal was on the books, so everything goes legit. The government's walking with twenty-six percent off your number. $260,000 divided by thirteen equals $20,000 per man. After taxes, the $260,000 divided by thirteen came out to $14,800."

"What the fuck ..." Uno shook his head.

"Fucking bureaucrats," Rand added.

"Wait a second ..." Bunny got the circle's attention. "Anybody see New Year standing here?"

There were loud groans before Rigor Mortis yelled, "What's that supposed to mean?"

"Well, it means the guy left on like day five, bro, no offense, but that ain't seventeen. And where is he now? On the day of Nolan's fucking funeral?"

"Bunny, what the fuck?" Rand rubbed his forehead. "This ain't right, man."

"No shit," Rigor Mortis said, incredulous.

"Of course you've got his back," Bunny said, "your attendance wasn't exactly perfect either."

After Rigor Mortis lunged for Bunny's neck, and the fight was immediately broken up, Cam shouted, "Enough!"

Order was restored. They straightened out their jackets and ties.

Cam said, "This isn't a fucking democracy, Bunny, all right? Thirteen went up, thirteen get the cut. Nolan's is going to Kara. Here ..." He fired the pre-wrapped stacks around the circle. Besides allowances for Nolan, Cooter, New Year, and Spoons, other smaller stacks remained. "I'm not sure if anyone here is ready to hear this," Cam said, "but Nolan and Ledo, on top of the all-or-nothing suicide contract, also had another wager."

"That motherfucker ..." Rand said.

O-Zone smiled and nodded. "The boy-toy millionaire lost his ass, didn't he?"

"Nolan was so worried about this fucking debt ..." Cam sorted the stacks. "It's blood money but everyone gets a slice."

Dead silence.

"The side bet was $80,000. And the only reason I even knew to collect on it was because he told Elias."

Rand looked at Elias but remained silent. Everyone did, because they suddenly wondered who else knew what.

"Since it's Nolan's bet," Cam continued, "the money actually belongs to Kara. But unlike the tax issue, even if the Pierce job gets judged against Nolan's company, the LLC and bankruptcy puts Kara out of reach. After we talked, she said you all earned it in the first place and wanted everyone to take a piece fair and square. That comes to $6,153 and again, Nolan's cut goes to her." Cam tossed out another round of stacks. They each looked at their money.

Cam closed the briefcase and cracked a beer. "I hate to beer and run, fellas, but I got to get back to my wife."

The nine of them tucked away their cash.

"All or nothing ..." Rand said. "Fucking guy had no middle gears."

Cam looked at Rand, O-Zone, and Elias. "What're you guys gonna do now?"

O-Zone shrugged.

"Jesus, Cam ..." Rand was speechless. "I don't have the slightest clue."

"Elias?" Cam sipped his beer. "What's up? You looking for work? The offer's open to all of you."

"Maybe. But I need to get out of here for a month or two, get the fuck away from all you glory-holes."

"No shit." Rand finished his beer and opened another.

"$80,000 ..." Bunny reflected. "If he had lost that bet ..."

"It wouldn't have mattered," Cam said. "Losing out on that contract was going to finish him either way ... why not bet the house or end it altogether?"

"Turns out he would have made it, though." Elias raised his beer. "In the immortal words of Team Bean, to *El Grande Jefe*."

"And Cooter and Spoons," Cam added.

Nine bottles collided in the center.

———

Two days later, Rand, O-Zone and Elias met at Kara's apartment. Afterward, the snow started falling on them in the parking lot.

"I think it's a great deal," Rand said. "We all know I ain't no owner, but you'll be a good boss."

They lit up a round of cigarettes as O-Zone said, "You really think so?"

"Sure."

"You're the one that wanted lead-guy pay," Elias reminded him. "Welcome to the show, Big-Time."

"I just hope it isn't a mistake."

"So what if it is?" Rand exhaled. "Then you just sell everything and jam."

"She gave you a great price ..." Elias flicked ash. "Truck, trailer, and tools for $140,000 ...? Hell, he paid seventy for the truck alone and it ain't even a year old."

"Don't forget," Rand said. "You got the Mexicans on board. If shit heads south, you could let them buy into the partnership to lessen your nightmare."

"I got a feeling you guys will be back," O-Zone said. "And your jobs will be waiting for you when you do."

"I appreciate that, bro." Rand hugged him and clapped him on the back. "I got to get going. My bus is pulling out in an hour."

"You got twenty grand in cash," O-Zone said, "and instead of heading to a beach somewhere warm, you're headed to Wyoming in the dead of winter."

"Mom's birthday's coming up. It's been a long time." Rand glanced at Elias and then they both seemed disheartened. "Take care of yourself, brother." Rand threw his arms around him. "We'll rally up soon enough. I got your number."

"You need to get a fucking license, man."

Rand laughed, but it must have been the same for all three.

"Mr. Zone, peace out, brother." Elias hugged O-Zone as O-Zone said, "Where you gonna go? Sure you don't want to stay on with me and Team Bean?"

"I'll be back." He looked at both of them and said, "Don't be strangers, man. After everything, that would be the worst."

Rand blinked into the falling snow. "Fucking A. See you when I see you."

They lingered a second longer before the swirling snow and gray-black clouds poured into the valley. Ski season, after all, was already under way ...

EPILOGUE

Buena Vista, Colorado
September 2001, Ten Months Later

After leaving Spring Valley, Elias dodged the winter in Lake Havasu City, Arizona, before meandering on a northeast course through the state the following spring. He hopped on with a roofing crew in Verde Village, helped fix cattle fencing in Fort Defiance, and worked for an asphalt company in Green River, Utah. There, the Roan and Book Cliffs provided a spectacular backdrop roaring out of the ground like giant battleships stacked in line.

He would have stayed on but once again felt drawn into the mountains. After visiting the Collegiates on many occasions with Rand, Elias packed the Skylark on the July 4th weekend and headed east. With ten grand still in the bank, he arrived in Buena Vista, Colorado, rented a trailer on the Arkansas River, and went to work at a sawmill west of town. With no ski resorts or tourist windfall, jobs were scarce, so he felt lucky to be employed.

He called Spring Valley every couple of months and heard Cooter's reattached fingers remained stiff and half-functional, but the therapists still promised a full recovery. He and New Year were planning on leaving for Texas, but not until Cooter was medically clear to close the workers compensation case. In the meantime, both were working with O-Zone and the Mexicans, and the money, while not like the old days of hurry up, was adequate for all involved.

Elias had also spoken with Rigor Mortis who, surprisingly, sounded pleased to get the call. After several minutes of niceties, Rigor Mortis told him to get his ass back to Spring Valley because he needed a fresh moron to abuse.

"Besides, I'm looking for a new way to make money," he cracked.

"Riggy—"

"And since you're a pansexual—"

"Dear God."

"—and I got a new camera—"

"Oh please stop."

"—I'll even rent a monkey, that way you can experience someone of your own species. *Monkey! Monkey! Monkey!*"

On the other hand, getting in touch with Rand Holmscomb was impossible. He had no phone or address and popped Elias a call every couple of months. At last check, he was somewhere near Kodiak Island, Alaska.

As for Team Beaver, Spoons still healed. He and Lizzie tied the knot as scheduled two months after the accident, but the rehabilitation of his leg and shoulder took another twelve weeks. Hence the photos of a drunken Spoons zipping around his own wedding reception in a wheelchair. In his absence, the Soldano brothers and Uno solidified the nucleus and monitored his gradual return to work. Cam had Bunny full-time now and swore his tutelage of the man-child would not be in vain.

On the phone with Elias, an offer of employment was again extended as Cam sounded genuinely concerned. "It's just not good for the public interest," he said, "to have both you and Rand running around on the loose. Why do you think Bunny's still here? It's sure as fuck not because he knows a goddamn thing about carpentry."

Elias smiled because he could hear Bunny yelling insults in the background. He told Cam he would be in touch and thanked him for the offer.

At the sawmill, work slowed and he was cut from five shifts down to three a week. So he picked up odd jobs, and after befriending one of the locals, bartered his framing skills for weed. The guy, John Grabel, needed a skylight installed in his remodeled bathroom, so Elias quoted him out at two-and-a-half ounces of kind bud. On top of dealing, Grabel also ran a financial consulting business out of his house. After Elias cut open the roof, Grabel, already overly loquacious, stood below and talked and talked while dodging the falling debris. Generous by nature, he kept Elias stoned and fed and even dragged a TV into the bathroom doorway.

On the roof, it was a bright sunny morning until Grabel burst into the room.

Elias, wrestling with the skylight, frowned at the disturbance below. "What's up?"

"I just turned-on CNN in the other room ..." Grabel whirled through the channels. "One of the World Trade Center's just exploded."

"*What?*" Elias flopped the window onto the roof and knelt down at the exact moment the second plane arrived.

"Oh my God." Grabel was in shock. "This has to be some kind of hoax, right?"

A lifelong New Yorker, Elias had been living downtown in 1993 when that attack occurred. His family, his former life, all of it came flooding back in an instant. He did not need to watch what followed because he knew there was nowhere else to go but home.

Newport, RI
March 2006

March 28, 2006

Note to the reader—

In an effort to shield the inhabitants of certain locations, the towns of Spring Valley and Brush Creek, along with the whole of Salinas County, are fictional.

The National Preservation Society and the National Ecological and Geological Association are largely based upon the work of the Nature Conservancy and NatureServe, respectively. In fact, much of the information about conservation easements came directly from their published material and websites.

The burning of Peak Four Resort on Mt. Pershing is based upon actual events that occurred at Vail Ski Resort on October 22, 1998. The Earth Liberation Front subsequently claimed full responsibility for the fire.

Socorro National Park in New Mexico, as well as Devil's Gorge, Mt. Lassiter, Blandings Pass, and Peak Four in Colorado, are fictional. The author has otherwise attempted to recreate the landscape and settings in Colorado, Utah and Wyoming.

And, most importantly, all characters are fictitious.

Excerpted Song Lyrics:

Don McLean, "American Pie," *American Pie*, United Artists, 1971.

Bloodhound Gang, "Fire Water Burn," *One Fierce Beer Coaster*, Republic Records, 1996.

The Carpenters, "(They Long to Be) Close to You," *Close to You*, A and M Records, 1970.

Special thanks to Leila Trabulsi, who illustrated all of the images in the preface. Thanks also to Ray Trabulsi, a guiding force.

Tremendous thanks to the primary editors—Adam Dunn, Adam Felts, and Rachel Coakley.

Thanks as well to those who read the manuscript and offered insight—Deb Perretta, Lisa Wolfe, Anthony Perretta, Steve Beaureguard, Mathew Gillespie, Katie Sauber, Mike Dawson, and Nicole Vitello.

ABOUT THE AUTHOR

Tom Trabulsi was born in the Midwest and attended high school in Rhode Island. After college, he worked as a bike courier in Boston and New York City. He moved to Colorado and worked construction throughout the Rocky Mountains. *Sandaman's Riposte* was his first novel. *Forked Head Pass*, a story about the Colorado land rush in the late 1990s, followed six years later. Currently, he is a firefighter in Pawtucket, Rhode Island. *The Fire Service of Sachem City*, his third novel, has already been completed.

CPSIA information can be obtained
at www.ICGtesting.com
Printed in the USA
BVHW050855050223
657899BV00029BA/1032